OLD TOWN

LIN ZHE

OLD TOWN

translated by
GEORGE A. FOWLER

amazoncrossing

Text copyright © 2006 by Lin Zhe
English translation copyright © 2009 by George A. Fowler

Published by AmazonCrossing
P.O. Box 400818
Las Vegas, NV 89140

Library of Congress Control Number: 2010918614
ISBN-13: 978-1-611090-07-9
ISBN-10: 1-611090-07-5

Old Town was first published in 2009 by Writers Publishing House, Beijing, as *Waipode Gucheng*
Translated from Chinese by George A. Fowler and published in 2010 under the title *Riddles of Belief...and Love*.
This English edition published in 2010 by AmazonCrossing.

CONTENTS

TRANSLATOR'S NOTE

Lin Zhe (pen name of Zhang Yonghong), is the author of *Grandma's Old Town* (*Waipode Gucheng*—Writers Publishing House, Beijing, 2006), renamed *Old Town* in this English translation. She was born in 1956 of Han Chinese parents then serving in the People's Liberation Army in Kashi (Kashgar), a small frontier city in what is now Xinjiang Uyghur Autonomous Region. After graduating from the Chinese Language and Literature Department of Fudan University in 1980, Ms. Lin worked as a reporter and editor for *Women of China Magazine* in Beijing. She has written fourteen novels that focus on women's issues relating to marriage and personal and family life. In addition, before publishing *Old Town*, Ms. Lin wrote three dramatic series for Chinese television unrelated to this novel.

The first, rather small edition of *Old Town* quickly sold out, and its enthusiastic reception prompted Tang Min, one of the country's most prominent film producers, to buy the rights to adapt it for television. The series, called *Army Doctor*, featuring well-known actors, began broadcasting in China in May 2009. Before production of *Army Doctor* had been completed, Tang Min commissioned Ms. Lin to write an additional television series based on the novel. Production of this series, named *Bygone Days in Old Town*, is now in its final stage, and is expected to be broadcast to Chinese audiences in early 2011. In addition, the Chinese publishers of the novel will be coming out with a second edition in the near future.

Of all her works to date, *Old Town* was the book that Lin Zhe had long wanted to write: a portrait of ordinary Chinese people from the aspect of faith—that system of beliefs and values, spiritual strength, if you will—that sustains people in difficult times. China certainly has suffered horrendously difficult times over the past century, and faith there has been clothed in very differing raiment indeed. Lin Zhe's parents, for example, were firm believers in communism and the stability it would surely bring to their afflicted country. In sharp contrast, Lin Zhe and her generation, who were still children during the Cultural Revolution, learned by bitter experience to believe in nothing whatsoever except themselves. Lin understands that while her generation may have gained a fierce clarity of sorts, they lost the spiritual strength that had been the precious heritage of the generations that preceded them.

Nor was this solely the result of disillusionment and cynicism from coming of age during the Cultural Revolution. Over the past sixty years alone, it is said, China has gone through the unimaginable equivalent of change that the West took two hundred years to experience and adjust to. As she has said to me, "Because of this enormous process of change, our traditional system of values has been severely impacted, and as a result we are the most lost and chaotic of generations. I felt it was my responsibility as a writer to record this history, and in my writings I have expressed our generation's confusion, especially the confusion suffered by Chinese women."

It is in this context that we approach and understand the recurring voice of the narrator, for this book is really her story: one of emptiness and despair, recollection, and, ultimately, a kind of illumination and salvation.

My longtime friend Lars Ellström, of Beijing and Oaxen Island, Sweden, unexpectedly and enthusiastically thrust *Old Town* on me in 2007. Lars and I first met in 1970 at Nanyang University in Singapore, where we both were studying Chinese, I the rankest of beginners and he already impressively advanced. When I telephoned Lars to discuss a certain literary translation project I was then considering, he interrupted to tell me of the book his friend Yonghong had recently written, and "never mind" the one I had called about. The result of that telephone conversation is now in your hands.

I had to make several key decisions in bringing this novel to a non-Chinese readership. Primary among them was how to deal with the predominant use in the text of relationship titles rather than proper names for members of the extended Lin and Guo families. Addressing and referring to close family members with relationship titles and not names is a living tradition in Chinese culture and society. And Chinese relationship titles embed precise terms that can clarify, for example, whether an uncle is on the father's or mother's side of the family and what his age is relative to one's mother and father. Thus, while Chinese readers would have had little difficulty in identifying and keeping track of these relationships in the original text, my concern was that the readers of this translation might find all of this rather bewildering. However, rather than requesting Lin Zhe to invent new proper names for this translation I have decided to remain faithful to the source text for several reasons. First, bringing a plethora of new names into play would surely cause more confusion than clarity. Second, such relationship titles in this book are actually rather limited in number, and I have provided family trees as a reference for the non-Chinese reader. Mainly, however, I saw retaining these titles as a way to draw us out of our world and into one that is very Chinese.

It is common in China to address friends by prefixing "Old" or "Young" to their surnames. This is generally a reference to the friend's age relative to a speaker, even if the difference is not that great. Thus, Dr. Lin's former medical adjutant, Li, continues to be "Young Li" across the years of their relationship, and Dr. Lin himself is referred to as "Young Mr. Lin" by Mrs. Yang, the widow of his former classmate in Shanghai, even in both of their old ages.

The given names of Chinese children are frequently made diminutive by adding an "er" sound to them. Thus, rather than "Little Hong," or "Little Su," etc., which are perfectly correct, but to my mind slightly cloying, I have simply transliterated these as "Hong'er," "Su'er," and so on.

Apart from the stylistic changes inevitable in rendering the Chinese source into English, I have faithfully mirrored the structure and narrative flow of Lin Zhe's original work in my translation. In particular, I have tried to evoke the flavor of the many proverbs and sayings in this book without obscurity or literalism. The striking array of allusions drawn on Chinese history and literature of all genres across the millennia, so typical of educated Chinese in their speech and writing, is also richly deployed in Lin Zhe's novel. I have provided footnotes rather than paraphrase or simply delete these proud jewels of the Chinese language. I hope readers will find these clarifying and illuminative of how profoundly China's history and culture reverberates and ever accumulates in Chinese self-reference.

On one specific historical note, in the sections of this novel dealing with the Great Proletarian Cultural Revolution, the reader will come across many references to "rebel factions," far more, in fact, than to Red Guards. As explained to me by Lin Zhe, while the Red Guards were largely student activists, the "rebel factions" were, by contrast, oppositionist organizations made up of nonstudents, i.e., factory workers, political cadres, teachers, etc. The armbands they wore would indicate their particular affiliations. The motivations and actions of these rebel factions were more a reflection of political conditions at the local level than any unified ideological stance or strategy, and they not infrequently engaged in armed clashes with each other. Lin Zhe recounts all of this in her novel.

In her citation of verse two of Psalm 78 in the Old Testament of the Bible as the frontispiece inscription in the Chinese edition of her novel, Ms. Lin foreshadows all the wondrous (and often terrible) deeds and "mysteries of old" related in her story. As I read *Old Town*, this evocation of "mysteries" struck me as touching something both existential and universal, notwithstanding the very specific twentieth century China setting of this novel. For riddles abound in the telling of *Old Town*: Who or what force directs our lives? Is it fate? Divinity? If it is divinity, then how to understand the confluence of events that impact and shape human existence and all too often bring suffering? And what holds life together in desperate circumstances – is it belief in God, Bodhisattva Guanyin, or a political system such as communism? Or is it love – whether of another person, one's family, or even one's country? And, seemingly above all, how is it that some people are nourished and sustained by that mysterious association, marriage, while others are somehow doomed to be poisoned by it?

In *Old Town*, the love of Ninth Brother and Second Sister for each other is like the bloom of an indomitable rose bursting forth in a climate of desolation, terror, and despair. The narrator, by contrast, is baffled and bitter over the failure of her own marriage and her pointless love affairs. Most poignant of all, though, is the mystery of the generations that preceded her. But this is beyond her understanding, for the world and age that shaped those generations is now closed to her forever. And if that is so, then who, really, is she? These are among the questions, the riddles that the narrator ponders throughout her long meditative recollection of her family in Old Town.

Finally, as we stand on the threshold of Old Town, a note on architecture. In the traditional houses of the educated and reasonably well off in coastal South China, the kitchen would be in the far back, next to the back door. In the old days, servants could pass in and out only through that back door, not through the front gate. Inside the main gate of an Old Town home is the "sky well," a smaller version of the more spacious courtyards of North China. Smaller, I would guess, because of the vastly greater rainfall in this region of the country. Passing through the sky well, you will arrive in the main parlor. Here are placed the ancestors' pictures, memorial tablets, and various and venerated heirlooms. Here also is the family dining table. By the side of the sky well of Ninth Brother and Second Sister's home is a little room that will later be converted into a simple clinic. Their residence at West Gate is rather small, not very typical, and certainly a far cry from the "three-courtyard-deep" mansion of Ninth Brother's boyhood, when old dynastic China had breathed its last and something new and unknown was just beginning to take its place.

Background Dates and Events in Modern Chinese History

1911 – Uprisings of republican forces in South China topple decrepit Qing dynasty. Sun Yat-sen elected first provisional president of the Republic of China.

1912 – Guomindang ("Chinese Nationalist Party") founded and assumes leadership of China's republican revolution. Provisional president of the Republic of China now Beijing militarist Yuan Shikai.

1916 – Death of President Yuan Shikai. Chaotic warlord period commences in many parts of China.

1921 – Communist Party of China (CCP) founded. *The True Story of Ah Q* by Lu Xun published in serial form.

1926–1928 – Northern Expeditions by Guomindang armed forces in coalition with CCP and other leftist factions to unite the country by defeating the warlords. Commander-in-Chief Chiang Kai-shek brutally purges the Northern Expedition of its communist and leftist elements in Shanghai in April 1927. CCP goes underground in cities or flees to rural areas of south China. Red Army formed in Jiangxi Province.

1928 – Capital of unified China established at Nanjing, Jiangsu Province, under leadership of Generalissimo Chiang Kai-shek, chairman of the National Government in Guomindang one-party state. Series of encirclement and annihilation campaigns launched against CCP-controlled areas.

1932 – Japan sets up puppet state of Manchukuo under Pu Yi, last emperor of the now-defunct Qing Dynasty. Manchukuo becomes springboard for Japanese aggression in North China. Other relatively small-scale Japanese provocations in China since early 1930s.

1934–1935 – Withdrawal of embattled CCP forces from southern China to Shaanxi Province ("the Long March").

1937 – The Second Sino-Japanese War formally begins with the Marco Polo Bridge Incident (July 7), followed by the Battle of Shanghai, aka, "Songhu Battle" (August–October), the Battle of Nanjing and the Nanjing Massacre (December), Guomindang government commences graduated migration to Chongqing, Sichuan Province, far up the Yangzi River. Guomindang government under Chiang and Communists under Mao Zedong sign agreement for a joint war of resistance against Japan.

1945–1946 – End of the Second World War in Asia. Negotiations between Guomindang and Communists on a coalition government fail. Open civil war resumes in July 1946.

1949 – Civil war ends in Communist victory. Portions of Guomindang army and numerous government officials, business figures complete retreat to Taiwan. Mao Zedong proclaims birth of People's Republic of China at the Gate of Heavenly Peace in Beijing (October). Chiang flies to Taiwan from Chengdu, Sichuan Province (December).

1950–1953 – Korean War. Chinese forces enter Korea to prop up collapsing North Korean army. War ends in stalemate along the 38th Parallel. Ceasefire and armistice signed by commanders of UN Command, Korean People's Army, and the Chinese People's Volunteers on July 27, 1953.

1956 – Hundred Flowers Campaign starts, critical views of party policies and government leadership encouraged by top leadership. Motivations for this still debated.

1957 – Anti-Rightist Movement quells all criticism of party in society at large and strives to purge society of "anti-revolutionary" elements.

1958 – "Great Leap Forward," the name given to the Second Five-Year Plan, aims at rapid industrialization and development of agricultural sector.

1958–1961 – Years of widespread famine result from major policy errors underlying Great Leap Forward, exacerbated by natural disasters.

1966–1976 – Period of Maoist "Great Proletarian Cultural Revolution," also known in China as "Ten Years of Catastrophe." While the Revolution's aims are complex and contradictory, many of Chairman Mao's ideological rivals and personal enemies are eliminated. Precipitous rise to power of Jiang Qing, Mao's final wife and the leader of the "Gang of Four" radical ideologues.

1968 – Mao orders "Down to the Countryside" campaign for urban youth who make up the increasingly violent and fractious Red Guards and nonstudent "rebel factions."

1971 – Death of Marshall Lin Biao, Chairman Mao's appointed successor, amid rumors of coup and countercoup plots.

1976 – Death of Chairman Mao Zedong, downfall of Jiang Qing and rest of the "Gang of Four." Deng Xiaoping commences rise to paramount power.

1977–1979 – "Beijing Spring" and "Democracy Wall" period. Deng Xiaoping repudiates excesses of Cultural Revolution period and effectively ends exclusionary class background system. "Democracy Wall" closed down when demands for greater democracy in China grow strident.

1980–1981 – Deng appoints Zhao Ziyang as prime minister and Hu Yaobang as party chairman. China's "Opening Up" to the world proceeds along with far-reaching economic and political reforms.

I shall open my mouth and speak in allegory,
the mystery of bygone days shall I tell,
Of what I have heard and know,
and of what our forefathers have told us,
These we shall not hide from their children and grandchildren,
So future generations shall be told of Yaweh's goodness and might,
and of his marvelous deeds.

—Psalm 78

GUO FAMILY

"Boss" Guo
m. Miss Huang "Old Lady Guo"

Daughters   **Sons**

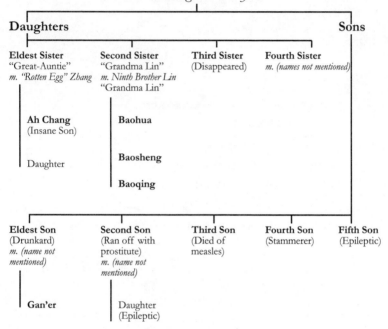

Eldest Sister
"Great-Auntie"
m. "Rotten Egg" Zhang

Second Sister
"Grandma Lin"
m. Ninth Brother Lin
"Grandma Lin"

Third Sister
(Disappeared)

Fourth Sister
m. (names not mentioned)

Ah Chang
(Insane Son)

Baohua

Daughter

Baosheng

Baoqing

Eldest Son
(Drunkard)
m. (name not mentioned)

Second Son
(Ran off with prostitute)
m. (name not mentioned)

Third Son
(Died of measles)

Fourth Son
(Stammerer)

Fifth Son
(Epileptic)

Gan'er

Daughter
(Epileptic)

LIN FAMILY

Great - Grandfather LIN
m. four wives

Eldest Brother	**Fourth Brother**	**Ninth Brother**	**Six Other Siblings**
m. "Big Sister-in-Law"	*m. (name not mentioned)*	*"Grandpa Lin"*	*m. (names not mentioned)*
		m. Second Sister Guo	
		"Grandma Lin"	

First Son

Second Son

Baolan
m. Ah Jian

Baohua
(Two Marriages)
m. "Reporter/Secretary Xiao"

Hong'er (Narrator)
m. Chen Chaofan

Beibei

m. "Big Zhang"

Maomao (Adopted)

Baosheng
m. (name not mentiioned)

Su'er

Baoqing
m. Fangzi

Wei'er

Daughter

Map of China

CHAPTER ONE — A FORGOTTEN OLD TOWN

1.

RAIN...PITTERING, SPLASHING...THE ETERNAL rainy skies of Old Town. I am sitting at that ancient Eight Immortals table in our parlor, staring blankly, my chin in my hands. As I look out at the drenched streets of the West Gate neighborhood, at the dripping eaves of the houses and the trickling branches of the trees, I think of the world beyond this old southern town— of the world I long for. And I am thinking, *What am I doing here in Old Town? What am I doing living in this house?*

This is something I can never figure out. I long to leave Old Town. It's like being homesick for somewhere else, and I've often felt the worst kind of sadness sitting in this house at West Gate. I'm like a traveler in exile who has no idea of where she will ever find a home.

Into this drenched and soaking street scene suddenly barges a familiar shape—Chaofan! He stops abruptly and peers inside. He clearly sees me. But his look is so strange. He doesn't know me. He has never known me. He's just happened to bump into a silly girl staring blankly, chin propped up in her hands. He lets his momentary curiosity pass, and is on his way again.

This picture doesn't feel very logical. It is like some badly edited scene in a movie.

Chaofan, why don't you recognize me?

I want to shout to him, but the sounds just won't come out.

When I opened my eyes, I was in a moving railway car. The wheels rolled along, cling-*cleng*-cling-*cleng*. The coach swayed and rocked and the green window curtain rested on my shoulder. I remained in a kind of trance, thinking of Chaofan on the rain-soaked streets of Old Town, but whether I was still dreaming or not, I couldn't tell.

The young man who had been sitting at my side returned to his seat, holding a glass brimming with steaming tea. He was with two others just like him, who sat directly across from me and chatted away in the Old Town dialect as if they hadn't a care in the world. Something about making some money up north by reselling dark glasses and fake name-brand watches smuggled in from the coast. In the late 1970s and the early 1980s, the term for smuggling, "running private-channel goods," was relatively new in China. My first impressions of this sort of thing had been positive. Private-channel goods were the genuine article at a fair price, and people who ran such items were unusually resourceful. Right! They even asked me if I wanted to buy a Rolex. I had no idea what a Rolex was. They said it was Switzerland's very best wristwatch and had been imported "privately" from Taiwan. I knew only that Titoni watches were from Switzerland and my mother wore one. I had heard that my grandfather, her father, gave it to her as part of her dowry. The watch core was inlaid with seventeen diamonds and I used to wish it would break so that I could get those seventeen diamonds, though I had never in my life seen a diamond. The three "private-channel elements" spoke to me in Mandarin, taking me for a "northern guy."

Old Town people thought I grew up looking more and more northern. I had a round face, fair with the slightest tinge of red, and I was taller than most of the girls in Old Town. Grandma looked at me anxiously once and said, "You mustn't grow any more. If you get any bigger, you might have a hard time getting married." And the blood of northerners really *does* course through my veins. I was born in the little town of Kashgar, far away on the Xinjiang border. The father I had never seen was a northern guy. From his photograph, I knew I looked like him. I looked like him a lot.

The train suddenly slowed and the fellow holding the glass of tea was caught off balance. As he staggered, boiling tea poured onto my leg and I yelled out in pain. The three young men said, "Sorry," all together in their Old Town-accented Mandarin.

My head cleared up completely under all this pain. But my hand didn't reach down to soothe my scalded thigh; instead, it automatically felt for the envelope hidden at my breast. In that envelope was my university admission notice, while one hundred and fifty *yuan* were safely tucked in a pocket in my underwear. I finally believed this was no dream. I really was on a journey and leaving Old Town far behind.

Moving aside the curtain to look out at the gently swaying and pretty countryside, I breathed out deeply, as if letting go of a heavy burden. But immediately doubts and hesitation again weighed me down. I thought of Chaofan. The year before he had tested successfully for entry into the Beijing Institute of Art, and so Beijing became the realm of my dreams and reveries. Before setting out, I sent him a telegram. Our year of separation has made my love for him all the more incurable.

⌘ ⌘ ⌘

That's how I left Old Town.

In more than twenty years, I've returned only a few times. My grandparents, Mother's parents, were no longer living, and the old

West Gate home of my childhood has been razed. Old Town and all of China's other places are now undergoing similarly drastic cosmetic surgery. Work sites for this disembowelment are everywhere. Even though from my earliest years I had longed to leave Old Town, every time I realized my childhood home and my grandpa and grandma were lost to me forever, that uprooted and forsaken feeling would hit all over again. Maybe I dreaded returning home because of the nostalgic feelings I still held on to.

I kept on going. I went to the other side of the ocean, to a little place called Lompoc, California. The pressures of just staying alive there kept me from thinking too much of where I had come from or where I was going. I did not even have the time to see much of the sunshine and beaches only a stone's throw away. I almost forgot Old Town. I had come from Beijing and everyone in Lompoc took me for a Beijinger.

Within a brief few months, I had worked in every Chinese restaurant in Lompoc. When I was looking for my first job, I lied about "having experience." That evening the boss "sautéed my cuttlefish," that is, he fired me. After repeated cuttlefish sautés, though, I could justifiably say I was experienced.

One day, before yet another of those restaurants was opening for business, another girl and I were setting the tables, folding the cloth napkins into patterns and placing them in glasses. I was just taking some glasses from the pushcart, when suddenly, from behind me, came a loud voice:

"Reporter!"

Working here were also PhDs, medical doctors, professors, and actors. Before hiring staff, the boss would ask each person his or her original profession back in China, and then these became our names. I guessed that he got a special thrill ordering us around, for he hadn't had much of an education himself. "What's the big deal about being educated? Don't you still depend on me to keep you going?" He talked like that.

What had I done wrong? Was the boss about to sauté some cuttlefish? Inside, I felt inches tall.

The boss's big fat head stuck out from behind the counter, both eyes looking as if they were about to burst, "You're slacking off!"

Slacking off? How? Ever since I started working in restaurants, I had forced myself to quit drinking tea all the time because it kept making me run to the toilet. I now chewed dry tea leaves to keep myself energized.

I just stood there, gaping. I was holding seven or eight glasses. Next to me stood Violinist—the boss called her Performer—who quietly said, "You're not supposed to stick your fingers inside the glasses."

Right then the boss roared out, "Trying to wreck my business, eh?"

Performer relieved me of the glasses I was holding and wiped them clean, one by one, with a cloth napkin. Actually, the napkin was a whole lot dirtier than my hands.

I nervously stole a glance at the boss, trying to figure out whether it would be sautéed cuttlefish time again...

I was really pathetic. I couldn't help asking myself why I had to travel so far across the ocean just to end up here. When I was little, the only thing I wanted was to leave Old Town. I felt that I would find a real home somewhere far, far away from my old one at West Gate. But later, in Beijing when I set up on my own, I felt it still wasn't home. I threw away my job and dumped my daughter to go chasing off to America after Chaofan. Where else could I migrate to in this world? Where would I find a real home?

Lompoc's population was small but its vein of religious sentiment ran very rich and deep. There were always people knocking on doors and preaching. Chaofan would get really irritated at this and figure out ways to shut up their preaching. To the Buddhists he would say, "I'm a Christian," and to the Christians he would say, "I'm a Buddhist." If the believer persisted, Chaofan would then sternly warn them: "America's a free country and you're interfering with my freedom of belief." This always did the trick. Privately, Chaofan and I were both proud to be atheists. For him, "religion" was another word for ignorance and foolishness. I myself wasn't quite as extreme. I believed religion made people good. Perhaps someday later on, when I had a career that guaranteed me food and clothing, I would think about being a good person, but at the moment, I had too many problems and worries. Where and when would I have leisure enough to sing songs of praise for a god who didn't exist anyway?

Several days later, I found in a Chinese-language tabloid a job that I *was* uniquely qualified for. The only requirement was "fluency in the South China Old Town dialect." When my eyes latched onto these words, it was as if a thunderclap from heaven had exploded right over my head alone, and I reentered a history that I had severed myself from so completely and so long ago. Old Town, soggy Old Town, now reappeared fresh and alive in my memory. *Old Town, root of my existence, how could I ever have forgotten you?*

Lucy, my employer, a fair-complexioned woman with black hair and dark eyes, totally surprised me when she came out with a few simple words of Old Town dialect. My job was to look after her mother, a woman who had been born in the south of China, in Old Town, actually. Lucy's now-deceased father had once worked in China as a young man and had married a Chinese woman. Her mother, now nearly eighty years old, had been stricken the year before with some serious illness and was suddenly unable to understand English, or even Mandarin. All she could do was speak Old Town dialect in a squeaky, *yi-yi-ya-ya* way. Baffled, Lucy shook her head and said, "Before, my mother could read the Bible in English. When she was young, she and my father went all around preaching the Word, and she spoke very proper Mandarin."

The name of this peculiar old lady was Helen. Every day when I wheeled her out to take some sun and the neighbors all greeted her, she made no response whatsoever. Lompoc was quite small and the people there all knew each other, but she always asked me, "When did all these 'outlandish folk' (Old Town dialect for 'foreigners') get here?" She thought Lompoc was Old Town. And it's true, every time the skies grew overcast and it started to drizzle, the soaked streets exuded that feeling only Old Town had. I didn't ask her what her Chinese name was and just called her "Ah Ma" ("Granny" in our dialect). She paid no attention, but I persisted in calling her that. Ah Ma's three children lived and worked in other parts of the country. Lucy, the youngest, lived the closest, in Los Angeles, and going back and forth by car would take her about four hours. As far as Ah Ma was concerned, her children were of no great importance and she actually didn't recognize them. Her frail old body was in Lompoc, but her spirit had already crossed time and space to return to Old Town, back to her early childhood days. She called me Big Sister, Second Sister, and Nursey, or Flower, or Elegant. In Old Town, on every street, there were many girls named Flower or Elegant. I felt for her. I often couldn't help having a bout of self-pity out of kindred feelings. "A rabbit dies and even the fox feels sad," as we like to say. Wasn't Helen's *today* a preview of my *tomorrow*? I saw myself sitting like her in a wheelchair, unable to speak English, unable to speak Mandarin, and using the Old Town dialect that nobody could make anything out of, right up to my death of old age in a strange land.

Helen had her lucid moments, though. Every day at nine o'clock in the morning, she would ask very clear-headedly for me to read the Bible to her and I would do so in the Old Town dialect. After hearing a small portion, she would stop me and say, "Let's share this part of the text." She related very well to the lives of the twelve apostles, as if they had been her old acquaintances. But then, closing the Bible, she would revert to total incoherence. As I read the Bible to her, I would try to awaken her memories. "Ah Ma, when did you come to America?" "America?" She would squint and say, "I've heard of it. Never went there, though." "Ah Ma, who gave you your English name Helen?" "Helen? Such an interesting name—is it yours?" If I kept on with these kinds of questions, she would get irritated and say, "You haven't finished reading this part of the text yet."

Helen aroused in me many memories of my grandfather and grandmother. They too were Christians. Christians were good people, just like Lei Feng, whom we had been required to study in school when we were young.[1] This idea of them had been the full extent of my knowledge and understanding of Christians. My grandfather had read the Bible his whole life, as if it were some kind of encoded, mystical scripture that contained his fate. Even when he reached the end of his allotted life span, he still couldn't comprehend what was in that book very deeply or fully.

I read the Bible to Helen merely to earn a living. I wanted to support my artist husband and send money home for my daughter. Other than this, the Bible had no further meaning for me. In the

---

[1]   Lei Feng (1940–1962), an ordinary PLA soldier killed in a freak construction accident and transformed by a team of party writers (as it was revealed in the late 1980s) into an icon of model Chinese citizenship. The "Learn from Comrade Lei Feng Campaign," based on the entries in his putative diary, commenced in 1963 and became the focus of intense indoctrination of Chinese youth, who were urged to copy Lei Feng's selflessness and utter devotion to Chairman Mao's teachings.

upheaval of the times, our generation had developed the ability to stay cool in the face of great change. The Revolution was an endless act of rejecting. What you worship today you might be knocking down and trampling underfoot tomorrow. We didn't believe in any person or anything. We had no faith. We were complete atheists.

Every day as I watched over Helen, leaving Chaofan was the thing that preoccupied my mind. But that would have been harder for me to do than a mother abandoning her hopelessly sick child. From the time that we had been innocent playmates to now I've always loved him with my whole being. I followed him all the way from Old Town to Beijing and then on to America. Eventually and painfully, though, the whole thing became clear to me. I never really had him, not for even one day. Though we slept in the same bed, I didn't know where *his spirit* was. I never knew what he would do when the sun rose the next morning. I also thought of my daughter, Beibei, whom I had left behind in China. When I recalled the time she took her first tottering steps, I felt my heart would break within me.

I clearly remember the last time I read the Bible to Helen. My eyes were uncontrollably brimming with tears. Because I was going to quit, Lucy drove back to Lompoc, bringing her son, Joseph, with her. She wanted me to stay on and promised to increase my salary. When she found out that I had left my three-year-old daughter in China, she just heaved a sigh, a look of total bafflement on her face. After being together from morning to night for several months now, old Helen found it hard to part with me, just as my small child had. I really couldn't bear abandoning her like this, and even before I left I was already feeling quite concerned about her. That day there was so much to say to Helen, and over and over I told her, "Ah Ma, I am really sorry about this. But quickly recover your memory and understand English when someone speaks it to you. That way it will be easier to find someone to take care of you." Helen seemed to understand all this for I saw the tears glistening in her eyes.

Before parting, Lucy invited us all to pray together. We stood around Helen in her wheelchair, lowered our heads, shut our eyes, and prayed. "Heavenly Father, dear God, we three generations of the same family here offer you our gratitude...We ask you to heal Helen, my mother. Make her recover her memory. Make her able to speak in English in a way pleasing to you..."

I peeped open my eyes and looked all around. Whereabouts was God? When Chaofan was in a good mood, he would let proselytizing believers into our house and wrangle with them just for the fun of it. He would ask them, "If there is an almighty god, how come there is still war and poverty? How come you drive such a nice car while I can't afford even some old beat-up one? So! If you can't even believe in what you can see with your own eyes and hold in your own hands, how can you believe in a make-believe god of myth and legend?"

I looked out the window. All was unbroken gray sky and rain. Lompoc was mostly rainy in the spring. The soaked streets, the trickling eaves of the houses, the dripping tree branches: how familiar this all was. In an instant, a dense sadness welled within me, and having felt so disconsolate for so long, I found myself thinking of Old Town.

2.

EARLY ONE MORNING ten years later, as usual, I jumped out of bed and rushed to the bathroom to wash my face and rinse my mouth. Only when I faced the mirror and raised the lipstick to my lips did I remember that I didn't have to go to the office. The television advertising company I had slaved away at running for so many years now existed in name only, and my ten or so employees had all left to find other ways to support themselves. The people of this world are basically like birds in the forest—when big trouble comes upon them, off they go in all directions. Who can employ anybody?

By this time, I had reached middle age. In over ten years, I had experienced the whole gamut of feelings a single woman might experience. Though I thought I had the eyes to see through anyone, and more than able to emerge whole from emotional whirlpools, this most recent ending had left me so hurt I wanted to die.

Putting the lipstick back down, I looked at the neatly arranged razor and the electric toothbrush. I picked them up, stared at them for a moment, and then just swept everything into the trash can. How many times had I been discouraged and depressed as I was now and thrown away the things left behind by men?

I gazed with self-pity at myself in the mirror. The unkempt hair and the haggard face—only a woman who found no joy in life could look like this. Then I thought of my mother. I had always disdained Mother's spinelessness, her utter passiveness in the face of difficulty. There was no joy in her life—she merely existed. She was a warning to me. When I was very small, I was determined to lead a life totally different from hers. But now, all I too had left was mere existence. I felt such a vast sadness. Looking in the mirror, I watched as the rims of those dark and lusterless eyes grew redder and redder before tears gushed forth from them.

I can't remember how many days I simply stayed inside. The next time I picked up the lipstick and faced the mirror again, it was for my meeting with Lucy's son, Joseph.

After leaving Lompoc, Lucy and I kept in contact by corresponding once a year. She had provided me with brief news of Joseph and Helen in her letters, so I now knew that after Joseph had resigned from television he had become an independent filmmaker and that old Helen had peacefully returned to heaven one summer day several years ago.

A few days ago, Lucy, for the first time, telephoned me to say that Joseph would be coming to China to complete a project and that she hoped I might be able to help him.

Joseph arrived. We had met just that one time in Lompoc and neither of us made much of an impression on the other. It must have been our sixth senses at work, for we instantly recognized each other at the coffee shop we had chosen for our meeting.

If my company were still hustling and bustling with one hundred and one things going on, I might have taken the time to invite Joseph to go out for a meal together. But that would have been purely to show off how the one-time female servant fluent in the Old Town dialect had transformed herself into a successful Beijing woman. Or I could have arranged for my assistant to help him or sent my secretary to arrange his itinerary. But everything that I might have flaunted was a mirage, something that belonged to another, different lifetime.

"Has everything been good for you these past ten years after Lompoc?"

Such an ordinary question, but it felt like a dagger poking at the wound in my heart, and the sharp pain passed right through to every nerve ending in my body. I said, "Not good, not good at all."

I couldn't be bothered with vanity, and so I told him how I had gone bankrupt overnight, how, when I left Lompoc I didn't have a thing to my name, and how today once again I hadn't a thing either. And how, no longer being at that splendid age of twenty-eight, I hadn't the time or the energy to make my comeback and start all over. I was over and done with and without a hope in the world.

"Maybe you were so busy with your work that you drifted away from God. Now that you have time to reestablish a close relationship with Him, how can you say that you have no hope left?"

Where was "God"? I found myself glancing up at the ceiling. Just yesterday, my good friend Xiaoli had also tried to persuade me like this. It left me speechless, not knowing whether to laugh or to cry. She said, "I'll pray for you, and ask God to open the road ahead of you." I thought she had stayed in the US for too long and had become cold and detached. My daughter, Beibei, had gone to America to do senior high school the year before, and Xiaoli had volunteered for the tough job of keeping an eye on her. I was beginning to worry that Beibei too would become insensitive. Once when I was with her and had vented all my grievances, she just said apathetically, "Uh, Mom, I'll pray for you." Wasn't that about the same as saying that I had suffered for ten years and all for nothing?

Now, sitting right in front of me was a believer who knew nothing of life's smoke and flames. Believers may be charitable and mean well but they lack sympathy. If you were naked and starving, they'd be sure to open their purses and wallets to help you. But I wasn't some disaster victim in Africa and I didn't need emergency aid. My pain and suffering were the awkward predicaments that modern women are running into all the time and everywhere. Such people's responses were meaningless…useless, sort of like dealing with an itch by scratching your shoe.

What I needed was a friend who would be willing take a knife in the ribs for me, someone like Chrysanthemum. She was everywhere and doing everything to grease relationships so I could bring to trial the man who had driven my company under. The very one who had brushed his teeth and shaved where I lived. Chrysanthemum said we ought to "use evil to rule evil," and hire gangsters to teach that hoodlum cheat a lesson. Those were the days when sheer loathing kept me going. Chrysanthemum and I shared a bitter hatred of this enemy, and again and again we imagined pounding him into a pulp. I could become quite hyper as I longed for my triumphant vengeance. Chrysanthemum was a person who really came into her own in adversity. She was my true friend.

"Let's just talk about you, OK?" I said to Joseph. "Your mother said on the phone that you might need my help. I'll be glad to help you."

My heart, cold as dead ashes, was slowly warming when suddenly a crazy idea struck me: *Could Joseph's project in China just maybe also help my company come back from the grave?*

"Uh, yeah. Right now I'm planning a family image data service. Modern society is an immigrant one. A person can live his whole life all over the world and most people don't know anything about their ancestors. They don't even know much about their own father and mother. For a lot of people it's only when they are older that the desire hits to learn about where they came from. Take my mother, for example. All along, she's regretted never knowing much about her own father and mother, and now that they've both passed on, she has only limited information to piece together their story. This regret of hers inspired me to create something. As you remember, my grandmother was from Old Town. I'd like to begin with that place, and I was hoping you could go with me down south and help me there."

Hearing Joseph speak of Old Town, I didn't feel the quickened heartbeat of ten years earlier when I first saw that employment ad in the Lompoc newspaper. Old Town was not far off—a two-hour flight south from Beijing. All I had to do to return was stand up and just go there. But in my mind Old Town had been receding farther and farther into the distance. After Grandma passed away, I never went back. And in Old Town I'd see the same old predictable pattern of tall buildings and grand mansions. I'd walk back and forth there and wouldn't be able to figure out where, exactly, I was. In Guangzhou? Shenzhen? Wenzhou? Nothing ever stays the same, of course, but the magnitude of change was beyond all imagining. Old Town was like a reformatted computer on which not a single byte of the original information had been left. Faced with such twists and turns in life, I didn't know whether this made me sad or happy.

Last year, I brought my daughter to school in the US and, as a favor, asked Xiaoli to drive us down to Lompoc for a visit. The small town felt and looked unchanged from before. The street I once lived on had a little roast chicken restaurant. Just as before, the Mexican lady owner was all smiles as she greeted and attended to her guests, only now her face was powdered a bit more thickly. The Chinese restaurant I used to work at was still there. Through the full-length windowpane, I saw the fat owner behind the counter, head bowed as he went over his accounts. Just about no changes, then. The trees and buildings on both sides of the street showed no sign of being worn down by time. As if entranced, I felt it had been only yesterday that I had been strolling about Lompoc.

This was exactly the warmth and intimacy people long for when they return to their native place, the feeling that they had never really gone away. In this sense, my own native home, Old Town, had vanished, and I supposed then I'd never be going back there again.

At that moment with Joseph in the coffee shop, Old Town had no special meaning for me. What I cared about were this job's prospects and how we would work together. I was very happy to accept this offer since I needed a new way to make money. Given my current predicament, I had no alternative but to consider restarting my old line of work compiling sentimental and fluffy stories, or disguised versions of my own great passionate love affairs, for newspapers and magazines. I coped with my economic crisis by living off the money I earned from these submittals. In the more than ten years since leaving Lompoc and returning to Beijing, here I was again, "cooking words to feed starvation."

Joseph said, "If we work together well, later on I can give you all our China business. Right now, we still can't do too much long-term planning. I hope God guides us and makes our daily work productive."

"God"— what a fine cliché. If there really were a God who ran the universe, why should I be here begging you for a cup of soup? But I didn't dare express my skepticism.

I laughed awkwardly and bantered, "May Almighty God bless and protect you."

"Bless and protect *us.*"

Joseph suggested that we pray for the work we were about to commence. As he mumbled away, I worried about my meeting with Chrysanthemum a little later. She had helped me find a lawyer to sue those two companies that previously had a cooperative arrangement with me. I wanted to sue for the damages caused by their one-sided termination. If there really were a God, let him reach out with his justice and help me win my lawsuit.

Obviously, God hadn't heard the call from my heart. The lawyer made his purpose clear from the start and sternly advised me to raise a truly frightening sum of money for the process attorney's fee: twenty percent of the amount I was claiming. Only after a prepayment of fifty thousand *yuan* would he get to work. Before that, he couldn't be bothered even to hear my grievance. Whether or not the people involved had been treated unfairly was apparently not important. "If I'm taking your money it means we'll win this litigation. We lawyers are housepainters. We can make black white, and white, black."

If I had that much money, why would I have had to scatter my staff to the four winds? Money was the thing I most needed now. Beibei was in America studying at a private school, and I had to come up with the tuition for next semester. I was thinking of how to tell her to change to a tuition-free public school. The lawyer saw me hesitate and, putting down his business card, took his leave. Chrysanthemum and I just sat there, stupefied, before we recovered our senses. She patted my shoulder, saying, "This lawyer isn't sympathetic at all. We'll get another." My heart, which had been burning with a desire for revenge, had now cooled down. "No need," I said with a bitter laugh. Our expectations for sympathy from that lawyer had been a delusion. He spoke for his employer only, and it didn't matter if that person were a devil who wouldn't hesitate to commit the Ten Evils. Where had our most basic common sense gone to?

I accepted the check Joseph held out to me. It was as if I heard "Go!" at a racecourse. My work had now officially begun. The very instant I put the check in my purse I thought of the lawyer I had met the day before. If I didn't have this check I wouldn't be investing my time or energy in Joseph's venture. This world is run on money.

I thought I ought to tell him the truth—that I really wasn't a Christian—just in case my behavior exceeded propriety and offended him. For example, as everyone knows, Christians advocate "turning the other cheek." I couldn't do this. There was no way I would renounce an old grudge. If I didn't have the money for a lawyer and the lawsuit, I would still think of side-alley and backdoor ways to get back the profits I had lost.

"Joseph, I have to apologize. I've got to tell you, I am still not a Christian. But before I die, I would like to find a church and be baptized, because my mother's parents were Christians, and so is my mother. Just in case after death there really is a soul and I couldn't find them there, I would feel so lost and lonely."

Joseph stared at me wide-eyed. He looked just like his mother, Lucy, with that same pair of dark eyes. "How can you think that? How would you know when you're going to die? What if there's no chance of being saved? At this hour, at this very moment, you can accept Jesus Christ as your savior."

I shook my head firmly, "I haven't got what it takes to be a Christian. I'd rather not have God watching me."

Joseph seemed to be still thinking of something. I was worried that he would start some tiresome sermon, so I stole a march on him by asking, "You won't drop this arrangement of me working with you because I'm not a Christian, will you?"

"Of course not."

"I will seriously and sincerely deal with this question of faith. Let me think it over by myself. Is that all right?"

"I'll respect your wishes."

Joseph smiled as he gazed at me. And in that smile I read tolerance and sympathy. I knew that in the eyes of Christians, a person who had not accepted Jesus Christ the Savior was truly pitiable. Joseph's dark eyes radiated a mild and tranquil luster. His eyes were so clear and pure, I felt indescribably moved, as if a mute string had been plucked in the innermost depths of my heart. I had made a living out in the wide world for so many years now and had dealt with people of every shape and shade. I had gotten used to watching the greedy and cruel eyes of jackals and wolves pursuing their prey. I always had to be on my guard, but in spite of this, I still became a tasty snack for those beasts. No, this isn't saying it right. I too am one of those greedy jackals and wolves. I'd skin a flea for what I could get and take the meat from another person's mouth. I am a sorry loser in the arena of life.

3.

THE TRAIN SET off with a long blast of its whistle. Chaotic feelings of kindness and grievance, love and hate, stayed outside on the platform and gradually receded into the distance along with that forest-like cluster of buildings. My thoughts cut across time and space to linger on Old Town. It wasn't the little modern city I had seen five years ago. It was the kind you'd see in a faded old photograph, one from a more distant time in the pitter-pattering of that never-ending drizzly rain.

Let me close my eyes and search for the first impressions of Old Town. I see my grandfather standing by the little coal stove boiling cow's milk for me. In those days, each family could order only one bottle of milk. I often drank milk under the gaze of my cousins who were fairly drooling with envy. I didn't like the layer of film that congealed from the milk fat so Grandpa or Grandma always used their chopsticks to skim off the film. I didn't understand why the only bottle of milk had to be given to me. I still couldn't grasp that I received such special treatment because my life was special. With my parents divorced, Grandpa, Grandma, and my uncles felt an extraordinary tenderness toward me, their little orphan girl. Giving me the milk had been the unanimous decision of the whole family.

I can also recall impressions that were even earlier than those of drinking milk. I was playing by the side of the well. I wasn't much taller than the height of the rock wall around the mouth of the well. Stretching my head forward to look down into the well, I saw the faces of a little girl and boy reflected side-by-side on the surface of the water. The little boy's name was Chaofan. The year I turned three, Mother crossed the entire vastness of China and brought me all the way from the northwest frontier to Old Town. So I speak in a "northern guy" style. The little boy said, "This is a well. Your granny washes clothing here." The little boy took hold of the front of my jacket and repeated, "Clothing."

This was the first scene I captured and held in my memory. Chaofan walks out of my hazy memories, and, true to vivid life, appears right before my eyes. I see Chaofan in his childhood years. I see his sad eyes. His sadness has enveloped my fate from the start. Even though we have broken up for more than ten years now, I still can't shake off his presence in my mind.

For a long time I never mentioned to anybody this man who has haunted me my entire life. Only my relatives in Old Town who still live in the past suppose we are a devoted and affectionate couple. From time to time, I get a telephone call from Mother and hear her ask, "And how is Chaofan?" Invariably I go blank for a moment and then simply say, "He's fine." So far, I have never met the right man. So I am indifferent, too lazy to let people know that I have corrected my errors, lest during long and sleepless nights they should sigh over the tragic upheavals of my life. I am actually not too tragic or miserable. If I had wanted to get married, I could have done it ten times over these past ten years. Doesn't having a new boyfriend in each year of my single life seem excessive? Right! Legally I am still Chaofan's wife. I'm just too busy and don't have the time to take care of the various necessary divorce documents. I'm going to wait until I actually decide to get married again before processing all that red tape. Until now, no man has motivated me enough to go through all that.

Oh, heaven! What more should I say? To tell a holy and pure believer about my utterly chaotic private life would be just like blaspheming against the Holy Spirit!

Joseph was still mildly and calmly watching me. His eyes told me that in his world there was a real and true God. I envied him with an envy for all people who had a belief in the divine. It was just like I envied those frenzied soccer fans on the soccer field Those people interested me more than all those fit and vigorous soccer stars themselves. Every time I saw their faces smeared with color and waving small flags in tears of either exaltation or desolation for goals scored or missed, I truly envied them. I would never be able to reach their state of self-oblivion. To this day, I still don't understand soccer.

At the seashore, Jesus met two disciples who were casting for fish. He said, "Follow me." The two fishermen threw down their nets and went with Jesus. This made me remember first hearing about kidnapping when I was little. The old folks often warned little children, "Don't run wildly about. There are wicked people out there, kidnappers. They'll give you one good smack on the back of your head and off you'll go with them in a complete daze. Later they'll sell you away to some far-off place."

If you can make me believe in the existence of God, you're going to have to have the knack of these kidnappers. A slap to knock out the knowledge and experience stored up in my brain and return me—totally unconscious—to the chaos of the time of my birth.

⌘　⌘　⌘

Let me return to Old Town, back to my grandma's Old Town. It's also your grandma's Old Town.

The well was at the northwest corner of the crossroads by West Gate in Old Town. My grandma's house was at its southwest corner. In between ran a little street. Behind the well was a yard enclosed by a wooden picket fence. The yard was completely planted with flowers. There was a small church there. When I played by the well, I didn't yet know what a church was. All I saw was a pretty wooden building. Grandpa and Grandma and lots of people sang songs in that building. The old lady who played the organ was Chaofan's granny on his daddy's side. Standing on the platform speaking was his grandpa. People called him "Pastor."

The West Gate church had been gone for many years by the time I left Old Town. One day in Lompoc, as I was walking along a little road on my way to work at the restaurant, I looked up suddenly and saw a small church right in front of me. How familiar that wooden fence was, and inside it the yard with all the flowers in full bloom! They clustered thickly around the plain wooden building. It was as if I had already known every tiny thing about this place. In my distraction, I thought I was walking by the West Gate street corner of my childhood and if I turned around, I would see Grandma, standing in the doorway under the oleander tree, waiting for me to return from school. At the church door stood a wooden placard that said this church had been built in a certain year at the end of the nineteenth century. One hundred years. Anything in America with a one-hundred-year history would be exceedingly valuable. My West Gate church certainly also had a one-hundred-year history. But when the bulldozers flattened it, they did so without the slightest sentimentality or hesitation. Our history is too long and heavy. We don't need to commemorate it. Now West Gate is all tall buildings. The church has become a chunk of concrete ground called West Gate Square. Who would now link West Gate Square with a church?

Joseph, what will your Old Town trip get you? I haven't the slightest bit of confidence in all this.

You say you have already begun to get results…that from my narrative, Old Town is slowly emerging from faded photographs into something with three dimensions.

I suddenly feel like a white-haired old lady relating long-forgotten events. I am not really old. American women say that life begins at forty. But what monumental and earthshaking changes this forty-year-old China has gone through! I am lucky to have witnessed all of these. Awhile back, my daughter asked me, "Mom, if you could, would you be willing to trade your age with mine?" I said no, there had never been a generation that has gone through more than my own has. Furthermore, I am still not old. There's still more of life to come.

You know that Old Town has a two-thousand-year history. You have collected a lot of information about the place. These ice-cold words are saved in your computer, just like lifeless props placed on a stage that lacks an actor to play the leading role.

Let me tell you an Old Town story pieced together from several generations of one of its families. Not one of its members ever left any earthshaking deed in the green bamboo strips of historical record. They came into the world as plain folk and went out just the same. In the billion worlds of the endless universe, they were as inconsequential as drops of water in a vast ocean. Generation after generation of ordinary lives are just the cycle of comings and goings, but it is such people who keep ancient Old Town fresh and alive.

CHAPTER TWO – NINE LIVES

1.

CATS HAVE NINE lives. That's what we always said in Old Town. One day at twilight, Rongmei, the daughter of Grandma's mute neighbor, went out back to throw what looked like a dead cat onto the side of the city moat. Rongmei told me that cats have nine lives and that when this dead cat received the earth's breath it would come back to life. And as it turned out, early the next day when, school book pack on my back, I went to invite Rongmei to join me on my way to school, I saw the dead cat casually padding about under the sky well.

My grandpa also had nine lives. By chance, he was the ninth child born into his family, hence his childhood name: "Ninth Brother." Ninth Brother's mother bled to death after giving birth to him. One hundred years ago, there was nothing unusual about women dying as they gave birth. Perhaps this was why men in Old China wanted the proverbial "three wives and four concubines." The more wives you had, the greater your sense of security. Ninth Brother's mother was his father's fourth wife. For three days after he was born, Ninth Brother neither ate nor drank nor moved. He was just like Rongmei's dead cat. The family elders decided to place him in the coffin with his mother and bury both of them together. The story goes that the very instant the coffin was covered, Ninth Brother let out a weak cry. This cry from the coffin saved a tiny life.

One summer, when he was eight years old, Ninth Brother fell ill with a strange disease that infested his whole body with scabies and burned him with a high fever that just wouldn't come down. By this time, his father had already died and all the affairs of the household were in the hands of Eldest Brother and his wife, "Big Sister-in-Law." With three generations of a family of several dozen members all living under one roof, the little boy who would be my grandpa counted for about as much as a cat. He was nothing more than another bowl and another set of chopsticks on the dinner table. Although he had numerous stepbrothers and stepsisters, both older and younger than he was, Ninth Brother's mother had given birth to him only. Within the household, there were also Second Mother and Third Mother, but with their "dim eyesight," they could see only the children that they themselves had borne.

Ninth Brother lived in a small room on one of the sides of the back courtyard. He had already lain sick on his bed for several days before someone discovered that a little one was missing from the dinner table. That night, Big Sister-in-Law found Ninth Brother unconscious and in convulsions. She told the family's hired hand, Ah Mu, to move him to the little alley outside the back door to "receive the earth's breath." She said that if Ninth Brother couldn't survive this night, that was just his fate. Big Sister-in-Law was very much a skinflint by nature. In her Economic Plan, there were no medical fees and she used all sorts of bizarre methods to deal with the family's illnesses and pains. The most she was willing to do was provide a cheap, "thin" coffin. She said that when one's fate arrived, the most skilled doctor with the most marvelous medicines would be of no use. Ah Mu placed Ninth Brother on the ice-cold steps of the back alley. He probably didn't feel altogether comfortable doing this, so he also put out the household's tawny dog, Big Yellow, to keep Ninth Brother company.

That back alley ran between the residences on two thorough-fares of high repute in Old Town. In local parlance, these were called "lanes." Hence, Stipend Lane and Officials Lane. These were where the wealthy people of that time lived. There were no big gates onto this back alley where the back walls of one after another of the "imposing dwellings and spacious courtyards" of Stipend Lane and Officials Lane faced each other. Normally only servants went through narrow back doors into and out of this alley.

Big Yellow lay down on his stomach by the side of Ninth Brother and began licking his little master with a soft and warmly moist tongue. The dog licked him over and over, from the top of his head right down to the soles of his feet. Big Yellow was one year older than Ninth Brother. They had played together from their earliest years. Out of the entire household it seemed only Big Yellow was excited to see Ninth Brother every morning. It was as if they had been separated for months, not just one night. A few days earlier, Ninth Brother had gotten a scolding from Big Sister-in-Law for eating an extra half bowl of rice. When the boy went back to his little wing room, Big Yellow seemed to sense this unfair treatment, and he followed in and gazed mournfully at Ninth Brother. The boy hugged the dog, and said, "Big Yellow, Big Yellow, you're an orphan, just like me. Every day I never get enough to eat. Do you?"

Ninth Brother saw his mother come through the mirror on his wall. She opened her arms wide to hold him. In her embrace he gradu-ally grew smaller and smaller, as small as an infant in swaddling. He reached out his little hand to feel his mother's smooth hair and cheek. *Oh, Mother, you didn't die, and I didn't get big.* He fell into an untroubled sleep. In his mother's embrace, he would never open his eyes again.

It was midnight. Far off, from deep in the alley approached a man bearing a lantern on a pole. The lantern was just a pale yellow glow by the man's foot. The man passed the back door of Ninth

Brother's home but never saw the little boy curled up at the foot of the wall. Big Yellow knew all about humans. He seemed to sense in this passerby a ray of hope for saving his young master. Getting up, the dog stretched out his neck and let forth a mournful howl. At this, the man couldn't help turning about in midstep, and raising his lantern, saw the dog and the child.

In those days, Chinese men wore their hair in a long braid, and this fellow was no exception. But he was a foreigner. He was a preacher, come from some Western country. Old Town folk called him Mr. Qiao. From his braid, you could deduce that he had been in China for a fairly long time. Old Town was such a small backwater of a place that the arrival of this blond, blue-eyed foreigner several years before had caused quite a commotion. And for a rather long time the front of the place where he stayed was even livelier than what you'd find today at the panda house in the zoo. People crowded around on tiptoes and craned their necks as they gazed at him. Every step, every move he made, became for the townspeople the stuff of laughter and comment over a cup of tea or after a meal.

On this night, Mr. Qiao had been preaching in someone's home in Stipend Lane. The master of the house would in no way allow such an honored guest to slip out the back door. All the old buildings of Old Town were made of wood planking, so even a rat moving through them made scritching and scratching sounds. Mr. Qiao worried that in crossing through three layers of courtyards, he would disturb the old folks and children who were now soundly asleep, and so he insisted on leaving by the back way. Had Mr. Qiao gone by way of the Stipend Lane Main Gate, Ninth Brother's sleep would have been the eternal one this time. Mr. Qiao never thought that the door over there led into the child's home, but supposed that this was some little vagabond, fallen sick while begging on the streets. He gathered up the unconscious boy in his arms and rushed to the home of a doctor by Drum Tower. Several years before, under Mr. Qiao's direction, this doctor had dismantled the Buddhist altar in his home and converted to Christianity.

⌘   ⌘   ⌘

Early the next morning, Ah Mu opened the back door. The only one there under the wall was Big Yellow. Panic-stricken, Ah Mu dashed out to search every corner of the alley, but nowhere was there even a trace of Ninth Brother. It was raining that day, and, his whole body soaking wet, Ah Mu dashed back home and rapped on Big Sister-in-Law's door. She opened the door with an angry shout, her hair hanging lankly. "Whose death tidings have you brought?"

"Ninth…Ninth Brother's …gone," Ah Mu stammered.

Big Sister-in-Law went on casually combing her hair. "*Ai*! That was his fate. Go to the coffin shop on West Street and order one. Something made of fir planks will be good enough."

"Big Sister-in-Law, there's no one there! Ninth Brother's disappeared!"

"No! It can't be! Where could he have gone to? Go look in his room."

With a great rattle and clatter, Ah Mu crossed through the parlor and ran to the back courtyard. The door to the little wing was wide open and the little bed empty. Ah Mu turned around then and ran clatteringly back to Big Sister-in-Law. "He's not there. Last night I was the one to shut the back door and I also shut Big Yellow outside. This morning the only one there was Big Yellow."

Eldest Brother and Big Sister-in-Law sat at opposite ends of the tea table in the parlor, looking each other straight in the eyes. Then Eldest Brother's temper exploded, "This was all because of your devilish idea. A cat may have nine lives, but where has a person got that many?"

"How can there be somebody dead if there's no corpse! He's pulled through for sure. I've saved his life, but that ingrate left without so much as a by-your-leave!" his wife shrieked at him.

Afraid of more henpecking, eldest brother made no retort but just went quietly out the back door and, taking Ah Mu with him, braved the rain in search of Ninth Brother in all of the lanes and alleyways in the neighborhood. In Stipend Lane, the Lins were a big and prestigious family. For three generations back, they had all been literati and officials. Eldest Brother ordered the family members and servants to say only that the household dog was lost in case they ran into any of their neighbors. However, reports of how the Lins' Big Sister-in-Law tormented "the little uncle" still spread widely throughout the small town. People said that Little Uncle could no longer bear to live and so killed himself.

⌘　⌘　⌘

Ninth Brother suckled at his mother's breast. Once again, he stretched out his little hand to feel her hair and cheeks. He wanted to tell her that he had a scary dream in which he was an orphan child with no father or mother.

All of a sudden, Mother pushed him away with a cold look on her face. An instant later, she was nowhere to be seen. As he ran back and forth from the front of his home to the back in search of her, he heard the banging sound of the wooden floorboards beneath someone's steps. Abruptly raising his head, he bumped straight into Big Sister-in-Law. She berated him ferociously, "Have you lost your soul?" Ninth Brother replied, "I want to find my Ma." "Your ma's long dead. She died because you were bad luck for her!" "No! Ma didn't die! You're tricking me! You're all tricking me!" Ninth Brother's heart just tore within him, and with a loud cry, he broke into bitter weeping.

The next thing Ninth Brother saw, mistily and through tears, were two pairs of jewel-like, bright blue eyes. *Where am I?* He had heard of heaven and hell...that good people went up to heaven after they died and bad ones to hell after *they* died. *I haven't done anything bad, so I must be in heaven now, and in heaven the celestial immortals grow a pair of nice-looking blue eyes.* He wanted to find a mirror to see if his own eyes had now changed color.

Mrs. Qiao was just giving Ninth Brother some cow's milk to drink when she saw him open his eyes. "Thank God, you've finally come to!" she exclaimed in surprise.

Is this celestial immortal what my mother has turned into? Ninth Brother just stared at her, not daring to move or speak, ever so fearful that in the blink of an eye he would tumble back down to earth and land right in front of Big Sister-in–Law.

Mr. Qiao stroked Ninth Brother's forehead. "You're much better now, child. You'll soon become as strong as a young colt. Tell me, where is your family?"

Ninth Brother just kept staring wide-eyed.

"Maybe he doesn't understand what we're saying," Mrs. Qiao suggested.

Actually, their Old Town speech *was* pretty hard to follow. Next, they both conferred for a bit in some kind of language Ninth Brother couldn't understand at all. *Surely that's heaven-talk*, Ninth Brother thought.

Mrs. Qiao bent over and continued to feed him the milk while Mr. Qiao, with much "dancing hands and stomping feet," as we say, finally got it across to him. "Child, you're going to get better and we'll help you find your daddy and ma."

For a long time, this foreign couple took Ninth Brother to be a deaf and dumb child.

⌘ ⌘ ⌘

Two months later, the Lin family had more or less forgotten the ninth brother they once had. One day Ah Mu went to the West Gate Rice Shop. This shop sold old rice. In those years, only poor people lived in the neighborhood of the West Gate's city moat. Such people were willing to buy old rice. It was cheap, and when you cooked it, twelve *liang* of old rice could make as much as one *jin* of the fresh kind. Ever since Big Sister-in-Law had been managing the household, nobody ate fresh rice. So Ah Mu would always pass up the nearby places when going out to buy rice.

Mr. Qiao's residence was next to the West Gate Rice Shop. Ah Mu lowered a bag of rice from his shoulder, and, pretending to wipe away some sweat, looked in through the gate. Even after several years, his curiosity about this foreign couple continued unabated. Once he had bumped right into Mrs. Qiao, and saw that pair of crystal-blue eyes. When Mrs. Qiao greeted him with a smile, he beat a panicky retreat. Back home, he conveyed to the other servants his expert position on the subject. "Foreigners are werecats, but they still keep their cat eyes." This time, when Ah Mu looked through the gate, he saw a little boy sitting in the sunlight of the sky well. *Heh! There are even little foreigners here! But how come this child doesn't look like a cat?* Taking a closer look, Ah Mu almost fainted dead away. He thought he had bumped into a devil. *That child is Ninth Brother, clear as paint!*

After Ninth Brother's "death," the Lin residence had become ghost-ridden. The servant girl, Ah Hua, saw something with Ninth Brother's shape floating about in the cooking area one midnight, amid a din of banging pans, bowls, ladles, and spoons. They said ever since he was little he had never eaten a full meal, so that after death he had become a "hungry ghost." Big Sister-in-Law became extremely frightened when she heard this and ordered Ah Hua to put a bowl of cooked rice on the top of the stove every night.

Ah Mu stooped and shouldered the bag of rice. He wanted to get away but couldn't resist turning around for one more look. Ninth Brother was still there, leisurely eating a banana.

"Ninth Brother! Ninth Brother!" Ah Mu stepped boldly toward him.

Ninth Brother was transfixed in amazement. The banana he was eating looked like it would fall right out of his mouth.

"Ninth Brother, you never died, right?"

Just then, Mr. and Mrs. Qiao walked in from the street. They warmly greeted Ah Mu and invited him to rest for a bit and drink a cup of tea. Ah Mu just stood there stock-still, the bag of rice on his shoulder.

Mr. Qiao could see there was something peculiar going on and signed to Ninth Brother, "Do you know this gentleman?"

For weeks on end, day and night, Ninth Brother had never opened his mouth to speak in the presence of his saviors and bene-factors, for he feared being sent back home to Big Sister-in-Law. So he made the best of this misunderstanding and played the part of a mute. He frequently dreamed he was being sent home and each time he would cry himself awake. On this particular day, Old Town was enjoying rare clear skies, and Ninth Brother was feeling good. But Ah Mu's sudden appearance was really a bolt from the blue. His worst worry had finally happened. He didn't dare shake his head to say that he didn't know Ah Mu. First, the banana slipped out of his mouth and next, he burst into tears.

Ah Mu noticed the boy's ruddy complexion and neat attire and knew that Ninth Brother was doing all right. What's more, the people of Old Town all knew that this foreign couple were Living Buddhas, who helped lift the needy out of misery and distress. Ninth Brother was doing better here than he would at home and surely, he wouldn't want to go back there to be bullied again by Big

Sister-in-Law. So he said to the boy, "Don't be afraid, I won't tell Big Sister-in-Law. It'll be just as if I never saw you."

Ninth Brother looked at Mr. Qiao, then at Mrs. Qiao, and blurted out, "I don't want to go back home with him!"

So this child wasn't deaf or dumb after all! The preacher and his wife never imagined that a child could pretend to be deaf and mute for two whole months out of fear of going home. *What kind of a home was that?* With the appearance of this pathetic deaf-mute child, they had already begun to plan a school for deaf-mutes in Old Town.

Mr. Qiao took the little boy in his arms and said, "Never fear, you're our child."

The preacher lifted the big sack of rice from Ah Mu's shoulders and led him to the back parlor for some tea and a chat. And after hearing all about Ninth Brother's pitiful existence, Mr. Qiao's blue eyes filled with tears.

Ah Mu returned to the Lin household and for several days stifled his urge to talk. Then, finally, he could stand it no longer and told Ah Hua his strange tale. In turn, Ah Hua herself couldn't resist disclosing this to the servant girl next door. Word spreads quickly through a place as small as Old Town and eventually this reached the ear of Big Sister-in-Law. She now worried that Ninth Brother's return home would not only bring another mouth to the dining table, but, worse, she would have to spend money on his schooling. So she kept all this to herself and didn't tell her husband, Eldest Brother.

Meanwhile, Mr. and Mrs. Qiao found themselves in a difficult position. On the one hand, they had comforted the little boy by saying that they would protect him against suffering any further wrongs. On the other, they also felt that they ought to let his family members know that he was still alive and obtain their approval before formally adopting him.

Just when they were preparing to pay a call on Eldest Brother and Big Sister-in-Law at the Lin family home, Eldest Brother heard from an old friend that Ninth Brother had been adopted by foreigners. This was making real asses of the Lins and bringing discredit to the family's venerable name. He didn't bother going home to discuss this first with "the Old Lady," but headed right over to West Gate, and with his hands clasped in front of him in greeting he burst into the Qiao residence. "Sir, I have just heard that you saved a little brother of my household. I truly do not know how best to express my gratitude. You both are Bodhisattvas come back into the world." "Not Bodhisattva," Mr. Qiao replied, "but God, the Ruler Above All, sent us to help your little brother." Eldest Brother had not given much thought to how "God" and Bodhisattva differed from each other, but he wholeheartedly wanted to bring his little brother back home.

Eldest Brother took hold of Ninth Brother's hand. Ninth Brother neither struggled nor resisted, but it seemed with every step he took he looked back, eyes overflowing with tears, at Mr. and Mrs. Qiao.

⌘　⌘　⌘

Many years later, Mr. Qiao concluded his mission of preaching in Old Town and received an appointment by his church to head its theological seminary in Shanghai. By then, the men of China had already cut off their braids.

2.

THERE'S A CHINESE expression, "Fly the womb and change one's bones." It means "to undergo a complete transformation." Think of a boy molding a figure out of mud. He looks at it and isn't satisfied, and so he crumbles it up and molds a new one. My grandpa's Big Sister-in-Law still called Christianity "Foreign Buddha." Although she was full of doubts and perplexities and thought she understood what she really didn't, Christianity made her "fly the womb and change her bones." In other words, she totally remolded herself. There was a spirit above her, and this spirit watched her every step and every move. Big Sister-in-Law was afraid that her earlier harsh abuse of Ninth Brother would someday bring retribution to her, so now she was more loving and considerate of him than she was toward her own children. I've seen the portrait of her in her later years, all benevolence and goodness. It's hard to imagine that she had been so cruel as to cast a gravely ill eight-year-old child into the street.

Ninth Brother graduated from senior high school in Old Town and Mr. Qiao paved his way to Shanghai for higher education. Before he left, Big Sister-in-Law herself sewed a quilted silk jacket and leggings for Ninth Brother. In perpetually springlike Old Town, people there called anywhere else "the North." The North was cold, and in winter your nose could freeze and drop off. Shanghai was "the North" too. Big Sister-in-Law, afraid that Ninth Brother's nose would drop off, also specially sewed a foot-wide, silken quilted muffler.

She sat stitching away by the oil lamp. She sewed up all the scars on Ninth Brother's heart. "The wife of an elder brother should be treated like one's mother"—so she was his mother, and he was more filial toward her than were even her own real sons and daughters.

In those days, Big Sister-in-Law had engaged the matchmaker, Mother Sun, to tiptoe on her tiny bound feet throughout the length and breadth of Old Town to act as a go-between for Ninth Brother. Big Sister-in-Law wanted to settle his marriage before he went off on his long journey. She worried that Ninth Brother would be adopted into some Northerner's family as a son-in-law and take on their name. If that happened, the Lin family would lose a male carrier of the ancestral name and when she went to the other world, all the assembled ancestors and family forebears there would take her to task for this.

Mother Sun took Big Sister-in-Law and Ninth Brother around Stipend Lane and Officials Lane to meet various prospects. Though she now believed in Jesus, Big Sister-in-Law was still very particular about achieving an appropriate match. Stipend Lane and Officials Lane residents were all prominent and important families, and only the daughter of a grand family would do for a young master of the Lin family. Ninth Brother, though, was uninterested in the prospective partners being introduced to him. It was just that he couldn't bear opposing Big Sister-in-Law's good intentions. So, puppet-like, he accompanied Mother Sun to family after family to view potential spouses.

People in the West suppose that in feudal times Chinese marriages were totally determined by the parents and the matchmaker, and that the moment before the groom and bride entered the marital chamber, they knew nothing about the sort of person they had married. It's always like this in the movies. If that were reality, then Old Town had already become enlightened by the beginning of the twentieth century. Here the tradition always was to introduce prospective marriage partners to each other. These men and women met each other in the company of their parents and the matchmaker, and only afterward was it decided whether to proceed with a marriage.

When the man called on a prospective spouse, the woman's parents would serve him poached eggs. My grandpa ate poached eggs in a lot of houses, but in none of these did he ever see a girl he took a fancy to. As Big Sister-in-Law anxiously watched Ninth Brother's departure day looming ever closer, she invited a number of her fellow congregation members to the house to pray for his marriage. That evening, she called him to her and told him if he couldn't decide on a spouse, his trip would be postponed. "I can't believe that in all of Old Town there's not one girl who appeals to you." In fact, early on there *had* been a girl who had struck his fancy, a girl he often saw at services at the West Gate church. He knew she was the third daughter of the boss of the Guo Family Cloth Shop at Drum Tower. The church members called her "Third Sister." All along, Ninth Brother had wanted to tell Big Sister-in-Law to have Mother Sun sound out prospects with the Guos, but he was so timid by nature that he didn't know how to bring up the subject. Besides, he had absolutely no hold on any winning strategy. Big Sister-in-Law very possibly might refuse. How could that sort of small-time family measure up to entry into the Lin family? Ninth Brother stood in front of Big Sister-in-Law for a long while, his head bowed. Finally, he got the courage to say, "I am a Christian and I would like to find a girl who loves the Lord. Third Miss of Guo's Cloth Shop at Drum Tower loves the Lord." Although Big Sister-in-Law wasn't too satisfied, she didn't insist against it, and the next day she sent Mother Sun to discuss marriage at the Guo home.

Unexpectedly, "Boss" Guo had no intention to marry off Third Miss, at least not for the time being. He had four daughters and wanted them to leave home one by one in the proper order. Eldest Miss at twenty-two still had no "mother-in-law's home," as they say.

In those years, a twenty-two-year-old woman might already be a mother many times over. Mr. and Mrs. Guo were in poor health, and with several boys still very young, they depended on the two oldest daughters to manage the shop's business and run the household. For the past few years, their parents couldn't bear letting these girls go off in marriage, and it was with heavy and care-laden hearts that Mr. and Mrs. Guo now saw the two girls becoming unmarriageable old maids.

Mother Sun hurried back on her little toes to the Lin family with information. The bridge of Eldest Miss Guo's nose was too sharp, probably a sign of an ill-omened fate. Second Miss Guo's full-moon face signified great wealth and honor. In the neighborhood around Drum Tower, she was renowned for both her "civil" and "military" capabilities, being highly literate (her "civil" side) and able to wield a ladle and prepare a nine- or ten-table banquet (her "military" side). Big Sister-in-Law was pleased indeed to hear this, thinking that bringing a daughter-in-law like this into the home could save on the wages of two servant girls. She put on her embroidered-flower slippers and tried to drag Ninth Brother off to meet his prospective wife. Ninth Brother, however, stubbornly refused. Though he was an introverted person, he also had an indomitable and tenacious will. Once he set his mind on something, no one short of God himself could make him change it. That year, Old Town got its very first photo studio. In those days, this novelty was quite a sensation. Ninth Brother went to the studio and had his picture taken to leave with Big Sister-in-Law. He hoped that this photograph could substitute for him when she visited the Guo home. Whenever Third Miss Guo could leave home in marriage *and* be willing to marry the man in this picture, he would return home to finalize the marriage.

⌘   ⌘   ⌘

My grandpa set off to study in Shanghai, filled with an adolescent's worries and desolation about going so far away from his native place. In those days, getting to Shanghai from Old Town involved a three-day and three-night voyage. His fellow passengers were mostly young students attending school away from their hometowns. The blood of these small town and enormously smug young lords fairly boiled within them to be charging out of remote Old Town, where "the mountains were high and the emperor far off," and into the very heart of this stormy period of the early Republic. They grouped together on the boat, full of impassioned and noble sentiment, and longed for the future, as if each and every one of them grasped in his very own hand the lifeline of the world.

No one paid any attention to solitary Ninth Brother, keeping to himself and reading the Bible. From time to time, he would raise his head to gaze at the far-distant horizon, thinking of Third Sister whom he had left behind in Old Town. Her voice was really good and her hymn-singing a marvel to hear. Ninth Brother took it as a matter of course that Mr. Qiao would arrange for his study at the theological seminary. And when he thought of becoming a pastor who, together with Third Sister, would work for the Church, Ninth Brother became extremely happy.

Three days later, Mr. and Mrs. Qiao, from whom he had been separated for so long, met Ninth Brother at the dock. Straightway they took Ninth Brother to the medical college the Church had just opened. Mrs. Qiao said that they had prayed to God for his studies and that, one night in a dream, she saw Ninth Brother wearing a white jacket and treating sick people. Quite by coincidence the medical college was just then recruiting students. She saw this as a decree from God, for God understood Ninth Brother better than they did. It seemed more appropriate that this introverted and reticent child become a doctor rather than a pastor.

3·

MY GRANDMA'S OLDER sister, my great-aunt, is now 102 years old. Today she lives in the nursing home in Old Town. Physically, she's near the point of total collapse. Every day a nurse has to lift her onto her wheelchair and push her out into the sunlight. Her mind is still lively, though over the past twenty years she has borne to the fullest an inner torment. The fact was, during the decades of the government's single child policy, the five nephews on her side of the family produced only girl children. She herself had only one son who never married. If her husband's family line comes to an end, that's of no great concern to her. But her side has no male descendents and centenarian Great-Auntie dwells on this day and night. Maybe this is why her mind has stayed so sharp. Every day she puts on her "old age" glasses and sets to work on her correspondence. One of her letters can take ten to twenty days to complete, or even longer. In these she requests the government to allow the Guo family nephews to have more than one child, by reason of their descent from the Tang dynasty general, Guo Ziyi.[2] Previously the Guo ancestral shrine near Drum Tower recorded the history of the clan's proliferation and this was where her forefather's name appeared. Guo Ziyi belonged to one of the minority peoples. How did she know this? And how did she know about the government's policy of permitting the minorities to have a second child?

Great-Auntie wrote to Chairman Mao in Beijing, and when the nurse told her that the current chairman was named Jiang,

---

[2] Guo Ziyi (697–781 CE). Born in Huzhou, Shaanxi Province, Guo was instrumental in crushing the great An-Shi Rebellion and other western frontier conflicts during the Tang dynasty. He is revered in China as one of its greatest generals.

she thought that Chairman Mao had retired, and so readdressed the letter to Chairman Jiang. Occasionally, though, she would get mixed up and still write "For the attention of Chairman Mao." She also still wrote to the Old Town government and her many relatives. One after another letter was mailed out, and one after another came back. The nurse gave these returned letters to Great-Auntie's Little Daughter. Little Daughter was a retired professor. She hadn't told her mother that the chairmen had been unable to receive her letters. Nor did she tell her that all her nephews' wives had long since passed the age for bearing children. Every time she dropped by for a visit, Little Daughter would bring her envelopes, paper, and stamps, and encourage her in her letter writing and struggle on behalf of her nephews' "second fetus." Isn't this both a grand ideal and a fine way to spend time? And so the one-hundred-year-old lady's days at the nursing home are completely filled. Great-Auntie's eyes show more luster than those of the old folk around her who are actually many years her junior. She may have broken the Guinness Book of Records for life span and it was all for the sake of continuing the Guo clan line.

However, long before Great-Auntie came up with her genealogical arguments, the several generations of Guos who earned their livelihood at the little cloth shop at Drum Tower street corner had been the most unremarkable people in the Old Town marketplace. Grandma's mother gave birth to four girls in succession before going on to bear five boys, also one after the other. By the time the youngest boy had been weaned from the breast, Grandma's father was sick with all kind of ailments, and so Second Daughter took over management of the shop. This was because Eldest Daughter didn't know how to keep accounts, often measuring out a *zhang* of cloth but charging for only seven *chi* worth.

Second Daughter, or "Second Sister"—that was Granny. My grandpa had liked Third Sister, but through a strange and complicated turn of events married Second Daughter. Hand in hand, they sustained each other through many decades of life. I have never known a more deeply affectionate and loving couple.

⌘   ⌘   ⌘

The Guo daughters were celebrated for their intelligence and beauty. Eldest Daughter, even though no good at bookkeeping, could chant poetry and compose verse as well as write with a fine hand. Had she been young in this day and age, my great-aunt would certainly have been called a "babe" writer. Second Sister was keen-witted and capable. Both the "interior ministry" and the "foreign affairs" of the Guo home were totally in her hands. Then there was Third Sister, even more extraordinarily clever and intelligent, and looking like the proverbial celestial beauty that had descended to earth. Third Sister was her father and mother's darling.

But the Guo sons? Every one of them was an unmentionable "Ah Dou the Weak."[3] When they were young, they were stubborn, ignorant, and always making trouble. Grown up, they became hard drinkers, opium smokers, slaves of the flesh. People always said that there was something wrong with the *feng shui* of the Guo ancestral tombs. In those days, very few rich people sent their daughters to study in "Western" schools. Only by a stretch of the imagination could the Guos be considered a comfortably well-off family, but still they were willing to spend the money to send Third Sister to one of these places.

---

[3]   "Ah Dou" (Liu Chan) was the weak and incompetent son of the heroic Liu Bei, king of Shu-Han in *Romance of the Three Kingdoms*, China's beloved epic of the sixty-year civil war and chaotic political struggle following the collapse of the Eastern Han dynasty in 220 AD.

Before Granny left home in marriage, Third Sister suddenly got violently ill and died. I heard that my great-grandfather couldn't bear this shock and that winter he died coughing blood.

Granny's sister-in-law, the wife of the eldest of her brothers, scrupulously fulfilled her duties and responsibilities as Big Sister-in-Law. She hung over a dozen painted portraits of departed Guos on the four walls of her narrow little building in the courtyard. She lived through the change of the Qing dynasty and the downward spiral in the family's conditions. Though she led a desperate and uprooted life for several decades, these pictures accompanied her in their pristine state. Among these were portraits of my granny's grandparents, parents, and several departed younger brothers. There were also pictures of two younger sisters who had died when they were just babies. The only one who had no picture was Third Sister, the one that Grandpa liked.

What was she like, that Third Sister who could make Ninth Brother fall so deeply in love with her?

When I was little, Granny would often take me from West Gate to Drum Tower, to her old home, her own parents' home. The eating, drinking, whoring, and gambling of her wastrel brothers had finished this place off. The only thing left was a small rundown house filled with ancestral portraits. The street we walked along was called West Street. Not far off from Drum Tower, on the north side of West Street, was a dilapidated residence compound. From the main gate, you could look in and see the many households squeezed and crowded in there. Under the sky well, there were always clothes of every imaginable color hanging out to dry. Only a few dark red stone steps in front of the main door still looked smooth and bright from the years of buffing and polishing. Every time my grandmother passed by here she couldn't help slowing down and peering fondly inside. This compound had been her real home, where she had been born, and where several generations of Guos had likewise been born. Whether or not I fully understood, she just always wanted to tell me about all the bygone events connected to that place and her family.

Third Sister had been born in the small wing off the sky well. Her mother had already given birth to two girls. That the third birth also was a girl clearly made the Guo clan elders exceedingly disappointed. Her mother cried for several days and nights because of that belly of hers failing to meet expectations. She wouldn't let this infant suck at her breasts. In those days, getting rid of a female infant was no different from flinging out a newborn kitten or a puppy. She quoted the old maxim to her husband, "'Failing to give birth to a son is the worst way to be unfilial.' Just go and take a concubine to give you a son." Though my great-grandfather longed for a son in concept, he also truly loved his daughters. Early in their young lives, each one of them had shown unusual intelligence and charm. On their part, they seemed to know that being born in girls' bodies they were indebted to their parents. So they were all the more solicitous of their mother and father and worked to win their favor. It was the custom of Old Town that not until five days after childbirth could a husband visit his wife. When, accordingly, Great-Grandpa entered her wing of the courtyard, bent over, and saw the infant girl abandoned at the corner of the bed, at that very moment Third Sister opened her eyes for the first time in her five days of life. The look from her crow-black eyes told her father of the wrong being done to her, and curling her tiny lips, she began to cry softly. Immediately, her father was smitten by this daughter. He picked up the child and, holding her close to him, said to his wife, "We'll just keep her."

Third Sister had better luck than the other two girls in the family. When she was seven years old, Old Town got a "Western" school. Folk in Old Town called anything at all imported from the outside world, "Western things." "Coal oil"— kerosene, that is—was called "Western oil," matches were called "Western fire," and so on. Before the Western school, private teachers had tutored educated people in Old Town at home. Wealthy people would set up a study room and invite someone well versed in the doctrines of Confucius and Mencius to be the teacher. Or else the teacher would arrange a schoolroom at his own home and take in several children to learn to read and write Chinese characters.

The earliest Western school in Old Town was church-run. Nowadays it is a famous institution. Family heads consider it an honor for their children to study in this school. The history of that school building goes back more than eighty years and the children's loud and clear recitations have never been interrupted.

Little Third Sister saw the young ladies and gentlemen from the wealthy homes wearing their neat school uniforms pass by her doorway. She asked Eldest Sister, "What are they doing?" Eldest Sister told her that they were the pupils at the Western school. She asked Eldest Sister to take her to see just what sort of place the Western school was, and Eldest Sister did so. The school was built beside Little West Lake. There for the first time they saw a two-story, Western-style building and heard the sound of school lesson recitations wafting out from within, which greatly moved Third Sister. Returning home, she begged and pleaded with her father to send her there to school. By that time my grandma's two younger brothers had been born. The older of the two was almost three years old but he still couldn't speak. Second Younger Brother at one year old was a "nighttime crybaby," asleep all day long, and crying up a storm the rest of the time. There is a saying in Old Town, "Look at youth to foretell maturity." Boss Guo concluded that his sons would never amount to anything and so cherished his daughters all the more. And so he gave in to Third Sister's pleas.

West Street consisted of several hundred households, but of these there was only one pupil in the Western school, and that was Third Daughter Guo. Thereupon she became renowned on West Street, like a movie star of today. Every word she said, every move she made, was scrutinized by the people of that neighborhood. Every day she tripped down those dark-red stone steps on her way to school and, every day after school, she tripped back up those same dark-red steps. Such a pretty sight on West Street! From grade school to junior middle school, she grew more beautiful and digni-fied all the time. The womenfolk of West Street would get together and express all kinds of dire worries about Third Sister: whose home would be graced by this sort of a girl that everyone loved at first sight? Afterward, with Third Sister always in and out of the West Gate church, the West Street women said she was a Western sort of Buddhist nun. They all sighed over the beautiful girl with the unlucky fate. Still later, when people discovered that Third Sister was going from door to door with a male preacher, there was a mighty uproar throughout West Street. Women traded gossip and made up many scandalous stories about her: the "preaching" was faked; what was true was something improper; conditions at the Guo home weren't lucky; and Boss Guo had no face to meet any-body and so just stayed at home pretending to be sick!

As my great-grandfather Guo became more bedridden, he was taken care of by my great-grandmother and thus became increas-ingly cut off from the world outside his door. Since they stayed at home the whole time, all the commotion on West Street had not reached inside the Guo residence. Eldest Sister and Second Sister heard these sarcastic comments and idle gossip but didn't give any weight to them. Third Sister believed in the god of the Western people. She was always mouthing "God this" and "the Lord that." The two sisters were worried that the girl might go and become a

Western-Buddha nun, and so they took her aside and asked her, "If you believe in the god of the Westerners, can you still get married?" Third Sister replied that God is happy when people get married and have children," which was a relief to her two older sisters.

Chinese Medicine Practitioner Chen, who looked after Boss Guo, belonged to a family whose friendship with the Guos spanned several generations. When, one day, Mr. Chen came in response to a call for his presence, he did not immediately take pulses and make his diagnosis as he normally did. He just sat in the main hall on the old-fashioned wooden armchair drinking cup after cup of tea. By coincidence, Granny's younger brothers just then got into a scrap over something or other and tussled from the back courtyard to the one in front. Mr. Chen took this opportunity to raise the subject with his old friend of restraining and disciplining children. He began by praising Third Daughter's beauty and intelligence, and, with much meandering, touched on the various rumors about her. Boss Guo didn't say one word, but the fine porcelain cup he was holding suddenly shattered into pieces. Toward evening, when Third Sister returned from school, her mother and father rained blows on her head, and forbade her from ever again crossing the threshold out of the Guo home. Her mother brought in a widow from the countryside to live in Third Sister's room and ensure that the girl's virtue was well guarded. The widow never let her go out of sight. But Third Sister's good name was now ruined in Old Town and she could never get married. Her mother sent a message to an uncle holding some official position in a faraway mountain district "to find a mother-in-law" for the girl.

What a disaster! I can't think of anything to compare it to in accurately describing just how serious this all was. At that time, neither Eldest Sister nor Second Sister "had a mother-in-law" and Third Sister's bad reputation had certainly made the two of them despair of their own prospects. Did they feel anger and resentment toward their younger sister?

Grandma's uncle arranged for Third Sister to be the lesser wife of a wealthy yokel in his mountain district. This bumpkin sent a team of porters with the betrothal gifts, and so around West Street the Guo family was judged to have regained a little face. Not only was Third Sister going to be married, she was going to enter a good man's home. So many poles of gifts were brought in and deployed like impressive battle formations in the Guo home that all of West Street grew alarmed.

It rained heavily that night and the virtue-guarding widow slumbered deeply. By the time she awoke, Third Sister was nowhere to be seen.

This was an even greater disaster! The skies above the Guo home had collapsed.

Third Sister had "died." All the Guos could do now was to bear an empty coffin out of the house. However, this empty coffin couldn't put an end to all the conjectures and rumors of the West Street neighborhood. Just about everyone knew that Third Sister had eloped with "that man." West Street's several "Western religion" households said that she had followed the call of God to go off and spread the Gospel. But those who had quite different feelings about the Western religion considered such talk to be the same as the Guo family's empty coffin—the more that was hidden, the more was exposed, and that's all there was to it.

Old Town's photo studio was next door to the Guo Family Cloth Shop. There my grandma left more than a few memories of her youth. For sure, Third Sister also had many photographs taken. The Guo family refused to keep such shameful memories, particularly the wife of Granny's younger brother. Pure as the driven snow all her life, *she* would not hang any photograph of Third Sister on *her* wall.

4.

IT'S NEW YEAR'S now. The older members of the family have to give the festive presents of a little cash to the children. I receive a lot more money than my peers. My cousins almost don't know my granny's relatives, but I'm a member of this large clan. Because I am Granny's little tail, wherever she goes, I tag along behind.

I have two great-aunts and four great-uncles. First Great-Uncle is a muddled drunk. On the first day of the New Year when we meet, he still knows enough to fish out a few small coins to give me. There are numerous older children and they will all give me money.

That night, before falling asleep, I'm like a miser, counting this year's take. The total wouldn't have exceeded the equivalent of fifty yuan today, but for me then that simply would have been an astronomical sum. Counting money is really fun. Granny is at my side and, watching me with a smile, asks, "How much? Granny will make it a round sum." Suddenly I think I should also have a third great-auntie. Big Great-Auntie and Fourth Great-Auntie both give me New Year's money every year. Granny ranks second among them in age, so where has Third Great-Auntie gone to? How come she doesn't give me New Year's money? I ask Granny this. The smile on her kindly face doesn't change, just seems to add a trace of sorrow. "She left us when she was quite young." I don't ask the reason for this, and lower my head to continue counting the money.

Third Sister was dead. After a few years, the Guos no longer thought of that coffin as having been empty. People's memories have a way of rewriting history and creating stories.

When Grandpa was seriously ill, Great-Auntie lived in Hangzhou at her eldest daughter's home. When she found out that Second Sister's husband was about to enter the True World, that very night she rushed back to Old Town by train. Her daughter bought her a sleeping-car ticket but she never lay down for a minute. Instead, this eighty-year-old lady actually spent the entire night in the dining car writing a letter. Even when young, she had always liked writing letters. At that time, her husband's family as well as her own all rode the buses for no more than eight *fen*, but she preferred to spend that amount on postage stamps. Frequently she had to add another eight *fen* for overweight. Anyway, writing letters was her hobby. She hunched over the swaying and lurching dining table and wrote to Third Sister: *Second Sister's husband has traveled to the end of his human life.* Great-Auntie's memory restores order out of chaos. She thought of Third Sister and believed that she lived in this world in perfectly good condition.

> My dear Third Sister, Second Sister's husband, Ninth Brother, is about to return to his heavenly home. He has been the best doctor in the world, the best husband, and the most ethical and compassionate man. You don't know him, although you and he worshiped together at the West Gate church. Maybe you never paid any attention to him. But Ninth Brother knew you, because in those days you were so extraordinarily pretty. Ninth Brother liked you and hoped that he and you might form the Hundred-Year Happy Union. His big sister-in-law had a matchmaker visit us and discuss things. That was when Daddy couldn't bear the idea of your getting married and leaving home. Daddy doted on you the most. So why did Ninth Brother marry our Second Sister? It's a long story. I remember the first time I met him when he appeared on our gate steps. It was like the sun was in my eyes. I secretly hoped that he would become my husband. On the day he and your Second Sister were betrothed, I buried myself in a cotton quilt and cried and cried until my eyes were swollen...

Before our old place was razed flat by the bulldozer, every time I would return to Old Town to see relatives I always got to read the thick stack of letters that Great-Auntie had written. Her characters were packed tightly together, and everything was unpunctuated and without paragraph divisions. At the time when she was learning to read and write, Chinese didn't have punctuation. Probably I was the only person patient and serious enough to read those letters, for I was born a curious cat.

So it turned out Granny's Third Sister hadn't actually died. I was deeply fascinated by the story that Great-Auntie related.

⌘　⌘　⌘

Grandpa's Big Sister-in-Law got wind of the "empty coffin" story that blew about Old Town. She also heard the theory of her fellow believers—that the young lady had left for distant places to preach the Word. Although Big Sister-in-Law believed in Jesus the Savior, she also believed that a young lady who flaunted herself in public abandoned decorum by doing so. Inwardly she rejoiced that none of this disgrace touched the Lin family. If Ninth Brother had been betrothed to Third Sister, that empty coffin would have had to be carried out of the Lin home.

Grandpa's eldest brother had been an official of the Qing dynasty, as had several generations of family members before him. What we today would call our monthly salary was known then as their monthly "rations." They had to use a washbowl to hold the heavy, shiny silver *yuan* pieces. One silver *yuan* would be enough for a poor family to live on for half a year, so it was obvious how rich the Lins were. After the Revolution and the cutting off of the braid that men wore, Grandpa's big brother straightway became unemployed and a housebound invalid as well. His two sons idled about the house chanting poetry, painting, and raising songbirds. They were a pair of spoiled playboys who affected the manner of eccentric intellectuals. With a great fortune being thus frittered away, the family's days went from bad to worse. Big Sister-in-Law let Ah Mu and Ah Hua go. And even when all that remained was a cook, she planned not to use him either. Her two daughters-in-law had come from grand families and didn't even know how much rice and water went into the boiler. When the Lins' own girls left in marriage, Big Sister-in-Law could count only on Ninth Brother who was then away studying. If he brought a daughter-in-law into the home, this would help her prop up the tottering House of Lin.

During his third year's summer vacation, Ninth Brother received a letter from Eldest Brother and Big Sister-in-Law asking him to come home to get married. Just which girl was being arranged for him wasn't made clear. But surely it had to be Third Sister Guo. While in Shanghai, Ninth Brother had kept a three-volume diary for her, and even the barest of entries, like "Raining today. All day long bent over my desk studying," was written with Third Sister in mind. The diary itself was Third Sister. Every day, under the lamp she would quietly listen in on all of Ninth Brother's subtlest feelings. Unrequited love is a beautiful sign of sincerity. Studying all by himself in a strange place, Ninth Brother was never alone.

Ninth Brother took the entire surplus of what he could save daily from his scholarship fund and bought presents. Eldest Brother, Big Sister-in-Law, nieces, and nephews—everyone got a "meeting gift." For Third Sister Guo he bought a jadeite ring, which he wanted to put on her finger in the church with the pastor's blessing. At this time, Mr. Qiao had accepted the position of church pastor in Beijing. Ninth Brother wrote to Mr. and Mrs. Qiao to announce the happy news that during this year's winter break he would bring his bride to Beijing to visit his two benefactors.

The rich love and affections within his Old Town home and its joyful air of marriage arrangements intoxicated Ninth Brother. He never even asked anything about the bride. All he thought about was the coming night of the painted candles and the nuptial chamber.

One night, when he was reading a book in his wing of the courtyard, his eldest nephew walked in. Ninth Brother assumed he wanted to discuss brush pen script. Uncle and nephew were only about two years apart. They had both studied and played together from when they were little and their feelings for each other were sincere and generous. This nephew was keenly interested in brush pen script, and the gift Ninth Brother had brought him was a copybook of Song dynasty calligraphy masters. His nephew never let this out of his sight.

Nephew didn't bother with conversational amenities but came right to the point, "Ninth Uncle, do you know whose family your bride is coming from?"

"Sure I know. Boss Guo's Third Miss, from the cloth shop by Drum Tower."

"For the two days you've been back, I haven't slept once. Now I've made up my mind to tell you the real story."

"What real story?"

"Third Sister."

This definitely was *not* going to be good, and Ninth Brother was unwilling to listen any further. Shaking his hands right and left, he said, "Never mind what kind of a girl she is, I want her to be my wife."

"No. Your bride isn't the Guo's Third Sister. It's a distant relative on my mother's side, someone surnamed Chen."

What's this? Ninth Brother just sat there with a stunned expression, while in his brain played a scene, just like he had seen in the silent films in Shanghai. The new bride, veiled in red, sits by the marital bed. The groom comes forward, lifts the veil from over her head, and a strange face scares the daylights out of him.

Nephew said, "Ninth Uncle, if you're unwilling to go through with this, it's still not too late. This is exactly the reason I wanted to tell you this tonight."

After a long, stunned pause, Ninth Brother asked, "Why would Big Sister-in-Law want to do this? I said I would marry only Third Sister Guo, and I left my picture for her to take over there in my place when they discussed marriage!"

"Just don't think about Third Sister anymore, Ninth Uncle!"

"She's gotten married?"

"She's no more."

Ninth Brother's eyes reddened and tears seeped from them.

Nephew didn't say that the coffin borne out of the home had been empty. He was unwilling to insult the girl that Ninth Brother so adored.

How did Ninth Brother ever get through this long, dark night? Would he have raised his head to heaven and asked God: *Oh, Lord, God, why didn't you bless and protect Third Sister?* Tearfully, he packed up his traveling things and got ready to head back to Shanghai, never again to return to heartbreak Old Town.

By early the next morning, his sense of indignation and impulsiveness now settled down, Ninth Brother told Eldest Brother and his wife that if the bride wasn't to be Third Sister Guo, he wanted to arrange a meeting with new prospects. This was all he could say. Eldest Brother and Big Sister-in-Law were like father and mother and he should obey them. If he had any disagreement with them, he could get it across only in a roundabout way. Before Big Sister-in-Law could open her mouth, Eldest Brother had already agreed to Ninth Brother's request.

You can well imagine the results of this visit: Ninth Brother refused to be the groom of the Chen girl. Big Sister-in-Law again sought out her go-between, Mother Sun. A din of drums and gongs and lanterns on poles again filled the town announcing the search for a bride for Ninth Brother. He was dragged along to meet the girls of several families and in every instance he shook his head in refusal.

Very soon, the vacation would be over. All during this period, he still made daily entries in his diary. And every day, with tear-filled eyes, he would pour out his sorrows and melancholy to the now-dead Third Sister.

On the day that Ninth Brother purchased a boat ticket back to Shanghai, he couldn't help walking to West Street. He knew Third Sister's home was that courtyard with the dark red steps leading up to the gate. For quite some time he hung around in front of it, wanting to pay a call on her parents and just have a look at her memorial portrait. And maybe he could even manage to get a picture of her to keep as a memento. Just when he drummed up enough courage to climb the steps, my grandma, Second Sister, walked out. At first glance he thought she was Third Sister, her student uniform changed into a well-fitting *qipao*.[4]

Standing under the sky well, Second Sister asked, "Visitor, who are you looking for?"

"Third Miss."

Before, there were always some outsiders who could never tell Third Sister from Second Sister, but after the great scandal hit the Guos, it would have been rare for anyone to make this mistake.

"Visitor, where do you come from?"

Ninth Brother's eyes brimmed with tears. "I too used to worship at the West Gate church. Three years ago I went to Shanghai to study."

---

[4]   The Manchu-derived high-collar, slit-sheath dress, widely known outside China by the Cantonese term *cheongsam*.

Oh, a student. Second Sister now addressed him as "Sir." "Sir, you are mistaken. Our Third Sister has gone on a long journey. I am Second Sister."

Ninth Brother soared up to the heavens. He floated at the tip of "an eighteen-*li* cloudy mist," as they say, and, muddled as he was, asked, "May I enter your mansion to sit for a brief moment?"

Second Sister should have turned away this unexpected visitor. There were no adult men at home. A man and a woman should have no contact outside of marriage, it is taught. What's more, he was looking for Third Sister. Third Sister was a painful sore that the whole family feared to touch. But this student's face was delicate and unusually handsome. A pair of sincere and kindly eyes that seemed to radiate some magic power confused Second Sister's sense of principle. She invited Ninth Brother into the main parlor, and only while she served him tea did she remember that the shop boy was waiting to go with her to South Town to buy some goods. So she handed Ninth Brother over to Eldest Sister who was right there also, teaching her little brother to read. "Sis, serve another cup of tea to this gentleman."

Great-Auntie not only loves to write letters, she also loves to talk. And so, in the space of two cups of tea, the entire tragic fate of the Guo family was related to the visitor. Because of Third Sister's "elopement," Father, in grief and sheer exasperation, coughed blood and died, Mother and old Grandmother took to their sick beds, and in two years, not one person had come to the Guo home to discuss marriage.

Ninth Brother had already accepted the fact of Third Sister's no longer being in the land of the living. Now he found out that she actually *hadn't* died but had eloped. It must have been with a man she had been infatuated with. This was gratifying news. In Shanghai, Ninth Brother had absorbed new ideas and new concepts. He approved of free love. At this moment, however, he felt as if he had fallen into a bitter sea on a dark night. Each pounding of the violent waves was one blow to his heart. He couldn't hear Eldest

Sister's mournful chatter. He bowed his head and lost himself in his own world. As a Christian, he realized that he was sinning. Third Sister was now some other man's wife and he shouldn't be thinking of her anymore. He silently asked Jesus for help: *Lord, just let me forget Third Sister, and let me bless her from an ordinary heart.*

At some point, who knows when, the sound of Old Lady Guo's groans and moans brought Ninth Brother out his dark thoughts and back to reality. A doctor's sense of responsibility extricated him from his melancholy and he said to First Sister, "I'm studying medicine. May I have a look at Auntie's illness?"

First Sister wiped the tears from her eyes with a handkerchief and looked blankly at Ninth Brother, "Oh, yes, now I remember. You are Young Master Lin. One year, Mother Sun came here to discuss the possibility of marriage. But we Guos don't have good luck."

After Ninth Brother took pulses and diagnosed the problems of the two old people, he went to the only Western clinic in all of Old Town to get some medicine. When he retraced his steps to the Guo household, it was already evening. Eldest Sister responded to his voice and opened the gate. His gaze was absorbed by Second Sister sewing by the lamplight. Her needle-runs and thread-pulling were like a work of art. *Oh, so beautiful!* He knew that three generations of Guos relied on that pair of nimble and skilled hands. Day or night, Second Sister sewed and embroidered to pay for the doctors and the medicine for their mother and grandmother and for her little brothers' private tutor. Ninth Brother was filled with sympathy and tenderness.

Three days later, Mother Sun arrived at the Guo home with Ninth Brother's proposal of marriage to Second Sister.

Out of sympathy for the Guo family, Ninth Brother had made up his mind to become their son-in-law. Although he felt rather more inclined toward Second Sister, he really wasn't particular about which of the daughters he married. It was his Big Sister-in-law who decided on the choice of Second Sister. Second Sister's sewing art-istry was renowned throughout Old Town. People said that the *qipao* she sewed made fat women look less plump and thin ones not so skinny. How the Lins needed such an intelligent and capable girl to manage the household! They had three generations, over twenty mouths to feed, and no one who earned any money. Outwardly, they still had to maintain the dignity of a great family and a grand home. Grandchildren had to be sent to the "foreign" school. And on every festive occasion, the whole household had to change into new brocades and damasks. Big Sister-in-Law urgently wanted Second Sister to marry into the Lin family. She hoped Ninth Brother would alter his travel plans and extend his stay for nine or ten days to wed and consummate his marriage. After that, he would leave his bride in her mother-in-law's home. Before the bride had even crossed the threshold, Big Sister-in-Law had already mentally cancelled the additional outlay for that year's new clothes.

Ninth Brother did not fulfill Big Sister-in-Law's wishes, though. The Guos needed Second Sister more than the Lins did. These days, as he was treating his future mother-in-law's illness, he could see with his own eyes the difficult straits that family was in. He agreed with his future mother-in-law to wait for the eldest of the Guo brothers' betrothal before returning to marry Second Sister. He also agreed that he and Second Sister would take care of her younger brothers.

This marriage built on feelings of responsibility and sympathy gave Ninth Brother unlooked-for happiness. In Second Sister, he found all the fantasies and hopes he had invested in Third Sister. Many decades of the winds and rain of human life would prove that he and Second Sister were a loving union of man and wife matched in heaven.

CHAPTER THREE – HAPPY FAMILY PORTRAIT

1.

I NO LONGER go anywhere by train. Over the past few years, the market has been so hectic that I just take a plane from one city to the next for signing contracts and meeting important clients. So all these cities leave me with pretty much the same impression: airport, hotel, and banquet room. Time being gold and with the money state of mind so urgent, I haven't got the time or inclination to sit and watch the countryside pass by from inside a swaying train.

The itinerary that Joseph had arranged for our journey south would take three days. I thought he did this to economize. Many Americans will buy grand homes and big-name cars but they are strict when they budget small financial matters. To save a few pennies, they'd drive way out of their way to fill up with cheaper gas. This is by no means uncommon and nobody thinks it odd. I told Joseph I could buy half-price plane tickets that wouldn't be much different from the train fare. This came as a big surprise to my travel companion. He said he thought that going by train cost a lot more than by plane. But that's in America, where the railway industry is like some decaying aristocracy. Even though its prospects grow more and more bleak, it still keeps its prices high. But Joseph's choice of going by train had nothing to do with price. He just wanted to watch the changing scenery as the train moved from north to south.

Ours is a slow train that invariably stops at every station it comes to. The male protagonist of the Old Town story has already cut off his long braid when, puffing and panting, our train is about to enter Tianjin.

On the platform, I get a call from Chrysanthemum She has just received reliable information that one of my university school-mates is about to take over the top position in an American media group's Asia-Pacific division. She wants me to drop everything and get right back to Beijing. There I am to launch a diplomatic offensive to capture the agency rights to produce one or two programs. "We'll be partners," she says, "and split the equity fifty-fifty." Give her thirty percent of the colors and Chrysanthemum would be gutsy enough to open a dye works. She has operated at least five different companies, all of which went broke. Lately her work has not been going too well. Her relationship with her boss is very tense and she's consumed once again by the idea of running her own show.

This news arrives just a bit too late. Joseph has bought two boxes of Tianjin-style fried dough twists and with a grin calls me back onto the train. I really do want to say that I can't go with him to Old Town, but I just don't have the strength to get the words out. It's hard to get off when you ride a tiger, and this slow-moving train is the "tiger" I can't get off.

We have just moved past the platform when Chrysanthemum again chases after me. She thinks I am now on my way back home after ditching Joseph and that this evening we can arrange a "Hongmen" banquet to sew up that top executive.[5] When she finds out that I am still riding the tiger, she gets so wrought up she can

---

[5]   A whimsical reference to the infamous banquet at Hongmen (206 BCE) in present-day Shaanxi Province where a *Macbeth*-like treachery was planned.

barely breathe. I can well imagine the spit flying out her mouth and all her facial contortions, her one hand holding the phone, the other waving about in great agitation. "You've gone totally nuts! Have you gotten all confused by that mixed-blood guy?" I run to the connecting section between the train cars and make a gentlemen's agreement with her. At this moment, my company will be recommencing operations and for the period I'm away she has full authority in any and all business matters. With her youth and good looks, Chrysanthemum is very sure of herself in tackling key relationship issues. As far as I'm concerned this is just a delaying tactic on my part. I don't want to come across with a beggars-can't-be-choosers expression in front of my old schoolmate. So I have Chrysanthemum convey to him that right now I'm working for another American media company.

Joseph seems very interested in Third Sister. "Third Miss Guo never went back home? Unless she really had died, she must have gone back to pay a visit to her parents."

I have the impression, from where I don't remember quite clearly, that later on, Third Sister did return home and was refused entry by the master of the household at that time. Maybe that was how Great-Auntie wrote it in one of her letters, but Grandma told me more than once that her big sister could never keep imagination and reality straight and that a lot of what was in her letters was just made-up stuff.

Following Old China's rules on virtue and propriety, when the older generation of males of the Guo family were no longer alive, the oldest son would have been the master of this household. The oldest of my granny's younger brothers was not yet eighteen years old and already a hopeless drunk, so it was his wife who became the master of the household in every sense of the word. She had been only fifteen when she married into the Guo home and two days into the marriage she went down to the kitchen to prepare the meals. At that time, she wasn't very tall, so she used a bench to stand on beside the stove as she stir-fried the vegetables. Obedient to her husband, caring and filial to her mother-in-law, she was in every way the "dutiful wife and loving mother" prescribed by Confucius. She had the authority to represent the Guo family in refusing to welcome Third Sister when she returned.

Joseph said, "She could have gone looking for her two older sisters."

"I don't know whether she did so or not. If there's time, I can take you to the old folks' home to ask my great-aunt."

"Oh, I definitely want to go to the old folks' home. That's where you can find living history."

Does Great-Auntie have the ability to think clearly, apart from that business of the Guos' "second fetus"? I doubt it. *Way back when I was in Lompoc taking care of old Helen, your grandmother, the Bible was the only thing she knew clearly. Other than that, she didn't even remember her own name.*

Why are you so interested in Third Sister? Are you connecting her with your grandma's own experiences? That's not possible. Such coincidences happen only in trashy pop novels, or in my great-aunt's own mental mishmash of the real and the unreal. So don't try to look for proof at the old folks' home. That'll make you even more brain-soft than someone one hundred years old.

⌘   ⌘   ⌘

Second Sister was forever working her needle and thread in the lamplight. Completed *qipao* and men's long gowns were always piling up like mountains beside her. During festival seasons, she had to work the whole night through to get things done on time. She really had no time for long-winded discussions about matters of the heart. Every evening, after putting everybody else to bed, her big sister would stay by her side. She really wanted to help Second Sister, but she created more work than help. Her simplest lockstitch and button sewing would make Second Sister spend even more time redoing her work. Eldest Sister's eyes weren't good—maybe it was excessive myopia—and even when she brought the needle and thread right up to the tip of her nose, her stitching was all over the place. When Ninth Brother sent his first letter to Second Sister, it was just a few simple words of greeting. Eldest Sister urged Second Sister to write a reply. Second Sister said casually, "Just send back a few words for me," and First Sister happily set about grinding ink and writing the letter. This was what she was best at. So the two sisters squeezed together under the lamp, one busily sewing, the other ghost-writing a love letter. Every time Second Sister saw Eldest Sister writing on and on, she was amazed: *how can she make so much out of just those few words I spoke to her?*

Ninth Brother's own letters became longer and longer and the envelopes these were stuffed into felt very heavy. And the love in this frequent correspondence steadily grew. When he held the pen to paper an endless affection swelled up in him, just as it did when, several years earlier, he had bent over his desk writing entries in his diary for Third Sister. Second Sister and Third Sister now had fused into one person.

For several decades thereafter, Great-Auntie took pleasure in talking about her letters to her sister's husband during those years. Right up to her old age, when her mouth had only four or five teeth left in it, she could still remember what particular Tang verse and Song lyric she had quoted in her letters. When speaking of the fun in writing this correspondence, her smile would transform that wrinkly old face into a blossoming chrysanthemum. Her own marriage had not been a happy one. She bore a lifelong grudge against her mother's bias in favor of Second Sister. My great-grandmother hadn't followed the order of precedence in first letting her eldest daughter find a husband, causing Great-Auntie to miss catching Ninth Brother, who turned out to be such a good husband. Still, she would be forever grateful for her father's turning away the Lin family's marriage overture for Third Sister on the grounds that he had to arrange his eldest daughter's own marriage first.

When I was a child, Great-Auntie was a frequent guest in our home. Whenever she could no longer stand her husband's browbeating and bullying, she would pick up her little cloth bundle and come to our house to escape the storm. In summer, as she enjoyed the coolness, and in winter, as she warmed herself in the sunlight, she told me many, many stories that were true and many others that were simply fluff. Among these, she related how my grandfather really should have made her his wife. At the time, I was still only a work-in-progress, an innocent little girl. I thought she was revealing to me the heaven-shaking secret that *she* was my real grandma.

Looking back at history, those were not peaceful years for China, what with the chaotic fighting between warlords and gun smoke rising on all sides. But thanks to the myriad streams and mountains shielding Old Town, its people led a comparatively serene existence. The Guo Family Cloth Shop was open as usual. Second Sister's handiwork became ever more renowned. Elder Sister now had a mother-in-law, and her husband came from a thriving family in South Town. The first Guo brother married and his fifteen-year-old bride stood on a small bench cooking for the entire family. The Lin family princelings still delighted in their calligraphy scrolls and songbirds. The family kept on eating up its ancestral fortune and it was clear that their holdings in the countryside were going piece by piece. Big Sister-in-Law was worrying herself sick, and every other day or so she couldn't get out of her bed.

My grandfather's two ears heard nothing that was going on outside his own window. The duties of a doctor made him feel perfectly at peace about distancing himself from current politics. He had learned on the job at his church-run hospital in Shanghai. There, with his own hands, he had treated the wounded from the Northern Expedition,[6] but he never tried to understand the difference between this war and the earlier tangled warlord conflicts. His greatest aspiration was to return to Old Town and open a clinic. Old Town lacked both doctors and medicine. In his opinion, those herbalists were not real doctors and he recognized that he had been orphaned precisely because of those quacks. Throughout his life, Ninth Brother stubbornly held to this prejudice. In his letters to Eldest Brother and Big Sister-in-Law, he asked for details of the sickness that had caused his mother's death and learned that she had been infected with puerperal fever. If Old Town had a Western doctor then, his mother would not have died. He wanted to return to Old Town to practice medicine and to get married and have children. Second Sister was waiting for him. A wife was the husband's bone of his bones and the flesh of his flesh. In marriage, the separated flesh and bone could reunite and achieve the completeness of human existence. As a Christian, this was his view of marriage.

⌘   ⌘   ⌘

In Grandma's treasured photo album, the wedding photograph of her and Grandpa was the picture that went back furthest in time. It had been taken amid all the blooming flowers in the yard of the West Gate church. Grandma wore a white wedding dress. Grandpa stood stiff as a pen in his Western suit. Photographed together with

---

6   Two major Guomindang ("Nationalist Party") -led campaigns (1926–1928) initially in coalition with the Communist Party of China and other leftists that started in southern China and moved north against the regional warlords, and had the overall purpose of unifying the country politically under the Guomindang. In June 1928, the Nationalist Revolutionary Army captured Beijing, then still the capital of China.

the bride and groom were Pastor and Mrs. Chen and their one-year-old son, Enchun. On the back of the photograph was the following in my grandfather's handwriting: *Taken in early summer, 1930.*

The three Chens had come from Beijing.[7] In the spring of that same year, they had accepted the invitation of the Old Town church organization to take up the resident pastorate of the West Gate church, and there they stayed for the rest of their lives. The Chens and the Lins have had a friendship that spans three generations. In my daughter Beibei's veins flows Lin and Chen blood, but I don't suppose this comes with any blessing from God, but rather from the curse of some mysterious crime, a thing I have been unable to free myself from my entire life.

Next, the album shows my mother and my two uncles. The young "Western" doctor and his beautiful, young wife embrace and hug three lively and adorable-looking children—a happy and perfect life recorded in a faded photograph.

Ninth Brother's first clinic was established at Drum Tower, actually in what had been the Guo Family Cloth Shop. As the oldest Guo son was drinking himself into a perpetual stupor, he was incapable of handling the business. Nor could there be any great expectations from the other sons, so Second Sister's mother let Ninth Brother turn the shop into his clinic. In the winter of their second year, they had a daughter. A father for the first time, Ninth Brother showed a fervor and enthusiasm that raised eyebrows among both the young and old in the Lin family. He actually stopped business and closed up the clinic to be with his wife during her month of confinement. The whole day long he would bury himself in the dimly lit room holding

---

[7]   Technically, the name of the city during this period should be "Beiping." In 1928, Chiang Kai-shek's Guomindang government in Nanjing ("Southern Capital") renamed Beijing ("Northern Capital") "Beiping" ("Northern Peace") and it officially remained as such until 1949, when it was renamed "Beijing" by the new government of the People's Republic of China.

his child, unable to let go of her. Once in a while, though, he would have no choice but to leave to take care of some seriously ill person, and this was hard on him. From the Lin residence to the clinic was about a fifteen-minute walk, but he couldn't bear even this short fifteen-minute distance from his wife and daughter. When the baby girl had completed her first full month, the young couple broke free of the big family residence and moved into the floor above the clinic. There they had two other children.

Happy lives are mostly all alike. Unhappy ones all have their own unhappiness. This was the famous saying of the Russian writer Leo Tolstoy. The several years following their marriage were the happiest times my grandparents would have in their whole lives. There were only a few "tales of marvels" that could be passed down to us in the later generations, and even Great-Auntie, who loved to tell stories, couldn't say the reason for this.[8] Although Ninth Brother insisted on giving free treatment to poor people, the clinic's income wasn't too bad. Second Sister still did some needlework handicraft to contribute to her mother's household budget. By this time, she had already been baptized a Christian and every Sunday the family in all its neatest and most attractive attire went to the West Gate church to sing hymns. The doctor's wife and the pastor's wife often took turns in hosting demonstrations of the culinary arts. And very often the doctor and the pastor would discuss everything under the sun over a pot of warm, watered-down wine without ever exhausting all the topics they wanted to discuss.

The ancients longed for the Land of Peach Blossoms, beyond our mundane world, but that place was not more idyllic than all of

---

[8]   Tales of Marvels (*chuanqi*), was a prose genre that became formalized during the Tang dynasty (618–907 CE). As a distinct literary genre, such Tales evolved from traditional anecdotes, *chansons de geste*, not to mention *amour*, and usually contained strong elements of the supernatural.

this. How could anyone expect that one day this happy existence, like a beautiful dream so cruelly interrupted, would vanish, never to return?

The Happy Family Portraits could be counted on our fingers. The several old and young members of the whole family, or even the several dozen of them, sitting neatly and evenly in the photo studio for a remembrance portrait, meant there were among them those who were going away. And whether this departure was for good or for ill no one could foretell, so in some places it is commonly considered taboo to take Happy Family Portraits. Grandma and Grandpa and their three children's earliest Happy Family Portrait was a foreshadowing of the upheaval and calamities to come.

In the winter of 1937, Ninth Brother brought the entire family into the photo studio at the Drum Tower. In the solemn expressions of all five family members were clearly traced anxiety and bewilderment. Behind them was the studio's backdrop of painted scenery but prominent above all else was the army uniform Ninth Brother was wearing. He was tightly holding his daughter to him. This precious daughter was the thing he most loved and worried about all his life. Their young sons weren't yet five years old, but they seemed to know that a great disaster was looming over them. Their brows were furrowed in an expression that showed that tears would soon fall.

What force could have made frail bookworm and sentimental, family loving Ninth Brother, husband and father—who didn't even know what was going on outside his own window—cast aside the wife and children he felt he never loved enough, and head for the battlefront?

2.

WHEN NINTH BROTHER told his wife that he wanted to go to the front lines up north as an army doctor, she supposed he was just expressing some kind of general wish. She also knew that war was going on in the north, and Ninth Brother had lived in the north and so inevitably, he would be rather more concerned and worried than someone who had never left Old Town. *But that was the north, after all. Wasn't everything just fine in our Old Town?* This had always been a blessed place. The many epochal changes during the dynasties had never brought the clash of arms here. People in Old Town believed that even if the sky collapsed, it wouldn't fall on their heads.

Everything in Old Town, with its eternal spring weather, followed the prescribed order. Children grew older by the day. That summer their daughter Baohua entered primary school. Ninth Brother bought a bicycle and every day he would use it to take her to and from school. In those years, bicycles may have been even rarer and more prestigious than today's BMWs. Ninth Brother rode it none too steadily and so he would have to push Baohua along the bustling streets to school. He said that by the time the two boys went to school, his bicycle-pedaling skills would be excellent and he could take the three of them on it, just like he'd seen at a street-side circus in Shanghai. How could he have possibly forsaken his children to go off to those distant parts?

Right up to when Ninth Brother received his uniform from the local government office, Second Sister thought he had just gotten some official sinecure or another, like those people on Stipend Lane and Officials Lane who once "ate the Emperor's grain," as they used to say. Every day he would go out early and come back late, and this family stayed as tight-knit as tight could be.

Only when Ninth Brother proposed taking a Happy Family Portrait at the photo studio did Second Sister actually feel that matters weren't as simple as she had supposed. Returning home, she asked her husband, "Would you really leave us?" Instead of answering her, Ninth Brother just turned to look out the window. She saw pain in the contours of his clear-cut profile. *Yes, he really is going.* She drew in a breath of cool air through her parted lips to stifle a cry. She had been wallowing in bliss over the past seven or eight years without the slightest doubt that these days would continue all her life, and that no power short of death could snatch away her happiness. Then, all of a sudden, her sheep-like, good husband had changed into a hard-hearted man she no longer knew. She wasn't a woman given to crying. After her father had died and life became so difficult for her family, she hadn't shed a single tear. But on this day the floodgates burst.

Ninth Brother must have gone crazy, or, as the Bible says, "been set upon by Satan." That same night she went to the West Gate church and even before the pastor and his wife had brought her upstairs into the sitting room, Second Sister again choked back her sobs. "Pastor, Mrs. Chen, I beg you, pray for Ninth Brother and ask God to save him!"

"Dear Heavenly Father, dear Lord Jesus, your child asks you to comfort the heart of our sister Guo. Let her no longer be sorrowful. Help her pass through the pain and suffering of being separated from her husband. Bless and protect Brother Lin with a safe departure and a safe return."

This prayer uttered by Pastor Chen greatly surprised Second Sister. She plucked up her courage to look at him and then at his wife. *Why weren't they asking the Heavenly Father to keep Ninth Brother from going? Surely they didn't support the idea of his forsaking wife and children? Uh...Pastor Chen, don't you say in your sermons that a husband should not leave his wife?* The words coming from the pastor's mouth were the will of God, and she didn't dare to oppose this. Second Sister held back her tears.

As Ninth Brother's good friend, Pastor Chen knew full well that Ninth Brother's decision was no overnight impulse. He had seen with his own eyes how this thought from deep within Ninth Brother had formed into something resolute and strong, as a tiny seed grows day after day into an unshakable tree.

The second year after Ninth Brother's return to Old Town, China's three eastern provinces fell under the guns of the Japanese. After this, the war moved south and Shanghai fell. Ninth Brother had several schoolmates and good friends in Shanghai who threw on military uniforms and rushed to the Song-Hu Battle.[9] One of these perished in battle as he was rescuing the wounded. How China's armies lacked doctors! And they especially needed Western-style ones on the battlefield. As he thought of the world beyond Old Town, Ninth Brother could not put words to his feelings of restlessness and distress. Here was a happy family as though from some tale of heaven: every evening his wife sewed in the lamplight of the parlor and the three children would sit around him in the sky well under the liquid moonlight. His daughter in her colored skirt sang country lyrics, "Shiny, shiny moon / shine on the parlor / bring out a bench for Dad / please, Dad, hear me sing a song." The sweet, lovely voices of the children were like honey, like grape wine, intoxicating him, entrancing him, so he couldn't tell heaven from earth. This was the peak of happiness and satisfaction for him. But every time he was alone, guilt, like poisonous vines, crept round and tangled

---

[9]   Another name for Japan's assault on Shanghai in August, 1937.

in his heart. Countless nights Ninth Brother remained sleepless. While Second Sister breathed evenly beside him, he would sink into deep self-reproach at his life in this cowardly fool's paradise. The only person in all of Old Town who could listen attentively to his inner struggles was Pastor Chen. Over these past few years he had wanted to go north to fight but didn't. It was as if he realized that there would come a day when he would break the hearts of his wife and children, and so he especially treasured every day he spent with them. He wanted to give them a kind of advance overdraft account of all his love for them.

In the summer of 1937, the Marco Polo Bridge Incident ignited the general explosion of China's War of Resistance against Japan. Old Town's own evening paper published the entire text of the National Government's Declaration of the War of Self-Defense and Resistance. It covered the entire page in boldface and read as follows:

"China today seriously declares that its territorial sovereignty has been flagrantly violated by Japan's aggression. 'The League of Nations Treaty,' 'The Nine Power Treaty,' and 'The Non-Aggression Pact' have been completely wrecked by Japan...China is determined not to give up any part of its territory. In the event of aggression, China will meet it by carrying out its innate right of self-defense."

The newsboy delivered the paper right into the doctor's hand. At the time, there was one patient in the clinic. The doctor held the paper and dumbly stood there, tears streaming from his eyes. For a long time the patient didn't dare disturb him.

From this day on, Ninth Brother's behavior became somewhat unusual, but Second Sister ignored this. That night he didn't open his mouth in prayer. Previously, before going to sleep, husband and wife always said their prayers together. There was actually nothing they wanted or needed; it was only to give praise and thanks.

Second Sister was so tired that she was already asleep when it came time for "Amen." Ninth Brother sat on the bed, silently praying. When Second Sister had fallen asleep, he was still sitting there. Ninth Brother loved the Lord. Second Sister felt a sense of inferiority toward him, so she didn't think too much of his odd behavior.

Ninth Brother's silent nighttime prayers grew ever longer. He begged his Heavenly Father to make him strong, to make him no longer so blindly loving of his snug little family, to rid him of his cowardliness and sentimentality. He was a doctor, so he ought to go to the bloody sacrificial battlefields and save lives. He said to Lord Jesus: *If it be according to your will, please lead me by your hand out of Old Town.*

All through that autumn, he prayed. Finally, God gave him clear permission. A military officer came with his orderly to the clinic to be treated for a stomach disorder. He was the commander of a coastal defense division here and was just about to lead his troops to the northern front. He and the doctor discussed everything about the war situation—the fall of Nanjing and the shift of the Guomindang government to Chongqing.[10] The commander predicted that in the end Old Town would not escape the war. He said that his troops desperately needed doctors. When Ninth Brother replied that he could help find a doctor, the commander was overjoyed. He gave Ninth Brother his contact address and said that he would appoint such a doctor head of the division medical station with the rank of major. At that time, Ninth Brother's daughter, Baohua, was in the clinic, playing and darting about by her father's side like a little swallow. She prattled endlessly at him and he patiently and indulgently answered all her simple and silly questions. That he doted on her was plain to see. This didn't sit at

---

[10]   The Guomindang government withdrew from Nanjing in December 1938. The Japanese army then entered that city and commenced a period of atrocities against the

all easily with the division commander, a man accustomed to life and death in the war zone. He never thought this delicate-looking doctor who was as sentimental as a woman would be the one to go off to war with him.

Ninth Brother believed that God himself had arranged this and that he would surely bless and protect him on his long journey and the family he left behind in Old Town. The next day, he located the division commander using the address he had been given.

On the eve of his departure, Ninth Brother projected a certain hard-heartedness. He kept very cool and calm as he systematically shut down the clinic and moved his wife and children back to the old Lin residence on Officials Lane. He organized his medicine, his instruments, and his personal papers. On many evenings, when he thought that Second Sister was sound asleep he would get up and burn his diary and some letters. For sure, he wanted to get rid of all he had written for Third Sister in his diary. If he were to fall on the battlefield, he didn't want his wife to be shocked when she went through his personal effects.

Even though the pastor and his wife said a lot of things to Second Sister, she still didn't really understand. So she too started to pray silently without her spouse knowing it. At night, when Ninth Brother would tiptoe downstairs, she would sit up and pray. *O Heavenly Father, Lord, thank you for giving me this good husband. Now he wants to leave home. Lord, please let me keep him, for we need him here.* But she got her answer from Ninth Brother's determined and stern expression. God wasn't keeping her husband from going. She believed this was fate. Fate was God's plan for everyone. She bore the pain and accepted what was real. She never said no to her husband.

---

defenseless citizens that the world now knows as the Nanjing Massacre. It was also during that same month that the government announced its move to Chongqing, a city in Sichuan Province situated on upper reaches of the Yangzi River.

Separately, the husband and wife prepared for the changes in their family life. Second Sister stopped working on the New Year's orders of *qipao* and rushed to sew a silk and wool vest for Ninth Brother. Although there was no lack of clothing in the army, she still worried about how terribly cold it got up north. Could her fragile southern scholar stand the winters there? Ninth Brother had taken care of his personal matters, and was busily running to the people at West Gate whom he had treated. They were poor people and Ninth Brother distributed pills to those who might have use for them, leaving instructions on dosage and storage.

The moment of departure and farewells came imperceptibly. One morning at 4:30, Second Sister heard in her half-asleep state the sound of light footfalls. Opening her eyes, she saw there was candlelight in the children's room next door. She got out of bed to look in on them, only to see Ninth Brother in his army uniform holding a candle and standing by Baohua's bed as if under a spell. Today was the day of his departure. But Second Sister still actually fantasized that maybe in some innermost part of him, seeing Baohua would make him change his mind at the last minute. She was again disappointed. He came out and said to her, "The Chens are waiting for us. Let's go to the church and say a prayer together. At six o'clock, the division commander will be sending over a vehicle to fetch me at the West Gate corner. Let's put everything in the hands of our God."

Ninth Brother rode Second Sister on his bicycle to the church. He wanted to leave the bicycle with Pastor Chen. With all his preaching hither and yon, the pastor badly needed something to get around on, something other than just his two feet. Ninth Brother's bicycle-riding technique was by no means up to par. On the road he wobbled right and left in a most alarming and dangerous manner, but luckily there weren't yet people walking along the streets. The two of them frolicked their way to West Gate like kids playing some risky game.

Pastor Chen and his wife had been kneeling in prayer for two hours already when the Lins arrived. Tearfully they beseeched God to allow Dr. Lin to return to Old Town without the slightest harm, for Old Town needed him.

Second Sister heard Ninth Brother say, "O Lord, your child still begs you to give him strength and courage. Make him always pursue what is right without turning back." She thought of Ninth Brother as already being indomitable and unyielding. She almost didn't know him anymore and she silently prayed to God that after the war ended to give him back to her as she knew him before, as that loving family man, Ninth Brother.

At six o'clock, an army truck arrived. Ninth Brother got up into the cab and the vehicle roared off. He did not cast a single glance back at Second Sister, standing there by the roadside.

3.

ALL HER LIFE, Grandma never could understand Grandpa's enormous act of going off and leaving his family behind. After he passed away, she found a photograph of him in his military uniform, and she was just as perplexed as ever. Putting on her old-age glasses, she scrutinized the picture and said to me, "Look at this, your grandpa looks just like a student in that uniform. In his whole life, he had never killed a chicken or a fish. How could he have ever dared go off to war?"

I was in high school when I learned that my grandpa had been a Guomindang army officer. I had applied to join the Communist Youth League. "Communist Youth League member" was a synonym for outstanding student—it was an honor and a glory. I wrote out many applications but they never accepted me. A student who was a member quietly took me aside and told me: *Your family is very complicated. Your grandfather on your mother's side was a Guomindang army officer, a major, even.* She said a lot of other stuff too, but I didn't hear a word of it. The blood surged from my heart to my head and blocked my eyes and ears. *How was this possible? The grandpa who warmed up cow's milk for me to drink every day turns out to have been a reactionary officer?* I imagined the way Grandpa wore his uniform and his sword. That was just so funny, funnier even than those foreign tourists renting gowns of imperial yellow to wear when they have their picture taken in front of the Forbidden City. *Major, how many revolutionaries did you kill?* But the year before last when our cat died, Grandpa was red-eyed from sorrow. He was much more easily moved to tears than my grandma. Returning home, however I looked at it, my grandpa didn't seem like someone who had worn a military uniform. I could completely understand Grandma's puzzlement and surprise back then.

Later, I had the opportunity to sneak a look at the résumé that my grandfather had written. In those years, people had to complete so many résumés each year. His own was really complicated. Just for the War of Resistance alone he had written two pages. He really was a reactionary military officer. And I suffered over this for a long time.

Later on, people in China no longer saw any shame in anyone of the older generation having been an officer in the Guomindang Army. Those old soldiers who went to Taiwan and now returned to visit their relatives became an honor and glory for the ancestors. I really wanted to write about my grandpa. He and Grandma were the people who had influenced me the most in my life. But every time I would start to do so, after a while, I always gave up. The most I ever wrote was about fifty thousand words. I couldn't write about them, because always in the end I couldn't connect all those "tales of marvels" with the grandpa who used to stand by the little coal stove heating up cow's milk for me.

My great-aunt had another version of my grandpa going north with the army. According to her, when he had been a student up north he had been on intimate terms with someone, someone who, with her "intoxicating aroma and seductive sleeves," as she put it, had been his companion during the period of his studies. They had a child together, and she and the child were waiting for him. And Great-Auntie said she was very pretty, a reformed woman from "the world of smoke and flowers."

Great-Auntie's tale out of the Arabian Nights spread fast throughout the Guo household. Granny was the last one to hear it though. Normally she would smile such things away. When they were children they had grown up sharing the same bed, and the stories her older sister composed didn't stop at one thousand and one.

Had these all been written down, they would have been as tasty, if not more so, as those popular tales about Ming Dynasty city folk by Feng Menglong and Ling Menchu. But without any letter or money for housekeeping from Ninth Brother for so long now, Second Sister found getting through these days very hard. Feeling on edge without any clear idea what was happening, she really couldn't endure any stimulation of this kind. So right away, she called a rickshaw to take her to South Town and her older sister, to have her clear all this up. Only when the rickshaw man pulled up at her sister's gate did Second Sister come to her senses. *How could I ever have taken Big Sister's crazy talk seriously?* She didn't get down, just told the puller to turn around and go back home.

The town's old folk had a saying: "A man shouldn't be allowed to read *The Romance of the Three Kingdoms* and women shouldn't read novels." Reading *The Romance of the Three Kingdoms* would turn a man into someone sinister and ruthless, while novels would give a woman all kinds of wild and silly ideas. Take, for example, Great-Auntie, who had certainly read lots and lots of novels. In her days, love between "women of the smoke and flowers" and gifted scholars was the hottest theme in novels about ordinary city people. My Great-Auntie missed her calling—she was a natural-born writer. Too bad.

No one corrected Great-Auntie's erroneous mental creations. Over the past few decades she forgot that she herself was the author of these stories and that she had treated them as historical fact. She firmly believed that Ninth Brother had another family up north. When my grandpa died, Great-Auntie had words to say to my uncles for not informing those people. She knew I was at university in the north, and, quietly pulling me over to one side, she said, "You ought to go see the people in that family. They are also your uncles and aunts." Fortunately, we all knew that she was an old crackpot and such rumors never led anywhere.

When the army truck took Ninth Brother away, it was as if a little boat had been rowed into the middle of the water and abandoned just like that by the helmsman. And while the woman and children left on board were at their wits' end, a great tempest was following close behind. Their situation was much more awful than they had ever expected, and it grew steadily worse.

For the first three months, Ninth Brother's letters and remittances came regularly. In them, he promised his wife that every month at the very least there would be a letter from him telling her that he was all right. And that, except for two silver dollars of spending money, he would be sending the full amount of his payroll home to her. After the postman delivered three remittances to Second Sister, Ninth Brother seemed to have dropped into the sea like one of those ritual clay oxen at springtime. There just wasn't any news from him at all. Before this, neither of them had expected the war would sever the postal routes. Coming without warning, this disaster caught Second Sister totally unprepared. Far into more nights than she could count, she thought of the very worst possibility: that Ninth Brother would never return home. If it hadn't been for the children, there's no telling what she might have done.

The Lin household split up and formed six little family units. Six dining tables were set up in the sitting room closest to the kitchen. The daily three meals were ordeals for her children. Three pairs of eyes watched the red-braised meat. Their mouths drooled, but the children didn't dare move their chopsticks. When Second Sister thought of this, it was as if her heart was being cut by knives and pierced by needles. Afraid that her relatives would see something odd, she moved the table into her room and told her sisters-in-law that this made it easier to teach the children to behave.

There was that plate of meat a few days before, set out right in the middle of the dining table and enticing with its aroma. Three pairs of bulging, greedy bug eyes were rolling in their heads. While Second Sister's attention was elsewhere, the older boy, Baosheng, stealthily gripped a piece of the meat with his chopsticks and stuffed it into his mouth. Then he took another piece and put it into his brother Baoqing's bowl. Five-year-old Baoqing's long eyelashes drooped low as he stared and stared down at that piece of meat. Then, swallowing his saliva with difficulty, he put the meat back on the serving plate. The daughter, who was a bit older, knew what her mother had in mind. "Ma's afraid other people will see we can't afford to eat meat. So now that the dining table's been moved inside, we can just go ahead and eat." Her little brother stubbornly resisted this enticement and, pursing his little lips said, "We ought to let Daddy eat the good things first. I want to wait for Daddy to come home before eating."

Second Sister was standing by the door and saw all this. Again, she couldn't help feeling the pain of a knife carving into her breast. The three children were all sweet little angels but that little one was an angel among angels. He understood best of all how things were and showed the greatest concern for her. When he was only two years old, Second Sister's mother had said, "This little one will be your and Ninth Brother's support someday."

She came forward and embraced the little boy. "Baoqing, eat now. When Daddy gets back, there'll be even better things to eat."

Baoqing's eyes couldn't disguise his joy. However, holding a piece of meat with his chopsticks, he didn't cram it into his own mouth, but brought it to his mother's mouth first. "Ma, Daddy's not home, so you should begin before us."

Such good children. She felt hope as she gazed at these little angels. This somewhat softened the pain of having no word from her husband.

⌘　⌘　⌘

That summer the postman became the object of Second Sister's longing. Every morning at ten o'clock he passed by Officials Lane. She calculated the time she should come outside. The Lin family had already split up with each housewife managing her own household. Second Sister would go out with her vegetable basket pretending that it was all coincidence. Looking very far off, she could tell at a glance from the postman's pudgy face that today, once again, she would be without hope. She dawdled along the side of the street, getting a grip on her sadness. She bought some food and odds and ends. Every fourth or fifth day she would buy a bunch of fresh flowers. Ninth Brother liked flowers. After they were wed, their home was never without fresh flowers.

Actually, she no longer felt much like looking after plants and flowers, but she didn't want her sisters-in-law to see that there was no news from her husband. They all envied the shiny silver coins she received every month. To keep up appearances, Second Sister went to a tailor's shop and collected some sewing to do quietly at home. And every so often she had to cook some meat dish to let the whole compound smell its aroma. That way they would know that "Old Number Nine's" household was doing all right. At times when she was feeling especially fragile, she would find some quiet place where she could cry for a bit. When she really couldn't stand it any longer, she would go to the West Lake church to ask the pastor to help her pray. She believed that his prayer had more power than hers and was more likely to move the Holy Spirit. In the end, it was from God alone that she could look for guidance and support. *O Heavenly Father, Ninth Brother loves you. You also love Ninth Brother. You will bring him back to us all safe and sound, won't you?*

Grandma's infatuation with the postman continued for just about one year. In the second year, right on the day of the Dragon Boat Festival, Second Sister brought the children back to her old Guo home. It was right on this day that the postman delivered a letter to the wife of their old neighbor, Ah Liu. Ah Liu was a soldier up north, and it had been several months since there had been any news of him too. "When fighting goes on for three straight months, a letter home is worth its weight in gold," the saying goes. Ah Liu's wife shouted and yelled in raptures that filled the entire street when she got this letter. She was illiterate, and so, catching hold of a refined-looking fellow in a long gown she pleaded, "Sir! You look to be skilled in reading. My husband has sent a letter from up north. Help me read it. What does he say?" This passerby looked down and glanced briefly at the contents of the letter. Then, with a grave expression, he stared long at Ah Liu's wife without saying a word. Urgently, she pressed him, "Did he send money? Tell me he's been gambling again and lost it all! He should be sliced a thousand times! If he doesn't send any more money, I'll sell his two sons!" The man returned the letter to Ah Liu's wife. "Elder Sister, I can't read this letter. Please forgive me." Then abruptly he walked off without a further glance at her.

Ah Liu's wife was a real termagant among the common townsfolk. With her hands on her hips, she poured out abuse on the man's mother as he walked away. "Wasn't the little money your family spent on your learning so you could read books?" She came out with more foul-mouthed comments that only Old Town's lower class of people say. Then she turned around and stopped a young man. "Younger brother, could you trouble to help Auntie read this letter? Auntie gets bullied because she can't read. From the look of you, if you don't place first in the imperial exams, you'll do well in the provincial ones. Help Auntie read the letter." The young fellow looked as if he had been called on by the teacher to read from a textbook. Every word and every pause came through clearly. In fact, this was a notification letter of death in combat. It praised Ah Liu's patriotic sacrifice in heroically resisting the Japanese. Before the youth had finished reading the final inscription, Ah Liu's wife let out a shriek that traveled the entire length of West Street. "Ah Liu! You unlucky devil! You've done it to me this time!" The young fellow raised his head from the letter and turned pale in alarm to see her flat on her bum in the street, beating her chest, stamping her feet, and wailing.

Row upon row of gawkers pressed around. "Ah Liu's dead!" West Street people all knew each other. It was as if everybody could tell an Ah Liu story. The old wife of the Zhang family lifted her cane and pounded the ground. "Today's Dragon Boat Festival. Just one year ago Ah Liu ate rice dumplings made at our home." An old gaffer of the Li family said that even when he was little, Ah Liu used to carry water for many homes on this street. His water buckets were bigger than other people's, and he got less for his work than other people did. "Good old Ah Liu! And you say he's gone now? Ah Liu went off to be a soldier so he could send money home. He wanted his children to go to school...didn't want them to have to sweat and slave to support a family like he did. Poor old Ah Liu!"

Second Sister was scrubbing and cleaning the area under the sky well. She was using the same water she had cooked the festival's rice dumplings in to scour every nook and cranny. People said that doing this could lessen the number of summer mosquitoes. She wasn't a person to run into the street to see what the fuss was all about. But someone came rushing in through the doorway telling about the woes of Ah Liu's wife. Second Sister knew that Ah Liu was in the north as a soldier, so naturally this led her to think about Ninth Brother. Shaking the water from her hands, she just stood there blankly for a while, unsure of what to do next. Finally, beside herself with worry, she stepped across the threshold and went over toward the crowd of people.

Her knees went weak when she heard about Ah Liu's wife. So what the postman delivered weren't always ten-thousand gold-piece letters. Sometimes the postman was the envoy from hell who would cruelly say to some woman, "Your husband's dead! From now on you're a widow."

After Dragon Boat Festival, Second Sister no longer bought vegetables as an excuse for "running into" the fat postman. When things had come to this, her greatest hope was to get no news at all from her husband.

One rainy day, while she was sewing, she heard a clattering sound on the floorboards in the front parlor. Then a person called out her name in a loud voice. She realized that the postman had come to her house. She lifted her hands from her sewing and locked them on top of her head. Ominous black clouds rolled down from the sky to sweep her into a vast abyss.

A nephew leading the postman pushed open the unlocked door. "Ninth Aunt, there's a letter from Ninth Uncle."

Second Sister's hands were still raised above her head and, panic-stricken, she asked, "In Ninth Brother's handwriting?"

"Correct, it's his handwriting."

Only then did she get up all a-fluster and, forgetting her manners, snatched the letter from him. Then, turning away, she covered her face and sobbed.

That day she signed for three letters and two remittances. From the letters she found out that Ninth Brother had sent far more than just these. *Ah well, never mind, that's just money lost and gone.* Even if she had received but one word from Ninth Brother, that would be enough to bring her dead heart back to hope and light. Now she was thinking more about setting off a string of firecrackers by the gateway to tell the world that Ninth Brother was still alive! This really wasn't news. All the relatives in the Lin family thought that Ninth Brother had been sending money back every month. If any of the sisters-in-law were hard up, Second Sister was the first person they'd go to for rescue. She quietly closed the door, and fervently dropped to her knees. *O Heavenly Father, Lord, thank you for deigning to hear your daughter's unworthy prayer. She still entrusts Ninth Brother into your hands.*

The children returned home from school. Second Sister opened her arms and clasped them all in her embrace, "Daddy has sent money and letters!"

Baohua said, "I want to buy a pair of leather shoes."

Baosheng said, "I want to eat three bowls of meat all in one go!"

Baoqing said, "I'd like a pencil. I can write and I want to send a letter to Daddy."

Their mother had a lot she wanted to say to these children. She wanted to teach them to know their Father in heaven, to be grateful to him for protecting Ninth Brother on the battlefield. But she couldn't say a single word. She only nodded her head, as tears streamed down from her eyes.

Chapter Four — A Christian at War

1.

On and on the monotonous wheels of the train roll and turn. My consciousness drifts into a haze and then gradually clarity returns.

Those children under the seat, not yet ten years old, are Chaofan and me. We're curled up like little mollusks and playing poker. Around us are pairs and pairs of swollen feet and, with them, pair after pair of dirty shoes all packed and piled up together. This is the first time that I remember leaving Old Town and the first time for me to ride on a train. My grandpa is being banished to a far-off mountain district. Grandma could have chosen to stay behind but she wouldn't even consider that, and so she boarded the train, taking me with her. Chaofan's own grandpa is no longer alive and his parents are still in the "cow pen," so there was nothing left for him but to go with his grandma, also in the ranks of the exiled. The whole train is filled with people being sent away for labor reform. In total contrast to the desolated, baffled, or resigned-looking adults are the children in the passenger cars. For them, totally ignorant of the outside world, traveling so far away from home is an ecstasy and excitement beyond measure. It doesn't matter to them if they know each other or not, they just squirm this way and that and band together to play in the stuffy, crowded cars. Grandma doesn't stop me from wriggling under the passenger seats. She is no longer telling me that "girls are golden branches and jade leaves," or that when you stand or sit you must do so properly. Her eyes gaze far out into the distance but don't see a single thing, not even the muck on Grandpa's and her own shoes. Shoes that never before had a speck of dust upon them. Chaofan and I are playing "winner," a kind of poker. In the dim light, I see the corners of his mouth curl into a pleased and wicked grin and I know that he's lucked out on a winning card. That wicked grin on his mouth and the melancholy in his eyes just fascinate me.

That young woman is the newly wed me, sweetly sleeping, my head pillowed on Chaofan's arm. We're on our way back to Old Town to see our families. We bought two sleeper-berth tickets but squeeze together into just one and are never apart the whole trip. The person I am then is so happy, so content. I guess I had come into this world just to find him, to be his wife, wash his clothes, cook his meals, and bear his children. The person I am then is such a loser. No enterprising spirit, no grand aspirations. Chaofan is a genius. This is not blind hero worship on my part. His graduation work has just won the top national prize. In his presence, I feel myself all dull and dreary. Every time I nuzzle up against him in sheer happiness, I could just die. This was probably because I had such a poor image of myself. I was terrified of losing him.

Scene after scene from the past is just like the uncut version of a movie flashing kaleidoscope-like before my eyes and I feel a sadness that penetrates to my very marrow. Such emotions are so unlike me. Over the past ten years, I merrily laughed at the world, and railed angrily at it too. I thought only silly women like Lin Daiyu[11] could feel brokenhearted when those memory-evoking seasons roll around again. The utter monotony of the train wheels is again making me foolishly melancholy.

---

[11]   The sickly, doomed female protagonist in Cao Xueqin's eighteenth century literary classic, *The Story of the Stone* (also widely known as *Dream of the Red Chamber*).

I'm doing my best to control myself from expressing this inner weakness. I tell myself it is only the conditioned reflex of my subconscious, because every scene connected in my memory with trains holds an image of Chaofan. This reminds me of the doorsill of Grandma's house. After I finished university the house underwent a renovation, and the newly fixed doorsill was now higher by one inch. I can't tell you how many times I tripped on that one inch. I know very well that the sill is now higher, but even when I lift my step I still trip on it. A scientist has said that the holding capacity of the human subconscious is thirty thousand times greater than that of full consciousness. In such an enormous space are warehoused my saddest and innermost feelings—toward Chaofan, and the height of Grandma's doorsill—just like dust-covered debris. In the aura of specific scenes, such feelings are ready to be inventoried. I'm clear-headed again now, and it's obvious that the conflicted feelings between Chaofan and me have long since been razed flat, like Grandma's home. There isn't even one little bench left behind.

⌘　⌘　⌘

During the eight years of the War of Resistance against the Japanese, the Guomindang army fought twenty-two major battles, suffered eighteen defeats, and lost almost one hundred general-rank officers on those battlefields. The name of the division commander who went to the clinic in Old Town is on that long, long list.

I don't know his full name. In my grandpa's "Confession Materials," he's labeled "Bogus Division Commander Zhang." He was a hero in the war, but during the so-called Great Cultural Revolution, he could only be called a "bogus division commander." Nowadays, we can again openly and grandly honor him as the hero he was. How could I ever explain to you that crazy time when everything in life was as unpredictable as the skies in April? After the "Bogus Division Commander" sacrificed himself for our country, there came a period in Grandpa's personal history for which he had no one to attest on his behalf. If you couldn't come up with someone to vouch for you, even frank and candid confessions were taken as lying attempts to cover up some misdeed. He was suspected of having been a Japanese collaborator, a secret agent, a spy—every crime in the book could be written onto this blank page of his history. Way back in 1954, the new regime launched a movement to liquidate counterrevolutionary elements, and Grandpa accordingly began his "Confession Materials" about this unexplainable period of his history. In all the many political movements that followed, he would be given this same writing assignment. It was something that could never receive a final approval. At our home, there was a big wooden box with a bronze lock on it. Once, it had been stuffed full with "Confession Materials." It wasn't until Grandpa realized his own Great Day of Departure was approaching, that, sick as he was, he burned those papers. Personal history confessions wouldn't be needed in heaven. I wonder what he must have felt as he watched the flames consume those papers with all his handwriting on them.

⌘   ⌘   ⌘

As the army truck started up to leave West Gate Street in the pale morning mist, Ninth Brother stared into the mirror on the outside of the truck. He watched as Second Sister covered her face and crouched down on the ground crying. Second Sister was a strong woman. Ninth Brother fully appreciated her strong character. Though the head of the house, he really didn't exercise the authority of a husband and a father but, always with a grin, would join the children in calling her "Ah Ma." The people in the household thought he was just joking around, but in, fact, he was seeking in her the mother's love he never had when he was little. Second Sister's tears didn't just get flicked away. Second Sister's tears had the greatest weight. And at this moment each teardrop was a bullet shot straight into Ninth Brother's heart.

The vehicle turned the corner and there was no more Second Sister in the mirror. When he thought this may very possibly have been his final glimpse forever of her, his tightly held willpower of the last few days dissolved entirely. Instantly the tears were rolling down his cheeks and he quickly took off his barracks cap and covered his face with it. He wavered, suddenly doubting the choice he had made. *Me, this mere weakling of a scholar, compared to the vastness of our country, I'm just a small drop of water in the ocean. But for my wife and children I am the sky above their heads. When Baohua wakes up in a little while and finds her daddy gone, she'll cry for sure and she won't be riding the bicycle to school anymore.* Of the three, she was the most like her daddy. A worrywart, brittle, and quick to cry—and always burrowed into some corner soundlessly pouring out her tears. Thinking of his little crybaby girl broke up Ninth Brother inside.

What am I doing? When God created people, he gave them different kinds of gifts. I am weak and incompetent, only fit to open a little clinic to support my family with. Why do I want to go do something that is so far beyond me? The division commander said that Old Town would have a hard time escaping this disaster. I should stay behind and protect my family.

With this thought, he stopped his crying and pulled the cap away from his face. He now decided to make a humble apology in person to the division commander and beg to be forgiven his cowardice.

The military camp in the northern outskirts was awaiting Dr. Lin. The troops, fully kitted up and ready to set out, lined up on both sides of the road. Opening the truck door and seeing this mighty sight, Ninth Brother was seized by panic. An open car was parked in the middle of the little road. Division Commander Zhang grasped Dr. Lin and pulled him up. "Brothers! Welcome Dr. Lin to the War of Resistance!" There was deafening applause and cheering. Ninth Brother stood at the side of the division commander, as dumb as a wooden chicken. *Am I dreaming? Are they filming a movie?* Division Commander Zhang was an educated man who spoke very eloquently in a voice as resonant as steel balls and bronze cannons, as the saying goes. He waved his arms about in his warm praise of Dr. Lin's patriotic forsaking of his family. He said that when he saw Dr. Lin's tenderness toward his child in the clinic, he really couldn't bear recruiting this loving father into the army. But Dr. Lin himself had a firm grasp of right and wrong. He knew that no egg could remain intact if the whole nest were overturned. *If there were no country, there would be no home!* Division Commander Zhang used this welcome for Dr. Lin to buck up the troops' spirits for the coming battle. If his speech was like a torch setting their hearts ablaze, the fervor of the camp sent flames raging into the heavens.

Ninth Brother was moved. Here in this great sea of faces, was there anyone who didn't have worried family members back home? *My life is no more honorable or respectable than theirs. If they can bathe in blood at the front, why can't I?* He closed his eyes and uttered a prayer to Jesus. *Oh, Lord, you always reveal your great power in the weakness of men. I ask you to take away my weakness and grant me a soldier's daring and courage. Amen.* Jesus said, "My grace is sufficient for you, for my power is shown perfect in man's weakness."

Division Commander Zhang patted Ninth Brother's bony shoulder. "Now you say a few words, Doctor!"

Ninth Brother was stupefied for a moment and then said, "I...I'm just a scholar who couldn't truss a hen, but I will work hard to learn from you all, and I can live and die with you."

The doctor's humble and sincere attitude had the unexpected effect of adding fuel to the fire. The applause and cheers the troops gave him were long and loud.

The army set out in a vast and mighty surge. Division Commander Zhang made the doctor sit beside him and stuck a little silver pistol into his belt. "I took this on the battlefield. German-made. I am giving it to you."

Ninth Brother gave the gun back to the division commander. "I'm a Christian. I cannot shoot someone."

The other let out a great roar of laughter. "Remember, you're going into battle and it's easier to kill a man there than to kill an ant. If you don't kill the enemy, the enemy will just kill you. Take it!"

Ninth Brother put out his hand to ward it off. "I have a sacred responsibility to rescue the wounded and dying and absolutely *not* to kill people."

"If the enemy was standing right in front of you, and he had a gun in his hand, what would you do?"

"I'd rather he kill me than me kill him."

"OK. I will help you achieve your beliefs. I hope I can protect you until this war is over, and when the time comes, I'll send you home myself. I liked Old Town quite a bit. I'll buy a house there later and be your neighbor."

That man would rather die than sacrifice the principles of his belief. Once again, the division commander looked at the doctor with new eyes. *This scholar isn't the weakling he seems.* The division commander was older than Ninth Brother by a few years. Later on, in the few days left to him in this world, he looked after and protected the doctor just as he would his own younger brother.

Though his home receded farther and farther into the distance with each passing day, Ninth Brother still lapsed into feelings of weakness. In camp, he would often secretly cry out of homesickness and he would pray all the harder just to keep on going.

One night, Ninth Brother went out to pray on a little hillside next to camp. The sky was so close and the clusters and constellations of stars so sparkling and brilliant, it was as if he could just reach out and touch them. He believed that the Lord Jesus was by his side. Without even opening his mouth to pray for himself and his family he immediately felt a great weight being lifted from him.

A gentle voice came floating to him on the wind: "O my child, I have already given you and your family the power to become the sons and daughters of God. You are immortal and, in the end, you will gather together in heaven. Your separation is now but for a little while."

"Yes, Lord," Ninth Brother said, "I shouldn't be so worried and unable to bear the separation from my children's love."

The year Ninth Brother turned eight, Mr. and Mrs. Qiao introduced him to Jesus. From that time on, no difficulty or obstacle could bring him down. Jesus was his lifelong source of happiness. Speaking with Jesus brought ease and serenity to him. There, on that hillside, no longer enmeshed in distressful thoughts about his family, he considered the world beyond his family. How were Mr. and Mrs. Qiao getting on? And how were his old Shanghai schoolmates? Since Beiping and Shanghai had fallen one after the other, there had been no word from them. *O Lord, please watch over them.*

There was no pity on the battlefield and death spread like a plague. Many people could not be saved and were going to plunge into the darkness. *O Lord, how should I save them? Mr. Qiao once told me of a ship sinking into the icy sea. It was a passenger liner that hit an iceberg and split open while sailing out of Europe for North America. Death came upon the surging waters and pressed in on the three hundred lives aboard the ship. A pastor stood up and called upon all the Christians at this final moment of their lives to launch rescue operations. "Believe in Jesus and you will have eternal life." When they drowned, the pastor and many of the Christians were still struggling amid the ice floes, searching for those who still had not had the chance to hear the Good News of Jesus.*

Division Commander Zhang, getting up in the night, saw the doctor's quilted sleeping bag still neatly folded on his bed. *Now what's that bookworm up to? Let's hope the night watch doesn't shoot him by mistake. Last time, in the Jiangxi Western Mountains, the sentries almost shot him for a black bear.* More than a few times the division commander heard the lower ranks saying how Dr. Lin wasn't quite right in the head. The division commander would just give a snort of contempt at such talk, for the doctor was a man of faith. He himself had no beliefs at all. When he was young, his greatest ideal was to lead troops in battle. He could have given his life for Sun Yat-sen and could have done the same for Yuan Shikai,[12] but he respected men of faith and principle. At military school, one of his very best friends believed in communism, and Division Commander Zhang saw in him the power of belief. If they hadn't lost contact with the outbreak of war, it was very possible he himself could have been brainwashed into becoming a follower of communism.

The division commander put on his military greatcoat and went up the hillside. He knew the doctor was praying and he didn't disturb him.

"Lord, I offer this prayer to you for Division Commander Zhang and the entire division, officers and men. Please protect ~~them and give th~~em peace. And, please, move the heart of Division

[12] Born in Henan Province in 1859, Yuan Shikai was by turns a top military commander in the last days of the Qing dynasty, a brutal power broker with the new republican government, its provisional president, and would-be founder of a new dynasty. He died, repudiated by all, in 1916. China's fragmentation into warring fiefdoms ensued, ending to some degree with the capture of Beijing by the Guomindang Revolutionary Army in 1928.

Commander Zhang. Make him get to know you and let him receive eternal happiness and bring happiness to the officers and men."

The doctor's fervent prayer moved Division Commander Zhang. All along, he had thought that the doctor was cowardly and weak and that he sought the god's help as a protective charm, like those men and women believers all burning incense in the temples, knocking their heads on the ground, and praying for blessings and wealth for themselves only. As the doctor said, "Amen," and got up to return to camp, the division commander called out to him.

"Dr. Lin, your god still hasn't moved me, but you have. Thank you for asking for blessings and peace for me. All right then, let's have a talk about your god. Can he really do anything? And how's he any different from Bodhisattva who's worshipped by the common folk?"

The doctor felt his heart turn over. *O Lord! You heard my prayer and have answered my request!*

"Division Commander, if you have been moved, that was nothing at all of my doing. It was God, Jesus, who moved you."

With great feeling, the doctor told the story of Jesus, of how that infant, born in a manger, redeemed the sins of men with his own blood. He is the Way, the Truth, and the Life."

The division commander only half-believed all this. He thought: *In over ten years of military life, I've killed men like flies. In the world of men, I am a hero of outstanding achievements. But if there really is a heaven and a hell after death, how will I be dealt with then? When the day comes that I get in the way of a bullet and bite the dust, will the vengeful spirits and wandering ghosts of all those who died under my rifle come looking to settle the score? Since Jesus can forgive sins, why not just believe in him?*

"Doctor, I suppose you have to go to church before you can believe in Jesus?"

"No, at this very moment you can believe in him. If in your heart and voice you just receive Jesus as your savior, you can gain everlasting life."

"OK, I believe in Jesus with my heart and voice."

The doctor prayed happily for the division commander. Raising his head, he gazed at the early light breaking magnificently across the horizon. *Surely, that is the Lord Jesus showing his approval of me. The Lord has sent me to the army not only to save the lives of the wounded but also to bring more people to everlasting life. This is such a great mission.* Ninth Brother felt for a moment he had changed into something extraordinary.

This day on the march, Ninth Brother wrote a letter to Second Sister, telling of how he had wavered in doubt, how every day he had cried thinking of her and the children who were now all alone. This showed how weak his faith was. He had forgotten what the Bible said: "Everything is God's will." God led him to join the army in order to use him. Ninth Brother asked his wife to pray fervently, and in her prayer to remember him, to make his faith all the more steadfast.

2.

WHEN THE TROOPS marched into Shandong, they received their battle orders. A division of the Guomindang Army, trapped by Japanese artillery fire, had suffered heavy casualties and was in grave danger. Division Commander Zhang had to lead his troops into an attack from the south and break through the enemy forces to rescue his brother unit.

The battle command post and the medical station were set up in the home of some local moneybags. That man and his family and everybody in the village had all fled. The sounds of rifles and artillery were now nearby. Ownerless chickens, ducks, pigs, and dogs were running crazily about on the dusty dirt roads.

This was Dr. Lin's first time on a battlefield and, in his inevitable terror, his hands couldn't stop trembling as he set up the temporary first aid station. In his appointment by the division commander as head of the medical station, his only orderly was "Young" Li. Moving with the army up from the south had taught Young Li some rough knowledge of battlefield surgery. In medical college, Dr. Lin had specialized in internal medicine, but would he be able to cope with this? As he looked at the white bed sheets spread over the few camp cots, he thought of the bloody scenes to come when the wounded were brought in with their shattered limbs. Cold sweat beaded on his forehead as a feeling of helplessness spread through him. Ever since he was little, Ninth Brother had feared the sight of blood. When he was an intern honing his skills in the surgery practicum, the moment the senior surgeon's scalpel made its incision and blood spurted out of the cut in the patient's abdomen, Ninth Brother's stomach would revolt and, with a sensation of floating, he'd just about keel over. Now that he was a military doctor, he realized seeing blood would be a far more serious test than just thinking about home.

Young Li quickly finished the work at hand and, coming to attention in front of Ninth Brother, said, "Reporting to the station head. Everything is now in proper readiness!"

Ninth Brother said, "Let us both say a prayer."

Ninth Brother had nurtured Young Li into becoming his first fellow believer in the army. As a child, Young Li had known only misery and suffering in a mountain district near Old Town. He had never gone to school. It was only because Station Head Lin was a good man that he had been willing to follow his beliefs.

"O Lord, please bless and protect this little medical station. And please give us the fortitude and ability to give the very best treatment to every one of the wounded."

"Amen," said Division Commander Zhang as he walked in. "Brothers, neither of you have seen real battle, right? Don't be afraid. You'll be safe with me here. Even if something unexpected happens, we can always meet in heaven."

When he said, "Heaven," the mouth of the division commander spread in a mocking smile. He still only partly believed.

A bomb exploded not far off. All around was in utter confusion. The roof beam, doors, and windows shook with each blow. Dirt and waste fell and thickly layered the newly spread white bed sheets.

The two armies were exchanging fire. The bloody battle had started.

Just as the division commander was about to head out the door, the first stretcher was brought in. The wounded soldier was covered in blood, just like someone pulled out of a vat of dye. The doctor had no idea where he had been hit and, with his scissors, cut through the blood-soaked uniform with delicate and refined motions. Watching alongside, the division commander stamped his foot in growing agitation. "What the...! You're an army doctor! This is a battlefield! Don't act like some big girl stitching flowers." And as he said this, he reached out and wiped off some blood from the soldier's face. "He's no longer breathing! So quit the useless work!"

His hands covered with fresh blood, Dr. Lin just stood there blankly. He felt angry and hurt at the division commander's insensitivity. *This was someone's life*!

The pungent smell of blood was a poison gas that made his heart race double time and his head giddy. The division commander saw his face turn ashen and the sweat drip from his nose and this just added to his fury. "I really never thought you'd be so useless. What made you think you had it in you to do this sort of thing? Just go home when the battle's over!"

The second stretcher was carried in. The soldier's legs had been blown off and these, with parts of their shoes still on them, had been placed alongside him. Blood was still spurting out of him.

The doctor clenched his fists and shouted, "Help me, Lord!" The words were no sooner out than it was as if some force thrust him aside, making him a bystander, and, as the saying goes, "watching a battle from the ramparts." He saw a pair of bright red hands pick up a forceps and lightly probe this way and that searching for the blood vessel in all the gore. After he had finished ligating and sewing, the doctor's face was covered with a film that spread all over in a dark red scab.

The third wounded soldier suddenly sat up on the operating table and fell over dead.

The fourth one's stomach had been split open, his intestines flowing out over the entire stretcher and stinking to the high heavens.

The division commander was just then in the rear courtyard pacing back and forth inside the command post. Looking abruptly into the first aid station set up in the front room, he saw the curtain, bed sheets, and the doctor's overcoat all dyed red with blood. The doctor was holding the gleaming white intestines in both his hands, his face totally without expression. He looked like a professional butcher. *Where did that scholar suddenly get this courage? Just a moment ago, he was shaking and shivering all over.*

Stretchers with their wounded covered the ground. One by one, those with serious injuries died. Late that night, combat faded away and stopped. The doctor looked at one after the other of the stiffening corpses, thinking that as strangers dying in a strange land, they would become solitary wraiths and wandering ghosts. He felt guilt and pain that he had not been able to save their souls.

⌘ ⌘ ⌘

This battle was one of the defeats. After their encircled fellow unit broke out, the division commander received the order to withdraw. Immediately afterward, the several dozen hamlets surrounding the village they had set up in were occupied by the Japanese.

The doctor was totally unaware of the military situation and supposed that their own soldiers were driving off the Japanese troops and everything was safe and sound here. Before withdrawing, he took Young Li with him to the well and got water to splash off the bloodstains inside the building. The division commander, who had been waiting impatiently in his vehicle, rushed in and hauled the doctor out, calling him a bookworm.

The gunfire to their rear was now continuous. The doctor asked the division commander, "How come fighting's still going on?"

"A company's been left behind to cover us."

"Then what about the wounded?"

"This is what's called 'losing a few to save the army.' They're in heaven's hands now."

"I should stay behind. I'm a doctor and I've learned a bit of Japanese. They shouldn't do anything to me."

"Don't talk nonsense. I'm not about to let you leave me!"

"If the battle isn't over yet, why are we withdrawing?"

The division commander laughed harshly, "You know the saying: 'A scholar meets a soldier—reason can say nothing to force.' Here I am, a soldier, meeting a scholar, and I'm the one who can't say anything. Just let's get going out of here!"

After several hours, their unit regrouped and rested by a small river. Both officers and men stripped bare and washed in the stream. The doctor waded in, still wearing his uniform. An officer with a northern accent shouted out, "Hey, doc, strip off yer duds!" Several guys laughed and reached out for him, scaring him so much he ran several yards off. Northerners seemed to have a kind of primitive frankness about their own bodies. Twenty or thirty men could strip naked and sleep all bunched together on one *kang*.[13] At night it wasn't uncommon to see a totally naked man relieving himself by the base of a wall or on a tree root. The first time he confronted "sky bodies" in the camp was when there was a midnight emergency. Still half-asleep, the doctor bumped into a row of men on a large *kang,* none of whom had a stitch on. He was so embarrassed he blushed like a girl. Backing out the door, he told them to put on some clothing. For a while, this incident became a big joke throughout the unit. Nowadays, although he was no longer shocked by such things, he still couldn't manage that kind of "frankness and sincerity" with them.

---

[13] A kind of brick-oven bed used in the cold North China climate.

The doctor went over to a shady spot under some nearby trees and, wading into the water, washed away the bloodstains from his body. A streak of red spread and drifted on the surface of the river. Looking at the blood clots he was scrubbing from the ends of his hair, he wondered: *Whose blood had that been? Is he now dead or alive?* In two days, he had seen far too much fresh blood and too many dead men. His ability to be so unmoved at the reek of blood surprised him. It was just war, brutal war. In just one day, it could take a person and forge him into someone else.

He sat on the riverbank and took out of his haversack the half letter he had written before the battle. He purposely changed to a fountain pen with dark ink. "Dear Second Sister, here is a letter which I didn't finish writing. The fighting began, and for two short days and nights, I passed between life and death. With my own eyes, I saw the evil and destruction of this world. I am a different person now, it would seem. I want to tell you everything, bit by bit, to make you mentally prepared; otherwise, someday later on when we meet, you won't recognize your husband. The bloodletting of war knows no pity. Anything at all could happen. You are a strong woman. If only you would become even stronger and not be afraid. We Christians have always seen death as a return home."

Mail was still flowing between Old Town and Jiangxi Province. But leaving Jiangxi, there was nowhere to post the seven or eight letters he wrote along the way. Nonetheless, he persisted in writing something to her at every place they stopped.

3.

THE TROOPS THAT had marched out from Old Town continued their way north. They fought and marched and marched and fought the whole way. Every battle they were ordered to fight in was still little stuff, cut-and-thrust flanking attacks, and never anything head-on with the Japanese army. The generalissimo wanted this force to conserve its strength and then rush into Henan Province to lead a major attack.

While the troops were stationed in a small market town on the Anhui and Henan provincial border awaiting orders, each meal in the camp was like the Last Supper—no one knew what the next day would bring. "If this morning we have wine, this morning we'll drink it," as the saying goes, and life became one great debauchery of eating, drinking, whoring, and gambling.

The division commander seemed to realize that Henan would be his burial ground. Every evening he would invite the doctor for a heart-to-heart talk over cups of wine. After he had passed his test of fire, this scrawny student of a doctor was no longer the object of the division commander's scorn. In fact, as time passed, the more the division commander trusted him. There was nothing, affairs of state or matters of home, that they didn't touch on in their discussions.

One day they talked about the current political situation. The division commander lowered his voice, "Do you know why 'Old Chiang'[14] has his heart so set on Henan?"

The doctor shook his head.

"That's where the communists' influence is stronger than ours. The old boy just doesn't live in reality."

---

[14] Chiang Kai-shek (pronounced "Jiang Jieshi" in Mandarin).

"Haven't the communists and the Guomindang agreed to work together against the Japanese?"

"You're still the bookworm. What emperor of any dynasty was ever willing to clasp his hands in front of him and cede half the land? Just you wait, sooner or later, those two sides, the Guomindang and the communists, will start fighting each other."

"You mean there'll be a civil war? Would you join in a civil war?"

The division commander took off his barracks cap and flung it aside. "Don't know."

The doctor respectfully raised the wine cup in both his hands. "Eldest Brother Zhang, listen to my word of advice. Don't go and fight your own countrymen. It's a sin and it will keep you out of heaven."

"I can't think that far ahead. Who knows the day I will join the ranks of the martyrs? *Ai*! I have no father or mother. Right now, you're the one I am most concerned about. If I die, just go on back home! There'll never be another senior officer who would look after you the way I have. Some are wilder than bandits. If they're in a bad mood, they'll shoot you and make up some report against you to their superiors. And then your family wouldn't even be able to get the condolence pension."

From what the division commander said in such a casual way, the doctor reflected on his most weighty relationships. Having been born into a big family, he had a multitude of siblings and Eldest Brother was thirty years older than he was. But he had never known any brotherly relationship as deeply affectionate as this one. When he imagined the division commander fallen in a pool of blood, the rims of his eyes reddened and he said in a breaking voice, "I will pray for you and ask the Lord to have mercy on you."

The division commander let out a great laugh. "So! Your guts can still churn. I thought that in your heart you were now the Indestructible Adamantine! Hey, can't we still meet again up there with Jesus? Right! There are a few small gold pieces in my leather handbag. When I take my last breath, they're yours. Don't forget to buy a little wine from time to time and have a drink on me."

The doctor wanted to follow up with something funny, like *In heaven there are fine wines and luminous cups*, but he couldn't squeeze a smile out of his tight expression.

Those bandits acting as soldiers that the division commander spoke of were everywhere. One time there was a battalion commander who wanted to be treated for a headache. When Young Li was a bit slow in moving, the officer suddenly pulled out his pistol and brought it up against the orderly's head. To meet such an enlightened, chivalrous, and kindhearted officer like Division Commander Zhang was really a blessing sent from heaven. *O Lord, please bless and protect Division Commander Zhang. This unit couldn't do without him.*

⌘　⌘　⌘

The Carnival of the Doomed in this little market town went on for about a month. The war had become distant and hazy and officers and men freely squandered every last bit of their pay. The postal routes had been paralyzed for several months now, so there could be no remittances home. The soldiers knew full well that hundreds of miles beyond the flames of war their families waited to put rice in their cooking pots and they wanted to help them, but they couldn't. So it would be better just to use what time was left to have as much fun as they could. Physically they lived in drunken debauchery; spiritually they were already dead. The doctor took Young Li with him and went canvassing up and down the ranks, telling everyone that death was another kind of beginning, that with the Lord Jesus there was forever a tomorrow. All the officers and men laughed at them and called them crazy. A drunken captain had heard that Jesus could perform miracles. He laughed wildly from a gaping mouth of yellowed teeth. "Have Jesus make me a woman to sleep with and I'll believe!"

One day, the division commander discovered that the hard grain liquor he had been drinking was watered down. Bored and irritated, he wanted to pick a quarrel and blow his stack, so, taking his orderly along, he went into town looking for the little shop that had sold the drink. Running the shop was a young widow, not bad looking and charming indeed. In no time at all, she had laid low this fierce tiger, this hero of a hundred battles, in her little garret. Thus were struck the sparks of love between the solitary man and the widow.

Love made the division commander turn his back on the life he had pursued for over thirty years. He took off his uniform and put on the homespun clothing such as the yokels wore. Every day he hung around the young widow. When she sold drink, he handled the receipts. When she cooked, he kept the kindling fired. When on those rare occasions he would return to division headquarters, he would sidle into the medical station, sit before the doctor like a patient, and vividly describe his love life. From the young widow the division commander learned to hum a few ditties of Anhui's popular "Yellow Plum" operas. The story of the fairy lady coming down to earth for love was classic Yellow Plum: "The birds on the tree pair up / Conjugal affections are both bitter and sweet." He sighed that the world still did have days that were good enough to bring envy to a fairy lady's heart. He said, "Younger brother, pray for me, OK? Pray that the bullets and shells have eyes to see me so this insignificant life might be saved to enjoy a few days of a woman's love."

The world gets drunk and only I stay sober. During those days, the isolation the doctor felt would have been hard to put into words. Thoughts of home bit at his nerves like locusts. He was never at ease for even a moment.

This military force, held back from taking part in any action, was a chess piece intended for a decisive move on the generalissimo's chessboard. But the Japanese had never once taken their eye off that piece, even before the generalissimo lifted it for the attack. There had not been the slightest warning sign of the combat that took place on the evening of that day. The North China Plain in deep autumn was at its most serene. The fifteenth day of the lunar month had just passed and the full moon shone extravagantly over the treetops. At night, it was even more peaceful, but the village dogs were the first to smell the gunpowder, and suddenly wild barking broke out, rising here and falling there.

The doctor was just then reading the Bible by lamplight. He copied a section of Epistle to the Romans into his notebook: *Tribulation engenders patience. Patience engenders experience. Experience gives birth to hope.*

Suddenly, there was a thumping sound. The division commander, his unbuttoned tunic hastily thrown about him, burst in. "The battle's started."

The doctor quickly woke up Young Li and they got everything in readiness.

The artillery fire moved closer and closer. By the time the eastern skies had lightened, groups of Japanese fighter planes came swarming at them. Again and again they circled tightly over the buildings. Probably they still didn't have reliable enough intelligence to bomb the frontline command post, so countless bombs were dropped on the small town. Piece by piece the buildings collapsed. In the dense fog of dust and smoke, you couldn't clearly make out anyone's face beyond two steps away.

The doctor heard the division commander call out for help. He didn't know how this battle had started, but he supposed that, as the division commander said, the main attack had commenced. With no idea just how critical and perilous the situation was, he lost himself in a single-minded concentration on saving the wounded. With his battlefield training, this physician was already the match of expert surgeons. He could rapidly find shell or bullet fragments, sew up blood vessels and wounds, and accomplish neat and smooth stitching. During some fleeting moments, he let his mind wander to Second Sister and those two skilled hands of hers. When the war was over, he intended to surprise her with a flower embroidered by his own hand.

Those of the ordinary civilians who could run, all headed for the rolling hill country to the south. The aged, weak, sick, or impaired couldn't flee and so just waited to die. That young widow, with her agile body and long legs, also stayed behind in the town. When her little shop collapsed from the impact of the bombing, she crawled out from under all the rubble and ruin, her entire body covered in lacerations, and threaded her way on her hands and knees through the gun smoke to division headquarters. When she heard the division commander roaring and raging she was so frightened she just quietly hid in a corner.

Line after line of forward defenses was attacked and destroyed. The final line was close by while reinforcements were still miles away. The senior division officers discussed the situation under showers of dirt and dust. Division Commander Zhang accepted his chief-of-staff's suggestion that the unit should split up into two divisions and break out of their heavy encirclement. Then, after merging with the relief force, they would turn around and counterattack. They all knew the price of this would be many lives, but continuing their dogged resistance would only lead to the annihilation of the entire force.

The doctor received the order to redeploy. With the help of the logistics company and taking the wounded with him, he withdrew in the direction of the fleeing civilians. His superior officer gave him only twenty minutes. The doctor didn't ask many questions—military orders were like a falling mountain. By the time he had made simple dressings for two of the wounded, the medical station had already been cleaned out.

The division commander walked to a little knoll at the entrance of the town to survey the battlefield. The young widow, shrouded in dirt, cautiously came forward. She wanted him to know that she had not abandoned him and run off by herself. This was to show him how much she loved him. But what she got instead was a roar.

"What're you doing here? Is this the place for a woman like you?"

"I ..." Her tears mixed with the dust on her face.

"Get the hell out of here!"

Holding the first aid case, the doctor stood off to the side, not daring to utter a single sound. He wanted to remind the division commander to take his medicine. This old pal of his had a stomach problem that was getting more and more serious. If it were not for the extraordinary times, he should have been under treatment in a hospital.

The division commander turned his glance to the doctor and roared at him too. "Why're you still here?"

"You should take your medicine."

"Of all the times...still fussing like some woman. Get going and take her with you. The farther the better!"

"Division Commander..."

The division commander's hand went to his holster and with the other he pointed at the doctor. "Keep up your blather, and I'll shoot you for disobeying military orders!" And then he pointed to the young widow. "And the same goes for you too. Stay one minute more, and I'll shoot *you!*"

By this time, the doctor had some faint inkling of how bad things were. He observed this good "elder brother" of his searchingly, and then said to the young widow, "Let's go."

On the battlefield, the division commander was a ferocious lion. No matter how careful the doctor was, he could never avoid the other's rage. Whenever the fighting was over, the division commander would always make up for it with him. Once, the division commander had let fly with some really foul language. Even though the doctor had not forgotten Jesus' teaching that you had to be patient and magnanimous, afterward, he could not maintain the same intimate rapport with the division commander as before and he had refused their daily chow time, buddy-to-buddy gab sessions. When chow time came, he took his mess tin and buried himself in a corner of the room to sit facing the wall. The division commander came up to him bursting with good spirits. "I'm not used to you not joining me at chow." The two men looked at each other and with a laugh all grudges vanished. From then on, the lion's fury no longer intimidated the doctor.

The doctor and the young widow reached the hilly countryside to the south. Line after line of the wounded waited there. He soon was busy with his endless surgery and was unable to look after the division commander's woman. Five days on, the fighting came to an end.

The newspaper and radio reports of that time all called this campaign a great and total victory, though, unfortunately, Division

Commander Zhang had fallen in battle courageously defending the country. While the top military command in Chongqing had already heard the reports, the doctor and the young widow still had no idea of this death.

After the firing had died down, the medical station reopened in the same market town. This time there wasn't a single continuous stretch of the city wall left. It was scorched earth as far as the eye could see and corpses were lying everywhere. The doctor hung a tent between two withered trees to treat the seriously wounded. The battlefield was being cleaned up and there in a pile of the dead they found soldiers who were still faintly breathing and these they sent to the station. The officers and men who had fallen for good were taken to an empty space nearby.

The young widow made her way through the smoking ruins in search of her lover. She had no idea what his rank was. She just called out his name as she went along, and moved and shifted the terribly mangled corpses one by one. The division commander's orderly recognized her and took her to the open space where bodies had been laid out. When he lifted away the blanket covering Division Commander Zhang, she let out an agonized shriek and burst into a storm of weeping.

The doctor had finished with one of the wounded when he heard a woman's terrible cry. Only then did he remember that the division commander had entrusted the young widow to his care and he hadn't seen her at all for many days now. He lifted the flap of the tent and looked out. Immediately he knew what had happened.

"Young Li, Young Li..." The doctor's voice went hoarse.

Young Li was over on the side lighting a fire to sterilize the surgical instruments. Looking up and following the doctor's gaze, he was so dumbfounded for a moment that he dropped the top of the pot he had been holding and in tears rushed outside.

The doctor thought of saying a prayer for the division commander, to ask the Lord to have mercy and forgive him for all the sins he had committed in this world and to receive him back into his heavenly home. He had opened his mouth and said, "O Lord," when everything within him fell apart and he sobbed and wept bitterly. He told himself not to cry, that Christians see death as a going home, that he shouldn't say good-bye to the division commander in tears, but no matter what, he couldn't contain his grief.

CHAPTER FIVE –
WHEN THE LOQUATS RIPEN

1.

GRANDMA SAID THAT when the Japanese planes appeared in the sky above Old Town, the streets were covered with ripe, golden-yellow loquats. Our Old Town was in one of those regions abounding in rice, fish, and fruit, and the Old Town folk were very particular about what they ate. Fruit, vegetables, and seafood were consumed only if fresh and in season. Oranges, bananas, loquats, "dragon eyes," and litchis—each of these fruits spelled a season of the year. Farmers and their wives shouldered pole after pole of fresh and plump fruit along the streets and through the alleyways. They all had their own piece of territory and could bring their baskets right under the sky wells of the homes of old customers. The friendships between some of these buyers and sellers had continued for generations.

When the loquats ripen, early summer has arrived. Three generations of my grandmother's Guo family all ate the fruits sold by Ah Shui. He was still a little boy way back when he and his father did their trade at West Street. By now, he himself had become a grandpa. Because Second Sister Guo married into the Lin home on Officials Lane, Ah Shui brought his trade there too. Second Sister, being the good-hearted person she was, would often give him clothes for his children. And Second Sister's husband—Ah Shui called him Uncle—had treated his little boy without charging a single *fen*. Every time Ah Shui came back into town, the fruit he would give Second Sister was the very pick of the crop, the very best of all.

Ah Shui asked Second Sister, "Is Uncle doing all right up north there?"

"He's fine, very fine. Only, he's thinking of home and his three children."

Second Sister was again packing up some clothing to give to Ah Shui's children, and she stuffed in a few copper coins. The last time Ah Shui had brought home such coins he got a good scolding from his old lady. He removed the coins from the cloth bundle.

"Second Miss, I can't accept your money."

They were both going back and forth over this when suddenly the air raid siren sounded. Ah Shui practically died from fright, and as he trembled and shivered, some of the coins fell clattering onto the flagstones.

Second Sister said, "Don't be scared. It's only a drill."

Starting the year before, from time to time the constables and the heads of several household groups would come to people's homes to provide instructions on how to protect against air raids. They ordered the residents to paste strips of white paper on the glass windows of their houses. Now, more than a year later, the white paper had all turned yellow. Second Sister had just decided to do a big cleanup and scrape away all those depressing paper strips.

The ear-piercing shriek of the siren sounded more and more urgent. Now the slack and easygoing folk of Old Town couldn't help feeling ill at ease. People dropped whatever work they were doing and ran into the streets, flustered and whispering rumors to each other. *What's this all about? Are the Japanese really coming?* Many of them were looking into the skies, using their hands to shield their eyes from the sun's glare. They still didn't know what it meant for airplanes to be flying about. Someone said airplanes were as big as eagles. Another had it that they were bigger than buildings, and these two, each sure he was right, went on and on about this.

Right then, the skies resounded with something the people of Old Town had never heard before—the thunderous roar of engines. These were just like floodwaters or wild beasts surging and raging everywhere. The siren's sound now sounded weak and ineffective in this great deluge.

The wolves had come—the wolves had really come! The Old Town folk stared dumbstruck at the planes over their heads. *Is this for real? Would Old Town, which for hundreds of years had never seen soldiers or weapons, now really be plunged into war?*

This wasn't just one or two planes; it was a whole swarm of them. They circled about in a dense mass, like some flock of crows gone mad. And from the crows' bellies fell black eggs of iron, one after the other, making the earth shake and the skies quiver!

Ah Shui said, "Second Miss, bring your children and come with me to hide in the countryside for a few days. My old lady'll fix up a clean room for you."

Second Sister thought about her three children. If they had to die, she wanted to die with them. She pushed past Ah Shui and dashed off to South Street. That was where the children's school was. She had to find them. As she ran, she murmured, "O heaven! O God! It's not life or death we care about. Either we all survive, or none of us do, and we all die!"

The people who had been milling about out of curiosity in an instant all vanished and the streets were now deserted. My grandma ran on wildly like a terrified doe, her hair bun all disheveled and her *qipao* flapping. She had no idea of how desperate she looked, nor did she care in the slightest. There was only one thought that kept her going—to die together with her children!

The contingent of people running in the same direction grew larger. Mothers converging from all directions raced toward South Street. They had the very same feeling as Second Sister—if anything had happened to their children, they just wouldn't go on living.

She saw the school now. The old banyan tree by the school entrance still stood there, calm and serene as always, and to her ears came the sound of children reading. She didn't realize this was a hallucination. Her pace slowed as her legs weakened under her. *Nothing's happened. I'm just too worried and upset.* Since Ninth Brother had gone, she was always seeing a snake's shadow in the reflection of a bow, as the saying goes, and always imagining the worst of any situation. Pastor Chen admonished her, saying that this was wrong. *The pain and suffering God gives you will in no way be more than you can bear. Jesus said, "My grace is sufficient for you."*

She pressed her violently heaving breast, and gasped for breath through her open mouth. *Nothing had actually happened anywhere... just foolish me creating problems for myself.* And if nothing happened, that was good.

A bomb glanced off the banyan tree as it fell into the school and exploded with an enormous roar. Then it was as if some giant's iron hand just swept away Second Sister and many of the other parents. As she lay flat on the ground she thought that she had been hit squarely in the bombing and was dead, for sure, and her children gone as well. But she felt strangely at peace. God in heaven had granted her prayer to let her die together with her children, and so there was nothing more to regret. She would take her three little angels back to heaven and wait for Ninth Brother there.

Everywhere parents were crawling up from the ground, keening and howling like wraiths or wild beasts. Second Sister raised her head and discovered that she was alive and in one piece. She rolled over, sprang up, and flung herself in the direction of the school, now in a fog of thick smoke. "Baoqing! Baosheng! Baohua! You can't leave your ma all alone!"

The explosion had smashed all the doors and windows of the classrooms, and bits and pieces of shattered glass covered the ground. Desks and chairs were strewn about every which way. The old fellow who rang the school bell told them that the students had all been moved into the cave on Stony Mountain beyond South Gate. Second Sister turned and went rushing off there with the rest of the crowd.

The air raid alert had been lifted and several hundred children emerged from the cave. The fathers and mothers waiting there frantically searched for their own children among all the others. And, as if finally reuniting with the survivors of some calamity, they wept from the depths of grief and the heights of exultation.

Baoqing was the first to rush into his ma's embrace, with Baosheng and Baohua right behind him. Second Sister squatted down, and pinched first this one and then rubbed that one to make sure that not a single strand of hair on their heads had suffered mishap. Only then did she break down in tears. "My children, my little dears, your ma will never let you go even one step away again."

The children were too young. They didn't understand how the adults could have gotten so panicky and lost their self-control. Baosheng stepped on Baohua's little leather shoes and the two of them started quarrelling. Baosheng said, "Ma likes you the best. When there's nothing to eat at home, she still buys you shoes." Baohua said, "The money that Daddy sends is all for me!" But Baoqing, who was not yet seven years old, was like a little grown-up. Stretching forth his chubby hand, he wiped away his mother's tears and said, "Ma, don't be scared. When I grow up I'm going to earn a lot of money and buy you flatcakes and clothes to wear, and leather shoes also for Big Sister." Second Sister took Baoqing in her arms. The relatives all said that she loved her little son the best. He was the little man of this family. Many times, he would quite consciously assume a father's role, comforting and supporting his mother. This little boy was so accommodating and good at understanding what other people wanted, how could his mother not love him until her heart just ached?

⌘   ⌘   ⌘

The people of Old Town had never seen real guns or cannons and couldn't bear this sort of fright. Though not a single person died from the air raid's explosions that day, several people died out of sheer fright. There was one eighty-year-old lady on Stipend Lane who had a son who was an official. When she celebrated her great sixtieth birthday, he gave her a coffin of the very best wood. This coffin was a great delight to her. Every year she had a painter come and lay on a fresh, full coat of varnish. But all the upheaval and chaos of war made her worry that she wouldn't get the chance to enjoy the use of her beloved coffin. Three days after the air raid, the old lady hanged herself and was laid out in her coffin and put to rest in the ground, all before Old Town itself was destroyed.

The Japanese planes had gone but they left behind a miasma of terror, and it was this terror, like an unstoppable plague, that brought Old Town down. By spreading the wings of their imagination, and treating imagination as absolute fact, people quite unconsciously did everything that would magnify fear. Rumors arose on all sides. Everyone suffered from such rumors and yet everyone invented them. Today it was reported that the Japanese were approaching from the sea. Tomorrow it would be said they had already arrived at Old Mountain. Old Town had relied forever on those endless mountain ranges to hide from war. Because of the airplanes, Old Town no longer had this protective screen. Several people back from the north told vivid and graphic stories of how the blue-faced and long-fanged Japanese raped and killed women, cooked and ate children, and how they chopped old folks into mincemeat and threw their remains into the rivers to feed the fish. Up north there was a big city called Nanjing that experienced just such calamities. There, after several years, the river waters were still running red.

The old sayings about cranes crying out at the whistling wind and enemies seen in every bush and tree describe just how jittery everyone was. For several days, the air raid siren at the corner of West Street would perversely go off, crazily sounding out several blasts from time to time, and even if it was just for a fleeting moment, this could lead to devastating panic. Men and women, the old and young, would dash about pell-mell, covering their heads with their arms.

The great catastrophe was approaching. When they see a bow, birds will fly off in all directions. One by one, the six tables in the back hall of the Lin home now became empty. Big Sister-in-Law and Eldest Brother Lin left Old Town for a mountain district about a hundred miles to the north where a serving girl, once part of Big Sister-in-Law's dowry, now lived. Second Brother Lin and all of his household sought refuge in the home of his wife's aunt. This woman's husband was working in a porcelain kiln near the border of another province. The ways of the world were all changing now. While "such-and-such" may have been the case previously, now things were totally different. In the past, country cousins were a burden on their moneyed relatives, and just thinking about them was enough to bring on a headache. Now, though, having relatives in the countryside was the greatest bit of good fortune one could have. Being the first to wrap up one's valuables and escape disaster was as enviable as going up to the capital to take the old imperial examinations.

Grandma could have chosen quite a few places to go to. Before she herself fled, her big sister had sent her rickshaw puller over to her home, but Second Sister didn't want to leave. Ah Shui, the loquat seller, also tried to persuade her to go to his home. Her own family members had sent any number of messages welcoming her and her three children to stay with them. But she declined with thanks one invitation after the other, and closing the doors and watching over her three children, she calmly faced life or death. Underneath the kitchen cupboard there was a little jar of white arsenic, quite enough to end ten lives. If the Japanese really did come to their door, she would lead her children out of this world.

Several decades later, when speaking of that jar of arsenic, Grandma's face still took on a heroic and stern look, as if that poison had been a magic sword that could destroy calamity and ward off harm. By that time, she was already more than eighty years old, but she didn't actually feel lucky or proud about having reached this age now that my grandfather was no longer alive. Every day she awaited the Lord's call. Sometimes she would resent God for having forgotten her. She had a group of old card-playing friends and they often got together to play *paijiu*. This group of more than ten old folks diminished one by one. Today someone might be at the table getting all worked up over winning or losing a few *fen*. Tomorrow that person may no longer be there. My grandma was one of the people in this little group who had lived the longest. She told me that during that earlier time she had felt no hope at all, what with my grandfather having been away for more than three years. She thought that only by going to heaven could she see him again.

⌘ ⌘ ⌘

The Lin mansion was like a theatre whose audience had all left. Removing her costume and going on "actors' strike" gave Second Sister an unaccustomed feeling of relief. From the time that she had first made up the lie that Ninth Brother was doing just fine out there, every day she had to create new lies to cover up and maintain the first one. Now there was no longer any need for lying. Now she didn't have to force herself to beat her cheeks swollen to look well fed, or put on a big act of buying a little meat to keep turning and frying to send the fragrance wafting out of the pan until it was almost ruined before letting the children eat it. No need to scrunch under the oil lamp at night to do sewing to earn a little change and still pretend to be to the manner born. Every time her relatives came to her for help to cover their daily needs, she would tuck her coins and small bills into her clothing and take these to a money house to change into big bills. Big bills would prove that Ninth Brother was still sending money home every month. With the burden of children to care for, if she broke off a tooth, so to speak, she just had to swallow it. And that was the way she made it through those three or four years. Now, though, she was really just too tired. She didn't have the strength to become a homeless destitute, a refugee.

All the tailoring shops along the streets were now closed. With no sewing work to be had, Second Sister extinguished the lamp and went to sleep much earlier. Her mind was a blank and so she slept very soundly.

Suddenly, the front door opened with a creak. Next, footsteps sounded on the hall floorboards. This she found quite puzzling. The doors and windows had been shut for several days now. *Don't tell me that naughty Baosheng has slipped out to play and forgotten to close the door.* As she was thinking of going out to see for herself, the door to the bedroom was pushed open and in came Ninth Brother, wearing his military uniform, and looking very angry. He sat down in the cane chair by the bedstead, his barracks cap held in his hand.

She didn't feel this was any soul-stirring reunion. It was as if her husband had just returned from treating some patient. She said, "Ninth Brother, are you hungry? I'll make some sweet rice dumplings for you."

Her feet had barely touched her soft-soled embroidered slippers when Ninth Brother stopped her in his grip.

"I never thought you'd be so cruel as to actually consider poisoning my children!"

Second Sister was stunned. Dimly, the thought of the arsenic under the cupboard registered in her. But she couldn't remember whether or not she had already poisoned the children. She ran barefooted into the next room. The two boys were curled up like a heap of prawns. Baohua was on the other bed, just turning over and softly grinding her teeth. Retracing her steps, she said with some resentment, "Ninth Brother, you frightened me almost to death."

The cane chair at the head of the bed was empty. There simply was no trace of Ninth Brother. Second Sister was so scared that her teeth chattered. *It's all over. Ninth Brother's dead. That was his ghost floating across the many leagues of rivers and mountains to return to this house.* She slid down the doorframe onto the threshold. *No, no! We are God's children. When we die, we return to our heavenly home. We won't be stranded in this world as lonely spirits and wandering ghosts. Surely, our Heavenly Father sent the Holy Spirit to tell me: "You have no right to end the lives I have given to you. You must patiently wait for your husband." I was out of my mind, I think. I was really out of my mind. How could I, with my own hands, have poisoned my three little angels? Even if it was just a fleeting thought in my mind, it was an unpardonable sin. O Heavenly Father, forgive me that moment of weakness.*

When dawn came and the children got out of bed, they saw that their mother had already fixed four cloth bundles. When they realized this meant a long trip, each of them excitedly chose favorite toys and stuffed them into the bundles.

Second Sister's own mother and younger brothers hadn't any plan to flee the coming disaster. For them death was no great matter. Such indomitable spirit truly still reflected something of the General Guo Ziyi style. The mother could not bear to part with the old Guo residence. "Monks can flee the monastery, but the monastery can't run off too," she said. If she were going to die, then she would just die in her own house. Second Sister's first younger brother couldn't stand the idea of no more strong drink for him if they fled. He would rather stick around West Street. "Wine is for drinking" is how he looked at life. His wife had used her dowry money to open a small variety store in front of their house. There was enough wine in stock there for him to drink for a year and a half. As for Second Brother, after hitting it off with a girl from the pleasure quarters, he vanished from the scene, to where no one knew. His wife took their daughter and returned to her own home. People said she suffered from "peach epilepsy," for when the peach flowers were in blossom, she would fall senseless. Grandma's third younger brother was the one that had won their mother's heart. Not long after Ninth Brother had gone off, this young man was about to be married when he suddenly died of the measles. This was a heartbreaking event for Second Sister and all her family. Second Sister's fourth and fifth brothers were still quite young. Normally, First Brother's wife handled the household affairs, but whenever she encountered any important problem, Second Sister would have to step forward bravely to play the mainstay role. When all her sisters-in-law were hard up for money, it was to Second Sister that they would go. If the sky fell down on the Guo home, Second Sister was the one to prop it up. Up to that time, no one at her old family home knew that she hadn't received a single bit of news from Ninth Brother in over two years.

Second Sister returned to West Street, bringing her children with her. There was no need to discuss anything. People who assume responsibility have the authority to make decisions. "Let's go. We'll head west to the mountain district and look for Uncle." "I'm not going," her mother said, "but you go ahead and take Fourth Brother and Fifth Brother with you." Second Sister didn't waste any more words. She just rolled back her sleeves and set to rummaging through boxes and closets and organizing the valuable items.

All the arrangements were completed. Second Sister wanted to go to the church to say good-bye to Pastor Chen as well as to go outside West Gate to find sedan chair carriers. With those tiny, three-inch bound feet her mother would surely need a sedan chair.

As always, Pastor and Mrs. Chen prayed for Second Sister. Second Sister left her uncle's address with them and urged them to make early arrangements to get out of Old Town. As she was writing down the address, Second Sister thought of Ninth Brother. *If Ninth Brother returns and can't find his wife and children, he would definitely go to the Chens.*

⌘　⌘　⌘

On the road, the little column of Guo family refugees had not yet passed through the city district when First Brother had already drunk a little flagon of liquor to the last drop. He roared out and staggered around with the empty vessel clutched in his hand. "I'm not going on...Nothing more to drink...I...I can't make it...The little Japs...This guy won't make it."

Second Sister made the sedan carriers stop and asked his wife, "What do you think we should do?"

"Let him stay. Just look at him! He can't go for one minute without drinking. Even if we go on five or ten miles, he'll be making a lot of fuss about wanting to go home." The woman glanced at the sedan chair. Her son, six-year-old Gan'er, was sitting with his granny. "Second Sister, please take Gan'er for us."

"Don't worry about Gan'er. If you two aren't coming with us, you'll need to find a place to hide."

"Bombs may not get him, but without something to drink he'll die for sure. It's really no good at all. I'll take him back to my home. All in all, it should be a bit safer in the countryside than in town."

First Brother's wife's own home was in the countryside east of the Yangzi. There, most people lived by raising silkworms, and groves of mulberry trees shaded all the buildings in the villages. *Could they get lucky maybe and escape the awful war?* Second Sister thought of how straitened her own finances were. There was no way they would be able to buy drink for him along the way, so she hardened her heart and said, "All right, just take him to your home, and bring all the drink you have in inventory with you. Take good care of yourselves."

Mother Guo stuck her head out of the sedan chair, "What's going on with First Brother?"

"Nothing. They're both going back home to get some things. They'll be catching up again in a little while."

And with that, Second Sister waved her hand at the carriers. "Lift the chairs. Let's get moving."

2.

As THE SUN'S rays slanted from the west, all the Guos, young and old, rested by a brook at the foot of Old Mountain. This was Old Town's scenic spot, with its emerald-green mountain range and its limpid streams. Many-hued goose-egg stones under the water glowed in the light of the setting sun. Ninth Brother had loved mountain streams. When they were newly wed, he would take Second Sister rambling through all the nooks and crannies in Old Town's outlying districts. It was on one of those huge goose-egg stones that Ninth Brother, eyes filmed over in a kind of intoxication, had embraced her and, with much head-bobbing and swaying, chanted poetry improvised by him then and there.

The sight of this place struck a chord within her and her eyes grew misty as she recalled Ninth Brother. She sat on the goose-egg stone and absentmindedly wetted a towel to clean her children's faces. Baosheng was playing with his slingshot off to one side. Second Sister had wiped his face repeatedly.

Just then, Gan'er wanted to suckle and, not finding his mother, burst out crying. At six years old, this child had still not been fully weaned. Whenever he thought about it, he would run into the kitchen and lift up the front of his mother's blouse to take a few sucks. The old lady in her sedan chair did magic tricks producing olives, haws, and mung bean cakes, and the most appetizing of all, pork floss. One by one, these were popped into Gan'er's mouth, but none of these quelled the racket he was making.

Clumsy and lumpish Gan'er was the heart's delight of Old Lady Guo. Gan'er was already three when he took his first tottering steps, and only when he was four did he say "Dad" and "Ma." In those days, no one knew about proper pregnancy and birth care, or that alcohol in the father's blood could sear the child's brain cells. In her lifetime, Old Lady Guo had had her heart broken by her several sons. Her daughters, though, had given her more good luck than she could enjoy, but that was not enough to make her change her view of the primacy of boys. She said Gan'er's difficulty in opening his "golden" mouth was a sign of great fortune and honor later on. She also said that ten "thousand gold pieces," that is, ten girls, could never match even one idiot son.[15] A few years earlier, she had favored Second Sister's two boys. Whenever there were a few tasty things around, she would tuck them away for these grandsons to eat. She would often quietly call them into her room and, with a trembling hand, reach for snacks at her bedstead that she would give them behind Second Sister's back. But now that she had a grandson bearing her own married name, the ones who didn't were, in her mind, well-named as "outside" grandsons. Whenever the three children visited their grandma's house, they often watched with staring eyes as their granny stuffed all kinds of good things into Gan'er's mouth, while not even a crumb went into theirs.

Baoqing stood to the side, staring spellbound at a few wisps of pork floss lying on the ground. "Granny, some pork floss has fallen down. I'll help pick it up, all right?" Picking it up he wanted to stuff the floss into his mouth but he didn't dare to. Clicking his tongue and swallowing his saliva, he then loudly said, "Granny, the floss is all picked up."

The old lady grabbed the floss from Baoqing's hand and put it into Gan'er's mouth. Baoqing sucked at the fragrance left on his fingers and said, "Granny, when I get big, I'll buy you pork floss to eat."

Like two little birds lured by food, Baohua and Baosheng flew to the side of the sedan chair, chirping to be fed.

---

[15]   Traditionally, the Chinese termed girls "one thousand gold pieces." Boys, though, were referred to as "ten thousand gold pieces."

Their granny hesitated for a bit, shredded some floss, and gave this to Baosheng and Baoqing.

"I want some too," said Baohua.

"Go away, go away! What's a girl like you doing, adding to the fuss?"

Crying, Baohua brought this grievance to her mother. Second Sister was upset over this incident, and shouted ill temperedly at her mother, "Ma, can't you just give Baohua a little something to nibble on?"

"Don't indulge a girl's gluttony," the old lady said. "Now, you're still treating her like something precious. I've really never seen anyone forsake loving a boy, yet revere a girl like an ancestor."

"Our Baohua is Ninth Brother's very life's blood."

"Don't Ninth Brother this and Ninth Brother that with me. I may be old but I'm not addled. There hasn't been any word from him from the beginning, am I right or not? If he really had money to send home, would your days have been as difficult as they have been? As for him, if he hasn't died along the way, he's ended up as the son-in-law in someone else's home."

"You, you..." Second Sister had painstakingly concealed her secrets of these many years. Now that her mother had so easily exposed them, it was like a scar on her heart had been ripped open and pus and blood were flowing out. She opened her mouth to say something, her chin quivering, when she suddenly burst out, "Ninth Brother, You've hurt me! Oh, you've really hurt me!"

Laboriously the old lady moved on her "three-inch golden lotus" feet to her daughter's side. "Second Sister, you're just too competitive and too concerned about saving face. You should have cried a long time ago."

Second Sister couldn't hear a word her mother said. She lay face-down on the goose-egg stone, overwhelmed with grief.

The children had never before seen their mother so distressed and sorrow-stricken. They just crowded around her there by the stone, as dull-witted as three simpletons.

Their grandma seized hold of Baosheng and Baohua. "Your ma is having a hard time of things. You have to be loving and respectful of her." She turned her gaze at Baohua and said, "When your father was with us, you were the 'thousand gold pieces Little Miss.' Now, with times as difficult as these, you're just going to have to save your ma a mouth to feed. When you arrive at the mountain district, get Uncle's wife to find you a mother-in-law. You'll have to change your 'Little Miss' temper though."

Baohua did not really understand everything that Granny was saying. She was vaguely aware that maybe her daddy wasn't alive now. In her mind, she saw Daddy pushing her to school on the bicycle. She had been half-aware of people on the crowded streets casting envious glances her way. Those were such happy times. Ever since her daddy left, she no longer felt real happiness. Even though Ma was very good to her and, at least on the surface of things, was even better to her than to her two little brothers, there was something of an effort about this on Ma's part. It wasn't like the deep, deep love that poured from the bottom of Daddy's heart. Clutching her handkerchief, Baohua ran behind a tree and wiped away her tears. Over the past few years, she had often hid alone in a corner, letting the tears wash her face whenever she thought of her daddy.

Through her own tears, Second Sister recalled the faith that Pastor Chen spoke of. He said that often a Christian's faith weakened under Satan's attacks. *All these years, no matter how hard it became, I have fully believed that Jesus would look after Ninth Brother and me. But today how could I have caved in at Mother's words to me?* She stopped crying and, finding the little mirror in her bundle, intensely set about combing her hair and cleaning her face. Having restored her wondrously feminine freshness and shining beauty, she took her two little boys by the hand and went looking for Baohua.

Baohua opened her red and swollen eyes, "Ma, tell me, has my daddy died?"

Second Sister crouched down and hugged her daughter. "Wherever did you get such an idea? Daddy is a child of God, and all our family are his children. None of us will die."

"Will Daddy come back home?"

"Daddy will definitely come back home. And he will buy a new bicycle for taking you to school again."

The day was getting on now. Second Sister hailed the carriers and told them to continue on their way. They had to reach Big Mountain by this evening. There they would spend the night at the postal relay station. The next day they would change to a new sedan chair and continue the journey.

Gan'er was sleepy. He snuggled and burrowed into his granny's chest to suckle at her breasts. When he opened his eyes and did not see his mother, he threw a tantrum even more terrible than the one before. Old Lady Guo tipped out the contents of her little satchel and tried all kinds of little snacks and dainties on him, but it did no good. Really, there was nothing else to do, so she actually raised up her blouse and thrust a pitch-black and flaccid nipple into the child's mouth.

Second Sister was walking alongside the sedan chair at the time and she heaved a deep sigh when she saw this happen. In the Guo ancestral temple on the street behind Drum Tower were recorded the many heroes and brave men the ancestors produced. Today, though, every male of the Guo clan was a feckless Ah Dou. If the previous generations now under the earth came to know of this, how would they feel? *When Father was still alive, he often said that there were problems with the feng shui of the ancestral tombs. Oh, really now, what feng shui problems? The problem was the Guo women themselves. When Second Sister was small, Great-Grandmother was still alive. From Great-Grandmother, to Grandmother, to Mother, all of them, right down the line, prized boys over girls. They were the ones who spoiled their sons and grandsons.*

Of her two younger brothers who were fleeing with them, Fourth Brother spoke with a stammer. This too was the consequence of her mother's doting. When he was little, he copied a relative's stammering. Her mother not only didn't stop this but even spoke with him using double sounds and double words. Fifth Brother was a sickly little sprout. Ninth Brother said this was because he had been too long at the breast. By that time, her mother was already more than fifty years old and her milk was too thin and without a bit of nourishment. But she couldn't bear weaning him.

The rise and fall, the life and death, of the Guo family has already reached the critical point. When peace again reigns in Old Town, I'm going to give First Brother's wife a good rapping. I want to tell her: "On you is the heavy responsibility for the vigor of the Guo family. If you don't discipline, restrain, and instruct your sons, you are the sinner of this Guo family."

Baoqing was nodding off as he walked along. After one stumble when he almost fell down, he moaned piteously, "Ma, I want to go to sleep."

Second Sister looked down at her little boy. He was older than Gan'er by only a year or so. It had been originally planned that the several children would ride by turns with their granny in the sedan chair. At this time, it wouldn't be impossible to put him inside, but she steeled herself and said, "Baoqing, these mountain roads are so dark. Maybe we'll go round a corner and run into a tiger. If you were asleep, and the tiger ate your ma, then what?"

Baoqing was clearly a bit worried when he heard about tigers. He bent down and picked up a length of a stick, and thrusting out his little chest, said, "Ma, don't be scared. If a tiger comes, I'll beat it to death." Baosheng took out the slingshot from his pocket. "I'll get him on the first shot." And as he said this, he turned to face the mountainside and shot off a stone.

"Good boys! That's more like my good sons!" Second Sister stroked their heads. She felt a wave of warmth flow inside her. Perhaps this was God's kindness. *With Ninth Brother away, it's these difficult times themselves that are raising my children.*

3.

NANJING[16] WAS ABOUT ninety miles from Old Town by mountain roads. It was a pretty little mountain town that today has become a popular travel and holiday destination. Travel agency ads call Nanjing, the little Switzerland of China's south. One of my sophisticated friends has gone to Switzerland and to Nanjing and what he said was even more fatuous: "In what way is Switzerland better than Nanjing?"

However, in later years, whenever Grandma mentioned Nanjing a look of pain would come over her. Her facial features seemed to clench up, as if she were having a toothache. Her head would tremble slightly as she said, "It's really such a long story. If I had known that place was called Nanjing, I should have realized that it was all going to be 'a long story' and never would have gone there looking for trouble."[17]

At the end of the 1960s, the Old Town government posted a bright red "good news" announcement. The name of my youngest uncle, Baoqing, was included on a list published by the revolutionary committee of those cadres being sent down to work at the grassroots level in the countryside. In those days, this was an extremely great honor. It meant that the people on the list had already passed a rigorous investigation. If by sheer good luck you got through this, you could once again put on the laurels of a "comrade."

---

[16] Not *the* Nanjing (or "Nanking") in Jiangsu Province, the former Guomindang capital of China up until 1949, but a small town in Fujian Province.

[17] Here Grandma is making a pun on the near-homophonous "Nanjing" and the Chinese expression "*Yi yan nan jin*" ("It would be hard to relate this in one word," or, as it is translated here, "it's a long story").

Among those places accepting cadres being "sent down" was this county town of Nanjing. Uncle Baoqing still remembered that beautiful little mountain place and so out of sentimentality picked Nanjing for himself. But before making his final decision, he came home to ask his parents' opinion. The moment Grandma heard "Nanjing," her "toothache" hit again, and, shaking her head, was much against Young Uncle's going to that "It's a long story" place.

On the final stage of this first journey there by the Guos, the sedan chair carriers were men from the county town of Nanjing who, with customary expertise, brought the refugees from Old Town to the residence of Master Huang. Master Huang was Second Sister's uncle and her mother's brother. He was a county official who had established a certain good name for himself locally, but the carriers said that his wife was even more famous. In Nanjing County, everyone knew her, from the county head down to the smallest peddler. Along the way, the two carriers seemed to want to go on gossiping about Huang's wife, but Old Lady Guo would have none of it. Many years before, she herself had been to Nanjing and knew how awful the local word of mouth was about *that* woman. And she herself had shed tears over it. The Huang family had only this one younger brother now to burn incense for the ancestors and, having left home and family to live far away, had gotten a fierce-tempered woman as his old lady. This was worse than his being a "live-in son-in-law" and a misfortune for his family.

"*Ai-ya-ya!* Actually I was hoping you would be coming!" Second Sister's aunt, Huang Ah Cui, then pulled a handkerchief from out of her sleeve and dabbed at her eyes, going through the motions of wiping away tears. "Quite a few days ago I prepared a meal to welcome your arrival. But I really couldn't keep it. Look—I just had the servants help us eat it."

She then stood by the side of the dining table. There hadn't been enough time to put away a few empty bowls and bit of salted vegetables on small plate. There wasn't half a drop of oil on the table.

Second Sister's mother paid no attention to her, but in great distress dragged over the younger brother she hadn't seen in so many years. "How come you've gotten so skinny? You're getting more and more skinny! Pretty soon you'll turn into a dried sweet potato."

In contrast, Huang's old lady was really tall and corpulent. When husband and wife stood together, one of them looked like a hairy gourd that hadn't grown right, while the other looked like a big winter melon just fallen off the vine.

"You Huangs eat but don't get fat," Ah Cui said, "Whatever was good to eat there, you never gave it to him first!"

"Who says he wasn't fat? When he was born, he weighed seven and a half *jin*.[18] The fat just rolled all over him. Take a look for yourself—now what has he become? A mere skeleton!"

The sister and her brother were twenty years apart in age and she was like a mother to him. Without realizing it, Huang Ah Cui put herself in the position of a mother-in-law.

"Big Sister, are you saying that I have treated one of you Huangs harshly?"

Standing off to one side, Second Sister was feeling uneasy and fidgety. She hastily took out from her bundle a silken floss jacket and gave this to her aunt. "Auntie, try this on to see whether it fits or not."

Auntie Huang took the jacket between her fingertips and dropped it on the back of a chair. "Later, when the day cools down I'll try it on."

---

[18]   A *jin* (or "catty") is the equivalent of 0.5 kg or 1.125 lbs. So Uncle Huang weighed almost 8.5 lbs at birth.

It was clear to Second Sister that the other woman saw this present as something frivolous. Then, turning away, she slid the jade bracelet off her wrist. "Auntie, this jade bracelet was especially chosen for you."

Auntie Huang raised the bracelet and bathed it in the full sunshine. The space between her eyebrows that had been knitted together now relaxed. "Oh, Second Sister, I heard that Uncle is away being a big official. You are truly lucky, unlike your own uncle cooped up here in the mountain gullies, serving as an utterly insignificant one. Ah, I suppose there's no hope for me in this life."

Hearing her aunt's words, Second Sister couldn't help feeling nervous. Luckily, at that moment, her mother was engaged in a lively chat with her younger brother about family matters, otherwise an argument between the two sisters-in-law would have been unavoidable. Their days as refugees still barely started, and with such naked hostility between her mother and her aunt, neither of whom would give way to the other, how would they all manage to live together under one roof?

Auntie Huang took Second Sister to the room that had been prepared for the Old Town relatives. A servant followed them to put the traveling bundles inside. When the servant had withdrawn, Auntie Huang said in a lowered voice, "Uh, Second Sister, if you have brought with you any valuable things, things that are worth money, it would be best to give them to me and Uncle. Our home has a cellar for storing precious objects."

Over the past few years, Second Sister had been continually selling off a large amount of her jewelry. Of what she now carried on her person nothing had been more precious than that bracelet. Now seeing Auntie Huang's scorching eyes, she didn't dare tell the truth about the awkward predicament of the Guo and Lin families. After Auntie Huang left, Second Sister sat on the bare-plank bed and stared vacantly into space. For the past two or three years those embarrassing times when she had slapped her own cheeks to plump them up had been really frightening. Could it be that now, having fled, she would live those days all over again? Lodging in this place, she would have to spend money and incur all kinds of personal obligations that would have to be fulfilled. Why not just rent two small rooms outside?

⌘   ⌘   ⌘

At dinner, some fried peanuts had been added to half a small plate of diced salted vegetables. These peanuts were kept in a glass bottle with such a narrow mouth that you had to stick your chopsticks straight down into it to laboriously pluck out just one peanut. Gan'er, who was sitting at the table, dragged this glass bottle toward him and spilled out a good part of the contents.

Auntie Huang stared wide-eyed at this from across the table. Her husband concentrated on eating his rice gruel. In ordinary times, Gan'er's granny would have certainly corrected him. Now, though, she pretended to take no notice. Auntie Huang's eyeballs moved in a slow survey of the Old Town relatives.

Second Sister could stand it no longer. "Gan'er! Put the peanuts back inside!"

Gan'er didn't want to.

Second Sister lay down her chopsticks and said with a stern expression, "Did you hear me? Put the peanuts back inside!"

Gan'er looked at his aunt, Second Sister, and, letting out a howl, went into a fit of crying that no one could do anything with. He jumped down from his chair and rushed to the doorway, shouting that he wanted his Granny "Ah Ma."

Cajoling her grandson, she put the blame for this all on Second Sister. "Why did you set off my little ancestor?[19] Gan'er, be good now, and Ah Ma will go out and buy you peanuts..."

Second Sister sat at the table pondering all this. She had already decided to rent a home outside as soon as possible. It had been difficult to speak out about this before, but now was her big chance.

"Uncle, Auntie, we have fled here and we don't know how long we will be staying. These children have all been spoiled in Old Town and I am afraid that they will be a big nuisance for you. I think that if we rented a place outside to stay, that would be the best thing to do."

Auntie Huang loudly opposed this. "Nowadays there are lots of people fleeing here to Nanjing, and not just you Old Town people. They also come running from over there in Zhejiang. Rents are getting more expensive, while our house has many empty rooms. I had originally also thought about renting them out. So, if you feel uncomfortable about it, just give me a rental payment."

"No. We would rent somewhere else. You have no idea how noisy Gan'er can be."

Uncle still kept his head down as he ate his rice gruel. Auntie Huang poked him with her chopsticks, "Hey, say something, you!"

Uncle hemmed and hawed, "Sounds good, sounds good."

"What?" Auntie threw down her chopsticks and then turned back to Second Sister, "You're burning your bridges behind you! Here we've taken you in, and now you want to go pay rent to someone else for a place to stay!"

Over on the side, the old lady heard about making rental payments and she hobbled on her little feet back to the dining table.

---

[19] Obviously not her real "ancestor," merely an affectionate term for a male descendent who would carry on the family line

"Now, Little Brother, we, your older sister and your brother-in-law, fostered your education and supported your becoming an official. But now that misfortune has hit your older sister and she comes running to you, you now want to charge rent?"

By now, Gan'er's tantrum was reaching a whole new level, and over here the sisters-in-law were quarreling. But Second Sister felt relieved and realistic about things. *This kind of a situation would have happened sooner or later. Rather than procrastinating to the fifteenth day, as they say, why not just lance the boil at the very outset?* She took her three frightened children, who had now lost their meals here, and went back to their little room.

⌘　⌘　⌘

Very early the next morning, Ah Cui decked herself out to the nines. Bubbling over like an elated matchmaker, she told Second Sister that she had now found a good house for her and she praised Second Sister for her wide range of knowledge and her farsighted-ness. She said Second Sister was very sophisticated and worldly wise. "I really can't bear your moving out. They say things smell more fragrant the farther off they are, while those that are nearby stink. If I were to force you all to stay here, afterward we wouldn't be so close. I'm still thinking of coming to Old Town to live out my last years. When that time comes, I will be relying on you."

Second Sister had been in the middle of a dream when Ah Cui arrived. When she opened the door, Ah Cui's high spirits hit her straight on. But for a moment she didn't react.

Ah Cui came right up to her, and lowering her voice, said, "You ought to leave your jewelry, silver dollars, and all your valu-able things here. Your uncle and I can take good care of these for you."

"Oh, I didn't bring much in the way of valuables."

"How can that be? The doctor's family is so rich."

Second Sister considered this for a moment. "I was afraid we'd run into bandits on the way, so I buried all the jewelry and silver dollars in the Lins' back courtyard."

Ah Cui stooped over and, slapping herself on the thigh, shouted, "*Ai-yah-yah*! How could such an intelligent person like you have done such a foolish thing? The Japanese toss out one bomb and everything goes flying sky-high in the explosion. When you get back home there'll be nothing at all!"

This kind of talk was not very propitious and Second Sister felt somewhat disgusted, and as she hesitated, she saw Ah Cui's enthusiasm abruptly fading and coldness oozing from her pores.

"The house I found for you, the rent's cheaper than what the market's charging. This was a personal favor to me and I'll hand over the money. Every month ten strings of cash, to be paid every three months."

Thirty strings every three months...this is no little sum of money. Along the road from Old Town they had seen people marking children for sale with wisps of straw. A little girl of seven or eight was selling for only ten strings. Second Sister had originally supposed that with a monthly payment of three or four strings, she could rent a reasonably good house.

"Or, I'll just go with you to take a look at the place?"

"If you don't believe me, then don't. But who *can* you believe?"

Just then, her mother asked from the back, "What are you two talking about?"

To smooth things over with Ah Cui, Second Sister handed the money to her without her mother's knowledge. Then she immediately got everyone out of bed, and the bundles, which had just been opened, were now tied up once again.

4.

WHENEVER I THINK of Grandma, she's always standing in the doorway beneath the oleander, wide-eyed and anxiously scanning everything within view. She's waiting for me to return from school, or for Grandpa to return from labor reform, or for the postman to deliver a letter from my mother or my two uncles. If whatever she was expecting didn't arrive on time, she would fall into an even greater state of worry. Each year the oleander grew taller. Each year Grandma was one year older. And throughout it all, worry and anxiety had become her constant companions.

"Prepare for rain while the weather's good" was my grandmother's motto. All her life she ran the home with great frugality without ever losing the grand style. In her later years, she became especially petty and stingy, and got all the more so as time passed. Saving became an incurable obsession for her. She saved coins, ration stamps for grain and cooking oil, and every kind of worthless coupon or ticket. She saved rice, soybeans, and peanut oil. She couldn't bring herself to eat any kind of food that hadn't been stored to the point of moldiness. The wives of my two uncles voiced some words about their mother-in-law and my older uncle's wife once launched a big cleanup. All the old and no longer edible foods were put into the garbage cart. Grandma became so angry she got sick and took to her bed. My aunt supposed she had done a good deed that would benefit the health of the family, but all she got was a stern reprimand from my uncle. Big Uncle had anguished memories of all the tough times the four of them had gone through together. He fully understood his mother and dearly loved her. After Grandma was eighty or so and could no longer go out and spend money, my two uncles still gave her money every month that they specially changed into small-denomination bills. This made a very thick wad for a hand to hold, which all the better imparted a sense of dependability and security to their old mother.

⌘ ⌘ ⌘

Nobody can predict what kind of crisis or calamity he or she will confront in life. Even though my grandma was more clever and sharp-witted than many women, the predicament she got into in Nanjing blindsided even her.

That little wooden house halfway down the hillside, with the drafts blowing in through all its four walls, belonged to one of Ah Cui's relatives. Ah Cui rented it and then sublet it to Second Sister. When Ah Cui came to collect the rent for the second time, the money in Grandma's purse was down to less than half the amount she had carried with her from Old Town. Her precious silver dollars had rapidly melted away, for everything had exceeded her original budget. The rent, the prices of firewood, rice, cooking oil, and salt were like boats on a rising tide as people fleeing the war swarmed into the county town.

Second Sister copied the local people and planted vegetables all around the house. She bought a piece of fatty pork, smeared it with salt, and hung it in the kitchen. When frying vegetables, she would take it down and rub a few globs of the fat in the hot pan. She also learned how to marinate salted vegetables and make pickled cucumbers. Every day her two younger brothers would take Baoqing and Baosheng fishing at the little brook. Once in a while they would catch something, and the whole family would be more excited than even at New Year's. And so the days passed in great liveliness. It was only in the stillness of the night that Second Sister would fumble with the money in the darkness, calculating what little remained and thinking of the war and of Ninth Brother in it. Then she would be engulfed in an indescribable cloud of grief and confusion.

One day, when the family was all sitting around the dinner table, waiting for Baoqing's trout to emerge from the cooking pan, two open "carry-chairs" stopped at the doorway. This kind of conveyance was a feature of the locality. Ever since Nanjing had become a place of refuge from the war, some people earned a living by lashing two wooden poles to a cane chair, thus making a kind of sedan chair for hire. A man and a woman stepped down. The man had an unkempt beard. Second Sister was just opening her mouth to make an inquiry, when the man, choking and sobbing, shouted out, "Second Sister!" It was the Guo family's long-lost Second Son. And now, accompanied by that pleasure-mansion girl with whom he had run off, he had found Nanjing. Earlier, he had returned to his home in Old Town. Many buildings on West Street had been destroyed by bombs, though the Guo residence was still there, untouched. And so was Eldest Brother, still keeping close to all those wine jars and unwilling to leave Old Town.

The chair carriers were waiting impatiently by the door and shouting, "Mister, you haven't paid us yet!"

Second Brother said, "Second Sister, pay them a string of cash for me."

Second Sister was stunned. "You don't even have that little bit of money on you?"

"If I weren't at the very end of my tether, do you think I'd have swallowed my pride and come looking for you, Second Sister?"

This younger brother of hers was still an incorrigible wastrel. No money, but he would still visit someone riding on a carry-chair.

It was just like back in Old Town, when he would take in the opera and gang about the brothels—it had to be by sedan chair.

In an instant all the happiness and joy of reunion after such a long separation was just wiped clean away. It was as if a millstone pressed with all its heaviness on Second Sister's heart. She paid the money and said to Second Brother, "For those who have fled here, eking out a living isn't easy. Don't parade your wealth or put on any more airs. Today you're riding on a carry-chair, tomorrow you may have to carry one."

Her brother guffawed, "Second Sister, you wouldn't let me do coolie work."

Second Brother's woman was a sweet talker. "Ma" came loudly from her mouth almost every other word. Old Lady Guo paid no attention to her, but she really didn't mind, and, cool and composed, she picked up her chopsticks and went straight for the fish's maw.

The old lady reached across with her own chopsticks to stop her. "The fish maw is for my grandson."

The woman twisted her expression into a brittle smile, "Then I'll just eat the fish's head."

Old Lady Guo again wielded her chopsticks to block her. "The fish head is for my other grandchildren."

The woman, still showing no sign of irritation, slurped down three bowls of melon porridge.

Second Sister had still not come to the table. There was almost nothing anymore in the cooking pan. She went outside and sat on the hillside. She wanted to pray to the Jesus her Lord to help her, but suddenly her faith weakened and dejectedly she looked up to the heavens and said, "O Lord Jesus, where are you? Have you abandoned our family?"

⌘　⌘　⌘

They watched helplessly as the plight of hunger drew nearer each day. Second Sister, who normally placed great importance on appearances, could only "tear her face" and go out to look for work. One day, Ah Cui was in a tailor shop in the county town when she happened to see Second Sister just then measuring a customer. She rubbed her eyes in astonishment. On this street, all the shop owners knew her, and everyone was rather in awe of Madam "Official's Wife." And now here was one of her Old Town relatives laboring away. This really *was* a disgrace. Ah Cui quickly covered up her face and left. Second Sister, turning around, caught sight of Ah Cui leaving. Ah Cui had not come forward to say hello.

Every day she went out early and came back late. Although this was hard on her, at least they had income now. The wages she earned were transformed into enough rice for the stomachs of ten people. The three children saw how difficult this was for their mother and became all the more considerate. They took over and divided up all the housework. The littlest one, Baoqing, would burn firewood and cook food. Every day, three meals a day, he would get next to the stove and blow on the fire. His cheeks, which originally had been fair and spotlessly clean, now looked like those of an actor in the opera. Baosheng's skill with his little slingshot grew more expert with each shot. He would go hunting for pheasants in the mountains and get fish in the brooks. Thus the supply of meat dishes on their dinner table was never interrupted. Baohua was responsible for cleaning the clothes, though the brook flowed turbulently and often clothing got washed away in it. But her mother never scolded her for this.

The third day of the sixth month of the lunar calendar was Second Sister's birthday, and her three children secretly prepared a "long-life banquet" for her. Baosheng set off deep into the hills in the middle of the night to grope about in the pheasant nests for a few eggs. He returned at noon and then went into the brook to catch fish. Baohua plucked flowers and blades of grass so that all the bottles and jars in the house were filled with colors of every kind. And Baoqing – all day long he blew on the fire in the stove until all the hair in front of his temples was singed.

Second Sister returned in the evening. She was just stepping across the doorway when she saw the table laden with all those good things to eat, including a bowl of "long life" noodles on which were placed two tiny pheasant eggs. She suddenly recalled that today was her own birthday and she was overwhelmed in a tempest of emotions. Caught in midstep, she just leaned against the door and wept. At that moment, she thought of someone for the first time in a long time. *How could I have ever said that Jesus had abandoned our family?* She thought too of Ninth Brother. After fleeing from Old Town, she no longer believed that there would ever be a day when she and Ninth Brother would meet again. Still in tears, Second Sister suddenly turned around and ran back outside, her three children running after her. They were surprised to see their mother kneeling there on the hillside, her head raised to heaven saying, "O Lord, Jesus, You haven't abandoned me. It's I who've abandoned you. Please forgive me!" The wind blew by and she heard Ninth Brother's voice hovering in the sighing pines.

Second Sister, you must have faith.

"Ninth Brother, I know you wouldn't leave your wife and children behind and go on alone to your heavenly reward." She wiped away her tears and hugged the three children surrounding her.

The children looked at each other. *Hasn't Daddy been alive all this time? What did Ma mean?*

When the four of them returned to their little wooden house, Second Brother and the woman were already standing there, picking their teeth clean. The only thing left in the bowls and on the plates were bits of thick soup and some gravy. Baosheng said angrily, "Today is my mother's birthday. This was for her, but she hadn't even sat down at the table. How could you have eaten everything all up?" Second Sister, though, just smiled and said, "Your ma knows what was in your hearts, and that is more beautiful than eating anything."

From that day on, Second Sister resumed her morning and evening prayers. She also wrote a letter to Pastor and Mrs. Chen in Old Town. In it she asked them to locate that fat postman and, if there had been any mail from Ninth Brother, to please collect it on her behalf and forward it to her. Before she left, she hadn't made this clear for fear that she would sink into a hope when there was none.

⌘   ⌘   ⌘

They had a place to live in and food to eat. That was good enough for Second Sister. She reckoned that they could thus survive in this fool's paradise until the end of the war. However, disaster always suddenly hits when people are least prepared for it.

Old Lady Guo now bickered with Second Brother's woman every day. Countless times, she asked Second Sister to kick her out, but Second Sister would always be noncommittal and just let such talk go in one ear and out the other. It was nothing more than just one additional mouth to be fed, and every day another set of clothing to be cut.

How could she have known that this pair was fooling everybody and smoking opium? The county town's one opium den was in a little alley just behind her tailor's shop and they often followed right behind Second Sister when she went to work. She never had the slightest inkling of all this. She didn't even know that they had already stolen the last three silver dollars she had sewn into her ragged quilted jacket and had smoked these away. They also stole the old lady's few pieces of jewelry for the same purpose. They had begun to smoke on credit at the den, and then when they couldn't get any more credit, they suddenly hit on an idea about Baohua. The woman told a landowner she had met there that the husband of her man's older sister was a big official in Chongqing. As she told it, Second Sister was having a hard time as a refugee and wanted to find a good local family to take in her daughter as a child bride. Later on, when the war was over, the husband would return to formally recognize the marriage and help his son-in-law become an official in the capital, Nanjing. Three generations of that landowner's family had hoped to become officials but had never succeeded in doing so. Now he in turn placed this hope on his own son. The moment he heard of this good thing, he immediately jumped up from his pallet and gladly agreed to the woman's asking price of four silver dollars. Four silver dollars could buy ten girl children along the road who could work, so it was obvious how much the landlord expected from this marriage connection. Second Brother and the woman took the money and then returned home where they tricked Baohua. "Your ma is going to make you new clothes and wants you to go to the shop for a fitting." Baohua was very fond of looking pretty and, when she heard that there would be new clothes to wear, she set off with them in high spirits.

Old Lady Guo had once joked that Baohua was always losing wash in the stream and that one day the girl would go floating off after it. This idle jest made Second Sister uneasy. Several days before, she had heard that there really had been a woman swept away while washing clothes. This so frightened her that she immediately and repeatedly gave the order that Baohua was not to go out to wash clothes.

The whole family was sitting around the table waiting for her to return so they could begin dinner. Only Baohua was missing.

Second Sister's heartbeat immediately quickened. "Did Baohua go out to do the wash?"

Baoqing said, "Big Sister went to your shop to try on new clothes."

"Who's given her new clothes?"

"Uncle said that you wanted to measure her for clothes."

Perhaps those two were just feeling bored and took Baohua off somewhere to play. Second Sister sat down and started serving out the bowls of rice when on second thought she felt there was something wrong. *Why tell a lie if you're just going somewhere for fun?*

Fourth Brother then stammered out, "Tha...that...wo...man... took...the bun...bundle..."

She asked her mother, "Ma, did you give that woman another hard time?"

Fifth Brother said, "Today those two were nicer than ever. Second Brother even brought back a piece of sticky rice cake to show his respect to Mother."

Cloth bundle, sticky rice cake, new clothes...these few words spelled out a fearsome plot. Second Sister brought her bowl down with a heavy thud and rice gruel went spattering all over the table. "Something's happened."

The old lady said, "The farther away that woman goes, the better!"

Second Sister rushed to the little room next to the kitchen. Her brother's and that woman's clothes were nowhere to be seen. She rushed to her own room. She pulled out the cloth bundle from under her bedding and felt all around the old jacket. The coins were gone!

"Damn that cur and bitch!"

Never before had Second Sister blurted out such rough words. "Something's happened! Something's *really* happened!" Everybody threw down their chopsticks on the table and came crowding into her room. The old lady saw Second Sister clutching the jacket close to her and immediately realized just what that cur-bitch pair had done. She hobbled on her little feet over to the bed and opened the cloth bundle on the pillow and with trembling hands reached inside the pile of clothing. The several gold rings hidden within a red stomach binder had flown off without the aid of wings. The old lady flopped down on her rump and beat the sides of the bed. In a cracked voice like tearing silk, she cried out, "You should be slashed a thousand times, whore! You stole my son, you even stole my rings...my mother's and my mother-in-law's dowries!"

Second Sister yelled in a hard voice, "Stop crying, what are a few rings? Something's happened to my Baohua! That woman's sold her into a brothel!"

Total perdition had hit them, but Second Sister stayed calm and cool headed. She reflected that the county town was surrounded on three sides by mountains, so there was only one way to get out. She gave orders to Fourth Brother and Fifth Brother to go after them in that direction. Baosheng, gripping his slingshot, declared he wanted to go out after his older sister too. Second Sister herself rushed off to the county town with all the speed she could muster. There was a brothel in town called the Gorgeous Fragrance Mansion, whose lady boss had once had a *qipao* made at the tailor's shop. This brothel was separated from the town by an ancient bridge. On her way to this bridge, Second Sister realized that Baoqing was by her side. Taking her little boy's hand, she said through clenched teeth, "Son, we just have to find your sister!"

At the doorway of the Gorgeous Fragrance Mansion was a crowd of brothel sisters on the lookout for business. Because their faces would always be thickly caked with white powder, the local name for them was "little white faces." Second Sister called out to one of these white faces, and, stuffing a small amount of money into the other's hand, asked if today the madam had bought a little girl from Old Town. Little White Face put it this way:

"These days, 'the monks are many, but the gruel's scarce.' The Mansion's eight or ten girls aren't pulling in two customers in a day, and the boss would like nothing better than to sell us. So how can you talk about someone new being bought?"

Second Sister only half-believed this, and went right in to look for the madam. But this one had the same story and, sucking on a water pipe, added lethargically, "Every day there's always someone coming to sell me girls. They don't want money, just a meal. In this way, I don't keep anyone. So go look elsewhere, why don't you?" Second Sister believed *this*. So Baohua was surely out on the road somewhere and maybe right now was crying and screaming to go home. Fourth Brother and the others would quickly catch up with her. Then she realized that a woman from a good home should get away as quickly as possible from a dirty place like this. Immediately she flushed red, and, pulling Baoqing by the hand, she ran from the Gorgeous Fragrance Mansion as if her very life depended on it.

Mother and son hurried along their way. By now, it had grown dark. A crescent moon over the mountain peaks shot forth its light with dazzling brightness, for it was almost Mid-Autumn Festival now. This would be the fourth Mid-Autumn Festival since Ninth Brother had gone off. *Oh, Ninth Brother, have you thought of how we have all suffered through these four years?*

Baoqing, noticing his mother wiping away her tears, raised his little head up at her. "Ma, Elder Brother is sure to catch up with Sister. Don't be so sad."

Second Sister gripped her son's hand, "Baoqing, your ma is thinking of Daddy. Do you still remember what Daddy was like?"

"I do. Daddy could ride a bicycle."

"Son, when Daddy returns, we'll get him to teach you how to ride one. When the time comes, both you and your big brother will ride your own bicycles to school."

She looked up at the moon over the mountain. *Jesus, if you really are all-powerful, please tell Ninth Brother about all of this. Make him come home. I am just too tired now. My shoulders can't carry all the people of this family.*

"Ma, Daddy has bought a bicycle up north. He's riding it back home right now."

Such words were clearly moved by the Holy Spirit. In her excitement, Second Sister stopped right there and squeezed her son to her breast. "Yes! Yes! Your ma sees!"

Baoqing was beside himself with joy at having made his mother happy. The two of them spoke about Daddy and bicycles as they hurried along. Following the mountain road, they went right through a little hamlet. Up ahead they could make out what looked like a few people on the road. Second Sister went up close and saw Fifth Brother lying on the ground, spitting out frothy saliva and panting for breath. Fourth Brother was by his side, distraught and agitated.

Fifth Brother's epilepsy! Second Sister went up to him and pinched the midpoint of his upper lip. When he came to again, she remembered Baosheng. "Baosheng?"

Fourth Brother stuttered and stammered but couldn't say what had happened.

Baohua had not been found. Baosheng had run off to who-knew-where. *Oh, heaven! I can't go on living!* Then it was as if an enormous black curtain had unraveled in the sky and had fallen over Second Sister's eyes. In the midst of all this dazzling moonlight, the world in front of her was as dark as lead. Her body was like a leaf that had floated down from a tree and was lying helpless on the ground. She sat there absolutely frozen in stillness.

A short time later, her two brothers found her, still in this state of oblivion.

Second Sister felt she was soaring up into the sky. She saw everything down below. She saw Baoqing crying as he shook his mother's shoulder. "Ma! Ma! Wake up! I'm scared!" She really wanted to fly on and say, "Son, don't be afraid! Fly with your ma. Fly north to find Daddy!"

5.

I CAN TELL from Joseph's expression just how much he wants to know how Grandma found her two children, but that's where I interrupt the story. For I've just recalled how, many years ago, Beibei and I got separated at the Summer Palace. In that brief twenty minutes I underwent the most excruciating torment. I became a mother animal whose cub had been stolen by hunters. Crazed, I elbowed and barged my way through the flow of people. If our separation hadn't been twenty minutes, but twenty days, could I have survived that long? I am now filled with guilt toward Grandma. I always made her stand under the oleander, her eyes anxiously watching for my return. After school, for example, I would impulsively detour to play at a schoolmate's home. I didn't understand why my grandma could get so worried if I wasn't on time. When she had aged to the point of senility, I was still trying to stop her stinginess and petty-mindedness. I wasn't like Uncle, giving her big fistfuls of small-denomination bills. I only bought her real things. She would always ask very lucidly how much each item cost, converting the cost of a piece of clothing or a pair of shoes into its equivalent in rice. Separated by the wide expanse of our years, I would gaze into her eyes. Her anxiety-filled look stabbed deep into me.

The cell phone rings and when I hear "Hello!" I know that Chrysanthemum's diplomatic efforts have been totally successful. And by now she surely has taken her bath and is wearing a loose negligee as she sits cross-legged on the sofa, all settled in for a long conversation with me. That's my style too. We can always keep our ends of the conversation going until it grows light in the east. Now, though, I keep saying, "OK, that's it for now," but Chrysanthemum seems to have no intention of stopping. I made the excuse of the battery running low, but she says, "There's a power outlet underneath your table." She had a cheap boss who let her use the train only for out-of-town business, so she knows train coaches like the back of her hand. All I can do is to patiently accompany her on this marathon phone conversation.

Chrysanthemum has "nailed down" my schoolmate. It looks as if there will be no problem in our earning a bit of money by taking on a few projects. What she wants to chat about, though, isn't our upcoming business, but rather her feelings toward this man. All along, she has favored men with full faces, darkly whiskered but clean shaven, just like a certain Hollywood star. She says our future partner's looks and temperament are just what she had always yearned for day and night in a man. Chrysanthemum is puzzled why I have never taken a fancy to this guy. I tell her that back then he was nothing special, and to be perfectly honest, the only impression he left with me was that they made amazingly tasty steamed dumplings at his home. Often on Sunday evenings, he would carry over a bamboo steamer of them to the girls' dormitory. "I remember a lot about you at university," Chrysanthemum says. "There was the time you climbed up on the wall to get back to the dorm and couldn't get down and he was the one who rescued you. Maybe at that time he was secretly in love with you? Just look at yourself! You missed out on such a good man! You don't mind my targeting him? To enjoy a guy like that for a week or a month would be worth one year of my fleeting youth. Hello? Aren't you listening to me? Have you got something going there? Does that guy have what it takes?" "Oh, heavens, Chrysanthemum, what are you saying?" I nervously look at Joseph sitting across from me as if he was some angel sent down from above. The bantering fun and abuse that

Chrysanthemum and I are used to would simply be dirty talk in his presence.

I also had my days of angel purity. I had loved Chaofan with a purity and innocence for so long. I supposed that he would be the only man in my whole life and I never looked at any other man. Even if I ate that other guy's steamed dumplings every day, he'd never have gotten more than a glance from me. That summer, when Chaofan's symphonic composition, "The Dream of a Chinese Child," was selected for participation in the Youth Music Conference, I would travel from one end of Beijing to the other, in rain or shine, to listen to his orchestra rehearse. I quietly buried myself in some far corner of the rehearsal hall watching Chaofan at work. For several hours, I had almost no chance to speak a single word to him. As I stared at his back, I would think of early childhood, of all the many things in our innocent friendship, and long for our rosy future. Beat after beat of happiness surging within me made me both giddy and agitated. I hadn't the slightest doubt that my lover was one of those rare and peerless geniuses and that the name "Chaofan" would finally resound in history. Such ardor and devotion wasn't much different from the reverence that true believers feel for their god.

I can no longer relate in detail how, bit by bit, my own "god" faded in radiance. Maybe I've already said too much. Every time I speak of it, the feeling dulls a little, until I find I can't even be bothered to mention it. I once wanted to tell my daughter something about her father, since I was about to take her to San Francisco to meet him. "I truly loved your father then." She was inspecting several pimples on her face with a little mirror and replied without much enthusiasm, "Oh, yeah?" Obviously, corny old love stories didn't have the attention-holding power for her that those few pimples had, and I discovered that I too was uninterested in rehashing such old things.

Beibei and I reached San Francisco a day before we were to meet him. I knew that my "rare and peerless genius" of old now supported himself by selling his art on Fisherman's Wharf. He was able to bring the entire wharf to life in an amazing way with his solo electronic band performances. According to one of his friends there, a part-time portraitist, Chaofan was making pretty good money. And that he was very popular with women. There was usually some unattached woman – the race varied —standing there listening and patiently waiting for him to pack up and take her home with him. Chaofan has not told me how he supports himself in San Francisco and I haven't given his secret away. That evening I deliberately sent my daughter off somewhere and slowly made my way on foot to Fisherman's Wharf. While I was still several blocks away my ears suddenly picked up the melody of "The Dream of a Chinese Child" and, as if by conditioned response, my heart beat with a wild throbbing. For one instant, that long-gone feeling of happiness and well-being was rekindled within me. But a moment later my pulse returned to normal and casually my steps moved along in time with the music.

I sat down beside a flowerpot behind Chaofan. It was a foggy and damp night without many tourists. Two or three would walk by, stop and listen for a while, and then move on. Only one enthusiastic white woman kept wiggling and twisting to the music. The moment the music stopped, she spoke a few words with the artist and when the music started again, she started to help out by collecting the money for the CDs he sold. *Would he take her home tonight?*

It was still "The Dream of a Chinese Child." I didn't know what dream it was he had back then. Nor do I know whether he still has dreams now. But I couldn't help missing those days of infatuation and craziness, and I shed a silent tear for all that. I quietly waited until he packed up, and indifferently watched that woman help him load his instrument into a van. I saw her sit on the driver's side. These two solitary souls brought together by chance now moved, talking and laughing, out of my sight. San Francisco is a beautiful city but the air is chilly. I've heard that single men and women there need only exchange a glance for one of them to take the other home. Did Chaofan suffer with a smile as his vagrant and drifting life led first into one stranger's embrace and then another's?

I clearly remember, after that little van was now loaded with the stranger and the synthesizer, just how empty and bereft I felt, but not because of any shock at what I had just seen. Actually, after leaving Chaofan, seeing him again like this was so totally devoid of any of the feeling from our past, I couldn't even figure out what I had been so passionate about then. But no longer believing in love, no longer having a man to be infatuated with and drive me wild, has desolated me. I feel I am sinking or drifting away. Maybe I really should believe in something, worship something, and offer my long-stifled passions to whatever it was I worshipped and believed in. But what could that be?

Chapter Six — The Road Home

1.

MY GRANDPA HAD a dream he cherished over a long period of his life but never realized, and that was to take Grandma up north to the place where he had served in the army during the war. He wanted to pay homage to Division Commander Zhang, the officers and men, both known and unknown, and to that widow who had been so pretty then. Such an idea came to him at the close of the civil war, but during the 1950s, his own questionable history made it impossible for him to escape the never-ending waves of revolutionary movements. During "Eliminate Counterrevolutionaries" he was almost shot dead. In "Anti-Rightists" he only just avoided being made into a "Big Rightist." My mother and my two uncles lived in a constant state of fear and anxiety over him. Even so, their own future prospects dimmed considerably by association with him and they would never be promoted to important positions.

The early 1960s were famine years for China. My grandpa reckoned that after this everything would be fine again and so he began his plan to take Grandma north on his nostalgia tour. However, during those years the third generation of the Lin family began arriving in quick succession, and Grandma, having just taken care of one daughter-in-law during her parturition and first month laying-in period, had to do the same for the next one. In 1965, the old couple finally set their departure date. Then, my youngest uncle's wife suddenly had a miscarriage, and Grandma just had to return the ticket and stay to take care of her. Grandpa went on by himself, thinking that later on they'd still have the chance to go north together. However, he didn't foresee that an even harsher Great Revolution was already then in ferment. That was the disaster that was preordained for him. He never fully weathered that ten-year-long catastrophe.

At home, we had an old-style 120 mm camera. It documented Grandpa's travels north in the autumn of 1965. In the pictures, he is still looking lean and wiry, but wearing his Sun Yat-sen-style suit, which was just like the military uniform of that period, and made his body a bit more filled out. He is standing on a piece of farmland where Division Commander Zhang and two hundred officers and ordinary soldiers are buried. The local townspeople seemed to have gradually forgotten the trauma of war and pretty much forgotten as well all those who had fought against the Japanese. My grandpa had the habit of keeping a diary. During the "Great Cultural Revolution," he burned over twenty diaries. In the final years of his life, he would write poems to express his deepest feelings. I have no way of verifying what Grandpa must have felt as he stood in that field, but I believe he certainly must have shed tears from all the different feelings welling up within him.

On that trip north, my grandpa stayed at the home of a local fellow, though he never dared mention that he himself had once been stationed here in the army. That would have been the Nationalist army. Anyone, even the most politically uninvolved country bumpkin, who spread it around that Grandpa had been a Guomindang soldier, would have stirred up feelings of caution and hostility. Grandpa told this oaf that a relative had entrusted him with the task of locating a young widow who had run a small shop in those days. Division Commander Zhang had mentioned that he had a few small gold pieces and, before the battle, had given a leather bag to Young Li. Afterward, when they retreated with the army, at first, neither Grandpa nor Young Li had known that there was gold inside the bag. Those few gold pieces miraculously saved their lives on the road back to Old Town after they deserted. My grandpa never felt easy about this, as if he had deliberately seized what should have been someone else's property, and so he brought along with him a not-inconsiderable amount of money to give to the widow.

The oaf went asking here and there and did find out what had happened. That winter, after the army had withdrawn from the town, the widow hanged herself on an old dead tree above Division Commander Zhang's grave. You can well imagine just how Grandpa felt when he heard this. The widow had died and he had survived. If he had given the gold to her then maybe it would have been the other way around. That night, he paced back and forth on that field, telling Jesus of the feelings of guilt he harbored. Was it, after all, because heaven favored him? Or had he been wrong in doing what he had done?

The day before Ninth Brother left this small market town in central China, his host slaughtered a laying hen to give his guest from afar a send-off dinner. Grandpa unobtrusively stuffed a few silver dollars in the *kang* of the house. Ten dollars was an enormous sum for a peasant only able to earn a few *fen* a day. The oaf was simply terrified by this amount of money. Could this southerner with his Sun Yat-sen suit perhaps be a secret agent sent from Taiwan? He rushed to report this to the commune office, taking the money with him.

The long-distance bus station was in the county town, a walk of almost ten miles. Grandpa had gotten almost halfway there, when a horse cart stopped beside him and out jumped several men. They seized him and brought him to the commune's armed force department for questioning. Fortunately, he had with him the travel document issued by his street committee in Old Town. In those days, no one in China had any concept yet of traveling for its own sake. Someone aimlessly wandering about would have been considered not quite right in the head. The commune's armed force department released this skinny, not-quite-right-in-the-head southerner.

⌘ ⌘ ⌘

The doctor and the many officers and men were incorporated into another unit. Hu, the division commander of this unit, was a man who had come up in the world by banditry. Young Li had heard more than a few stories about him. Just last night, some bumpkin's dog next door had disturbed this Hu fellow with its barking. Hu jumped up stark naked from under the covers and, taking his pistol with him, rushed out the door and shot the dog dead. He had also killed two adjutants in the same rash way—afterward they were accused of having been deserters. The first time the doctor saw Division Commander Hu was at a pep talk. This big, dark-skinned fellow, his ferocious face covered with lumps and swellings, stood there, one hand on his hip, the other gesticulating vehemently. On average, for each minute he talked, he would come out with at least three curses and swearwords so filthy you could hardly bear to listen to him. The doctor buried himself out of sight within the rank and file. He couldn't help deeply missing Division Commander Zhang and the brotherly affection they had shared in those days. Division Commander Zhang had once told him: *If there comes a day when I can no longer protect you, just light out fast for home and take Young Li with you.* The doctor now really did want to go home. And it was during

Division Commander Hu's wild and incoherent pep talk that the thought of doing so first sprang into his head, though he immediately squelched it. Desertion would be shameful when there was such danger to the nation hanging over everyone.

Division Commander Hu's hometown was only a little more than thirty miles away from this garrison, so his three wives all moved in and became his camp family, each occupying a different civilian residence in the neighborhood. These were the days when there was no smell of gunpowder, no wounded soldiers, and when there were so few visitors at the medical station you could net sparrows at the door. But the doctor wasn't really just taking it easy. Day and night, night and day, the commander's three old ladies had all sorts of minor ailments, and would send someone to call the doctor to come and treat them. This was especially so with Third Wife. Whenever the commander didn't spend the night at her place, she would come down with something.

Third Wife would always wait, all powdered and rouged, at the warm end of the *kang* with tea prepared. She wanted the doctor to sit down, chat with her, and keep her company. But the doctor wouldn't buy this and always kept a few feet away from her, staring blankly ahead. He never uttered a word or responded on any matter that wasn't connected to medical treatment. Even so, Third Wife still said a lot. She was a southerner, from Jiaxing in Zhejiang Province, the child of a family that had produced scholars for generations. Because her father had died young, to help her mother raise her younger brothers and sisters, Third Wife had no choice but to seek a livelihood in Shanghai. A married man with children tricked her into going up north, and in Loyang she met Commander Hu. Her eyes glistening with tears, she would often ask the doctor, "You're a southerner too. Don't you ever think of home?" And every time she asked him this, he would feel all broken-up inside, but he just gritted his teeth. He would have none of that line of talk.

On one cold and breezy night, Third Wife again called for someone to get the doctor. The doctor put on his uniform, but after pacing back and forth in his room for some time, decided against playing this pointless game. He gave his emergency treatment kit to Young Li, and told him to take her temperature and do a diagnosis. If Third Wife really had something wrong with her, there'd be time soon enough to treat her. When Third Wife heard that the doctor was unwilling to come to her, she flew into a rage and smashed the pot of tea. Later, Young Li returned, chuckling and scuffling in with his soaking wet sandals, to make his report to the doctor. By fixing a problem that had vexed many hours of his time, without hurting someone's feelings, the doctor supposed that his approach had been a smart one.

Unexpectedly, the very next morning, Commander Hu suddenly appeared at the aid station, pistol in hand. He knocked over the table standing between him and the doctor. Thrusting his pistol against the side of the doctor's head, he snarled. "You've got nerve to treat my woman like that!" The doctor thought he was a dead duck and would end up just like the barking dog who fell before this gun. He closed his eyes and silently prayed, *Lord, I'll be meeting you now. If your child has committed any sin, please be merciful and forgive him. And I entrust Second Sister and the children into your hands.* Commander Hu was puzzled, seeing that not only was the doctor not scared but that he looked positively radiant. From the time he was twenty years old and had straggled into a local bandit gang, he had killed men beyond number. In most cases, he never sneaked up to attack from behind. Toying with the person he was about to kill was what he liked best. He again bashed his pistol barrel against the doctor's temple and roared, "You know you're about to die!" "I know it," said the doctor. "And you're not afraid of that?" The doctor looked straight at Commander Hu and thought: *O Lord, is even this brutal man one of your lost sheep that you would never forsake?*

Commander Hu yelled at him, "Oh, so you're looking at me now?"
The doctor answered him calmly, "Commander, don't be angry.
Nobody can choose when he dies. Today, I'll die at your gun. That
was set long before I entered this world, wouldn't you agree? I am
just sorry to have made you kill one more person." Commander Hu
was like someone who had been tickled on the sole of his foot. In
spite of himself, he just burst out laughing so violently that spit
went flying out in all directions. He put away his gun and said,
"Now that's a good one. I've never met anyone less scared to die.
You dainty little prig, though...how come you're not scared of
dying? OK, I won't kill you, then!"

Just then, Young Li returned from performing some job. His
eyes widened in amazement when he saw the overturned table and
the commander in a good mood. He just couldn't imagine what
had happened. If he had returned one minute earlier, he would have
fallen on his knees and begged for the doctor's life. He might even
have said something he shouldn't have, and bullets from the barrel
of the commander's gun would have gone straight through the doctor's head for sure. Actually, Young Li shouldn't have gone out on
this day at all, but having done so, shouldn't have dillydallied for
such a long time. Just now, he had been next door. When a mess
worker had been drawing water, the rope broke, and Young Li had
been busy helping the fellow retrieve the bucket.

Just what force arranges all the small things in life?

The thought of going back home now flared up enticingly in
the doctor's mind once again. And the reality that surrounded him
only added fuel to the flames and reinforced the idea of desert-
ing this army. Over the past few months, the infirmary had been
unable to get the medical supplies it had requisitioned. There was
no alcohol or surgical cotton and the doctor had to buy distilled
grain spirits and boil bed sheets to prepare for the urgent needs of a

battle situation. Payroll was months late. Everyone, enlisted men as well the officers, knew that Commander Hu was embezzling their silver dollars, and though all of them were angry they didn't dare say anything. Every day there were incidents of desertion and anyone caught on the road was brought back and shot. *This was clearly a bandit lair and a slaughterhouse, so why not just go home?* The doctor asked himself this question day after day.

He had heard the news that Old Town had been bombed. He didn't know whether his family was dead or alive, but he continued to send letters to Second Sister. Even if only one out of a hundred letters reached her, it would be worth the effort. Day in and day out, he sat in the lonely medical aid station writing letters, telling his beloved Second Sister of his indecision about leaving. *Maybe God has not bestowed upon me the grace to "govern the state and bring peace to the earth." I ought to pay attention to my own moral growth, guard my own home, and just be a good husband and father.* Occasionally he would insert a cartoon in his letter, a sketch of Old Town and the three children that he missed so much. He would draw a scene of his return to the old Lin residence: Baoqing, raising his little head and gazing at his returning father with unknowing eyes, "Uncle, who are you?"[20] The Baoqing in this cartoon was how he remembered the child from three years ago.

Commander Hu then took a fourth wife and threw a big wedding banquet. Theatrical troupes performed for three whole days and three nights. Young Li came running over, excitedly called the doctor to watch the performances, but the doctor burst out in a fury and slammed the table, shouting, "And you *still* feel like seeing

[20]   This is an echo of Tang dynasty poet He Zhizhang's most celebrated poem, "Homecoming" (*Hui Xiang Ou Shu*): "I left home young, I now return old / My accent is unchanged, but my temple hair is sparse. / The children do not know me. / They smile and say, 'Visitor, where are you from?'" It is a beloved trope of popular nostalgia in China.

plays!" Young Li had never seen the doctor so angry, and just stood there, afraid to move. He felt so unfairly treated he wanted to cry. The doctor came forward, sat him down, and apologized. "Young Li, you know our Old Town has been bombed. Even Old Town is no longer peaceful and tranquil. With the world war as grim as it is, to hold a wedding banquet for a concubine is a real sin! And if we joined in all the revelry, that would be a sin too. Lately, all I've been thinking about is whether or not to go home." Young Li's eyes brightened, and he said, "Then let's go home! I'll go with you! I know the road leading to Anhui. And it would be easiest for us to get away during these two days." The doctor rested his head in his hands and muttered, "Let me think about this."

Young Li knew that when confronting such a heavy decision, the doctor needed to calm his heart and pray, so he quietly withdrew from the room. He had just reached the street corner when he saw the town's mute carrying a blood-soaked body on his shoulders. The fellow rushed toward him, crying for Dr. Lin in his strange *yi-yi ya-ya* voice. In the few villages near division headquarters everyone knew that the doctor surnamed Lin was a Living Buddha, someone who worked miraculous cures and would always help anyone in need. Young Li turned right around and rushed back to the medical aid station to assist Dr. Lin with the bloody person the mute had picked up on the road. It was a young woman who was hemorrhaging from a miscarriage. When he had finished treating her, the doctor recognized her as Second Wife's serving maid, a girl only sixteen years old. It was all too obvious. This was surely the evil doings of Commander Hu. Second Wife had taken a red-hot steel needle, stabbed the girl in the stomach to kill the fetus, and then had driven her out of the house. Because of the shortage of medicine, in the end the doctor could not save her.

What more reason was needed for going? With finality, the doctor addressed Jesus: *Oh Lord, if you agree with my going, then open the road for me. If not, then let the sentries shoot me dead.*

That evening, with lustrous stars filling the whole sky, the doctor and Young Li walked out of the camp, their hearts at ease. Along their way, they passed any number of sentries, but not one of those fellows blocked their path.

2.

DURING THE WAR of Resistance, China was a cake cut into pieces. Some of these had fallen into Japanese hands. Others were the "red bases" of the Communist Party and areas still under the Nationalist government. Still others were the roosts of collaborationist "Han traitors" and local bandits. The doctor's road home would pass through all the pieces of this cake. He had to become like a chameleon, so that only by constantly shifting his protective coloring would he not recklessly court death. But the doctor had barely the slightest inkling of the dangers that might possibly befall him. During these years in the army, he had been cut off from the larger events of the world. If anything, he now sought all the more refuge in his books.

The pair of deserters made good time on foot for about ten miles. It would now soon be daybreak. Off in the distance in the rays of the pale morning light could be seen a little town still deep in slumber. Young Li joyfully stripped off his uniform and flung the pieces high in the air. "So long, Commander Hu!" he shouted.

The doctor sat down right where he was, his thoughts flying back to Old Town. Now should be the season when litchis were brought to the markets. He squinted and faintly caught the clean scent of this fruit. He saw Ah Shui bringing his fresh litchis. Second Sister was loading the fruit into a wooden bucket, and the children were jostling each other as they picked out the biggest ones, peeling them, and plopping them into their daddy's mouth. *Oh, can such beautiful times have only been a dream?*

Young Li pushed and shoved the doctor. But the doctor didn't want to open his eyes. "Right now I'm eating litchis! My little girl has peeled a big, sweet one. It tastes so nice!"

Young Li had no mind for dwelling on the litchis of home with the doctor. "We've got to think of a way to get hold of two sets of ordinary folks' clothing. Otherwise, if people see we are deserters, we'll get caught and turned in."

Although they had thrown away their barracks caps and rank insignia along the way, all it would take was one look to tell they were soldiers.

They followed little paths between the fields and entered a tiny village where twenty dwellings clustered, each one poorer than the last. In the whole village, there wasn't one extra set of clothing. Two brothers sharing one pair of trousers was nothing remarkable here. The doctor almost forgot the reason they had entered this hamlet. It was as if he were an envoy dispatched to help the needy and the distressed here. He gave a little money to each of the families so that the old people and the children who were sick could see a doctor. After staying for two days, Young Li borrowed some tattered rags and went into the market town and bought two sets of old clothes.

They discarded everything that people might associate with the army. Among these was the leather bag that Division Commander Zhang had left behind. When Young Li turned the bag upside down and gave it a few good smacks, the lining came loose and out fell several pieces of gold bullion the size of rubber erasers that schoolchildren used. The two men just gaped.

Division Commander Zhang had said he had a few gold pieces, but the doctor hadn't taken this seriously and when they left that war-ravaged town, he gave the little widow an amount of money, the equivalent of two months' pay. Had he discovered this gold at the time, he would have given the entire lot to her. Now they were sitting on the brick *kang* of some yokel's home. The gleam of the gold pieces lying on the grimy cotton batten was very captivating to the eye. Young Li said, "Mr. Lin, Division Commander Zhang was very fond of you, so these should go to you." The doctor shook his head, "They should go to the little widow. Division Commander Zhang certainly had this in mind at that time."

"Let's just take them now and when the war ends, we'll both come back up north to find her," said Young Li, and he bound the gold pieces into his waistband.

One of the locals wordlessly led them out of the village. In his hand was a vegetable leaf of some kind and when they arrived at the road, he said to the doctor, "Sir, you're so fair and clean looking, it's going to make people suspicious. Women in the cities and towns rub the juice of this leaf on their faces to avoid bad things happening to them."

Young Li said, "Quite right, and if anyone asks, just say you're my older brother, and I am taking you to a doctor."

The doctor lowered his head in submission and let the fellow apply this makeup on his face.

Half a month later, they had meandered to Wuhu.[21] They didn't go into the city, for on the way there they had flagged down a long-distance bus headed for Nanjing.[22] Exhausted by the journey and unshaven for days, the doctor really did look like a person at death's door from some terrible sickness. On the Wuhu-Nanjing road, the bus encountered three different bandit gangs, but they lost only the bit of money specially prepared for such occurrences. Each time, Young Li wept and wailed that this was the money he needed to save his brother's life. Afterward, all in all, he couldn't help feeling secretly pleased at such a brilliant performance.

When they saw Nanjing's ash-gray city walls, the most difficult and dangerous part of the journey had been completed. Now that they were in Nanjing, Shanghai wasn't too far away. And from

---

[21] A very old city on the Yangzi River in southeastern Anhui Province.

[22] That is, the former Nationalist capital in Jiangsu Province, at this time in the story the capital of the collaborationist government under Wang Jingwei.

Shanghai's Sixteen Wharf Landing they would board a ship, and that would be about the same as putting one foot on the threshold of the Old Town gate. Then, going home to eat litchis would no longer be just a dream! The doctor, much affected by these thoughts, gripped Young Li's hand. Young Li felt the doctor's hand trembling and softy asked him, "Sir, are you really sick?" The doctor's eyes reddened, and in a choking voice, he replied, "We're almost home."

Young Li absentmindedly looked out the bus window. Under the city gate, the scene was all in tumult, like a farmers' market. He could faintly make out women's high-pitched cries and shouts, and from all sides speeding vehicles were getting bogged down and jammed up along the side of the road. Their bus also slowed down. He had a presentiment of something bad about to happen, but he didn't dare tell the doctor.

Their battered and travel-worn bus came to a stop. The doctor and Young Li followed along in the flow of people to the city gate. Many people were holding aloft small cards that had faded yellow. Young Li asked a man beside him what these were. The man was astonished that these two fellows didn't know about "Loyal Citizen" identity cards and said in a lowered voice, "Get out of here fast! Even people with cards are searched and questioned. Without cards you'll be taken for communists from up north of the river." Young Li had no time to relate this to the doctor for Japanese soldiers with rifles locked and loaded were already standing in front of them. He quickly made a show of searching through his pockets for the document, turning not only his own pockets inside out, but also the doctor's. He shook open their bundle from which fell two pieces of old clothing and several dried buns. Then, smacking his chest and stamping his feet, he cried out, "The cards are gone! Someone's stolen them!"

Young Li reached the very acme of the acting profession with this performance but it couldn't change reality. They were pulled out of line by the Japanese and thrust into the clump of people who had been searched and were considered suspicious. All around was face after fear-contorted face. The women were crying loudly. The men were heaving deep sighs and groans. The doctor finally realized that he was facing the worst calamity of all. Most probably here and now outside the city of Nanjing he would "meet his Waterloo." Suddenly, he very much did not want to die and a strong will to survive that he had never before felt roused within him. He closed his eyes and prayed. *Heavenly Father, Lord Jesus, I beseech you to help your child to pass through this danger and let him return home for just one look at Second Sister.*

Several Japanese soldiers escorted the twenty or thirty "suspect elements" to the outskirts of the city. Young Li and the doctor dropped to the very back. A Japanese soldier holding a rifle was walking beside them. As they were making their way through a grove of trees, Young Li suddenly held up three gold pieces in both his hands in front of the soldier. The soldier took one of them and weighed it in his hand. His eyebrows gave a jump and immediately he grabbed the other two pieces. *A deal!* Greatly excited, Young Li dodged behind a tree, dragging the doctor with him.

The doctor hadn't seen the transaction carried out between Young Li and the Japanese soldier. He thought that the soldiers would chase after them and mow them down with a volley of fire. The sounds of footsteps grew fainter and fainter and then disappeared. There were only a few birds singing a monotonous tune in the loneliness of this forest. Young Li kept shoving the doctor. "Sir, we're safe and sound now!" The doctor gazed at him in a kind of a stupor. "Why did the Japanese let us go?"

"Division Commander Zhang's gold bullion saved us! *Aiyah!* I'm so stupid, giving him three pieces. Actually, one would have been enough to do the deal!" When the doctor finally figured the whole thing out, he wept tears of gratitude. *This clearly was God's miracle. He deigned to hear my cry of desperation and fulfilled my wish to survive.*

⌘ ⌘ ⌘

The fright they experienced below the city gate shattered their dream of returning home to Old Town. They had just now cried for joy over their narrow escape, but now they fell right back into pessimism and despair. There was no way into Nanjing, and originally they had planned to take the train from there to Shanghai. But this road was totally blocked. What other road could they take to go south?

From their experiences during the earlier part of their journey, they knew they would have to go into the countryside again. It was safe for them only in those areas of sparse population. Just as in the backcountry of Anhui where they had sought assistance from peasants and country folk, the rural districts here would minimize the dangers they were in. They decided first to find a peasant's home to stay in, and then make a move as soon as they could. It was now a windy, moonless night. There were a few weakly flickering lights way off in the distance and they thought these must be a village. After walking for about five miles, they heard the sound of water slapping against a riverbank. The glow they had seen came from fishing lights on a river. By this time, the two men had neither eaten nor drunk anything for more than a day, and each felt so hungry it was as if the skin of his belly was stuck to his backbone. Young Li just sat down on the ground and declared, "I can't take a step more." Daybreak was almost on them and, once again, moving about recklessly held many disadvantages and few advantages for them. The doctor distractedly walked toward the river's edge and, standing on the levee, saw fish breaking the surface of the water from time to time. He felt a real envy. *If we could become fish, we could just follow the water downstream all the way to Old Town.*

A small boat anchored next to the riverbank bobbed and swayed on the waves. The doctor was standing less than ten steps away from it. On the boat, a fisherman was just then building a fire and the doctor moved forward to greet him, "Good morning to you, countryman."

Startled, the fisherman scrutinized this outlander. The doctor asked him where he lived and whether business was good. The fisherman answered these questions with an ambiguous shake of the head.

Hearing voices, Young Li ran up the side of the levee and, smelling the fragrance of the fish soup, straightway made mewing sounds like a cat begging to be fed. The fisherman beckoned them to come on board. Young Li took the doctor by the hand and waded in the waist-deep water to clamber aboard the boat. That pan of mushy, under-seasoned, and overcooked fish broth was as good as old Zhu Yuanzhang's soup of pearls and jadeite.[23] The taste of it was something the doctor would never forget as long as he lived.

The fisherman never asked his guests where they had come from or where they were going. As the two deserters sat under the boat's shelter discussing new plans in the light of changing circumstances, they discovered that the boat had lifted anchor and was speeding toward the middle of the river. Young Li shouted, "Uncle, we don't know how to swim!" The fisherman worked the scull and said with a smile that curled the sides of his mouth, "Could see that!"

"So may we trouble you to take us back on land in a bit?"

"You looking to die there? The Japanese kill people just like you."

---

[23] Zhu Yuanzhang (1328–1398) was the founder of the Ming Dynasty in 1368.

Young Li and the doctor glanced at each other, wondering what kind of people the fisherman supposed they were. The man had not asked anything about his visitors, but was quite willing to tell them all about himself. He had been born and raised on the little fishing boat. After his parents died, he had led this lonely and solitary life. Young Li had been calling him "Uncle" at every point, only to later find out that this fisherman—with a face filled with all the twists and turns of life and whom he had taken to be fifty or sixty years old—had been on this earth only a bit more than thirty years.

The fisherman's two visitors stayed on this small boat. These two Old Town "land ducks" learned how to toss and retrieve the fishing net and to work the scull. Every time the fisherman went ashore to sell the fish, they would take the vessel far out in the stream for safety's sake and wait for the fisherman's return before sculling back to the riverbank to meet him.

The doctor's skin darkened and he grew more robust. Calluses formed on his hands. Now the urge to return home gradually flagged and faded. He forgot that he was, as the poet said, "but a guest here."[24] Life on the water passed day by day. Only occasionally in a half-dreaming, half-awakened state did he realize he was floating on a river, and then dejection would take him.

One day, the fisherman came back from the riverbank and quietly said, "This evening there's going to be a steamship carrying goods down to Shanghai. One of you can go first."

The doctor was stunned. Young Li asked, "How do you know we want to go to Shanghai?"

The fisherman said evasively, "The first day I saw you I knew where you had come from."

---

[24] From the poem "Waves Washing on Sand" by the "Exiled Emperor" and renowned poet of the Southern Tang, Li Yu (Li Houzhu, b. 936 d. 978).

"And where was that?"

The fisherman raised his hand and jabbed it in the direction of the north. So all along he had taken these two men to be communists from "north of the river."

"'People often go by water to Shanghai. That steamship is still helping 'up north' to send its goods. Don't worry, it's reliable.'"

Actually, he had been making discreet inquiries about the route for some time. It was only that these two men were much too fair and clean looking. He worried that they would never make it through all the checkpoints along the way.

What the fisherman said made the doctor feel ashamed of himself. Even though he had left Division Commander Hu totally out of a sense of justice, he was, after all, a deserter. He hadn't even tried to find another army unit truly prepared to bathe in its own blood in order to fight the Japanese.

They both went at it long and hard about which one should go first. Young Li became quite agitated. He stood at the prow of the boat and said, "Sir, if you make me go first, I'm just going to jump into the water right here and feed the fish!"

The doctor said nothing. He just sat stock-still under the awning. The hope of returning home had kindled anew within him, but why wasn't he feeling any joy? He couldn't bear leaving Young Li. Though he had not yet been separated from this capable assistant who had been with him day and night, the doctor already felt unbearable pain. Nor could he bring himself to leave the fisherman. Once they parted, they probably would never have the chance to meet again. When he thought of the fisherman, floating all alone on the water, growing older and dying of some disease without a single person to ask about him, the doctor's heart broke within him.

Sculling his boat late that night, the fisherman found the steamship and came up alongside the larger vessel. The doctor looked at Young Li and the fisherman, unwilling to leave. The master of the steamship reached out and hauled him straight up on board. Just as the vessels were separating, Young Li thrust two gold pieces into the doctor's hand. By the time the doctor realized what had happened, Young Li was already out of reach.

The steamship's engines throbbed to life. Young Li cupped his hands over his mouth and shouted, "When I get to Old Town I'll go to Officials Lane and look for you at the Lin residence. If I can't make it back, please look after my ma! We live in Li Village, Tongpan District, out in the east!"

The doctor fought to hold back his tears but in the end shed a few furtive ones. He was so choked up he couldn't open his mouth, and just stood there gazing at the little boat rapidly moving farther and farther away.

3.

ON A BLAZINGLY hot summer's day, my grandfather was making his way through a mass of porters and climbing the steps of Sixteen Wharf Landing, a bulging hemp sack balanced on his shoulders. Shanghai had been a second home for him when he was a young student, and after returning to Old Town, he often longed for the day when he could take Second Sister and the three children to tour all those places of his earlier life. But never did he think that returning to his second home would be like this. The load on his shoulders weighed more than he did. Although over the past two months the fisherman had deliberately made him do heavy work, and made him bare his arms so they would be burned dark by the sunlight, he still had trouble bearing such a heavy weight. He was bent forward almost horizontally and both legs trembled with each step. From the way he looked, you might think he was some pathetic person who insisted on working in spite of being sick. Surprisingly, he wasn't stopped for an identity card check as he passed through the inspection hatch. But he never made it with his sack to the nearby warehouse. Only a few steps past the hatch his legs gave way under him and he feebly collapsed to the ground, the big sack pressing down on him. He tried to push it away but couldn't move. Some unknown carrier helped him get his load into the warehouse. There grandpa lingered until about evening and then followed the group of workers going off shift and returning to their homes in Shanghai.

The big buildings and mansions of Shanghai were just as before, but this was no longer the Shanghai he had known. The sight, as he remembered it, of Mr. and Mrs. Qiao standing on the dock to welcome his arrival more than ten years earlier came vividly back to him. The last time he had corresponded with them, they were in Beiping, but contact had been lost for quite a long time. *Where were his two saviors now? They were getting on in years. If only they could safely return to their own hometown and live out their remaining days in peace and ease.*

Looking up abruptly, Ninth Brother saw a ragged beggar right in front of him and automatically he quickly stepped aside to avoid him. The beggar did the same. Stopping to take a closer look, Ninth Brother realized he was in front of a shop's display window and that beggar was him! He looked at the window for a long time. The free and easygoing young student in his long gown and mandarin jacket of those earlier days had become the figure in front of him now. This was just what people meant when they spoke of the transience and vicissitudes of human existence. He didn't know if the sea lane from Shanghai to Old Town was open. What identity papers did he need? He might have to stay here four or five days. He thought he ought to buy a set of clothes and then go to Zhabei[25] to see a former classmate, one of his best friends then. He also ought to buy some small gifts for the man's children.

As Ninth Brother stepped into a small shop, the owner standing behind his counter shouted, "I've got no money for you!"

Oh, that so-familiar Shanghai speech! In a voice filled with an excitement he couldn't restrain, Ninth Brother said to him in Shanghainese, "I'd like to buy something."

"Buy what? You got money?"

"I've got silver dollars."

Immediately a dazzling smile appeared on the shop owner's face. Ninth Brother reached down to unbind his waistband. But looking down, he discovered that the long cloth strip around his

---

[25] A district of Shanghai ravaged by fighting in the War of Resistance against the Japanese. Previously spelled "Chapei."

waist wasn't there. He stood there dumbstruck, just gripping the ends of his shirt. The shop owner put on a long face, thinking this yokel was playing a trick on him. "Go on home, and when you've got your money then come back!"

The two pieces of gold Young Li had given him had been wrapped in the waistband and when the steamship docked, he had specially tightened and retightened that cloth. Earlier on the wharf, his stumble and fall had dazed him and once inside the warehouse he had untied the band from his waist to brush off the dust that covered his entire face and body. Then he had dozed off against a stack of cargo. When he left, he had forgotten about his waistband. However, while there were still some silver dollars in his trouser leg, he wasn't sure how much a silver dollar was worth. Enough to buy a boat ticket back home? He bent over and pinched at his trouser leg. The silver dollars were there, safe and sound. By this time, he had no desire to buy anything and he slunk away under the sarcasm and ridicule of the shop owner.

Ninth Brother remembered the address of his old classmate and found his home. Ten years before he had been invited to a dinner party there. This classmate, surnamed Yang, was slightly older than the others, and so they all called him "Old Yang." By then Old Yang was already married and his wife had a fine hand at cooking.

Mrs. Yang did not recognize her husband's good friend. She thought he was some beggar, and said with ill grace, "You've come to the wrong place. I'm starving to death here myself!"

"Mrs. Yang!" Ninth Brother called out. She took a closer look at him but still didn't dare believe that he was her husband's good friend Young Mr. Lin. "Mrs. Yang, your wine dumpling soup was really delicious." When she was sure he was the refined and genteel Young Mr. Lin, her lips trembled and she began to cry. Old Yang was also an army doctor and had already been gone from Shanghai for five years. Three years ago, his last remittance home had come down from Shanxi Province. After that, there had been no word. Now, at the sound of the woman's tragic sobbing, Ninth Brother thought of his long-separated Second Sister. *Oh, Second Sister, useless and incompetent as I am, I overrated myself and thus I abandoned home and family. I thought I could share the cares and sorrows of our country, but have ended up as a vagabond bum. Second Sister, you've suffered so. I can't face you from shame.*

The Yang household consisted of all ages. Old Mrs. Yang's mind was confused and she mostly kept to her bed. Every day Mrs. Yang herself coughed incessantly. As an internist, Ninth Brother could tell there was something seriously wrong with her. What worried him even more was that because of the straitened circumstances of their family, the two children had stopped going to school. The thirteen-year-old son was hauling heavy sacks at the train station to make ends meet at home.

His face washed and teeth brushed, and wearing Old Yang's clothes, Ninth Brother restored some measure of his graceful bearing of those earlier years. Two days had passed and he hadn't mentioned the matter of his returning to Old Town. The few silver dollars might perhaps be just enough for travel expenses, including the cost of the necessary travel permit. But the circumstances of the Yang household were right there in clear view. *Since God has let me see the difficulties they are in and he even wants me to stretch forth my hand to help them, how could I just pack up and walk away?* Ninth Brother struggled with this problem. He had already given Mrs. Yang two silver dollars and that very evening she sent the money to the land-lord's home. There was more than half a year's rental in arrears and the landlord had given his ultimatum: if she couldn't hand over the rent he would put them on the street with nothing but the clothes on their backs.

At this moment, Ninth Brother was sitting in a cramped little room. Mrs. Yang and the two children were away. Only Old Mrs. Yang was there, lying on her bed, babbling endlessly. On the wall, there was a printed picture of the cross. As Ninth Brother gazed at it, all sorts of feelings welled up inside him. He closed his eyes and prayed: *O Heavenly Father, thank you for watching over me at all times, and letting me get through all the dangers in this perilous journey. Without your great love, my life wouldn't be worth that of an ant. O Heavenly Father, it is from your blessings that all along the way I have met good people. Today my steps are resting awhile at the Yang family. You know better than I the difficult circumstances they face. I would really like to help them, but even if I did everything within my power, it would be just a cup of water poured out on a cart of burning firewood. Tell me what I should do.*

That evening, Mrs. Yang returned from doing the washing at someone's house. She sat in a chair, coughing and coughing. Ninth Brother suspected she had caught tuberculosis. When he urged her to seek treatment at a hospital, Mrs. Yang glared coldly at him. That look made it impossible for him to hold on to the remaining silver dollars—four of them in all. He handed her three of them and kept one, thinking that tomorrow he would go to the hospital where he had once practiced and get a prescription for her.

He had no travel fare now. And the road back home was a very long one. But, in fact, Ninth Brother's heart felt at rest. On this night, as he and the older Yang boy squeezed into the little attic, he slept better than he had for the past several days.

Quite early on the second morning, Ninth Brother had just gotten on the electric tram headed for the hospital, when, looking up, he saw a familiar face, a former classmate from Hangzhou in the church school. The two men were overjoyed at this chance meeting. This fellow had just moved from Hangzhou to Shanghai and he was on his way to work at the very hospital that Ninth Brother was going to. When he found out about the Yang family, he gave his full assurance that he would look after Mrs. Yang and the two children. This Hangzhou classmate was from quite a prosperous family and for him to assist the Yang family hardly required any effort on his part. Before alighting from the tram, they had arranged everything. Ninth Brother was so happy he made a total spectacle of himself. Standing in the streetcar, he grasped his two hands together in front of everybody and exclaimed loudly, "Thank you, God! Thank you, Lord Jesus!"

Several days later, the Yang family totally broke free of all their difficulties. Mrs. Yang and her old mother-in-law received the best medical treatment and the two boys were back at school. All the problems of the travel money to return home and the identity documentation were no longer problems. Ninth Brother was ecstatic, like a happy child that is eager for praise and approval after doing something that pleased an adult. When he went to Sixteen Wharf Landing to buy the boat ticket he said to his dear Heavenly Father: *Your child is incapable on his own but thanks to your great power he helped a family in need. Maybe this was your intention—for your child to stay in Shanghai. Helping others fills my soul with happiness. And I see the Yang family's lives just as if I were seeing the difficulties Second Sister and the children are going through. I beseech you, Heavenly Father, to protect the homeward path of your child. Your child will all the more love the wife and children you have blessed him with.*

Whenever my grandfather got elated, he would radiate a kind of childishness. He would do this even in old age. I still remember normally taciturn Grandpa standing under the sky well, playing at squirt guns with my little cousin. These were rough-and-ready toys made from plastic bottles. Grandpa and grandson paid not a bit of mind to the difference between them in age but played together quite happily. At the time, I was extremely surprised since most of the time my grandfather was rather stern and never said much. His final years were not an easy time for him.

Ninth Brother, a childish smile on his face, stepped lightly up the steps of the ticket sales office, only to be told that three days before the Japanese had sealed off the sea route to Old Town— sealed it off indefinitely!

How to take such a direct blow? And how could he go back to the Yang family in Zhabei? Mrs. Yang had prepared a few small dishes and invited the Hangzhou classmate for Young Mr. Lin's send-off dinner. They waited until past ten o'clock at night, and only then did Young Mr. Lin appear, so drunk he could barely stand up. They rushed forward and asked what had happened. Leaning on the wall, he pulled over a chair and sat down. He opened his reddened eyes and stared first at Mrs. Yang and then at the Hangzhou classmate. Then he said something that seemed to make no sense at all: "When the nest overturns, how can the eggs remain whole?"

Chapter Seven – Grandma's Guardian Angel

1.

GRANDMA SAID THAT everyone has a guardian angel. You can't see an angel with your physical eyes, but not even your tiniest hair escapes the angel's notice. When Grandma got so old she could no longer take care of herself, our family arranged for a nursemaid to come in. This nursemaid discovered the old lady had one peculiar failing: she was unwilling to take off all her clothes when she bathed. The nursemaid would tell her, "At your age...and anyway, we're both women, so why be shy?" My grandmother would say, "I don't want the angel to see me so old and ugly." Bewildered, the nursemaid looked all around the room and asked who this angel was. "You can't see it. In my whole life I have seen it just one time," was my grandma's reply.

Grandma told a lot people about the time her soul went soaring off as proof of this angel business. She believed that the angel took her up into the heavens, supporting her in the palm of its hand and rescuing her from painful reality. Grandma supposed that after she died she would be sent back to the world to be somebody else's guardian angel. So early on, she prepared a complete, shining white angel's outfit: a many-plaited hat trimmed with lace, a jacket and trousers set, and a pair of soft-soled shoes. When I arrived home for the summer break during my third year at the university, Grandma had her "old-age glasses" on and was busy sewing. I was the one she was the most worried about, she said. In time to come, she would definitely request her Heavenly Father to let her be my guardian angel. The angel outfit lay in the trunk over the years. Every time I ran into Grandma, she would always say to me with a sigh, "Has the Heavenly Father forgotten me?" She lived to be ninety-five years old before finally putting on that spotless white angel outfit and going to heaven.

My great-aunt was one of those surgeons of the thought revolution. She worried that Grandma's testimonies about the angel would lead us children astray. Once, behind Grandma's back, she called all the cousins together and explained this angel. She said it was a temporary amnesia, the body's self-defense mechanism. It was just like someone who lost consciousness while suffering an extreme level of pain. She added a whole lot of other scientific facts that sounded dull and dry to us. Compared to these, we were happier listening to Grandma's mysterious stories.

⌘   ⌘   ⌘

The good-hearted yokels of the area helped Fourth Brother take Second Sister and the stricken Fifth Brother home. Little Baoqing followed at the rear of the crowd, wiping his tears as he walked along. Soaring high above, Second Sister saw everything in a vast panorama. "Baoqing, don't be sad, Ma is here." Baoqing couldn't hear this. He wiped his face with his sleeve, almost already totally soaked with tears...

Second Sister's mother hobbled to the end of the bridge, Gan'er in tow, to await the news. *Everyone in this family, from the youngest to the oldest, is like a migrating bird, laboriously carrying grass in its beak to build a nest. No sooner do they stop to catch their breath, when yet another deadly blow falls upon them. The three generations are scattered in all directions, like birds spying a bow. Will they find Baohua? And can Second Sister bear up under this shock? If Second Sister breaks down, this family will be totally done for. Second Sister believes in the Foreign Buddha, doesn't she? Ah, Foreign Buddha, consider this husband and wife who have always believed in you, and make your presence felt.* However, at this point, what Old Lady Guo wanted to do above all else was to go to the temple and burn a pillar of incense. There was a temple on the distant mountaintop, but her little feet really couldn't move any farther.

Gan'er was cranky from lack of sleep. Old Lady Guo just sat right down on the spot and, holding her grandson, gazed helplessly at the far end of the bridge. When two carry-chairs appeared, she didn't dare believe that it was Second Sister and Fifth Brother seated on them.

Second Sister saw her mother and told the carriers to stop. Looking surprised, she asked, "Ma, it's so dark now, what brought you here?"

Baoqing realized his mother could speak now and a smile broke out on his little tear-streaked face.

Second Sister helped her mother onto one of the carry-chairs. When they returned to their house, she casually greeted the local folk and went in to wash and drink some water. Pulling Fourth Brother over, the old lady softly asked where Baohua was. Fourth Brother gave a look of total bewilderment. After sending off the visitors and putting Baoqing to bed, Second Sister boiled water, washed her hair, and bathed. Then she changed into some loose-fitting clothes and, picking up her wicker sewing basket, sat by the lamp and began to sew. "So late and you're still not sleeping?" Old

Lady Guo probed. "I'll go to bed when my hair's dry." She was too normal, so much so that her mother and the two younger brothers grew frightened.

⌘   ⌘   ⌘

Gripping his slingshot, Baosheng walked with rapid steps in the dark night. He was wearing his Old Town primary school uniform, the pockets filled with small but quite heavy stones. Flames of anger flared in his breast and it was as if some high-powered engine were driving him swiftly on.

Ah, my good son. Young as you are, you are showing the heroism of a true man. Of the three children, Daddy especially loved Baohua. Ma tended most toward Baoqing. Ever since he was little, naughty and mischievous Baosheng had not been particularly endearing to people, and both Second Sister and Ninth Brother had used the switch on him to make him behave. But Baohua and Baoqing had never received as much as a stern look from their parents. Now, though, his mother regretted this deeply. *Ninth Brother, do you see this? Our Baosheng is a really fine fellow. Each one of our three children is the pride of their parents. We must love them equally and not show any favoritism.*

The next evening, Second Son Guo stood drinking beside the counter of the postal relay station. As he drank and drank, he suddenly burst into a fit of tears and sniveling. The woman at his side was worried that Second Sister would come after them and kept urging him to get on the road. Number Two bent over the counter as loose as mud but with a tongue so stiff it could hardly move. He lashed out at her, "Stinking whore, you bad luck star. You've brought death and ruin to my family. Oh, Mother, your son is ashamed to face you. When you die, I won't be there to cover your head or pay my last respects. Second Sister, oh, I am so sorry."

Usually, the woman led Number Two around by the nose. When she wanted to go east, he would never dare even glance to the west. Once in a while Number Two got drunk and behaved atrociously, but she could put up with it. She stared dully at her man and thought about abandoning him and just ending all this, but then a feeling of despondency overpowered her. In this world of chaos where could she go? *People age and pearls lose their luster.* The little bit of money saved up in their earlier days had all been squandered. All she had now was this down-and-out, good-for-nothing princeling. *But I'll stick with him. Good or bad, at least he's somebody to be with.*

The postal relay station was a little wooden structure out in the middle of nowhere, its sparsely planked walls letting out the dim glow of its lamps. That was what caught Baosheng's notice. He remembered the time they had come there from Old Town when he had rested his weary feet and changed sedan chair carriers. *Since it was too dark now to find carriers, could those two rotten eggs be spending the night inside?* He knew that there were guest quarters on the second floor and the steps were next to the kitchen. All he had to do was block those steps and they couldn't run away. A watchdog was tied to the main door. Baosheng nimbly circled round to the rear door leading to the kitchen. When his small form suddenly charged in, the night watchman let out a yell of frightened alarm. The sound of this had barely faded when it was followed by two cries of pain. Second Son and that woman were each hit by a stone from Baosheng's slingshot. Second Son shielded his head. The woman covered her heel. They both rolled around on the ground in agony.

Baosheng stretched the slingshot and aimed right at his uncle's eyes. "Where's my sister?"

The woman cursed and yelled as she leapt forward in an attempted counterattack. Baosheng then let fly with a stone that hit her right on the bridge of her nose. Immediately she was dripping blood.

The watchman thought that a robber had entered and he took hold of a vegetable cleaver from the kitchen. In an instant, Baosheng let fly again. *Clang!* The cleaver fell to the floor. The watchman was just about to bend over and pick it up when Second Son cried out, waving his hand. "Don't touch that deadly thing! Don't hurt the child! He's my sister's son!"

These words softened Baosheng. Everyone said uncles loved their nephews. "Even if a bone gets broken it is still linked to the tendon," the saying goes. Among Mama's own family, Second Uncle loved him the best. Second Uncle had never thought he was naughty. Sometimes they would even play practical jokes together. The year before last during the Dragon Boat Festival races, he had sat on Second Uncle's shoulders. Recalling this, Baosheng slackened the tautly pulled slingshot. "Give me back my sister and I'll let you both go!"

Second Son's woman was lying facedown on the floor regaining her strength. Suddenly, she sprang up and opened her blood-smeared hands. *Bam! Smack! Bam!* She boxed Baosheng's head on the left and the right and he was soon covered with blood. Second Son stood there stupefied for an instant then dashed forward and the three of them got all twisted up into a pile. After a while, when the woman discovered that the person hitting her was Second Son, she let go of Baosheng and grabbed hold of her man's collar, shrieking and cursing until she was hoarse.

This uproar disturbed the lodgers upstairs. Almost all of them came out from under their quilts and gathered at the top of the steps to watch the melee. Was it a fight between husband and wife? Then why was the child's face beaten all bloody? A bespectacled youth with a questioning look on his face went up to Baosheng and took hold of the boy's shoulders in both his hands. "You look very familiar. Are you from Old Town?"

Baosheng recognized this young man as Pastor Chen's son, Enchun. Baosheng's nostrils quivered and he wanted to burst into tears, but he just clenched his teeth.

The pastor and his wife came over and asked, "Baosheng, how come you're here? And your ma, where is she?"

Fuming with rage, Baosheng pointed to the man and the woman still pummeling each other and said, "They tricked my big sister into going with them and then they sold her!"

The pastor's wife quickly blocked the main entrance and shouted, "If you don't hand over this boy's sister, we won't let you leave this place!"

Second Son recognized the pastor of West Gate church and his wife. Weeping, he knelt down before her. "Oh, Mrs. Pastor, I am too ashamed to face Second Sister. Please tell her that I ought to die. Baohua's at some rich guy's home. The boss of the opium den in town knows where it is."

One hand covering up where her clothes had been torn, Second Son's woman poked him savagely on the head. "These days a girl is cheaper than a cat, and over *that* little wench you're beating me!"

Pastor Chen asked for a clear account of all this and, bringing Second Son up to his feet, said, "You don't have to face your sister, but you do have to take us to find Baohua. I'll give you whatever money you'll need."

This repulsive-looking pair hadn't spoiled the mood of the pastor and his wife, who, full of affection, said to Baosheng, "Child, be at ease. Our Heavenly Father has always watched over your sister and brother and he sent us here to help you. I'm sure your sister will return safely to your mama's side."

The situation in Old Town was really going downhill. People said that the Japanese had taken a fancy to this well-situated and resource-rich place and wanted to make it into an air base. With the Old Town people scattering far away in all directions to escape this calamity, the place had become still as death. One rich merchant of Old Town who had contributed funds for the building of a church in Qingpu County sent someone to invite Pastor Chen to preach there. Qingpu and Nanjing were adjacent counties and the relay station where the Chens were resting on their journey was right at the boundary line. The evening before they actually had not planned to spend the night here, but Mrs. Chen had been suddenly seized with a violent case of dysentery at the road crossing ahead of them and was unable to go on. This appeared to be a coincidence, but in the eyes of Christians, all coincidences reflected God's good purpose. Mrs. Chen, who was never sick, no matter when, had been stricken at the gate of this station. Not only that, but the moment she stepped into the building, they ran into an old practitioner of Chinese medicine who was also stopping over here and this doctor soon had her all fixed up. Last night they had expressed their gratitude to God for making them find this place and meet the doctor. Now it was even clearer that the power of God far exceeded anything they could imagine. God himself had led them to help Dr. Lin's family when all along they had been concerned about the Lins. How could they not feel an overwhelming gratitude at this fortuitous encounter with Baosheng?

Second Son didn't believe in God, but he did believe that Pastor Chen wouldn't deceive him. When the sky grew light again, he got the pastor to hire him a carry-chair and he went back to Nanjing to look for Baohua. Second Son's woman was still angry and said fiercely that she wanted to make a clean break from him. "If I never see him again, I'll shed no tears at my death." But the moment they lifted the carry-chair, she chased after him.

2.

BAOHUA WAS LED off by her future "mother-in-law." Second Uncle had said, "This auntie is a relative of ours. Your ma is visiting at her house." The county town was a peaceful place of little streets and alleys amid the surrounding hills and streams. After passing through town, they got onto a mountain road. Now Baohua began to feel afraid and said she wanted to go home. "Mother-in-law" tightly gripped her by the hand and humored her, "We're almost there. Your ma is waiting for you." After going a few more steps, at the foot of the mountain a big and burly fellow leapt up, and in one swoop took up frail little Baohua into the crook of his arm. Then, with vigorous strides, he hurried toward the mountains, as if on wings.

The only resistance that Baohua could make was to cry. For two days and nights, she neither ate nor drank as she squatted in a corner and wept incessantly. The landlord's whole family "knelt down and paid homage," as the expression goes, to this young miss from the high official's family, and took more pain in caring for her than they ever did in attending their own ancestors. Day and night, the several women of the house took turns keeping Baohua company. They took out cured meat, salted fish, and bright white rice, things they normally couldn't bear to eat as being too extravagant, and brought these all steaming hot to her. The little serving maid who brought the food smelled the tantalizing aroma and salivated mightily. The staple food of folk in the mountain districts is sweet potatoes and several years might pass before they could eat a bowl of white rice. The serving maid forced down her saliva and coaxed Baohua to eat. "Such delicious rice, such nice cured meat and salted fish. In the master's house, it's only during the New Year that we get to eat this kind of food. On New Year's Eve we servants are able to eat just a small mouthful of rice. So why aren't you eating? In whose home are you the thousand-gold-pieces young lady to make our master treat you so well?" Baohua, like a little dog, loyal and faithful to its own home, but now unfortunately gone astray, curled up into the corner silently shedding her tears. These flowed inexhaustibly. Her eyes were so swollen she couldn't open them, but her tears still gushed out endlessly.

⌘　⌘　⌘

By the time I came forth into this world, my mother's kidnapping was an incident long past. But I can imagine her all curled up in a corner weeping. My mother was the biggest crybaby I've ever known. She rarely cried out loud but always just bowed her head and silently let loose with her tears. My deepest impression of Mother was of her going back to her old home holding a bag embroidered with flowers. Each time she had no sooner entered and before saying even one word, she began to cry. That affecting and pathetic style inevitably made people think of Lin Daiyu in "Dream of the Red Chamber," so I've never liked Lin Daiyu. Maybe it's a case of "excess leads to reaction." Mother's tears nurtured my own hard-as-nails temperament. I rarely cry. I treasure tears like gold.

Throughout her life, my mother always made the wrong choices in marriage. This was the secret anguish that my grandpa and grandma harbored and were never able to dispel. Before my grandfather passed on, he called me to his sickbed. Stretching forth his thin, almost transparent hand and feebly drawing me to him, he said, "You must show concern and love for your mother. Later on, when you're able to, be sure to bring her into your home." After she turned ninety,

Grandma grew more and more confused. Sometimes she would awake with a fright from some dream, put on her shoes, and rush outdoors, mumbling and muttering that she had to find Baohua.

Mother would mostly return to her old home in some snit over her husband. Her second one was a fierce-tempered northern cadre who stayed fierce-tempered right into old age. He would overturn tables at the drop of a hat. Just let him hear one word he didn't like and he'd grab whatever was near at hand and dash it to the floor. When Grandma and Grandpa were no longer alive, Mother would take a little bundle of her things and seek refuge with Baoqing. Both my uncles would try to persuade her to leave that volatile man. No matter how many times Baohua would swear never to see her old man again, after no more than a few days she couldn't stand up to his nice words and would again return to washing his clothes and preparing his meals.

When Mother was young, the experience of divorcing my father gave her a sense of inferiority and shame that stayed with her throughout her life. In those times divorce was extremely rare and furthermore something to be extremely ashamed of. Now with everything changed, divorce is no big thing. But she never emerged from the shadow of that divorce. Without holding fast to the slightest principle she would make excuses and overlook my stepfather's bad temper, which was growing all the more heedless of any propriety. My grandmother always said that her pretty face is what did Mother in. She was exquisite, a good-looking, pocket-sized babe. If it hadn't been for her pretty looks she certainly would never have married either my natural father or my stepfather. These two were both high-level cadres who did whatever they said would. When they met her, they just had to marry her.

Grandma and Grandpa both dearly loved Pastor Chen's son, Enchun. While Baohua was still a child, they had imagined a match between the two of them. Baohua was so delicate and high-strung that giving her to honest, good-natured Enchun would relieve them of all their cares and concerns. God never brought this match to pass, but through many strange twists and odd turns, their own children were marked down in the marriage book of heaven. My union with Chaofan pleasantly surprised the old folks of both families. But they would never know what an absurd life we led. If Grandma really were my guardian angel, encircling and closing round me, she certainly would have wept a tear in sadness.

⌘   ⌘   ⌘

By the third day, Baohua was clinging to life with breath as slight as gossamer. Only her tears were still flowing copiously. "Father-in-law" worried that his future daughter-in-law was ill-starred. If something untoward happened, her father might later come with troops to remove his head. So he changed into clothes he wore only at the New Year and rushed to the county town to find out where Old Lady Guo's younger brother lived. Second Son had once told him that Master Huang, the county official, was his dear uncle on his mother's side. Dangling a lively hen, "Father-in-law" knocked on the door of the Huang residence. Ah Cui heard that someone had come calling for "Great-Uncle," and "Great-Auntie." Seeing the oafish-looking fellow, she concluded that it was one of her husband's poor relatives and told him in no uncertain terms that he had knocked at the wrong door. She then called a servant to relieve him of the chicken and send him on his way. Right there and then, "Father-in-law" decided that he had been tricked. He had spent four silver dollars to buy a girl who would be completely useless as a servant. It was for these four silver dollars that he stood there on the street beating his breast and stamping his feet, spit flying all over the place as he cursed and called names. China was poor then. The small landlords who were able to accumulate a few *mu* [26] of barren fields all got to where they were by abstemious living. As head of a household, this fellow could eat white rice only twice a year. Four silver dollars could buy many, many *dan* of rice. [27]

"Father-in-law" returned home, crestfallen and indignant. Seeing "Mother-in-law" just then spooning rice porridge into Baohua's mouth, he rushed forward and snatched away the earthenware bowl and flung it to the floor. "Let her die! Let her die!" he screamed.

"Mother-in-law" was kind-hearted. She was afraid that this girl, insubstantial as a bean sprout, would get slapped to death by "Father-in-law," so she put Baohua in the hay shed next to the pigpen and left with her some of the sweet potatoes cooked on the previous few nights.

That night, "Father-in-law" tossed and turned, unable to get to sleep, so he woke up his old lady and the two of them sat discussing how to deal with Baohua. Since neither of them could bring themselves to use a lamp, they held their meeting bumping about in the dark. The husband said they had to sell the girl and get back what money they could out of it. His old lady said, "Keep her for a few more years and then decide. This delicate and fine-skinned girl looks city-bred. Maybe she really *is* some big official's "thousand gold pieces" after all."

Suddenly, the barking of dogs sounded in this lonely mountain village. Since they wouldn't pay for dog food, they didn't raise dogs. It was the barking of other people's dogs that put them on the alert. Who would be barging into the village at the third watch past

---

[26] A *mu* is a measurement of land equivalent to about one-sixth of an acre.

[27] A measurement of harvested and dried rice equivalent to about 50 kg.

midnight? They both puzzled over this. Then they heard footsteps coming close on the other side of the courtyard wall. Next came the voice of their great-nephew from some distant branch of the family calling out, "Great-Uncle! Great-Aunt! There's someone from town here to see you!"

"Mother-in-law" lit a small oil lamp and asked who it was. Hearing that it was the man from town who had sold the child, she pressed up close to the crack in the door and looked outside. There she saw quite a few people standing in the moonlight. She supposed that it had to be the relatives of the big official. Not daring to open the door, she returned to the room and told her husband, "Uh-oh, the relatives have come to see the girl!" The landlord was so terrified he trembled all over, and it took him the longest time to get his shoes on.

When the pastor and his wife entered the house, Baohua had already been shifted from the hay shed to the big bed in the main chamber. They could scarcely believe that this straw-plastered bag of skin and bones was Baohua. The pastor gave the landlord four silver dollars and without awaiting his reaction, Enchun took up Baohua on his back and disappeared into the darkness of night.

Second Sister was still at her embroidery. Four full days had gone by and she kept on embroidering. She heard her son shout, "Ma! Ma! They've found Big Sister! Big Sister has returned!" She glanced up and looked distractedly at Baosheng, as if just awakening from some great dream. "Where have you been? Up to your tricks again? Why are you so covered with dirt? And where are your shoes?"

Baosheng stared at his filthy feet. The night before last, he had lost his shoes fighting with Second Uncle's woman. These two days he had gone about thirty miles in bare feet, *but why would Ma start asking me about my shoes at this time?* From over beside the stove Old

Lady Guo gave him a wink, but he still couldn't understand what was wrong with Ma.

"Ma, Big Sister's been found. Uncle and Aunt Pastor and Enchun are all here now!"

Enchun entered, still carrying Baohua on his back. "Auntie Lin, don't worry. Baohua's safe and sound."

The moment Baohua started to cry, Second Sister came fully to her senses. Throwing down the sewing in her hand, she embraced the girl, crying tears of grief and joy all mixed together. Baoqing and Baosheng clustered round them, and all four of them held each other tightly. And Baosheng, who hated crying the most, for the first time cried as if his heart would break.

3.

BAOHUA BIT THE end of the lead pencil. Her eyes, fringed with long lashes, gazed intently downward at the table before her. She was concentrating on a coarse bamboo paper workbook containing neatly written arithmetic problems. Having been out of school for so long, she found even second-year arithmetic problems beyond her.

Enchun sat beside her. The pastor and his wife had left him in Nanjing Town to tutor the three Lin children. Enchun was a second-year student in the lower-middle school and was fully up to the task of being a home teacher of young students.

"If you give it some more thought and take it slowly, surely you can figure it out." The inspiration of Enchun and the misty breeze outside spurred Baohua on.

Off to the side, Second Sister was ironing clothes. Although they had fallen to the level of refugees, she was still unwilling to wear clothes that were even the slightest wrinkled. Even if they were the old clothes worn at home, they had to be neatly ironed. She paused in her work and gazed at Enchun, saying to herself with a sigh, *Oh, what a good fellow. Even long ago, when he was little, Ninth Brother had his eye on him. If only Baohua could marry him someday, what a stroke of good fortune that would be.*

Abruptly, a feeling of desolation arose within her. She realized how long it had been since she had last thought of Ninth Brother. Ever since Baohua had been lost and then recovered, her zest for living had almost burned out. Now it was with fear and terror that she watched over and guarded her three children as if they were the wildest hope she could have, as if her happy lot in life might incur Satan's jealousy. Day and night, she expressed ardent feelings of gratitude to her Heavenly Father in every word of praise she could think of. Only in this way could she avert disaster.

Baosheng and Baoqing came in, each carrying on his back a bamboo wicker basket filled with melons and other vegetables. A family on the mountain behind them had opened up some wild land for planting and now the harvest was ready. The two boys were just back from buying vegetables in the market and loudly gabbling and yakking away about something Second Sister couldn't understand in the slightest—then realized to her surprise that they were speaking the local dialect! She took another look at her two children in their bare feet and rolled-up trouser legs. They looked just like real buffalo boys. She recalled how they had previously looked in Old Town with their polished shoes and hair combed neatly at the part. Of what people called the twists and turns of life, nothing could be greater than this.

Is it possible that I've grown so old I'll die in these "long story" gullies and ravines? That my children have taken new root here? The mental balance that she had sought in fear and trembling over the past few months was now undone. As she thought of Old Town, of her life during the peaceful years, a powerful longing swept through her in all its turbulence, like floodwaters bursting the breach in a levee. She lifted her eyes to gaze into the distance, letting the iron she unconsciously gripped in her hand drift back and forth over a piece of clothing.

I want to go home. I want to go back to Old Town, and even if I die, I want to die in the place I was raised. I want to take my children with me and look for my husband just like Meng Jiangnu did in those ancient times.[28] Rather than just muddling through a shameful life here, she would face artillery fire and rifle bullets to search for her husband

---

[28] Men Jiangnu's husband had been press-ganged into the building of the Great Wall during the period of the Emperor of Qin (259 BCE–210 BCE). Having no word from him and fearing for his survival, she made warm clothes and set out to locate him. Upon finding him dead, she wept so bitterly that a portion of the wall collapsed. Impressed with this paragon of loyalty, the Qin Emperor offered marriage to her. Her grief unassuaged, she however threw herself from a precipice near the place she had chosen for her husband's burial.

across ten thousand leagues. She thought of looking for the provincial government when she returned to Old Town and demanding her husband from the governor. If he couldn't give her an answer she would take her children with her and find Chiang Kai-shek! At this point, she was so agitated that her whole body shook. *O heaven, I should have thought of doing this a long time ago!*

Fourth Brother pointed to the iron in Second Sister's hand and stammered, "Sec-Second Sister…bu-burning…!"

She dropped the iron and called her children over to her. "Do you miss Old Town?"

"Yes!"

"Do you miss Daddy?"

"Yes!"

Old Lady Guo quietly took away the smoking iron and thought, "Has this Second Sister fallen sick again?"

"Your ma wants to take you to find Daddy. We'll leave this place for good!"

The three children cheered and hopped about like sparrows.

That night, Second Sister ordered her highly excited children to go to sleep early. Then she went by herself to the side of the mountain and spoke to her angel. *I know you are watching over me. I'm not asking you if you approve of my decision. I only want to ask you to help me do what I want to do. If this is the road to my death, I just ask you to let the children and me die at the same moment.*

⌘　⌘　⌘

Whenever I'm at a low point in my life, my mind turns to Grandma during the War of Resistance. The picture that emerges in my memory is not the hardships she fled; rather, how she brought her old mother, children, and brothers back to Old Town after its catastrophe. I see her entering through East Gate, entering an Old Town now changed beyond all recognition, destroyed buildings everywhere, the banyan trees withered and charred. She mentally prepares for the worst: they would go first to the Lin residence in the middle of town. She visualizes the dilapidation of that home. The kitchen in the rear courtyard and the living wings at the front had originally not been solidly built and so very possibly these had collapsed. The scores of glass windows and roof tiles may have been shattered in the explosions. Rebuilding the gardens would take months and months of time, and maybe even longer.

The reality, however, far exceeded my grandma's powers of imagination. The Lin residence and the two homes on either side of it were simply no longer there. The Japanese bombs fell indiscriminately on the roof beams of the Lin residence and the buildings caught fire. All those deep halls and spacious gardens, which had lasted almost one hundred years, were totally destroyed. The well, which had nourished generations of the Lin family, was like a mirror inlaid on blackened ruination.

Baosheng bent over and as he sifted through all the rubble found a shoe that Baohua had worn when she was little. He also found a stethoscope and medicine bottles that his daddy had left behind. From time to time, he would whoop in excitement. He was still too little. He couldn't take in what this scene really meant.

My grandmother stood there, one hand holding Baohua, the other holding Baoqing. Beside them was the well with its eight-foot-wide mouth. A family jumping hand in hand into it would not have hit the sides of the well. I don't know whether or not at that moment she was thinking of this.

⌘　⌘　⌘

Grandma would describe this scene in a very calm voice. At that time, I had flunked my university entrance exam and my future stretched out bleakly before me. I really thought of dying. Grandma said that heaven won't totally block someone's purpose in life. She said, "At the time I returned from Nanjing together with my three children, my house was gone and I had nothing. I thought that heaven wanted our family line to end. This year you didn't pass, next year you can test again. If you can't get into the university, it would be quite all right to study at the polytech. Staying in Old Town and becoming a primary school teacher or a nurse and leading an easy life would be even better."

When I returned from Lompoc to Beijing, I reckoned I could still go back to my job at the newspaper. I was informed, however, that I had been unenrolled there. There were new students living in my 110-square-foot room at the staff dormitory so I found a small hotel where I could stay. Entering that semi-basement with its pervasive odor of mildew, I sat down hunched over my unopened baggage and broke down in tears. When I had had enough of crying, I got up and tried hard to remember Grandma's stories. As I thought about every detail of her and her whole family standing in the midst of the ruins, my tears stopped flowing. I was so many times better off than Grandma had been then. My bank account held more than three thousand U.S. dollars saved up from my salary. On the strength of that money, the idea of becoming my own boss first sprouted in my head. Later on, I really did become a boss and at one time had assets worth several million. Then, when I had no choice but to declare bankruptcy, I also thought of Grandma's stories. In very Ah-Q fashion,[29] I told my friends that I now finally had time to exercise and work on my looks, even though all the time I was dreaming of making a comeback.

You probably don't know who Ah-Q is. It's not important. But, in short, I rejoice that I possess the genes Grandma bequeathed to me. I have persistence in abundance.

⌘ ⌘ ⌘

Baosheng was still treasure-hunting: a whole porcelain bowl, an inlaid picture frame with the family portrait. When he found a silver necklace with little bells, he went running over, all excited, to claim a reward. "Ma, look, wouldn't this be worth money?"

Ninth Brother had a silversmith make this when Baohua completed her first full month of life. That day he shook the bells all the way home, his complete joy so plain to see. Grandma felt more like weeping over the gardens that had been destroyed and for the happy life that had now vanished, but she didn't shed another single tear over them again.

The Guo compound at West Gate was still intact and Old Lady Guo cried in joy for this. She stood at the doorway and, clasping her hands together, thanked heaven and earth and all the various spirits and Bodhisattvas for the virtues of the Guo family ancestors that brought lives of ease and comfort to their descendents.

The gateway was unlatched. They supposed that Eldest Son and his wife were inside. Gan'er pushed the door open and rushed in. In the sky well sat a strange woman sorting vegetables. Old Lady Guo wondered: *So Eldest Son and his wife have money enough to hire a servant woman?* The woman asked who they were looking for.

---

[29]   Ah Q is the eponymous antihero of Lu Xun's ferocious satire *The True Story of Ah Q* (published episodically between December 1921 and February 1922). One of the great losers of literature, Ah Q is a bullying coward who always tries to persuade everyone including himself that he has actually come out on top, morally at least, in all the calamities that befall him. All except the final catastrophic one. Saving face was Ah Q's game.

Fifth Brother said, "This is our home." The woman craned her neck around and shouted, "Mr. Fan, Mrs. Fan, your relatives have come!"

This family has changed its name to Fan?

Mr. Fan walked out. Second Sister recognized him as the owner of a local tea company. This fellow, Boss Fan, didn't extend a single word in conventional greeting, but just turned around and went back inside. Then he came right out again, now bearing a title deed in his hand.

Second Son had sold the house!

"This is impossible, absolutely impossible!" Old Lady Guo pulled open her jacket and snatched out her stomach bib, an item of clothing that had never before left her body. "I haven't even told Second Sister, so how could that have flown into your rotten-egg hands?" But what the trembling old lady had gropingly reached for turned out to be nothing more than two sheets of coarse straw paper! She gaped, unable to make a sound. Then, lifting one three-inch foot, she stamped the ground and fell with a crash on the steps by the sky well. At once blood began to drip from her.

Second Sister did not come forward to help her mother up from the ground but raised her eyes to the blue, blue sky and cried out angrily and resentfully. "Oh God, what sin has our family committed that you should punish us so?"

4.

THE HOUSES OF Old Town, especially those of the poor, were all built of flimsy wooden planks. Just one artillery shell would have been enough to destroy a whole street of such dwellings. Those who had fled Old Town were now continuously returning, but many came back to their native place after long and arduous journeys only to find that they had no home to return to.

The West Gate church was filled with people living there who had experienced the painful loss of their homes, and among these were the three generations of the Guo family. Pastor and Mrs. Chen gave the big upstairs room to Second Sister, while the three Chens themselves squeezed into the little room at the foot of the stairs. The religious activities of the congregation began to return to normal. Since the church hall was now packed with the old and the young, the sick and the crippled, every Sunday the congregants sang hymns in the yard.

After living in the church for several months, the sound of prayer, hymns, and the organ played by Pastor Chen's wife lingered always in her ears, but in her heart my grandmother had gone far away from her angel. She refused to take part in the services and every Sunday would go to the tailor shops. Three shops employed her and she could do these jobs at home so she intentionally arranged to pick up her work on Sundays. When Pastor Chen and his wife invited her to pray together with them, she said she preferred to pray alone. But she secretly said to her angel, "I'm no longer asking anything from you. I have been afflicted with so many misfortunes, and you watched unmoved as these happened. From now on, you can just shut your eyes and no longer watch over me.

When I go to heaven, I am going to register a complaint about you to our Heavenly Father, that you did not fulfill your angel duties and responsibilities."

Eighty-year-old Grandma was sewing her angel outfit and when she got to this part of her story, she chuckled and removed her old-age glasses.

Nor can I help being amused. It all makes me think of a young girl in love who's throwing a little temper tantrum. I myself often acted like this when I felt wronged. I would ignore Chaofan, while actually expecting to be loved even more passionately. Just before one summer vacation, I was sulky and annoyed with Chaofan. I think I was just being jealous of that pretty little violinist who had put a piece of chocolate into Chaofan's mouth. I was standing off to the side and they didn't see me, like I was the Invisible Man. In the middle of the night, I bickered with him and told him I was going back to school. Chaofan didn't try to get me to stay. Furious, I stomped out to the gate and turned around, expecting he would come chasing after me. Instead, I discovered that the light in his room was out. He had actually and calmly gone to sleep! The hurt I felt was beyond all description. To the present day, I'm still angry over it.

I asked Grandma, "You've never thought that your angel didn't really exist?"

"Not really exist? How can you say that?" She again took off her old-age glasses that she had just put back on and looked at me in wonder. "It's just like your neighbors or your relatives. You might not like them, or you might be angry with them, but you can't say they've never existed. That second brother of mine, I never forgave him, and never saw him again either, but he did exist. Oh, that's not the right comparison. The angel knows what I mean and won't be angry."

"Grandma, you've really got a lot of guts to make an angel mad at you."

"True! And I don't even understand why. Even though very many of the buildings in Old Town had burned down, those were, after all, still in the minority. My mother-in-law's house was destroyed and my own family home was lost to us. Men who went off to become soldiers would send some news home to tell whether they were alive or dead. I saw some widows who suffered injustice call out their husband's name in their bitter tears. I wanted to cry but couldn't because I didn't know whether my husband was alive or dead. I thought I was the most wretched woman in the whole world."

⌘　⌘　⌘

Not long afterward, when the municipal government and the Guomindang Party office came back down into Old Town from the mountain district, you could say that Old Town swallowed a tranquilizer. There was still fighting going on in the world outside, but lucky Old Town achieved a kind of limited peacefulness. The signboard of the municipal government was rehung, and all the merchants who were watching which way the wind blew then hurriedly opened for business.

Second Sister began devising a "Spring Flower Barges into the Magistrate's Court"[30] stratagem, in which she would bring both her mother and the three children bursting into the government office and demand her husband back. Unexpectedly, however, the government made the first move and found Second Sister. They ordered her out of the church. At the time, Pastor Chen was there and he tried to find out the reason for this but was sternly reprimanded by two

---

[30] The name of a popular opera in South China.

plainclothesmen. She was pushed blindfolded into a car, and only after some time finally got out. Such details made her think of how they caught communists. The Lins' neighbor had a son studying at teachers' college who had been picked up like this. She had seen with her own eyes an identical car drive out of Officials Lane, and ten days later, the family recovered the corpse from the government office. She wanted to say, "I am a respectable woman and no communist," but her tongue had gone stiff and her teeth were chattering as if she had malaria. She couldn't get out a single word.

When she realized that death was the worst that could happen to her, she immediately freed herself from her terrors and she started thinking clearly and vigorously.

Angel, I've offended you, so you are punishing me like this. You aren't a good angel, but I want to tell you, I'm not afraid to die. I have lived enough. I have now brought three children back to Old Town. Pastor and Mrs. Chen can look after them well. Don't think that I would be broken-hearted out of concern for them. I will return to my heavenly home joyfully and with an easy mind.

Second Sister was brought to a special organization of the Guomindang. This organization was quite mysterious. There wasn't even a sign at the door. Once the black cloth that had covered her face was removed, she saw sitting behind a wide desk a middle-aged official in a Western-style suit. She thought he would perform the interrogation by pounding the table and demanding that she turn over the Communist Party people she knew. She deliberated how to best respond. She couldn't say she didn't know. If you said you didn't know, that was the same as protecting communists. The best approach was to act like some hellcat woman weeping and raising an uproar over her unjust persecution. However, she really didn't have the strength to make any kind of uproar. Furthermore, she was annoyed with her angel. She believed that the angel was there

within that high-ceilinged, gloomy room and she didn't want it to
see the ugliness of her weeping and sniveling.

The official's expression hardened. He jabbed his finger in the
direction of a chair and told Second Sister to sit down. She was
stunned and didn't dare believe her own ears. He again pointed to
the chair, "Just sit down." He then looked down and opened up a
folder of documents. "Where is your husband?"

Second Sister had just sat down, but now she sprang up again,
holding onto the desk for support. "My husband? Did you say my
husband? Is he dead?"

"Sit down, you! I ask. You answer. And don't talk nonsense.
Where is your husband?"

"You're asking *me* where he is? That's what *I* want to ask *you*!
My husband went to war to fight for your government. There hasn't
been the slightest bit of news from him for several years now. Even
if he's dead, you should have issued a notice to me."

At this point, Second Sister became unable to control herself.
She took out a handkerchief and covered her tear-filled eyes.

The document folder in the official's hand contained none other
than the letters that Ninth Brother had sent home from various
places up north. So, well before the Japanese bombing of Old Town,
this organization had been keeping its eyes on him. The reason
was an extremely simple one. In their routine sample-checking
of mail, they had discovered that in one of Ninth Brother's letters there was no writing, only a cartoon sketch. The inscription
on the envelope merely consisted of two written characters: "He
Nan."[31] The greater part of Henan Province belonged to the communists. Ninth Brother had been recruited into the army directly
by Division Commander Zhang and the local government had no

---

[31]   The province adjacent to and northwest of Anhui. Henan's name, "South of the
River," refers to the major part of this province, which lies south of the Yellow River.

record of this. They couldn't identify this man's family status and therefore suspected him of some entanglement with the communists and thought that the sketch was code related to the underground movement. Although during the War of Resistance against the Japanese, officially the Guomindang and the communists were cooperating, the Communist Party was not allowed to grow and spread in the Guomindang areas. This special organization picked up and retained every letter from Ninth Brother. More than half of these consisted of cartoon sketches that he had done to strengthen the ties between him and his children. Probably this officer also could see that these were nothing more than ordinary letters home and had early on decided to ask Second Sister about this just to close the case. What with the bombing and everyone fleeing, though, the matter had languished until now.

"What was your husband previously? Where did he join the army?"

Startled and suspicious, Second Sister looked at the official. "How is it that none of you knows this? If you're asking this, do you mean that if my husband is dead, he died in vain?"

"I ask. You answer." The official's tone of voice was much milder now.

"My husband is a doctor. Old Town's first Western-medicine clinic was opened by him. When the War of Resistance first started, a Nationalist division commander came to the clinic for treatment and he then took my husband off with him."

The official asked a number of inconsequential questions and then closed the documents. "All right, you can go now."

Second Sister was astonished. "What does this mean? Are you letting me go?"

The official nodded.

Second Sister took a few steps in the direction of the door, and then abruptly turned around and firmly sat back down in the chair.

"Sir, I am not going. I had originally intended to come to you. I want you to tell me: is my husband dead or alive?"

"This is not something I handle."

"If you don't handle this, then who does?"

The official hesitated and pondered this for quite some time. Then, from the documents, he drew out two pieces of letter paper and slid them over to Second Sister. "Here, take a look if these are your husband's letters. If they are, then he's still alive."

My dear Second Sister... These four characters were like thunderbolts knocking her flat. This was no time to be irritated with the angel. With a loud cry, she burst into a violent fit of weeping. The official told his subordinates to get her into the car and set her down in the vicinity of West Gate.

Her hair bun had come undone and the tear-soaked ends of her hair were disheveled in every which way. She gripped the several late-arriving letters from Ninth Brother and wept bitterly as she ran back to the church. Dashing upstairs and crying uncontrollably, she threw herself onto her mother's breast. She cried so hard that the very colors of heaven and earth vanished.

Old Lady Guo said nothing to console her daughter, just quietly stroked her hair. This news of Ninth Brother's death came as no surprise as far as she was concerned. She ached for her daughter. *All the daughters of the Guo family are intelligent and beautiful. And all of them are sow-thistles. The eldest's husband is a wife-beating scoundrel. Fourth Daughter's husband is a useless loafer-princeling. Only Second Sister had married a good man. Ninth Brother respected the elderly, cherished the young, and was cultivated and sensible. But now he had died young. Does all this mean our Guo family has no good luck? Or that those Lin ancestors had done some awful deed?*

She also thought of Third Sister from whom there had been no news for so long. Many years back Third Sister had once secretly returned home. The old lady had not met with her but had ordered Big Brother's wife to drive her away. Now having gone through so much wartime chaos and disaster, the old lady's heart was no longer so inflexible and she felt regret and sadness when she thought about Third Sister.

The pastor and his wife also supposed that death news had descended on them. They ascended the stairs and stood behind Second Sister hand in hand, praying with tears in their eyes. "Oh, Lord, we ask you to come and comfort Mrs. Lin. We ask you to take away her pain and bitter suffering and infuse her heart fully with Your great love." They also thought of their many friends in the West Gate district who had received Dr. Lin's help. They ought to hold a memorial service for him.

The three children were scared out of their wits by their mother's grief. It was quick-thinking Baosheng who saw the letters in his mother's hand. He went up and very carefully and gently took them from her. He saw a line of writing: "Is Baosheng still naughty?"

This was Daddy's letter! He raised the letter in front of Pastor Chen and his wife, saying, "Here's a letter from Daddy!"

Mrs. Chen helped Second Sister get up and, seating her comfortably, began combing her hair. She didn't stop her from crying. "Go ahead and cry, Mrs. Lin. In the bosom of God draw from painful experience and give free vent to your tears. You are an unusual woman. You have 'supported the old and led the young by the hand' and endured irredeemable disasters one after the other. O Lord, thank you for leading her through the valley of the shadow of death. Let her rest by the grassy banks of the stream. Let her husband safely return so that united, husband and wife will never be separated."

A few days later, that same postman, for whom Second Sister had once so eagerly waited, appeared, his whole body dripping sweat. He had heard here and there that Mrs. Lin was living at the church and now he placed in her hand a letter from Dr. Lin, postmarked "Shanghai."

CHAPTER EIGHT — REVOLVING MONTAGE

1.

TO ENTER INTO my grandmother's stories is to leap across space and time. All those long-ago events come gushing out, just as if they were my yesterday. On the other hand, the reality of today, the age I live in, then becomes something fuzzy and chaotic.

It's only after a long string of words comes from Beibei on the telephone that I come back to my own space and time.

"Ma, where are you now? How come I hear train sounds?"

"Uh, you're right—I'm on the train."

"On the train going where?"

"Back to the old home in Old Town."

"Where've you got the time to take a train to Old Town?"

Beibei doesn't wait for my answer, but immediately moves on to other things. She doesn't care about Old Town. She had lived there only for a while when she was quite small. Later on, at home in Beijing, when she answered telephone calls from Old Town, she'd report these to me in the voice of a complete outsider. "Your uncle called. Someone from your old place is trying to get in touch with you."

Your this...*your* that. None of it has anything to do with her. At that time, she considered herself nothing less than a real Beijinger, and though to this day she can speak fluent, American-style English, being a Beijinger is what she's proud of.

Her father is also *"your"*…*"your* former husband." I've corrected her by saying that he and I have not divorced. Her little mouth is a curl of disdain as she says, *"Hai!* So how's it any different from being divorced?" I congratulate myself at having made the big and wise decision early on to raise Beibei by myself when I got back from America; otherwise, for her I would have only been "the woman who gave birth to me."

I took over raising Beibei when she was four years old, the year that I returned to Old Town. She didn't recognize me. She just hugged the legs of my cousin's wife and wouldn't pay any attention to me. My cousin's wife said to her, "This is your mama. Your mama has come to take you back with her." Beibei suddenly turned and climbed up on the bench and from the counter took out a framed picture. "My mama's in here." There was a heartrending black humor in this adorable, childlike logic.

These past two years her perception about her father has deepened. I've noticed the change in how she refers to him. She now calls him "The Artist," rather than "The Bum."

"School vacation starts in two days and The Artist said he would drive me to the Grand Canyon. Also, two young overseas students will be going along with us."

I haven't told Beibei about my predicament. Business hasn't been profitable and I can't pay for her study at the private high school anymore. She loves that school so much that even on the weekends she can't bear to change out of her uniform. It is like the mark of aristocracy and she walks along the main road wearing it, her chest swelling with pride and proudly accepting the admiring glances that come her way. I really can't find it in me to disappoint my daughter and I think of discussing this with The Artist, but I know what he'll say. From the very beginning, Chaofan didn't at all go along with the idea of Beibei attending a private school. He wasn't happy with a lot of other things about Beibei, not just that. There had been ten years of separation between father and daughter before the two of them managed to reunite. He's a stranger to Beibei and Beibei is a stranger to him. They probably can never bridge the vast gulf between them.

Let Beibei discuss tuition with her father. Perhaps this will produce results. Just as I am on the verge of saying, "Beibei..." I change my mind. It would be better to hold back on the bad news. Wait until the last day and then tell her.

Beibei seems to sense something. "Ma, it sounds like something's bothering you. What's up? Has someone in your family in Old Town gotten ill?"

I hesitate for a moment, then decide to reveal a bit of the news to her. "Beibei, your ma has had some problems at work."

"Anything serious?" Beibei's raised voice betrays her disquiet.

"Yes, maybe something serious."

"So, just how serious?"

Visualizing my daughter's anxious expression, my heart melts. "Don't get too worried. At the most, I won't be the boss."

"Do you mean that your company...has gone bankrupt?"

"Just about bankrupt. But there's still some hope. It's not that there's no hope at all."

"Hmmm..." Beibei pauses for a second. "I've got a classmate whose father did something at the bank and two weeks ago got arrested. She managed to get through this semester, but doesn't know what she'll do for the next one. She's really pathetic. Ma, you haven't done anything illegal, right?"

"No. Our operations are very normal. Don't even think such silly things."

"That's good."

As always, before hanging up we exchange our usual icky words: "I love you." "I miss you." "Here's a hug and a kiss." Putting away the phone, I lean against the connecting corridor between the passenger cars, basking in great happiness and feeling deeply touched. *My daughter is sixteen years old. She's getting big now and understands the way things are. She knows about loving her mama.* I've always complained to the high heavens while bringing her up. Only now, though, do I know that being a mother doesn't just mean paying out. I see that all that laborious plowing and cultivating produces a rich harvest. In the midst of these reflections, the phone rings again.

"Ma, how come I feel uneasy? Are you very sure there's nothing wrong?"

"Dearest daughter, you really are thinking about this too much. Ma's OK. If you don't believe me, call and ask Auntie Chrysanthemum. It's just that the company's finances have met with some difficulties. It's not the end of the world. At the worst, I'll have to go back to work. Right now, in fact, I am helping someone with a job."

"Ma, if there are problems, next semester I'll transfer to public school. I can still get The Artist to give me a bigger allowance."

Surprised, I'm a little choked up. "Beibei, you love your school so much, and Ma is still making a big effort. I wouldn't lightly make you give up your..."

"It's no big deal. Haven't I been studying here for two years now? I know all about the top schools. It's been enough."

I'm sure that she is shrugging her shoulders and crinkling her nose at the other end of the phone, the way she acts when showing total disinterest.

"Dearest daughter, no matter what, Mama is grateful for your understanding."

⌘ ⌘ ⌘

Does Beibei feel depressed by all this? Would she still be able to have a good time during this vacation?

While I am trying to figure out whether Beibei might become depressed, I myself am extremely depressed. My thoughts wander and I question the reality of the whole situation. Not so long ago, the company's splendid prospects had dizzied me and that light-headed, walking-on-air giddiness still hasn't left me. Several big-name brands signed letters of intent with us and we might have earned fantastic profits. Just how we could have spent all the money by the year's end is something that's kept Chrysanthemum and me awake nights on end. We had plenty of opportunities to prevent the crisis. If we had just exercised the slightest caution about that man, if I myself had asked how our customers were doing…if, if, if…

I realize that I have gotten myself into a dead-end alley. Since my proverbial rout from the city of Mai,[32] I frequently get trapped in this kind of no-win situation.

So, think about Grandma's stories again. Think about her, that woman, the mainstay of the whole family, standing in the ruins of the Lin mansion, with everyone gathered around her. Now that really was a time when the sky collapsed and the earth caved in.

Maybe I've become like the man of Qi who feared the sky would fall. Beibei learned in her sixth-grade textbook this saying: "The man of Qi worried about the sky." From that time on, "The man of Qi worried about the sky" became her fall-back line. Whenever I grew anxious about her schoolwork or her behavior, she would just give a merry laugh and say, "Ma, there you go again, the man of Qi

---

[32] A defeat suffered by Guan Yü (160-219 CE), one of China's great historical figures who was immortalized in Luo Guanzhong's fourteenth century historical classic, *Romance of the Three Kingdoms*.

worrying about the sky." Beibei grew up under my very eyes, but many are the times I've realized I don't understand her. I wouldn't admit that I was getting older, but the generation gap between us was plain to see. When she was very small, she had this kind of disinterested temperament. She never allowed herself to show she felt embarrassed. Whenever she got into some awkward situation, she'd always find some consolation. Once, when she only got 70 percent in mathematics I asked her why. She laughed in a self-mocking way. "The teacher gave me only 70, but I wasn't the worst. There were a whole lot of people who did worse than me." When I was young, once even I slipped up and, quite coincidentally, also got a 70. I was so ashamed. I slunk off to bury myself in my quilt and dampened the pillow with my tears. For a long time afterward, I never dared raise my head and look anyone in the eye.

My young staff members were like Beibei too: they didn't care about anything. They never tried to connect with the boss in any personal way. All they cared about was their pay. If I wasn't prompt in awarding a salary increase to good performers, they might vanish from the office at any time. They are a generation of wide-awake pragmatists and, I admit, more than a match for me.

The image of Beibei smiling disdainfully appears in my mind. The relaxed sound of her voice lingers in my ears. "Hey, Mama, aren't I doing all right?"

I laugh with relief just as the conductor patrolling the coaches passes by. He's surprised but grins courteously at me.

2.

IN RELATING THE difficulties of our own generation's lives, in the long river of history these twenty or thirty years are a mere blip of time. And in this mere blip of time how many totally different lives have we had? We have been pupae hibernating underground and we have been butterflies fluttering amid the flowering shrubs. From pupae to butterflies, from butterflies to pupae...with each bump of time we pass through an illusory and unfathomable change of human existence. It is impossible for me to say for sure whether we are pupae or butterflies.

I envy my grandparents' and parents' generations. They were sustained by a kind of belief their whole lives, whether it was the lifetime of pupa or of butterfly. I also envy the generation after me, the generation of Beibei and those young employees of mine. They don't have any neat, uniform beliefs or standards. Each one fights solitary battles and takes life as it comes.

⌘ ⌘ ⌘

I arrived in Beijing. As I stood timidly on the railway platform clutching my university acceptance letter, at that very moment I was merely a pupa newly awakened from hibernation, excited and bewildered in this transformation of my destiny.

The waves of people around me gradually receded and I saw Chaofan...Chaofan, who had been in my every thought, day and night. He stood over there, not far away, but not close either, his arms folded. He appeared calm and self-assured, as if he were pondering some far-reaching course of action. He looked neither this way nor that for the girlfriend from whom he had been separated for so long. Rather, it was as if he had been ordered to the train station to meet a stranger and he was passively there awaiting the stranger to come forward and claim him.

When there were just the two of us left on the platform, and he walked toward me, I could see nothing in his eyes of the passion of a long-awaited reunion. For an instant, I really felt I had been a reckless greenhorn in coming here. When he reached out his hand, I thought he would take me in his arms, but instead he just bent down and picked up my baggage. It was an unwieldy roll of bedding. Grandma had been afraid that I would get chilled to the bone in freezing and snowy Beijing and had someone fluff up a cotton quilt weighing eight *jin* and a mattress weighing six. Scornfully, Chaofan hefted the weight of this roll. "Beijing's winters aren't a bit cold. There wasn't any need to bring such heavy bedding." I discovered that his pronunciation had also changed. We Old Town people can't manage those "er" sounds that Beijingers add at the end of some words, and when we try we come across stiff and tongue-twisted.

What kind of a place is Beijing, that in only one year the Chaofan I grew up with could have changed into such a stranger?

I endured it for a long while, but finally I pricked up my courage and asked him, "Chaofan, has your heart changed? Don't you love me now?"

He laughed as if I were an ignorant child who had asked a grown-up some impossible question. He hooked my arm into his and said, "How could I not love you? It's just that I understand love differently now. Soon you'll understand it differently too. You'll realize that Old Town with all its one thousand years is simply a thousand-year-old mummy —it's totally dead. So get a good taste of life in Beijing. It's only in Beijing that you can say you're living."

The philosophy of Jean-Paul Sartre was just then all the rage on campus. The philosophy espoused by this old French guy is called existentialism, and to this day I've never understood what it goes on and on about or why it should have been so glamorous then. He raised the lid of Pandora's box in the hearts of the young, and set free all kinds of passions and cravings that feasted themselves wildly like insatiable locusts.

Chaofan lent me a few of Sartre's books, and *The Second Sex* by Sartre's mistress, Simone de Beauvoir. Their books really are seductive and beguiling. After I returned the books to him, I never again asked such silly questions such as "Do you love me?" We devoured each other's young and sexy bodies. Every time we met, it was like a going-away party. We imitated Sartre and his mistress and made no commitments for tomorrow.

Perhaps deep inside I am a conservative person. I had no eyes for any man except Chaofan. I frequently wandered about in the little grove of the campus by myself, all worked up, guessing whether Chaofan had other girls.

After Sartre, I encountered books that even more "departed from the classics and rebelled against orthodoxy," as some would put it. Reading Nietzsche's pronouncement that God was dead, I couldn't help closing the book to deeply reflect on this. My grandfather and Chaofan's grandfather lived for God all their lives. They were dead now. If their souls are in heaven, would they be sighing deeply at all this?

I lived in Beijing for a period but, unlike Chaofan, I couldn't categorically say that Old Town was a lifeless old mummy. I missed Old Town's warmth, its fragrance, and its moods. I missed those childhood days that he and I had spent together.

I suspected that all those books and theories were just gimmicks that he unsuccessfully tried to hide behind. He had changed.

That melancholy, concentrated gaze that once so intoxicated me just to think of it, now became evasive, drifting, and projecting the lost bearings and desires of a provincial youth in the big city. When I listened to my professor analyze the lust-driven youth, Julien Sorel, in *The Red and the Black*, I would think of Chaofan.

But I loved him just the same. Just have him appear before me and my reason would totally collapse. I couldn't imagine losing him. My principles and basic standards kept falling back in complete retreat. I even put up with his endless love games with different girls, since that's the way Sartre and de Beauvoir had been. They had tolerated each other's lovers.

⌘ ⌘ ⌘

Memory is like a virus-infected computer that can no longer form complete pictures. It's also like an exposed film on which the slightest trace of image has disappeared.

Cut that exposed film—the story's male and female protagonists have already become an unhappy couple. One summer we were at an open-air café next to the Bay Bridge. I held a thick stack of bills in my hand: Beibei's school tuition and living expenses, entertainment and travel outlays, dental bills for her braces. At the time, this little bit of money was a mere drop in the bucket for me. But I had crossed the Pacific Ocean to find him and demand repayment of the advances he had gotten from me. Over the many years that he had spent filling in with various bands, he hardly earned a cent and he was without any fixed place to stay. I felt not the slightest sympathy toward him.

"Your daughter…I'll put it this way, it's like Beibei and I have no blood relationship. I am just the hired nursemaid or the home tutor."

"Your daughter's underbite is serious. She needs a year of teeth straightening. Each month her braces have to be changed and this costs quite a few hundred dollars."

"I've got no money," he said. "So just let the teeth of a poor man's daughter stay the way they are. Please tell Beibei that her father in America is a poor artist, and not to think that there's gold lying all over the place here."

I said, "'For thirty years fortune stays east of the river, then thirty years to the west of it'—every dog has its day. Everyone now knows that there's no gold just for the taking in America, but maybe there is in China now. You ought to go back and take a look at the friends we were close to before. See what kind of a life *they're* leading."

Even though I was taking my adversity with a smile as I led the aristocratic life-style of a single person in Beijing, I only had to think of him and I would be filled with resentment and grievances. Many times, I've had my head turned by the success of my "great achievements." At this point, though, if I looked back I would see only my own pain. With a great effort I held my tongue, and swallowed the sharper words I wanted to come out with: *You are one total loser of a man, an irresponsible wrecker. You've wrecked Beibei's and my happiness. You also wrecked your own future.*

He slouched in his seat the whole time, his eyes wandering everywhere but at me. Indeed, I was the last person he wanted to see. The bills in my hand and the resentments in my heart were his golden headache headband.[33] To see Beibei he had to meet with me. And he loved Beibei a lot.

---

[33]   From Wu Cheng'en's classic Ming dynasty collection of tales entitled Journey to the West. "Golden headache headband" refers to the magical golden band Bodhisattva Guanyin persuaded the uncontrollably mischievous monkey, Sun Wukong, to put around his head. What Sun Wukong didn't know was that it could never be removed and was intended to tighten painfully whenever he got up to his sublime pranks.

"I'd like to have Beibei come live with me. As long as I've got something to eat she won't starve."

I laughed coldly and pointed to a tramp sitting by the water. He had just taken out a piece of sausage from his jacket and was feeding it to his dog. "You want to make Beibei lead your bum's life, just like that dog?"

He turned around and stared at me. "I never thought you'd change like this. The lowest lowlife's got more class than you. I've got to think up some way to take back my daughter. I can't let her have bad influences like you in her life!"

And then he dropped a few dollar bills and left in pompous anger.

As I watched him go off, an aching emptiness and desolation overcame me. My work has taken me everywhere and I've had lots of experience with people. I had supposed that never again could a man hurt me, but every time I met with Chaofan, I got hurt, badly hurt.

3.

IF CHRYSANTHEMUM INVITES me to have dinner with her, it means that yet another man has been put out to pasture. The moment that Chrysanthemum fails in love—though she claims not to believe in it—she becomes like a bug that has lost all its internal heat. Even in Beijing's summer heat, which gives most people rashes, she would scrunch up her shoulders and hunch over like she was warding off the cold, the very image of some pathetically delicate and sickly person. It's true that ending an affair of the heart is a lot like undergoing major surgery. The man who gets her all worked up then becomes a tumor that's got to be cut out at all costs. The tumor's excision drains her of all vitality and she usually needs about three months of careful recuperation to regain it. After those three months, she would again enter all-ablaze into another foray of love.

Normally before dinner, we take a cup of coffee or some other drink. As always, she carelessly stirs the coffee, or whatever it happens to be, with a little spoon, heaving one sigh after the other. "There's not a single man worth loving." Lately she has come out with an updated version: "There's not a single man worth going to bed with."

The first time I met Chrysanthemum was at a business dinner. After all the food and drink, a group of us set off for a cabaret. While the men were busily cuddling and hugging the gorgeous hostesses, the two of us made an unobtrusive and embarrassed retreat. At that time, Chrysanthemum was in a "recovery period" from a particularly bad wounding. She invited me to have coffee at the revolving Western-style restaurant on the top floor of a hotel. I thought she wanted to talk about our business collaboration but, surprisingly, she launched right into an attack on men. Her sharpness and candor produced a good feeling in me in spite of my surprise.

Along with the updated theory, Chrysanthemum also updates her action. She was already impervious to sword or spear, as if she had girded herself with helmet and armor. As usual, she sat facing me, twirling her coffee. Before saying anything, she laughed and raised her chin in a silly grin. "The moment I woke up there was still a man's warmth beside my pillow, but I already couldn't remember what he had looked like!" As she saw it, there were only two kinds of men: those who were worth going to bed with and those who weren't.

Chrysanthemum is like a blurry mirror. Although there is some degree of exaggeration and distortion, I can make out my own image in it. And so, for this very reason, it was "love at first sight" between us and we became the best of true and trusted friends.

⌘ ⌘ ⌘

Leaving Beijing is to leave the magnetic field and momentum of our lives. It's like walking off a movie screen and sitting down in the dark with the viewers on the other side to watch a series on urban women. A lust-filled city and lust-driven women... so many of the details give me goose bumps. As they run wild and hit rock bottom in their search for happiness, as they laugh uproariously and endlessly over their coffee, their scars show through all the makeup.

This woman from Old Town is more than equal to the task of drifting with the tide. But somewhere within she keeps the clear-sightedness of the outsider. At some deep level of her soul there hides a small-town girl who loves to dream. Who had sat at the ancient Eight Immortals table, gazing out foolishly at the rain-soaked streets. And just as in the past, she spins romantic dreams of innocent love and longs to be with her beloved from the days of their childhood games right until white-haired old age.

The wrist of the hand holding Chrysanthemum's little spoon that's stirring the coffee forever bears a three-inch-wide silver bracelet. Under the bracelet are three lines of scars, like three little worms flat on their bellies. They are a souvenir of her one brief marriage. She shakes her head as she laughs about the past. "Can you believe it? I was still a real virgin when I got married!" This is as ridiculous as those old wives who even now hoard their grain and pork ration coupons. It was quite by chance that she met the man who made her die a living death. Now she shakes her head more fiercely. "It was really just too ridiculous...to end up being ruined by such an utter bore!" In order to erase history's branding from her wrist, she has searched everywhere for doctors and medicines, and over the past few years has spent incalculable sums. But she is still going to have to keep relying on the silver bracelet which, "the more it conceals, the more it reveals."

But, for such women, isn't all that letting go and gaiety perhaps just a futile attempt at covering up?

I hear the heartbeat of that half-grown girl from Old Town. She is not happy. Since leaving Old Town, she has lost the happiness she had. She is full of anger and resentment at the man who brought her out of Old Town and onto a road of no return.

Why is it that every time I meet with Chaofan I am always so strong and aggressive? Why can't I just express a woman's tenderness and longing? Why can't I release that Old Town girl imprisoned within me, and weep and moan for those trampled and violated feelings?

Right now, I can feel my own weakness. My hardened heart is like a lump of ice in the sunlight, rapidly melting away.

CHAPTER NINE – ENCHUN

1.

THE MAN FROM the special investigation team had come again. He was a dark, thin, bald fellow in a plain uniform and he glowered fiercely as he sat at the Eight Immortals table. He was now a frequent visitor at our home and would always sit himself at the place of honor, usually reserved for my grandfather at mealtimes.

When I was seven or eight years old, my two uncles, my stepfather, and quite a few other relatives were put under surveillance and control by "special-case investigation teams" of the various rebel factions. They were all locked up in the "cowshed" to make an accounting of their crimes. All kinds of these teams had come to make my grandfather and grandmother verify certain aspects of their personal histories. My grandfather also went into a cowshed.[34] The mother of the neighborhood revolutionary committee director had once been his patient—when the old dame was young she had caught tuberculosis. If it hadn't been for Dr. Lin, she wouldn't have survived to get married and have children. So Dr. Lin had been her savior and benefactor. After she asked her son to give his mother's savior and benefactor special treatment, Grandpa spent less than a

---

[34] In the urban areas, these would not have been real cowsheds. "Cowshed" was just a term for any basement or makeshift structure used for holding "counterrevolutionary elements" for coerced confession and self-criticism sessions.

week locked up in the cowshed, and then returned home to write out his "confession" there.

Yesterday we received a visit from the team investigating my stepfather; it included a very fat northerner who had long been my stepfather's subordinate. He would always go to the kitchen to pour some boiled water or pretend to use the toilet in order to get away from his colleagues, and would quietly say to Grandma, "Don't worry. He's out herding the cows. He's very happy." My grandmother would stuff into his satchel the cigarettes and grain spirits she had collected in advance. When the team members were wearing themselves out in all the places they had to go to investigate my stepfather, he himself would be sitting carefree and relaxed on a hilltop, smoking and having a drink of liquor as he kept an eye on the equally carefree and relaxed cows.

But this dark and thin baldy was in charge of the team investigating Enchun. From his stern attitude and the frequency of his visits, you could get a sense of how serious Enchun's problems were.

During the War of Resistance, Pastor Chen's son, Enchun, was active in the communist underground, and he transmitted his communist beliefs to the three young Lin children. If he hadn't done this, when the Guomindang government withdrew from the mainland, these children would surely have gone with their school across to Taiwan and joined the thousands and tens of thousands of students in exile. Enchun's beliefs even convinced my grandfather that communism was the beacon of hope for China and Jesus' plan for saving its suffering people. In the summer of 1949, the Lins had a nephew, a government official, who sent his ninth uncle and his family five boat tickets to Taiwan. Grandpa refused these without the slightest hesitation.

Who could have foreseen the so-called Great Cultural Revolution in the 1960s? Or that not one of the former underground party members would have the good luck to escape being "secret agents"?

Ferreting out "Secret Agent" Enchun was like taking hold of a single grape and dragging out the whole cluster. The group of underground party members he had developed was made up entirely of supposed secret agents. And tracking each one of these was a special investigation team. Sometimes those other teams as well would appear at our house. That was because on the eve of Liberation, Enchun had used the West Gate church to mask his involvement in the underground revolutionary movement. A good number of these "secret agents" had been sworn into the Communist Party Youth League at the West Gate church.

The special investigation teams were masters at composing detective fiction. They suspected Enchun of developing an organization of secret agents to infiltrate the Communist Party for the Guomindang. Lying on firewood and tasting gall, as the saying goes, these "secret agents" had strictly disciplined themselves and wormed into low- and high-level positions within the Communist Party—and doing all this while coordinating plans for the Guomindang counterattack against the mainland. Thereafter, they would reemerge in a trice as distinguished and meritorious officials of the Guomindang.

What an absolutely hair-raising suspense novel this would have made!

My grandfather sat on that patched-up, old rattan chair, eyes half-open, occasionally pointing to his ear to show that he couldn't hear. During that period, we all supposed that he had gone deaf. All he could do was pretend to be deaf and dumb in responding to those special investigation teams coming in from everywhere, for he was historically "stained." If he were to say anything at all, he might make things even worse for family members already locked up in the cowsheds.

Grandma sat behind the rattan chair, and whenever a person on the team asked something, she would shout it into Grandpa's ear.

"Did Guomindang people ever go looking for Enchun at the church?"

"Enchun caught pneumonia."

"We didn't say anything about pneumonia."

"It was pneumonia!"

That's how he would answer the questions no one had asked him.

One morning, Pussycat, who had been lost for days, suddenly appeared on the top of the sky well, its whole body badly mangled. It must have just barely escaped ending up as something tasty in a family's cooking pan. After this narrow brush with death, Pussycat had made it to the top of the wall of its own home, but hadn't the strength to jump down. My grandfather was the first one to hear its weak mewing, and we brought out a ladder and rescued it.

I quietly said to Grandma, "There's nothing wrong with Grandpa's ears."

Grandma made a tense shushing sound and ordered me never, ever to tell anyone this.

During that period, my grandfather wished he *were* deaf and blind. He never stopped praying for God to take away his eyes and ears, and even his life.

His good friend, Pastor Chen, could not wait for God's call. He ended his own life, dying in the well that he himself had dug in front of the church door. Twenty years earlier, when the young pastor first arrived at West Gate, he saw poor people along the city moat eating, drinking, washing, and brushing their teeth in the water from that stinking ditch, so he appealed to his fellow believers to donate funds to dig a well. Not long after Pastor Chen was no more, the well dried up. My grandfather kept wondering what that could have meant. He also wondered whether the Heavenly Father had forgiven Pastor Chen and had opened the gates of heaven for him.

Whenever the teams did not come visiting, Grandpa just sat on that patched-up, old rattan chair. He would sit there all day long, day after day, his eyes closed and his body completely motionless. He just couldn't comprehend the revolutions occurring in the world. Everything was upside down...everything was in a complete mess.

How could Enchun have become a secret agent of the Guomindang? And why, when they were catching secret agents, did all the calligraphy and books have to be burnt up? And why did the shops and taverns have to completely change their names? Those names had lasted for over a hundred years and now were turned into things that were "red" or revolutionary.

The name of the city moat behind our house was changed from City-Protecting River to Redness-Protecting River. The family's grandchildren also clamored to change their names. Su'er became Fanxiu—short for Oppose Revisionists—since the Soviet Union (Sulian) was revisionist and the betrayer of communism. My name, Hong'er—Little Rainbow—was still all right though. You just had to rewrite the "insect" part of the written character as "twisted silk" to change Rainbow to Red. The sound stayed the same. Grandpa had chosen the names of his grandsons and granddaughters but he never told anyone that all of these came from the Bible. Su'er commemorated Jesus (Yesu). Hong'er referred to Noah's covenant under the rainbow in the Old Testament. One day, Su'er, the eldest grandson, came home and my grandfather called to him, "Su'er..." The grandson replied, "Gramps, I'm not called 'Su'er.' I'm called 'Fanxiu.'" To Grandpa this sounded like a simple announcement: "I'm not your grandson. I'm another family's grandson." Grandpa no longer paid any attention to him. Fanxiu called him "Gramps," and my grandfather just shut his ears and didn't hear it.

He secretly read the Bible, hoping to find answers there, but he could get no explanation. Neither Moses nor Jesus told him why Enchun became a secret agent. Was it because the channel of communication between him and God was blocked?

This was all extremely painful for him.

2.

HE WAS ALREADY a white-haired old fellow. As always, he wore glasses for his severe nearsightedness and buried himself in that room piled high with books and magazines, continuing his research on socialist economic theory. If you paid a call on him, he would receive you from afar with great feeling and excitement. He would sit you down on the room's single high-back chair and, dragging that leg of his that had been broken in the Cultural Revolution, he would dig up a long-unused glass from out of the piles of books and papers, and after disinfecting it with alcohol, brew some tea for you. Then he would sit on the side of the bed—also piled high with books—and you'd have a long chat with him. His words outnumbered his books, so you'd have to be patient. He was so very alone. Many saw him as an eccentric freak or some worthless piece of junk from an archeological dig, and nobody wanted to have anything to do with him. In all these years, his only son had been unwilling to give Enchun even a telephone call.

Holding the alcohol-tinged tea, I sit in this landscape of books and papers. How many years has it been? That copy of *Capital*, crammed with his own handwritten notes, is still on top of the desk. At the corner of the table, an old-fashioned alarm clock is still stopped at five-fifteen. If it weren't for his facial appearance that showed the passing years, I'd think it was only yesterday that I had last come to see him. Actually, we see each other every four or five years at least. But in the four- or five-year intervals, the world goes through titanic changes and our lives do too. Only he himself has kept a small place where he lived in solitude, stuck outside of time.

Once all the fuss of receiving a visitor is over and done with, he sits down and discusses Marx's economic theory, and the fixed law of the inevitable destruction of capitalism. He never complains about the terrible things that have happened to him. Tolerantly and optimistically, he'd say that all this was normal. Christianity had a two-thousand-year-old history and, if you added the period of the Old Testament, it was closer to four thousand years. And how many upheavals from heresies and rebellions had there been? China's socialism was only a few decades old, still in its infancy. So, traveling a few winding roads was normal.

He is playing his lute to the cows, for my thoughts are like those cows meandering about in some far-off place. I stare at him, trying to find Chaofan in his face. Father and son look extremely alike in their noses, chins, and ears. I grieve for him. He still doesn't know that his son just up and left the orchestra during his first performance abroad and doesn't want to come back. After so many years, he thinks his son is still in Beijing composing music. Becoming another Chopin had been his own ideal and he bought a transistor radio so he could hear his son's music. Every evening he falls asleep listening to symphonies. He never asks his son to come home to see him. One's pursuits are demanding and his son's pursuits are as important as his own. He wants to devote every bit of energy left in his life to writing a book on China's socialistic economy. He wants to do this to prove the correctness of his beliefs.

I wonder if Chaofan would also devote his life to proving that going to far distant lands and living freely with no beliefs at all had been the correct thing to do. He doesn't read any news from his native land and he has never stepped a foot back in China. I still think about Pastor Chen, already a misty figure in my memory. Pastor Chen had watched the people in that rebel faction at the West Gate church all grow up. They had tried to help him survive under false principles: if only he would declare at the general meeting that, from that day on, he no longer believed in God. But that he couldn't do, and went right out to throw himself down the well in front of the church.

The inflexibility of the men of the Chen family runs down a direct line.

On the Winter Solstice in 1947, Enchun, a student of the Old Town College of Commerce, turned eighteen. Early that morning, just as he was walking out the door on his way to school, his mother said, "Today is your birthday, so after classes come right home. Dad and Ma have a present for you, something we've prepared for eighteen years."

Enchun stopped right there and gazed at his mother. He wanted to tell her not to celebrate his birthday, but he was also afraid of going against their good intentions. Hesitantly he nodded his head.

He had in his book bag a rice ball for lunch. The school was not far from West Gate, and previously he had always gone home for his noon meal. Now with food supplies so scarce, his father made him stay in the classroom and read. In this way he could conserve his energy and cut back on food consumption.

There were quite a few beggars with their children waiting for him at the school gate. They knew he would divide up his lunch and give it to them, so seeing him coming, they immediately swarmed around him. Enchun had just taken out the rice roll when a small girl, beating all the rest to the prize, snatched it away and in one quick move stuffed it into her mouth, her two cheeks swelling up like balloons. Several small boys tried to pry open the girl's mouth with their filthy hands.

Enchun couldn't bear to watch any more of this scene. He gritted his teeth and, extricating himself from the crowd of beggars with difficulty, walked away. Every day he wanted to bring a little more food, but things were very tight at home. His father always relied on the congregants' donations to live, but these days they all were having a hard time too. Sometimes what he received in a whole month wouldn't even buy a few *jin* of hulled rice. One day there really was nothing at all in the cooking pot. His mother sat in front of the organ and prayed: *O Lord, we have nothing to eat now. Our family of three can only boil water to drink. Even so, our faith will not waver. We know that you see us from heaven and that you will not forsake us.*

Just then by chance Baohua ran over to ask about something in arithmetic. When she saw there were only three glasses of water on the table, she turned right around and ran back home, a place across from the church the Lins had now rented after the war. A little while later, Baohua returned with a huge "sea" bowl of hulled rice. Mrs. Chen was beside herself with happiness and, her eyes brimming with tears, sang a hymn as she played the organ. She gave thanks to Jesus the Lord for hearing her prayers and sending Baohua over with the rice. Enchun felt pity and sadness for his mother.

He walked with his head down, avoiding the stares of the beggars who came at him for food. Suddenly, someone patted his shoulder. It was the math professor, Teacher Zhao. Teacher Zhao was just the person he wanted most to see today.

"Good morning, Teacher Zhao."

"You feel bad about not being able to help more people, am I right?"

Enchun nodded.

Teacher Zhao was from Beiping. Enchun's family came from there too, and Pastor Chen and his wife had once paid a call on this fellow from their hometown. They invited him to hear the pastor preach the Word at the church, hoping that the teacher could receive Jesus' saving grace. The teacher and his student had become quite close from this time on, and Enchun also became the head of the study group that Teacher Zhao had launched. This little group professed to be tutoring in mathematics, and math books and workbooks were displayed on the table, but what Teacher Zhao talked about was the Soviet Revolution, communism, and the leader of all those making "an about-face for liberation" in North China, Mao Zedong. Teacher Zhao had never said he himself was a communist, but Enchun believed he was. It was said that over the past two years, not a few of the people taken to be shot on that piece of barren land outside of West Gate were communists. Clearly, the Communist Party was in Old Town. Eighteen-year-old Enchun made a big decision: he was going to join the Communist Party. If he couldn't find the party in Old Town, he would leave home and go up north to look for it. Today he wanted to tell Teacher Zhao of his decision.

As they walked into the school grounds, Enchun stopped and with a grim look on his face said, "Teacher Zhao, today is my eighteenth birthday."

Teacher Zhao warmly shook his hand. "Happy birthday! Let me invite you to lunch."

"Teacher Zhao, I couldn't sleep all last night. I have made a decision that involves the rest of my life."

"Oh?"

"Please introduce me into the Communist Party."

"I…Let me think about how to do this. I have a friend who may be a communist."

"This society is like a boat lost in the darkness and it could run aground and sink at any moment. I can't wait any longer!"

"You know it's very dangerous. You could be caught and shot at any time."

"Rather than being tormented in all this darkness, I would prefer to die opposing it. Teacher Zhao, if you can't help me, in ten days I'm going to disappear from this sealed jar of a little town.

"You can't go, Enchun. Old Town needs young people like you who are attracted to the light."

Around dusk, Enchun met again with Teacher Zhao. Teacher Zhao said that he had now been with that "friend" and the "friend" had agreed to accept his application. So from this day on, Enchun was a probationary Party member.

Evening at Winter Solstice comes early. The teacher and the student strolled about Little West Lake. Neither could see the other's face clearly, but at this moment Enchun felt a ray of light come pouring out of the clouds and enveloping him fully. He saw his own heart throbbing in the light.

⌘ ⌘ ⌘

Today, Pastor and Mrs. Chen wanted to give their eighteen-year-old son to the embrace of Jesus. They had completed the preparations for Enchun's baptism, and in the very center of the church was a big wooden barrel filled to the brim with clear water on which had been sprinkled flower petals. Naturally they couldn't do without all five of Dr. Lin's family to share in the blessings and happiness. Enchun was very close to the three Lin children and after today they would also become brothers and sisters in the Lord.

Enchun sought out the candlelight as he entered the church. Mrs. Chen immediately began playing the organ and the three Lin children sang the hymn "Jesus, Lead Me," which they had just learned. "Lead me, Jesus. Lead me, Jesus. Jesus, lead me by your hand day by day..."

Mrs. Chen led her son by the hand. "Enchun, today is your eighteenth birthday. You're now a grown-up. We know that from the time you were little you have loved the Lord. Surely you are willing to tell Jesus with your own voice that you long to be his child, and with your own voice will ask the Lord Jesus to forgive you your sins."

Enchun had never expected that the gift his mother had spoken of would be his baptism, and for several moments he was at a total loss. Stiffly he went with his father to the side of the barrel.

The pastor asked: "Are you willing to accept Jesus as your eternal savior?"

Everyone being baptized would hear the same question and, fervently nodding, answer "Yes." He then asked Enchun: "Do you admit that you are a sinner?"

Enchun silently shook his head.

Pastor Chen hadn't noticed his son's expression. Just as he was about to ask the third question, Baosheng yelled out, "Uncle Chen, Big Brother Enchun doesn't want to!"

Abruptly Mrs. Chen stopped playing the organ. Her hand was raised in midair. *What's the matter with my son? Has he been attacked by Satan?*

Enchun really wanted to tell his parents that starting today he was a completely new person and that his heart belonged to something else. He wanted to struggle for his beliefs his whole life.

"Dad, Ma, I'm sorry. Please forgive me."

"Son, are you ill?"

"Ma, I am fine...better than ever."

"If you are in your right mind, you must tell us the reason for this. From when you were little you knew Jesus. Why don't you accept his redemption?"

Enchun drew himself very erect. "Ma, I can't tell you why now. But in the future, even in the not so very distant future, you will certainly understand. And, not only that, you will support me."

Holding the Bible to his breast, Pastor Chen leaned against the pulpit. Over the past decades the number of people he led to Christian baptism was uncountable. How was it he couldn't lead his own son? He felt heartbroken and defeated.

⌘　⌘　⌘

Standing off to the side, Dr. Lin saw this as nothing accidental or unforeseen. He vaguely sensed that Enchun may have accepted communist ideas. It was easy for decent and upstanding young people like Enchun to be attracted by communism. In Shanghai, he himself had several classmates who went rushing off to the communist-liberated areas. All of them were decent, upstanding youths. He also had a classmate who called himself a communist sympathizer because communism and Christianity had no essential differences between them. The basic ideas of communism were to level the differences between rich and poor, the equality of all people, and food for people to eat. Wasn't this exactly the New Heaven and New Earth sought for in Christianity? And there were many records in the Bible of the early Church advocating that everything be shared in common, to each according to his need.

The doctor told his wife to take the children home and asked the pastor's wife and Enchun to leave them. He then discussed his own views with Pastor Chen, but before opening his mouth he addressed a silent prayer to Jesus: *O Lord, the wisdom of your child is limited. If your child's thinking is wrong, please correct it.*

Pastor Chen heard the word "communism" and tiny beads of sweat started oozing from his forehead. His mind formed a gruesome picture: Enchun, with his hands bound behind him, being led to that barren field outside West Gate.

The doctor's sympathy toward communism and his understanding of it made the pastor feel for the first time his own poverty and dull-wittedness. He didn't know whether making an analogy of communism with Christianity would offend Jesus. An even greater worry arose from the selfish heart of a father. Enchun had still not been baptized. In the event of some unforeseen disaster, he could never enjoy eternal life in heaven. The pastor spoke of these worries and the doctor said he would try to influence Enchun. The doctor loved Enchun as his own son.

Several days later, the doctor arranged to delve into the subject of communism with Enchun. They were like two underground activists secretly contacting each other, and they had a long talk in the pavilion at Little West Lake. The doctor came straight to the point. "I don't know if you are a communist or not, but I would like to know what communism is." Enchun told him that communism represented the interests of the broad laboring classes. As the doctor saw it, Jesus was the spirit that watched over the toiling masses. Jesus had said, "It is harder for a rich man to enter heaven than for a camel to pass through the eye of a needle." The more he pondered this, the more he discovered similarities between the ideas of communism and those of Christianity. The darkness of society's realities aroused his sense of justice. He expressed to Enchun his own willingness to be a Christian who supported communism. At the same time he still tried to persuade Enchun to be baptized. "Political parties are only the work of this life, but by accepting Jesus you can gain eternal life. The two should not be contradictory." Enchun smiled but made no reply.

3.

HAD YOUNG MISS Baohua also sat at that Eight Immortals table, cupping her chin in her hands and gazing out at the drenched streets, lovesick and moonstruck over her Big Brother Enchun?[35]

The owner of this building and his whole family had moved to Indonesia during the War of Resistance. Here the Lin family would live peacefully and contentedly for half a century. Undoubtedly this was God's plan. Dr. and Mrs. Lin had prayed the whole night through in their tearful gratitude at this. Although they were often so bad off that "in pulling down their sleeves, the elbows showed," compared to the separation and chaos of the war period, they felt heavenly splendor and joy every moment of every day.

Baohua was still the pearl in the palm of her father's hand and he continued to speak to her in soft and gentle tones as in years past. Whenever he had the time, he would still escort Baohua to school himself. But he had not realized that now that she had grown, something was weighing on her mind.

Enchun's behavior on his eighteenth birthday had hurt his parents' feelings and hurt Baohua's. One month earlier, she had begun to prepare a gift for him. Every evening, she would hide herself away in her "lady's quarters" to knit a scarf. Her hands were not as nimble or skilled as her mother's, so she often missed loops and had to undo double stitches. She also embroidered a heart on one corner of it. She believed that when Big Brother Enchun wore this scarf he would have a clear sense about her good feelings for him. That evening she didn't have the opportunity to give him this present,

---

[35] It has always been the custom throughout Asia for sweethearts, married couples, etc. to address each other endearingly with such family relationship terms.

though, and for several days following when she pretended she was going to the Chens' home to ask about problems in mathematics, she never ran into Enchun there. But she did hear that every night he was very late in returning home. The main doors of the College of Commerce and the Women's Teachers' Training College faced each other and these days "free love" was the big thing. *Would he be doing this free love?*

Baohua looked at the mathematics workbook spread out in front of her. Without Enchun beside her to guide her, she couldn't make sense of even the topic headings and as she thought and thought, tears fell from her eyes. Her two younger brothers who were also there doing homework secretly glanced at each other in amusement. Baosheng teasingly said, "Big Sister's sums are scarier than wooly caterpillars, aren't they?" Holding her workbook close to her breast, Baohua went back to her room and slammed the door shut.

Her parents were both sitting off to the side. Daddy was reading a medical book and Ma was sewing. They smiled as they gazed at their three children and never intervened in their squabbles. Even if the children yelled fit to raise the roof, this also was all part of family happiness.

No one understood what was weighing on Baohua's heart. She felt very much alone and as she sat in the darkness, her hands clutching that scarf to which had been entrusted a young woman's feelings, she let her tears pour forth freely. Would he do this free love? If he did, then he was a heartless person. She decided to creep out this evening and wait by the church door for him to return. Even if she waited until dawn, she had to find out the answer.

Holding an oil lamp, Daddy knocked softly on the door. "Good little Baohua, go to sleep. Good night."

The house was absolutely quiet. Baohua slipped out on tiptoes. She crossed the street, entered the churchyard and sat down on the steps. Now that her nervous tension and excitement had passed, the sluice gates of her tears opened up yet again. When she was small, Ma had often said that Enchun was the Lin family's "half son," though Baohua didn't know what "half son" meant. Baosheng said, "This means that you and Big Brother Enchun are going to marry." She thought that the marriage between her and Big Brother Enchun would be arranged by the parents. There was nothing wrong with arranged marriages and she was willing to live a lifetime with Enchun.

Around midnight, Baohua, dozing on and off, heard Enchun's footsteps. She was as familiar with their sound as she was of those of everyone in her own family. It was a cloudy night, so dark that your five fingers stretched out in front of you would have been invisible. She jumped up and walked over toward this sound and by the side of the well she collided against Enchun's chest.

Enchun grabbed hold of Baohua. "What are you doing out on the street this late at night?"

"I was waiting for you."

"So, you couldn't work out the math homework?"

"Mmmh."

"This late do you still want to do homework?"

"There's something else I wanted to ask you."

"Which is...?"

"Why are you coming home so late every night?"

"I'm also tutoring math."

"Don't trick me!"

The tears that Baohua had been holding back coursed down again.

Enchun led her to the railing around the well and they sat down. He laughed. "You've got more tears than this well has water.

You're going to have to stop being Lin Daiyu. Society will now no longer welcome girls like Lin Daiyu."

"I know *you* don't welcome me."

Enchun heard this and realized she meant something quite different and so, very cautiously, he asked her, "Are you angry with me?"

Baohua covered her face and said nothing. The scarf she gripped in her hand fell down.

Enchun picked up the scarf and put it over Baohua's shoulders. "Good Baohua, go home and go to sleep. I no longer have much time to do your homework with you. I am going to be doing things many times more important than mathematics, but I still care for you and like you. From the time we were both small we've been the very best of friends, right?"

Baohua pulled the scarf from off her shoulders. "I knitted this for you for your birthday. Every day I have brought it with me looking for you, but I couldn't find you."

Enchun accepted the scarf. "Thank you. Now I won't get cold coming home at night."

"I didn't knit this to keep you from getting cold!" Baohua said angrily.

Enchun felt quite alarmed. He was aware that Baohua had grown up. When he had been small, children could say whatever they wanted and no one would take it seriously. He had told his mother, "When I grow up, Baohua and I will be married." He had even told Baohua, "When you grow up, do you want to marry me?" If Baohua was in a good mood at the time, the answer was "Yes." If not, then "No." Now she was grown up, but he had already changed into another, totally different, person. Revolutionary ideals and fervor completely possessed him, body and soul. He was prepared to spill his blood and lose his head for the sake of the birth of the New China.

He took a closer look at Baohua, wondering whether or not he could impart revolutionary truths to her, but immediately he stopped this thought. She was a pampered and willful little miss, like a piece of fine porcelain that always had to be handled delicately. He discovered that his own feelings toward her had changed. His tender and protective feelings had changed to worry and anxiety. The dawn of the New China was already appearing on the horizon. When the thunder of the revolutionary age sounded, would Baohua be weeded out and rejected? He felt more in common with the new woman who opposed feudalism and sought progress. In his reading group there was just this new kind of woman. She was healthy and enlightened, her cheeks were always rosy, and her eyes burned with ardor. She and he both could selflessly go to their deaths for the sake of the New China. Ever since accepting revolutionary thought, Enchun was often subtly aware of his own changes. At this moment he once again marveled at these changes. His thinking had changed. His vision of everything had changed. Indeed, he had become quite a different person.

"Good Baohua, this world is going to experience gigantic change and you will have to keep up with these new times. Don't be a shrinking violet. You've got to be the weeds and thorns by the roadside. Wildfires can't destroy you and when the spring winds blow then you'll come to life again. All right?"

Baohua said, "I don't understand what you're saying. You've changed. You're no longer the way you used to be."

"'Changed' is right; and perhaps someday you also will change into a new person."

"Do you practice free love?"

Enchun laughed. "Baohua, what are you thinking of?"

Baohua was sensitive. She felt how Big Brother Enchun with whom she had grown up had become a stranger to her. She could no longer demand him to do this and that just as she pleased. Her tears changed from an intermittent misty drizzle into a cloudburst. She suddenly ran off crying and dragging the scarf behind her.

Enchun sat by the side of the well. He thought about chasing after her and taking her by the hand and kidding her until she stopped crying and started laughing. From when they were small, he used to kid her like that, but now he hardened his heart and just sat there. The revolution was cruel. Every day, at any moment, someone could be mounting the chopping block. In order not to hurt Baohua, he had to control himself.

Baohua ran home and at the gateway turned around to look. A heart more fragile than porcelain had been shattered.

CHAPTER TEN –
GOLD YUAN CERTIFICATE DAYS

1.

"WHEN YOUR GREAT-GRANDFATHER Lin was an official during the Qing dynasty," Grandma told me, "he would have to take a washbasin to hold all the silver dollars he'd receive on his monthly payday. And one washbasin of silver dollars could buy a very nice house." She also said, " On the day that Grandpa went to collect *his* salary, he had to hire a rickshaw to haul it all back, and a rickshaw fully loaded with paper money was still not enough to buy a sack of hulled rice."

It was only after finishing university and reading a history of modern China did I learn that these were not just *Tales from the Arabian Nights*. One thing I learned: in 1937 one hundred *yuan* in paper currency could buy two cows, but by 1947, that same amount could only buy one coal briquette. One year later, one hundred *yuan* couldn't even get you one grain of rice!

⌘　⌘　⌘

Today, Dr. Lin received his final salary and piled a rickshaw high with the paper money. Pulling this rickshaw for him was Shuiguan, who lived beside the city moat. More and more refugees had crammed together along the two sides of the moat. All of them had come to Old Town with their children and old folks to escape famine, and they supposed they could beg for their meals in such a prosperous town. They would pick up a few pieces of wood planking along the way and build little shacks all cheek-by-jowl, like so many pigeon coops, just for something their lives could perch on. Shuiguan was one of these people. Half a year before, he had started earning money by moving things for Dr. Lin. When this particular day arrived, he went to the door of the public hospital to meet Dr. Lin. The doctor put the paper money in the rickshaw and chatted with Shuiguan as they walked back home. Whenever they came to an uphill part of the way Dr. Lin always wanted to help push.

Shuiguan said, "Next month we may have to make two trips."

Dr. Lin laughed bitterly. "Next month we'll be drinking the northwest wind."

Shuiguan didn't pay any attention to this comment but just continued his bantering. "In the rice shops it's one price when the rice goes on the scale and then another when it comes off. This is how they are going bankrupt, one by one."

His shoulders sagging, the doctor walked alongside Shuiguan without hearing a word the fellow was saying. He had been fired today, the third time this had happened since coming back to Old Town after the war. Old Town had only three hospitals, so he wouldn't be finding work anymore. This afternoon a critically sick person came to the hospital with family members, none of whom had any money. The three children knelt in the hospital courtyard desperately knocking their heads on the ground. Without proper authority he did what had to be done to save this patient. The patient survived but his own job didn't. On the two previous occasions, he had lost his job because his sense of sympathy had displeased his superiors. But he had no regrets. If to keep his rice bowl filled he had to watch a life pass away before his eyes, he would never be at peace again. The only solution was for him to open his own clinic. But that would require an investment in medicines and equipment. All the family's money was in Shuiguan's rickshaw and he still had to get to the rice shop at West Gate as quickly as he could to change it into rice.

What was the world coming to? The doctor looked up at the dark and overcast sky, and spoke to his God. *Heavenly Father, is this your will? Is this your way of telling us that you are unhappy with the Guomindang government? That you want the common folk to rise up in support of the communists?*

The shop at West Gate was closed. Many people carrying baskets of paper currency suspended from shoulder poles were loudly and angrily wishing the owner an unpleasant death. Shuiguan pulled the rickshaw to a halt and looked questioningly at the doctor. Dr. Lin heaved a big sigh. "Let's go. It's not easy being the boss of a rice shop."

Second Sister had the three children with her as she waited at the gate. When they saw their daddy coming home—escorting a load of paper money—they rushed forward to greet him, whooping with joy. The doctor's gloom immediately vanished like mist and smoke.

Why should I get so worried? Our Heavenly Father brought me back alive from the war. Through all those perilous rivers and mountains beyond counting how many miracles did I bear witness to with God at my side? God is too kind and good to let our family die of starvation.

He didn't tell Second Sister about losing his job. As always on paydays, they invited Pastor and Mrs. Chen over for dinner. In the kitchen were two eggs that had been kept for a month now. Second Sister beat these together with the pulp of a gourd and fried a large, golden-yellow omelet. She also cooked some bean curd soup into which she mixed sweet potato starch, giving it a very thick and hearty look. They had no more rice wine so they made do with tea. The Bible teaches that all things work together and always bring good to those who love God. All their sufferings and hardships could be the source of instructive discussion whenever they gathered to eat together. The pastor's wife said that over the past few months, whenever there were days when they had nothing to cook, God would send someone over with rice and other food. He had already sent over Baohua, the boss of the rice shop, and many others whose names they didn't know. Even if they didn't manage to eat a tasty or filling meal, they never went longer than a day with nothing at all.

The adults of the two families didn't realize that Baohua's disposition had turned peculiar. She suddenly interrupted the talk by saying, "God has never cared about us."

Traditionally, at the Lin home children weren't allowed to speak at mealtime, but the upheaval of the war had done away with family rules. Dr. Lin's love for his three children had reached the stage where he would wink at this sort of thing, and so he said with a smile, "If God isn't helping you do your math assignments it means that in the future you won't need mathematics in order to eat. You can teach Chinese language and literature in primary school, or even become a nurse. Then, when you get married, you can help your husband teach your children."

Pursing her lips, Baohua put down her rice bowl. "I'm not getting married!"

With that, she left to shut herself in her chamber and cry in the darkness.

Dr. Lin rushed cheerily in there after her but spoke about other things.

These were extraordinary times. The parents of the two families knew that Enchun's position was special. Without needing to say anything to each other, they had kept the plan of marriage between him and Baohua a deep secret. Pastor and Mrs. Chen were still heartsick about their son's rejection of eternal life and they prayed for this with great earnestness and urgency.

A prayer at the end of their gatherings was essential. They prayed for Enchun's salvation, and Mrs. Chen tearfully said, "Heavenly Father, we beseech you to take pity on and forgive our young son Enchun's error. Please lead this lost sheep back to the fold."

As long as they sought Enchun's entry through Jesus' gate of eternal life, even if tomorrow gunshots outside West Gate signaled the moment of his death, their hopes would not be shattered, for they would know that their son had gone to heaven.

As Mrs. Chen was calling out "Heavenly Father...Heavenly Father," suddenly the sound of a wildly driven automobile interrupted their prayers. You could count the number of autos in Old Town on your two hands. Plowing heedlessly through the crowded streets were mostly police vehicles grabbing people: communists, unauthorized holders of gold and silver dollars, small-scale merchants and peddlers hoarding rice, spreaders of discontented views... Any ordinary citizen might offend the government and land in prison in shackles and chains.

The sound of the motor cut off abruptly. It seemed to be just outside their door. Mrs. Chen took hold of her husband's hand, and with both their hands trembling, the pastor said, "O Lord, we don't know why the automobile is there at the door, but you know, and we place Enchun into your hands."

Mrs. Chen stood up and the pastor gently pressed her back down. "What should or should not happen is with the permission of the Heavenly Father. The only thing we can do is to pray."

The doctor said, "I think Enchun's situation may be dangerous, but also that nothing's happened to him yet. If it had, they wouldn't have come to West Gate. Our child is under God's protection. Don't be too worried."

Would Enchun return home at this very moment and walk right into the mouths of guns? Dr. Lin quickly called Baosheng and Baoqing to take off their shoes, muss up their hair, and unbutton their shirt collars. "One of you go to the Drum Tower and the other to Little West Lake to look for Enchun. When you find him, have him go around beyond West Gate and hide at Shuiguan's house by the river."

Baosheng and Baoqing realized that they were getting involved in a thrilling game, and went running off, both nervous and excited.

After the two youths had left, the others joined hands and continued to pray for Enchun and for the two Lin brothers.

Baoqing was the first to return, at dawn. He had gone from the East Street corner of Drum Tower to South Gate and then returned, feeling bad about his lack of success. Baosheng followed right behind. From the way he wiped his sweat with his sleeve it was clear that he had accomplished the mission his father had assigned to him. And Daddy rewarded him with a roll of paper money to buy some deep-fried dough sticks.

Next, the two families saw that in both the ground and upper floors of the church, there wasn't a single thing that was still in its original place, from the bowls and chopsticks of the kitchen to the flower garden in the courtyard. It was as if a cyclone had passed close by. Before setting about to put everything back in place, they said a prayer of thanksgiving. The shocking scene before them seemed to tell them, "An enormous disaster has brushed by you here." How could they not shed tears of gratitude?

2.

BAOHUA AND BAOSHENG were both students at the public middle school. The Three People's Principles Youth Corps, a Guomindang organization was active at this school.[36] To prevent the students from being corrupted by the communists, the doors of the Youth Corps were open to all, and appearing in their class photograph was sufficient for the students of each academic year to be considered to have joined this organization. Baohua's class picture had already been taken, but that was on the very day that she had skipped her math test by pretending to be sick at home. In this way she became the only student in her class without a party affiliation. Because she was introverted by nature and not much of a mixer, her classmates and the Youth Corps leaders never discovered that some "element" had slipped through the net. She even received a copy of the class photograph with the inscription, "Souvenir of Y Class of X School Joining the Three People's Principles Youth Corps."

In one more day, Baosheng's class was to have its picture taken. That evening, when the whole family was seated at the dinner table, he suddenly remembered that to be in the photograph he had to wear the school uniform. Earlier that day he had gotten his shirt collar torn fighting with a classmate. Daddy was saying grace. Baosheng barely waited for the "Amen."

"Amen—Ma, my clothes got torn. Could you mend them for me?"

---

[36] "The Three People's Principles" ("San Min Zhu Yi")—Nationalism, the People's Government, and the People's Welfare—were the focal points of a broad political philosophy developed by Sun Yat-sen and adopted as the state ideology by the Guomindang ("Nationalist") party, which at this point in the story was at least nominally governing China.

"You've grown again. What you have are too short. We'll go buy some material in a couple of days and Ma will make you some new clothes."

"There isn't enough time. Tomorrow the school is going to take our picture."

Daddy asked, "What's the occasion? Why the photograph?"

"For group membership in the Youth Corps," cut in Baohua.

The doctor put down his chopsticks, and fixed his gaze on Baosheng. "You're not to join."

Baosheng thought this strange. *Didn't Daddy all along tell us to obey the school teachers? Joining this is what everybody does at school. Why is Daddy against it?* He concentrated on shoveling rice into his mouth and never dared say another word.

Second Sister also felt puzzled. *Since it was something the school teacher ordered, what could be wrong with it?* As soon as the children withdrew from the table, she said to her husband, "Baosheng's sensible now. Since he started lower-middle school, generally he hasn't made his teacher angry. If he was as naughty as before, surely the teacher wouldn't have let him join that group."

The doctor also realized that he had reacted too strongly. He felt astonished at how extreme his feelings had been. With a forced smile that signified just how complicated his feelings were, he looked over at his wife.

This glance conveyed the retraction of an order by the head of a family. After cleaning up the dinner table, Second Sister then took out her sewing basket and mended Baosheng's shirt.

The doctor sat on the rattan chair deep in thought. Enchun was still at Shuiguan's home. Into that little coop were crammed all three generations of a family. He ought to think of how to find the young man another place of refuge. Up north the Communist

Party was rapidly expanding its power and influence. According to a newspaper analysis of the situation, in the future a divided rule might be formed, north and south, using the Yangzi River as a natural boundary. *Could Enchun continue to stay in hiding like this? Where did his future lie?*

He couldn't sit still as he pondered these thoughts, and picking up his little medical bag, he went out the back door to the river to see Enchun. An old mother at Shuiguan's had taken sick. The neighbors thought that Dr. Lin had come to see a patient.

⌘   ⌘   ⌘

On the following day, Baosheng went off to school wearing the school uniform his mother had mended and ironed for him. When the teacher ordered the students to move the benches to the sports field to prepare for the photographs, Baosheng, acting on a sudden impulse, slipped away. Across from the school was a new bookstore where he wanted to take a look at *The Romance of the Three Kingdoms*. At home Daddy didn't let him read this book. There was no need to fear the teacher would put him on report. It felt good not having to worry about this.

Baosheng took out a crumpled one hundred *yuan* bill and, pointing to *The Romance of the Three Kingdoms* on the book rack, asked whether this amount was enough. The shop owner laughed warmly and told him to look at it as much as he pleased and that it didn't matter whether or not he had money.

"Young man, aren't you playing hooky by running over here?"

"It's not hooky. They're having their pictures taken at the school, but I'm not joining in."

"I know that's for group membership in the Youth Corps. How can you dare not to take part?

"Uh, my daddy doesn't like the idea of my joining it."

"What does your daddy do?"

How come this shop owner's talking so much? Baosheng, absorbed in the part about the "Peach Orchard Oath,"[37] felt a bit impatient.

The shop owner took the hint and kept his mouth shut right up until when the school bell sounded the end of classes and only then did he say, "You can take it home with you."

Baosheng stared at the rental deposit written on the book jacket. "I don't have enough money."

"I won't charge you anything. Let's become friends. Later on you can just go ahead and take any book you want to read."

The owner pushed the hundred *yuan* bill back into Baosheng's hand.

Suddenly, such an unexpected friend had burst into his life. Baosheng was delighted with this unexpected good fortune. "Really?"

"'Once a word leaves the mouth, a team of horses can't overtake it.' My name's Bai. You can call me Big Brother Bai. And yours?"

"Lin is my family name."

"Younger Brother Lin. Good. We'll swear our Oath of Brotherhood in the shop."

Baosheng raced joyfully home with *The Romance of the Three Kingdoms* tucked into his shirt, intending to tell Baoqing about this at the first chance he got. He hadn't the slightest idea that this was one of those turning points that happens in a person's life. A book made Baosheng a sought-after and locked-in target of the communist underground organization.

---

[37] The immortal opening scene of *The Romance of the Three Kingdoms* when the three heroes, Liu Bei, Guan Yü, and Zhang Fei, swear an oath of brotherhood in Zhang's peach orchard to defend the collapsing Han dynasty against the forces of insurrection.

3.

IT WAS SUNDAY again and the faithful came to the church for the worship service. Nobody knew about the ransacking that had hit this place a few days before. Everything was as always. Mrs. Chen sang and played one hymn after the other. The sunlight outside the window shone down on her densely wrinkled face. Everyone could see that she was as joyous as a bird on the end of a branch. The pastor at his pulpit also similarly exuded joy and gladness. Today's lesson was "God bestows blessings on our children and grandchildren." He gave examples from the Old Testament and told about the sons and daughters of many of the faithful who had escaped all their dangers. He most of all wanted to tell Enchun's story, but this he couldn't do.

Originally, Enchun was to have led that evening's study session, as Teacher Zhao was going to the outskirts of Old Town to provide guidance to a newly established youth study group. Late that afternoon, though, Teacher Zhao suddenly sprained his foot. In all the years of going up and down the steps in front of his house, he had never once suffered a sprain. But such a thing would have to happen just at this time. Immediately his foot became so swollen he couldn't move, so all he could do was to have Enchun substitute for him. As a result, Teacher Zhao and several students were all caught on the spot, while Enchun escaped a calamity as a result of this unforeseen turn of events.

Here was another coincidence. The pastor and his wife sensed this was God's special love for the faithful and they accepted His reward for their lifelong resolve to spread the Good News. More than once did the Bible mention that Jehovah invariably brought blessings on the people and their descendants who believed in Him. The Bible was the word of God. It was the covenant between God and His people. And God could be trusted.

Every word of the pastor's sermon fell into the deepest recesses of the doctor's heart. Today he wore the Western-style suit that he hadn't put on for so long. He brought his three children with him, intending to lead them into Jesus' fold early in their lives. With the times the way they were, Baosheng and Baoqing would sooner or later join this party or that faction. As long as they were God's children, their parents could rest easy about them. At home the night before, he had coached them on how to respond to the pastor's questions, explaining why such-and-such had to be the answers. He said a lot and the children had no idea what he was talking about. They only knew that from when they were little, Daddy and Ma were Christians in the same way that they knew Daddy treated people who were sick and Ma sewed marriage dowries for people. They didn't have any special longings, but they wanted to obey their father and make him pleased with them.

When the pastor in his pulpit called upon the "new people," the brothers and sister of the Lin family stood up in a row. Dr. Lin became all worked up and grasped his wife's hand. She glanced over at him and saw the reddened rims of his eyes. Her own eyes reddened too. This event was the most valuable gift that the husband and wife received in this life.

⌘　⌘　⌘

On Sunday afternoons, the Lin parents would usually take the children to spend time with either the Lin or the Guo elders. These relatives had all settled down in every corner of Old Town. Old

Lady Guo and her drunkard first son lived above a provisions store at Drum Tower. Big Brother and Big Sister-in-Law Lin had moved into a little wreck of a place at South Gate.

Second Sister was rushing to finish a bridal trousseau. Her husband had lost his job and again they had to rely on the livelihood from her sewing. Ninth Brother sat beside her to keep her company. Sometimes he even helped her with some stitching, so his battlefield-trained craftsmanship once again found a use for itself.

The house was peaceful and quiet. Baohua had tucked herself away into her lady's chamber. One of the boys had been sent out to look in on Grandma Guo and the other to visit their uncle, Big Brother. Baoqing brought over some watered-down spirits to his alcoholic uncle. Second Sister had stored away three bottles for him. While she couldn't bear the idea of actually drinking this herself, she wanted to bring relief to her brother. Whenever he was too long away from the smell of strong drink he would just sit there on the street and burst into loud lamentations. The municipal government was at Drum Tower too. Several times, empty bottle in hand, he had wanted to barge in and demand the mayor give him something to drink. Though the liquor that Second Sister supplied to her brother became increasingly diluted, the inebriate never sensed how his big sister was dealing with him. He would drink and complain, "The morals of this world have gone to the dogs when even liquor no longer tastes like it used to."

This gave husband and wife a source of conversation that never ran dry. They imagined her drunkard brother guzzling up what Baoqing brought him and blinking at the thought of how the morals of this age were changing. They just laughed and laughed. Indeed, Old Town folk had this saying: "When bad luck hits, wine wouldn't ferment." The final years of the Qing dynasty had been hard times to be a wine merchant in Old Town.

There was still much for them to discuss about the chaos of the war and their own separation at that time. When the children weren't around, Second Sister would ask with a pretty pout about Shanghai. "What happened there?" After Ninth Brother had returned, the widow often wrote him. In all these letters she said she missed him. Second Sister would "eat the vinegar" of jealousy, and every time she showed it, Ninth Brother would swear up and down about his faithfulness—which would then arouse an ineffable sweetness in her. Over time those old Shanghai stories became the seasoning and spice of their married life.

Ninth Brother gazed spellbound at Second Sister passing the thread through the eye of her needle. He often did that, and on every occasion his heart could not help but beat a little faster, as if it were the first time he was seeing this woman. The children had all grown and she was still so beautiful. He couldn't keep himself from cupping her face in his hands to kiss her. Startled, she shied away from him, pointing to Baohua's room.

At this moment of marital intimacy, Pastor and Mrs. Chen suddenly arrived, together with a girl who looked like a student. Mrs. Chen's face wore an expression that was hard to read as she said, "This young lady wants to find Enchun. Does Dr. Lin have any news of him?"

Dr. Lin didn't know how he should respond to this and cast a beseeching look at his wife.

Second Sister kept on sewing as if nothing at all were amiss and, glancing with eyes half-closed at the girl, replied, "It's been quite a few days since we last saw Enchun. If *you* see him, tell him to drop by and spend some time with us whenever he has the chance."

"Dr. Lin, I've heard Classmate Enchun speak of you. My name is Huang Shuyi. He would certainly be willing to see me. I need to meet with him before this evening."

Baohua emerged from her lady's chamber. Full of hostility, she sized up Huang Shuyi. *Isn't this a girl student of the Teachers' College? What's her relationship with Big Brother Enchun? She isn't the least bit good looking.*

Abruptly, Dr. Lin took up his medical bag. "You all stay here. I have an appointment with a patient."

He didn't leave from the back door. Only after making a round-about circuit on the street to confirm that no one was tailing him did he go by way of the moat to Shuiguan's home.

When Enchun heard Huang Shuyi's name, the dark eyes behind his glasses immediately lit up.

The doctor didn't ask much. He guessed the girl was a communist messenger coming to coordinate something with Enchun. He told Enchun to change into the old clothes Shuiguan wore when he was pulling his rickshaw. Then he led him through the back door into the kitchen.

Baohua saw her daddy motion the girl student to go to the kitchen. Neither he nor Ma accompanied her there, but sat with Mrs. Chen at the Eight Immortals table looking terribly mysterious. Curiosity drove her to see what this was all about. When she saw the girl student sitting and talking with Enchun at the stove, their heads practically glued together, she was so enraged she started to tremble all over. The thing she could still do was to cry, and burying herself back in her room, she did just that—a whole river of tears.

Only a sheet of wood separated the lady's chamber from the kitchen. At every minute, at every second, Baohua's ears were zeroed in on Enchun and the girl. They were about to set out. Her mother lit the fire to cook something for them. Her father also helped by squeezing together rice balls for them to eat along the way. She didn't know where they were going, or for what purpose. She only felt that they both were like a pair of eloping lovers. And the people helping them elope were none other than her own parents. Her closest and dearest people had formed an alliance to betray her. In agony and despair, Baohua just wished she could die.

When dawn came, the doctor discovered his precious daughter was running a high fever and babbling wildly. After this there was no end of her illnesses, serious and minor. The only thing for her was to leave school and stay at home.

CHAPTER ELEVEN –
IT'S NOT THAT I DON'T UNDERSTAND

1.

THE REVOLUTIONARY MARTYRS' Cemetery in Old Town was not far from our primary school. Every year during the Qingming Festival,[38] the school would organize a visit to the cemetery to sweep up and offer flowers. On a wall in the cemetery's Memorial Hall were displayed photographs of the Sixty-One Martyrs. I clearly remember that number. The Revolutionary Martyrs' Cemetery was on a big piece of sloping land outside West Gate. There the pine trees were blue-green and flowers were in bloom the whole year round. It was also a good place for us to play hide-and-seek. The old custodian of the cemetery watched over the place strictly but we always had a way of slipping in. For example, we would send a boy student to make a frontal attack to distract the old fellow's attention, and then our large detachment of troops would pass behind him in single file. Once we were inside, if he wanted to find us, it would be like dredging the sea for a needle.

---

[38] The traditional Qingming (literally "Clear and Bright") Festival occurs close to the spring equinox. While it is intended primarily to celebrate the coming of spring, it is also the time when Chinese families visit the burial plots of their departed family members and ancestors in a gesture of filial piety.

I hid countless times in the Memorial Hall in some corner or the other, but no matter in which one, I could always see that wall. The Sixty-One Martyrs looked at me. I looked at them. It was like our saying, "Well water won't seep into river water."—*I'll mind my business if you mind yours.*

⌘ ⌘ ⌘

When Cousin Su, the one who changed his name to "Oppose Revisionists" Lin, was fifteen years old, he was sent out to do labor in the countryside. He never had the chance to attend university, but today he is the richest of his generation of Lins. Nobody remembers "Oppose Revisionists" Lin. Because of my grandfather's wrath, the name lasted only three months. At the mention of that old matter of the name change, Cousin Su just gives a big laugh. Nowadays he doesn't oppose revisionism; if anything, he's only afraid there won't be enough of it.

Cousin Su took me to his *other* home, the one for his mistress. It was where a young chick who had once been a beauty contestant in Old Town now lived. He wanted me to see how good he was at moving back and forth between his two homes to make two women feel content with their lives. Starting in the early nineties, a man would keep a mistress to demonstrate how successful his endeavors had been and to show off his ample wallet.

As we walked into the building complex, somebody's speakers were just then blaring out a popular rock song of the day in which a singer shouted until he was hoarse, "It's not that I don't understand, it's just that this world is changing too fast."

So true...Every morning bright and early when you open your eyes, today's sunshine isn't the same color as it had been yesterday. Everything is changing so drastically there's no time to make any sense of it, and if you try you're already l eft behind.

Just before we arrived at Cousin's "grand mansion for beloved women," I suddenly felt a bit hesitant as I thought of his wife. She was a good and capable woman and loved by one and all in the Lin family. I had just decided to entrust Beibei to her, so how could I deceive her by going to visit my cousin's other woman?

I mentioned this worry to him, but he just planted his hands on his burly waist and laughed and laughed.

"You're such a hick. Are all Beijing people hicks like you? I tell you, unless your husband proves totally worthless, you'll need to learn how to be the Number One and put up with his little concubine. I wouldn't hurt my wife, nope, not the slightest little hair on her body."

Actually, I was annoyed no end about my own husband's other woman. Chaofan was already in America. He still had that pretty violinist who had left the orchestra with him. I never dared mention to my Old Town relatives that he had now left China, or that I was at a crossroads in my own destiny—looking back, ahead, and all around—indecisive about what direction to take.

Cousin Su misread my glum expression to mean that I was feeling some ethical or moral pressure. He took out a mobile phone as bulky as a brick and called his mistress to tell her that the visit had to be cancelled due to an unexpected event. A woman's affectedly sweet voice carried from the hand phone. "What a bore."

⌘   ⌘   ⌘

The land this complex stood on was right where we children used to play hide-and-seek. At that time several square miles of the hillside were all part of the cemetery. Since then, though, the martyrs' domain had been swallowed up piece by piece and was now dense with new properties for rent or for sale. All that was left was the stone Remembrance Tablet and the Memorial Hall so pitifully hemmed into one little corner.

I said I would like to visit the Memorial Hall to see the photograph of a newly added martyr, one who had borne the crime of being a counterrevolutionary. It was only after thirty years in the Nine Springs of the netherworld that he had been rehabilitated. He had been Enchun's leader in that long-ago time. He had also been the older brother of Enchun's wife.

Remembering the origin of the relationship of this martyr with my family and especially with me, Cousin Su shook his head. "For someone dead for so long...she just had to get him a martyr's name. But, really, what was the point?"

I knew he meant Chaofan's mother. In order to overturn the judgment against her brother, she had bitterly struggled on for fully thirty years and more. She lost her job, her family broke up, she was treated as a rightist, she went to prison, but as long as there was one breath within her she insisted on going to Beijing to register her grievance. And when her yellow petitions[39] were turned down, she cried out this injustice to the entire country.

"Foolish." "Silly." This was Cousin Su's judgment on our parents' and grandparents' generations. Of the whole Lin family only he had penetrated to the true meaning of life, that is, getting money and seeking pleasure. And, whatever you do, never shortchange yourself.

Chaofan says the same thing. When he was at university in Beijing, his mother was still there seeking redress but she never

---

[39] Traditionally, the solemn color of yellow, associated with the emperor and written prayers to the gods, was the color of the paper used by people who traveled to the capital to present their petitions.

disturbed her son right up until her brother's remains were transferred to the Martyrs' Cemetery. Then she wrote her son a long
letter in which she extolled the heroic vision of the party. For more
than thirty years her loyalty and belief in the party had kept her
going. There were seven or eight densely packed pages of this. Her
son only glanced at the letter and with a cold, mocking laugh tossed
it all into the wastepaper basket. This woman, who disappeared
three days after giving birth to her son, never received that son's
pity and forgiveness.

⌘   ⌘   ⌘

The displays inside the Memorial Hall were just the same as when
I was young. Then, when I stood before the pictures of the martyrs,
their gazes seemed to come alive and touch me deeply. Their average age had been only twenty-two years. When their pictures were
taken, they knew that the moment of death had come, but there
was no look of terror on their faces, rather, they looked calm and
collected. The oldest among them was that one there: he had suffered injustice for several decades and was no more than thirty years
old. He looked out at the world with a disdainful smile.

Maybe they had been happier than us. Just then I was rushing
about madly, getting set to leave China. Crowds thronged the
embassy district in Beijing all year long regardless of the season.
Many people had passports simply so they could leave China. If
they couldn't get to one country they would just go to another.
Those receiving visas would go wild with joy. Those who were
refused visas were like people mourning a death in the family. I
belonged to this latter group. Sometimes I would be startled awake
in the middle of the night thinking about where my life was going.
I couldn't keep from feeling frighteningly devoid of any substance.

I had to leave because I couldn't find anything with greater meaning here. After Chaofan had gone, my life became utterly chaotic. I wanted to bring Beibei back to my old home down south and then go meet head-on a life that was even more chaotic.

Cousin Su, standing beside me, expressed a different sort of regret as he pointed to a martyr who had only been nineteen years old. "To die so young...I'll bet he had never even met a woman. Look how handsome he is. If he had been born in this age he might have become some youth idol and made a major bundle."

For most people nowadays, money is the measure of everything. While feeling real pity for these figures, Cousin Su congratulated himself at his great luck in becoming such a favored son of the times.

Maybe I'm the incompetent one, with almost no salary to speak of and not enough money to use for measuring right and wrong. I never told my cousin that I envied these martyrs who had died so young. I envied them for their fulfilled lives.

It's not that I don't understand, it's just that this world is changing too fast.

There's another saying too: "The moment humanity starts to ponder, God just laughs."

Standing in the gaze of the martyrs, I tried to reflect on philosophic theories of human life, but I became even more confused than before.

2.

THE CONTINGENT AT the gate of the U.S. Embassy on Xiushui Street were now lining up earlier and earlier, so I also set my bedside alarm clock earlier and earlier. But even if I got there at five o'clock in the morning, I could no longer stay ahead of everyone. A lot of out-of-towners simply saved on hotel money by throwing on army greatcoats and spending the night beside the iron fence.

The day I was first called in for an interview, I had been waiting in the snow for exactly seven hours. The consular officer was a white man, a left-handed guy. He ran his eyes over my material, glanced through the glass window at me, and then the rubber stamp in his hand came heavily down on my passport: "Visa Refused."

I had expected this. I've never been a lucky person. That's why I've never bought lottery or raffle tickets. Even if the winning rate were eighty percent, for sure I would be one of the hard-luck cases of the other twenty. I had heard beforehand that a certain left-handed consular officer was really tough and, of course, it had to be me who got him. I wasn't brokenhearted, just numb, so that those fellow sufferers lined up through the doorway couldn't tell whether things had gone well or badly. Lots of people crowded around me to get a sense of their own prospects.

The newspaper where I worked was pretty close to the embassy district. I also had fellow sufferers at the office awaiting my news. Young He's new husband had gone to Japan and she was now hard at work studying Japanese, just waiting for him to earn enough for her tuition. Young Ma's husband had already received a scholarship at NYU and she wanted to offload her baby son she was still breast-feeding so she could study with him there. Young Wang's husband had a lover who came to their home and made a big fuss, and now Young Wang was thinking of just walking away from the whole thing. When our director wasn't around we all eagerly discussed leaving China and our husbands.

As I pushed the door open, three pairs of eyes all swiveled in my direction. The look on my face rendered them as subdued as cicadas on cold days.

After quite a while, Young He passed me a cup of hot tea and said, "Never mind, fragrant herbs and exotic plants are always somewhere out there on the horizon. How about going with me to Japan?"

Young Ma said, "Getting a visa to the U.S. from Japan would be much easier."

I was thinking of Chaofan, imagining that at this moment how the snowflakes were floating in the skies on the other side of the ocean and of him and that violinist warming themselves by the stove. This was a scene straight out of Hollywood and I supposed that was life in America. No matter who, once people got to America they could lead a fine, upper-class life-style. I thought that if I could just get a visa I could chase the violinist away from the stove. A rubber stamp shattered that dream.

Young Wang was always the last one to make known her views. "You've got to ride a horse when you're looking for a horse. First get a lover, and then all the other problems will slowly take care of themselves."

She herself was one of those persons who practiced what she preached. When she discovered that her husband was being unfaithful to her, her first reaction was to reconnect with those men who had previously shown her their affection. Spreading and scattering her feelings all around, she got three "ABC" lovers.[40]

---

[40] "ABC," Chinese slang for "American-born Chinese."

Whenever she felt bored, at least one of these three would have the time to keep her company, to make love to her. "Having tasted the bone's marrow, its savor grows"—lovers became her narcotic. She didn't seem too hard-pressed to leave China. When, after much rigmarole, an invitation letter finally arrived from Germany, she put it in a drawer and never did apply for her visa.

Soon afterward, my second round of Operation Visa got under way. I even got in line at three o'clock in the morning. Again that rubber "Visa Refused" stamp.

Walking out of the embassy gate, a man took hold of my hand. The night before, it had rained and a stranger behind me had taken off his windbreaker to shield me from the weather. He told me that his wife had been in the United States for three years now and that they had been together only half a year. As we spoke about our own experiences, suddenly he put his arms around me. "Why should we be wasting our youth like this? For you and me, wife and husband are only abstract concepts. And here we are suffering such physical and mental torment over this concept. It's really crazy! Come with me—let's go, right now!" he said. I said I was also thinking of trying my luck, though I clearly knew there would be no good luck for me.

We were called separately to the windows and almost at the very same time our applications were refused. This was the sixth time for him.

With great urgency he pulled me after him as he jumped on a bus and for more than half an hour we never uttered a single word. I followed him obediently without the slightest sense of needing to be on guard. I did feel a little aggrieved, but also a little gratified in some indescribable way. It was a small, dust-filled apartment. A wedding picture hung on the wall. The bride looked quite happy in all her wedding finery. He closed the door and, turning around, took me by the waist and threw me onto the bed. I closed my eyes and let my body be trampled and slaughtered by this man, this stranger. Chaofan's image was what filled my head...my body, my head...lying in two different places...

This was how I had my first lover. We often met clandestinely, made wild love, and never spoke of the future.

One day he told me he still wanted to stand in the visa line at Xiushui Street. I wasn't surprised. In fact, I was involved in some secret doings of my own. Chaofan had now obtained a green card and I would be going to America as his legal wife. I heard that the violinist had married a Taiwanese restaurant owner. Having already gone through all that mental anguish, I didn't much care now. What I didn't see couldn't hurt me. I never verified with Chaofan whether she had really married anyone. But even if they were still snuggling up in front of the stove, so what?

3.

As I GAZED out the window of this thumping old Ford at the thick fog blanketing the mountain tops, I thought, "So this is America. America, I'm here." Out of the corner of my eye, I stole a glance at Chaofan, just then engrossed in his driving. Since leaving the airport, I still hadn't looked him straight in the face. I was feeling guilty, as if I had stolen something and he had been its owner.

The tour-group members could not dispel my pain of separation. During the trip I thought of little Beibei and again and again tears would whirl and dance in my eyes. What would she think if Mama wasn't there when she woke up? I also wondered about the man who had been my partner in support and comfort at the time we had needed these most. When he was refused a visa for the eighth time, his wife initiated divorce proceedings against him. Tearfully, she asked him to be humane. He accepted the reality of the divorce but made no effort to keep me with him as a result of it. When we parted, we embraced each other, sobbing bitterly like a loving husband and wife being forced apart. *Would he soon have another sweetheart?*

In order to find a parking space where he didn't have to pay, Chaofan drove round and round the fog-shrouded streets. This wasn't his style. He had always been free and easy with money, never giving a second thought to where it all went. He would look at me scornfully whenever I haggled with a peddler or stall owner. In those days the summer grasshopper attitude was normal with him. If he had no money at the end of the month, he would sell his wristwatch for ten or twelve dollars, and go on calling all his friends in to drink and pontificate for hours.

After stopping the car, we walked for about ten minutes to Chinatown.

"Things are cheap here," said Chaofan.

I finally struck up the courage to look at him straight-on. I saw a pair of exhausted eyes devoid of all vitality. *What kind of a place is America that could change this wild and intractable person into something so dejected and dispirited?*

The roadside food joints would remind you of the sidewalk food stalls in Guangdong from which the songs of Taiwan's song prince, Ch'i Ch'in would blare: "I'm a wolf from the north, prowling the boundless wilderness."

So this is America? The land of freedom worth abandoning family and career for?

There were no romantic, coldly beautiful snowflakes, no stoves with their dreamy warmth and fragrance. As we sat in the greasy restaurant, I just had to laugh at myself.

Chaofan bought a newspaper and sat there poring over it. From time to time, he circled something with his pen. I couldn't imagine what news absorbed his attention so strongly.

The next thing I know, some real news almost knocked me off my chair—*he's looking for an apartment!*

Where had he stayed last night? And how had he spent all those hundreds of nights before that? Suddenly at that instant I just lost all hope. I felt like I was being oxygen-deprived or poisoned. Right then and there, everything turned black before my eyes and I could feel cold sweat spreading across my back.

After walking streets, threading alleys, and looking at so many places, we finally put our feet down in a room we sublet from a Mexican guy. The only thing in it was a mattress. Totally dejected, I sat on the floor and started to cry my heart out. I longed for Chaofan to reach out and hold me to him, to tell me that everything would be getting better, that there was still bread to eat, milk to drink. When I had been in Beijing awaiting my visa, my "lover" often comforted me in this way, and I did the same for him.

Not Chaofan, though. Instead he got irritated and scolded me. "What are you crying about? You come to America. Someone meets you, finds a place for you, and gives you food to eat. Those people who come here without a soul to turn to, how do *they* make it?"

I stopped my sobbing and looked at him. *If I had no one to turn to in America, why would I have come here in the first place?*

The suitcases were still unpacked. I had already decided to fly back home as swift as an arrow. I didn't utter another word.

Upstairs was our landlord's bedroom. All of a sudden wild thumping sounds came from our ceiling, like someone was wrecking the place. The couple above us was making love, earthshaking and heaven-splitting love, totally unmindful of anything else. Their animal roars rent the stillness of the late night.

We were lying side by side on our improvised bed, each of us occupied with our own thoughts. We stared at the shaking ceiling whose collapse seemed imminent. Neither of us wanted to touch the other.

I don't know what he's thinking, and he doesn't know what I am thinking.

Several days went by and our landlord's earthquakes were occurring every night. Still feeling inhibited, we kept an arm's length from each other. I was planning my return to China every minute of the day and night. Also, for "humane" reasons, I wanted a divorce.

The bed had to be placed against the wall. This was the only habit that remained from before. He would want to sleep on the inside, like a big kid all curled up in the corner of a room. I didn't know if he still had those nightmares. These made him more touchingly feeble than a lamb. In his fright he would whisper into my ear what he would never be willing to say in the daytime. He'd make me believe that our lifelines were linked together, and no one, no matter who, could separate us.

As if I were afraid of this happening, I was always very careful to sleep glued to the far side of the mattress.

I had already contacted my good friend Xiaoli, and she was driving up this weekend from Lompoc to fetch me. I wanted to go there to get a job and earn enough to pay for my return fare to China. But before this plan could be carried out, I had no sooner escaped from this disaster when Chaofan dragged me back into the mire.

Early one morning, a damp and hot body awakened me. Breathing heavily, Chaofan had burrowed into my breast, both his hands tightly clasped around my shoulders. This sent me back into the past, to that old familiar feeling. I kissed his forehead, his neck, and his thick, hard ears. "Dearest, don't be afraid. I love you, I'm here." He was choked with sobs. "I love you too. Don't leave me." My body worked its own will, forgetting all resentment and grievances as it ecstatically went to greet him. We had been just like that in our younger years. In his fright and weakness began our first derailment.

As I stroked his sweaty back, I was as forgiving and tender as any mother, loving him until my heart ached. I knew that he would always live in the shadow of Pastor Chen's suicide. That day a seven-year-old Chaofan stood by the side of the well, utterly terrified by the scene of the rebel faction hauling out his grandfather's body. Iron hooks had pierced the pastor's eye sockets and from these hung his two eyeballs. From then on nightmares like wronged ghosts have haunted him. Sometimes he would even walk in his sleep. That's why he had to lie next to a wall. His granny would guard him. Every night he would pray, right up until when he was a grown man.

In grief and sorrow we made tearful love, again and again, as if to make up fully for the time lost during our separation. Of course, this didn't mean that he didn't have other women. Early in the morning of the very day he met me at the airport, he had left a woman's bedroom. His sexy sad eyes were so good at getting women. But with the women of those duckweed meetings on flowing waters he has to put on helmet and armor and disguise himself as a bandit or knight. He cannot let the slightest weakness show through.

This man at my breast was another child of mine. Even though he was strong and big, even a bit bigger than me, he was just my child. How could I have forsaken him?

CHAPTER TWELVE — HUNGER IN OLD TOWN

1.

MY GRANDMOTHER WAS an attractive woman and she kept her looks throughout the various stages of her life: an attractive young woman, an attractive wife, and after she reached old age, an attractive old lady. Only a wall separated Old Town's first photo studio and the Guo Family Cloth Shop. The studio owner would take Second Miss Guo's pictures for free, provided that she let him display them in the studio. That antique camera kept taking pictures of my grandma for thirty years, right up to when the camera and its owner retired.

In the autumn of 1948, the photo studio owner heard that Dr. Lin's clinic was now open for business, and so, equipment on his shoulder, he went to add his congratulations and lend his support to the opening. The so-called clinic was merely that room in our home facing the street to which had been added a door, a coat of white paint, and a counter and table. That was all. The photo studio owner set up his camera, and took a picture of Dr. Lin sitting in the clinic with his stethoscope hanging from his neck. He also had my grandmother stand by the gate under the oleander tree for her picture. His head was burrowed under the dark cloth as he looked through the lens. But no matter how he looked, the person in front of him just didn't seem like Second Miss Guo. Even though she had a bit of makeup on, it couldn't disguise her pallid and haggard appearance. He wanted to ask, "Are you sick?" Then, on second thought, he realized she was probably just famished. In this time of hunger, it was difficult to keep body and soul together, even in a doctor's family. Somewhat hesitantly he clicked the shutter. Afterward he told Second Miss Guo that the photo had been overexposed. By the next time he arrived at the doctor's home to take pictures, Old Town had come back to life again and everybody had things to eat. He gave the photo to Second Miss. The doctor's wife scrutinized it and breathed a deep sigh: *The Communists had come just in time.* No one could have then imagined how Old Town might again starve for two years.

When Second Sister stood under the oleander to be photographed, she had gone hungry for quite a few days already. During all that time she had only a bit of thin rice gruel. She didn't dare tell her husband that the bottom of the rice jar was now showing. After the photo studio owner left, that normally would have been when she lit the fire and started to cook. The three children, their stomachs churning with hunger, were coming home soon.

She sat in front of the stove, her chin cupped in her hands, worried and wondering whose house she could go to for a bit of rice. She thought of all the relatives and close friends, but who of them had extra rice left in their own rice jars? Almost every day now, Pastor and Mrs. Chen's meals consisted of only a few glasses of water. Her own old mother living at Drum Tower was already so starved that her whole body was bloated with edema. Of all her relatives, only Elder Sister's home still enjoyed "tasty food and strong drink," but she had no wish to see that utter scoundrel of a brother-in-law. A few days back, Elder Sister had made off with a few *jin* of hulled rice from her mother-in-law's home (where she lived) to give to her own mother's family. Her husband then beat her so badly that her nose was bruised and her face all swollen.

Second Sister said to her angel, *"O Angel, please tell the Heavenly Father that Second Sister has no rice to cook for her husband and children."* The rickshaw man, Shuiguan, carried his wife on his back to the clinic. She had been washing clothes when she just suddenly keeled over in a faint. The doctor bandaged the wound on her head, and, going into the house, asked Second Sister to fill up a bowl of some rice gruel for Shuiguan's wife. Second Sister shook her head uneasily. The doctor thought she was holding back and his face reflected a faint displeasure. Even if the last bowl of rice gruel was all that was left in the house, she should give it to his patient unstintingly. He reached out and lifted the cover off the cooking pan. It was totally empty. Then he bent over and opened the rice jar. That too was totally empty. "The Complete Man keeps his distance from the kitchen," Mencius once said.[41] For many years the doctor had not entered the kitchen and he never thought supplies would run so low. He glanced apologetically at his wife.

Second Sister felt rather hurt. After Ninth Brother had become unemployed they depended on her sewing to somehow or other survive. But Ninth Brother's reputation had spread far and wide. Well before the clinic opened for business, their home had become a real clinic, with patients sitting right down on the dining table seeking treatment, like students lining up before the inner halls of knowledge. The little bit of hard-earned money from her needlework mostly went to buy medicine. Since these were all poor people from the neighborhood, the clinic didn't collect a single *fen*. Dr. Lin even often sent food and clothing to the patients' homes. A Christian

---

[41] Not out of snobbery or sexism, but rather from compassion for the animals that were killed there and the horror at hearing their dying cries.

should love his neighbor like himself. She didn't dare dissuade him from doing this.

O Angel, you've seen how the rice jar hasn't even one grain left in it. Could you turn it into a pot of fragrantly steaming rice for me?

As she prayed, she fell into a confused sleep in which she dreamed she saw herself at someone's wedding banquet. She was eating her favorite "eight joys" meatballs, and even taro paste and sticky rice cakes. She took a bit of something from each course with her chopsticks and placed it in the bowl next to her hand. She was thinking of wrapping it all up and taking it home to her children.

"Second Sister, Second Sister..." Elder Sister barged most inopportunely into her dreamworld, calling and calling her name.

Second Sister realized that she was dreaming. *Even when I'm dreaming I can't get a full meal.* Reluctantly, she opened her eyes and suddenly discovered Elder Sister standing by the side of the stove, her face wreathed in a smile. This made Second Sister feel a certain unreality. For how many years now had Elder Sister come running to her from some terrible thing, crying to the heavens and wiping away her tears? *What was she up to today? Can I be just fainting from hunger?*

"Second Sister, I've never before seen you sleeping the day away. You're all tired out, for sure."

As she spoke, Elder Sister opened up a bundle she was carrying, revealing a stack of neatly piled thin noodles. "Thin noodles" were a specialty of Old Town. Ordinary people could eat them only on New Year's Day and birthdays.

Am I still dreaming? Second Sister rubbed her eyes.

"The sun rose in the west and your brother-in-law has gone mad. He told me to bring these noodles over to you."

Has that devil-fiend suddenly turned kind and generous? That really would be a miracle. This is the angel's doing, for sure. Second Sister thought of her prayer just now. She had prayed for the angel to give her a pan full of cooked rice, and instead got this big pack of noodles. Pastor Chen once said that God gives you far, far more than you can imagine.

"Thank the Lord. Sis, to tell you the truth, today our family was going to go hungry."

"Is your family's foreign Buddha working his powers for you? This morning *he* asked me how the doctor gets by now that he's out of work, and I said he depends on Second Sister's pair of clever hands. He told me to bring over a pack of noodles, so I quickly wrapped up this bundle and came right over, before he could change his mind. As I was going out the door he said to be sure to invite you over tomorrow."

Second Sister left Elder Sister and went into the bedroom and closed the door. She knelt on the floor and uttered a prayer of thanks to her Heavenly Father.

When the children returned they saw bowls of steaming rice-flour noodles on the table. They stared at each other in amazement, unable to guess whose birthday it must be today.

⌘　⌘　⌘

Second Sister supposed that her brother-in-law's invitation to visit them and delivered in this way was merely out of courtesy or for form's sake. She took out a silken floss vest from the trunk and got it ready for Elder Sister to take back with her, one gift for another. Unexpectedly, though, after breakfast, two sedan chairs arrived at the door with the word that "the boss" had sent them over to fetch the Mrs. and Young Auntie, that is, Baohua. This put Second Sister in a bit of a spot. It had already been several years since she had last seen this brother-in-law, and that was before she had fled Old Town as a refugee during the war. One day, Elder Sister had scorched the rice, and when her man came to the table and smelled the burnt smell, he snatched up the rice bowl and smashed it right against Elder Sister's nose, causing blood to spurt out all over. When she then ran off in tears to seek refuge in Second Sister's home, Second Sister made up her mind that Elder Sister should make a clean break from that son-of-a-bitch husband. She told the older woman, "I'll take care of you. If I can't take care of you as long as you live, my children will take over from me." When Brother-in-Law Zhang came for his wife, Second Sister wouldn't let him in, and as he stood outside cursing and swearing in language that was painful to hear, Second Sister brought a bucket of cold water from the well and dashed it over him. Spineless Elder Sister went home again with her husband, all the same. Her child was there, so there was nothing more that her younger sister could say on the matter. But from that time forward, the Guo family had broken off all contact with this in-law of theirs.

As she sat at her dressing table, the thought occurred to Second Sister that there was something a little peculiar about the whole thing. Her brother-in-law's family were surnamed Zhang, not an Old Town name, not originally. The Zhang ancestors had fled to Old Town from famine up north. They were proficient at arms and boxing and they brawled their way into top control of the whole area. By the current generation, the several brothers had gone from bad to worse. At the top they colluded with the police, and at the bottom they ganged together with local bad hats and riffraff. The year before last, when the price of rice shot up, the Zhangs hoarded food supplies and made a major killing on the prices. The government plastered the streets with notices against private holdings of gold and silver, but the Zhangs brazenly made large-scale purchases.

The night before, Elder Sister had secretly told her that under the floorboards of the Zhang mansion it was all gold and silver.

Second Sister was still hesitating when Ninth Brother came into the room. She told him, "I really don't want to go."

Ninth Brother moved in front of the mirror and gazed at his wife admiringly. "Just go. We shouldn't hold grudges. Maybe he's changed now. If Jesus could forgive the men who nailed him fast to the cross, what person couldn't be forgiven?"

To keep the Guo family face, Second Sister didn't mention the history of the Zhangs, and at this moment she found it impossible to talk about her own misgivings. There was so much about the people and things of this world that Ninth Brother would never understand.

⌘   ⌘   ⌘

When the sedan chairs arrived by the moat at the southern part of Old Town, Brother-in-Law Zhang, all smiles, and holding a gold-plated water pipe, greeted her at the door. He had grown very corpulent—the House of Zhang had prospered and grown fat during these hunger years.

"Oh, Second Sister, you're as pretty as ever. Does your husband give you some elixir of life to keep you from getting old? Just look at your elder sister—she's looking ancient enough to be your mother!"

"Second Sister's husband doesn't have any fairy elixir, only a good temper. If Brother-in-Law's temper were good, Elder Sister would surely turn young."

Second Sister was straightway invited into the dining room where a sumptuous repast was set out on the grand twelve-place dining table. It was just like the wedding banquet she had dreamed of the night before, where there was everything she could ever wish for. Elder Sister also seemed a bit bemused, and she whispered to her younger sister. "This could be a Hongmen banquet."[42] Second Sister had never read as widely as her sister and didn't know what "Hongmen banquet" meant, but she did sense Elder Sister's unease.

As he pulled on his water pipe, Brother-in-Law Zhang kept on praising Second Sister's good looks. Back then, he said, if the Guo family had not insisted on marrying off their daughters starting with the oldest, it would have been Second Sister who entered the Zhang home, and that's for sure.

"Brother-in-Law, in our family we are all one line of sons and daughters, and I am not pleased with this kind of talk. Your invitation today should be for some other, respectable matter, should it not?"

"Of course! Second Sister is exceedingly intelligent. Eat, eat! First eat! Second Sister's husband lost his job so things at home can't be all that easy for you. I have given special orders to the kitchen to prepare more good things to eat so that you can take them back with you. The children can satisfy their craving for delicious things."

I'm sure he holds a grudge against me for splashing cold water on him, and today he wants to take advantage of our hunger to shame me. "These days, how many people could compare to the Zhang family? Brother-in-Law has invited me alone to eat all these exotic delicacies, but wouldn't it have been better to cook a few buckets of rice gruel and set up a tent to provide relief to poor people? Doing good deeds has its own rewards."

"What do poor people have to do with me? They're poor because that's how fate predestined them. Listen, Second Sister, your

---

[42]   That banquet with the Macbeth-like treachery explained in Footnote 5.

brother-in-law is no Bodhisattva. Today I've invited you here not to provide you with relief. This isn't just a friendly banquet. I have a money-earning matter that I would like to ask your help with."

And as he spoke, Brother-in-Law drew out from inside his lapel three silver dollars. "Take them. Consider it a prepayment."

Second Sister grew even more puzzled and ill at ease. "What can I, one woman, do to help the Zhang family?"

Brother-In-Law lowered his voice: "My big brother has a business going with Old Ridge and needs a woman to pretend to be a rich wife taking goods back to her family home. Leaving Old Town isn't the problem. And at the other end, receipt of the goods has been all arranged. It's only one portion of the road midway there that we can't be sure about."

"What can I do?"

"You're that rich wife! Go one trip and get this amount." Her brother-in-law opened three fingers. "Loudly clinking, real silver dollars!"

Second Sister had not yet touched her chopsticks. If up to then she had behaved out of a feigned reserve, now she couldn't eat at all. She didn't even know what kind of goods were to be escorted. Her heart beat wildly, *pu-tong, pu-tong*. The name Old Ridge was an extremely sensitive one. Enchun and that girl student were there. Whoever had anything to do with Old Ridge would be committing the crime of "contacting communist bandits," and that brought with it a beheading. The Zhang family was doing business you could get beheaded for.

No, I am a respectable woman from a respectable family. I haven't the courage to run goods for you. These unspoken words were on the tip of her tongue but in her mind also floated the image of that rice jar so starkly bare. The noodles that Elder Sister had brought over would take care of three days at the most. After that, where would they get their food from? And the children's school fees had to be paid soon. Where was the money for that? Three silver dollars were right before her, radiating their enticing gleam.

"Now, Second Sister, Brother-in-Law wouldn't hurt you. You come across quite proper and very prosperous. There's no need to make you up to look like some rich fellow's wife. It's sure to be extremely safe. After you make a few runs, your family will not worry about food or clothing."

"Let me think about this..."

Second Sister got up and went into the back garden where she sat on a bench. First of all, she needed to decide whether or not she would be violating a commandment. Under Ninth Brother's influence, she saw the communists through different eyes. *The Zhangs are selling to the communists and earning the communists' money. I am just helping deliver goods, nothing our Heavenly Father would blame me for, surely? But I can't discuss this with Ninth Brother. If I let him know that his own wife was taking a desperate risk and breaking the law, all for a few measures of rice, his male dignity would be hurt.*

After turning this over and over and reasoning this way and that, Second Sister decided to earn this money. For this she made a prayer, asking for the Holy Spirit to protect her and give her a safe trip.

She returned to the dinner table and asked, "When do I leave?"

"This evening."

"To and from, how long does it take?"

"Three or four days."

A woman from a respectable family who does not return home at night was a big matter, indeed. No matter what, she had to get some word to Ninth Brother. She got up and said good-bye.

Brother-In-Law said, "When the time comes, a chair will be by to fetch you."

Along the way, Second Sister thought up many excuses and pretexts. Elder Sister wasn't feeling well and wanted her to stay with her for a couple of days. *The Zhangs had a relative who wanted a trousseau made...No, that was no good. Lying was a sin. How could I avoid lying and not offend Ninth Brother's sense of dignity?*

Returning home, she put it to Ninth Brother in this way: "Someone over in Old Ridge is bringing in a batch of goods through the Zhangs and they need a woman to help deliver it."

"Why would they need a woman?"

"Wouldn't a wife returning to her old home want to bring nine or ten shoulder poles of goods as a pious gesture to her parents?"

Ninth Brother lowered his head and said nothing. The newspaper often carried reports of encirclement and extermination campaigns against Old Ridge. *The guerrilla bands up in the mountains certainly must be having a hard time of it.*

Second Sister sensed Ninth Brother's lack of opposition, so she hurried off to the rice shop before it was nightfall. Paper *yuan* was worthless, but silver dollars still had value. She spent one of these and bought a stock of emergency food supplies and items of daily use. She gave one silver dollar to Ninth Brother so he could buy medicines for the clinic. Ninth Brother didn't ask where this money came from. It didn't matter—this was a blessing from heaven. Second Sister concealed the other silver dollar. This was the first time that she hid household funds from Ninth Brother. *O Angel, forgive me. I have to keep a little emergency money for this family, for these three children.*

2.

FOR SOMEWHAT MORE than half a year, the Zhangs would send a sedan chair every month to fetch Second Sister and take her "back to her old home." She never concerned herself with what had been loaded beneath the seat of the sedan chair or packed at the ends of the porters' shoulder poles. It was as if the moment that she saw those goods with her own eyes she would offend heaven. Not knowing was no sin. She scrupulously avoided sinning to gain this hard-earned money and so before each trip she would very calmly pray to her Heavenly Father to keep her safe.

One woman leading a group of brawny men climbed mountains and crossed ridges, pushed through Guomindang military police checkpoints, penetrated the haunts of bandits and wolves, and were beset by all manner of perils. With every step they took they might have plunged to their deaths in lonely ravines. What kind of courage and audacity did this woman possess?

Time changes everything. Delivering goods for Old Ridge's guerrilla force eventually became a special honor and glory. All kinds of people connected with it floated to the surface, either taking credit for others' achievements, or seeking to use this to expiate crimes they had committed. The boss of Old Town's biggest silk factory had funded those shipments and thus became a "red capitalist" and a member of the Chinese People's Political Consultative Conference. Elder Sister's two Zhang family brothers-in-law were put up on charges of homicide. They both should have been marched, hands tied behind them, to the execution ground, but they appealed to the new regime on the grounds of their revolutionary merits and so escaped death.

There once was a playwright of Old Town-style opera who tried to bring to the stage the story of the Old Ridge guerrillas. He had interviewed the red capitalist and laboriously tracked down my grandmother. Before meeting her he had already formed the strong impression that she was some fabled heroine and he had hopes of writing a revolutionary masterpiece.

Comrade Second Sister Guo was clearly a disappointment to this playwright. She insisted that she was just a woman. Her husband had lost his job, and to keep her family from starving to death, she just had to perform that arduous task. She didn't even know what was in the packages the porters were carrying with their shoulder poles. Nor did she know who the people were who received the goods. The playwright prompted her by saying that it had been rifles and ammunition for the guerrillas and that she had accomplished a great deed for the Revolution. But Second Sister stubbornly argued, "I didn't know, I really didn't know. I was only doing this to earn a little money for rice!" The playwright didn't realize that Second Sister was just then pleading her innocence to her angel, and he thought this ignorant housewife was a bit deranged. And so, reckoning the whole thing to be hopeless, he closed his notebook and left.

In talking about the past, especially those times when Elder Sister came running to them for refuge, the two sisters would gab on and on about that wicked fellow who beat his wife even in his old age. Elder Sister said her husband actually wasn't all bad. "He had helped the communists and helped you Lins out." Second Sister let out a snort of disgust. "The Zhangs *still* owe me for two trips. They are just plain black-hearted. Imagine cheating a woman out of payment for which she risked death!" As for helping the communists, Second Sister had her own views on that. She once told Elder Sister, "That year when the communist's head was hung on the South Gate city wall, it's very likely the Zhangs had betrayed him." Elder Sister turned pale and cried out in fright, "Never talk such rubbish!" Second Sister apologized, saying that she hated that brother-in-law so much she just didn't know what she was saying.

Older people remember when the communist was beheaded and publicly displayed. His head on the city wall became for the timid and conservative people of Old Town a nightmare they couldn't shake off. Second Sister didn't know that this also set off a ruthless internal purge by the communists. Nor did she know that some people were unjustly blamed for it, among these Huang Shuyi's older brother. Second Sister was a housewife who kept well away from all the political whirlpools but this ordinary housewife had witnessed the astounding affair. Her reasoning and conclusions may have been the closest of all to what had really happened.

⌘   ⌘   ⌘

It was almost the New Year and "the rich wife" was again about to return to her family home. As Second Sister sat in the sedan chair, she discovered there was a new face among the shoulder-pole porters and clearly not someone who had grown up in a home where they did heavy labor. She imagined that, like Ninth Brother, the fellow was some out-of-work scholar. Because of her sympathy for him, she would glance at him from time to time. She also found that the shoulder-pole loads seemed lighter than previously and that the chair itself fairly floated above the ground.

There was no avoiding the South Gate inspection post. This was within the Zhangs' sphere of influence and they had often passed through it without ever being stopped for checking. The atmosphere today was very different. Far off down the middle of the road Second Sister saw several policemen poised for action. The damp and rainy air was heavy with ill omen. She quickly took out the Zhangs' fake road pass. That was the travel request from her "high official husband" to the military police along the way. With rifles held at the ready, the police swarmed forward. She forced herself to sit calmly and motionlessly in the sedan chair. She saw them ransacking a few trunks. These contained bottles and cans of no worth at all. *Were the Zhangs doing this death-defying business for such stuff?* She took special note of the baleful look of one policeman as he appraised that scholar. *Is he going to be called out for a frisking?* Just as she grew worried about this, that policeman waved his hand to let them pass. The chair was lifted and Second Sister closed her eyes and endlessly thanked her angel. *O Angel, please protect me. Protect me one last time. From now on I will no longer risk my life to earn this money. Even though the Zhangs are sitting on my pay, I want to forget all about it.* Then, on second thought, she said to herself, *Since I've decided to give up my pay for those last two times, why not decide right here and now to turn around and go back home?*

She was going to halt the chair carriers while she seriously considered abandoning the thing halfway there. Before she could open her mouth though, the second inspection post came into view. Suddenly from the side of the road burst forth a group of policemen just as ready to open fire as the earlier one. And with precision and accuracy they pounced on that scholarly looking fellow and, pulling a great hempen sack down over him, threw him into a black automobile. The porters hadn't even had time to set down their shoulder poles before that car just left them in a cloud of dust. The whole group of them stopped right in the middle of the little road for who knows how long a time. Only when a file of people passed by and yelled at them to get out of the way did Second Sister realize she was still sitting in her chair on the carriers' shoulders.

"Let's just go back." she said. "We no sooner leave the city gate when something bad happens. Well, that's as far as we're going."

Not a single one among them seemed opposed to this and in one motion they all picked up their shoulder poles and headed back to the city. Second Sister carefully scanned the South Gate inspection post. The police that had been there earlier were all gone off now. The two policemen now on duty were just dozing there.

Second Sister brought the frightened porters with her and knocked on the big gate of the Zhang residence. In spite of the magnitude of the incident that had just occurred, surprisingly not one of the Zhang brothers got out of bed. They seemed not to be concerned in the slightest about their possible involvement in the incident. Nor did they seem worried about the damage to their goods. Brother-In-Law sent Elder Sister out with the message that the loads were to be carried into the back courtyard and after New Year's they would calculate what pay they owed her.

⌘   ⌘   ⌘

On the twenty-eighth day of the twelfth lunar month, Old Town celebrated "Little New Year," and a human head was hung from the South Gate wall. Old Town's newspapers carried photographs of the communist. He had been that porter taken off by the police. Rumor had it that this mysterious figure had been an important communist from the north and the person who betrayed him had received a big reward.

Second Sister was just setting the table and getting ready to cook when the newspaper in Ninth Brother's hands drew her attention as if it were a magnet. The solution to the puzzle was right there in the words, "big reward." *Correct, they definitely picked up a big reward. The Zhang brothers would do anything for money.*

Ninth Brother looked dejected and dazed as he propped the newspaper up in his hands. Second Sister didn't dare to give voice to her own thoughts on this matter. She knew that her husband was mourning that communist who had been beheaded.

When the children came to the table they saw that their daddy was feeling low, and so no one dared to say much. They hurried through their rice gruel and each went his or her own way. His book bag pressed under his arm, Baosheng said he was going to a class-mate's home for after-school lessons and homework assignments. Lately he had been finding this or that reason to go out and it would be late at night when he returned.

What homework do you have that you can't do at home?" Second Sister asked him. "Don't go out today!"

"Just let him go," said Ninth Brother.

After dinner, Ninth Brother again picked up the newspaper. So that he could be by himself quietly for a while, Second Sister collected a pile of dirty clothes and went to the side of the well to wash them. This evening had been one of those rare days of good weather. The glittering stars seemed to brighten the whole area. The street crossing was unusually quiet as Second Sister sat on a small bench scrubbing the clothes. A host of thoughts kept going back to the bloody scene at South Gate. *Almighty Father, you know better than we do whether the Zhang brothers took the bounty. Please judge them yourself.*

...This is Baosheng's blue school uniform. Ever since he was small he has been running around. I always have to pay extra attention to his cloth-ing. Second Sister discovered an ink stain on his lapel. *Where did this come from? It's been a long time since he last used a brush pen to practice his calligraphy.* Looking more closely, she also saw a few lumps of paste on his cuffs. *What has Baosheng been up to?* She couldn't help thinking of the frequent appearances of antigovernment slogans on the street. Everyone said that the communists were making the students do this. *Don't tell me Baosheng is also involved with the*

communists! She hadn't seen with her own eyes the head on the wall at South Gate, but at this very instant a crystal clear image leapt before her. *O heaven! Might Baosheng get into trouble this evening? This child is such a bother and always has been ever since he was little. Raising him's been no easy thing for us. I have to go find him, and right now!* She knew that Baosheng was close to the boss of that bookstore. *That fellow has led my son astray, I'm sure of it.*

She dropped the half-washed clothes, went into the house, took off her apron and oversleeves and put on a knitted wool jacket. Ninth Brother seemed transfixed, his eyes closed. Whenever he was feeling down, he would close his eyes, as if to escape reality this way. She didn't want to alarm him and so she went out the door very softly. Suddenly he said to her, "Where are you going?"

She hesitated about telling him her worries, but she felt she was losing control of herself, "I want to find Baosheng. This child is going to get into trouble. Starting tomorrow, the three children will not be allowed to take one step out of the house. The way things are nowadays, it's no use being educated. The people getting executed and killed are all the educated ones."

Ninth Brother pointed to the chair beside him. "Sit down and calm yourself a bit."

"I can't be calm. Do you know what Baosheng is doing every evening, coming and going like a shadow?"

Ninth Brother's tone of voice was very steady. He said, "Sit down. Let us just pray for him."

Second Sister lowered herself slowly into the chair. "It seems you already know. Why don't you keep him in line? It's been so hard for the five of us to get to where we are today."

"It's not easy for anybody. Don't all families have a father, a mother, sons and daughters? Our children have been given to our Heavenly Father. So don't worry so much."

Second Sister stared at her husband, a furtive tear trickling down her cheek. "Oh, you! Normally you can't bear to step on an ant. But where it concerns your son's life, you aren't worried. You're too rigid in your feelings toward your own family."

Ninth Brother heaved a great sigh and, closing his eyes, said, "I've already known for more than a month now, and during that time every night Baosheng never came home. And I can't sleep at all."

Second Sister wiped her tears and her heart ached as she looked at her husband. She knew that lately he hadn't been sleeping very well and thought it was because his body had become overheated. Today she had boiled some cooling green bean soup for him.

"Why don't you stop him?"

Ninth Brother still kept his eyes closed. "The child's grown now. He's beyond our control. Let's just pray for him."

Second Sister couldn't stop the terrified images from piling up in her mind. It was as if it all were actually happening in some corner of Old Town. She stood up. "I still want to go find Baosheng."

Ninth Brother took hold of her. "Let's just pray."

The oil lamp burned dry and the flame was out. Their prayers still went on.

3.

THE MORE SHE thought about it the more uneasy she felt. But she felt it impossible to express her anxieties and hidden resentment to her husband. Ninth Brother was full of compassion for the world. His own family was only one part of the world and he didn't see them in a different light just because they were his wife and children. As the head of a family he possessed absolute authority and could totally prevent tragedy from happening. But he seemed unmoved, as if he were indifferent to Baosheng being one of his children. The three young ones were all flesh of her flesh. She would not stand by and watch any one of these being hurt in any way. She was going to launch a "protect the calves" campaign right under Ninth Brother's own eyes.

During that period, Second Sister became a bit neurotic. Every night when Ninth Brother had fallen asleep, she would softly get out of bed and make her way in the darkness as if sleepwalking to count her children. Baohua had the habit of grinding her teeth at night. Standing in front of the door she would listen to the little gnawing-rat sounds the child would make. She would then feel her way to her sons' room. Every time he turned over in his sleep Baoqing muttered incomprehensible words. Baosheng was still falling asleep like that before taking off all his clothes. She pulled back the cotton cover and took off his dirty clothes and socks. As usual, as he shifted from place to place, he would snore like thunder.

Turning over, Baoqing said, "Wait for me, bro." These words were said very distinctly and Second Sister heard in them a danger signal. Who knows how many plots and deceptions these two little kittens were hatching in this small room behind their closed door?

She climbed up into the little attic before dawn. That was where the owner of the house had piled up all kinds of things. Up and down she carried bucket after bucket of water until finally the place was clean.

The first lunar month had not yet come to an end and Old Town folk held it taboo to do any major cleaning up during this month. Ninth Brother, seeing her busying away, covered with dust and dirt and the sweat soaking her back, asked, "What gave you the idea to do all this cleaning?"

"Baoqing is big now. He should have his own room."

Ninth Brother had never paid much mind to folk customs and was not overly suspicious, so he didn't see that Second Sister was just then doing things her own way, even if it meant deviating from accustomed thinking and practice.

Who is more important, the husband or the children? Second Sister really couldn't tell, but relying on her maternal instincts, she opened up mother-hen wings to shelter her chicks from the winds and the rain.

When Baoqing came home from school his mother brought him up to the little attic. "Son, you know Ma loves you the best. You have to obey and from today on come back home right on the dot. And in the evening you're not to take even one step away from home."

"Ma, this evening I want to go with Elder Brother to read books at the bookstore."

Second Sister secretly congratulated herself on taking this timely measure. "That's just what I mean! You can't go running around with Elder Brother. Now...Obey!"

"He hasn't done anything bad."

"I don't care what he's done. I'm not letting you hang around with him! Do you want Ma to go on her knees before you?"

This frightened Baoqing and he quickly replied, "Ma, I'll do as you say!"

After eating dinner, Baosheng signaled to Baoqing that it was time to go out. Baoqing shook his head in refusal.

Second Sister picked up the laundry bucket and followed Baosheng out. She walked past the street crossing and stopped him. "I'm not asking you where you are going, but I want to tell you, you are making Daddy and me lose our sleep every night."

Baosheng lowered his head and, looking at the tips of his toes, said haltingly, "I'll come home a little earlier."

"Your Dad doesn't control you. I don't control you either. Don't involve your sister and brother in this. Son, the trials and tribulations this family has gone through, you yourself ought to remember. Something unexpected and unpleasant can happen in the family to no matter whom."

Sobbing, Second Sister was unable to go on.

Baosheng came forward to support his mother. He put down the little bench for doing the laundry and sat her down on it. "Ma, you've forgotten. I can use my slingshot," he said with a laugh. And with that he drew from his pocket the little catapult and several glossy little stones. "This is my rifle. Whatever flies in the air or runs on the ground with two legs or four, one shot will lay it low for three days."

"Oh, you! So big now, and still this naughty." Second Sister laughed, bitterly shaking her head. "Legs grow out of your body and you just go wherever you please!"

Baosheng came close to his mother's ear and said, "Ma, the daylight is coming. And when the day breaks everything is going to get better."

Second Sister raised her eyes heavenward. The sky was just getting pitch black. *What kind of craziness is this child talking?*

"You're not to stay out until daybreak!"

Baosheng left. Second Sister was standing there blankly when she saw Elder Sister, a bundle coiled in her hand, approaching West Gate from the southern part of Old Town. *I'm sure she's running from his temper once again.* Second Sister straightened up and was about to rise and greet her but then sat back down again. Elder Sister loved to talk and always wanted to get to the bottom of things. She also loved to make things up out of thin air. If she discovered any "spider threads and horse hoofmarks"—clues, in other words—about Baosheng, and after a few days made peace again with her husband and went meekly back to the Zhang household, there's no telling what she would then say. *No! I can't let her go back home.*

⌘　⌘　⌘

Elder Sister bent over the Eight Immortals table, tears pouring out of her. Her scoundrel of a husband had again beaten her over the usual petty matter. Off to the side, Second Sister listened to the end of the story and then gave her a hot towel.

"You came at just the right time. Fourth Sister has taken ill. It's still not too late in the day for us to go see her, and it would be even better if you could stay a few days with her."

When Elder Sister heard that her fourth sister was sick, she forgot all about her own heartbreak, and, giving her face a good wipe, picked up her bundle and was ready to set off.

Two days before, Second Sister had gone to see her mother. There she found out that Fourth Sister had miscarried and was in an extremely weak condition. Fourth Sister's husband never lifted one finger to help her, so the sick woman still had to wash the clothes and cook the meals. That family really did need someone to help out.

So I really haven't told a lie, Second Sister thought.

Two hours later Second Sister returned home. Ninth Brother was sitting by the lamp reading the Bible. He asked her, "Why hasn't Elder Sister come back with you?"

"I had her stay to take care of Fourth Sister for a few days so she wouldn't have to sit around here doing nothing and feeling worse."

"That makes good sense."

The way Ninth Brother looked when he praised her made Second Sister feel a bit guilty. *Have I gotten used to telling lies now?* She took up her sewing and as she squeezed in front of the lamp, silently said to the Angel, *"O Angel, forgive me. Actually, I was only hiding some ideas from Ninth Brother. If that offended you, please go easy with me."*

4.

BAOHUA STEPPED INTO the classroom just as the bell for classes rang. She had been like this ever since she was little, always arriving late at a languorous pace, and rushing off in a hurry. When she reached the third year of lower-middle school, she wouldn't have been able to call most of her classmates by name. Everyone, including the teachers, called her Little Miss Dainty. In fact, she had an inferiority complex and took on an unsociable and eccentric air to cover up her feelings of unworthiness. Because she was exceedingly petite and delicately built and because she couldn't get the hang of mathematics, she refused to make friends in school.

The atmosphere in the class that day felt somehow different. More than half the desks were standing empty. When the bell rang, the students were still chirping and twittering among themselves— the place sounded like a vegetable market that had just opened. The Chinese language teacher stood by his lectern, at a total loss.

Baohua went to sit in her usual place. Beside her a girl student was saying to a friend, "Are you going to the general student demonstration today?"

They whispered together for a while, then stood up and left. The teacher pretended not to notice, and this in turn encouraged a great crowd of those restless and undecided students to leave the classroom with a noise like the rustling wind.

The teacher said, "I don't know how to teach you remaining four or five kittens. Just study by yourselves and if there's anything you don't understand, you can come and ask."

Several girl students gathered together and boldly expressed their views. Some said that there was going to be big trouble today, while others said, no, nothing big was going to happen. That long-haired student, the daughter of the boss of Old Town's cigarette factory, said that the communists would be coming soon, and that they were especially against the people with money, so her family was moving its wealth to Hong Kong and she herself was about to go there to study.

Baohua sat all by herself off to one side, listlessly turning the pages of her schoolbooks. Hearing of the imminent arrival of the communists she felt a bit of excitement. When the communists came Enchun could also return to Old Town and continue his studies. She felt confident about taking the exams for the teachers' training college. The gates of the Teachers' Training College and the commercial college where Enchun studied faced each other across the way. They could go to school together again every day, just like they used to. Enchun would ride his bicycle, and as she fantasized riding on its top bar, her back glued to Enchun's chest as they raced forward into the wind, Baohua felt all beautiful inside.

The bell sounded. The Chinese language teacher at his lectern pretentiously cleared his throat and announced the end of his class. Next was math class. Baohua dreaded math and the math teacher. *Since the teachers weren't bothering about those skipping classes today, why don't I just skip out too?* She collected all her schoolbooks and followed the Chinese language teacher out of the classroom.

She bought a few olives at the grocery shop at the street corner. As she chewed she thought about going to East Street to take a look at what was happening. She was a naturally timid girl and not someone who liked to join in any excitement, but she longed to hear more news about the communists. The communists were now closely linked with her happy life. Putting the last olive into her mouth, she abruptly made up her mind, turned about, and bravely headed for East Street.

⌘ ⌘ ⌘

At this very moment, an unexpected visitor arrived at the Lin home—Enchun's friend, Huang Shuyi. Had Baohua decided instead to go home, she might have run into her quite by chance, and perhaps in later days the trajectory of her fate would have been completely different. Ninth Brother had left to make house calls, so Second Sister received this girl. The girl said that she and Enchun had left Old Ridge three months earlier and were now teaching school in a little market town more than sixty miles beyond Old Ridge. She herself had rushed home this time to attend her old grandmother's funeral and had been entrusted by Enchun with a letter and gifts for his parents and all the Lin family.

Second Sister exchanged conventional greetings with the girl and asked about Enchun. When the girl spoke of him a blush spread over her cheeks and Second Sister could tell that she liked Enchun very much. She supposed that they shared many goals in common and that, later on, when they became man and wife they would become even more congenial. Enchun had been a well-behaved and good boy ever since he was a child. So Ninth Brother early on saw him as a "half son" and hoped that when he and Baohua grew up they each could get positions as grade school teachers and live out their lives in peace and security. He never expected Enchun to be so discontented with his lot in life. Second Sister had already given up this "half son" because her Baohua was a weak and shy child, unable to stand the bumps and jolts of life.

The girl, Huang Shuyi, took her leave without waiting for Dr. Lin to return. Second Sister opened the presents. There was a piece of gambiered fabric from Guangdong Province, enough for a summer outfit for each member of the Lin family, and a small red paper packet for Baohua, with a silk handkerchief and short letter inside. In the letter Enchun welcomed Baohua to spend some time with him during the vacation period.

Second Sister put the handkerchief and letter into her pocket. While she was cooking lunch, she sat in front of the oven, took these items out and looked at them over and over. She wondered… if Baohua saw this letter, would she be willing to wait for her vacation to go find Enchun? She was that headstrong and willful. When a contrary mood struck her she was uncontrollable. Second Sister knew that last year when Baohua had been sick and had to quit school, this was connected to Enchun. Whatever else, they had to avoid any further trouble. She decided to hold on to the letter.

⌘   ⌘   ⌘

Baohua took a shortcut and hurried to East Street. The demonstrators had already reached the gate of the city government at Drum Tower and there were only a few people who had not yet dispersed from watching the uproar. On the ground were many placards. Baohua picked one up that read "Oppose Hunger." She assumed that this demonstration had nothing to do with the communists. By the side of the road were a few people whispering to each other that over by Drum Tower the police had come out in force and scattered the demonstrators, and that a lot of students had been seized. Hearing that the police were arresting people, Baohua immediately took off for home. As she was nearing West Gate she happened to run into Mrs. Chen just then seeing Huang Shuyi off. Her heart felt as if it had been scalded. *Had Enchun come home?*

Turning around, Mrs. Chen caught sight of Baohua. "Is school out, Baohua?"

"Hello, Auntie. Who was that woman?"

She didn't know that Baohua had met Huang Shuyi. "That's your Enchun's colleague. I just found out that Enchun is a grade-school teacher in another part of the country. Thank the Lord, this is really very good news."

"Does she teach together with Older Brother Enchun?"

"Oh, yes. And in two years you too can become a grade-school teacher."

"How is it that Older Brother Enchun hasn't come home?"

"He should soon. He can be back during the next school vacation."

Mrs. Chen had Baohua wait a bit while she cut some roses for her to take home. When she came back out of the house with the clippers, Baohua was gone without a trace.

Under a tree beside Little West Lake, Baohua wiped away her tears. She never expected that the relationship between that girl student and Enchun would have been so close. Last year she had been really shocked when those two had left Old Town together. Later she knew that Enchun was in trouble and had to leave and at the time she thought that girl student was just helping him get out of Old Town. It was only today that she discovered they had been together all along. They had gone together to Old Ridge and then together had gone to some distant place to teach. Enchun had entrusted the girl with visiting his father and mother. This implied something very special, for sure. However, this time Baohua wasn't so fragile. She decided to cut the bond of affection between them in one stroke and never pay any more attention to him. She vowed that someday she would marry a man who was more handsome than Enchun.

This day was unusual for the three children of the Lin family. Baosheng and Baoqing both took part in the demonstration, and Baosheng was also a subleader of this particular student movement.

The eldest of the Guo sons saw all of this happening from the street at Drum Tower and, all stirred up, he shouted out slogans along with the students. During the previous year, before there had been any student demonstrations in Old Town, he had himself attacked the government office. By then, his home had been out of liquor for days. He really hated the government.

Suddenly, at the very moment the police began to move in, he spotted his nephew Baoqing among the student demonstrators. Out in the front ranks it was utter chaos. He lunged forward and seized Baoqing by the ear. "You come home with me!"

Terrified, Baoqing begged for mercy. "Uncle, please, whatever you do, don't tell Ma! Tomorrow I'll send you over a bottle of liquor."

When he heard there *was* liquor, Eldest Brother Guo was even less willing to let go of him. "I'm your mother's brother and I can't stand by and watch you court death. You've got to come with me!"

So, in this way, Baoqing was dragged home by his drunkard uncle.

Everything was quite peaceful at West Gate. Second Sister still didn't know that the students had taken to the streets. After making lunch, she waited for the children to come home.

Eldest Brother Guo didn't betray Baoqing. He wheedled his way to a bottle of watered-down grain spirits, and went off muttering and swearing to himself.

Baohua also returned, the same as always.

Baosheng got hit by a police baton at the gateway of the city government. One-half of his face was all a great bruise. When he got back home he told his parents that he hadn't been watching where he was going and had bumped into the south wall. That morning Ninth Brother had gone out on house calls and heard about the student demonstration. Afraid that this would worry

Second Sister, he didn't mention it to her. In words pregnant with meaning he ordered his son, "Be careful when you go out on the street." His father's gentle and concerned glance made Baosheng so choked up he couldn't eat.

5.

THE CORNER AT West Gate had several sights which always moved me and left me with deep impressions that remain vivid and alive to this very day.

Every day, a middle-aged man, lean and lanky, holding a bamboo broom taller than he is, sweeps the street back and forth without a trace of expression on his face. He does this in every season of the year and from sunup to sundown. My grandmother and Mrs. Chen frequently bring him water to drink and move out a small bench for him to rest on. He hears and sees nothing. It is as if he were sweeping a city totally devoid of people. People say that he had been a professor in the history department of Old Town's university, sentenced to sweep the streets during the Cultural Revolution. From that point on, he never tired or grew bored doing this.

A fat little frizzle-haired guy is always standing under the lamp at the intersection with his hands clasped behind his back. He rouses the West Gate folk from their dreams every day at the crack of dawn, just like a rooster crowing at the daylight. He has quite a resonant voice and had once been recruited into the army's performing artist troupe. He was in uniform for a few months but then for some unknown reason had been sent home again. From that time on, the West Gate intersection is the stage he performs on.

There's a woman, a compulsive rag and junk collector, pushing a little bamboo cart. She picks up whatever she sees lying around. Her home is on the other bank of the city moat, but she likes to sleep out in the open all around West Gate. Time and again her people haul her back home, and even married her off to a bachelor in the mountain district, but she's still got to run back to rag-pick around West Gate.

There's another woman—who doesn't show up every day—who's like a migratory bird, for only during a certain season does she come to linger briefly around West Gate. She looks like a porter, for on her shoulder there always hangs a towel of indeterminate color. She stands far off in some dark and gloomy corner near the rice shop, and the way she looks at you is equally dark and gloomy. I always feel that she harbors ill intent and every time I run into her I feel uncomfortable all over.

One time I was watching Chaofan and my younger cousin at the intersection flicking marbles. Suddenly I raised my head and found myself looking straight at that woman whose ghastly stare seemed locked right on me. At the time I was holding on to my little cousin who had barely learned how to walk. I was afraid this woman was going to snatch the little girl from me and run off with her, so I went home and called Grandma. Grandma's expression told me that she knew that woman, but when she walked over there, the other woman left in great hurry. Grandma chased after her a ways, but that woman kept on running.

Grandma told me that the woman was Chaofan's mother, someone called Huang Shuyi. I was so startled at this news that my eyeballs just about popped out of my head. I had always supposed that Chaofan didn't have any mother, just like Rongmei next door, whose own mother had breathed her last when Rongmei came into this world.

Grandma said that when Huang Shuyi was young she had stood out from all the rest. She had dimples in her cheeks and she smiled so very sweetly that no one expected her to develop a mental disorder. A perfectly fine girl from a respectable family had become a wraith-like vagrant. Grandma's head was buried in her sewing as she mended one of my cousins' socks, when suddenly out of nowhere she said, "Enchun was ill-fated. Your ma was too."

⌘   ⌘   ⌘

People laugh at the blind man feeling the elephant. In fact, in this confused and tumultuous cosmos of a billion universes, who *isn't* a blind man feeling an elephant? Each person can stand at only a certain perspective and interpret the world based on his or her own cognitive powers. My grandmother, using her own, decided that Huang Shuyi was mentally deranged. Later on, I had the opportunity to "feel the elephant" from a different angle and came to the opposite conclusion. Huang Shuyi wasn't mentally deranged. Her nerves were as tough as steel rebar.

That girl who smiled so sweetly had been a student in the music department of the Teachers' Training College and was the offspring of an illustrious and influential family. Her father had been a student the government sent to study overseas during the early years of the Republic. Her family owned Old Town's sole electric light company. Her elder brother, Huang Jian, brought Huang Shuyi into the Communist Party and he himself was one of the leaders of the Old Ridge guerrillas. In the winter of 1947, she and Enchun received orders to leave Old Ridge and go to a little town on the seashore and, using teaching as their cover, engage in underground work. At that time she was secretly in love with Enchun and she thought that Enchun was secretly in love with her, and that it was only because of the Revolution that he had temporarily put aside the love of a boy for a girl. The Revolution was about to succeed. The Guomindang government and the Communist Party were confronting each other across the natural barrier of the Yangzi

River. If only this line of defense could be breached, China would enter the heavenly Communist Age. When that time came she would ask Enchun to stay on in this beautiful little town, teach, get married, and have children.

⌘ ⌘ ⌘

Huang Shuyi had brought a radio from her home. Plugging it into an electrical source, she heard the female broadcaster screeching at the top of her lungs that the Yangzi was an unbreakable natural barrier and that recovery of the north was imminent. Enchun's reaction was to reach over to turn it off. But Huang Shuyi stopped him.

"When you listen to the Guomindang radio broadcasts you've got to turn everything around. When they say "unbreakable," it means "the situation's critical." This is the just the reason I wanted to bring this radio with us."

She raised her head and gazed with a deep look on her face at Enchun standing beside her. "The Revolution is about to succeed. Have you thought about life afterward?"

"I may go back to school and continue my studies. What about you?"

"I'd like to stay here. I'll ask for the piano to be shipped over, and then have seven children. Every evening they'll gather around me and sing as I play. Don't you feel that would be heaven on earth?"

Enchun heard the overtones of this particular melody, blushed, and laughed awkwardly.

Huang Shuyi liked best of all the way he would blush, and she didn't let him off the hook. "I'm going to name the seven children after the seven notes of the scale. What do you think?"

Enchun blushed even more deeply.

⌘   ⌘   ⌘

The days when they taught by the seaside were the good times that Huang Shuyi would never forget. Every day she listened to the radio and longed for the beautiful vistas of the communist heaven. The seventeen-year-old Teachers' Training College student thought of communism as a magic bottle gourd that could make everyone realize his or her own dreams.

That night at midnight, the radio transmitted the news that the Yangzi "has fallen." Huang Shuyi sprang out from underneath her covers and rushed barefooted to knock on Enchun's door. Then she ran dragging him to the seashore and shouted out, "Oh, victory!" The two young revolutionaries went crazy with happiness. The naturally bashful Enchun, very much out of character for him, joined her in singing and leaping about.

However, a completely unforeseen misfortune was awaiting Huang Shuyi. One month before, the sound of a rifle shot on Old Ridge had announced, unnoticed, the prologue of her mortal struggle with destiny.

Our story again has to return to the beheaded and publicly displayed communist. Huang Shuyi's brother, Huang Jian, had been ordered to make a special trip to Old Town to meet this fellow and bring him into the mountains. The arrangement was for the newcomer to go to the Zhang home as a porter, and according to plans, Huang Jian would go with him to Old Ridge. As it happened, though, just at this time Huang Jian's old grandmother became seriously ill. That communist who gave his life had been a high-level leader. When he found out about the grandmother, he gave permission to Huang Jian to stay in Old Town for a few more days. Three days later the grandmother's condition took a turn for the better and Huang Jian immediately hurried back to Old Ridge. The moment he arrived at the mountain pass he was tied up by his battle-ready guerrilla comrades, locked up in a cave and interrogated. He wrote report after report. He had suspected the Zhangs, but the only person who could vindicate him could no longer speak. Who would believe him now? When the news of the public display of the beheaded communist arrived from Old Town, immediately Huang Jian was shoved out of the cave and shot dead.

When Old Town was on the eve of Liberation, Huang Shuyi's father chartered a boat to go to Taiwan and made a special stop at the little seaside town to meet his daughter. There were six boys in the Huang family and only that one girl. The father could have abandoned his oldest son, Huang Jian, but could not bear losing this daughter. The boat waited in the bay for two days and two nights. And for two days and two nights the father and the daughter argued fiercely. The mother brought in several serving maids and she and they all lined up and knelt down in front of Huang Shuyi. In tears herself, Huang Shuyi knelt down in front of them. Seeing that their daughter was bound and determined and there was nothing further that could be done, they wiped their tears and departed.

Four months later, Old Town and the little seaside town simultaneously announced their peaceful liberation. Huang Shuyi wrote to the provincial leaders seeking their help to locate her elder brother. The answer she received was this: "The traitor and special agent Huang Jian has already been executed by gunfire." That was the start of the long, long and bitter journey to overturn her brother's verdict.

CHAPTER THIRTEEN — LONGING FOR PASSION

1.

CHRYSANTHEMUM RAMBLES ON listlessly, skipping from one topic to the next. "Where are you now?" "I suppose you haven't slept at all tonight." "Is that mixed-blood guy fun?"

She gives me no chance to reply. One question mark is followed by yet another. At this very moment she is sitting in that coffee shop on East Chang'an Avenue, absentmindedly stirring her coffee as she gazes out through the plate glass wall at the heavy flow of traffic outside. If she is wasting her time all by herself in a coffee shop, it's a sure sign that she's hit a low point. But she's not in any hurry to tell me what's happened.

Has our grand scheme totally fallen through? I am beginning to get a bit anxious. In business, the duck will often fly right out of the pot even after it's cooked. How much more so when we haven't yet even gotten hold of a single duck feather? Wouldn't the sure money-maker my schoolmate held in his grasp also be attracting swarms of business raiders? He could say to Chrysanthemum, "OK, I can give this whole program to you," and say the same thing to someone else. So long as there's no contract, social talk is like a ship passing by without a trace. You can't take it seriously.

The train's public address system is just then announcing the Yangzi Bridge in Chinese and English. Joseph is glued to the window taking pictures and recording an audio explanation of the scene. "This is the famous Yangzi River. The Yangzi divides China into north and south..."

I'll go along nicely with this boss and maybe I'll not only be well looked after but can also keep up with my daughter's tuition payments. I'm suddenly feeling a bit tired of it all, like I've lost the drive to cope with all the winds of change in the market.

I want to say this to encourage Chrysanthemum: "Never mind! Haven't you already started several companies? You know all about making money and about losing it too. You've got to keep your cool when things change."

Chrysanthemum's question has nothing to do with what I am thinking. "Answer me this and tell the truth: I've gotten old, haven't I? Have I lost my appeal?"

For a second I am at a complete loss and it takes awhile for my brain to start moving again. "You sounded so serious; I thought something big had happened."

"A woman loses her appeal—isn't that big enough?"

"This isn't your style. Ms. Chrysanthemum's appeal radiates in all directions, so always have faith in yourself."

"No, I'm done for. To tell you the truth, I just had my thirty-sixth birthday."

"You're thirty-six. So?"

"I haven't had a baby yet. I'm thinking of marrying any old cat or dog I meet so I can have a kid."

"What's wrong? What's made you this negative all of a sudden?"

"Do you know, yesterday evening that classmate of yours actually asked me, 'How old is your child?' And then he took his daughter's picture out of his wallet. O heaven! And to think of all that French perfume I sprayed myself with for nothing!"

I just can't help it. I laugh so hard I double up. "Hey, everybody fumbles it sometime. It's not that big a deal."

"This has been a signal. It tells me that men no longer look at me from an aesthetic angle. I don't have any aesthetic worth now. I went back home, washed off the makeup, and as I stood in front of the mirror, I counted on my fingers how old I am. After thirty-six comes thirty-seven. How could I be thirty-seven? Forty isn't far off, and that's what scares me!"

I sense that Chrysanthemum is really upset and I don't know what I can say to comfort her. Sometimes I too can feel awful about the passing of my own youth and then a vast inner emptiness always spreads within me.

After a long silence, Chrysanthemum continues, "Our pal is actually willing to work with us. All we need is for you to get back so things can start moving. But how come I can't feel happy about this? What's the real point of making money? Let's say we make mountains of silver and gold, we're still going to get old and die."

I ought to be happy about the news she's conveyed, but I stay with her train of thought.

"So just go ahead and include marriage and a kid on your agenda."

"And marry whom?"

"That Ah Mu who fixes your computer…hasn't he always been nuts about you?"

From having her computer fixed, Chrysanthemum got to know an upright but not terribly scintillating fellow. She calls him "Ah Mu." Ah Mu likes her. For him it's sweetness itself to be able to run around being her male housemaid. Whatever is broken or not working in her home, with one telephone call Ah Mu is at the door, tool kit in his hand. He doesn't say much. When he arrives he just silently sets to work. In two years he's said only two things to express how he felt: "I've been divorced for five years and have no child," and "I think of you every day."

"Him?" Chrysanthemum shouts. "Oh, right, thanks a lot! You've got me entering the church in my wedding dress, hand in hand with Ah Mu? If my previous boyfriends and my former husband found out that I married that blockhead, I'd be laughed to death..."

"Or else advertise for a partner?"

"Advertising is even more hopeless. Does a good man have to go to a matchmaking center?"

"Then I just don't know what you should do."

"I never counted on you to tell me what to do. Just listen to me gripe and moan. That'd be good enough. The sun will go on rising as it always does, the days will pass as before, and after a while I'll just go and register the new company. Which of us two do you see being its legal representative?"

"You just go ahead and take full charge of the business matters, and it wouldn't be a bad idea to hire another person."

"You've got your own thing going. Have you been kidnapped and gotten all mixed up? *Ai*, these days if I could only get all mixed up like that, I'd be happy. Go ahead with your own thing."

⌘　⌘　⌘

Now that I've shut off my phone, I'm just sitting here in a depressed daze. Chrysanthemum always treats me as the receptacle for all her bad moods, the place where at every turn she dumps her mental garbage. Maybe by now she has already recovered her usual smugness and high spirits, while my skies have been blanketed by all the trash she has left behind. It always takes me a long time just to break free of it all.

The Yangzi Bridge has receded far into the distance without my noticing it. I find Joseph sitting beside me, and apparently he's been here for quite a while now. He is looking closely at me, his eyes showing genuine concern.

"It looks like you're not too happy."

"It's nothing. Really, it's nothing."

I force a smile, then suddenly everything goes blurry. I quickly shift my glance to what's outside the window. It's at this moment I discover the weakness I hid within me for so many years now. The ambushes and open attacks of this world no longer hurt me, but I haven't the strength to resist a warm gaze.

⌘   ⌘   ⌘

Chrysanthemum says that the next time she marries she definitely wants a church wedding ceremony. Although she hasn't the slightest idea what religion is all about, she has a special fascination for the wedding ceremonies she sees in the movies. Every time the pastor on the screen asks the groom, "Are you willing to love her forever, whether in wealth or in poverty, or in sickness or in health?" she is so moved that tears stream down her face. Instantly her normally sultry expression disappears as if it never existed and she is as enchanting as the purest angel.

She once loved a married man, someone who was rich and successful, and she wanted to be his bride. So she went to the Lama Temple to burn incense and to the North Church on Ganwashi Street to sing "Alleluia," a Buddhist rosary on her wrist and a chain with a cross on it hung around her neck. For the first time in so many years, she had met a man worth talking marriage to. It was also the heaviest blow she ever suffered in a lost love. But she still has not abandoned her dream of someday having her own church wedding ceremony.

Chrysanthemum likes successful men and doesn't see this as vulgar snobbery. She says that every cell on a successful man's body just glows. But men who are beaten down and frustrated by life she finds as stifling as the air during the plum rains. Without a shred of pity she runs away from one plum rain season to another, including that husband of hers who made her love him so much she slashed her own wrist.

If she ever really does stand in church beside a groom who is both rich and in good health, she would say to the pastor with teardrops in her eyes, "I am willing" to love him forever, whether in poverty or wealth, or in sickness or health. She is entranced by the solemnity of religion. She doesn't realize that when you stand in front of God, "one promise is worth a thousand pieces of gold." But just let the day come when he is no longer wealthy or in good health, she'd say he isn't lovable anymore, or that he's turned into something hideous. She'd have a hundred reasons for leaving him.

2.

A GARAGE CONVERTED into a cabin was my home in Lompoc. It was also Chaofan's studio. It was as if he had decided to pitch camp here and bury himself in composing. He believed that a "foreign Bo Le"[43] would surely one day discover "a thousand league horse" in him.

Our landlords were an old retired couple. They'd tell everyone they met that their new tenant was "a great artist" and they were delighted no end to have such wonderful music to keep them company in their lonely twilight years.

Several years before, I had esteemed my husband even more than did this honest and simple old couple, almost to the point of adoration. Every day our Beijing home had plenty of "wonderful music." Even if he played just some casual little piece, I could easily listen to it a hundred times without feeling bored. But Lompoc's "garage music" felt like a dish of vegetables that you had to force yourself to swallow, and it was loathsome to me in the extreme.

After slaving away at my job all day long, I would drag my heavy feet to our home, and see the thread of light shining out from behind the doorframe. This late at night he still had his earphones on and was fiddling with the synthesizer. I would then sit down a ways off beside someone's flower bed and savor the bitterness of these wretched, poverty-stricken days. My inner balance was gone. I'd rather linger on the street than go home and share the joys of his composing. I wished the light in the doorframe would go out and that he would fall into sweet slumber. Then I would grope my way into the room without saying a word, and close my eyes

---

[43] Bo Le was a legendary judge of superior horses and could identify one able to run a thousand leagues.

till tomorrow and another day of toil. And I would still be slaving away on all the tomorrows after tomorrow. I saw no hope. I simply didn't believe that any "foreign Bo Le" would appear. How many times had I thought about unplugging the electricity and bringing him back to reality by saying, "You should get a job. Even if it's washing dishes or pushing a broom, it'd be worth more than your art!" I knew that were such words to come out, it would be the total collapse of everything. Though I still didn't want to go down that road, every day I gave myself a reason for leaving Lompoc and this husband who could never again give me a happy life. I could find over a hundred more reasons.

After Xiaoli and her husband, who had stayed behind in China, had divorced, she rushed off to marry a white man, an engineer. To attend her wedding, I pulled all my clothes out from the dresser and trunks and scattered them on the pallet we used for a bed. I tried this one and that, but they were all things I had brought over from China and none were appropriate for the occasion. After almost one year in America, I hadn't spent one cent on clothes or cosmetics. *What kind of days had these been? How could I have fallen so low?* Flinging away the clothes I was holding, I threw myself down sobbing on the messed-up pallet.

Chaofan stopped what he was doing and turning toward me, said coldly, "There's no reason for you to be so brokenhearted. You're still young enough to be someone's bride again."

I tightly covered my mouth to keep myself from speaking. A whole chain of words that could maim and kill were right on my tongue. Even if the whole lot poured out they wouldn't have plumbed the depths of my disappointment. I knew that deep inside him, he felt the same too. He probably missed that violinist. She had been secretly helping him out all along by forever sending him all kinds of musical material and equipment he needed for composing. That synthesizer, worth more than $10,000, was one of the things she had sent.

I bought myself some new clothes and makeup, and, all bright and fresh looking, stood prettily beside the bride. When Xiaoli and her newly appointed husband slipped the rings on each other's finger, I could no longer hold back the tears. I could feel that pair of feet inside me chafing to run off from my own marriage.

As always I labored and toiled away at my job. And with each passing day I was mentally traveling farther and farther away. At night I often still sat by myself along the road, counting all the reasons I had for leaving.

I don't possess Chrysanthemum's candor. I have never dared admit to myself that I also love successful men. *This* man, though, could no longer satisfy even the least of my vanities, so I was going to leave him. Rather hypocritically, I always made myself out to be the innocent one.

⌘   ⌘   ⌘

We would often run into the same old couple in front of the coffee shop that Chrysanthemum patronized. The old fellow pedaled a little cab in which his old wife sat. In the summertime they would be out riding around just for the fun of it, and in the winter, to take in the sunlight. The two of them chattered on and on with each other. Separated by the glass wall, Chrysanthemum stared at them as in a trance. "How do you suppose they could be inseparable for a whole lifetime?" I thought, *because they didn't know that a marital relationship can be abandoned. They are just like my grandmother, who never imagined that she could get another husband in place of Grandpa. My grandfather was impoverished half his life, but in Grandma's eyes he would always be the noblest and best head of the household there could be.*

3.

A WHITE MAN will say to his wife, "I love you," and send her flowers. Every Valentine's Day, Xiaoli would receive flowers and a card with tender and affectionate words on it from her husband. But even during their honeymoon, Xiaoli suspected she had married the wrong guy. For many years, there would always be a few days in every month when she thought seriously about getting divorced. Every month, the two of them had to spend a lot of time sitting at their big round dining table doing the accounts. The table would be covered with credit card statements. After separating the billings that he himself had to pay, her husband would always very generously select a billing for some dinner out together or a charge from the supermarket. "Here, this'll be my treat." Thoughts of divorce would always flare up in her every time he said this, like an overgrowth of weeds making her mind run wild. Her husband never knew the anger in his Chinese wife's heart at moments like those. Plucking up the voucher for that "treat," tender-eyed, he would wait for her exaggerated expression, "Oh my dear, that's so kind of you. I love you."

When the U.S. economy slumped one year, Xiaoli's company went under and she lost her job. So she packed up her personal effects at the office and brought them home. When she walked in the door she threw herself into her husband's arms and told him about losing her job and said she might not be able to get another one. Her husband's mild and gentle gaze never changed and he caressed her hair. "Don't worry. You can borrow from me." He kept kissing her teary eyes, and then added, "You don't have to pay your share of the mortgage this month." The house had been purchased with a loan and every month Xiaoli had to hand over several hundred dollars for the mortgage. Her husband waited for her tears of gratitude, but to his surprise Xiaoli shoved him away from her. "Let's just divorce, OK?" This white husband thought the shock had unhinged his wife.

Over the next two or so years, I had no news whatsoever from Xiaoli. When I did run into her again, she hadn't divorced after all. She said this was because "she had found another love." At a low ebb of her life, she had walked into a church not far from where she lived. That evening the church choir was rehearsing Christmas carols and the unaccompanied choral singing was just so beautiful. She never knew that the human voice could make such wondrous sounds. She felt transcended and purified, and before she knew it, tears were streaming down her face. The choir director noticed this Oriental woman, and walking over, brought her up to the choir loft. And so this was how Xiaoli became enthralled by hymn singing and how she began her "love affair" with God.

I couldn't see the god that Xiaoli loved so deeply, but I did see that over these years she indeed was like a woman who was perfectly satisfied in this affair. She was sparkling and radiant with joy. She still sat down regularly with her husband to split up the bills. But she no longer got angry.

⌘　⌘　⌘

I brought the divorce agreement signed by Chaofan back with me to Beijing. But because I couldn't find our marriage certificate, I wasn't able to register our divorce at the courthouse. I thought I would wait until I remarried before going through all those complex legal procedures. That day has yet to arrive. I've tried hard to get married again, and even registered at a matchmaking center.

I received computer "matches" and again and again went out on the blind dates, full of curiosity and hope. And again and again I would return home disappointed. I don't remember which blind date it was, but afterward I went right back to the matchmaking center and told them to delete my personal data from their computer.

Xiaoli said everyone has flaws and that a person's love is always conditional. If this person's just too mean-spirited for you, you might end up changing him for someone who's even more unbearable. Only God is perfect. God's love is unconditional.

I don't know "God," and deep inside I don't believe "God" exists. But I am obsessed with the idea of being loved unconditionally and I long with the fervor of a religious believer to love a man who has no flaws. I'm looking...I'm waiting...

CHAPTER FOURTEEN – NEW HEAVEN, NEW EARTH

1.

A GIRL SOFT and gentle, restrained and reserved, still not betrothed, and living in her maiden's chamber…and then, overnight, a communist bride. This was Old Town in the summer of 1949.

Much of Old Town was totally in the dark about what was happening. Now the word spread all around West Gate that the communist army from the north was linking up with the guerrilla band at Old Ridge. They were consolidating their strength and awaiting orders as they prepared to attack Old Town. People supposed that bloody street fighting would bring the war right to their doorsteps. The timid and conservative city folk all showed surprising initiative in readying food and water. Then they shut their doors and gates and quietly awaited the arrival of the new era.

Dr. Lin and Pastor Chen had discussed what they would do. The moment gunfire sounded, the West Gate church would become the first aid station for the areas of combat. The doctor had already placed inside the church all the emergency medicine, supplies, and instruments that they would require.

This evening, Second Sister locked the gate from the inside, picked up her sewing basket and sat in the main parlor. She was standing night watch, listening closely for any movement by Baosheng and Baoqing. She hadn't invited her husband to be an ally in her "protect the calves" campaign, and so Ninth Brother groggily stepped out of the bedroom to call Second Sister to come to sleep. She told him she was rushing to make some baby clothes in advance of Fourth Sister's month-long confinement.

As the night wore on, Second Sister was overcome by fatigue and she dozed with the sewing still in her hands. Suddenly the front door creaked and she woke up in a fright to see Baosheng about to go out, taking Baoqing with him. Running after them, she scolded, "Go back! Get back to your own rooms!"

Pulling Baoqing along as he moved out the gate, Baosheng said, "Ma. Daybreak is coming! Don't worry anymore!"

And, with that, her two sons dashed past her and disappeared into the blackness of the night.

Once again Ninth Brother awoke from his dreams, and, groping his way into the parlor, discovered Second Sister's sewing basket fallen on the floor and the front door wide open. Second Sister's figure was standing motionless as a statue outside the doorway under the oleander. He approached and took hold of her arm. "Just stop worrying and come to bed now."

"How can I possibly sleep?"

"What should or shouldn't happen is beyond us."

In the darkness tears rolled down Second Sister's face. She couldn't pour out to her husband all the worries filling her heart. She knew that Ninth Brother would just reason with her by saying things like "If we allow ourselves to get worried and anxious it means we don't trust in the God we worship."

Husband and wife went back into the house. Second Sister put some more oil in the lamp and resumed sewing. Ninth Brother sat silently by her side. When light appeared in the sky and roosters began crowing all around the neighborhood, neither of them had said a single word.

⌘   ⌘   ⌘

The early morning at West Gate was as peaceful as ever. As Baohua stood on the steps under the sky well lazily brushing her teeth, her alcoholic uncle came in, a liquor bottle in his hand.

"Oh, Baohua! How come you're still at home? The students are all out on the streets greeting the communists. Didn't you know?"

Baohua rinsed out her mouth. "Uncle, there's nothing for you to drink here, not one drop."

The eldest son of the Guo family pointed the bottle straight at Baohua's nose. "The communists have arrived! This liquor now tastes again like it used to. Here, have a sniff. Now that's real liquor!"

Baohua pushed the bottle away. "When the communists get here you're going to have to swear off drinking!"

"Impossible!"

Then he sat right down in the parlor and as he drank from the bottle he nodded his head in time to a little tune he hummed.

Second Sister came out of the kitchen and was surprised to see her brother there. "There's going to be fighting, and here you are, still gadding about!"

"Fighting? Who's fighting?"

"The communists are already at Old Ridge and are about to come down to attack us!"

Her brother exploded with laughter. "Second Sister, all you people out in the sticks here in West Gate, you didn't get the news. At this very moment, the heavens above already belong to the communists!"

Second Sister peered up through the sky well. The sky was very blue and wisps of clouds were slowly scudding by. It looked no different from yesterday.

"Oh, you! So early in the day and you're so drunk you have no idea of what's going on around you. Go right home and tell my sister-in-law to store away a few bottles of liquor. In a couple of days, if they start fighting, the wine shops will be closed, and then what would you do?"

Her brother laughed all the louder and the drink in his mouth went spraying all over. "Second Sister, you don't drink but you're the one who's really all fuddled. The communists have already taken over the government offices at Drum Tower. Go downtown and take a look. There's a whole sea of people there just waiting to greet the communists!"

Doubtfully, Second Sister looked at her brother and then abruptly turned around and shouted, "Ninth Brother, the communists are already here in our Old Town!"

Ninth Brother walked out of the clinic. At the same moment he heard young people passing by the door saying that Old Town was liberated. In such a flash of time had the new heaven and the new earth arrived.

"Liquor knows best of all. When times turn bad, it turns into stuff that tastes plainer than water. Poor me, drinking water all these years and only now smelling the aroma of liquor. For just this reason alone, I'm going to raise both hands and welcome the communists!"

This oldest son of the Guos hugged the liquor bottle as if it were a dear one who had gone through the separation and the chaos of war. Joy and sorrow mixed together had him all choked up.

Second Sister glanced at Ninth Brother and saw that he too seemed ready to break into tears. She had no idea what the communist heaven would look like and couldn't comprehend why her husband and children longed so much for the new era, but she clearly heard a voice within her say, "Second Sister, your family will be at peace from now on." That heart of hers, tightly compressed by cares and worries, little by little unclenched and relaxed. A totally strange kind of fatigue came over her. She limply sank down and slumped over the table, her eyes closed and she fell fast asleep.

Her brother stretched his neck back and drained the last few drops of liquor from the bottle and wandered off muttering and mumbling.

The house was absolutely quiet. Ninth Brother stood beside his wife, staring at a patch of the blue, blue sky above a corner of the sky well. Inside he felt all stirred up and at the same time, a sense of doubt. *Is this true? Has the communist era begun with such peace and quiet?*

Impulsively, the doctor thought of going to the East Street intersection to see for himself just what was happening. He went to his daughter's room. Baohua was just then revising her assignment in preparation for her application to the teachers' college.

"Baohua, the communists have come to our Old Town."

Pencil in her hand, she leaned back to look at her daddy. The radiant smile now on her daddy's face showed a childlike innocence. He was truly happy today. "Daddy, when did you join the Communist Party?" she teased him. "And how come I never knew about it?"

"Communism is good. Everyone is equal. Everyone has work, and food to eat. This is the spirit of Jesus."

Baohua thought of Enchun. Had he returned to Old Town? Then immediately she thought of that girl from the teachers' college who had been together with Enchun. Baohua felt a dull ache within her. She forced herself to smile at her father, and then lowered her head and continued with her reading.

The doctor reached out and took away the book. "Daughter, today is not for reading books. Come on, let's both go over to East Street. We too should make a brief appearance, wouldn't you say?"

He took her by the arm out through the gate. The two of them were still on West Street when they heard the sound of drums, gongs, and firecrackers loud enough to split the heavens.

The doctor stopped where he was and like some demented person shouted, "It's true! It's true! It's *true!*"

At Drum Tower the streets were mobbed with people and Baohua and her daddy got separated along the way. Like a little loach, her slight figure wriggled with ease into the middle of the area. Then she saw with her own eyes the tawny uniforms of the communist soldiers. They had come from out of the north like a surging tidal wave. Every face under a military hat was Enchun, for she believed that he was in their midst. Even though she had vowed countless times to forget him, this moment of inner agitation inevitably gave rise to flights of fancy. She fantasized she saw Enchun stride out of the ranks of the communists, and grasping her, say, "Baohua, the world is at peace now. I can go back to school and resume my studies." In total contrast to her normally shy aloofness, she couldn't help following the citizens of Old Town along the side of the road, whooping and cheering together with them in the general jubilation.

The tawny uniformed ranks gradually receded into the distance. A lion dance commenced at the street intersection by Drum Tower and the sound of gongs, drums, and firecrackers kept on and on. Baohua's whole head was drenched in sweat as she squeezed her way out. She wanted to go to the West Gate church to ask for news of Enchun.

At this very moment, Dr. Lin was in the church together with Pastor Chen writing slogans on brightly colored paper: "Love the Lord, Love the Communist Party," "God Bless and Protect Communism."

Mrs. Chen was standing on a bench polishing the church windows, helped by a fellow congregant who rinsed the cleaning cloths. This person said to her, "Your young prince has rendered a great service to the Communist Party. He's going to be a high official in the new government and that's for sure."

"Our son loves the Communist Party just as we Christians love Jesus. But he doesn't seek for his own interests. When communism has succeeded, his ideals will be realized. Maybe he'll just teach school out by the seaside for the rest of his life."

Baohua stood behind them and just when she was just about to address her auntie, the helper asked, "Your prince should now be at the right age for marrying. Have you all approached anyone about this?"

Deng, deng, deng, pounded Baohua's heart wildly, and the fire in her cheeks spread right to the tips of her ears. She expected Mrs. Chen to say that they thought highly of the Lin family's "thousand gold pieces."

The pastor's wife stood on her tiptoes as she polished the glass. "These are new times. It's no longer the fashion for the parents to arrange everything in marriage. We haven't had news from him for a very long time. Everything's been put into God's hands."

"Maybe the day will come when your prince will return home, bringing along your daughter-in-law and their children."

The mother chuckled happily at that and turned to look out the window, as if little grandchildren just learning to walk were tottering toward her.

Seeing the happy smile on Mrs. Chen's face, Baohua pictured Enchun and that girl student from the teacher's college coming in from the other side of the wooden fence carrying their children.

They would be unaware of her presence. Just like at this very moment, when everybody was busily coming in and going out and unable to see her. This made her feel extremely sorry for herself. She went over to the well beside the church door, leaned over and stared at her own reflection. The image of the girl floating on the surface of the water was so delicate and pretty. Looking at her you would think she was a sixth-grade student. No one would believe she was already a big girl of seventeen or eighteen. The entire neighborhood around West Gate saw her as the "little one" of the house, and even her two younger brothers humored her as they would a younger sister.

Totally dispirited, Baohua turned from her reflection and, rocking back and forth on her feet as she stood up, she found her gaze directed toward the far-distant mountain peaks. She thought, "I'm going to do something that will amaze everyone!"

Two months later, Baohua really did do something that utterly confounded everyone's impressions of her.

2.

WHEN THE COMMUNIST army came down from Old Ridge, the Guomindang's Youth Corps organized a withdrawal of the students of Old Town's two technical colleges to Taiwan. These students were now waiting at the docks of the fishing harbor for boats to take them there.

Late that night, the bookshop owner, whose identity as the local department head of the Communist Party's ministry of youth work had already surfaced, rushed to the harbor, taking with him a group of progressive young people to persuade the students to return to their homes.

The two Lin brothers were told to quickly get in the group at the head of the West Floodwater Bridge. Beyond the bridge was a market town, and beyond that was the bay. There, by the side of the dock were some twenty or thirty small vessels packed with students. A number of other students had already been taken to the small island opposite the harbor. The students didn't know that a life of exile was now beginning and that hereafter they would forever be separated in life and death from their families.

In one night, the boss of the rice shop at West Gate lost two sons who had been studying at the technical college. Then, after enduring more than twenty years of bitter waiting, he and his wife both hung themselves. Many years later, the two sons returned to Old Town. They knelt right there in the street in front of the door of the rice shop, wailing and lamenting. There was no one at West Gate, man, woman or child, old or young, who failed to shed tears at this scene.

❋ ❋ ❋

Baoqing went aboard a pitching and rocking small boat. Following his leader's instructions, he cupped his hands around his mouth and shouted at the students. "Old Town has been peacefully liberated! There won't be any fighting! Whatever you do, don't go into exile with the Guomindang! Just go home! Your parents are waiting there for you!"

He didn't know that at the other end of the craft, the boatman was already moving the scull. The students in the boat were all bigger than he was and nobody paid much attention to what this boy was shouting.

On this evening the wind was in their favor and the boat moved fast. Baoqing shouted and shouted. Then abruptly he turned his head and discovered how far away he now was from the docks. He ran from the prow to the stern of the boat to find Baosheng and figure out what to do. When he realized that his older brother wasn't on this boat, he felt totally helpless. "Uncle, I want to go home. My ma is waiting for me," he said mournfully to the boatman.

"Just sit down in the boat nice and quiet and wait for me to send the students to the island there, then I'll take you back home," the boatman replied.

"No! If I don't go back with my older brother, my ma will be worried crazy!"

Baoqing' face was all twisted up and he was just on the point of tears. The students sitting behind him let out a roar of laughter.

With the wind behind it, the little boat scudded along in good time. The docks of the fishing harbor were now far off in the gray first light of dawn. Baoqing stood frozen there beside the boatman. He thought of his mother's worry-filled eyes. He thought of that nightmare when his sister had been kidnapped and sold in Nanjing County several years before. *No! I can't let my mother suffer another shock.* He went to the side of the boat and looked down at the billowing waves and then again at the distant docks. He took a deep breath of air and threw himself over the side. But just as he was in midair, the boatman grabbed hold of him by his collar and flung him back onto the deck.

"You want to die, huh? Jump in and let the fish eat you up so that there won't even be one bone left for your ma?"

Baoqing rolled over and sprang up from the deck. "Uncle, when can you bring me back home?" he pleaded.

"The quickest would be tomorrow afternoon. But if a storm comes up, it's hard to say."

Baoqing lowered his head dispiritedly and for the very first time he thought of God and of praying for a safe return home. He remembered his mother teaching him that when he prayed he had to say "In the name of Jesus the Lord."

Suddenly, a girl student stood up in the middle of the boat and came over to Baoqing. "Baoqing! Are you Baoqing?"

Baoqing looked blankly at this pretty student. *I haven't even started praying yet and God is already showing his powers?*

"Baoqing, I'm Baolan."

Imagine meeting one's own relative in the midst of danger! Much against his will, Baoqing's eyes filled with hot tears.

Baolan was his cousin, the only daughter of his father's third brother. She had distinguished herself by her intelligence ever since she was little, and she excelled in chess, calligraphy, painting, and plucking the *qin*. Even in grade school her writings were frequently published in Old Town's afternoon news. The children in Dr. Lin's family greatly admired this gifted female scholar-cousin of theirs, though these past two years they hadn't seen much of her. Now the two cousins were on the same small boat and had almost not recognized each other.

"Baoqing, how come you've jumped on board this boat?"

Baoqing remembered his mission and hastily drew himself up with as much dignity as he could muster. "Baolan, sister! Old Town has now been peacefully liberated! Whatever you do, don't go to Taiwan with the Youth Corps! If you do, you'll never see Third Uncle and Third Aunt again!"

Baolan gazed transfixed at the water. She had left Old Town only yesterday afternoon and by the time the evening skies darkened she was already feeling homesick. She had always been somewhat lacking in animal vitality. All year round her hands and feet would stay cold. Every evening her mother heated up a pan of water for her to put her feet into, and she would sit there reading a book as her feet warmed up in the hot water. She would do this until her whole body was glowing with heat and only then blow out the lamp and go to bed.

Baolan went back among her schoolmates. "How come I've got the feeling something's not quite right? The school brought us out to escape danger. If there really had been fighting and chaos and we needed to seek refuge somewhere, we ought to have been with our parents and families. If we now go away for a few months, or even a few years, and can't get back, then what?"

Baolan had a lot of influence among her schoolmates. The words she just spoke were like drops of water falling into a red-hot frying pan, for they burst like bombshells on board the vessel.

Taking advantage of the changed situation, Baoqing came up and fanned the flames: "Peaceful liberation! No fighting! Let's hurry back home! Don't, whatever you do, go with them to Taiwan!"

Somebody shouted at the boatman, "Turn around and go back!"

The boatman let go of the scull. "Think hard now. There's still time to go back, if you want to."

Baolan raised her hand. "I've decided to go back!"

A male student who was then pursuing Baolan immediately raised his hand to follow suit. Out of twenty or thirty students, the majority clearly indicated that they wanted to return home. The rest of them mostly had come from other places to study in Old Town and as far as they were concerned, it didn't matter where they went.

The boatman furled the lofty sail, and with a laugh took Baoqing by the ear. "Little brother, today you can go back home to pout and make eyes at your ma!"

⌘　⌘　⌘

Nor was it at all peaceful for Baosheng on his boat. A Youth Corps student pushed him off the boat, and Baosheng, thrusting himself out of the water, grabbed him and pulled him in, and the two of them grappled with each other in the shallow depth next to the dock. As they tussled fiercely, Baosheng realized that their boat was moving and, breaking free of his opponent, turned and climbed back on board. Then he dashed over to the boatman and tightly grabbed hold of the moving scull. The Youth Corps student, following close behind, now rushed forward and the two of them began pushing and shoving. The vessel rocked back and forth like a cradle and the female students on board shrieked in terror.

The boatman watched in bemusement as the fierce struggle went on in front of him. He didn't know what was going on in the outside world. Over the last few months the people of the fishing villages no longer put out to sea for fishing but were busily transporting people and cargo to that small island opposite them where big cargo ships waited to take them on to Taiwan. While the several dozen small craft of the fishing villages were thus sculling back and forth, did no one give a thought to what this was all about? The dynasties come and go, but these people whose livelihood was the sea never changed from one generation to the next.

No one knew whose blows first drew blood, but now that the faces of these two students fighting each other were streaked with it, the boatman saw this as bad luck. People like these fishermen whose lives depended on the sea were very superstitious. In such villages, every household worshipped Guanyin Bodhisattva and believed that she manifested her divine powers at sea. Every time before setting out, the whole household would burn incense to Mother Guanyin and kneel in prayer beseeching her for a safe voyage. No one could say or do anything that was inauspicious and the sight of blood was inauspicious to the extreme. So without the slightest warning the boatman exploded in rage, and with a great roar pulled apart the two students and thrust them aside. Baosheng and that other student each fell overboard from either side of the boat.

At this time, there were boats continuously returning to harbor. Those young people still standing around at the bay swarmed down to the shore. One of the boatmen shouted out, "Don't! Don't go! Soldiers are going to seal this place off. Once they do that, we won't be able to get back home!"

When Baosheng once again pulled himself back on board, the vessel had already cast anchor near the shore.

⌘　⌘　⌘

Grandma said she slept right through Liberation. She never knew how she got from the parlor to the bedroom, nor did she remember waking up several times during that period. The one thing she clearly remembered was that long and gentle dream of her father. He seemed to be holding a little child. He held her on his knees and said, "Second Sister, you are my good daughter." She wanted to look around and see her father's face clearly, but for some reason she wasn't able to do this. Grandma guessed that was her Father in heaven whom she would someday meet face-to-face.

That evening, Second Sister opened her eyes in a tumult of sounds. The house had always been quiet. Such loud noise was against the rules of a home "fragrant with books," as the dwellings of the scholar-gentry were often described. Off and on she heard a lot of terms like "communism," "revolution across the land," and "liberate the entire people." *Had Baosheng and his revolutionary party friends come home to hold a meeting here? The voices are so loud...aren't they afraid of getting their heads chopped off? This child is getting bolder all the time.* She hurriedly put on her jacket and going outside, was surprised to see Ninth Brother sitting animatedly in the midst of a group of young people. She also saw that the front gate was wide open, and panic-stricken she rushed out to bar it shut.

When Baolan shouted out, "Ninth Aunt," it took awhile for Second Sister to recognize her. "Baolan, are you a communist too?" Then she rushed over to Baosheng. "Your third uncle's family has only this one daughter, Baolan. If..."

Baosheng laughed. "Ma, there's no need for 'if.' This is Liberation now!"

"Liberation" was a new term. Second Sister pondered long and hard over what it might imply.

Ninth Brother couldn't keep from bursting out laughing. "Look at you! Sleeping like that right from one dynasty to the next!"

She vaguely recalled—was it yesterday? Or the day before?— her drunk of a brother arriving to say that the communists had taken over Old Town's government.

Baoqing guided his mother to a place where she could sit down. "Ma, good times, peaceful times, have begun. From now on you'll never have to worry again."

Baolan told her ninth aunt all about what happened the night before last out in the bay. "If Baoqing had not dropped out of the skies like that, I don't know when I would ever have been able to see Ninth Uncle and Ninth Aunt again."

Second Sister gave a stunned look at Baoqing. "What were you doing going out to sea? Heavens! If that boat had been unwilling to turn back...

Reaching beneath the table, Baoqing gave a few tugs on the end of Baolan's jacket as he interrupted his mother. "Aren't I all right now, sitting here right beside you, without having lost a single hair on my head?"

The children went on talking all about the new "dynasty." She couldn't understand what they were saying. After a while she felt sleepy again and started yawning. Ninth Brother led her to the bedroom to go to sleep.

⌘　⌘　⌘

All during that period, my grandmother suffered from what medical science calls "hypnopathia." Day and night, she was overcome by an extreme lethargy. It was as if a machine that had been overloaded for a whole year long just fell apart the moment it stopped operating. When the doctor, my grandpa, was at wits end on how to deal with this, he just quietly took up doing the housework. He began by going into the kitchen to learn how to light up the oven. Later on, the breakfast we ate at home was always done by him, right up until that time of his life when he could no longer get out of bed. On the occasions when he had nothing in particular to do, he would sit by the bed gazing at his wife in her deep slumber. Scene after scene from the silent movies played before his eyes: Second Sister anxiously watching for that fat postman, Second Sister bearing up the young and the old of her family in their wartime flight, Second Sister standing on the ruins of the Lin ancestral residence, now destroyed by Japanese bombs. All this was another kind of exchange between him and his wife. His heart overflowed with love and gratitude. *Such a good woman...such a good wife. Thanks be for this favor from on high.* He began to think about which of them might leave this world first, and more than once with tears in his eyes did he say to his Heavenly Father, "If we can't return to the Kingdom Come together as man and wife, then just let me go first." A life without Second Sister was simply inconceivable for him. He begged his Heavenly Father to forgive his weakness and selfishness.

Grandma's hypnopathia lasted until that year's Mid-Autumn Festival. From the middle part of August when Old Town had been peacefully liberated, she was in her state of hibernation for more than two whole months. During this period, Dr. Lin reregistered his clinic business, Baosheng began work in the regional government as a political cadre, and Baohua passed her entrance exam at the teachers' training college. Baoqing, who just kept on skipping grades, entered the commercial college—becoming the youngest student there in its entire history. The weather was favorable and crops were abundant. The beautiful peace of every aspect of Lin household life was more than they had imagined possible. Every day my grandmother and grandfather expressed their gratitude and blessings for the new society.

3·

ON THE MORNING of the Mid-Autumn Festival, my mother, Baohua, her book bag on her back, passed the West Gate church on her way to school. As she had the habit of doing, she slowed her steps. Every day at this time the pastor's wife would be in the yard clipping the flowers and plants in her garden and Baohua would always stand on the other side of the fence to greet Mrs. Chen.

"Good morning, Auntie!"

"Good morning to you, Baohua!" Mrs. Chen cut several gorgeous red roses and passed these across the fence to Baohua. "It's Mid-Autumn Festival today. Here are some flowers for you to give to your teachers."

Baohua brought the roses to her nose to smell their fragrance and as she looked up to thank her, suddenly her expression totally changed. She saw Huang Shuyi. Huang Shuyi was sitting on the steps of the church lost in thought. And right then Baohua also saw through the church window the form of Enchun quickly passing by.

So Enchun really had brought a daughter-in-law back home!

Baohua wanted to go in to confront and embarrass him, but she turned around and ran off.

"Oh, Baohua, your big brother Enchun is back. Come over this evening for a reunion dinner at Auntie's house."

The pastor's wife had her head buried in the plants and flowers and she went on speaking for quite a bit before she realized that Baohua was nowhere to be seen. She stood up and gazed far off into the distance, then turned around and looked Huang Shuyi up and down. *The girl's face has distress written all over it. Is she going to go on being so distressed and anxious?*

The night before, Enchun had brought Huang Shuyi home with him and explained to his parents that the two of them were "comrades in the Revolution." And as Huang Shuyi now had no home in Old Town, he asked if they could spare some small corner as a place where she might stay. In the middle of the night, Mrs. Chen heard the girl sobbing in the guest room. Carrying an oil lamp, the woman went to her son's bedside. "Enchun, you and the girl Huang have been together in the Revolution for two or three years now. I know you have been together day and night. If you are guilty of any transgression, neither I nor your father will blame you for it. Only, you are going to have to take responsibility for your own actions. You have to be responsible for the girl Huang." After a long pause, Enchun, his arms wrapped around his knees, replied, "Ma, I have committed no transgression, but my conscience tells me to reach out and help her. She is all alone in the world now. A year ago, the brother she most looked up to and loved died unjustly."

"How are you thinking of helping her?" asked Mrs. Chen. "Will you marry her?"

Enchun gravely nodded his head. His mother left her son's room and roused the pastor from his slumbers. Then the two of them prayed for Enchun.

They didn't know all the ins and outs of what had happened, only that their hearts were filled with doubt and misgivings. From the very beginning these two children had risked their lives in joining the Communist Party. Now, to general acclaim, the Communist Party was in control of all under heaven. So why did these two now seem so care-ridden?

The whole West Gate neighborhood said that Enchun had done great things for the Communist Party. The pastor and his wife had not hoped their son would return to his home a high official and with all that went with it, only that he would be happy and at peace. But when they looked at his face they saw neither peace nor happiness.

Mrs. Chen had cut a few exuberant chrysanthemums and was going to call Enchun to go with them to pay a call on the doctor, when glancing around she saw Huang Shuyi wiping tears from her eyes.

"Shuyi, are you thinking of your family?"

Huang Shuyi looked blankly at her for a moment and then hastily wiping her tears with a handkerchief, said, "Oh. No."

"From now on, Enchun's home is your home too. His father and I will consider you our own daughter."

Mrs. Chen put down the flowers and the clippers and was going to take the girl into a warm embrace, but to her surprise Huang Shuyi stood up with a cold and forbidding expression on her face. "Auntie, my parents belonged to the exploiting class. I and my older brother broke off completely from them several years ago. If they were still living in Old Town I would deliver them myself to the judgment of the people's court."

A shiver coursed through Mrs. Chen's heart. She had by now realized that the new society talked about class struggle and she and the pastor were trying hard to understand this principle of the Communist Party. However, whenever they met with a specific example affecting someone or something, she still could not accept it. Now worry for her son began to grow in her. If he married this cold and rigid girl, what would his future be like?

⌘　⌘　⌘

The pastor's wife did not pick up the chrysanthemums she had placed on the church steps but with a heavy heart just walked over to the doctor's house. She forgot that she was a messenger of God. At this moment she was only an ordinary mother, a mother who saw the dangers latent in her son's fate. A sense of wanting to help but being unable to do so bore down heavily on her.

The doctor's clinic was very busy. Patients filled all the available space on the benches. Mrs. Lin had just gotten up and eaten breakfast and was beginning to feel tired all over again. The pastor's wife sat at the Lins' Eight Immortals table for a while. She mentioned Enchun's return rather flatly and invited all the Lins to join in the reunion dinner and to enjoy the Mid-Autumn moonlight that evening in the churchyard. Mrs. Lin accepted enthusiastically. She didn't see the worry or anxiety on Mrs. Chen's face. How could there be anything to be worried about in these peaceful and prosperous times?

⌘　⌘　⌘

That day, Baohua skipped classes and just scuffled aimlessly along the streets, her book bag on her back. A thought grew in her mind, joint by joint, like spring bamboo shoots after rain, and was almost about to burst through her skull. *I'm going to leave West Gate, and I'm going to leave Old Town!*

She went to the army recruiting office, right by the main gate of the city government at Drum Tower. Behind several long tables sat some soldiers. In front of each table stood a little card on which was written the name of a particular military region. She mingled with the bustling crowd of people there and lingered around the various tables: Nanjing Military Region, Changchun Military Region, Lanzhou Military Region... She had studied geography and she knew where these places were located within the territorial domain of China. The Xinjiang Military Region table had the fewest people of all standing beside it. Baohua stopped right there, quickly locating Xinjiang on the map spread out in her brain. Old Town was on the southeast coast, Xinjiang was on the northwest frontier. There was nowhere farther away than Xinjiang.

A worker in a military uniform said to Baohua, "Little girl, what grade are you in at school? How come you're not there studying now?"

Baohua squinted angrily at him and kept on staring at the card on which was written "Xinjiang Military Region." An irresistible mystique and allure caused a burning feeling in her chest. She imagined returning to West Gate in uniform and announcing to everyone that she was going with a great military force to Xinjiang! She saw Enchun's glasses falling to the ground and one after another of the funny, wide-eyed and tongue-tied faces. This was the effect she craved, even in her sleep.

"I want to enlist," Baohua said, enunciating each word clearly and distinctly.

"How old are you?"

"Eighteen."

"Little girl, your revolutionary enthusiasm is extremely praiseworthy. But you're too young. Study for two years more and when you've reached lower high school, then come back and talk about enlisting."

Baohua said with great seriousness, "I am a student at the Teachers' Training College and I want to be a soldier and go to Xinjiang!"

The three military people sitting on the other side of the table glanced at each other, and one of them, looking rather incredulous, slid a form over to Baohua.

⌘　⌘　⌘

Late in the evening, it was already very merry and lively in the churchyard. Dr. and Mrs. Lin had arrived neatly attired. Mrs. Chen had also invited some of the lonely old people of the neighborhood, including the rice shop boss and his wife. Baosheng and Baoqing had rushed over much earlier to see Enchun. Baohua's absence went unnoticed.

The well-intentioned doctor was earnestly comforting the couple from the rice shop. He said the communists had come down to Old Town from the north for only a little more than a year. Now with the recovery of Taiwan clearly imminent, surely next year at this time their sons would be back home. Tears streamed down the face of the rice shop "boss-lady." From the beginning she had been so afraid that the two sons would be beheaded for joining the Communist Party that day and night she never took her eyes off them. Who could have imagined that they would disappear overnight to Taiwan? My grandmother drank tea endlessly. She had to resist with all her might the urge to drop off to sleep. Baosheng and Baoqing crowded around Enchun for great long palavers. Neither of the two brothers realized that Enchun had just suffered a setback that would have been unbearable for any ordinary person.

Huang Shuyi shut herself up in the small room writing out the documents of her appeal. Earlier that day, she and Enchun had gone to the provincial government to find the local head of the Organization Department.[44] Teacher Zhao, who had led them in their underground work, had given up his life in the cause of the Revolution, and now there was no one who could vouch for their earlier entry into the party. When Huang Shuyi mentioned her brother Huang Jian, the department head sternly admonished her

---

[44]   An enormously powerful organ of the Chinese Communist Party Central Committee, responsible for career positions in post-1949 China.

to have faith in the party. He also said she would not be allowed to undertake the overturning of a verdict of a traitor. Huang Shuyi was not intimidated and when she caused a fierce emotional scene, he called in the soldiers on duty to escort her off the premises. Enchun urged her to see that the Revolution had succeeded. "Whether or not our own merits and achievements are recognized is not important. Compared to all those fallen martyrs we are already very fortunate." Gnashing and grinding her teeth, Huang Shuyi stood by the side of the street and vowed that as long as she still had a single breath she would seek to rehabilitate her brother's good name. At the time, she certainly had no idea that this litigation would become her lifelong work and that only after a full thirty-five years would Huang Jian's name be engraved on the Remembrance Tablet at the Martyrs' Cemetery.

Pastor Chen's family still kept the traditions of old Beijing. Anytime there was a festival they wrapped dumplings. The steaming hot dumplings were now brought to the table and their open-air banquet commenced. In the moonlight, the little church courtyard immediately became still and quiet as Pastor Chen stood up by the dining table and said the blessing: "Dear Heavenly Father, we give you thanks for granting us this good life we have. And we thank you for this sumptuous feast..."

Just then, Baohua appeared behind Pastor Chen, head to toe in full military uniform. The pastor's wife had just said "Amen" when she opened her eyes to see a female soldier of the Liberation Army. "Welcome, Liberation Army soldier, and join us in our Mid-Autumn Festival banquet!" Mrs. Chen greeted her in delight.

Her lips pursed in a tight smile, Baohua fixed her stare on Enchun who was sitting directly opposite her.

Enchun's glasses slipped down his nose little by little. "B-B-Baohua?" he stammered.

Baohua plucked off her army hat and shook out two long braids of hair.

The doctor had fished out a dumpling with his chopsticks and was conveying it to Second Sister's plate. He was just about to tell her a funny story about he had wrapped dumplings during a Mid-Autumn Festival back in the army camp in Henan. He had gone to the mess kitchen to help, but he just couldn't get the hang of wrapping them. The few pathetically misshapen dumplings he managed to squeeze together and put in the pot all burst apart, spilling out their meat stuffing. Hearing somebody call out Baohua's name, he didn't pay any attention. He just assumed she had been there all along.

"Ma, Big Sister is a Liberation Army soldier now!" Baoqing yelled.

The doctor turned his head and saw his uniformed daughter. The dumpling clamped between his chopsticks fell onto the table. Then he smiled. *Surely this child is playing a joke.* Normally taciturn, Baohua occasionally played little practical jokes that would take people totally by surprise.

"Baohua, where did you borrow the uniform? It looks very good on you."

"Dad, I've joined the army."

The doctor smiled as he used his chopsticks to pinch up the fallen dumpling. "Very good! 'Hua Mulan Joins the Army.'"[45]

Second Sister looked at her daughter. Suddenly it seemed that a cold wind blew straight into her face. In that instant her lethargy and muddled state of mind were completely gone. Intuition told her this was no joke. A storm was descending on their peaceful and quiet lives. She stood up.

---

[45]   During the Northern Wei dynasty (CE 386–584), the girl Hua Mulan joined the army disguised as her aged father to fight nomadic invaders on the frontier. This beloved tale of filial piety had already been filmed several times in China by the time this Mid-Autumn Festival banquet took place at the West Gate church.

"Baohua, your audacity knows no limit. Such a big matter and you never discussed it with your parents!"

Before Baohua's smiling expression could rearrange itself, tears just rushed down her face.

The doctor laid down his chopsticks. His daughter's tears told him that she wasn't playing any joke. *This really is something unforeseen.* He had never thought that one day Baohua would fly off far away. Now it was his turn to be totally confused.

Second Sister said, "Let's go. I'm taking you to a senior officer of the Liberation Army. Right now! You're not strong enough. You're too delicate. You can't be a soldier."

"Parents can't prevent their children from joining the Revolution!"

Baohua ran home, wiping away her tears.

The doctor guided his wife to a chair. They forced themselves to keep up a cheerful front until the banquet ended so as not to spoil this happy occasion.

⌘　⌘　⌘

All alone in the house, Baohua slumped over the Eight Immortals table weeping. She began to feel the panic and fear of a small child who had unintentionally made a terrible mess of something. Xinjiang was so far off. Her superior officer said that the wheels of a truck setting out from Old Town would roll along for up to two months before they got there. And it was extremely cold in Xinjiang. The moment you weren't careful your nose could fall off from frostbite. A big gate opened wide in front of her. How she hoped that Enchun would come forth from the gathering darkness and say, "My good Baohua, don't be so willful and throw one of your childish tantrums. Huang Shuyi is only my comrade!" If

Enchun did this, Baohua would go back to school the very next day and accede to her father's wishes to be content with staying in Old Town as a primary school teacher.

She yearned for him, but Enchun never appeared. Perhaps this was due to the humiliation of being told just that day that he would not be accepted in the ranks of the Revolution. Maybe his sympathy and worry for Huang Shuyi prevented him from ever again diverting any attention to Baohua. Right up to when Baohua left Old Town with the army, he never came to see her, not even once.

⌘ ⌘ ⌘

After the banquet was over and everybody had gone home, Dr. Lin and his wife paced back and forth irresolutely along the street in front of their house.

"Ninth Brother, no matter what, we have to stop her. The child has gone mad!"

The doctor just continued walking along without saying anything.

Second Sister sensed the struggle going on inside her husband. *Don't tell me he would agree with Baohua becoming a soldier?* Thinking about the War of Resistance when Ninth Brother abandoned home and family to perform his "noble deeds," she realized that this was no impossibility. And in this highly agitated state, for the first time she began shouting at her husband.

"Physically and temperamentally Baohua isn't suited for the army. You've got to oppose this thing firmly."

Ninth Brother still said nothing. Actually he was trying hard to convince himself to accept this reality. As far back as when his daughter was still an infant in swaddling he had hoped that she would study at the teachers' college and become a school teacher in

Old Town. Baohua's acceptance this summer at the teachers' college was the fulfillment of that dream. The day she started classes he wanted to send her to school himself, but Baohua was afraid the other students would laugh at her and strongly refused this. But he followed her secretly and from a distance stood outside the main gate of the college and watched as his daughter's form faded into the campus. His sense of elation had still not slackened. Then when Baohua suddenly and perversely went off the tracks and joined the army, Ninth Brother's feeling of loss was hard to explain, but then he thought of how he himself had expressed over and again his fervid advocacy of the Communist Party. If he opposed his daughter joining the army, wouldn't this be not practicing what he preached? *Our Lin family daughter is finicky, but aren't the daughters of other families like that too?*

Second Sister could read her husband's inner soliloquy, and in a fit of anger she walked off from him and went straight into their daughter's room.

"Baohua, if you don't heed your elders you'll be headed for misfortune. Ma totally opposes your joining the army. Don't obey now and you'll regret it later!"

Baohua embraced her pillow and said nothing. The mother saw on the daughter's face a decision to bet all on a single throw. Ninth Brother was like that in those days when he informed his wife he had decided to leave them in Old Town. Both father and daughter had that same weak and bumbling appearance and both had the same ironclad will. In the face of her daughter's determination the mother just hit a wall and disintegrated. She sank feebly down beside her daughter and in voice filled with misery said, "Baohua, you're so skinny, how could you ever carry a rifle?"

⌘　⌘　⌘

Two months later, the doctor received their first letter from Baohua and only then learned that their precious daughter had gone with the army to Xinjiang. His mind was in a daze as he held the letter and for several days the idea of eating and drinking never entered his mind.

CHAPTER FIFTEEN – EMPTY NEST

1.

GREAT-AUNTIE STEPPED THROUGH our gate flashing her toothless grin. My earliest impressions of her have always been those of a corny old biddy. When she was young she had a fine set of teeth, but less than two years into her marriage her husband had bashed out all the ones in front. These she fixed with a whole row of gold teeth and then Zhang pulled these out one by one, roots and all. But when she arrived this day grinning as she did, the scars of all those ravages weren't to be seen. Her bright look made you think of a child waiting to be handed red packets of cash from the grown-ups on Lunar New Year's Eve. She didn't mention that vile husband of hers, nor did my grandparents ask about him. Over the decades, Great-Auntie had learned early on not to wait for Zhang's fists and feet to land upon her but to run straight over to our home at West Gate.

Whenever she came to stay, she would stick tightly by me. Every morning she accompanied me right up to the school gate, and when school was let out in the afternoon, she waited at the junction with a little bag of broad beans or popcorn. Grandma controlled my consumption of snacks quite strictly, so Great-Auntie and I would do "bad things" behind her back and have a great time enjoying our secrets. I repaid her by listening all-ears to her stories. That toothless mouth was an inexhaustible source of tales of spirits and evil forces in heaven and on earth. Though she repeated many of these stories, every version had something new in it.

Great-Auntie spoke of Second Sister with great pity. As she put it, all the pain she herself suffered by being trampled on by her evil bully of a husband paled into insignificance compared to the trials and tribulations of Second Sister's life with her good husband, Ninth Brother.

She said that it was during the War of Resistance that Grandma suffered the most, but then she also said that Grandma's hardest time was when the Guomindang issued the gold *yuan* certificates. One day, meeting me after school and sitting together sharing popcorn by the city moat under the old banyan tree, Great-Auntie lowered her voice and said, "I've never told you, but actually your grandma's greatest days of suffering occurred long after Liberation, in 1954. That was a few years before you were born. Your grandpa was almost taken out and shot." Suddenly looking very agitated, she scanned the area all around us and then raised a finger against those wrinkled lips of hers. "Whatever you do, don't tell anyone. And especially don't go and ask your grandma. This was by far and away the greatest heartbreak she ever experienced. She and your grandpa loved the Communist Party the same as they loved Jesus. Let's say, for example, all your life you go to church to worship, but all of a sudden Jesus turns his face away and says, 'I don't know you,' and orders you cast down into the infernal regions. This is the way I'd put it. Can you understand what I mean?"

I both nodded and shook my head—this was all way beyond me.

"At that time, your mama was in Xinjiang, your younger uncle had gone to fight in Korea, and your older uncle had been assigned to a mountain district to the north of us. Now your grandfather had been taken away under arrest and held who-knew-where. The government was then eliminating counterrevolutionaries and every day these elements were being shot. You could casually point out someone on the street as a counterrevolutionary and the next day that person would never be seen again. It was really scary, just like the bombs the Japanese dropped, you never knew on whose heads these would fall."

My fingers kept kneading a few bits of popcorn instead of putting them into my mouth. I suddenly felt my heartstrings pull taut. From what I had learned starting in kindergarten, I didn't hesitate in the slightest to conclude that Great-Auntie's thinking was counterrevolutionary! She was standing on the side of the counterrevolution to attack the Red mountains and rivers of our country. Great-Auntie's shriveled, sunken mouth and her odd expression made me think of the wolf in the tale of Little Red Riding Hood. In order to eat the little girl, that wolf first devoured her grandmother and then put on her clothes and kerchief. Its aim was to trick Little Red Riding Hood into letting it get close to her and then in one bite gobble her all up. The teacher told us that man-eating wolves might be right beside us and that they were counterrevolutionaries who hated our new society. They were secret agents from Taiwan who lay hidden, just waiting for the moment to work their destructiveness. Using all kinds of tricks, they would rope in and corrode ignorant young people and help the enemies of the people bring down the inheritors of the Revolution. So we always had to pull tight on the strings of the class struggle.

We actually never relaxed our revolutionary vigilance. Not long before this, my two cousins and I had gone to play around Little West Lake. There we saw a sad-looking middle-aged woman sitting all by herself on a bench in a clump of trees. She just sat there like that from morning to evening. My older cousin said there was something wrong with her. She might be a female secret agent sent over from Taiwan waiting for another agent to secretly contact her. We hid behind a holly tree, and the longer we peeped out through the mottled leaves, the more it seemed that she was a secret agent. Just like the secret agents in the movies, she let her wavy hair hang down to her shoulders. She was also thin like them and had a ghastly look about her. We decided to wait for the other agent to contact her and then dash out and take them both alive to the local police substation. The evening light faded in the west, darkness gradually came on, and the moon crept up behind the tree branches, but no other agent appeared. The woman slowly got up and as she bent over to throw a crumpled-up piece of paper under the bench, my cousin sprang out from behind the holly tree and shouted, "Stay where you are!" Horribly frightened, the woman let out a shriek that scared my cousin so badly that he fell right down on his little bum. Dazed, we watched this "female secret agent" vanish into the night. When our nerves had settled down a little, my cousin pulled out the crumpled-up piece of paper from under the bench and smoothed it open. There was nothing on it at all. It was only a strip of bathroom tissue, a little bit damp, perhaps from the woman's tears. Still, my cousin decided to take this tissue paper over to the substation by the side of the lake. The policeman on duty heaped praise on us, and we returned home lightheaded with excitement and ready to ask for our reward for this deed from Big Uncle waiting for us at home.

What we received, however, was sheer misery. The grown-ups had been worried sick at the disappearance of the three children and when they saw us return perfectly safe and sound so late at night, their worries immediately turned into uncontrollable rage. Big Uncle leaped out of his chair, and grabbing a feather duster down from the wall, without any explanation laid it on elder cousin's backside. We two girl cousins both got a slap. But physical pain didn't make our revolutionary vigilance waiver and letting the "female secret agent" slink away like that gave us something to brood over for quite a while.

I stared closely at Great-Auntie and my eyes must have been filled with vigilance and hostility. She noticed me still kneading the popcorn in my hand. "Doesn't it taste good? Well, today it got scorched. I was originally going to buy you some broad beans." And as she spoke she reached inside her lapels to feel for some coins in her tightly bound stomach halter. "Here, go buy some broad beans with this."

Great-Auntie took me by the hand to go to the street where an old lady, as toothless as she was, ran a stall. This old lady used pieces of old newspaper the size of your fist to make triangular containers filled with peanuts, broad beans, or popcorn, each for two *fen*. I stood there glued in place swallowing my saliva as the nice aroma of the broad beans drifted into my nostrils.

"Or else," Great-Auntie paused for a moment, as if making a hard decision, "I'll buy you a piece of taro cake?"

Taro cake was my favorite. One piece cost five *fen*, so Great-Auntie was investing really quite a bit of capital to cozy up to me.

A great struggle went on within me as I followed her for a couple of steps. Then I looked up at her. "Great-Auntie, why do you want to spend so much money on things for me to eat?"

"So much money?" Great-Auntie opened her cavernous mouth and laughed, her two sunken eyes blinking oddly. "You call this money? You don't know! Great-Auntie was rich when she was young, and under the floorboards of Great-Uncle's home gold was lying everywhere. If we had saved up a few gold bricks then, life today wouldn't be so difficult, when you have to think long and hard about buying a piece of taro cake. *Ai...*"

Teacher told us that in the old society workers led lives of great misery and distress. Clearly Great-Auntie belonged to the exploiting classes. Maybe she had taken up a whip and flogged her little housemaids, like they did in the movies. *So could I eat the taro cakes of the class enemy?* This really was a severe test. However, in the end I couldn't resist the temptation. I accepted the fragrant and glistening taro cake that Great-Auntie bought for me straight out of the frying pan.

She broke off a small corner of the cake and put it in her mouth. Her two lips wriggled about for quite a while. "This taro cake isn't as fragrant as they used to be then. In those days, the restaurant next to the Zhang home would send over two pieces specially made for me every day. They used fresh oil to make them… so crisp and flaky…"

After finishing the last bite of cake, I immediately rejoined the Revolution. I wiped my mouth a couple of times and then addressed her with severity, "Great-Aunt, you are not permitted to attack the new society!"

"Attack the new society? How could Great-Auntie attack the new society? The new society is good. Those rotten egg Zhangs are scared of the new society and no longer dare show their fangs and stretch out their claws. Your great-uncle is afraid of the Communist Party. After Liberation his fists got a lot softer."

I got confused all over again. *What* was *Great-Auntie's class background?*

"All her life your grandma loved to keep up appearances." Great-Auntie sat down beside the moat under an old banyan tree and wiped away some perspiration with her handkerchief.

That day Great-Auntie had spent seven *fen* on me, first buying me popcorn and then a taro cake, so I had to listen to her weave her stories with more than my usual patience.

"Your grandma loved keeping up appearances. No other woman loved keeping up appearances more than she did. And no other woman was more strong and unyielding. At the time no one realized that your grandpa had been arrested. For several months there was no news of him at all. It was very possible that he had already 'eaten a bullet.' She told all the Guos that Ninth Brother had gone to Shanghai to visit friends. I myself supposed that was where he had really gone. As for the story of your grandpa in Shanghai, I'll wait until you've grown up before telling you more about that. Your grandma was all alone in the house, but she was so clean and particular about things, even if she cooked at home, the clothes she wore were starched with rice water and ironed stiff and smooth. *Aiya*! At that time it was really my fault…your great-uncle was blowing his stack practically every other day, so I ran over to your house and as always burst into tears in front of your grandmother. I'm old now and my tears have all dried up. But when I was young my tears could be worse than your mama's. One night your grandpa all of a sudden returned. I was the one who opened the door. Just guess what I saw!"

Great-Auntie's tense and mysterious look made my little hairs stand on end.

"What?"

"A ghost! A shadowy figure stood there in the moonlight, as dry and thin as a scrap of paper and with a shaggy clump on top you couldn't tell was beard or hair. I was so shocked when this figure called me 'Big Sister' in Ninth Brother's voice. As I grabbed the gateway for support, my legs just went soft under me and I keeled over. That was the only time in my whole life that I fainted. I felt like the lightest of light feathers floating away in the wind. I saw your grandma lighting an oil lamp and coming out of her room— your home still didn't have any electric lights at the time. 'Ninth

Brother, is that you?' your grandma asked. When your grandpa saw Second Sister, he threw himself like a little child into your grandma's arms and began to cry. What it was...your grandpa's name had already been listed as one of those to be shot. Suddenly a high government official checking names released him. The foreign Buddha protects your grandfather. With him, calamity always changes into good luck."

I was so captivated by this story I hardly breathed. "What crime did Grandpa commit that he got taken away to be shot?"

"It was the movement, the Eliminate Counterrevolutionaries Movement."

"Oh!"

I didn't ask any further. Even though I was still a kid, I already knew that a "movement" was a time of emergency and any unforeseen thing could happen. There was neither reason nor logic to it.

2.

ONCE AGAIN THE postman had become the person Second Sister most longed to see, for she was awaiting letters from her three children. There was no rule to Baohua and Baosheng's letters. Sometimes several would come in quick succession and sometimes two or three months would go by without a single word from either of them. But Baoqing, off to Korea in the army, ensured his parents had a letter from him regularly each month. Whenever she wasn't doing something at home, every morning at ten-thirty she would stand in the gateway respectfully awaiting the postman. Usually the only thing he handed her was *The Old Town Daily News*, which Ninth Brother had subscribed to.

On this day, it was still just the newspaper. Watching the back of the postman as he pedaled off, Second Sister again couldn't repress a twinge of disappointment.

She took the newspaper to the clinic and handed it to her husband. "I thought today we'd receive Baosheng's letter. Oh, that child, still heartless as ever."

The doctor had his head in the newspaper. "You know he's heartless, so don't get all wrought up by it."

As there weren't any patients for the moment, Second Sister just sat down at the examining table and waited for Ninth Brother to discuss the latest important political developments reported in the news. This was right during the "Eliminate Counterrevolutionaries" period. Floods of print were devoted to "eliminating counterrevolutionaries," and again a number of these elements "had fallen into the nets of heaven and the snares of earth."

The doctor looked up, perplexed, "Are there really so many counterrevolutionaries?"

Three years before, because Second Sister was literate and the dependent of a soldier of the Revolution, she had been elected a cadre of the residents' committee and a representative of the neighborhood women. She frequently participated in senior-level organizational meetings and her ideological consciousness was now fairly high. "That's why the district cadres all say we have to wipe our eyes clean and heighten vigilance. The reactionary forces are always trying to overthrow the new society."

The doctor's expression grew even more puzzled. "Everyone repeats the saying, 'The superior ones are those who know and understand the times.' How come these *other* people just won't grasp reality? Nowadays, everyone has work; everyone has clothing and sufficient food to eat. So what's the matter? Isn't this exactly the peaceful life that ordinary people wanted?"

As he saw it, the so-called counterrevolutionaries and forces of reaction weren't abstractions but real and living individuals.

Second Sister reflected on this. She thought of the new term "class struggle" that she often heard at the most recent meetings, and parrotlike she said, "This is probably the class struggle that the leading cadres talk about."

When the work groups were being divided into separate classifications, the Lin family was designated as "urban poor," defining them as part of the proletariat class. The rice shop boss at West Gate was classified as "small capitalist," which meant one of the exploiting classes. After going to Taiwan, their two sons had broken off all contact with the family, and the owner's wife grew seriously ill from pining for them. Dr. Lin often went to her home to treat her and the two families became very close indeed. *How does this business of class struggle come into the picture?*

"The class struggle is very complicated," Second Sister added.

The doctor gave a laugh. "I see that you don't understand it very well either. Go to the meetings more often and keep on raising your ideological level."

He strongly supported Second Sister's participation in social activities. In this way she could divert her thoughts and worries about her children. She was one of those people who couldn't bear to be idle for very long. The busier and wearier she got, the greater her vitality. After Liberation, if there hadn't been the residents' committee work, it is very possible she might have fallen chronically ill, just like the rice shop boss-lady.

"I'll go cook now. In the afternoon I'm off to another district meeting."

Second Sister stood up and was just leaving the clinic when the doctor said to her, "Second Sister, our friend at the rice shop's been doing a bit better over the past couple of days now. The best thing you could do would be to take her along to your meetings. If you could make her a group head or something to handle various family matters like you do, her health would benefit greatly."

Second Sister turned to look at her husband and gave him a thin smile. But inside she was thinking, "Oh, Ninth Brother, you're so naive. The rice shop boss-lady is from the exploiting classes. She has to be controlled and changed by the proletariat. How could she possibly emerge as cadre?"

Unaware of his wife's thoughts, Ninth Brother went on, "Her sickness is entirely due to psychological factors."

"Ninth Brother, I think you also ought to join in these meetings. You're too behind in your thinking.

"And what does *that* mean?"

"The woman is classified as a small capitalist. She's not the same class as us."

"What's all this class business? Now it's all joint private-state ownership. So they're proletarian class too."

"The government doesn't put it like that."

"Second Sister, don't forget, we Christians preach that everybody's equal."

Second Sister couldn't utter a single response to this. She was still a devout Christian who never missed worship on Sundays. Every night she would fall asleep in the midst of her prayers. Even so, she had never linked her work on the residents' committee with "the Word of God."

"As members of the proletarian class we can't be arrogant and look down on other people," said Ninth Brother, looking appraisingly at his wife. "Just think for a minute; if it hadn't been for the Japanese bombing the Lin family ancestral home, or if the Guos hadn't produced wastrels and drunks, how would we be classified now?"

Yes! How would we then have been classified? On the eve of Liberation, Elder Sister's three Zhang brothers-in-law all had a falling-out and their fighting bankrupted them. After Liberation, they too were evaluated as "urban poor" and, luckily for them, proletarian in class. The government even gave Elder Sister's husband a comfortable job as a dispatcher at the bureau of industry, and in two years more, he could take his retirement money and live out the rest of his years at home.

Second Sister considered her own ideological level to be higher than Ninth Brother's, but when she tried to help him her thoughts would hit a wall and progress no further, like that rusty old clock on the wall in their house. Every time it reached five-fifteen the clock would just stop abruptly. She gave an awkward laugh and asked, "Would noodles be all right for lunch?"

Ninth Brother nodded yes.

⌘   ⌘   ⌘

Before leaving the house, Second Sister changed into the clothes she had ironed the night before and stood in front of the mirror to put on some light makeup. She was going to take part in a big awards meeting for the model dependents of soldiers. Feelings of honor and pride surged within her. In the beginning she had done everything she could think of to keep Baohua from joining the army. Two years before, Baoqing had put on a uniform and went off to fight in Korea and she was now no longer an ordinary housewife. As a women's representative of the residents' committee she knew that the country's interests stood higher than all other principles. At his send-off party she wore a red flower for Baoqing. The photographers took pictures of that moving scene and she framed this page from the newspaper and hung it on the wall. Distinction and glory calmed her yearning for her youngest son. Baoqing was her very lifeblood; however, she hadn't shed a single tear at their parting. But several times Ninth Brother had cried late at night when he prayed for Baoqing and all the soldiers who had gone to Korea with the volunteer forces.

At fifty years of age, Second Sister still looked youthful and pretty. She walked into the clinic and told Ninth Brother, "I'm off to the meeting."

Ninth Brother was treating some old fellow from the neighborhood and was just then taking his pulse. He looked up at his wife and said, "Off you go then, Director Guo."

Over the past few years, people at West Gate who knew them well now called Second Sister, "Director Guo." Ninth Brother himself often jokingly called her that too.

His patient was a woman of about the same age as Second Sister, but her face was haggard with cares and grief and all her hair had turned white. She said with a sigh, "Director Guo gets younger with each passing year. Just look at me—still breathing but already halfway into the grave.

"She's always trying to improve her mind, that's why she doesn't get sick or look old. She's able to accept whatever happens and always see the good side of things. When she has free time she helps with government in various ways. On Sundays she goes to the church to hear Pastor Chen's sermons..."

Just as the doctor said these words, he suddenly felt there was something he wanted to say to Second Sister. He turned his head and watched as she practically flew across the intersection. Smiling, he shook his head and said to his patient, "That's her for you— already fifty years old, but when she walks the wind still flies out from under her feet."

"Director Guo has good fate. Her husband is kind, her children are proving their worth, and she's still healthy."

"She ate bitterness to the fullest earlier in her life. Now that there's no more bitterness, sweetness has taken its place."

The doctor prescribed some medicine for his patient, and again dispensed a basketful of soothing words to her. After several decades of practicing medicine he knew full well the decisive influence of the spirit on the body. He always did his utmost to get patients to let out whatever pent-up grief or anger they held within them and he did whatever he could to guide the reconciliation of their innermost troubles.

⌘　⌘　⌘

At the district committee hall Second Sister once again wore a large red flower. Over the past few years, one of their drawers was filled to overflowing with the certificates of merit and red flowers she had accumulated. She had been invited to mount the chairman's rostrum, and facing several hundred revolutionary army dependents, she spoke of her own journey in pursuit of progress. The secretary of the neighborhood committee had prepared the text of her speech and she read it through once beforehand. But when she was on the rostrum she delivered her speech without it in a cool and controlled manner.

"Originally, I was an ordinary housewife. Raising children was entirely for carrying on the ancestral line, to look after me in my old age, and to see that I would be properly buried. When my daughter Baohua joined the army in 1949, every day I wept and grieved."

The secretary had instructed her to be sure *not* to say she had blocked her daughter's enlistment into the army —that would have been too reactionary. She was just supposed to tell how she couldn't bear giving her daughter up and that she cried with a broken heart, and nothing else.

"When the war to help Korea and oppose America erupted, Imperialist America's artillery shells landed right at our gate. At that time, I only had my youngest son, Baoqing, with me. He had graduated from the technical college and was just about to get a job and earn some money. But for the motherland I myself sent my son to the battlefield."

Applause interrupted Second Sister's speech again and again. She was now thoroughly intoxicated with her own words. Letting her mind drift a bit, she remembered the words her father had said to her several decades before, his face sad and full of regret. "Second Sister, it is just too bad that you have a woman's body. If you were a man, with your intelligence and ability you could become a big official for sure." *If Daddy were alive to see me standing in the district government hall making this report, oh how happy he'd be!* Her mother had died just last year but she had shared in her daughter's splendor. The old lady would tell everyone she met that her family's Second Sister was now a big official. Whenever her little grandchildren fought with the neighborhood kids, she would hobble as fast as she could with her cane over to their doorsteps and warn their mothers, "Our family's Second Sister is a government official. So don't you bully my grandchildren!"

After it was all over, Second Sister did not remove the red flower when she went to her drunkard brother's home nearby. His wife, now over forty years old, had again added a boy to the Guo family and her month of post-parturition confinement had not been over for very long. The government was promoting births, for with many people came great power, and if the people were many they could defeat American imperialism. She was going to encourage her brother's wife to keep up her efforts to continue raising the descendants of the Revolution.

Her oldest nephew, Gan'er, who had barely managed to pass out of grade school, now dug in his heels and refused to study anymore. But the drunkard had never forgotten the ancient precept of studying to become an official, and just then he was at home drinking and smashing crockery onto the floor trying to keep his son in line and continue studying. Second Sister kept thinking about going home to make dinner but was unable to get away for the moment and stayed on to adjudicate the matter.

⌘   ⌘   ⌘

When he had sent off the last patient, the sky was already darkening and still there was no sign of Second Sister. As he gazed across the intersection he smiled and repeated to himself the old saying, "Having too much fun to long for Shu, having too much fun to long for Shu."[46] He walked into the kitchen where the fire in the oven had

---

[46]   Ninth Brother's whimsical allusion to an event in *Romance of the Three Kingdoms*. The last ruler of the state of Shu, the feckless Liu Shan, surrendered to the kingdom of Wei and went into exile in Loyang, where he behaved as if he had forgotten he was the lord of a defeated state. On one occasion he was given a banquet by an important Wei minister, who insultingly ordered the musicians play traditional Shu melodies to gauge his reactions. Liu Shan's entourage were saddened to hear these and asked if he, Liu, did not miss Shu, to which Liu replied, "I'm having too much fun to long for Shu."

gone out. They had just begun to burn coal balls at home and these never burned right. He had to keep relighting the fire almost constantly. He put the little coal burner by the gate and used some old newspaper and small pieces of charcoal to get the fire going. People passing by invariably stopped to ask, "Dr. Lin, what are you doing making your own dinner?" The men in Old Town didn't go "down" to the kitchen. They carried their teapots with them and waited for their wives to serve the rice and vegetables. The doctor couldn't care less about what other people thought of this. He saw doing the housework as a repayment to Second Sister. He owed her so much, so very much, in this life, and however much he did for her, these were trifles hardly worth the mention.

This evening he intended to invite Pastor Chen over to enjoy a few cups of wine with him. Lately the pastor had seemed in low spirits. The pastor had really appreciated the bean curd potage that Second Sister made for him and the doctor got ready to feel his way through recreating this dish. By then, though, the vegetable market had closed so he went straight to Shuiguan's house beside the river to ask for some bean curd. For two years now, Shuiguan's wife had been running a bean curd stall. Nowadays, with each of their children gone off to seek a living from doing handicrafts, the husband and wife were enjoying a relatively prosperous life.

When the doctor arrived at his house, Shuiguan was hugging his teapot and waiting for his wife to serve dinner. Now he excitedly guided the doctor back outside. That very day Shuiguan had bought a new three-wheeler pedicab, and so now he just had to take the doctor out for a spin. Along their way, Shuiguan jingled the crisp-sounding bell as he pedaled the doctor all around the streets of West Gate. All this really appealed to the "little kid" in the doctor and he asked Shuiguan to let him pedal. As he had never learned to pedal anything well, this three-wheeler turned out to be even more intractable than a bicycle. The doctor had no sooner climbed aboard when it just took off and narrowly missed hitting a tree.

As might be expected, when the doctor was walking back home with the bowl of bean curd he was in excellent spirits and along the way he hummed a hymn. Then he looked up and saw the gate wide open. *Oh, Second Sister's back. I'll just get her to lead me through making bean curd potage.*

"Has the heroic mother come home now?"

Suddenly a policeman and a man who had the look of a cadre popped up from the Eight Immortals table. *They must have come looking for Second Sister.*

"Director Guo has gone to the district meeting and hasn't returned yet."

The policeman's face was taut and grim as he said, "Counterrevolutionary element Lin Bingkun, you are under arrest!"

For so many years now no one had ever addressed him by name, so the doctor felt the situation must be rather serious. He put the bowl down. "Comrades, aren't you making a mistake? I'm classified urban-poor."

"Cut the gab and let's go!"

"Now?"

"Get moving!"

The doctor thought about his having once worn a Guomindang army uniform, but that history had already been explained countless times. That was his ineradicable stain. *Once I go away, will I be able to return? Oh Second Sister, you have just enjoyed a few days of happiness and now troubles are back again.*

"I'd like to leave my wife a note."

The policeman and the cadre glanced at each other and neither said yes or no to this. The doctor found some paper and a pen and wrote: "Second Sister, the government has come here to invite me to go to make a report on some problem. You know I back the Communist Party. Don't worry, and take care."

⌘ ⌘ ⌘

My grandma returned and opened the door. The house was totally dark. She supposed that Ninth Brother had gone to the church to chat with Pastor Chen. She lit the lamp and first of all saw the bowl of bean curd on the table. She wondered whether Ninth Brother was perhaps waiting for her to make bean curd potage for the pastor's dinner invitation. Next she saw that note. Immediately she realized that a catastrophe beyond all redemption had descended on her home. In that instant it was as if she had plunged from the end of a cloud into a deep abyss. This shock was too great. All the other calamities she had experienced, homeless wandering during the War of Resistance, hunger during the gold yuan certificate days, were nothing compared to this. She didn't know how the government would deal with Ninth Brother, but *she* had already been given the death sentence. The note that Ninth Brother had left for her was the written verdict of that death sentence. A sharp pain and a chill spread from the depths of her heart throughout her whole body.

3.

HOW OFTEN SHALL I sleep like this every night, waking up every few minutes? And every time I awake I plunge into fog and mist. Has something bad really happened to Ninth Brother? Second Sister reached out and felt for the icy cold pillow. It was the pillow that he had used for seven or eight years now and the embroidered flowers on it had worn off. She held the pillow tightly to her nose to smell his scent. And then awareness would come to her once again. *It's true, something bad's happened to Ninth Brother. Oh, Ninth Brother, where are you at this very moment?*

Sometimes she would kneel in prayer but just couldn't help feeling perplexed. *Is there really a God? O God, if you really are everywhere, why do you still let Ninth Brother suffer such injustices? Could it be this husband and wife still haven't suffered enough in this life?*

Opening the gate in the morning was the hardest thing. In those days Old Town folk did not close their gates during the daytime. If someone's gate was shut and windows fastened during the day, the neighborhood would think that something had happened to that family. Beyond the gate was a vast ocean of shame and disgrace. Everybody would look at her with contempt and rejection. *So all along this revolutionary army dependent was secretly a member of a counterrevolutionary family!* And people would sigh over how complicated the class struggle was. In all the misfortunes she experienced in her fifty years, losing property and relatives had never hurt her dignity, a thing more valuable than life itself. But this calamity swept her dignity through the dirt. She thought of long-lost Third Sister. Over the intervening decades she had finally come to understand how her father felt at that time, unable to bear up under the shame Third Sister brought the Guo family. *Could I then go on living if I had to wear the hat of a counterrevolutionary family member?* Second Sister thought of dying. If a bullet ended Ninth Brother's life, she couldn't live one single day longer.

Ninth Brother's message was "You know I back the Communist Party." *Yes, long before Liberation he backed the Communist Party. But he did, after all, wear a Guomindang army uniform. According to government policy he could be considered as having engaged in the old-line counterrevolution. It didn't matter whether it was the old-line one or the current one, once you wore the counterrevolutionary hat, that was that. Could our three children's joining in the revolution cancel out Ninth Brother's crime?* Though she had always possessed surpassing intelligence, Second Sister realized that she was actually extremely stupid. She couldn't figure it out at all. She just couldn't understand it. And the more she tried, the more mixed up she got.

That picture of her sending off Baoqing to war was still on the wall. Second Sister had the red flower in her hand and her smile was more eye-catching than the big flower. Every one of her tiny wrinkles proclaimed her happiness to the world. Beside that picture was the "Happy Family Portrait" taken in 1937 at the Drum Tower photo studio, before Ninth Brother went to fight in the War of Resistance. Who would have expected that out of the family of five, she would be the only one left? She stared blankly at the picture and over and over asked herself, *Ninth Brother, you scholar, too weak even to truss a chicken, why did you have to become a soldier? They always said a good man doesn't become a soldier. How could you have abandoned a perfectly good family to do just that? How much misfortune has that uniform you wore brought to this family? We managed to survive hairbreadth escapes from death and thought we'd seen the end of it all. Who could have known that the real disaster lay hidden all along until it fell out of the heavens today? Can we survive it again?*

The gate had to be opened, even if she dreaded seeing anyone. She forced herself to comb her hair and dress neatly, and she was more selective about what she wore than when Ninth Brother was at home. To disguise her haggard expression, she put on a little powder. Every day patients came looking for Dr. Lin and if it were just small ailments like headaches or slight fevers, Second Sister would wrap up a few "Somedon" pills for them. "Somedon" was a new medicine and Second Sister saw it as an all-purpose balm. No matter where the pain was, you just took two of these. This attachment lasted until she was over ninety years old. She couldn't tell Baosheng from Baoqing, but she still remembered to call for "Somedon." She told everyone who came looking for the doctor that "Dr. Lin had gone traveling." People would say, "Oh, he's gone to see his daughter" or, "Oh, he's gone to see his son." To all of these people she just gave a vague smile.

Harder even than opening her gate every day was attending meetings. She didn't know if she was still qualified to attend meetings, and in order to avoid awkward situations, she sent a leave request to the leader of the West Gate neighborhood. Above the residents' committee was the neighborhood committee, and above that was the district committee. The bookstore "boss" who had earlier brought Baosheng into the Revolution was now the deputy district head. That same day, this deputy district head went to the neighborhood committee to check on its work. When he asked about "Revolutionary Mother" Second Sister Guo, the neighborhood leader gave a full accounting of her circumstances. The deputy district head then said, "I believe she can make a clean break from her husband. Her son is in Korea defending China and at any time might give his life for our motherland. We can't see her as an enemy." The neighborhood leader then asked whether or not to let her continue with her committee tasks. The deputy district head expressed no opinion on this matter. All of this occurred at the height of the political movement and even someone as highly placed as he had to be extra cautious. The neighborhood leader had even less dared lay a finger on such a sensitive case. They revoked the positions of two other committee cadres and shelved the matter of Second Sister. Therefore, around West Gate there was no news about Dr. Lin and everyone believed that he was off traveling somewhere.

Second Sister mustered up all her courage and opened the gate. Shuiguan jingled his bell as he flew by on his pedicab. "I guess Dr. Lin'll be coming back soon? If he sends a cable with the date of the boat, I'll go fetch him. He didn't ask me to take him when he left. That's not the way friends should be!"

"If there's news, I'll be sure to let you know! But before, when Dr. Lin went traveling, he never cabled when he would be coming home."

"Dr. Lin's kind of funny that way. Now with him gone, if you need anything, just call me!"

Then Shuiguan rode off, jingling away. As she watched him go, Second Sister thought, "Shuiguan, if you knew that Dr. Lin was a counterrevolutionary, would you still be this good to him?" She really thought of asking him directly.

Everyone would inquire about Dr. Lin. Second Sister knew that every word she said was a lie, but there was no way around it for her. The longer it went on, the more frightened she grew. You can't wrap fire in paper. At any time the paper could get poked through, and how would you fix something like that?

The postman brought the newspaper and a letter from Baoqing. Second Sister looked calmly at her son's letter and then spread the newspaper out on the dining table. She placed a magnifying glass on top of it and painstakingly searched for Ninth Brother's name. *As long as his name doesn't appear in a newspaper, it means he is still alive. So up to today he is still alive and maybe even has been pardoned by the government.* This was Second Sister's last hope.

Far off in Korea, Baoqing somehow sensed that things had happened at home, for the last letter had been written by his mother. He didn't ask about anything happening to his daddy but filled the letter paper with concern toward his mother. He said that she and he had gone through so many difficulties and dangers. "Ma, you took us through every step of the way. I don't believe that anything could bring you down. Everything can become things of the past."

Tears streamed down her face as she held up Baoqing's letter. Just at that moment, Elder Sister arrived. She didn't ask her younger sister why she was so brokenhearted. *Probably she's thinking of her son.* Well, she herself was the one with the hard lot in life and she sat down and chattered endlessly on about her own troubles.

Elder Sister's only son had been insane for several years now and her oldest daughter who had recently been admitted to university suffered another breakdown and was persuaded by the school to return home. Elder Sister thought all this was retribution for all the many evil things the Zhang family had done. "I am their mother. I never did anything wrong, so why should I be the one to be punished like this? Back then Daddy preferred you and gave you away to Ninth Brother and married me off to the Zhangs."

Second Sister grew so irritated she couldn't stand it anymore. "Elder Sister, I'm not in the mood to hear you go on and on about ancient disputes."

Momentarily stunned, Elder Sister said in an injured tone of voice, "Now that you're in the Revolution you've become an official and earned a lot of glory. I'm not worthy of being your older sister now."

"*Aiya*! Elder Sister, can't you see how upset I am right now?

Elder Sister cast a glance at the newspaper framed on the wall. "Who told you to be so heartless in sending Baoqing to Korea? I hear that a man's lifeblood can freeze inside him there. Would it have been worth it, trading a son's life for a newspaper picture?"

"Don't talk nonsense!"

"All right then. And what about Ninth Brother? I've been having fierce headaches lately. Please ask him to come over and treat me."

"Ninth Brother's away. He's off traveling."

"He's gone to Shanghai, am I right?"

"Mmh."

Elder Sister had just stood up. Immediately she sat right back down again. "Now *this* is really something. *Ai,* so many years have passed and he still hasn't forgotten Shanghai. You're very generous, still letting him go to Shanghai. But what would you do if he didn't come back?"

Second Sister was clear about where Elder Sister's crazy mind was headed, and just looked at her, not knowing whether to laugh or to cry. "I have something I need to do. You stay here and read the newspaper."

"Are you going to a meeting?"

"Mmh."

Elder Sister clucked her tongue and shook her head. "And you still have the heart to go to meetings."

⌘ ⌘ ⌘

Second Sister walked up to the church fence. She wanted to go in and tell Pastor and Mrs. Chen about what had happened at home and to ask them to pray for Ninth Brother. She hesitated for a moment, and then walked on. The pastor and his wife weren't feeling very much at ease either. Enchun had married Huang Shuyi and troubles had been never ending over the past three years. Huang

Shuyi was going everywhere in pursuit of her appeal, and several times en route to Beijing by train or ship, had been escorted back home by public security personnel. How could their Enchun have married such a restless and dissatisfied girl? He had risked his life for the Revolution, but now, after Liberation, why had he become so mute?

Second Sister passed by Little West Lake and without realizing it had walked right up to the neighborhood office. This startled her and she quickened her pace. Elder Sister said Ninth Brother had gone to Shanghai. Actually this wasn't a bad pretext. Second Sister decided that evening she would write the three children and tell them that their daddy had gone to Shanghai. If Ninth Brother really had gone to Shanghai then it was all right, even if a woman was waiting for him there.

Up ahead were the commercial college and the Teachers' Training College. Dimly in her mind she saw Baohua and Baoqing, each wearing their school uniforms, walking over toward her. *How good it had been in those days.* Second Sister sighed deeply. *Perhaps Elder Sister wasn't wrong in saying I shouldn't have sent Baoqing to join the army. Baoqing isn't headstrong like Baohua. If I hadn't agreed to this he wouldn't have gone.* She felt deep regret over this, like a knife stabbing into her breast.

Just then a man pushing a bicycle came toward her. Second Sister quickly wiped away her tears and stepped to one side, but the bicycle kept coming in her direction. She looked up and saw a familiar face. They say that when a hard-luck type tries to drink water it sticks between his teeth. What you fear is what you'll end up seeing. And if you are afraid of meeting someone you know, there's no way you'll ever avoid that person. Furthermore, this was no ordinary familiar person—it was Deputy District Head Bai, "Big Brother" Bai who had owned the bookshop.

"Aunt! It's been a long time."

"Oh, District Head Bai, greetings!"

"Don't call me 'District Head.' I'm Baosheng's friend, you know. He's gone away to work, but we're always in contact."

Maybe he doesn't know about Ninth Brother yet, otherwise he wouldn't be this polite to me.

"Oh. Please keep helping him. Well, you're busy, so I won't bother you."

Raising her hand in farewell, she turned around and walked away.

"Aunt!" Deputy District Head Bai called after her. "I know about Uncle's matter. I will definitely look into this. You must believe that our party would not treat a good person unjustly."

A good person? Did the district head say that Ninth Brother is a good person? Does that mean he doesn't see him as a counterrevolutionary?

O God! O Lord! This is surely someone you have sent to comfort me. You know I am weak. You know I can no longer hold myself up. Stretch forth your hand and support me and don't let me fall.

Second Sister ran into the thicket beside her and knelt down with her eyes raised to heaven. "O Lord, I love you!"

She wept the whole way home and wept again at the Eight Immortals table right in front of Elder Sister. Elder Sister kept handing her hot towels and never stopped sighing. "You think you know a person, but you really don't. I expected Ninth Brother would have forgotten Shanghai by now. Does he think about that child there? You're to blame for sending the child away."

In the midst of her sobbing, Second Sister began to titter and giggle.

Elder Sister thought, "Our Second Sister is done for!" Dropping a towel that had just been used she embraced Second Sister. "Oh, my wretched, unlucky sister!"

4.

MANY, MANY YEARS later, the secrets of the "Eliminate Counterrevolutionaries" period were no longer secret. My grandmother could take an audience's perspective and relate from every possible angle the details of the play. Of course the tickets to this particular play were far too expensive. They almost "caused her spirit to depart on the execution ground," and they deprived my mother and two uncles of their bright career prospects. To dispel the fog enveloping the Lin family, my two uncles worked like Sherlock Holmes for over ten years searching everywhere for "spider threads and horse hoofmarks." But after endless complications and setbacks they were still unable to detect the chief culprit in all this.

Grandma wept tears of gratitude as she thanked heaven and earth for the deputy district head's calling my grandfather a good man. Still, she didn't dare entertain any extravagant hopes that this chance meeting could bring Ninth Brother back from the dead.

The deputy district head had heard Dr. Lin was suspected of being a special agent, but he let this go in one ear and out the other without paying it any mind. At noon on this day, he had taken some spare time to go home to see his mother, with whom he never had the chance to share a meal, being so busy with the current movement. However, after running into Aunt Lin on the way, he didn't go home but pedaled to the district government building and went right into the "Eliminate Counterrevolutionaries" office. There he took out Dr. Lin's file. The doctor had already been reported to the city government as an entry on the list of those to be shot. His crimes were his having been a Guomindang army officer and now a hidden special agent. In his file was a letter anonymously signed by

"The Revolutionary Masses" that stated, "Previously Dr. Lin secretly slipped back to Old Town from the army with a special commission from the secret police organ in Chongqing. In Old Town he developed an underground anticommunist organization and, like a spider's web, this organization has already spread to every corner of Old Town. On the surface he runs a medical clinic and treats patients, but in reality this is where he draws people into his organization. He has even managed to get his children inside the Communist Party."

Before Liberation, Deputy District Head Bai had dealings with the Lin family and he concluded these accusations were pure fabrications. He took this file right to the city government and sought out the leader of the local "Eliminate Counterrevolutionaries" movement. The deputy district head didn't dare say that he himself could prove that Dr. Lin wasn't a special agent, only that this case was "complicated." If what the anonymous letter said was true, this man could not be shot, at least not right away, but should be handed over to the national security organ so they could uncover his underground organization.

When the movement leader took a glance at the file, his eyeballs looked like they had been scorched, though he immediately regained control of himself and carefully read the details of the material.

This man's name was Li, and, in fact, he was the Young Li who had been with Dr. Lin so many years before up north with the army.

While Dr. Lin was meandering his way back south, Young Li had sought refuge with the communists' New Fourth Army. Now, not too long ago, he had transferred out of the army to civilian work and returned to Old Town where he held a double position as head of the Organization Department and director of the "Eliminate Counterrevolutionaries" office.

Department Head Li kept Dr. Lin's file. He didn't mention his own relationship with Dr. Lin to the deputy district head and in an official tone of voice said, "This is a phenomenon well worth our serious attention. We ought to be on guard against those enemies who in their evil intent confuse our line of vision. I will be investigating this case myself."

The next day, Department Head Li saw Dr. Lin at the detention center. Although the doctor's hair and beard was all one big clump and he had turned thin almost beyond recognition, still, in one glance he could recognize the Dr. Lin of long ago in that man by the courtyard wall pulling up weeds. The doctor was squatting on the ground conscientiously pulling up weeds and piling them up all very neatly beside him. This was just how Young Li would watch the figure of Dr. Lin in the battleground first aid station. So many old things welled up in his heart. He held back both his tears and the impulse to step forward and identify himself to the doctor.

Ten days later, my grandfather was released from the lockup. He didn't know why he had been arrested or why he had been released. As he stood on the street corner at West Gate in the middle of the night as if in a trance, he supposed this had all been a dream.

What happened next was my Great-Auntie thinking she was looking at a ghost standing at the gate and my grandma just then coming out with a lamp and so frightened she started shivering all over.

Grandpa had once again mysteriously dodged a calamity, but the Lin family's bad luck had by no means run its course. That anonymous letter writer went on writing letters. He sent one to Uncle Baosheng's work organ and another to Uncle Baoqing's army unit. Nor did my mother in far-off Xinjiang have the good luck to avoid all this. Uncle Baosheng's position at that time was section chief. He never got promoted any higher. Younger uncle returned to China from Korea, was discharged, and sent back to his home in Old Town. And because of this, my mother was abandoned by her husband who had ambitions of becoming an officer.

Who in the world had the Lin family offended so badly as to put us in mortal danger? Every holiday, the two Lin brothers would come home to West Gate and convene a meeting. They each found a lot of clues, but overall it was as ineffective as dredging for a needle at the bottom of the ocean. The impact of these anonymous letters on the Lins was deep and far reaching. They were a sword hanging over every family member. Every time there was a political movement that sword would descend to claim their lives. This went on right up to the early 1970s when my cousin registered for military service. He hadn't been in uniform for three days when he was discharged. The reason given was that his grandfather and father were suspected secret agents.

Grandma had suspected it was her brother-in-law Zhang. If the Lin family had any enemy at all it could only have been him from the time when she had dashed the bucket of cold water at him. She arranged to have her sister bring over some of his handwriting and Baosheng submitted this to the leader. But the answer they received was negative. So who else could it have been?

With the catastrophe of the "Great Cultural Revolution," my two uncles no longer held any hopes of political advancement. They grew used to the burden of "suspicion." Because it was only suspicion, they were still fortunate enough to survive, and, in fact, not do all that badly. Since they were unqualified to join those who were "making revolution" during that period, and the rebel factions had their hands full over those two years, Baosheng and Baoqing each stayed at his own home and raised chickens. Every Sunday the two brothers would return to West Gate, each holding a handsome rooster which they would release to fight under the sky well, with the loser ending up in the cooking pot.

One day at the end of the 1970s, when I was returning home from school, I could see far off a number of people crowding around our gateway. Grandpa had departed this world not too long before and I was feeling extremely vulnerable. Immediately I thought the worst—*Grandma had died! O heaven, I can't lose my grandma!* Like a crazy person I squeezed through, pushing aside people, but what I saw was Grandma sitting calmly at the Eight Immortals table. Then I turned my head and saw a crazy person, a real one, standing under the sky well hurling curses and abuse at our Lin family, his frothy spit sputtering all over the place.

"Lin Bingkun was a counterrevolutionary special agent. He received a special commission from Chen Lifu in Chongqing.[47] They bought out the doctor and shut me up in the nuthouse because of what I knew..."

I was just about to open my mouth to chase that crazy person away when my grandmother called me, "Hong'er, get a glass of water for your elder cousin, Ah Chang."

Was this Great-Auntie's son, Ah Chang? I knew that Ah Chang had been in the nuthouse for over ten years.

"What you said is very important and you should report it to the government right away. Sit down and drink some water while I go get some paper and a pen. You write it down and Second Auntie will be sure to give it to them," said Grandma to Ah Chang.

---

[47] Together with his brother Chen Guofu, Chen Lifu (d. 2001) headed what was known as the CC Clique of the Guomindang Party, undoubtedly its strongest and most influential political faction and one that represented the most conservative and uncompromisingly anticommunist elements of Chinese society. Chen Lifu also headed the dreaded Central Bureau of Intelligence and Statistics, one of the two main police bodies in Guomindang China.

Ah Chang drew out from his breast a much wrinkled letter. "I wrote it all down in the beginning. The doctor was bought out so I couldn't send it."

"Give it here to Second Auntie. Second Auntie supports you and will help you send it."

"No, you're the secret agent's old lady! I can't give to you. I want to arrest you all myself and hand you over to the police!"

Grandma told me to go to the substation and call over a policeman.

Grandma, are you so angry you've taken leave of your senses? After all, this is a crazy person you're playing games with! I didn't know the story of the anonymous letters and my two uncles had long ago given up their detective work. I was hopelessly confused by all of this.

This was the way that the case, which had been suspended for over twenty years, was solved. When Uncle Baosheng rushed back home upon hearing the news, the police had already put Ah Chang back into the asylum. Though my uncle had lived at peace with this "suspicion" and had been a steady and reliable minor section chief, now he just blew up and cursed, using a crude term he had never used before. Threatening to knock that crazy man flat, he turned to go after his cousin in the insane asylum but Grandma stopped him with a rap of her hand on the table. "You don't think he has suffered enough retribution? Or that he isn't more miserable and wretched than you?" Uncle Baosheng sat down and lit up a cigarette with hands that were trembling violently.

Grandma poured Uncle a glass of water and sat down next to him. "Don't just think how he hurt our family. You want to reflect on how we benefited in all this disaster. If it hadn't been for that anonymous letter, the three of you might be scattered to the four corners of the earth to this very day. Three generations of our family are able to gather together and we can thank him that you and Baoqing never became big officials. What happened to all the big officials? Weren't the ones who were 'struggled' to their deaths all big officials?"

When Ah Chang was little he fought with Baosheng after getting hit by my uncle's slingshot, so he remembered the Lin family. As for Zhang, Second Sister had once thrown a bucket of cold water on this rotten-egg brother-in-law because of his foul mouth and that event had rankled within him for years. After Liberation, Second Sister's fame caused him no end of teeth-gnashing. Though he would often vilify the whole Lin family, he really never thought of doing them any actual violence. He just said this to satisfy his craving for such empty talk. He didn't know that Ah Chang, then in junior high school, was already insane. But Ah Chang remembered each and every bit of these slanderous stories his father made up. Later when his madness became something terrible and he was tied up and committed to the asylum, he thought he was being persecuted by an organization of special agents. Late at night he would frequently burrow under his cot in the ward to write anonymous letters.

After more time had passed, my Great-Auntie's husband became terminally ill. After lying in bed for more than two years, he was covered with sores. Again and again he would seem to die but would always manage to recover, and each time he came to, he would say to his wife, "I will be a good person in my next life. I will never hit you. I won't raise even a finger against you." When people are about to die, their words are kind and good. Although Great-Auntie's heart had softened, she truly feared remarrying this man in the next life. Panic-stricken, she waved her hand at her husband. "Don't wait for me. Whatever you do, don't wait for me. In the next life I am going to be a nun and follow the Buddha. I'm not marrying anyone." She was secretly determined to live another twenty or thirty years, by which time he would have returned to earth, gotten married, and had children, lest in a moment of carelessness she bump into him again. In the moments before his death, Great-Auntie's husband would often mumble, "Ninth Brother was no counterrevolutionary secret agent." These words astounded her, as she had been in the dark about this all along. Although she often fled to West Gate, my grandmother had never divulged this family secret to her. After Zhang was laid to rest, Great-Auntie came to West Gate and mimicked him, making a joke of all this. Grandma laughed it off.

⌘　⌘　⌘

When I left Old Town and went north to study, the West Gate home once again became an empty nest. Grandma was the only person there. Reminiscences about the past became her daily nourishment.

"I never expected your grandfather to go before me. His fate was an extremely hard one."

I had returned on vacation and Grandma was poaching a bowlful of eggs for my welcome home. As she sat down she muttered to herself and I knew she was plunged into memories. Even though she saw me and was poaching eggs for me, her memories went on uninterrupted.

"Back then, small as he was, he got very sick and they threw him out into the street. Even a dog couldn't have endured it, but he survived. The Japanese killed so many people. He was shoved against the mouth of a rifle but didn't die.

"That's right! And during 'Eliminate Counterrevolutionaries' he almost…" But then I remembered Great-Auntie bringing her finger up to her withered lips and commanding me never, ever to tell anyone, and above all not to ask Grandma, for this had been her greatest heartbreak and caused her greatest loss of face.

Grandma brought over her sewing basket, put on her old-age glasses, and not without some self-satisfaction said, "He was a good man. Unless Jesus himself came to take him, nothing could harm him in this life. It's just that Jesus has forgotten *me*. I've waited year after year, but there's been no news. When the time comes, I don't know if your grandfather would still remember that we had been husband and wife here on earth."

The layered jacket in her hand was being sewn for Ah Chang. Ever since that rotten egg of a brother-in-law had died, Great-Auntie depended on her daughter to support her and she didn't have any money to buy clothes for Ah Chang. Now every year my grandmother made several sets of clothes for him. Ah Chang was still in the insane asylum and he continued to burrow under the cot to write letters reporting that the Lins were special agents.

5.

I HAVE SET out with utter confidence on my trip across space and time. I consider myself able to describe those times I never lived through. I clearly see Ninth Brother's sad childhood. I see tiny Ninth Brother, his whole body covered with scabies, thrown out at the foot of the courtyard wall by the Lins' back door. I see his body writhing in pain, a long-untended braid spread out on the slippery stone paving. I see Mr. Qiao approaching with his lamp pole, that gentle glow of light moving back and forth...

Coming closer and closer, as I approach periods of time less distant, the film projector in my head seems to malfunction and the faces of those people who once lived and those who are still alive are all becoming blurry. Or it's like a computer attacked by a virus and the screen showing nothing but gibberish. I can't make out clearly right from wrong, blessing from calamity. My thinking is devoid of all logic.

You're staring at me with a thirst to know that shines evermore from that pair of blue eyes.

When Great-Auntie told her stories she loved to whip them up in mist and mystery, and then always stop just at the most important point. I would tug at her blouse and eagerly ask, "And then what?" And then she would use her imagination to continue making it all up and breathe life into whatever she was saying and make it more real than real. For example, she firmly believed that her husband had been reincarnated as a black cat. That cat had run to her place and she could do nothing to chase it away. So she kept it and called it "Blackie." Blackie had the very worst temper you could imagine. Any day it didn't get fed fish, it would claw its mistress.

Great-Auntie uncovered all the scars on her arms. "You see, you see! He was condemned to be an animal but still hasn't let go of me! I told him, 'You probably can't even become a cat in your next life! I'm sure your soul is like a saw jammed in a block of wood. It can't go forward and it can't move back. That's the way you are, helpless and stuck.'"

I don't have the unbridled and soaring talents of Great-Auntie who, in spite of her limited cognitive powers, can endlessly create marvelous stories. I discovered that when I tried to solve the riddles of Old Town objectively, with accuracy and depth, though I wanted to with all my heart, I simply didn't have the strength. Now, as far as you're concerned, that would be an unfathomable "book from heaven." And how much more so could it be said for me?

"And then what?" (*You finally can't hold back anymore.*)

I give a wry grin. "And then, Grandma lived to be ninety-five years old. One day she told her nursemaid that she needn't cook for her anymore. She just went that calmly. Great-Auntie at 103 is still in the old folks' home, energetically wielding her pen for her Guo family who were without anyone to carry on the family line.

"Is that all?"

"If you still want to hear, say a prayer to your god to give me inspiration."

This was said rather mockingly. Such a cynical tone reminded me of Chaofan. He always cared about nothing and ridiculed everything. I also thought of that Guomindang army rabble saying to my grandfather, "Have your god make me a woman." Then I felt guilty.

You still show such sincerity as you reflect. "I am extremely moved and give thanks to God for letting me hear such a beautiful story."

Outside the window in the drizzly rain stretches the watery countryside of China south of the Yangzi. Perhaps back then Grandpa went along that little road where the mountains and rivers are changeless and where generation after generation of people hurried by.

"God had an extraordinary love for your grandfather and grandmother."

"Is this your opportunity to preach to me? Let me tell you something. I'm an atheist *and* a pantheist. I wouldn't favor any single religion."

I vigilantly erect my defense works.

"Every person believes in God and it's all because he or she is touched by God."

"So I guess I'll just wait for God himself to touch me."

I pick up the phone that is lying on the dining car table. The sixteen unanswered calls are all from Chrysanthemum. She definitely has come up again with some new move to prove her charm, or else, while bored out of her mind from stirring her coffee, has hit on something that's perked her up. This bad lady is on record for having spent the night with total strangers. I've warned her, "If you go missing, I'm not going to report it to Public Security, and no one will know that there's one less Chrysanthemum in this world." Chrysanthemum crinkled up her nose and wailed mournfully, "Am I so pathetic?" This joke was a little cruel but has a lot of truth to it. This is why we long to find husbands. Who doesn't fear being alone?

I am just about ready to return her calls. This character who never plays her cards in turn always provokes, but also satisfies, my curiosity. The phone in my hand suddenly rings. A "long-time-no-see!" telephone number pops up on the screen like some specter. I grasp the phone as if it were a burning charcoal and, panic-stricken, I want to hurl it out the window. For the past two years I have been changing my telephone number and every time I terminated it is because of this one's appearance. I deleted all the contact details related to this person from my address list. But the terror etched into my heart hasn't faded in the slightest. Even to Chrysanthemum have I never told the plain truth about this period of history. I preferred her laughing at me for being so old-fashioned and moronic, and concealed my broken heart and shame as if this were a top-secret plot.

I had thought at one time this was true love. The moment this man appeared, life was snapped off right at midpoint. The previous first love of two little innocents, a love marriage linked by flesh and blood and torn up by the roots, together with its broken history, had long turned to ashes. I returned to the time when love is first awakened. Blissful and scorched, I awaited his telephone call, awaited the sound of his footsteps, awaited his passionate embrace and kisses. That passion more ardent than flames would have been enough to melt a thousand-year-old glacier. He has a wife and child and on his hand he wears a diamond ring that he said she bought for him on their tenth wedding anniversary. This love which arrived so abruptly was like a tornado and a tidal wave that swept away every last bit of judgment I possessed. No ethics or morality could restrain such a "Great Love." I had no doubt whatsoever that the day would come when he would remove this ring and put on another one for me.

I don't have it in me to relate that extended process of evolution. All the memories that remain about that married man relate to my initial passion and final madness.

Arguing—endless, ceaseless arguing: over his marriage, over a telephone conversation with a man about work, over a day when my every movement wasn't in the palm of his hand. "Great Love" is a demon camouflaged as a beautiful woman that reveals its hideous face. What is called "passion" is actually insane possessiveness. In his case human possessiveness led to extremes in taking possession of money, wealth, and women. He checked the addresses listed in my phone and the e-mail box of my computer. He lay in wait for me at the hotels and guesthouses where I had business meetings to see if I was being "immoral" with other men. A man picking up a silk scarf of mine that had fallen on the ground and helping me wrap it around my neck—such insignificant trifles became indelible evidence of guilt. That evening, when everything in the house that could be broken was broken, filled with pain and grief I ran for my very life.

Every bit of information connected with that history is like a devil from Pandora's box that can arrive at any time to torment me. Sometimes when I am feeling humble I reflect on the bad things I did, and can do nothing but accept my punishment. If there really were a god that could pardon sins, I would kneel down before him.

CHAPTER SIXTEEN – THE FISH THAT ESCAPED THE NET

1.

AFTER MY GRANDFATHER got back from Shanghai during the War of Resistance, he went more than once to Li Village in Tongpan District in the eastern outskirts in search of Young Li's family. Young Li's widowed mother had passed away during the war. The old people in the village only knew his young friend was in the Guomindang Army. After Liberation, Grandpa again went to Li Village where everybody supposed that Young Li was now in Taiwan.

The medical orderly and the doctor had gone through thick and thin together in the flames of the War of Resistance. Many times each had offered to the other the chance to survive in the face of death. The closeness of this kind of friendship surpassed even blood kinship. I imagine Department Head Li could hardly wait to go to West Gate to pay a visit to Dr. Lin—just like those stirring, emotional scenes in the movies, when two people meet again after a long separation and shed tears of sorrow and joy at having both survived some disaster.

⌘　⌘　⌘

One morning, Second Sister was on her way out the gate to greet the postman as always. She had reached the sky well when she saw a man wearing a hat and a surgical mask looking in. She approached him and asked, "May I ask who you are looking for, comrade?"

"I've heard that Dr. Lin's medical skills are very great, and so, attracted by his fame, I have come to be treated."

"Dr. Lin has gone out on a call. Please sit down for a while in the clinic."

"Are you Mrs. Lin?"

"Yes."

He looked at the red paper with its black characters pasted on the gate. "Glorious Military Dependent."

"Your son is in the Liberation Army?"

"Both Second Son and the daughter are in the Liberation Army. Eldest Son is a revolutionary cadre who is currently away participating in land reform," Second Sister proudly replied.

"Very good! Very good!"

Second Sister beckoned the patient to sit down in the clinic and when she went out to get the newspaper she discovered him standing in the front hall, lost in thought as he gazed at the picture on the wall, that " Happy Family Portrait" taken in 1937.

"This is the only family portrait we have. I don't know when the whole family will ever again be able to go together to the photo studio."

"Time is passing by very quickly."

"Oh, yes, time is passing by very quickly."

The fellow paused for quite a bit and then asked, "Dr. Lin is in good health, then?"

Second Sister kept looking at the pair of eyes above the surgical mask. She felt this patient was a bit strange. *Don't tell me, when you come to be treated, you also ask about his health?*

"He looks thin and frail. Lately after coming back from a trip, he's gotten even thinner. But he's not sick or anything."

"The clinic's revenue is all right?"

Second Sister didn't answer right away and again kept looking at that pair of eyes above the surgical mask. Everybody who came here to be treated was from nearby neighborhoods. Very rarely were there any strange faces among them. In taking care of them, Dr. Lin was often "paying rather than being paid." She had her own thoughts on this point, but had never revealed them to anyone. Here was a stranger, but precisely because of that she had a sense of security. She laughed in a slightly mocking way. "What revenue?"

"Business is no good?"

"He doesn't see treating sick people as a business. There's nothing to be done about that. Luckily our children are all filial. Every month they send us money."

"Oh."

This stranger was Young Li. He didn't say anything more. He understood Dr. Lin and he understood Mrs. Lin sitting before him. Back then, he and the doctor had shared the same *kang* to sleep on and he had heard a lot of stories about Second Sister. He even knew that Third Sister had been the one the doctor liked most at first.

He lowered his head and considered whether or not to wait until the doctor returned home. Or whether or not he would identify himself to the doctor. This was a big question and one that he had not settled right up to the moment he stood in the Lin family gateway.

After Young Li had parted with the doctor on the Yangzi River, the fisherman assumed he was a communist and sent him north. And so in this way Young Li became a fighter in the communist-led New Fourth Army. At the time he was not yet fully eighteen years old. His courage and natural martial qualities came repeatedly to the attention of his superiors and when the Liberation Army crossed the Yangzi he was now a battalion commander. No one had asked him about his history before his eighteenth birthday and he himself felt strongly that period wasn't worth mentioning at all. So, with the growth of experience, that history gradually became a millstone around his neck. He was a revolutionary cadre who had not only been in the Guomindang Army, but had moreover hidden his past. If such treachery ever came to light, he would never be able to wash himself clean of this, even if he jumped into the Yellow River. He had seen with his own eyes many comrades-in-arms who had fallen from the saddle due to "historical problems," and he shuddered each time it happened. He had seen Dr. Lin's file. In the résumé completed by the doctor, the section on the period of his army service during the War of Resistance cited two persons as references, Division Commander Zhang and Orderly Li. Zhang had died on the battlefield and Li's whereabouts were unknown. The doctor knew Li's family home but barely mentioned it. Young Li sensed that the doctor had protected him and gratitude filled his heart.

He thought about telling Dr. Lin that "Whereabouts Unknown" Young Li now was a top-level Communist Party cadre. He also thought about inviting the doctor to his own home to meet his own beautiful and gentle wife and two adorable children, but that was a history that could never, ever be touched.

Second Sister saw the patient's downcast expression and thought that he was feeling the pain of his illness. "Comrade, just bear with it a bit. I am going to call Dr. Lin."

"Thank you, Mrs. Lin, but I think it would be better if I don't bother him."

"How could a patient in need of a doctor be a bother to him?"

And as she spoke, Second Sister stepped out the room. By the time she and the doctor had hurried back, he was gone. They asked the girl selling firewood by their gate and were told that he had hailed a pedicab and left. The doctor thought he must have gone for treatment at the hospital. From Second Sister's description of him, such a decision had been the right one, for he needed a chest fluoroscopy.

⌘   ⌘   ⌘

A few days later, the postman handed Second Sister an official letter from the district health bureau. The doctor's name was written on the envelope.

Ninth Brother tore open the letter and after giving it a scan, laughed, "This is someone's joke, I suppose?"

It was an offer of employment. The health bureau was offering Dr. Lin the job of head of internal medicine at the district's People's Hospital, with the remuneration of a state cadre.

In the early Liberation period, for some doctors, running a private clinic was the only option. Such doctors either had "historical problems," or else had not received a standard education and were viewed as quacks, what was called "Mongol doctors."

Dr. Lin had once taken the competitive test to qualify for employment at the People's Hospital. Because of his age he came in "after scholar Sun Shan," or in other words, he failed to place. Now he was over fifty years of age. If he enjoyed the remuneration of a state cadre, in a few more years he could take his pension and retire in his old age. Was such a good thing really possible?

This was all rather queer. Second Sister came around behind her husband and saw the big red stamp of the health bureau employment letter. After some thought she burst out laughing. "You have me and our children to thank for this. Because we have been positive in seeking ideological progress, the government now sees a backward element like you differently."

"Oh, so the backward element now basks in the glory of the positive ones. Thank you all very much!"

But he thought, "What Second Sister said was true. The Communist Party really is very magnanimous in granting me such a big favor."

He pulled Second Sister by the hand to pray together. They gave thanks to the Communist Party and to the Lord Jesus.

⌘　⌘　⌘

The doctor didn't know that in Old Town there was a department head named Li. He was even less aware that this piece of stuffed pastry that seemed to have fallen from heaven was the gift sent by Department Head Li. Afterward, when even odder things happened, he still remained in the dark.

2.

THE DOCTOR COLLECTED his first salary. This was his reward for working for the new society. As he clutched the thick wad of cash he felt ineffably moved and happy, and for some reason he thought of his father. His father had died way back when he was seven years old. The deepest impression he had of his father was the portrait hanging on the wall. Now his father stepped out of the portrait—as alive now as he had been before—sat down in the old-style wooden armchair, and softly called him. Ninth Brother came forward. His father brought out from an inner pocket several warm silver dollars and pressed them into Ninth Brother's hand. He remembered that he was only slightly taller than the arm of the chair then and it was New Year's Eve money his father had given him.

The trials and hardships of more than half a century were nothing compared to this sense of total ease and comfort. The doctor forgot that he himself was now old, and for an instant he was a child once more. And just like some naughty student he idly kicked the small stones on the street as he walked all the way from the hospital gate right to the department store on East Street. He wanted to use this first salary to buy something that would be worth remembering. As he strode through the main door of the store, his gaze immediately fixed on a new model Everlasting bicycle. He had never properly learned how to ride a bicycle when he was young and that was his greatest regret. He paid no attention to any of the other things in the store, just that! (*"With the Everlasting brand, we will have everlasting happiness under the leadership of the Communist Party!"*) The sales attendant brought out a model for him to try, but he waved it away. "I don't need to try it out, I'll just buy it."

Pushing the bicycle, the doctor took the long way around to a secluded spot beside Little West Lake and there he tried it out. His left foot thrust down on the pedal, but his right foot hadn't yet left the ground, and he took a big tumble. He paid no attention to the scrape on his wrist as he got back up, but hurriedly pushing the bicycle to a place with more light, he clucked his tongue with an aching heart when he saw the faint scratch on the handlebars.

⌘ ⌘ ⌘

Second Sister was at home lighting the fire to cook dinner. When it came time to eat, Ninth Brother had still not returned so she put down what she was doing and stood by the gate peering out in all directions. Over the years, whenever anyone at all in the family was late in coming home, she would wait anxiously like this by the gate. By the time blackness was streaking the sky, the bright, crisp ring of a bicycle bell came closer and closer, and a man pushing a bicycle appeared at the street crossing. She was still tirelessly searching up and down the street.

Like a naughty boy, Ninth Brother rang the bell even more loudly as he passed by Second Sister. She wondered what kind of problem this person could be afflicted with. Ninth Brother stopped and started laughing.

"My old lady, here is my first month's pay. I am giving it to you!"

Second Sister was amazed. This fellow who never acted his age, was it possible that he still wanted to learn to ride a bicycle? She knew that it was almost payday, and already had plans to give money to her several younger brothers. The eldest had sons for whom school fees needed to be paid. Second Younger Brother had returned to Old Town all alone without "that woman" and was expecting relief funds from his older sister. Still, she didn't begrudge her husband this purchase. Recalling the first Lin family bicycle back in the 1930s, Ninth Brother's purchase of a new one showed that his heart was at peace and ease. She pursed her lips into a half smile as she walked around the bicycle and said gently, "Do you know how old you are now? You never learned to ride when you were young...can you still learn now?"

"Just you wait. I'll learn this very evening. Later on I'll take my grandchildren to school on it!"

Ninth Brother hoisted the bicycle through the back door of the kitchen and went to the side of the moat to find Shuiguan. Shuiguan thought that some emergency had occurred at the doctor's house and, quickly putting down his bowl of rice, went running out. The doctor pointed to his brand new bicycle. "Shuiguan, hold me up on this thing. This evening I am going to learn to ride a bicycle!" Shuiguan was also enjoying this. "Dr. Lin, why bother to learn now? Whenever you need to go out, all you got to do is just shout for me."

"Later on I'll invite you to ride my bike!" replied the doctor.

When Second Sister brought the food in from the kitchen, Ninth Brother had already gone. She stood in front of the gate under the oleander tree. Ninth Brother had planted this tree with his own hands during the year of victory in the War of Resistance. Many times she would stand under it, pensive and care-laden, and straining her eyes as she awaited the late arrival of some family member. This time, though, sweetness filled her being. Only now had the good days really come.

⌘　⌘　⌘

These good days passed one by one and the happy events of the Lin family kept on coming. The doctor's three children had all married, and their first grandson had now been born. The doctor named this boy Su'er. People outside the family supposed that this word was the "Su" in the term "Su Lian," meaning the Soviet Union. In those days, people spoke of the friendly relations between China and the Soviet Union. Only he and Second Sister knew that "Su" here meant "Ye Su." The one small regret that blemished these happy times was that the doctor never did learn to ride the bicycle. When Baoqing returned from Korea his father presented it to him as a welcome home present.

And so the doctor walked unsuspectingly into a new "movement," this one called "Freely Express Views." He saw many articles in the newspapers addressing views to the party, but he didn't feel these had anything to do with him. Those writers were all well-known figures, while he himself was merely a poor Old Town scholar. Had there been no Communist Party there would have been no good days for him. He loved the Communist Party.

The waves of this movement washed into the People's Hospital where the doctor worked. On this particular day, the hospital closed early and held a big meeting. There the head of the hospital and its party secretary each made his self-examination. Following this, they mobilized the entire workforce to present views and opinions to the leadership. Dr. Lin was so moved by the sincerity of the two leaders that he grew misty-eyed. He had no views to present with regard to the party, but he always had views about the hospital leadership. It was just like he loved Jesus, but that wasn't to say that he completely accepted all the other members of the church.

The head of the hospital and the party secretary both were originally northern cadres assigned to the south. The head of the hospital had been in the army medical corps and the secretary had come up from the battlefield, but every time there was a consultation within the hospital, they both would make peremptory decisions. They would issue orders like "you just have to cure this patient!" to the chief physician. Dr. Lin felt their style deviated from scientific practice and had on many occasions presented his dissenting views directly to these leaders. These two clearly felt disgusted with him and for a considerable period of time he was not invited to take part in consultations. However, this year Dr. Lin's name was included on the list for promotions and salary increases. This surprised him and his colleagues, as well, and there were some who guessed that he was related to a leader at an even higher level. The promotion and salary increase really couldn't dispel Dr. Lin's bias against the hospital leaders. However, on this day under the party's leadership, the head of the hospital and the party secretary finally recognized their problems and humbly they requested the views of those present. It was their style of the "self-effacing true gentleman" that so moved Dr. Lin.

The meeting hall grew completely still. Old Town folk are timid and conservative. Normally they would do no more than to let loose with complaints in private. When the leaders solicited their views right then and there, everyone became as quiet as the proverbial cicadas on cold days.

When Dr. Lin slowly stood up, all eyes were upon him. Fighting back his tears, he said, "This is just the broad-mindedness that communists ought to possess. You—the party secretary and the head of the hospital—are human. All humans all have flaws and make mistakes. You are the heroes and statesmen of the Revolution, but curing sickness and saving people requires specialized knowledge and in this respect you are laymen. You frequently go against specialized conventions and interfere with the established treatment programs of doctors for their patients. I hope that from now on you can improve in this respect."

The party secretary straightway humbly expressed his acceptance of Dr. Lin's views and at the same time extolled him for "saying all you know, and saying it without reserve."

Then the floodgates opened and all the secret complaints came pouring forth. The clerk immersed himself in recording them, writing page after page. Up on the dais, the party secretary flushed red and the hospital head blanched waxen, and they both never stopped wiping away their perspiration.

Dr. Lin didn't feel good about this. Some people's views were excessively sharp. A very fat nurse in internal medicine who had been punished because of an accident in treating a patient became totally unbridled in voicing her dissatisfaction and in rapid-fire fashion, attacked the hospital head. Unable to put up with this, he shouted, "You've gone too far!" However, the emotions of the meeting had gotten out of control and no one heard him.

It was already late at night when the meeting ended. The two leaders left the meeting hall amidst swarms of people who still wanted their say. The doctor also wanted to go up and have a word with the leaders. He wanted to say, "Actually, your excellent points far outweigh your shortcomings." But after following for a few steps he saw he wouldn't get a word in and withdrew back into the hall where he sat dazed and all alone in a corner. His sense of having done something wrong filled him with guilt, but he just couldn't place what his mistake had been. The duty staff turned off the lights and shut the doors. But he still sat there in the darkness.

This evening Second Sister was frantic. She waited for Ninth Brother by the gate until her legs went numb from standing. Worry and anxiety entwined her heart like poisonous vines. She thought something had happened to him. His shape finally emerged from the darkness at the West Gate crossing. His body had returned, but his soul was lost who-knew-where. Tight-lipped, he refused to say what had happened. The next day he went to work as usual, but Second Sister had the strong feeling that something unknown was about to happen. Disasters often suddenly fell from the heavens at unguarded moments. She grew terribly afraid.

⌘　⌘　⌘

Two months later, the "Oppose Rightists" movement followed on the heels of "Freely Express Views." Again in that same meeting hall, the party secretary vehemently asserted that rightist elements were using the "Freely Express Views" movement to attack the party and socialism. "We have rightists in our midst, and, what's more, many of them."

Once again Dr. Lin stood up and the meeting hall went deadly silent. "At the time of 'Freely Express Views,' the views I presented to the hospital leaders were too extreme, but in no way was I attacking the party and socialism. Even so, if it is a question of investigating and prosecuting rightists, I should be counted as one of them."

This was quite unlike last time when "pulling one vine moves the whole mountain." Now he was standing utterly alone. Pair upon pair of panic-stricken eyes focused on him. *Why should they be so frightened?* He very much doubted that people's thinking could possibly be all the same. There would always be those who tended to the left and those who tended to the right. It was precisely the left and the right checking and containing each other that things never ended up in too great a deviation either way. He saw the fat nurse, her head buried in her arms. *Surely she must be feeling that her accusations at the earlier meeting had been too extreme, so why doesn't she stand up and big-heartedly recognize her mistake?*

When the doctor admitted he was a rightist, he felt a great sense of relief and after the meeting he went home in exceedingly good spirits. Along the way he bought peanuts and some of Old Town's aged rice wine. It had been several months since he and

Second Sister had sipped wine under the lantern. Today he finally felt unburdened of all he had been carrying since "Freely Express Views." He wanted to invite Second Sister to enjoy some wine and have a chat.

⌘ ⌘ ⌘

Day by day, the big character posters in the hospital grew in number. This new "rightist" designation steadily grew into something quite terrifying. You could almost say it in the same breath as "counterrevolutionary." Every day, Dr. Lin went around the outer wall of the hospital reading a string of big character posters. There in black ink on white paper was his name and the names of many others. Many people attacked each other as rightists.

What is going on here? Dr. Lin just couldn't figure it out.

On this month's payday, Dr. Lin was called to the personnel section where the section head gave him three months' salary and said, "The leadership of the health bureau is of the view that your work level does not reach that required in state hospitals. In accordance with the spirit of higher authority, we suggest that you take the initiative of resigning."

The doctor was at a total loss as he stood in front of the desk in the section head's office. When he had first received the employment letter he thought someone was playing a joke on him. Today he was being forced to quit and this also seemed like a joke. He had a vague sense that a pair of hands behind him was manipulating the ups and downs of his destiny. *Who could that person be?* Suddenly he laughed, "All right, all right. Good-bye."

He was still wearing his white smock as he left the personnel section office, and gripping the three months' salary, he walked straight out of the hospital. People at the gate greeted him, but he heard nothing and saw nothing. Despondently he implored Jesus. *O Lord, I truly am all confused. Why should people play such practical jokes on me? How will I ever explain this to Second Sister? She is so concerned about my work. I don't blame her. She's had a lifetime of the upheavals I have been entangled in. Before, I thought that when we got old I could finally give her "a high pillow" and a life free from care, but I am truly an incompetent man. O Lord, I beseech you to comfort Second Sister, and keep her from being too worried.*

The doctor looked up and discovered that he had now walked all the way to West Street. Half a century before, that was Mr. Qiao's residence right there in front of him. A wave of warmth swept through him and a feeling of gratitude like a sunbeam swept away the gloom of his bad feelings. *What do I amount to? When I was eight years old I should have died like a wild dog by the roadside. But I survived, had a family, built up a practice...my wife and children are perfect, so what does a tiny setback count for?*

He kept pinching the wad of paper currency he held in his pocket. Feeling much better now, he wanted to go home and play a joke on Second Sister. He would tell her that higher authorities had especially commended him and tripled his salary. The sight of Second Sister squinting as she counted the money would be just so adorable.

At the West Gate street crossing, the doctor stopped to take a look. There was no sign of Second Sister under the oleander tree. He supposed she had gone back to the kitchen to fill the rice bowl and bring out the food.

"Second Sister!" As he passed through the door he stopped in midstride. Second Sister, together with Baosheng and Baoqing, were sitting together at the Eight Immortals table, looking very stiff and formal.

Don't tell me they already know that I've lost our rice bowl...

"What brings you back here together?"

"Dad, Baoqing and I would like to have a word with you," Baosheng said.

Surprised at this, the doctor asked, "About?"

Second Sister stood up and interrupted them. "First, let's eat. Afterward, then you can talk."

"You sit down. I want to hear what they have to talk about!"

Although his two sons had already married and had families of their own, they still felt respect and awe toward their father. They looked at each other, and Baoqing said, "Bro, you just go ahead and say it."

Baosheng cleared his throat. "Umm, let me put it this way. Baoqing's and my salaries aren't too bad. We wish you wouldn't report to work or run the clinic anymore, but just stay at home with your grandchildren. Su'er often gets sick when he's placed in the child-care center."

Oh, so that's it. These two have come at just the right time.

The doctor asked Second Sister, "And what do you say?"

Second Sister hemmed and hawed. "I...I would like you to have work, and then retire after a few more years. And with your pension you could stay at home with the grandchildren. But what our sons are saying makes sense. The 'Oppose Rightists' movement's under way now and you're too frank and outspoken. Don't call some disaster upon yourself in your old age."

"What's 'Oppose Rightists' got to do with it? China, with its hundreds of millions of people, can't be all leftist, so I'm an ideologically conservative rightist."

Baosheng exclaimed in fright, "Dad, whatever you do, don't talk such nonsense!"

Baosheng looked down and paused for a moment, then with a grim expression on his face said, "Dad, just come back home, all right? For me and Baoqing. We guarantee that you and Ma will never worry about food or clothing."

That morning, Baosheng had met his old boss, Deputy District Head Bai, and found out that the hospital had a big character poster calling Dr. Lin its number one rightist. His old boss said to him in a flat tone of voice, "Persuade your father to resign and just go back home." Baosheng knew well just how much weight these words carried. His father's historical problems made his own promotion fail just when it was on the point of success. When Baoqing returned from Korea and was about to report to the military academy, he received his demobilization notice. If their daddy had one more charge against him, his sons and grandchildren would probably all be dragged into this.

The doctor felt his two sons were too chickenhearted and this disappointed him greatly. He spoke with studied reserve. "All right then, both of you go back home. I'll talk this over with your ma."

"Dinner is ready. Eat first and then go," Second Sister said.

"Let them go back to their own homes to eat!"

The two brothers looked at each other in stunned amazement and didn't know what to do.

Baosheng stood up. "Dad, we're doing this for your own good."

"Just go and leave me in quiet for a while."

Their sons left. Husband and wife ate without saying a word to each other. Then Second Sister cautiously put in, "Actually, you are a doctor. In the hospital just go ahead and take care of sick people. Why get involved in this rightist-leftist business?"

Then she noticed that Ninth Brother was still wearing his white smock. "How is it you've come home wearing your work clothes?"

The doctor removed the garment and took out the salary from his pocket. Then he played his joke on Second Sister. "I got a raise this month."

She counted the money. "How come it's this much?"

"That's right! And you still want me to quit?"

Second Sister thought this over for quite a while, the money in her hand. "Peace and security are the most important things. Our sons work in the government and know a lot more than we do. 'Wind doesn't just blow out of a hollow rock'...."

The doctor suddenly got all worked up. "I'm sorry, Second Sister. I'm always getting you involved. You've eaten so much bitterness in this life with me, and now that we're old, there's still no peace. Have you ever regretted marrying me?"

"What's the matter with you today?"

"Really, tell me, have you ever regretted this?"

"Yes, extremely. What about you? Have you regretted marrying me?"

"*Mmh,* yes, I have."

They both looked at each other and smiled.

The doctor said, "Heat up some wine. Tomorrow I won't be going to work. Let's drink a little more and talk a little more."

"You've decided, then?"

Two cups, then three cups of wine, warmed their stomachs. The doctor told Second Sister all about his resignation. The two of them pondered late into the night and still couldn't make any sense of the sequence of all these events that had come so quickly, one after the other.

3.

Su'er was just the kind of big-headed, big-eyed boy that everyone loved at first sight. Every day he would run about under the knees of his Granny and Gramps wearing his split-seat trousers and chirping endlessly, like a little talking magpie. Since coming into the West Gate home, he became the focus of Dr. and Mrs. Lin's love. A dense and enveloping family joy shut Dr. Lin off from the outside world. And at that moment, the outside world was all stirred up. Throughout the entire country, half a million people were designated as rightist elements. The provincial newspapers had just published this terrifying number.

At ten o'clock in the morning, the postman handed the newspaper to Second Sister. Glancing back, she saw Ninth Brother with their little grandson planting flowers in the sky well. Su'er was playing in the dirt with a spoon. She wanted to go over and stop him but she was moved by this scene of love between grandfather and grandchild. Hazily she recalled Baosheng and Baoqing when they were both very little. Then they had experienced more than enough of the chaos and dislocations of war and only rarely this kind of happy time.

It was now several months since Ninth Brother had resigned from the hospital. Second Sister, as always, held daily meetings in her capacity as director. She was all the more aware of how perilous a calamity their family had avoided, otherwise today Ninth Brother would be "Wearing the Rightist Hat." Perhaps he might even be sent to some distant and isolated mountain district for labor reform. *O heaven!* She shuddered to think of it. Peace and security were blessings. No amount of money could buy the happy scene of children or grandchildren playing at one's feet.

She placed the newspaper on Ninth Brother's desk and, remembering that she should renew its subscription for the next quarter, rushed into the sky well and said, "Gramps! Don't forget to go to the post office to renew the newspaper subscription."

After Su'er had come to them, they imitated Su'er's calling them "Gramps," and "Granny."

Ninth Brother kept on busily gardening. "No need to subscribe anymore. Gramps hasn't been reading it for a long time already. Gramps' ears aren't listening to what's happening outside and all I want to do is play with Su'er."

"I agree. Since your thinking will never keep up with the revolutionary tide, it would be better not to have any ideology at all."

"That's right, the little flowers and plants don't have ideology. Every day they wear pretty clothes. The birds in the trees don't have any ideology and every day they sing happy songs. Su'er, is Gramps right?"

"Gramps is right...and Granny's right too." Su'er had a nimble mind. He was not yet two years old and he already understood balanced diplomacy.

Ninth Brother laughed. "Su'er is the flower on the top of the wall that bends with each wind. When he grows up, for sure, he can't be a rightist."

"Don't keep going on about rightists and leftists. This is a very serious matter."

"You're the one who makes it serious. In our home, you're the leftist, I'm the rightist, Su'er is the middle-of-the-roader, and we're still near and dear to each other."

"Oh, you!" Second Sister shook her head and changed the subject. "How could you have given Su'er the spoon to play with?"

She somehow felt that, inside, Ninth Brother was very clear about everything and only pretended to be all muddled up as his way of escaping reality. In this she sensed great danger. She worried that he might boldly and self-righteously go to the government and announce that he was a rightist. Sometimes at meetings she heard air raid alarms going off inside her and was terrified that he was stirring up some calamity at home.

Taking the sewing basket, Second Sister sat down at the Eight Immortals table to make a little stomach bib for Su'er. As she sewed she pondered over whether or not she should come out straight about all this with Ninth Brother. She recalled that Pastor Chen had said that Christians had to submit to authority. Rightist elements did not submit to the government and so they had to be punished.

"Gramps, you can't keep saying you're a rightist. Submission to the government is the lot of Christians. If the government says rightists are bad people, then they're bad people."

Ninth Brother turned and gazed at Second Sister. He had something to say but he didn't say it, just silently lowered his head and went on gardening.

Second Sister saw that he had heard full well what she had said and the alarm abruptly stopped ringing inside her.

⌘   ⌘   ⌘

That afternoon, Second Sister went to a meeting at the neighborhood office and Ninth Brother took Su'er to soak in the hot springs. The hot springs of Old Town's eastern district were renowned. It was said that they could cure more than ten kinds of disease. Leading Su'er by the hand, husband and wife walked to Little West Lake before going their separate ways. The weather was pleasant and they were all in a good mood.

Grandfather and grandson passed by a little sundries shop and Su'er saw fruit drops in the glass counter. His eyes homed in on them and he swallowed several times. "Gramps, what are those?"

Ninth Brother gazed at his grandson in wonder. *Every day new continents can be discovered on this little guy. See how cunning he is? He wants to eat candy but doesn't come right out and say it.* He purposely teased Su'er. "That's medicine for curing coughs."

Su'er immediately started to cough. "I want to take medicine."

Ninth Brother couldn't help letting out a great guffaw. He reached down and fished out some paper currency to buy some candies which he placed in the child's pocket. Just then, a person called out, "Dr. Lin!"

Reflexively he turned around to look but it took a while before he recognized the woman with the frenzied and grief-ridden face as that fat nurse at the People's Hospital. In over half a year since he had last seen her she had lost a great deal of weight.

"Dr. Lin, how so very carefree you look taking your grandson out for a stroll."

"What's the matter with you? Have you become ill?"

"I've suffered a lot because of you!"

The nurse wept silently. With trembling shoulders, she whimpered about the tragedies that had befallen her. She had become the hospital's top rightist, her husband divorced her, and with a child only five years old, she had been assigned to work in some outlying rural hospital.

The day was still clear and fine but Dr. Lin seemed to be struck by a bolt of lightning. Unable to express himself, he just kept saying, "I'm sorry."

"What's the use of 'I'm sorry'? You're the real Big Rightist!" she screamed hysterically.

"Yes, yes. If there's any number-one rightist at all at the hospital, it should be me. I'll go there and tell the leader."

The doctor had no sooner said this than he was off, even forgetting to take his little grandson with him. Luckily, Su'er was a sharp lad, and letting out a bellow he ran to catch up. With Su'er in his arms, Dr. Lin went into the leader's office. The former head of the hospital had been transferred and his replacement called in a clerk to record what was said. "The nurse is still young," the doctor said, "I hope the leader can give her the chance to correct herself. If the hospital hasn't met its quota of rightists, then count me as one of them." The head of the hospital conscientiously took notes and asked him to return home and wait to be dealt with.

That evening when Su'er had fallen asleep, Ninth Brother told Second Sister all that had happened that afternoon. She stopped her sewing and raised both her hands high above her, holding them there for some time. Just today the alarm had been lifted from within her and now the bomb fell right on top of her. What more could be said? This fish that had escaped the net swam right onto the chopping board and asked to be cut up. She supposed that he was a dead man for sure.

His eyes tightly closed, Ninth Brother sat behind Second Sister in his rocking chair. Baoqing had given him this for his most recent birthday. Every day at noon he would doze off, holding Su'er as he sat in the chair. It gave him a feeling of satisfaction impossible to put into words. Thinking that he might no longer be able to hold Su'er as they rocked back and forth in the chair, grandfather and grandson daydreaming together, Ninth Brother grew tremendously afraid. He really wasn't a desperate and daring man, but every time he encountered some major issue, he would sense a force sweeping him along into making some extraordinary decision. It was as if he had received an irresistible order: *You must do this.*

He opened his eyes and sorrowfully addressed Second Sister, "Let's say a prayer together."

Second Sister, wordlessly and devoid of any expression, went into the bedroom and dug out some silk wadding and cloth and spread it out on the dining table. Her skilled hands then dexterously cut out padded jacket and padded trouser patterns for Ninth Brother. She had heard that Old Town's rightist elements were all sent to mountainous areas for labor reform. Since it had come to this, she had to plan for the worst and she hurriedly made several sets of warm clothing for him.

"Second Sister, this isn't something I want either. If you don't forgive me, I'll feel even more miserable."

Crick, crick, crick went the scissors. When Ninth Brother's padded jacket and trousers were done, she still had to make some for herself. She had steeled herself. No matter where Ninth Brother might be assigned, she would follow him, even to the ends of the earth. Residence committee director, glorious army dependent, all the honors that she had cared about she now tossed aside. Suddenly she felt her heart grow lighter. Actually, the terror and panic that people feel in confronting disaster more often than not is even more painful than actually going forward to endure the disaster. She had always been in a state of fear that the sword hanging over her head might fall. Now the very moment she relaxed her vigilance, the sword had fallen, catching her totally unprepared. All she could do was wait to be butchered. She'd take things as they came. After all, Second Sister was a woman who had weathered great storms before.

Ninth Brother stared intently at his wife. Finally, the shame and panic in his eyes moved her and called up her mother's tenderness. She put down her needle and turned to comfort him. "Don't think about it too much. It's just fate, your fate and mine too. We'd like to avoid it, but we can't."

Ninth Brother wanted to say something, but the corners of his mouth started to twitch and suddenly he was crying like a child.

⌘   ⌘   ⌘

They didn't tell their children of the dreaded event that might occur in the family. They treasured every day, every hour they had before that event happened. Second Sister requested sick leave and didn't participate in any more meetings. The two old folks brought Su'er all over Old Town, wherever there was a place for him to play, and they ate all over Old Town, wherever there was a place to eat. It was just at that time that Grandpa bought a 120 mm camera. Everywhere they went they took souvenir photos of the images of the family happiness shared by grandparents and grandson. Many pictures were candid snapshots that recorded Su'er's every expression, and these were extremely vivid. My grandfather had the pictures developed and inserted into photo albums. He was preparing this to console his moments of wistfulness and longing after he and Su'er were parted.

One month, two months, passed by. "Oppose Rightists" gradually became a term of the past. The reason was unclear, but the hospital leadership once again released the big fish that had thrown itself into the net. Grandma recommenced her committee work and was so busy going in and coming out of meetings that she was gone from sight the whole day long. My grandfather often held Su'er in his arms as he sat in the rocking chair late at night waiting for "the director's" return. Sometimes he would tease and joke with her. "If another "Oppose Rightists" movement starts up again, I would still throw myself into the net. In that way, every day you would keep me and Su'er company." To which, Grandma had this reply: "You're the fish that swims right onto the chopping board and asks to be cut up. The government has let you go. No matter how much work I do, I could never repay this immense favor."

⌘　⌘　⌘

After Grandpa passed on, Grandma gave that photo album to Su'er. She turned page after page, recalling the story behind each picture. "This picture is at Gathering Spring Garden Hotel. You were eating prawns. Here's one of you at Drum Mountain. You were all tired out from walking and lay on the ground and wouldn't get up." Su'er said, "Gramps and Granny really knew how to have fun, bringing a grandchild on their honeymoon." Grandma said, "Did you know? At that time a calamity struck our home. There was no reason to be happy. Nowadays, I think it's God who lets us be happy. Su'er, you just believe in God. I'll take you to church." Su'er was absorbed in admiring his picture when he was a child. "Look! I was already a handsome guy when I was this small!"

Grandma sighed. "None of you believe. Later, where will your Gramps and I go looking for you all?"

CHAPTER SEVENTEEN – CHANCE AND PREDESTINATION

1.

THERE'S SO MUCH chance behind just our births alone. Everyone arrives in this world as the result of a string of accidents, that's all. People find this idea discouraging.

If only Miss Baohua had not been so headstrong and felt she just had to go to far-off Xinjiang, if only my real father had not gone on an assignment to a small town on the border where he caught pneumonia, there would have been no me in this world. I am just so paltry and insignificant, so marginal.

Baohua thought that dropping out of school and joining the army was rather an earthshaking deed. The whole of West Gate would move heaven and earth for her, and all the Lins and their very near and dear Chen family would make a wall of their bodies to keep her from leaving Old Town. Actually, to her great surprise, apart from her mother, nobody else expressed opposition to what she did. At the time her father was closedmouthed and went around with a saddened expression. He loved her the most. Of all the family he was the one who wielded the most authority and had he resolutely opposed this, Baohua could not have walked out the gate. But he never once said no. How could he have been so hard-hearted?

This hurt and bitterly disappointed Baohua. The military vehicles carrying the new soldiers set out. As they sped along under towering mountains and over lofty ranges, Baohua suddenly realized that she had not at all been mentally prepared for such a journey and she started to blubber. Then the two other women soldiers traveling with her followed suit. Their troop leader was like a kindergarten teacher, cajoling this one and encouraging that one, telling jokes, and doing magic tricks. The women soldiers smiled through their tears and then a second later broke out crying all over again.

Baohua cried like this all the way to the border town of Kashgar.[48] There she worked as a medical orderly in a military hospital. Hearing that after two years of military service she could be demobilized and return home, she bought a kind of speckled broad bean and put seven hundred and thirty of these into a bottle. Every morning she would tip one of these out and just waited for the day when the bottle would be empty and she could submit an application for demobilization. Women soldiers at the base were rare birds. Every one of them had many suitors, and Baohua was no exception. However, she had made her mind up to return to Old Town and she consistently refused all those who were chasing her, including several leading cadres to whom she had been introduced through her organization. She made one very clear commitment: to get back south to Old Town, she would make sure not to fall in love and get married. Daddy also advised her like this in every one of his letters.

Very quickly the bottle was emptied of its last bean and that very day Baohua submitted her application for demobilization. This was refused by her superiors and they promoted her from medical

---

[48] The official Chinese rendition of this Turkic name is "Kashi." Xinjiang Uygur Autonomous Region was established on October 1, 1955, with its capital at Urumqi. This vast territory in China's far northwest is bounded externally by Russia, Kazakhstan, Afghanistan, Kyrgyzstan, and India.

orderly to nurse. Tearfully, she refilled the bottle with beans. Two years later she once again applied to be demobilized, and once again this was refused. But Baohua didn't cry this time. She pursed her lips and said to her leader, "If you don't release me to go home, when the weather gets warmer I'm just going to get in a truck and go home by myself." The leader let out a big laugh and didn't take her seriously.

Every woman soldier at this frontier base was petted and flattered. Frail and delicate Baohua was even more the object of tenderness. Though she had been a soldier for several years now, her "Eldest Young Miss" temperament hadn't changed one bit and she really did start planning to run away from the frontier. Between Kashgar and Old Town stretched the endless land and rivers of China, and in those days communications were primitive to the extreme. She would have to go seven days and seven nights by long-distance bus to the region's capital, Urumqi. Then she would take a plane to Lanzhou in neighboring Gansu Province, where there was a train to Shanghai. From Shanghai she would go by boat to Old Town. Baohua still needed to work for quite a while to be able to save up enough to pay for such a journey.

Just at this moment there was a patient in the internal medicine ward, a reporter named Xiao. The moment Baohua laid eyes on him, the medicine tray fell out of her hands onto the floor, for she really and truly saw Enchun. There had been no news of Enchun for several years and her father's letters never mentioned him. She thought that Enchun was now a big official in the Communist Party. He had taken part so early in the underground movement that these days he just had to be a high-level cadre in the party.

This patient, Xiao, was reading a book and the tray's fall startled him. When he looked up he saw standing in the doorway a little nurse whose eyes were brimming with tears. At that instant he felt she was extremely beautiful.

Even though they were looking each other right in the eye, Baohua still saw Enchun. Indeed, Enchun and Xiao strongly resembled each other. From a photograph taken of Xiao when he was young, he and Enchun both had the same big physical build and a similar bookish air about them.

Reporter Xiao laughed as he walked over from his bed and helped pick up the tray and the pills spilled all over the floor. "What did you see that scared you so much?"

His accent was very thick and Baohua couldn't locate it. Its strangeness roused her from her dream: *This isn't Enchun.* For some reason she cried brokenheartedly all the more. Sobbing, she dispensed the pills and took his temperature. Like a big brother, Reporter Xiao asked her all kinds of questions. Was she homesick? Was anyone bullying her? The more he asked, the more brokenhearted she grew. The next day, Baohua told him, "You look a lot like one of my older brothers back home." "Then just see me as that older brother," Reporter Xiao said.

When Reporter Xiao was discharged from the hospital he gave Baohua a letter. This was the first love letter that Baohua had ever received. Most of the women soldiers who came to the frontier were matched up within three months, so Baohua, who "guarded her body like jade," had long been the target of a multitude of enlisted men and officers, all vying for her. They'd ask their leaders to come forward as their matchmakers. All one of these would have to say was, "Ah, Miss Lin, let's just have a chat," and she would know— here was one more matchmaker. Report had it that a regiment-level cadre was lovesick for her, but up until now no one had ever wooed her with a love letter.

Reporter Xiao's love letter was elegant and polished and as gorgeous as a poem. Just above his signature he wrote, "I think

I have fallen in love with you." Suddenly she burst into loud and inconsolable tears of grief: for her distant home, for her father and mother who anxiously waited for her return, for the promise she had kept all these years that was now broken. She wanted to marry this young reporter so overflowing with talent!

Baohua's writing style wasn't too bad either. When she was little, arithmetic problems scared her but her marks in Chinese were always at the top of her class. As for verse, she could reel off Tang *shi* and Song *ci* backward. She now commenced a love-letter correspondence with Reporter Xiao, then in Urumqi. There was a letter every week, and every letter was several pages long.

Reporter Xiao's going to Kashgar to do interviews had occurred purely by chance. Until then he had merely been an insignificant night-desk editor at his newspaper. Reports about Kashgar's rural land reform not only had to appear as the headline in the first edition, these also had to be sent to the central leadership for their review and approval. Such an important, on-the-spot reporting mission couldn't be given to Comrade Young Xiao. But an "old revolutionary" senior reporter got sick along the way there and came back without accomplishing anything. A subeditor who set out had just met with a car accident and was now laid up in the hospital.

Young Xiao, although virtually an unknown, cherished lofty ambitions, and while normally a quiet person, he strived for the chance to show what he could do. Because the leaders fretted about having no one suitable to assign, here was his golden opportunity. He sought out the director of his newspaper for a talk and quite systematically presented his understanding of rural policy. This conversation achieved the intended effect. On the road the second day the reporter began to get sick. The weather on the desert was extremely changeable, with temperatures dropping more than forty degrees at night. A trip like this of seven days and seven nights was a test greater than the normal person could bear and his own physique was not as strong as that of normal men. But he knew what this trip across the desert meant for his future prospects, and pushing on to his destination he was put right into the hospital barely breathing. Though still sick, he did a splendid job in carrying out the assignment. His report of many thousand words earned him honors, and right afterward an important Party member selected him among all the rest to be his secretary. This position was a stepping-stone to promotion. Secretary Xiao now saw a brilliant career ahead of him: section chief, bureau head, department head, and positions even higher than these.

This string of chances and accidents was thus the origin of my life and, furthermore, set the course of my destiny.

I think that when Reporter Xiao fell in love with my mother, this was something real and true. Although extremely ambitious, at that time he was, after all, still young and exuded scholarly airs. Love, marriage, pregnancy and birth, all followed logic and nature. However, while I was still an embryo inside my mother, a time of nightmares and vexation began for my father.

One day, the organization's department head called him in for a talk. Secretary Xiao could barely hold back his ecstatic feelings. He thought he was about to be assigned some important mission, but during the brief twenty minutes he was in the department head's office, Secretary Xiao went through a terrifying ice storm. In one instant, the skies fell and the earth split. Baohua's father was suspected of being a secret agent! Those two words, "secret agent," at the time were more frightening than "AIDS" and "bird flu" are nowadays. Right away Secretary Xiao thought of divorce, but unfortunately he had just found out that his wife was now pregnant. And to keep them together as a married couple, the unit leader had transferred Baohua to Urumqi to work in a military hospital. She was already on her way there.

My mother told me only one small thing about my father. Pregnant with me, and after traveling hundreds of miles, she found Secretary Xiao, but he was unwilling to bring her home with him and in the end settled her into a guesthouse. That evening, crying and sniveling bitterly, he asked her to get an abortion, because, "Your father is suspected of being a secret agent, so I have to divorce you. We can't have a child."

How could touchy and headstrong Baohua have managed to get through those days? Did she spend the whole time bathing her face in tears? I've never tried to have a heart-to-heart talk with my mother. Maybe those experiences wouldn't have been as painful as I have imagined. Many people who on the surface appear weak and spineless actually are surprisingly tough inside.

In short, she really did go on the operating table, quite prepared to take out the child within her and then return, unburdened and unattached, to her family home in Old Town. As the doctor did his pre-op examination he heard the embryo's heart and he asked her, "This child is healthy. Do you really want to give it up?" These words made Baohua jump off the operating table, put her clothes back on, and leave. Secretary Xiao, waiting by the door, thought that the operation had been performed and even asked her to go out for a meal. He refused to share a room with Baohua, but apart from that he wasn't too bad toward her. He always helped whenever she needed him.

Not too long afterward, Baohua's stomach began to bulge, so he would just have to accept this baby. In accordance with the law, they waited until their child was one year old before going through the divorce process. That day they carried the child with them to a photo studio to take the Year Old souvenir photo, together they put the child in the nursery school, and together they went by pedicab to the bureau of civil affairs and got divorced. Their relationship did not undergo any further change as a result of the divorce though. Every day Secretary Xiao would go to see the child and he gave more than half his salary to Baohua. If Baohua was on night duty he would bring the child back to his own place. On holidays they would take the child out to play and take snapshots. They stood in front of the same backdrop and separately held the child for souvenir photos.

Baohua kept on submitting her applications for demobilization. When her child was three years old, she finally received her superiors' approval. That summer, when Secretary Xiao went with his chief to attend a meeting in Beijing, Baohua took the child in her arms and just quietly departed. After his return, when he went to see his child at the day care center with a cloth doll bought in Beijing, all he got for his efforts was empty air. Someone wrote to Baohua and told her that Secretary Xiao squatted down on the floor of the day care center, weeping and wailing and unable to rise.

⌘　⌘　⌘

I don't know whether or not I should despise such a man. Occasionally I'll think of the scene of my first face-to-face meeting with my father in Beijing. He had invited me to eat rinsed lamb, but he didn't eat a single bite of it himself, just stared at me as if dumbstruck. Suddenly he covered his face with his hands and started to cry loudly and plaintively, as if to show how difficult had been the decision he made so long before. Maybe he had cried and sniveled countless times in the same bitter way when he was all alone. Secretary Xiao's career didn't go as he had hoped. Throughout that time of political movements, with all the ups and downs, every movement was like gambling on horses. Who could guarantee winning every round or that all your stakes had been placed right? I heard that during one movement, afraid of being implicated in something or other, my father made some detrimental comments against another colleague. Later, that colleague became his leader and that's where his dreams of a career ended. He's rather pitiful, wouldn't you say?

2.

WHENEVER HUANG SHUYI appeared at the West Gate street crossing, she never escaped the notice of the former boss-lady of the West Gate rice shop. On this day she once again rested like a travel-worn bird of passage by the wall next to the shop. It was about a year since she had last been here, maybe longer. No one knew where she had been during all this time, what she had been doing, or how she had managed to keep herself alive. She came stealthily, took a look at her son, and then stealthily departed.

The rice shop had early on been taken over by the government but the former owner and his wife still lived on the floor above it. He worked there for several years and then retired. His wife was still sickly and stayed inside, year in and year out. Every day she sat at the window watching the street scenes down below. A long time before, she had sat like this watching her two sons go off to school. More than ten years had passed now and the luxuriant black hair of the woman at the window had gradually gone white as she gazed out longingly.

This former boss-lady knew everything that happened around West Gate but all those details she saw meant nothing. They were only small dots on a great stage set. If you compared the West Gate street crossing to a stage, her two sons would have been the main performers on it. And what's the use of a stage without the main performers?

The rice shop boss-lady had never connected this wretched vagrant woman with the daughter-in-law in the pastor's family. When that woman at the foot of the wall crossed her line of vision, she would tell her husband to give the wretch a little something to eat and one or two pieces of clothing. She aided not only this woman but also other pathetic people passing by at West Gate. She wanted to accumulate virtue so that she might live long enough to see the return of her sons.

In the summertime, Old Town swelters unbearably. The woman by the wall was wearing clothes given to her by the former rice shop boss-lady the year before. She sat on the ground wiping her sweat away with a towel. Her clothes were torn and she was even darker and thinner. The rice shop boss-lady roused her husband who was just then dozing off and told him to fill up a bowl of green bean soup and give it to that woman. Glancing back again she discovered that the woman was now leaning against the wall, looking bloodlessly pale and gasping for breath. The boss-lady reckoned that she had collapsed from sunstroke and immediately changed her order and told her husband to go and find Dr. Lin.

Right then, the boss-lady saw the pastor's little grandson, who had just learned to get about on his own, come running out of the house wearing a red stomach bib. The child's father chased wildly after him all around the back courtyard. She didn't know the connection between this scene and the woman at the foot of the wall, but it made her think of her sons in Taiwan. By now they should have gotten married and started their own families. *Do I too have a grandson now?*

Dr. Lin rushed over, but Huang Shuyi had already gone. The boss-lady stuck her head out of the window and said to him, "This is really odd. Clear as day, I saw her fall down. How could she have just totally disappeared before my very eyes?"

The doctor didn't give much thought to the vagrant woman. Since she had gone, it meant she wasn't that sick. Then the sight of Enchun inside the church fence caught his attention and in his fleeting glance he thought he was seeing Pastor Chen. *How could that child have aged so quickly?* After Old Town's liberation, Enchun returned to his studies, and upon graduation from the university he became a teacher. An academic paper on economic development resulted in his being designated a rightist element, and he had just returned after three years of labor reform. Dr. Lin dearly loved Enchun and he worried far more about him than he did about his own two sons. Every time he saw the young man, the doctor would think of his daughter in far-off Xinjiang and of certain images of the boy and girl when they were little. *Truly "a golden lad and a jade girl." Who could have expected that their fates would turn out to be so rocky?*

For more than ten years now, whenever he thought of Baohua, sadness would overwhelm him and he would pray silently for her to come home soon. Sometimes he stood at the gate watching the boss-lady who sat in the upper story of the rice shop like a wooden statue inlaid in the window. This would lighten his pain a little. *At least I know where my daughter is and at least every month I can receive my daughter's letter and remittance.* The long, drawn-out separation was making him hopeless and numb, when suddenly one day he received a telegram from her saying that she had already started on her way back home. The doctor held the telegram up before him and read it again and again. It was well over an hour before the tears slowed their course down his cheeks.

At this time, Baohua was already on the road. The doctor reckoned she would soon arrive in Shanghai. He went inside the church fence and silently sat under the parasol tree, patting the stone bench beside him as a signal for Enchun to come over and join him there.

The doctor and Enchun had held many important conversations under this tree. On the eve of Liberation, it was here that he had asked Enchun to tell him about communism, and where he himself had decided to support the Communist Party. During Eliminate Counterrevolutionaries, although the doctor had received quite a scare, they actually discussed how to understand and support that movement. Enchun had been designated a rightist, and before going to the mountain district for labor reform, the two of them had sat here under the tree facing each other wordlessly for a long time. The doctor said only one thing: "I'll come visit you." On Mid-Autumn Festival this year, he went all by himself up there to bring moon cakes to Enchun.

Enchun sat down, holding the child in his arms. The doctor stroked little Chaofan's face and said, "The first time I saw *you*, you were this big and wore a red stomach bib. Time passes so quickly… decades now…"

"Ah, yes, so quickly."

"Baohua is already on the way home now."

"Oh, that's really great! She's coming home for a visit?"

A few days after receiving Baohua's telegram, a letter arrived from her. In it she told her parents that she had divorced, and that she had a three-year-old daughter whom she was bringing back to Old Town. The joyous feelings of the past several days had been like clear and sunny skies. Now a mass of black clouds boiled up. Baohua wrote, "Your child has brought dishonor to the Lin family. I beseech my father and mother's forgiveness and acceptance of their unfilial daughter and her pitiful little child." These lines shattered the doctor's heart and he didn't let Second Sister read this letter, nor did he tell Baosheng and Baoqing about it. In front of his sons he always maintained his patriarchal dignity. In those years, divorce was without question a deep and burning disgrace. His precious daughter had divorced. He couldn't say a word of this to his own sons, and with Enchun it was like having a fish bone in his throat. His eyes dampened.

"She also has a child now, a daughter."

"Oh, is that so? She now has a child...I still think of Baohua as a young girl. Will she be bringing the child back with her?"

The doctor nodded, and lowering his voice said with some difficulty, "She's divorced."

Enchun looked as if he had been dealt a heavy punch in the chest. He sucked in a breath of air and held it for some time before saying, "She's coming home. It's a good thing that she's coming home."

"I really don't know if she'd been all alone in the border wastelands without a single friend or how she spent those many years. My heart aches to think of it."

The doctor loved his daughter the most of all and he loved Enchun next. From the year that Old Town was liberated, Huang Shuyi had begun to go everywhere in search of redress. Three years ago, after giving birth, she just disappeared without waiting until the completion of her month-long confinement period. The doctor heard that she had taken a train to Beijing to file her appeal and that she had once been put into an insane asylum, but afterward had run off again. He was never clear why Huang Shuyi had to pursue this litigation. Way back in the distant past, she and Enchun were ready to shed their blood, even lay down their lives, by taking part in the underground. How many times had they walked out of terrible dangers and lived on safely to Liberation? Furthermore, in Enchun she had a lover who became her partner in marriage. *What was it that she still couldn't shake off?*

"You also make my heart ache," he said. "Persuade Shuyi to come back and spend some time at home. Why does she have to go through all this pain and trouble?"

Enchun shook his head and bitterly laughed. He had done everything he could for Huang Shuyi. He made her his wife.

Because she was fond of Petofi's famous line, "Life is dear, Love is dearer,"[49] he had thought that marriage could build for her a harbor in which to escape reality. Before and after getting married, Huang Shuyi was always rushing here and there in her appeal against her brother's sentence and the nonrecognition of her party membership. She said that truth and justice were higher than life, higher than love, and higher even than freedom.

The doctor said, "Both of you come together to meet Baohua when she arrives. She was very close to you."

Awkwardly, Enchun said, "Uncle Lin, you see, I now..."

The doctor stood up with a stern look on his face. "Enchun, your Uncle Lin sees that you have grown up. You are an upright and fine young man. I love you and think highly of you, more than Baosheng and Baoqing. Heaven doesn't judge people by success or failure. You have to stand up and be a man!"

When the doctor had been investigated during Eliminate Counterrevolutionaries, he had been unable to find anyone to vouch for a number of details in his history, and he would say, "God knows that what I have stated is true." His investigator would strike the table and bellow, "You are not to spread religion and superstition!" And so from that point on, he began to change the word "God" to "heaven" when speaking to outsiders.

Enchun, his eyes hidden behind their glass panes, reddened slightly. His nostrils quivered and sniveled as he shouted, "Uncle Lin!"

Nestled against his father's breast, little Chaofan didn't understand what was happening, and his frightened, dark eyes stabbed deeply into the doctor's heart. The doctor thought of the grand-

---

49   Sandor Petofi (1823-1849), a famed Hungarian poet and martyred guiding spirit of the 1848 Revolution.

daughter he had never met, who was at this moment on the road, homeless and miserable.

⌘　⌘　⌘

Back then, Student Huang Shuyi had longed to give birth to seven children for her beloved and name each one after a note of the scale. And every day, with all seven of them clustering around her, she would sing and pluck the *qin*. Such a beautiful, storybook image of a heaven was forever on the horizon. But she had already abandoned that delusion as early as when she and Enchun went to the marriage registration office. She had called on her husband to become her battlefield comrade, to fight shoulder-to-shoulder with her and together bring redress to her older brother. Only by cleansing this injustice to Elder Brother Huang Jian could Enchun's and her party membership be restored. She had supposed that Enchun would do this. He had been an unflinchingly courageous warrior for the truth and for the New China, and now he would stand up for the truth in the same way, no matter what the obstacle. He had been her source of strength.

Obviously Enchun disappointed her. As she saw it, the Enchun she had married was an out-and-out coward. Passive and incommunicative in the face of adversity, his so-called academic research was nothing more than an escape from reality. So she just fought on alone. She visited offices to file petitions in person. She searched for proof that her brother had been dealt with unfairly. She set out to investigate the bloody event south of the city just prior to Liberation. Who could have sold out that high-ranking communist cadre and taken the reward in exchange for his head?

Before the Guomindang evacuated Old Town, they burned all their documents, but she was able to "trail the vine back to the melon," as the saying has it, and found the Zhangs. She actually met the husband of the eldest Guo daughter, but that rotten egg of a wife-beater played dumb and had three different ways of saying "I don't know" for every one question of hers. Had Huang Shuyi been aware of the family relationship between the Lins of West Gate and the Zhang family through that marriage, perhaps the mystery would have become clear as day, and a gleam of light might have shone over her gloomy fate. At the critical point, when she was one step away from escaping her mental labyrinth, she changed course and fell deeper and deeper into a blind zone. Her setbacks redoubled, but the more she fought the braver she grew. Her husband's attitude of total indifference roused Huang Shuyi's aggrieved feelings to a fever pitch. Almost every day, as if in a fit of hysteria, she used the worst words on the face of the earth to rail and hurl abuse at him. Divorce was inevitable. But after they divorced, Huang Shuyi discovered she was pregnant.

The child within Huang Shuyi was likewise a life that burst into this world by accident. His gramps and granny gave him the name Chen Xiaofan—"Little Ordinary Chen." They hoped that the Chen family's little grandson could pass through life safely and with little notice. When Xiaofan was two years old, Huang Shuyi went to the police substation and changed her child's name from Xiao—"Little," to Chao—"Transcending."

The very day she changed her son's name, she went into the West Gate churchyard and, standing on the steps, with stern and righteous indignation told the pastor and his wife, "I won't let you poison my son with your beliefs. That's spiritual opium. Enchun is a man poisoned by spiritual opium, and now he's passive and good for nothing. If that's what happens, I'd rather my son die young first!"

The pastor and his wife stared tongue-tied at this fierce and implacable woman. They thought of Miss Huang Shuyi in her student days, such a sweet and wonderful girl. *This child was definitely possessed by devils.* They firmly believed that here on earth all pain, trouble, and evils were caused by devils.

When Chaofan had been younger, Huang Shuyi came to West Gate several times to make off with her son, driven perhaps by longing for him, or perhaps consciously to make him a prop in her litigation. Once, with her sick child in her arms, she succeeded in stopping the provincial governor's special car. At the time, Chaofan was running a high fever and having convulsions. The governor had his secretary send the mother and the child to the hospital while he himself issued a memo requesting the appropriate department to investigate this woman's grievance. But several months later what Huang Shuyi received was an official notification disallowing a reversal of the case. Her elder brother Huang Jian could not escape implication in the homicide case south of the city. Therefore, Enchun's and her party membership would not be recognized.

Huang Shuyi immediately set out on a wandering northward course to seek out a higher level of leadership with whom to make her appeal. At that time she hadn't one *fen* to her name, so along the way she got jobs doing rough work, like breaking up quarry stones and carrying heavy loads at depots and wharfs. This stop-and-start journey from Old Town to Beijing ate up more than half a year's time.

3.

WHEN HE RECEIVED his daughter's telegram from Sixteen Wharf Landing in Shanghai, Dr. Lin just couldn't stay seated, but paced alone around the dining table, first this way, and then that, the message clutched in his hand. Second Sister had gone out to a meeting and Little Su'er was at the kindergarten. The doctor tried to calm himself down to say a prayer of thanksgiving to Jesus and the Heavenly Father, but as he lowered his head, he just sobbed, unable to say a single word. His heart beating wildly, *pu-tong! pu-tong!* he impulsively dashed into the street yelling, "Baohua is coming home! My daughter is coming home!"

The voyage from Shanghai to Old Town would take two days and two nights. He had suffered through the prolonged separation of over ten years but these last two days and nights were just too unbearable. How many times did he sit down? How many times did he stand up? He took Baohua's picture out of the photo album and guessed what she looked like these days and what his granddaughter looked like. The image of three-year-old Baohua emerged in his mind, dainty and delicate as he held her in his arms, as soft and insubstantial as a kitten. What was the child's name? He hadn't known he had a granddaughter. Back when he named Su'er, he had prepared a name to give to a future granddaughter—Hong'er—"Little Rainbow." A rainbow was the sign of God's covenant with man.

Mindlessly the doctor walked out the gate and over to the church where the pastor and his wife were tending the flower garden in the yard. The doctor stood at the fence and said rather idiotically, "Baohua will be home in two days."

The couple did not pause in their work. They knew that Baohua would soon be home. "Yes, this batch of flowers is waiting for Baohua's return. Look how gorgeously they're blooming!" said Mrs. Chen.

"She will be on board for several hours. Two days and two nights."

The pastor's wife stood up and gazed off into the distance. "When the railroad comes through here, I've just got to go back to Beijing to take a look. I'm really looking forward to a bowl of Dashanlan *douzhi*. It's been so many years now…"[50]

The three people all soliloquized at cross purposes. The doctor felt the host of feelings clogged up inside him was straining to get out. Turning around, he found himself looking straight at the boss-lady there in the window of the rice shop. She was just then combing her hair and the sight of that head of white hair in the sunlight startled him. Holding her comb, the boss-lady waved at the doctor. He really wanted to shout over from across the main street, "Boss-lady, my daughter's coming home!" But he swallowed the words that were on the tip of his tongue and instead said a silent prayer. *O God, thank you for bringing Baohua back to my side and please look with favor upon that poor mother there.*

The doctor sat in the bus without knowing where he wanted to go. Nor did he know what he wanted to do. Old Town had just this one bus route which crossed the city from West Gate to the side of the moat beyond South Gate. As he passed the provincial newspaper office gate he thought of his niece Baolan whom he hadn't seen in so long. He decided to get off the bus and look for her. He

---

[50] Dashanlan is Beijing's famed and venerable commercial street, just south of Qianmen ("Front Gate"). Some of its shops date back several hundred years. *Douzhi* is one of Beijing's signature dishes, a pungent soup made from fermented mung beans. Beijing people say it is only palatable to "real Beijingers." Not true.

would invite her to go with them to the dock at noon the day after tomorrow to greet Baohua.

Baolan's father and mother both left this world not long after Liberation. Ever since then she had been taken care of by that male student, Ah Jian, her boat mate on the night they returned to Old Town. He provided financial assistance to her so she could attend university in Shanghai. After she graduated, Baolan was busy with her career and unwilling to get married. Ah Jian quietly waited for her. The year before last at the New Year the two of them brought their wedding "happiness candies" to their ninth uncle and ninth aunt. Ah Jian had waited almost ten years.

To enter the newspaper building to find someone, he had to fill out a form at the gate house. The old fellow on duty saw Baolan's name and said, "This person has long since stopped working here."

"Where has she been reassigned?"

"A rightist. She went to labor reform."

⌘　⌘　⌘

Dr. Lin looked at him in shock. Every New Year, Baolan and Ah Jian would come to West Gate to offer the season's greetings to him and Second Sister. Baolan was still a well-turned-out person and always sparkling with laughter. It's true that she had lost weight and looked darker. He just supposed she had gotten sunburned from going to the countryside on reporting assignments.

It was impossible for him to believe this was really so and stammered out, "I'd like to look for Lin Baolan. The one you said was a rightist was named Lin?"

"Correct. Lin Baolan. Formerly the "Girl Genius" of this newspaper. She wrote a lot of articles."

"You haven't remembered wrong?"

The old fellow in the gate house office sent out a sneering laugh from inside the window, then turned away and went on with what he had been doing.

After who knows how much time passed, the doctor heard him say to someone who had gone into the room for a newspaper, "That person's looking for Lin Baolan. Do you know where she is now?" The other person said, "Oh, Lin Baolan's returned from labor reform. She's a worker at the printing plant." Coming back to his senses, Dr. Lin asked for the directions and immediately set off.

In a dingy factory building, every one of the old-style printing machines was pounding away fit to shake the heavens and shift the earth. Somebody told Dr. Lin that the woman in the corner moving paper sheets was Lin Baolan. He excitedly moved forward several steps, then suddenly turned and went back out the door.

Baolan had been a highly competitive girl. Under these circumstances, she certainly wouldn't have been happy to meet a Lin family relative. He withdrew a ways and stood under a tree gazing at her. She was loading the paper onto a little wheelbarrow and distributing it at each of the printing machines and then transferring the printed product to another corner. This was the kind of work for a husky fellow. She was bent over the whole time and, from the look of it, extremely tired. Dr. Lin's third brother and third sister-in-law had so treasured this girl, their only child. What would they have thought had they seen this scene? The doctor felt that he himself had a responsibility he couldn't shirk regarding Baolan's present fate. Originally it had been Baoqing who had intercepted Baolan and Ah Jian out at sea and brought them back home. Perhaps that had been a mistake. It was inevitable that Baolan, with her scintillating brilliance and all-too conspicuous talents, would become the bird that sticks its head out and gets hurt.

I didn't look after Baolan properly. I should have realized early on that she would stir up trouble for herself. Intelligent people are always going to be proud and stick their necks out. The Bible says it clearly: God will always block the way of the proud. Over the past ten years, I have been terribly worried about Baohua, but thought little about Baolan. I have been too selfish.

Seeing the girl laboring so bitterly, he wanted all the more to go forward and lend her a hand, but again decided against bothering her and forced himself to move on.

Now he especially wanted to meet with Ah Jian. In the Oppose Rightist Movement, many couples broke up, sensing the calamity about to hit them, but Ah Jian married Baolan *after* she became a rightist element. Dr. Lin, as a senior member of the Lin family, wanted to express his gratitude to Ah Jian directly.

Ah Jian taught mathematics at a high school. At this moment he was in his office correcting student assignments and was very surprised to see Ninth Uncle. The doctor didn't ask anything but merely said that Sunday was the exact day of Baohua's return and that he hoped that Ah Jian and Baolan would come by and see her. Then the doctor got up and firmly shook Ah Jian's hand. "You're a good man. Our Baolan was really lucky to get married to you. Thank you!" Ah Jian seemed to catch the drift of the doctor's words. "Ninth Uncle, rest assured, I'll spend my life looking after her."

⌘　⌘　⌘

When Second Sister returned home, evening was already well advanced. Ninth Brother was sitting in his rocker looking uneasy. He hadn't gone to the kindergarten to fetch Su'er, nor had he lit the stove to make dinner. *Something's happened, for sure!* She pulled over a chair and sat down beside him.

"Ninth Brother, what's wrong?"

Ninth Brother handed the telegram to her. "Baohua has already left Shanghai."

Second Sister smiled in relief. "Look at you, so happy that you don't even want your grandson!"

Ninth Brother forced himself to return Second Sister's smile, got up and left to fetch Su'er.

He had not mentioned to anyone, not even his wife, about what had happened to Baolan. His heart ached so much he couldn't bring himself to touch on it.

Baohua's arrival at the dock was quite impressive. The Lin family, the Guo family, and the three generations of Pastor Chen's family, several dozen people in all, had arrived early to wait by the water. Relatives that rarely got together were all gathered here today. The eldest son of the Guos dangled a liquor bottle in his hand and told amusing if incoherent stories about Baohua when she was little. He believed that Baohua would bring him a bottle of liquor as a meeting present.

China was now entering the period of the 1960s when many provinces experienced an endless series of natural disasters. Famine was spreading as quickly as a plague. Old Town, that lucky place, also began to show the symptoms of this. All foodstuffs began to be rationed according to coupons held by the population, but even so, supply still did not meet demand. In order to convert coupons into rice and pork, people started to line up in the middle of the night.

The liquor that eldest Guo son depended on for his survival was also hit by the famine. Whomever he met he would beg for something to drink. He could walk for more than an hour in the middle of the night to knock on his older sisters' doors. If his importuning didn't succeed, he would sit right down on the ground and just howl and wail like a brokenhearted child.

Baolan had now arrived. There in this crowd she stood out as she always did with her bright laughter and her tastefully selected outfits. Her relatives called her "Girl Genius" and "Reporter." That Guo alcoholic pestered her with his complaints and troubles. He wanted her to write an article to the government to report that the monthly ration of liquor even when diluted was still not enough to last him two days. Baolan, leaning on Ah Jian's shoulder, beamed her smile at him. "Ten *jin* of grain will only distill a little over one *jin* of liquor. Our country's in trouble now. You should just drink a little less," she said.

Ninth Brother closely watched every twinkle and smile Baolan made, almost forgetting Baohua who at this very moment was drawing close to Old Town. This morning he had asked Second Sister for coupons for ten *jin* of grain and one half a *jin* of cooking oil, ready to slip them into Ah Jian's hand a little later. With Baolan doing heavy work, he had to be sure she was eating well. Second Sister showed no haste in opening the drawer, a sign of the struggle going on within her. This really did put her in a difficult position. For several months now this aging couple had not eaten a full meal, and she had saved a few coupons in the event an even greater famine hit. Ninth Brother had steeled himself to ask for the coupons. Second Sister asked him whom these were for but he only said, "There are people who need these more t han we do."

At first he supposed that Baolan's smile hid her real desperation, and this was like a knife plunging into his breast. Ah Jian always held Baolan's hand. In conservative Old Town, even sweethearts madly in love with each other rarely held hands in full view. Ah Jian and Baolan's look of total intimacy was natural and it certainly wasn't intended to prove anything to others. They had always been this way, like Adam and Eve in the Garden of Eden, two lives fused into one. Gradually Ninth Brother's tension relaxed and a sense of relief washed over him. He thought of his and Second Sister's own happy marriage. No matter what awful things might happen in this world, a harmoniously married couple's home was like Noah's ark, or a harbor in a storm. Their own world of two was far more solid and strong than what was outside.

He handed the grain and oil coupons back to Second Sister. She looked at him, puzzled. "If you give them to me, I probably would lose them. You'd better take them."

Just then the boat docked with a long whistle blast. The doctor's heart felt as though gigantic forces were at play there. *Oh, my precious daughter, my poor Baohua! The day when I and Second Sister go away, who will look after this orphaned mother and fatherless child?*

⌘   ⌘   ⌘

My Great-Auntie was also there that day. She says that Mother and I were like real refugees. At that time there really were more than a few refugees on board fleeing to Old Town from the famine. Baohua, holding her child against her breast, her belongings packed on her back and pulled behind her, walked into the crowd of people. Among the dozens of people on the shore not one of them recognized her. Baohua and her child stood in the midst of her relatives, who were all looking off into the distance.

They had traveled this road for more than half a month. In Lanzhou, a piece of their luggage got lost, and they lost yet another piece in Shanghai. Neither mother nor child had changed their clothes in several days. But Baohua was too exhausted to feel upset about this. She was like some frightened mother animal carrying her baby in her mouth as she rushed down a road away from death, afraid only that she might lose the child. At night when they went to sleep she would tie one end of her belt around the child and the other to her own wrist.

She had made it home. Finally she had transferred the child safely to Old Town. Baohua slowly put the child down, tears streaming down her cheeks.

When Grandpa was certain that this weather-beaten, utterly travel-worn little woman was Baohua, he didn't go forward to draw his daughter to him and cry in each other's arms. He just stood there stunned for a moment, and then abruptly turned and went behind a pile of cargo, and, taking out a handkerchief, wiped the tears from his eyes.

Old Town folk express their feelings in this kind of self-controlled and restrained way.

4.

THE SUMMER I was ten years old, my body began to show some pecu-
liarities. On my chest there bulged two symmetrical little bags as if
I had been bitten there by venomous mosquitoes. I really supposed
that I had been bitten by mosquitoes. In a few days, the little bags
which were as big as peanuts grew to the size of broad beans. I was
now worried. There was a doctor in the family, and when I first
was able to read I was already leafing through medical magazines.
That's how I learned of a type of fatal illness called cancer.

At the dinner table I thought I was about to die and was so
frightened I couldn't swallow a thing.

"Ah Ma, I've got cancer!"

Grandma glanced at me. "Don't talk nonsense. How could a
little child get cancer?"

"Really!"

This was just at the time when the Great Cultural Revolution
was raging at its fiercest. Grandpa had been ordered to go to study
sessions. Great-Auntie was living with us. There were bruises on her
cheeks given to her by Ah Chang. The Great Cultural Revolution
had raged right into the lunatic asylum and all the crazy people ran
out. Ah Chang beat his daddy until he spit up blood and hit my
Great-Auntie so terribly that she was afraid to go home.

Great-Auntie was sitting right across from me and she could see
my dread. "Where do you feel bad?" she asked with concern.

I put down my chopsticks and bowl, and covered my chest with
both hands. "Two bags are growing here and they're getting bigger
and bigger every day."

The two old sisters immediately commenced to giggle and laugh. A chunk of unchewed rice ball moved out onto the corner of Great-Auntie's mouth.

I was going to die, and here they were, laughing at me! I was so mad I wanted to cry.

Grandma said, "That's not cancer. It's you growing up, and very quickly you'll become a big girl. From now on, when you stand you need to do so with the proper deportment, and when you are seated. And you can't play all those noisy games rolling around with Chaofan anymore."

Great-Auntie licked the rice ball back into her mouth. "It's the Revolution now and your thinking is still feudal. Never mind, Hong'er, you should still play your innocent 'green plum and bamboo horse' childhood games with the little Chen boy, just like in *The Story of the Stone…*"

"What nonsense," Grandma interrupted her.

I didn't know what these two old ladies' gorgeous and mysterious allusions meant and I wallowed all alone in my feelings of self-pity. I felt terribly isolated, as if cast aside. At that moment I thought of Chaofan and wanted to see him badly.

The West Gate church had long ceased to exist and a revolutionary committee name-board had been hung up on that little wooden building. Chaofan and his granny had been driven out of it to a small and awfully drafty hut beside the city moat. I told him I had something important to tell him and we both squeezed into the space under the bridge. With tears streaming down my face I told Chaofan that I was going to die. Grabbing hold of his hand, I made him feel the lumps of cancer on my chest. We knew how dark and scary death was. During the early part of the Cultural Revolution, Pastor Chen's suicide had been an enormous shock to us. Its inescapable shadow enveloped our young years.

I saw terror and hurt in Chaofan's tear-flecked eyes. That gave me great comfort and satisfaction. So I wasn't so totally insignificant after all.

Suddenly he shouted in a strange voice, "I won't let you die! I just won't let you die!"

"I don't want to die either. I'm scared!" I said, crying.

"If you're really going to die, I'll carry you on my back and we'll both jump into Little West Lake!"

In those days, corpses were often pulled out of that lake. A few couples had tied themselves together and jumped in there.

I believed that Chaofan would do that. A gust of strength blew into me, like a ball being blown up, and made me no longer afraid. I even felt a beautiful sense of tragic heroism.

⌘　⌘　⌘

That evening, Grandma went to the study session to see Grandpa. Study session was also called "being in the cowshed." It was now Shuiguan's son's turn for night duty there, so he would arrange for Grandpa and Grandma to meet. That day she had been cooking some good things for Grandpa to eat, like Tea Leaf Eggs, or Eight Treasures in Sauce. I tagged along for a taste of these delicacies.

Great-Auntie and I sat in the sky well, taking in the cool air. "Just go out and play, why don't you?" she said. "I won't tell your grandma."

At this time, Chaofan's granny had started looking after him. When Mrs. Chen moved out of the church she took the organ with her. During the day she went to the revolutionary committee to sweep the floor and wash the toilets. In the evening she went back to the little hut to teach her grandson to write characters and to practice playing the organ.

I again thought about my cancer. Without knowing it I rubbed my chest with both hands. Great-Auntie tapped me there with her big rush fan and giggled.

"What are you laughing at?"

"Ah, Hong'er! Those are women's secrets. You can't rub your breasts in front of people."

She had said "breasts," not "chest" or "cancer lumps." Suddenly I seemed to get a vague inkling of something. My whole body was starting to burn like ignited charcoal.

"You're starting to grow breasts. In two more years you'll be growing into a real woman. You can then have children. Your great-uncle's wife entered our Guo family when she was only fourteen years old. She was fifteen when she gave birth to Gan'er."

O heaven, this is much more serious than cancer. Today, I let Chaofan feel my chest and I raised my blouse to show him those two little red and swelling bags. But how will I explain this to him? In the darkness I curled up in a ball, so ashamed that I wished I could just die.

Great-Auntie chattered on nonstop. I think she was talking about things from *The Story of the Stone.* She said that a girl in her previous life had been an herb growing out the crack of a stone, and there was a boy who had been that stone in his previous life.

"I saw it all before. You and the Chen family's little grandson had unfinished business from your previous lives. The year we went to the dock to meet you and your mother, you saw that bunch of strangers crowding all around and you were so scared you started howling and crying. No one could coax or cajole you. Then that small boy handed you a little pinwheel. You looked at him and smiled. At that time I foresaw both of your future lives. And I've been guessing all along who owed a debt to whom in your previous lives ."

⌘ ⌘ ⌘

It's impossible for me to recall just what day of what year Chaofan entered my life, as if he were innate in what had been eternally predestined for me. Why, after all, would two apparently accidental spirits make an appointment to come to this world?

On one snowy day, Chrysanthemum sat in front of me stirring her coffee. This character had disappeared for several months, like the proverbial clay ox thrown into the sea, and I thought that she had found her final anchorage. But she came floating back up to the surface and drifted back into her previous groove. She drifted from one man's embrace to another's, tasting to the fullest the winds and dust of carnality and the vicissitudes of life, but she always believed that before she came to this world, God or the Holy Spirit, or some supernatural force beyond human comprehension, had already prepared her other half. They were searching for each other in the vast sea of humanity, a search that was bitter and painful.

"Now just think about this calmly." She stopped moving the little spoon in her hand as she earnestly looked at me. "Your other half stood right there blocking your vision when you were nothing but primordial chaos, so how was it you both got on so well, but then 'raised the bridle bits to take your separate paths'"?

Why indeed did we raise the bridle bits and go our separate ways? Why couldn't we have become like Grandpa and Grandma? In war, sickness, poverty, life, and death, nothing could separate them. When Grandpa died, Grandma prayed diligently every day, speaking with God and Jesus to let her return before much longer to heaven and be reunited with Ninth Brother.

Chrysanthemum went back to stirring her coffee. "It might be that you two are both going in a circle and that in the end you will get back together again. Isn't there some song that says that when you reach the end you return to the beginning?"

All I could do was to bitterly smile. Sometimes I would imagine my own declining years. I would always experience the beautiful and heart-stirring feelings in the form of those white-haired couples walking hand in hand in the evening's fading light. But by no means was that to be Chaofan's and my fate. We would only face each other in silence and count up the hurtful grudges we bore against each other.

CHAPTER EIGHTEEN –
PATHOS ON ISOLATED ISLAND

1.

GREAT-AUNTIE FELL SICK in the summer of her eighty-fifth year. She couldn't eat and would get bloated whenever she took even a little rice gruel. Looking in the mirror and seeing a face growing more emaciated by the day, she would remember her mother who died this same way. Old Town people called it the cut-off-from-food sickness, something like anorexia. The very first time Old Lady Guo ate a meal that held no savor for her, she announced that she was going to die because her own mother and her mother's mother had both died of this sickness. When Great-Auntie realized that her own time on earth would not be long, she grew both afraid and angry. Her husband had been dead for over three years now. *That devil just won't let go of me! He's probably already been reborn in some other person's family and is waiting for me to die and begin another life of retributive fate.*

The older generation's attitude toward life and death was more relaxed than ours today. They don't struggle with fate by going to a hospital for a liver or lung transplant. They all say that when the King of Hell calls your name from the register at three o'clock in the morning, you can just forget about dawdling around another two hours before reporting in. Although my Great-Auntie was scared and angry, she didn't resist. She pulled out a statue of the Bodhisattva from under her bed and started praying to it. Every day she would say, "O Bodhisattva, I don't know what form that devil is in his new life, but if he's a fish in the water, please make me a bird in the sky. If he's here as a human, please just keep me as a ghost in hell."

Apart from this, she wanted to lose no time in settling some matters long weighing on her mind. There were only two of these, and both were related to marriage. One was her worry over the Guo family's "temple incense sticks and candles," that is, the continuation of the family line. The government had started to implement its single-child policy. The third generation of the eldest Guo son was entirely female. Second Son's only child had been the girl with "peach epilepsy." Third Son had died young, Fourth Son had produced no issue, and Fifth Son had a boy who hadn't yet married. *We Guos are the descendants of General Guo Ziyi. The incense sticks and candles must be kept burning. Could we scrape together a little money for Gan'er to get another daughter-in-law? Or spend it on moving the Guo family cemetery to a place with better feng shui?* She always felt it very likely that one or two gold pieces had been left behind under the rotting floorboards of the old Zhang residence and she wanted her Guo nephews to know this secret.

There was another secret—one of the heart. All her life she had adored Ninth Brother. The many things she told him out of jealousy she ought never to have said. For example, she told him that long ago all the letters that Second Sister sent to him when he was studying in Shanghai came from her own pen. She also frequently brought up the subject of Third Sister. She said that Third Sister really didn't elope with anybody, but became a foreign-Buddha nun. Now, though, she wanted to be totally candid with Second Sister and seek her forgiveness.

Great-Auntie believed that my grandfather had secretly cherished Third Sister all along. Second Sister and he enjoyed a loving and affectionate married life, but that was just on the surface. He had never given his entire heart to Second Sister, for it had been carved up into several separate and unrelated pieces. Third Sister occupied one of these and his "family" in Shanghai, another. The evidence was irrefutable—ever since Ninth Brother returned to Old Town during the War of Resistance, he had always planned to take a nostalgic journey back to Shanghai. In the spring of 1965, he left Second Sister behind and went on his pilgrimage all alone, returning only at the end of the summer. Ninth Brother had gone to see the Shanghai woman. He had to see her. Only by doing so could he really show that he was a man of affection and good faith.

Great-Auntie started to write a letter and kept at it off and on for over ten days. She packed two letters into one big envelope and mailed it to Second Sister at West Gate. She wanted to make Second Sister carry out her last request never to rest until the Guo family's incense and candles prospered and flourished.

⌘　⌘　⌘

As she always did, Grandma stood outside the gate waiting for the postman. Sometimes she vaguely sensed that she was back in those terrible wartime years, waiting for Ninth Brother's letters. During the fiery and passionate 1950s, she longed for mail from Baoqing in Korea and Baohua in Xinjiang. Actually, nowadays only two people wrote to her. One was me, studying in Beijing, and the other was Great-Auntie in South Town. Great-Auntie was often at West Gate but she still wrote her letters. Letter writing was an addiction for her. Often in the morning she would put the letter in the mailbox by the gate and in the afternoon appear in front of Second Sister.

Two days after she received her elder sister's letter, Grandma finally put on her old-age glasses and tore open the envelope. *Nothing more than old sesame seeds and rotten grains trivia on top of her totally made-up stories!* It took some effort to read the cramped, fly head-sized written characters, and mostly she just skimmed over these pages and put them into her drawer for me to read when I came home for the summer. Grandma never understood why I would take any interest in an old woman's foolish ravings. Still, she saved those letters for me and was quite happy to chatter on about the memories they aroused. She would tell me, though, that such-and-such a thing was like *this* and not like *that*. These two old ladies could talk poles apart about the same thing.

Grandma saw only a few words throughout those ten densely written pages: *I, your elder sister, am suffering from the cut-off -from-food sickness. The women in the older generations of our family all died from this.* She stuffed the letter into a drawer, took out her bottle of cure-all Somidon, and then got on Bus No. 1. This bus set off from West Gate and stopped at Great-Auntie's gate right next to the station.

When Great-Auntie saw Second Sister, she was so happy that tears came to her eyes. "Second Sister, you've forgiven me? If not, it will weigh like a great stone on my soul, and I'll have a hard time avoiding that devil Zhang."

Grandma didn't know what Great-Auntie wanted her to forgive. When she saw the Bodhisattva set out on the dining table she felt very uneasy. Ever since Ninth Brother had converted her to believe in Jesus, she would always get an uncomfortable feeling whenever she saw a clay idol.

"Since when have you been worshipping Bodhisattva? Quick! Get a piece of cloth and cover it up!"

Great-Auntie took a face towel and put it over Bodhisattva's head. "Death comes to everyone. I've lived to be eighty years old and that's old by any account. The only thing I ask is never to run into that devil in my next life."

My grandma really believed that Great-Auntie wouldn't live much longer, for she had gotten so thin she was barely recognizable. The cut-off-from-food sickness would cook you dry, bit by bit. She actually didn't feel sad about this. After my grandpa went, Grandma eagerly looked forward to the Lord's call home. Regardless of who she heard had passed on, she would always softly complain, "How come it's not yet my turn?"

"He certainly isn't letting me go," Great-Auntie moaned. "He said that he would look for me to be his wife in the next life. The day he breathed his last, he gripped my hand ever so tightly...Oh, Second Sister, I'm really terrified about meeting him again."

Grandma felt it was her responsibility to help her elder sister escape disaster in the next life and she knit her brows to summon inspiration.

"Just believe in Jesus. When you believe in Jesus, your soul will rise up and enter heaven. *That* one's spent his whole life committing wicked deeds, so you can be sure he's gone to hell. There's no way he could find you."

Great-Auntie's wrinkled face broke into a smile. "That would be just wonderful! Ninth Brother's in heaven and I would meet him before you do. I would say to him, 'Second Sister's thinking about you every day.' Quick, tell me how to be counted a believer in your foreign Bodhisattva!"

"Jesus is not Bodhisattva. Jesus is God. First throw away that clay Bodhisattva and I'll go call Mrs. Chen to pray for you."

Then Grandma got up and hurried back to West Gate to invite Mrs. Chen over. The church at West Gate had just been restored.

Mrs. Chen, now also in her eighties, was bent over almost ninety degrees at the waist, but her zeal for preaching was now more exalted than ever. Every day, all bent over, she spared no effort in spreading the Good News everywhere.

Great-Auntie didn't get rid of Bodhisattva. She kept bowing to it and put it back under her bed, saying, "I am sorry, but because Rotten Egg is under your control, I'm afraid of going where you are and meeting him there. I want to go to the place run by the foreign Bodhisattva."

Two hours later, bent-over Mrs. Chen entered the Zhang home. The three old ladies held hands and prayed and Mrs. Chen sprinkled a little water on my great-aunt.

Great-Auntie was in good spirits as she waited to die. She took her fine silk clothes out of her trunk and every night would fall asleep exquisitely dressed. She thought that when she opened her eyes she would be in heaven and could then speak with Ninth Brother. But to everyone's surprise, she gradually recovered and she lived past one hundred years. She is still going strong.

Swishing her reed fan, Grandma looked at me as she sat on the special seat, Grandpa's venerable rattan rocking chair. "Your great-aunt has really taken leave of her senses. It was nothing of the sort at all. At the time you were still small, and your little cousins were being born one after another. I really couldn't get away. Your grandpa sent us a postcard from every place he stopped at. If you're staying for a while there're still more of these. Here they are, all in the drawer."

A pile of postcards now faded yellow recorded my grandfather's feelings on his nostalgic journey. It was obvious that he was in a fairly good mood.

At the beginning of the 1960s, China suffered a period of famine brought on by natural disasters. Then, finally, like a withered tree coming to life again in the spring, benign scenes of peace and prosperity appeared. The news media and public opinion, with an ardor fit to set the heavens ablaze, called for study of Lei Feng's selfless spirit. As Grandpa saw it, the Lei Feng spirit was the embodiment of the spirit of Jesus. The beautiful age of "Everyone loves me and I love everyone" had arrived. The injustices and terrors my grandfather and many others had suffered during the 1950s counted for nothing. *If you didn't go through the storm, how would you see the rainbow?* Communism was the rainbow in the sky after the storm had passed.

If you could say life still held just a few small undesirable things, these would be Baohua's marriages. Baohua wanted to marry again. My grandfather's journey avoided this very event.

Their future son-in-law was a northern cadre who had originally come south to liberate Old Town. Now he was the Public Security bureau chief in a district commissioner's office about thirty miles from Old Town. After Baohua transferred to civilian life and returned home, she worked at the hospital under the jurisdiction of that office. When this Public Security chief entered the Lin home for the first time, an army greatcoat thrown over his shoulders, right off my grandfather sensed with alarm that things did not bode well for his daughter. For some reason, he reminded my grandfather of Division Commander Hu. He had the same Henan accent, and the same loud voice. Even though the fellow tried his best to ingratiate himself with his future parents-in-law that day, Grandpa could also tell immediately he was a totally bad-tempered and unruly man. With Baohua as always so petite and delicate, one great roar from this Public Security chief might hurt her.

Grandpa arranged to talk with his daughter and tactfully asked her to carefully consider this lifelong choice. He had hardly finished one sentence when Baohua burst into tears. She said that if he didn't accept this man as his son-in-law, she would never again enter this house for the rest of her life. Grandpa believed that if his precious daughter said she'd do something, she would indeed do exactly that, and so the best thing for him was just keep his mouth shut.

My grandfather had been planning this trip for about ten years. Right when his daughter's marriage date was imminent, he abruptly decided to set out, even though my grandmother couldn't break away to accompany him or get him to change his mind. Grandma urged him to hold the wedding banquet for Baohua, and then go, but he said, "I'll pray for her while I am on the road. I'll ask God to bless her." Grandma asked him for that Swiss watch. Earlier, when they were preparing Baohua's dowry, they spent a lot to buy this watch right off the wrist of an Overseas Chinese. But my grandfather wouldn't hear a word of this. After many days on the road, though, he told Grandma in a postcard what corner of the bookcase the watch was hidden in. What was going through his mind during this period? It is very possible that in the course of this journey he realized that he was at fault for being prejudiced against this future son-in-law. He had looked down on this revolutionary cadre descended from some young cowherder, and so, painfully, he examined his own failings.

However, my mother Baohua's marriage, in fact, came as no surprise to my grandpa. Not long after the wedding, her tear-washed days began. The greater part of their lives was spent in quarrelling over utterly trivial issues.

2.

THE DOCTOR LEFT the train at Hangzhou, his first stop. During his student days he had gone there with a group of schoolmates and sat on a rock beside Three Pools Mirroring the Moon, writing in his diary for Third Sister Guo. That rock was still there, and when he saw it, the doctor felt as if he had crossed paths with an old friend again. He sat down and wrote his first postcard to Second Sister. He said West Lake was extremely beautiful and that he hoped that next year they could see it in the springtime together.

Brother Yu was the name Dr. Lin gave to that Hangzhou native who had helped him and Mrs. Yang during the war. After retiring, Brother Yu moved back permanently to Hangzhou, though his family members were all in Hong Kong. During the difficult times he had visited them annually and from there he would send Dr. Lin peanut oil and cookies. Dr. Lin's chief purpose in going to Hangzhou was to call on Brother Yu and thank him in person.

On the previous evening at the Yu ancestral home beside West Lake, the two old friends enjoyed a pleasant talk that went on long into the night and touched on many past things. Dr. Lin spoke of the experiences he had gone through in life: how when he was eight years old he had fallen seriously ill and been put out in the little back alley, how Mr. Qiao had saved him, and how that couple from England gave him the light of this life and hope for the everlasting one. He regretted that it was now almost thirty years since he had lost contact with them in the upheaval of the war. Perhaps they were no longer on this earth.

In those student years, the college held a weekly Bible class which Mr. Qiao taught. When speaking of his own life, Dr. Lin would naturally have mentioned Mr. Qiao, but he never in any way expected that Brother Yu, sitting across from him, could provide the sequel to his story.

There had been a pastor from the north who preached in the Hangzhou church. He said that the spirit of Jesus was one of self-less love, and he gave the story of Mr. Qiao as an example of this. During the War of Resistance, this northern preacher had been a high school student, and he and several schoolmates had been caught by the Japanese while fleeing the war. They were then locked up in the concentration camp at Weifang in Shandong.

At the time, Mr. Qiao, who had been preaching in Shandong, was in that same camp. During the daytime, they would be taken out in gangs to do heavy labor in the mine, and in the evening several dozen men would squeeze onto pallets in a small hut. That wasn't the bad thing. What made the deepest impression on these high school students was the hunger. Three times a day, each person received only one small, coarse cornmeal cake known as *wowotou* and half a bowl of thin rice gruel. Often bloody fights would break out and more than one person was beaten to death for snatching a *wowotou*. The future pastor and his schoolmates were the same. During meals they worked hard at guarding their pitifully small servings of food.

One day, Mr. Qiao quietly slipped into his hand a *wowotou* kneaded into a small hard ball. The boy just swallowed it down whole without bothering to see who had given this to him. The Japanese had treated this foreigner differently. When they doled out the food, they would give him an extra *wowotou*. But two months or so later when Mr. Qiao died, it was from hunger. He hadn't eaten a mouthful of solid food during that whole period, but had given all his rations to the children whose bodies were still growing. At that time, Mrs. Qiao was in the women's camp. She didn't make it to the victorious end of the war either.

Dr. Lin looked out the window at the bright moon. Many scenes of his childhood passed slowly through its hazy nebula. He dimly heard Mr. Qiao's gentle voice: "Child, we know you now miss us, but don't be sad. We are in heaven waiting for your return so that we can all be together."

The grief he felt receded little by little. He believed that God was now rewarding them in heaven because they really had practiced selfless love toward others. They were blessed.

⌘ ⌘ ⌘

At Brother Yu's home, Dr. Lin saw an old photograph, a group photo of their church-run hospital during that earlier period. When his glance fell on a young woman in the front row, he gave a start. *What was Second Sister doing in this photograph?*

Brother Yu was pointing out another young woman in the photograph as he related his own story. His first wife had been one of the new wave of women in the 1930s, and before the War of Resistance she crossed the seas to study in France. Two years later, he read in a newspaper the announcement of his wife's divorce. During the war, he had liked a nurse at the church hospital in Shanghai, but she was a confirmed celibate. He pursued her assiduously for many years.

"She went to Taiwan. She went to visit relatives there. Just before leaving she told me that when she returned she would give me a definite reply. I never thought that when she left it would be forever."

Dr. Lin listened patiently to the end of that story of the nurse and then, pointing to the woman in the picture who looked like Second Sister. "Who was this?" he asked.

"She was the wife of a pastor who had been hospitalized."

The pastor in the hospital was a white man and he was sitting right in the middle of the front row.

"Where were they from?"

Brother Yu shook his head vaguely. He was still immersed in his own story.

Might she have been Third Sister? Elder Sister Guo, my great-aunt, had told a lot of stories about Third Sister: that she had committed suicide rather than be married; that she was part of the new wave of free love people and had eloped. Another version was that she and a white missionary had gone to the north. In the doctor's mind Third Sister was already a distant myth and legend. He enjoyed such a perfect marriage with Second Sister that he even projected the illusions and fantasies of his youth onto his wife. She was Second Sister. She was also Third Sister. But at that moment he particularly hoped that woman who looked like Second Sister *was* Third Sister. And he hoped that she had a happy marriage, a perfect marriage.

⌘   ⌘   ⌘

He had originally supposed that these regrettable things in life would wait until the day he met with Jesus before receiving a full explanation, complete with annotations. But the nightlong conversation was like opening up the book of mysteries and deciphering the secret code of existence.

He sat at the Three Pools Mirroring the Moon and wrote a letter to Second Sister. He told her the story of Mr. and Mrs. Qiao's selfless love, compared to which they themselves still had a long way to go. He mentioned Third Sister. He was very definite in his choice of words. He said that she had been favored by God and became the wife of a pastor, and that during the War of Resistance she had done the Lord's work in Shanghai. He believed that this news of the past could be a source of comfort to the Guo family members.

3.

WHEN I WAS little, I thought that we had a relative in Shanghai. Every year that relative would send Grandpa and Grandma two letters, one at Spring Festival and another at Mid-Autumn. Shanghai was such a big and fascinating city that even an envelope from there fairly dripped with the chic and the in-vogue. The envelopes sold in our little shop in Old Town were made of coarse brown paper—cowhide paper, we called it, but Great Shanghai's envelopes came in all kinds of colors and were wondrous to see. The candies sent from there added a little more sweetness to the memories of my childhood years. Their garishly colored wrappers captivated me even more than the candies themselves, and I saved up many of them. I would boil these wrinkled-up things piece by piece in clear water, stick them on glass panes, and wait for them to dry. Finally I would insert them in books. After this treatment, the candy wrappers looked just like finely wrought gold or silver foil. I always felt pride and a bit of superiority whenever I would tell my little friends that we had a relative in Shanghai. Then I would take out those books with the candy wrappers stuck in them and show off my treasures to them.

Having said that, I am suddenly hit with pain. A stronger and deeper memory than how I possessed those treasures is how I came to lose them. During the early part of the Cultural Revolution, Shuiguan's son brought a rebel faction to our home to confiscate things. When I think about it now, it's as if it were all just a routine. They made a total mess of everything and then took away two old *qipao* that Granny hadn't worn for a long time already, for *qipao* were, of course, the curious and bizarre clothing of the bourgeoisie. After two or three years, our home experienced only one genuine search and confiscation episode. It seemed that my stepfather, Zhang, had some problem and this implicated his West Gate parents-in-law. It was a calamity, something really devastating! My grandfather's big earthenware pot was dug up from under the flowerbed in the sky well and carried away. I don't know what had been packed inside it, nor do I know when Grandpa had dug such a big cellar. Grandma had hidden her jewelry under the stove, but that too was tracked down and confiscated, including the bracelet from *her* grandmother's dowry.

However, Grandpa and Grandma's losses were really nothing compared to mine. I never expected it, but those enticing gold and silver foils didn't escape that catastrophe either. At the time I was hiding behind my grandmother and peering out in terror at the unexpected event occurring around us. At the last minute a dark-skinned, bald man discovered the two books that I had stuck the candy wrappings in and with one motion dropped them into a big hempen sack. Suddenly, like some cornered little mother animal, I angrily and fiercely leaped out, crying and tearing and pulling as I tried to grab my treasures back. Baldy flung me into the corner with a sweep of his hand, picked up the sack, and left. The "Ever Victorious" rebel faction then got in their beat-up truck and drove off in a cloud of dust. I crawled back up and ran outside after them. I chased them from West Gate toward Drum Tower, shouting myself hoarse like a crazy person, "My candy paper! My candy paper!" I never at all heard Grandpa and Grandma running after me and calling out my name. Many people at West Gate had been my grandfather's patients. They didn't know what had happened at the Lin home, or perhaps they thought that the doctor was chasing a cat burglar who was making off with a purse. But a whole lot of people joined in the chase. When I was just about at Drum Tower, I was picked up around the waist by a pair of arms strong as iron.

⌘   ⌘   ⌘

Why am I now bringing up my candy wrappers? Thirty years have gone by and I have almost never thought about this, but the sharp pain just now surprises me. I never knew that some corner of me could still harbor such bitter grief. Now I know that even though my grandparents did all they could to shelter me, like eagles protecting their chicks, the Cultural Revolution which has been termed "the ten-year catastrophe," still scarred my childhood.

⌘   ⌘   ⌘

What I want to relate is Grandpa's journey to Shanghai and the "Shanghai relative" he intended to visit—Mrs. Yang, the widow of his classmate. When I was little, she was the one who sent a steady flow of candies from Shanghai. It's too bad I never got to meet the old person who sent me the pretty wrappings and the endless pleasure and endless pain.

Great-Auntie didn't know that during the War my grandfather had found himself stranded in Shanghai, because Grandma was very tight-lipped about this with her. But she was unable to keep Great-Auntie from spreading the wings of her imagination to make up stories about Ninth Brother's other home and the other woman in Shanghai. With the sharpening of time, Great-Auntie became totally convinced that when Ninth Brother was studying in Shanghai, there was someone with "an intoxicating aroma on red sleeves," a woman of "the wind and dust" who had reformed herself for his sake. She raised a child and remained loyal and chaste her whole life. When Ninth Brother passed on, the Lin family never actually sent an obituary notice to Shanghai. Great-Auntie felt a deep sadness whenever she thought of an ageing woman in far off Great Shanghai still waiting for Ninth Brother.

My great-aunt's imaginative powers really did not transcend the logic of life. According to my textual research, Grandpa *did* have a Shanghai story that was unavoidably poignant and beautiful, but it didn't occur during his student years but rather during the wartime period. By that time he had more than his fill of the devastation of partings and death, and his hopeless stranding in Shanghai lasted for more than two and a half years.

On the first anniversary of Grandpa's death, the Shanghai relative sent representatives to Old Town to call on my grandmother: a woman of about the same age as my mother and a daughter about that of my own. This pair stayed at West Gate for over ten days and I have kept my friendship with that Shanghai girl to the present day. Neither the young Shanghai girl nor I knew just how in the world our two houses were connected and we were both curious about this. Together we would often sift through the evidence and piece together stories from both families. Now that we have both grown and experienced life, every time we meet we still talk about our respective grandmother's stories. Those repressed feelings, filled with tragic meaning, were experiences our own generation has no way of understanding.

More than twenty years had passed since their wartime parting. Although in their letters they frequently spoke of visiting each other, year after year passed by. Mrs. Yang had now grown used to treating this longing as merely something to be concealed in her heart. Then, suddenly, she received news from Young Mr. Lin that he was setting out for Shanghai. Now the old lady who had just completed her sixty-year cycle was like a young girl who heard that her fiancé was returning from a distant land. In an instant she was totally beside herself, her thoughts scampering like monkeys and racing like horses. She tossed and turned until past midnight, when gradually her mind cleared and she knew what she should do. Then she immediately turned on the light and set about straightening up her room.

She had all along kept traces of Young Mr. Lin. There was a photograph of him on the wall. Outsiders seeing this would suppose it to be the household's Happy Family Portrait. Old Mrs. Yang sat in the very middle, the younger Mrs. Yang and Young Mr. Lin stood behind her, while the three children clustered around them. This was Young Mr. Lin's souvenir photo taken when he bid farewell to Shanghai. This Happy Family Portrait was set in a frame and had hung there for over twenty years. Suddenly today it made Mrs. Yang feel a bit presumptuous and bashful. She took it down and hid it in the clothes cabinet and used a magazine picture to cover the mark on the wall where the picture had been hanging for all those years.

Time slowed down during those few days that Young Mr. Lin spent in Hangzhou. To keep herself occupied, Mrs. Yang scrubbed and cleaned endlessly. She also made a special trip to Nanjing Road to perm her hair and buy clothes. Returning home with her new outfit, she tried it on in front of the mirror but she felt these clothes were not appropriate and got back on the bus to exchange them. When she tried the new ones on, she felt *these* weren't suitable either, so she went back again to the store to make yet another exchange.

Her brain and her hands diligently organized the past. How many moments had there been during his long stay in Shanghai when Young Mr. Lin made her crack and crumble inside? Those moments were the crowning point of her entire life. Compared to them, what occurred before and afterward was prosaic and of no particular interest.

She saw that scene at dusk when Young Mr. Lin stepped into this stone gateway building. She was just then sitting beside the gate on a small bench worried about having no food to cook. She didn't know whether her son who had gone off to do his porter's job could bring some of his wages home today. He was only thirteen years old, and every day he shouldered hundreds of bales that weighed more than he did. Every month that black-hearted foreman pocketed the money earned by her son's sweat and blood. *What's the use of going on living like this?* The people with money had been able to escape Shanghai. She just hoped that a bomb would fall on their whole family so that all of them, old and young, would die together. She thought a beggar was coming over to ask for something to eat and she rudely scolded him.

How could she have known that here was an angel sent by God? In just a few short days her children were back in school with new books, her own and Old Mrs. Yang's illnesses received medical treatment, the rent was paid, and enough gleaming white rice bought to fill her rice jar right to the brim. She had also studied at a church-run school but the days of bitter troubles and despair had made it impossible for her to believe that there really was a benevolent God. That day she held the rice jar close to her and fervently knelt down in tears, thanking the Lord and asking for forgiveness.

Outside the gate was the world in its second great war. Japanese-occupied Shanghai still reeked of blood and terror but whenever Mrs. Yang washed and cooked the rice she had a deep sense of heavenly well-being and happiness. From then on for the next several decades, even though now in her twilight years she enjoyed a perfectly comfortable life and never had to worry about clothes or food, she would still watch the rice jar closely. Whenever the level of rice fell ever so slightly she would top it up. It was only when the jar was filled to the brim would she feel a happiness beyond all others.

Her children accepted this as some kind of unsettled problem from the war period. Actually, she was missing the time in heaven that Young Mr. Lin had given her.

After putting the Yang's family life in order, Young Mr. Lin had wanted to return to his own home. That afternoon, before going out to buy a boat ticket, he was in exceptionally good spirits and, stepping through the gate on his way out, he turned around and hugged the woman's little son and lifted him high in the air. "In Uncle's home there's a boy as big as you. Probably he won't recognize his daddy!" This was first time she saw the withdrawn and mournful Young Mr. Lin's face break into a dazzling and child-like smile. But the Japanese had unexpectedly closed down the sea lanes and he returned from Sixteen Wharf Landing looking dejected and distracted, just like a wave-ravaged sand castle that was crumbling. As he sat in the corner with his head down, weeping gloomily, his brokenhearted expression made Mrs. Yang think of an abandoned child. A maternal impulse stirred within her and she felt the strong urge to go over and draw him to her breast and comfort him.

In her whole life, Mrs. Yang had never cried in a man's arms, not even her husband's. When Old Yang joined the army, the situation hadn't been as grave as this. No one had realized that things could get this bad and certainly had no feeling of parting for the last time. Her bitterest weeping found a companion in Young Mr. Lin's tears, and he also put aside his man's mask more than once to cry and snivel in her presence.

Brother Yu in Hangzhou found a job for Young Mr. Lin at the church-run hospital. He brought medicine to the homes of patients and gave shots to those who despised the idea of being sick and thus might spread infections. One evening he came back especially late, and sat there silently in his usual corner of the room, seemingly preoccupied. Mrs. Yang guessed he must be thinking of home again.

She had heard many stories about Old Town and Second Sister off and on and could feel just how much Young Mr. Lin loved his family. She didn't know how to comfort him. Quietly she cooked dinner and brought it to the table, and quietly she brought out her sewing. She was sewing a lined jacket for him. She too had an agile pair of hands. She looked down, sensing that Young Mr. Lin's gaze was fixed upon her and this made her rather uncomfortable and flustered. There was the sound of a repressed sigh in the room. She put down her sewing and handed him a glass of water. "The Japanese can't close off the sea lanes forever. You'll be getting home soon. For now just consider this place as home and the three Yang children as your own..." She seemed to realize that it wasn't too proper for her to speak like this so she added, "You are their savior and they ought to look upon you as a kind of second father."

The little Yang boy was just then playing by the gate, and hearing sounds in the house he timidly went inside. Young Mr. Lin hugged him and let out a stifled sob. Mrs. Yang knew that something serious had happened. Was it his home and family in Old Town? Young Mr. Lin was always listening to the news from Old Town. In Shanghai there was an Old Town Fellow Residents Association and he often went there.

That night, after the children and the old lady had gone to sleep, Mrs. Yang led Young Mr. Lin to a nook in the little alleyway in back for a talk. They didn't dare go off too far. Once it was dark, Shanghai was like a dead city. The Japanese military police patrols grabbed anyone they saw.

Young Mr. Lin stood there facing the wall. He didn't have the courage to look at Mrs. Yang. This pathetic woman still didn't know her husband had perished a few months before in Shanxi. Brother Yu had gotten this news in some roundabout way and, unable to bring himself to face her with it, placed this difficult task with Young Mr. Lin. *Am I going to tell her or not?* A fierce struggle raged within Young Mr. Lin.

Mrs. Yang wanted to ask about Second Sister and the three Lin children. Young Mr. Lin never stopped sending off letters to Old Town though he never received any reply. *Did he finally get a reply today that brought bad news?* She didn't dare voice this question.

Young Mr. Lin finally turned toward her and drew out an envelope from inside his shirt. Packed in the envelope was money that Brother Yu had collected from various people. Young Mr. Lin didn't have the courage to say what this was all about, but simply handed the money to her. Mrs. Yang didn't have to open the heavy envelope to know what it meant. Her legs began to give way, her stomach knotted, and she crouched slowly down on the ground. Then she curled up and convulsed violently as if in a fit of malaria. Young Mr. Lin never expected that her instincts would have been so sharp. He didn't say a single word but just stood there numbly waiting for her to keen and wail. *She ought to have a bitter cry over this.* Seconds passed by, then minutes. She didn't cry. She just lay there contorted and trembling without making the slightest sound.

Young Mr. Lin stood by awkwardly and helplessly. "It is improper for the unmarried to have physical contact," the ancients taught. To avoid any suspicion of impropriety, he right then and there made up his mind to move out of the Yang home, even though here were Old Mrs. Yang and the children, the gate was left wide open during the daytime, and at night he slept with the eldest Yang boy in the little space under the stairs. There was nothing at all to be suspicious about, but he still felt he ought to move a distance apart from them. But now he was like an actor who had forgotten the plot and his lines. He stood there blankly on the stage, his mind floating back to Old Town and seeing Second Sister anxiously watching for him. *I have to return home alive for Second Sister's sake...*he told himself.

He heard Mrs. Yang sobbing next to his ear and felt that half his face was damp and hot. He couldn't figure out how she could now be in his arms. He froze for an instant then grasped her more tightly. Their heads touching, they cried together for a long time, a very long time.

The next day, life went on as it always had. They decided to conceal this entirely from Old Mrs. Yang and the children. Six months later when the old lady was dying, she held on to Young Mr. Lin with one hand and Mrs. Yang with the other. "I'm going now. My son is there waiting for me. He and I feel at ease with you both being together." They looked at each other in surprise. *Had the Old Lady borne the grief of losing her son in silence all this while?*

⌘　⌘　⌘

As she thought of this scene across the long passage of the years, Mrs. Yang, now with grandchildren surrounding her knees, could not help feeling her heart give a leap. At that earlier time, she was indeed like a wife tied by love to her husband and tied by love to Young Mr. Lin. It was a hopeless feeling. Young Mr. Lin was a man with a family. She had seen the Happy Family Portrait that he had carried concealed on him. His wife was so dignified and beautiful that she herself felt utterly unworthy. Shanghai during the Japanese occupation had been named the Isolated Island. Would the Isolated Island be forever cut off and all alone? She didn't dare think about the future, didn't dare imagine what this home would be like when there would be no Young Mr. Lin.

4.

THE GRANDDAUGHTER OF the Shanghai "relative" said, "When the news of Grandpa's death reached Shanghai, Grandma was just then sick and unable to get out of bed. She wanted me to buy a piece of black crepe. She sewed a black sleeve band and wore it for a whole year."

She called them Grandpa and Grandma, without adding "your" and "my." This confused me, as if my grandfather were actually her grandfather, and our family with our blood ties to him had instead become outsiders of no relationship standing. Impatiently I corrected her. "*Your* grandma wore black crepe for *my* grandpa." She laughed. "Ever since I was little I thought the person in that photograph in my grandma's room was my grandpa. Nobody explained it to me. I also just took it for granted that your family was another of Grandpa's families. Didn't all the men in the old society have several families?"

So, my grandfather held such an important place in a family with which I hadn't the slightest connection! Even though he left Shanghai and returned to Old Town, he was still that indispensable member of their family. Whenever I reflected on this, odd and mixed-up feelings would spring up in my head. It's hard to describe the sensation they produced.

I couldn't help being curious and speculating how my grandmother would have felt had she known all this. I remember that every year Grandma would buy some high-quality dried bamboo shoots and olives, and sew them up in cloth and hand them to Grandpa to send to the Shanghai relative. During the "Cultural

Revolution" when Grandpa was shut up in the study sessions, she even wrote replies on his behalf to the Shanghai relative.

Was Grandma ever envious or jealous? And that Shanghai woman, adoring and clinging to a man whose main thought was to return to his own home, who never for one instant forgot his own home, and who longed to be reunited with his beautiful wife—who could say what this tasted like for her?

The old-fashioned women of Chinese tradition were old, old books written in the classical style, deep and vast and far beyond our understanding.

⌘　⌘　⌘

Mrs. Yang received the news of Young Mr. Lin setting out from Old Town on his journey and supposed that he would be bringing his wife so that they could revisit all the old places together. In his letters he often said he wanted to bring Second Sister to Shanghai to meet her and the children. It was because Second Sister was going to brighten her home with her presence that she swept and cleaned the place over and over again, and over and over again tried on her clothes. That's also why she removed and hid all traces of Young Mr. Lin in her house. She fixed up the master bedroom for them and bought a complete set of brand new bedclothes. She herself planned to move into that little space under the stairs that Young Mr. Lin had lived in then. It still contained the single bed and the little dresser that he had used. For twenty years she had considered Young Mr. Lin as her own man, but she had never felt jealous or schemed to replace Second Sister. She just always humbly and modestly hid behind the figure of Second Sister and felt an inner admiration for this Old Town woman whom she had never met.

Sometimes back then a frightening idea had even flashed in her mind, a hope that the war would go on and on and the sea lanes to Old Town would be sealed off forever. Such thoughts were unforgivable sins and she would reprove herself severely every time she had them. But she never revealed any word or deed aimed at detaining Young Mr. Lin. She actively assisted him in his search for a road home. It was she who introduced the Old Town Fellow Residents Association to him. She even helped him to find out how to go overland back to Old Town. No matter what the day and age, there are always people brave enough to do business at the risk of their lives. Old Town's silks and specialty products could still be bought on the market and she relayed this discovery to Young Mr. Lin. It showed that in addition to going by sea there were other ways home. Together they leafed through maps, devising a return route. In those days there was a railway going from Shanghai to Hankou. From Hankou he could take a roundabout route through Jiangxi and cross over the mountains to Old Town. Such a way was very long and dangerous. She asked Young Mr. Lin to take her eldest son with him as a traveling companion. She told him to give the boy an education and send him back to Shanghai when the war ended. All this on her part actually made Young Mr. Lin hesitant. Every time the hope of returning home was kindled within him, he would immediately sink into sorrow over the idea of their parting.

Always after the children were asleep they would discuss important moves. At that time in Shanghai there were nightly blackouts so they would sit face-to-face at the dining table. The main room had a lattice wall of glass and on every small square of the lattice were pasted strips of white rice-character paper. With the weak rays of light from the small sky well penetrating through, they could still dimly see each other. Young Mr. Lin lowered his head and let out a deep sigh. She sensed that he could not bear leaving this family. That was all she needed to know, and tears of happiness and satisfaction flowed down her cheeks. She reached out and, grasping his pale and delicate hand in hers, comforted him and urged him to leave Shanghai.

⌘　⌘　⌘

My Shanghai relative's granddaughter and I surreptitiously conjectured about romance between my grandpa and her grandma, these two ill-fated mandarin ducks who had both lost their mates in the chaos of war. Did they, in occupied Shanghai, in their forlorn despair, in guilt and the reproaches of conscience, have "a flash of thirsty pleasure"?[51]

But let's not forget that they were both Christians. She and I were both studying history at university when Freud was all the rage, and we discussed sex frankly and without inhibition.

Actually, that was beside the point. Is there anything that touches the depths of one's being more than two souls who were so entwined?

Day after day, Young Mr. Lin struggled with his irresolution. Finally he decided he would go. They were divided in their views about taking the eldest Yang son. Mrs. Yang said that she wouldn't allow him to leave unless he took Number One Son. Young Mr. Lin said that he couldn't let a child risk this kind of danger. He told how he had been separated on the Yangzi River from his orderly, Young Li. If anything happened to this child, he could not face his former colleague Yang and Old Mrs. Yang.

---

[51]　Mandarin ducks are the traditional Chinese symbol of lifelong marital love and fidelity. "A flash of thirsty pleasure"—again Li Yu's poem, "Waves Washing on Sand." See chapter 6, footnote 24.

Just then, Mrs. Yang received a returned letter, one that Young Mr. Lin had written to Second Sister. Some good-hearted person at the post office in Old Town added a few words on the back of the envelope: "The Lin Residence at 26 Officials Lane has been destroyed. The death or survival of its residents is not clear." *Should I give this letter to Young Mr. Lin?* Mrs. Yang was extremely hesitant to do this.

That evening when Young Mr. Lin returned to the Yang home and the children all shouted out, "Foster Daddy!" he showed no reaction. Looking numbed, he straightway buried himself in his little space under the stairs. Mrs. Yang entered and saw him silently weeping as he held up his Happy Family Portrait in front of him. As it happened, he had just found out from the Old Town Fellow Residents Association that the Japanese had bombed Old Town a second time. Renowned Officials Lane and Stipend Lane now no longer existed! It was also said that the head of the Old Town Salt Monopoly Bureau and his family, more than ten people, had been blasted into bloody pieces. There was nothing left of them that could be identified with any certainty. And that family's home had been just on the other side of the wall of the Lin home!

Young Mr. Lin gazed wretchedly at Mrs. Yang. "Second Sister and the children wouldn't have been staying in the house, I suppose?" he said, seemingly out of nowhere.

Mrs. Yang's pocket held that returned letter. She knew what he meant. Crouching down beside him, she said, "Second Sister is such an intelligent and capable woman. She would know how to protect herself and the children. I'm sure she'd have taken them with her and escaped from Old Town early on."

"Where could she go? A woman with three children wandering in hardship from one place to the next. And without money. It's been a long time since I sent her money."

"The children are grown. They can look after themselves and look after their mother too."

Young Mr. Lin seemed willing to believe Mrs. Yang's reasoning and he calmed down some. A moment later his face grew all contorted again. "Second Sister looks soft and quiet, but inside she's strong and unyielding. She'd rather die with dignity than go on living without it."

Mrs. Yang got up and covered his mouth with her hand. He was crying his heart out in a keening and mournful way. She cried too but was it for unfortunate Second Sister, or for her own hopeless feelings?

⌘　⌘　⌘

For a while after that, they didn't mention Old Town. The days passed and Young Mr. Lin proved himself to be the man of this house in deed as well as name. Every day he went out to earn money. And every month he handed over to Mrs. Yang the exact amount of the miserable salary he earned at the hospital. Every evening Mrs. Yang sat under the lamp with its black cloth covering making clothes for Young Mr. Lin. Autumn had just begun and she was sewing a lined cotton jacket for him. She even dug out a piece of fine silk that she had from her dowry and was thinking of making him something for next summer. She was like an ostrich, her head buried in her own world, a world in which she supposed that Young Mr. Lin would stay with her, year after year.

The peace and calm of life in this home lasted until a navigation route to Old Town was opened. The news of this had just been made public and already boat tickets for the next three months had been sold clean out. The shipping company would no longer issue tickets beyond three months in the future. Young Mr. Lin, who had been beside himself in excitement over this development, now lost all poise in despondency over his inability to buy a ticket. His unmistakable change of emotions that day was like a pair of scissors cutting Mrs. Yang's delusional world into pieces. He was Second Sister's man. He was Second Sister's man every minute of every day. When it came time for the property to revert to its original owner, she was happy for his happiness and despondent in his despondency. Late at night she often cried herself awake from dreaming. They were two lives in adversity and tribulation adhering to each other. *I am in you. You are in me. We are indistinguishable from each other. Today if we were pulled apart—one inch, one centimeter—while still living, oh, I could never bear the pain.*

Sometimes she felt so very much alone in her unhappiness. Young Mr. Lin couldn't understand how she felt.

Young Mr. Lin resigned from his job. Now, early every morning, he would be at the dock under the moon and stars to wait for someone to return a ticket. When the sun sank into the western sky, the same scene played at the gateway: he would come home hanging his head and looking upset. She held back her pain and did the best she could to appear tenderhearted. She filled a pan of water for him to wash his face with and squeezed out a hot towel and handed it to him. She silently accompanied his incessant sighs.

On this day, Young Mr. Lin came back earlier than usual. Mrs. Yang was still in the little sky well washing clothes. Suddenly she saw a foot step in through the gate. She didn't look up to see the expression on his face, but with one wild beat her heart plunged a thousand feet. He stepped so high and so lightly and joy and happiness radiated out of him. Today he had bought a boat ticket!

He stood beside her pail of clothes wash and said in a trembling voice, "I'm going home! Tomorrow I can go home!"

She flicked off the water and soap from her hands and slowly stood up. Tears, which she was fiercely holding back, still broke through and appeared in her eyes, but she forced a smile. "That's wonderful! Just wonderful! I am so happy!" she loudly said.

Young Mr. Lin started to say his good-byes to the three Yang children. His spirits were still soaring. One by one, he took them by the hand and told them to obey Ma, to study hard, and when the war ended, "Foster Daddy" would come and see them for sure. Behind him Mrs. Yang was hanging up the wash to dry. Her face was wetter than the clothes in her hand. *He doesn't notice this. He really doesn't notice this.* After setting out the clothes to dry, she ran to the little alley in back and wept silently. She thought of her husband for the first time in a long while. She still hadn't cried this brokenheartedly for him. Was this a sin for which she should be punished?

That night Mrs. Yang put into Young Mr. Lin's leather suitcase several pieces of clothing that she had hurriedly made for Second Sister and the children. "I'm not sure whether they'll fit or not. Please have Second Sister accept these little gestures of my regard for her," she said.

Young Mr. Lin was stunned. He now remembered that the Lin home no longer existed. He didn't know whether his family was dead or alive. He didn't know where Second Sister and the children were at this very moment. His excitement abruptly faded and died away. He was still there, sitting at the dinner table in the dark night of the Shanghai blackout. Lowering his head, he said despondently, "I thought that when I returned to Old Town I would step through the main gate of the Lin family home and my son would ask me, 'Uncle, who are you looking for?' I forgot that the old Lin home is no more. I forgot that no one knows if Second Sister is alive or dead. I was a fool to have been so happy…"

Mrs. Yang again stretched out her hand and took his. *Will this be the last time I take his hand in mine?*

"When you return to Old Town you can surely find them. You must be confident. God loves you, and Second Sister too."

Young Mr. Lin grasped her hand strongly. "I'm sorry. I just have to abandon you and the three Yang children and go home. Right now leaving this family is as hard on me as leaving my Old Town one. If only I could split myself in two and leave one-half here. Stay well. Stay well. I will miss you."

These were just the words she had been waiting for over the past several days. She had only asked this little, little thing. She had never held any extravagant hope that this man with a family of his own would weigh her against his wife in his mind. She cried. There was both bitter anguish and sweetness in her tears.

He cried too. The lonely man and the widow of war's upheaval once again cried in each other's arms.

How could this anguish and heartbreak not have been "carved on the bone and engraved on the heart"?

⌘　⌘　⌘

When she sent Young Mr. Lin to Sixteen Wharf Landing and saw his figure fade into the sound of the ship's whistle, in her heart there arose both a hazy and a clear hope that, maybe, when he returned to Old Town, if his beloved family had been wiped out and Second Sister and their children were gone forever, in his heartbreak and despair he would think of the Shanghai family. Over the next several decades she had often dreamed of him returning, that little leather suitcase in his hand, walking with firm steps across the threshold, and tearfully falling into her arms.

5.

In the misty drizzle of the early morning, the train pulls slowly into Shanghai. I can hardly count the number of times I've come and gone from Shanghai. Today the two characters, Shang Hai, on the station signboard have a different flavor to them. I desert my traveling companion and go off a way by myself. In each of the train compartments scenes of reunited friends and loved ones are being performed. I think of my Shanghai "relative" in the 1960s. Had she stood here to greet the man she had been waiting for on such a misty and drizzly morning?

There are only a very few words in Grandpa's postcards about their reunion. You might almost miss the emotional colors. He went to Shanghai together with Brother Yu of Hangzhou. On the postcard it says, "Left Hangzhou this evening headed for Shanghai with Brother Yu." Later, Mrs. Yang joined their travels. The three of them went together by train to Nanjing. I am sure Grandpa took them to where he had narrowly escaped death along the Yangzi, told them the story of how he escaped under the muzzles of the Japanese rifles, the time spent floating down the river, and how he learned from the fisherman to cast a net and haul in fish. Perhaps he had a tiny hope of learning the whereabouts of the fisherman and Young Li.

Grandpa wanted to keep going north, to see the former battle-fields, pay homage to Division Commander Zhang, and to see the little widow. Mrs. Yang and Brother Yu did not accompany him on this northward part of the journey. When they took him to the train to Henan they stood on the platform and agreed to meet in

Old Town the following year, never suspecting that was to be their last farewell on earth to each other.

Two years after Grandpa passed on, the Shanghai relative followed him, and the bulldozer leveled the West Gate home. The few traces of them that had remained in this world thus disappeared. At that time, my grandmother was already muddleheaded. Who else would have been interested in the letters and pictures Grandpa had left behind?

We were. The granddaughter of the Shanghai relative and I. Every time we got together, we always had a laugh about the pathetic and invincible stubbornness of old-fashioned women. "My grandmother was extremely ridiculous. The day before she died, she suddenly rose out of bed and started rummaging through trunks and chests looking for things. My uncle's wife thought she was looking for her bank passbook, and she followed her around, all flurried and flustered. They said that if she really couldn't find it, they could go to the bank and report the loss. Who knew that what she was looking for was Grandpa's picture—oh, I mean *your* grandfather's picture. It was the one of him alone, wearing a long gown. The next day, she was gone. When we changed her clothes, we discovered that picture by her pillow. My mom placed the picture at her breast..."

I too had some funny stuff to share with my Shanghai relative's granddaughter. When Grandma was over ninety years old her body was still strong but her mind was totally gone, worse than her older sister, Great-Auntie. She had no sense of time and place whatsoever. She would often mumble and mutter to herself and talk with Ninth Brother about the weather, "It's going to rain today. Be sure to take the umbrella..."

I don't know why, but standing now in the misty rain on an early morning in Shanghai, I feel a little bit of self-pity and a little bit of melancholy. I have that achy feeling that comes just before crying. Sifting through the records and editing the sad story of an unknown Shanghai woman is like the indescribable attraction and loss you feel after seeing a tearjerker love story on the screen, and with one last lingering look you leave the theatre. The reason people create dreams and chase dreams on the silver screen is because real life is so humdrum and boring or even ugly. I just have to envy and admire my Shanghai relative. It's like I am envying and admiring the female protagonist in a love story. Most of her life she has no male partner, but all her life she has love. These days, many women change men like rides on a carousel but don't have love. Like Chrysanthemum. Like me.

CHAPTER NINETEEN – YEARS OF REVOLUTION

1.

OUR LIN FAMILY'S own Great Cultural Revolution occurred before the Red Guard rebellion. Grandpa was still traveling in the north when turmoil erupted in our home. The wives of my uncles Baosheng and Baoqing, both progressive-minded Communist Party members, in a sudden joint action came and took away my cousins, leaving me all alone at West Gate. I was then in first grade at West Lake Primary School. One day after school my mother showed up at the gate. She told me that Grandpa and Grandma were severely old-fashioned in their thinking and not fit to raise and educate Successors of the Revolution. That was why my two aunts had come to fetch my cousins home. "You should also leave West Gate, and Mama's now come back to take you away."

As I remember it, Mother was only a visitor at home, an outsider who didn't have much to do with me. The period of time she lived at West Gate was far shorter than Great-Auntie's, but I knew that she was someone who had the right to take me away from Grandma. The revolutionary action of her two daughters-in-law deeply hurt Grandma. On the day that my cousins all left West Gate, Grandma didn't feel like lighting the stove to make dinner and just gave me a few *fen* to buy myself a yam cake at the stall by the end of the bridge. This was something really, really rare, and even Granny Wang, who ran the stall, thought it strange. Everybody knew how strict the rules were in the Lin household, especially about letting little children buy snacks on the street, and most especially their gold branch and jade leaf granddaughter. I didn't forget the Lin family rules. I held up the steaming hot yam cake in front of me all the way to the gate before popping some of it into my mouth. Then I happened upon Grandma in the empty parlor wiping tears from her eyes. Before this, I had never seen my grandmother in tears. I gave a little gulp and timidly put the yam cake up to her mouth. Grandma embraced me, "Hong'er, don't you leave your grandma. No matter who comes for you, don't go," she said between sobs.

I wrested my hand from Mother's and right then and there stared down at my little leather shoes. These were a pair of red shoes with designs carved in them. In Old Town a lot of little kids ran around barefooted no matter what the season. Their parents couldn't afford even the cheapest cloth shoes for them, but ever since I was little I wore leather ones, pair after pair, all in different colors and styles. My clothes too were more fashionable and well chosen, compared to what other people's children wore. But my hair was where I most differed from them. Every day Grandma would change it to create a new style for me.

These weren't things that mattered to me. A little girl in first grade doesn't yet know how to weigh what was good and what was bad. What I did think about was that if I left West Gate I would no longer be able to sleep holding Grandma. I could never bear nights without Grandma. Mother used to take me to where she worked, and whenever she couldn't stand my crying tantrums she would send me back to West Gate. She didn't know why, once day became night, I would turn into an unreasonable little brat. I wouldn't tell her what was in my heart and even in my youngest years I shut her outside the world of my feelings.

Mother said, "Just look at what you're wearing. And your hair! It's no wonder your aunts say you're a little bourgeois missy. It's for your own good that Mama's taking you away."

"No!" I was like a small heroine in a glossy magazine. "I'm not going with you! No matter who comes for me, I'm not going!" I said coldly and defiantly, chest thrust out and head raised high.

Tears formed in Mother's eyes. She couldn't control her own "big missy" temperament and she became very upset. "If I had known that you'd turn out like this, I wouldn't have brought you to West Gate. I shouldn't even have given birth to you!"

I left her there and ran off for home to seek a reward from Grandma for all this. She didn't praise me, just looked at me forlornly and heaved a sigh. Like me, she certainly didn't understand this sudden and unexpected family *coup d'etat*. The Lins had weathered decades of tempests and the more difficult things got, the stronger their affections for each other would grow. How could she have thought that there'd be a day when her own back courtyard would catch fire, so to speak? She still was a cadre of the residents' committee and still brought home her endless awards and commendations. So how could anyone say that she was backward in her thinking and unfit to educate and raise the third generation of Lins?

⌘   ⌘   ⌘

Grandpa brought back lots of presents from his travels. The Lin family had now grown into a large household of over ten members and he brought something for everyone, including a pair of large-sized woolen gloves for my stepfather. This was to show that he accepted this northern fellow as a Lin son-in-law. He took out the presents from his travel bag and arranged them item by item on the Eight Immortals table, telling my grandmother that this one was for so-and-so while that one was for somebody else. I got a pretty pencil case. People say that to travel is to learn to be homesick. Thinking about his home in Old Town and about his dear ones there while on this trip, Grandpa knew just how happy and satisfied he was.

I don't know how Grandma told him about that sudden flare-up in our own back courtyard or what his reaction was to this. The next day I saw that all the presents had been put back into his travel bags which were then stuck under their bed and not opened again. The most obvious change was that they loved me all the more. This made me gladly endure whatever hardships there were.

How I miss that happy time. I was living like the Manchu imperial princesses you see on the screen. Every morning from the time I opened my eyes my grandparents would hover around me. Grandma washed my face and combed my hair, which by then had grown to be more than a foot in length. One day it would be braided, while the next it would be combed into hair buns. Off to the side, Grandpa blew on the milk to cool it down and then he would feed me the little cut-up hard-boiled egg. Every day these two old folks took me to school and fetched me afterward. I soon totally forgot about all the loneliness I had been left with after all my cousins went away from West Gate.

Meanwhile a great movement that was to overturn five thousand years of history was fermenting in Beijing. The people of Old Town had no sense of all this, and Grandpa who had not been reading the newspapers for a long time now supposed that people were still studying Lei Feng. The main focus of life at home at West Gate was whether I would stay there or go away, and about this I was totally in the dark. My stepfather was unable to make children and he had secretly stirred my mother up into bringing me back to their home, threatening to take this to court if she couldn't. Grandpa adamantly disagreed. He couldn't hand his tender and delicate granddaughter over to that uncouth northerner. It may have been that Division Commander Hu had left too deep an impression on him, but he felt that I would be in danger with them. So he wrote to his former son-in-law in Xinjiang and, winning him over as an ally, got him to issue the order for me to stay at West Gate. Grandpa's letter-writing friendship with this former son-in-law lasted for the rest of his life.

⌘   ⌘   ⌘

Every Sunday morning Grandpa went to the church to worship God and in the afternoon would go for a soak in the hot springs at East Gate. This was an ironclad rule. One Sunday morning, Grandpa had no sooner stepped out when my two uncles and aunts as well as my mother suddenly showed up at West Gate, and a family revolution concerning my hair then ensued. They wanted to cut my braids! It was just like the revolutionary movement in ideology going on at that very moment. Mother and my two aunts had previously always permed their hair, but on that day their heads were neatly cropped short.

Mother came out with a set of patched clothes gotten from somewhere or other, and in a pique shouted at me to put them on. In an effort at compromise, Grandma said that since wearing tattered clothes would make me "recall past sorrows and savor the joys of the present," I shouldn't also need to have my hair cut, though in the future she wouldn't change the styles, just comb it into two small braids. My two aunts' attitude was unexpectedly mild. In soft and cooing voices they did ideological work on Grandma and judged that this curly haired woman was also in the ranks of the Revolution.

Mother chased me all over the room to cut my braids and put on the old clothes. I whirled around and gave her a fierce bite. The awful shrieks of mother and daughter were like to raise the roof. She sat on my little bed and taking hold of my pillowcase wiped her tears. I rushed forward and snatched it away from her. "You're not to dirty my things. You're not allowed to sit on my bed!"

"I shouldn't have given birth to you. I shouldn't have wanted you!" Mother again said, choked with sobbing.

The elder of my two aunts came over and gently taking me in her arms asked me if I knew who Liu Hulan was. "When that fourteen-year-old revolutionary martyr was sacrificed she was wearing ragged clothes and her hair was cut so short that half her ears showed."[52]

I can't recall what methods she used to talk me into wearing those beat-up clothes and letting her cut my hair. Grandma sat at the Eight Immortals table watching my two aunts performing this makeover on me. Possibly afraid to leave me alone, she could only watch my hair fall to the ground. She had doted on my hair. How did she feel then?

Big Aunt brought me in front of the mirror. "Look! Now *there's* a successor of the proletariat class. The way you looked before was like a landlord's Little Miss Pampered."

I saw a little girl, a complete stranger. She looked like she had been made up into the model of a wretched child in a kindergarten program. This seemed really funny to me, and the face with the tracks of tears burst into titters and giggles at the mirror.

---

[52] Liu Hulan (1932–1947), a young girl in Shanxi Province beheaded by Guomindang forces during the Civil War for refusing to identify Communist Party members among her fellow villagers.

"See how much Hong'er looks like Liu Hulan!" Big Aunt loudly announced, quite pleased with herself.

If the rebel faction at this point had beaten their gongs and shouldered their weapons, none of this would have left an especially deep mark on me. It would have been merely a short skit of a harmless joke, nothing more. However, my younger uncle, feeling he hadn't fully expressed himself, just had to tie a dog's tail on a sable, as the saying goes. He brought over a pan of water and threw in a piece of dirty clothing. He wanted me to learn how to wash clothes, and, furthermore, to do so out by the gate! O heaven! I was to exhibit myself in my ragged old clothes in public at West Gate! The pan with the clothing, soap, and a little bench were set out at the gate under the oleander. All that remained was for the lead actress to mount the stage and begin performing.

I looked down at the patches on my clothing and thought of each and every one of the familiar faces of the neighbors around us. Dimly I imagined Rongmei's little eyes. She was always looking at me, my Shanghai candy wrappers, my leather shoes, and piece after piece of my fine silk clothing, in envy of something she could gaze at but never attain. All the West Gate children looked at me like that. Our family had money. Grandma's children were all government officials. From birth I wasn't like these other children. But today my clothes were shabbier than what Rongmei was wearing. How could I go out into the street? I had never before washed a single dish or handkerchief. Why did they want me to wash clothing?

Grandma was still looking at me with her silent and helpless expression. Big Aunt was quite confident she could bring me out there. Several mouths in turn poured sounds into my ears, but the whole thing was just impossible. At this moment I really did become the teenage heroine, Liu Hulan. I had never studied the words "Death before Submission" in school, but I had that "Death before Submission" spirit.

The battle of wills went on for quite a while. Big Aunt slapped the table top with her hand and got up. "Go out and do the washing! Today we'll see who's fierce, you or we grown-ups."

"I'm not going wash clothes! I'm not going to do it!" I dashed back into my room intending to change into my own clothes.

Big Aunt again came to coax and cajole me. I cried and wanted her to compensate me for my hair. I also hurled some bad words at her. Young Aunt angrily pushed open the door, picked me right up, and threw me outside the gate. My two feet had no sooner touched the ground when I leapt back into the house. Back and forth the struggle went. All this movement in our house attracted a lot of attention from people passing by. The tragedy I had most worried about now happened—Rongmei was standing under the tree looking in! When she understood what was going on, she rolled back her sleeves to help me wash the clothes. In a fit of total exasperation, I dashed my head against the wall. Younger Uncle lifted me up and, pressing me down on the bench, gave me a few good slaps. This heavy-handed repression fueled my resistance all the more. I jumped up and to everyone's surprise lifted up the heavy Eight Immortals table.

Immediately the whole house fell silent. Several faces were shaking in disapproval at me as if to say: "This child is done for. We can't save her."

Grandma bent over and picked up the smashed teacups from the floor. "You all just go now. Dad will be coming back soon."

My two uncles looked at each other. They still felt a little diffident in front of their daddy. "The Lin family problems come from Dad. The revolutionizing of ideology has to begin with him!"

⌘   ⌘   ⌘

When Grandpa returned, I was in my own room just crying and crying. The things that had happened today were just too brutal for a delicately brought up and pampered girl like me. In my grievance over the wrong done to me, in my misery and fright, I was like a little dog used to being petted and spoiled by its master but which now had been cast out into the streets. I couldn't figure out what was going on in this world. All along I had thought that my two uncles loved me more than they loved their own children. Whenever they came back from travel assignments they would give me gifts even better than what they gave my cousins. Their wives, my two aunts, often yelled at and even struck their children, but they always greeted me with smiles. I still didn't know there was a feeling called sympathy, but they sympathized with me for being a fatherless child. How come just overnight they didn't love me anymore? I felt hurt beyond measure.

A meeting was going on in the main hall which was separated from my room by a single wall. Their attitude toward Grandpa was very restrained, so I couldn't make out much of what was being said.

Suddenly my grandfather let out a thunderous, earsplitting roar. "Get the hell out of here, all of you! Get out! I don't want to see you again!"

I stopped my crying and sat up, terribly frightened.

My uncles and aunts left. Mother, after crying herself dry, finally went too. The house at West Gate was deathly silent.

⌘   ⌘   ⌘

Those days, my younger uncle, Baoqing, would come back to West Gate to give money to Grandpa and Grandma for their living expenses. Big Uncle Baosheng entrusted his portion of this allowance to Younger Uncle. Baoqing would call out "Dad!" whenever he came in and went out. My grandfather just sat there resting, eyes closed, cultivating an inner tranquility, and paid no attention to his son. I saw that when Younger Uncle turned and left he had flecks of tears in his eyes. I felt terribly guilty and regretted not obeying him that day about washing the clothes. I was sorry that I had blown the whole thing up into something so big that the family was split every which way over me. The veil of the Lin family's warm feelings of tenderness and affection had been lifted aside and the arrangements of life utterly changed. The heart of a little girl in grade one of primary school filled with contrition and guilt.

⌘　⌘　⌘

Only after Grandpa died did I hear about that conversation concerning faith and belief. The second-generation Lins were each and every one a Communist Party member. Even finicky and crybaby Baohua entered the party while serving in the army. They tried to educate Grandpa on atheism, and this enraged him. He is buried in the Lin ancestral grounds. That's where Grandpa's father and his father's wives sleep their long sleep. His Elder Brother and Big Sister-in-Law are also there. My younger uncle Baoqing bought a good-quality granite headstone for Grandpa and he asked the carver to carve a cross on it to show his respect for Grandpa's beliefs. As for himself, he hoped that when the day came, his son would give him a party flag. He was a loyal and sincere party member.

The affair was over and the situation changed. The incident of the clothes washing became a dinner table condiment every time I returned to visit my family and relatives. No one knew this had left an indelible mark upon me and became a personality flaw that I have never been able to overcome. I frequently, and in ways impossible to explain, plunge into compunction and guilt. Certain situations make me irresolute and hesitant and I always suspect that I have done things wrong. I've gone to psychiatrists and under hypnosis recalled every detail of that Sunday. I have cried myself red-eyed until my insides felt like they were being sliced to bits.

2.

HOME HAD GROWN cold and cheerless. More and more, Grandpa would just sit in the main hall, his eyes closed, in a state of spiritual recuperation. Our little pussycat was also old and didn't like to move around, preferring to nestle against its master's body and join in this eyes-shut repose. Every once in a while my grandfather's hand would unconsciously stroke the cat's back, and each time the animal would raise its eyelids sluggishly and repay him with a look of happiness and gratitude. Pussycat knew nothing of the affairs of the human world and could not feel the heavy clouds roiling and churning within its master nor the tense atmosphere around us. I was one year younger than the cat, but my every pore sensed the shapeless oppression that spread throughout our home. Grandma crept about as if on eggshells and when she spoke she frequently raised her index finger and put it to her mouth. This made everything all the more tense, as if Grandpa, sitting off by himself, eyes closed and spiritually gone away, were like some tiger gathering its forces before springing forth.

Red Guards and big character posters were out on the streets now. I still went to school every day, book bag on my back. I would invite Rongmei from next door to accompany me and we would go to the church to get Chaofan to join us. Not long after my short haircut, the church ceased to be a church. Families were now continuously moving in to take up residence there. Inside the wooden fence clothes of all colors had been laid out to dry in the sun. It was a scene of indescribable clamor and disorder.

Once beyond our gate I could feel my joys revive. I even felt more joyous than I had previously, for the teacher wasn't checking attendance or looking at assignments. We could arrive late or just skip school entirely. We lurched and staggered as we poked our way along. Along the streets was bonfire after bonfire into which people were throwing books, calligraphy scrolls, and fine silks and satins. Even though Rongmei's daddy was a mute, he knew about destroying the "Four Olds."[53] He took the home's drinking glasses with their painted little ladies and serving maids and smashed them publicly on the street. Chaofan, who had just begun to learn about stamp collecting, picked up many valuable stamps from these fires. I only had eyes for candy wrappers and I was able to get quite a few of these too.

Every day there were fresh and exciting things going on. The whole world had changed into a reckless playground where you could do whatever you pleased. People were pulled into the street to be "struggled." Among the surrounding onlookers we were like little fish darting in and out through the eyes of the net. We saw rebel factions cut the hair off of old ladies of the landlord class, and we followed along clapping and cheering. We were a little audience in a playhouse with no idea whatsoever that the plot on the stage would change the lives of our own families.

Red Guards came to West Lake Primary School to develop Little Red Soldiers organizations. Two rows of tables were set up along opposing sides of the athletic field and our classmates were racing to sign up to join. The chaos on the school grounds was wildly arousing. In the midst of such a commotion who wouldn't have worked hard to worm a way in? As I lined up, I noticed that the two registration points were different Red Guard factions. One called itself East Sea and the other, Front Line. The Little Red

---

[53]   Though destruction of the "Four Olds"—old customs, old habits, old culture, and old ideas—was one of the stated goals of the Cultural Revolution (1966–1976), this movement actually started in 1964.

Soldiers they recruited were also divided into two factions. Under the basket of the basketball court those two factions of Little Red Soldiers who had just received red armbands were viciously arguing with each other, each side cursing the other for being royalists, that is, supporters of the current leading cadres at all levels of government. I turned around to find Chaofan. I wanted to join the same group as he did. After some serious thought, Chaofan said, "'Front Line' sounds more revolutionary." So together we became "Front Line" Little Red Soldiers.

Once the armbands of Little Red Soldiers were put on, the games really got going. I joined in hooting and jeering and spitting at the East Sea Little Red Soldiers. We shouted ourselves hoarse reviling them as the royalist faction. It really felt as if I were feeding some craving! Grandpa and Grandma had painstakingly formed their granddaughter into their golden branch and jade leaf. At home even the word "I" could not leave my mouth—I had to call myself Hong'er. All these commandments and taboos were like a cocoon encasing my body and today I broke forth from that cocoon. The rebellious nature in my blood was completely released and, like a bird, went soaring along to its heart's content.

As I returned to West Gate, off in the distance I could see Grandma standing under the tree waiting for me. The bird soaring through the skies landed on the ground, came forward, and nicely said, "Ah Ma, Hong'er's home from school."

Dinner was served. As always, I called Grandpa to the table. He opened his eyes and looked at me. His stare at my arm quickly felt like a nail being driven in. "Take that off."

"Why?"

"Take that off!"

"No!"

Grandpa gazed at me impassively then closed his eyes again. He didn't come to the table this meal. Those days he often fasted. Grandma sat at the table to keep me company while I ate. She herself didn't touch her chopsticks.

⌘   ⌘   ⌘

Ninth Brother sat there, eyes closed but spiritually still in turmoil. His thoughts were as tangled as hemp. From time to time he would ask himself what he had done wrong to make his children raise the bamboo staves of rebellion. Sometimes anger would fill his heart. He saw Baosheng and Baoqing's so-called atheism not as something derived from knowing or thinking about truth, but from currying favor with those in power, and he despised such petty people.

That day Baoqing's wife, Fangzi, had said, "Dad, you have already harmed us badly enough. Every time our political backgrounds are checked, we just can't get around you. Don't harm us anymore!" These words enraged the doctor and he slammed the table, telling them to get the hell out of his sight. Those were just angry words that slipped out of him and he looked forward to the next time they all got together. That's when he would distribute the gifts stuffed under the bed and restore the atmosphere of harmony in this family. Several months had passed but the two daughters-in-law had not shown their faces at West Gate. Previously the Lins held one or two big family reunions every month. New Year's, festivals, the third generation's birthdays—all were pretexts for getting together. He never expected that the big Lin reunions would actually become such a vague and uncertain anticipation. He didn't speak to Second Sister about this. Toward Baosheng and Baoqing he still maintained his reserve.

Again it was Sunday. After the church had been disbanded, the doctor didn't stop reading the scriptures, praying, and praising God, and he was just then reading the Bible when Baosheng and Baoqing arrived back at West Gate.

Baoqing stood beside his dad and rubbed his hand along the rattan chair his father was sitting on. "This chair ought to be replaced."

The doctor accepted the olive branch of peace his son offered him and a current of warmth flowed through him. "No need to replace it. Just ask the rattan man to come fix it. This was your birthday present to me the year you returned from Korea."

This was the first time in several months his dad had said anything to Baoqing. Baoqing felt so grateful that his nose started to tingle.

Baosheng kept the fire going: "Dad, you've gotten thin. So has Ma. You shouldn't be so economical," he said.

In a flash, the ice pack in his heart melted. He stood up and went into the inner room to let his tears flow as freely as they would. He took that bag of gifts from under the bed, and all smiles, went back into the main hall and placed the gifts one by one on the Eight Immortals table. "This one's for Su'er, this is for Wei'er. Here, this is for you, and here's one for *you*..."

The two brothers looked at each other, at a total loss as to what to do. Today they had arranged to return to the West Gate home to carry out a thorough cleanup. Sooner or later, this house would be a target of a Red Guard rebel faction sweep, and they would be sure to find proof that the Lins were reactionaries. But now, with all of this in front of them, how could they get started?

The ice pack in his heart had thawed. The father and sons were reconciled. Second Sister joyfully rushed back and forth, conjuring up several types of appetizers and a heated wine pot. She waved her sons to come over and share some cups with their dad.

His face wreathed in his long-absent smile, the doctor brought out the photographs he had taken on his trip and told the stories behind each one. In one breath, all the talk that had been bottled up within him for several months now poured out.

This meal lasted for two hours. Afterward he took his towel and soap and got ready to go for a soak. It had already been a long time since he had gone to East Gate hot springs bathhouse.

The two brothers kept signaling to each other with their eyes. As their father was about to go out the gate, Baosheng screwed up his courage and said, "Dad, we want to have a chat with you."

The doctor sensed that something not good was connected with this visit by his two sons and his heart sank. He sat back down in the rattan chair and closed his eyes.

Baosheng and Baoqing spoke very carefully about the current situation in Old Town from the larger perspective of the whole country. They wanted to persuade their dad to agree to begin clearing out all the proof of his once having been a reactionary. To their complete surprise, he quickly nodded his head in agreement. Then the two sons opened a big hempen sack they had prepared for this task and began to go through all the trunks and cabinets. The "proof of reactionary guilt" of this family turned out to be far more than they had imagined: photos of dad wearing a Guomindang army uniform, the photo of him with the foreigners Mr. and Mrs. Qiao, a Guomindang Party flag, and Baohua's primary school Youth Corps group photo. Every piece of this evidence could land the Lin family members on the killing ground. As the brothers cleaned everything up, cold sweat poured out of them and they rejoiced at having caught all this in time.

The hempen sack was now stuffed full. Second Sister also found two big cloth bags and they filled those too. Now, how were they going to destroy all this evidence of their political crimes? If they hefted it on their shoulders and went out onto the street in the middle of night and happened to run into Red Guards, wouldn't that be the same as throwing themselves into a net? Nor would it be safe if they just tossed it out the back door into the city moat where somebody could quite possibly drag it out of the water. Second Sister thought of Shuiguan's son, Ah Ming. When Ah Ming was small, Ninth Brother had paid all his school fees. Now he was the leader of the West Gate rebel faction. Asking his help would be the safest thing to do. Baosheng and Baoqing remembered that on the eve of Liberation, when the Guomindang were catching members of the underground Party, Enchun had hidden at Shuiguan's house. The two brothers supported their Ma's suggestion.

Ah Ming came over and told them that several times the rebel faction had wanted to raid the Lin home, so he had just gone through the motions. He told his father to get this secret information to Uncle Lin. His father had said that since the Lins were a revolutionary family there would be no problem, and luckily the ideological consciousness of the two brothers was high. As he spoke, Ah Ming pulled a sleeve badge out of his pocket and put it on. The three of them together carried all the evidence out of the house and burnt it at the West Gate street crossing.

The great deed was now accomplished. While the Lin brothers and Ah Ming ate the stuffed rice ball soup made by Second Sister, Ah Ming told with great relish the news of his rebel faction. The day before, they had raided the house of a capitalist's concubine. When the concubine opened the door and saw the red armbands she was so terrified she peed in her trousers. Baosheng said that the personnel section chief of his organization was an old dame who took on a very severe look when lecturing people. Lately she was bowing to anyone she met and every morning she brought hot water to all the rooms of the office. When someone wrote a big character poster that said her behavior was unusually suspicious, she too wet her pants as she stood by the notice board.

They paid no attention to the doctor sitting off to the side, his eyes closed and in his spiritual repose. He had been sitting there all along, listening to his two sons and Ah Ming talking and laughing. He really wanted to stand up and tell them off, but to avoid an even greater worsening in family relations he just forced himself to bear with it, though it was like bearing with a knife stuck into his heart.

Baoqing's glance fell on the Bible that was clutched in his father's hand. This book had been with his dad for decades and because of its age should be among the Four Olds that had to be discarded. Thinking his dad was asleep he softly walked over and drew the book out of his hand.

The doctor opened his eyes. "Just what do you think you're doing?"

"Dad, you can't be reading this book anymore. It's dangerous."

The doctor's eyes bulged in fury. "Put it down. You aren't worthy of destroying it. I really never thought I would raise such dirty swine like you. That you would actually take pleasure in another person's terror...I don't know you!"

Baosheng said, "Dad, really, you can't leave this book around the house. If you don't want to burn it, just keep it at Ah Ming's home."

"Right, put it in our place, our home is the safest."

The doctor cut off Ah Ming. "Ah Ming, paste up a big character poster for me. I am breaking off relations with them. From now on, I want nothing to do with them!"

Baoqing handed the Bible to Ah Ming, who held it close as he stood there stunned for a moment, and then said, "I don't know what book this is, Uncle Lin, but whenever you want to read it, just come over to our home."

The doctor closed his eyes and leaned his head back against the chair. He raised a hand and weakly waved it. The two Lin brothers knew that this meant that their dad had come to terms with them.

Second Sister was holding her breath as she stood at the passageway to the kitchen. In her hand was a jar of white sugar from which she was about to give Baoqing another spoonful, for Baoqing loved to eat sweet things. *How had a storm again so suddenly erupted?* She stood frozen on the spot, but when she saw Ninth Brother wave his hand as an end to hostilities, she let her breath out as if a weight had been lifted from her. She understood her husband. If he felt cornered or pressed, he really would break off relations with his sons. If that happened, she could have no other choice but to stand beside him. But she loved her children. "The hearts of a mother and son were linked in the womb..."

The Lin family was lucky. Several days later, a real rebel faction came to their home. They raided the reactionary army officer's house, but all they seized were two old *qipao*.

3.

THE DAY SCHOOL suspended classes was dazzling with sunshine. Old Town tends to be fairly rainy, but after rain the skies are especially clear and bright. We still arranged to go to school together. On the main gate of the school was posted a "Classes Suspended—Stir Up Revolution!" notice and the school principal's struggle session was just getting under way on the athletic field.

With nothing to do, we roamed about the school grounds for a while. Rongmei said that today being so sunny we should go out and pick mulberry leaves, because if the silkworm babies ate the leaves on rainy days, they would poo a lot. In those days we all raised silkworms. There wasn't a kid in Old Town who didn't have them. We walked up the hill behind the Revolutionary Martyrs' Cemetery. The mulberry trees in the vicinity were always bare-limbed. The leaves that had just budded were picked clean. Every time we went to pick mulberry leaves it meant a springtime hike through the countryside. We crossed hills and ridges and went farther and farther on.

Chaofan's eyes suddenly lit up and he shouted, "Look!" On the hillside ahead of us was a mulberry tree luxuriant with leaves! In an instant, he was sitting in the crotch of the tree and the leaves were falling in wild profusion. Rongmei and I squatted on the ground, picking them all up. Our happiness and excitement of that moment was just like the Red Guards meeting Chairman Mao in front of the Gate of Heavenly Peace.

We threw all our texts and assignment books out on the hill-side and returned in grand procession to our own homes, book bags crammed full of mulberry leaves. When we got to the West Gate intersection, Chaofan made us hook our little fingers and swear not to tell anyone—including my own cousin Su'er—about our secret treasure. He said that if one day Su'er had nothing to feed his silkworms, he'd have to trade his marbles for our leaves.

⌘ ⌘ ⌘

On this very day, on the very day when we had been so happy picking mulberry leaves, something occurred at West Gate, at my home. Something big.

The headquarters of Old Town's rebel factions carried out a unified deployment of their entire forces throughout the city in a thorough revolutionary operation. West Gate's faction was sent to East Gate. North Gate's faction came to West Gate. There was a "Big Changing of the Guard" in the north, south, east, and west. When Ah Ming received his orders, he had no time to tell his father and mother that he wouldn't be coming home for the noon meal, but just took his troops and set out.

Pastor and Mrs. Chen were the first to feel the brunt of all this and they were dragged out into the street. Dressed in heavy fur robes under the blazing sun they were then struggled. The rebel faction cut their hair in front of everybody. On their scalps were patches of white where they had been shorn bare and clumps of black where there was still some hair. It was horrible to see. They bowed their heads and kept admitting, "I am guilty." The rebel faction then took a print of Jesus confiscated from the Chen home and tried to get them to confess to the crime of having illicit relations with foreign countries. Pastor Chen said, "That is Jesus." "Who is Jesus?" the rebel faction asked. "The son of God," he replied. Then the rebel faction pressed him to yell "Overthrow Jesus! Pull Jesus off his high horse!" But Pastor Chen, biting his lower lip, would not open his mouth, and ten broad leather belts with brass eye rings fell on him like a typhoon. Almost instantly he was a welter of blood and torn flesh.

At noon, the mass of onlookers broke up and went away and the tired rebel faction sat in the shade of trees, drinking water and resting. Abruptly, the bloody man lying on the ground crawled to his feet and made his way over to the church. His wife thought he was thirsty and was going home for some water. She herself was so giddy from being out in the sun so long she saw spots before her eyes. Stumbling and staggering, she followed after him. But when she got to the curb in front of the main gate of the church, the pastor was nowhere to be seen. Not giving this much thought, she continued on into the house where she filled a cup with green bean soup she had made the evening before and brought it outside. She saw the rebel faction standing around the well and looking down into it. Right up to that point she was still looking this way and that for her husband.

Nor did the Lin family escape this catastrophe. The rebel faction from North Gate hadn't been able to seize any proof of guilt, so they just started smashing things. All the furniture in the Lin home was overturned. The doctor was dragged to West Street and struggled at a public clinic. Other doctors who ran private clinics in the West Gate area were struggled along with him. It didn't matter if they had practiced traditional Chinese or Western medicine, all had placards saying "black reactionary doctors" hung on them. Dr. Lin wasn't only a black reactionary doctor; he had been an officer in the reactionary army too.

⌘　⌘　⌘

As we each returned to our own homes, the streets around West Gate were all buzzing with excitement. Such excitement was common in those days. I was both thirsty and hungry and was also afraid Grandma would scold me. Not coming home on time for the noon meal was really breaking heaven's commandments, so I hardly felt like seeing what all the uproar was about this time. I thought that Grandma would be waiting under the oleander searching for me with her worried eyes, but there was no Grandma there under the tree. Looking around I saw a big character poster on the gate, its ink still dripping wet. Suddenly my two legs felt like they were giving way. The characters I was able to recognize were Grandpa's name and "Guomindang Army Officer." I didn't understand how these words were connected.

Grandma was all by herself in the main hall, setting the tables and the benches back in order. As I stood there on the steps of the sky well, Grandma was straightening up the aftermath and ignoring me, as if I didn't even exist.

All the ferment in the street boiled over into our own home. The playhouse audience was being pulled up onto the stage to take the lead roles of the play. All kinds of calamities might happen to me. Grandma might be pulled out into the street and have her hair shorn. Grandpa might be flogged by the leather belts used by the Red Guards. Chaofan's stamps and my candy wrappers all might be burned to ashes.

Scene after scene played right before my eyes, vivid and pulsating with life. I bowed my head against the doorframe and cried. Grandma came over and took my hand. "It's nothing, it's nothing. The rebel faction came to check whether we had any of the Four Olds. They were going door to door. Even Rongmei's home, where they've all been workers for several generations, they checked there too." She said all this with a forced laugh.

Somebody had informed on Rongmei's granny for having taken some silverware from a Four Olds bonfire, so the rebel faction raided her home as well.

"Who was a Guomindang army officer?" I asked Grandma.

Grandma's reply came firm and clear. "I don't know. That is definitely a mistake. Our family is a revolutionary family."

I believed Grandma's explanation and, feeling relieved, I went into the kitchen to find something to eat.

⌘   ⌘   ⌘

We didn't know that Pastor Chen was now dead. His body was being hauled out of the well near the West Gate intersection. Row upon row of onlookers stood around the edge of the well. Chaofan, his book bag filled with mulberry leaves, squeezed through. Wide-eyed, he saw people using iron hooks to grapple his grandpa's corpse out of the well, then throw it on a flatbed cart and haul it away. Mrs. Chen was overcome with grief and pain. The only thing she could do was pray, and time after time she would faint dead away in the midst of her prayers.

Late at night she remembered her grandson and found him in a corner upstairs. He was using a scissors to cut up and mash all his live silkworms. He looked totally at peace, as if he were just an incorrigibly naughty boy doing his usual practical jokes. His granny came forward and took him back to his room to go to sleep. She told him that his grandpa had gone to a far-off place to do thought reform and it would be a long time before he came back home.

The sun was now far to the west. The North Gate rebel faction withdrew their troops and departed the battlefield. The black reactionary doctors still stood by the entrance of the West Gate clinic. They were smeared with black ink from their hands right up to their shoulders, their heads had been shorn, and on the placards that hung on their chests were written each person's name and crime. Dr. Lin had kept his eyes closed from start to finish, just as he normally did at home when he was recharging his spirit. Today had been the most painful day of his life, but not because he had been struggled or because his hair had been cut. He actually didn't know what he looked like at that moment. He shut his eyes and took refuge within his own world. Somebody else seeing him would have thought he was just a shell without a soul. Let the rebel faction wreak havoc upon him, they still wouldn't be able to hurt his inner self. What pained him, though, was that his belief in God was wavering. He couldn't keep from having this one thought: *O God, O Jesus. I have followed you most all my life. Do you really exist? If you are the almighty God why do you not stop all the things that are happening in this world?*

This thought flitted by lightly and was gone. It toppled the whole of his existence like collapsing dominoes. This kind of feeling was just too frightening. He did all he could to recall testaments to God's presence over the past decades. *It was God who sent Mr. Qiao to find me so long before on that wet, deep night. It was God who brought Second Sister into my life. It was God who let me escape with my life from under the barrels of the Japanese rifles...how could I still doubt God's existence?* But then another voice said: *Perhaps that was all just chance. Don't people who don't believe in God also have experiences that could be explained as pure coincidences?*

He tried to draw close to God, to recover the sense of being in God's bosom, but some force repulsed him and cast him out into the dark and stormy sea of night, all alone and helpless like a small boat which has lost its way. He was a mere bookworm, too weak to truss the proverbial chicken, but very rarely did he have feelings of fear and terror. That time when the bandit Division Commander Hu leveled the gun at his head, he hadn't shown the least bit of cowardice. During the Eliminate Counterrevolutionaries period when he had been taken to the execution ground with those who were really about to be killed, he had maintained a similar calm and composure. But today he knew terror and fear.

The black reactionary doctors all went home, each with his placard. Only Dr. Lin still stood there. A middle-aged man came over, bearing a cup of tea. The doctor had once treated him and his family. Today, on the way to work, the man had noticed Dr. Lin being struggled and so he parked his bicycle and lingered there right up to this point in time. At his work unit he also was a small leader of a rebel faction so it was easy for him to pal with his brothers of the same level in the North Gate rebel faction. Rather cryptically he let on that this scrawny Lin geezer was related to a leader at the top who was then very much in favor, and that his sons and daughter were all exceptional people. So, showing mercy would be the wise course of action. The person in charge of hair shearing was a female rebel. When she got to Dr. Lin's head she may have reflected on that leader at the top who was then very much in favor. Her hand weakened, the scissors fell to the ground, and she didn't bother to pick them up. They were still there under the doctor's foot.

"Dr. Lin, the rebel faction has gone off duty. You can go home now. But first have something to drink."

The doctor opened his eyes. He didn't recognize this middle-aged fellow who had brought tea to him, but it felt just like running into a dear friend in the midst of a battle. His heart melted, his throat constricted, and he couldn't speak. Right then someone else brought him some sweet rice broth to which extra sugar was added. They had been his patients. He couldn't call them by name, but he didn't need to know who was who. They were all the love he had sown over the decades. Today they were repaying him with love.

The middle-aged man wanted to see Dr. Lin home. The doctor looked at his own two hands that were as black as charcoal and politely declined. He thought that returning home looking like this would scare Second Sister and Hong'er. He wanted to find somewhere to wash himself clean, and, before going home, to go see Pastor Chen and tell him about his wavering faith in God. He would ask Pastor Chen to pray for him.

As he walked along he discovered that the middle-aged man was walking behind him. "I know where my own home is. Don't follow me!" he harshly told him.

The middle-aged man nodded his head and withdrew away. The doctor's odd attitude worried him. He had heard that the West Gate church pastor had killed himself. Might the doctor be taking this too hard? He followed the doctor at a distance. The doctor was not following West Road to take the direct way home, but was going around by Little West Lake. Although the lake's water was shallow, it had met the needs of the many people who intended to kill themselves. The middle-aged man wanted to rush forward and stop him, but he saw that the doctor was squatting casually beside the lake washing his hands. It didn't look like he was going to commit suicide. He stood behind a tree and continued to watch him. The ink, which had been baked by the sun, was hard to get off. The doctor patiently rubbed and cleaned it off, bit by tedious bit.

The sky darkened and a full moon hung from the tree branches. *He is still washing his arms. This doesn't seem normal. Could it be that he wanted to die but lacked that little bit of courage to do so?* The middle-aged man decided to come forward and try to have a chat with him.

"Dr. Lin…"

"Why are you following me?"

"You've treated everyone in our family. In times of difficulty you also gave us several *jin* of rice."

"Oh."

"You're a good man. You surely will be rewarded for that. Just whatever you do, don't take things too much too heart."

"You're afraid I might I kill myself? That won't happen. Ease your mind of that and just go on home. It's getting late."

"I'd like to see with my own eyes that you get back home."

The doctor smiled. Although his faith had wavered today, he still firmly held on to Christian principles. Life was God-given. Man did not have the right to take his own life.

"I just want to be quietly alone for a bit. I never expected you'd be this concerned over me. It makes me rather embarrassed."

"Today at noon, the pastor of the West Lake church committed suicide. He jumped into the well..."

"Do you mean Pastor Chen?"

"I don't know his name. I heard that the rebel faction used iron hooks to pull him out. It was really awful. It'd be better to live a lousy life than to die a beautiful death, isn't that right, Dr. Lin?"

"He's dead?"

"Yes, dead. What else? Before jumping into the well he had been beaten within an inch of his life."

O God! How could you allow such a thing to happen?

The middle-aged man didn't know about the doctor and the pastor's friendship and he gave a lively account of all the hearsay on the streets.

The doctor just sat there numbly, his mind a total blank. Suddenly he leaned over and fell into the water. The other man leaped in and pulled him out. Then, putting him on his back, he set out at a trot for the Lin home.

⌘　⌘　⌘

My grandmother wasn't at home, for she had gone to keep Mrs. Chen company. I was in my "ladies' chamber" playing with my candy wrappers and my silkworm babies. The bodies of several of these animals had started to become transparent. This meant that they would very soon be spitting out silk to make cocoons. This house had gone through a ransacking, but my treasures were safe and sound. Joy that had been lost and then recovered pulsated through me.

Someone was talking in the main hall but I wasn't paying any attention, thinking that it was Grandpa returned home. It was a stranger who was saying "Dr. Lin this" and "Dr. Lin that." I didn't know that Grandpa had been dragged out and struggled. Grandma said he had gone for a soak. Also, I hadn't played his spoiled little girl with him in a long time. He would have just gone off into his eyes-closed meditation that kept people at a distance.

The stranger was joking and trying to get on Grandpa's good side or else make him feel good. "Drum Tower isn't called Drum Tower now. It's changed to Red Tower. The other day someone asked my Ma the way to Red Tower. My Ma said, "What are the times coming to, with people still looking for white-face mansions?' I'm going to call the Red Guards to come and get you..."

The man let out a great laugh as he spoke. I couldn't get what was so funny. Old Town folk called brothels white-face mansions. That was a name I was hearing for the first time.

I can imagine my grandfather just sitting there, his eyes closed and waving his hand at the stranger, signaling him to leave.

The stranger said, "Dr. Lin, I want to wait until your family members return before I go."

⌘　⌘　⌘

I drifted off to sleep in the droning voice of that gabby man. In my dream I heard the sounds of someone's grief-filled and mournful sobbing.

The next day, everything was as usual. I told Grandma that the night before I had dreamed there was someone in the house crying and it had gone on for a long time. Grandma said that was a dream and dreams were the opposite of what was true.

Breakfast was rice porridge and deep-fried dough sticks. I was used to calling Grandpa to eat. Usually he waved his hand a bit. From the vigor of his wave I could tell what kind of a mood he was in. It might be, "Don't bother me!" or, "You go ahead and eat and don't wait for me." Today he paid no attention to me. I was anxious to eat the dough stick and so I called him quite loudly. His eyes were closed and he showed not the slightest reaction. My grandmother said, "Don't shout. Your grandpa's ears have gone bad. Beginning last night, whatever I said to him he couldn't hear." I took a bite of the dough stick but when I chewed it, it was tasteless, for I was looking with worry at my grandfather. *Would he become a mute person? Rongmei said her dad wasn't mute originally. The year her mother died, his ears suddenly went deaf, and later on he became a mute.*

Chapter Twenty — Absurd Joys and Sorrows

1.

Teardrops are piling up in Joseph's eyes. Suddenly he bounces out of his seat, rushes past the little tea service table, and lands right down beside me. He's all worked up and throws his arm around my shoulders. "I'm sorry! We didn't know you'd gone through such things. We didn't take good care of you."

I'm not sure what kind of a response I should make to this. If it were part of a plot in some movie, the director probably would want the woman to fall unresisting into the man's embrace and a romantic love would ensue amidst heartrending tears. But my heart's sending me a very clear message: *Refuse this sympathy. Compared to what we've gone through and what our feelings were then, white people's sympathy seems superficial and low-budget.*

When I made up my mind to leave Lompoc, the teacher and classmates of the language school where I studied were just amazed. *There's somewhere out there better than rich and beautiful California?* They came looking for me at the restaurant where I worked, hoping that I would think twice before making this move. At the time there were several Chinese movies that appealed to white people and had won prizes. My teacher supposed "that's China," but the distressed and disgusted expressions on the faces of these white people brought about the strongest reaction in me. Never before did I realize that I loved my country so much. I told them the story of the frog in the well and said that Lompoc was a tiny well. "You are frogs at the bottom of that well. You don't know the skies beyond your sky." That they couldn't save me made them all the more distressed and disgusted. It was both absurd and funny.

I lightly pluck Joseph's hand from off of my shoulder and, much against the prescribed scenario, burst out laughing, to his total mystification.

⌘   ⌘   ⌘

Everyone says that was a terrifying period when everyone feared for his or her own safety. But many of the pictures I have saved in "Memory" have comic qualities. Of course there are also tragic ones, those of the love that pierces me deep inside.

I don't know if Great-Auntie, now in the old folks' home, still can remember the big revolutions of the twentieth century. Those were the best days of her life: "When the Chinese People stood up," liberated and breathing air free of the old oppressions. There was also my alcoholic great-uncle. Inciting rebellion and raiding homes were his rich banquets. When he got hold of a red armband and followed the Red Guards through the streets and alleys, anyone's liquor could be his for the taking. Then there was me, along with tens of thousands, even hundreds of thousands of young schoolchildren. We threw away our texts and assignment books and savored the taste of total freedom. My cousin Su'er, then called Fanxiu, a wooden gun stuck in his belt, became the king of the kids. With great flair he devised strategies and plans in his general's tent and led the troops out to do battle and seize Chairman Mao badges. His father and mother made revolution at their respective organizations and at home after work would argue politics so much they wanted to divorce. They couldn't pull themselves away enough to control their son. Those two years were the most memorable period of Su'er's young life.

⌘　⌘　⌘

Great-Auntie arrived in a merry mood. She had come to West Gate to announce to Second Sister and Ninth Brother the happy news that her rotten-egg husband been struggled again yesterday. After Liberation, the many-courtyard Zhang family mansion had been confiscated, and more than ten households were now living in it. The neighbors' dislike of his bad temper and wife beating had been long growing. Someone organized a session to struggle him and this was arranged to be held in the main hall. Ordinarily that place was densely packed with the dining tables of all the various households. After dinner, these tables were put away and about one hundred residents of the front and back courtyards, men and women, children and oldsters, pressed chest to back as they squeezed in to commence the struggle session. Not knowing what crime would cover wife beating, they hung from his neck a placard reading "Zhang So-and-So, Rotten Egg." The neighbors supported Great-Auntie as she took the stand to make her denunciation. She exhibited her injuries: a permanent lump like a hard bread roll on the bridge of her broken nose, a forefinger on her right hand that could not extend straight, and a rather lame left leg. Great-Auntie's memory was good and she remembered the story behind each and every scar: this one from the rice being too hard, that one because she had taken a couple of silver dollars back to her family home—all just trivial matters. Because the ideological thinking of this mass of people was high, the regular troops of the rebel faction outside had no trouble in handing him over to them to deal with at the meeting. If Rotten Egg's real crimes had been brought up, it wouldn't have been too much to take him out to the execution grounds to be shot. By the time the neighbors had moved in, the Zhangs were already counted as urban poor and the revolutionary masses grabbed him only for the crime of beating his wife. When this rotten egg with the placard hanging from his neck was struggled, how secretly happy and lucky he must have felt!

Great-Auntie knew that Ninth Brother was now deaf. She sat down, took a drink of water, and wiped away her sweat. Then she pulled out a pencil and a small piece of paper from of her little cloth bag. As she wrote, she said to Second Sister, "Revolutionary rebellion is good. That rotten egg has changed. Last night he brought water to wash my feet with." On the paper she wrote a series of characters unseparated by any punctuation. "Last night fifth time Rotten Egg struggled Rotten Egg got scared washed my feet." She gave a few nudges to Ninth Brother who just then had his eyes closed and was in his spiritual retreat.

Ninth Brother opened his eyes. He glanced coldly and with some hostility at his sister-in-law as he briefly noted the contents of the paper. Then abruptly he stood up and walked into his room where he took down an old piece of work clothing hanging by the door, a dark blue denim shirt. Afraid he would go out and stir up some calamity, Second Sister had made a special trip to Shuiguan's home to get it. This shirt was Ninth Brother's protective talisman.

She raised her eyebrows to look at him. Lately he had been like this. He would sit there, his eyes closed and recharging his spirit, when suddenly something would occur to him, and he'd get up, put on his work shirt, and off he would go. When she asked him where he was going, he never answered. Second Sister suspected all along that he hadn't really lost his hearing. She knew his family said that when he was little, people often thought that he was a deaf-mute, because several months could go by without his saying a word. And looking at him they'd think he couldn't hear anything either. She followed him to the gate. "Don't go far. Come back early. With such disorder going on outside, I can't help feeling worried." Ninth Brother made no response to this but Second Sister believed he had heard her. Uneasily she watched him depart, and her worries grew as he walked out to West Gate.

The rebel faction took over from the residence committee. Now idleness became the thing that most bothered Second Sister. Every day she spent a good deal of time washing and cleaning up the home. When her elder sister came by, she was up on a ladder wiping the window panes. She had started the window washing after seeing Ninth Brother off. The two sisters, one up on the ladder, the other down below, chatted about Rotten Egg's scandals. Elder Sister said, "Rotten Egg doesn't have a temper and he's milder than Ninth Brother. Sometimes I feel he's just downright pitiful."

"You can still pity someone like that guy so steeped in evil and headed for damnation? They struggled him as gently as a breeze and more softly than tiny raindrops. He actually got off easy!"

"But he really didn't commit any counterrevolutionary acts," her older sister retorted.

"Now don't you go and protect him!"

⌘　⌘　⌘

The doctor walked out of West Street and passed through Drum Tower. He wanted to see that rightist nurse at People's Hospital. After returning from an outlying district, she worked in the hospital laundry room. During the difficult period at the beginning of the 1960s, the doctor traveled by long-distance bus to see her and brought her a moon cake. This forged between them one of those friendships where age difference does not matter.

Pastor Chen's death filled the doctor with anguish. He could not shake off a deep sense of guilt and remorse. After the rebellion started the two old friends had cancelled their weekly get-togethers over drinks and snacks. He always thought that compared to himself, the pastor was the more indomitable and the one who received more help from God. He never thought that he ought to take the initiative in showing concern for Pastor Chen, in encouraging and supporting him. From this experience there arose in the doctor a solicitude for the relatives and friends around him who were in difficult circumstances. He called on Enchun, his niece Baolan and her husband, Ah Jian. He also kept in touch with many of his former patients. Such people were the targets at struggle sessions. He knew that he himself was merely a little person of no real consequence. All he could do was to offer them a bit of insignificant concern. But in this extraordinary period of time, a warm glance at someone in despair might perhaps be a fulcrum, a pivotal point, to help them go on living.

As a rule, his two daughters-in-law did not come to the home at West Gate. Baosheng and Baoqing themselves arranged to return every ten or fifteen days. The two men separately participated in the rival organizations of Old Town's two big factions. Daddy now being deaf, they sat beside him and debated without any inhibitions. The doctor couldn't be bothered to distinguish between who was right and who was wrong. It all just meant that the two sons were doing all right in their lives and didn't need his special attention. The person who worried him was Baohua. Her husband's position was quite important. Probably he would escape calamity. One of these days he had to get Ah Ming to write out a travel pass for him to go see her.

The commerce bureau where Baoqing worked was not far from the hospital. It was now noon, time for getting off work. The doctor thought of his grandson Wei'er. A few days before, Baoqing had returned to West Gate and told Second Sister that the child often got sick in the child-care center. He was a brash little fellow who didn't know when to stop eating. When he was a bit over one year old, he could eat two big bowls of rice. When children got sick, it mostly came from their eating. He ought to warn the person in charge of the children to limit his food. *Now where is that child-care center? Would Baoqing and his wife have gone to fetch the child at this time of the day?* He reached the shady tree outside the gate of the Commerce Bureau and he strolled slowly along the wall next to the road.

Sure enough, Baoqing appeared in view. He was pushing his bicycle, and Wei'er, his head drooping, sat on the seat. *Was he sick now?* A few months ago, the fair and plump child had turned yellow and thin. The doctor was much disturbed. Baoqing's own head was also drooping. His wife, wearing a red armband, was at his side saying something or other with great feeling.

They were moving closer toward him and Fangzi's voice resounded from the main road. "I really had bad luck when I married into you Lins. Your father is a suspected foreign agent as well as having been a Guomindang army officer. Then there's your ma. Your ma's a real old witch. You've got to break off relations with the Lins!"

Baoqing's two feet came together and stopped. He gave his wife a look. He wanted to say something but didn't. He just continued walking.

The doctor read in his son's face an inexpressible grief and desolation. All along he had been prejudiced against his two sons for always lacking a certain spunk or grit in their dealings in the world. Now he felt remorse. As their father, he hadn't really shown concern and love for his two sons. When they were babies he had abandoned them. Dimly he saw in the big Lin courtyard three children, their mouths drooling as they stared at a pan of soy sauce-braised pork, but never daring to move their chopsticks. Second Sister often related this scene to him, her tone of voice revealing the joy that arises when bitterness has run its course and sweetness replaces it. It was only at this moment, as he ruminated over the past, that he sensed the bitterness in it. *I was never with the children when they were young. Now here I am again interfering with their futures.* The doctor's eyes glistened. He felt the impulse to go over to his son and say, "I'm sorry."

Fangzi turned her volume up louder and louder. "I won't let you go to West Gate! And I am not going to let you give our money to them. If you don't break off relations with them totally, then let's just divorce!"

Baoqing once again stopped dead in his tracks. His head now hung even lower. "Your background is good but now you're implicated in my life. Maybe getting divorced would be the best choice."

Fangzi's mouth dropped in stupefaction. A moment or so later, with a look on her face as if she had just lost her parents, she burst into tears. "Divorce! All right! For your reactionary parents you'd be willing to divorce me!"

Baoqing moved on, pushing the bicycle along slowly. Fangzi followed, crying, reproaching, hitting.

⌘   ⌘   ⌘

Gazing at this scene now steadily moving away from him, the doctor couldn't help but heave a deep sigh as he reflected on all of this. Baoqing and Fangzi's marriage was something he and Second Sister had pushed all by themselves. After Baoqing joined the army, a plain-looking girl student claiming to be his classmate would often show up at the Lin home. Every time she walked in she would roll up her sleeves and help Second Sister with the housework. Although she was nothing remarkable to look at, she spoke sweetly and was diligent. Ninth Brother and Second Sister liked her. The doctor wrote to his son that a classmate of his named Fangzi often came to the house to comfort his parents in their lonely empty nest. When Baoqing replied, he "put Zhang's hat on Li's head," mistaking Fangzi for quite a different classmate. Baoqing once sent home a photograph of a female soldier from the army song and dance ensemble. Second Sister was afraid that if her son married a northerner he would never get back to Old Town and she quickly obtained from Fangzi a picture to send to him. She hoped he would not let down a hometown girl. From then on, they often had Fangzi reply to his letters on their behalf.

It seems as if all that happened just yesterday. How could Fangzi have turned into such a cunning shrew?

He didn't know that Baoqing's marriage had been unhappy from the start. Occasionally, Second Sister had some veiled criticism to say to Fangzi, but Ninth Brother would always stop her. Fangzi was an extremely possessive and controlling woman. She brooded on that first abortive love Baoqing had in the army and she bore a grudge against Baoqing's attachment and obedience to his mother. She actually did love Baoqing but she longed to possess him totally. For many years now she had tested and tormented him every day.

The commerce bureau was also split into two factions, and Fangzi and Baoqing joined one of these, where she was a backbone element in it. Today the rival faction had stuck up a big character poster exposing Baoqing's reactionary lineage. Fangzi and the other leaders could but "flick away their tears and decapitate Ma Su"[54]— they posted a notice announcing Baoqing's expulsion. This calamity was Fangzi's golden battlefield opportunity to set about uprooting her husband's social relationships, and her mother-in-law was the number one enemy target for uprooting. That always elegant and poised woman was a disease in her vital organs. Because Baoqing always so deeply venerated his mother—for him there was no one in this world more pretty and capable than she—Fangzi had gnashed her teeth in hatred early on. She never expected to have to face this choice. To her surprise, Baoqing preferred divorce and to stick with his West Gate family no matter what its fate might be. How could this have not driven her crazy?

⌘   ⌘   ⌘

The doctor walked along aimlessly, like a withered leaf blown about by the wind this way and that. He had now arrived at the hospital, but he had forgotten why he had come in the first place. Uneasily he stood at the outpatient main gate. From his pallor he looked like someone needing to register as a patient himself.

It was the rightist nurse, just then sweeping the floor, who first noticed him. Coming up to him, she asked, "Dr. Lin, are you ill?"

"Don't take it to heart. Right! Don't take it to heart, couldn't it…"

The rightist nurse lowered her voice. "Dr. Lin, your Heavenly Father will be by your side."

---

[54]   Another reference from *The Romance of the Three Kingdoms*. Ma Su was a brilliant military strategist from the Kingdom of Shu, and much admired by Zhuge Liang, himself an incomparable strategist, who nonetheless ordered him decapitated for an arrogant blunder which cost Shu the battle of Jieting (228 CE).

In those years past, he had tried to get this same person to believe that there was an Almighty Father in heaven. That one would surely be blessed by relying on Him. But the rightist nurse to this day had not accepted any kind of religious belief. Right now she was just comforting the doctor by offering medicine when the disease was at its most critical stage. The look of despair on his face made her uneasy.

Heavenly Father? Dr. Lin trembled inside. It had been many days since he had prayed in earnest. He had not only closed his eyes and ears from the people around him, he did this to God too. He truly couldn't understand why, if people were learning from Lei Feng's wonderful millennium, all of a sudden the beacon fires had blazed forth on all sides and the entire world descended into insane chaos. *Pastor Chen had said that everything that happened was permitted by God. O God! Why did you permit all this?*

"Dr. Lin, you wanted me to go on living. Now I want *you* to go on living."

"Go on living, of course…"

Footsteps sounded in the corridor. The rightist nurse rushed off, broom in hand.

⌘   ⌘   ⌘

The doctor went to Old Town University where Enchun worked as a furnace stoker in the school's heating plant. The doctor by now had come here more than a few times to rendezvous with Enchun. In the most recent struggle session, the Red Guards had shorn Enchun's head. Today the doctor brought with him a pair of little scissors to trim what remained of Enchun's hair.

"Enchun, come, have a seat. I'll tidy up your hair a bit."

Enchun laughed good-naturedly and pulled over a broken wooden crate and sat down. "Actually, it doesn't matter. Nobody sees me, and I can't see me either."

The doctor stood behind Enchun and worked on his hair practically strand by strand. Until this point in time he still hadn't told him that Pastor Chen was no longer in this world. Enchun supposed that West Gate remained peaceful under Ah Ming's protective influence.

"Uncle Lin, after this, don't come and see me anymore. Don't leave West Gate. I am doing all right. Physical labor is the best rest for mental labor. Please convey to my daddy and ma to take good care of themselves and to look after little Chaofan."

"Mmmh."

"I'm studying socialist economics. Here I can continue my research. There are a lot of specialized subjects that have been denied right across the board. The professors have all burned their books. Compared to them, I count myself very fortunate."

Enchun had long been reading a tome thicker than the Bible called *Capital*. It was written by Karl Marx. The volume was inside the broken crate, and each time he added coal to the furnace he would then wash his hands clean with soap, take out the book, and continue reading.

"Enchun, way back then you described to me the beautiful vistas of communism. That truly attracted me to it. I really embraced communist…"

"Uncle Lin, don't be too pessimistic. Setbacks are inevitable. Our China is a backward, agricultural society. Ideological problems will definitely appear."

"Setbacks are inevitable." Enchun is always saying that. The doctor was profoundly moved by the persistence of Enchun's faith.

He always came to see Enchun out of deep compassion and pity. It was just like bringing a present, but one that was never handed over. Enchun did not need compassion and pity. The doctor thought of Baoqing. *My poor sons.* He had the impression that they never had a boyhood. It was as if from the beginning both sons were the men of the Lin family. He couldn't even remember ever having embraced Baosheng and Baoqing. What leaped before his eyes across the decades were scenes of Baohua wearing a little dress and little leather shoes, pouting prettily in his arms. "I should show my sons some love and concern," he thought.

⌘　⌘　⌘

This month Baoqing was a few days late in giving his parents the allowance for their living expenses. Ninth Brother noticed that when his son passed a heavy envelope to his mother his eyes appeared confused and shy. Second Sister dumped a pile of tiny denomination bills and a handful of coins out of the envelope. "How come it's all in small change?" she asked, puzzled. Baoqing didn't reply. He had stolen some of it from Wei'er's savings jar. He also sold old books and newspapers behind his old lady's back before being able to put together fifteen *yuan*.

Ninth Brother walked into the kitchen and brought out the Eight Treasures rice pudding, then warmed it in the stove, and placed it before his son and said, "Eat it while it's hot."

Baoqing tilted his head in surprise as he looked at his father. From when he was small until now his father had never personally served him food. Furthermore, of late his father had been paying no attention to him at all. Such tremendous warmth was hard for Baoqing to bear. He stood up, quelling the storm of emotions within him behind a fit of dry coughing.

"Dad, you eat too."

His father directed at him a friendly hand gesture and a glance filled with tender love and affection.

Second Sister was also so surprised that she forgot all about pursuing the question of the envelope full of loose change and small banknotes.

Under his father's gaze, Baoqing gulped down the pudding and wondered what this was all about today. He still couldn't get over receiving such sudden fatherly love.

Ninth Brother drew the money-filled envelope from Second Sister's hand and said to his son, "Your ma and I still have something left over from our inheritance, so use this money to buy something nutritious for Wei'er."

Baoqing looked down, not daring to move. His tears fell pinging into the bowl.

Ninth Brother stuffed the envelope into Baoqing's pocket. Then he went back to his rocker, closed his eyes and engaged in his spiritual recuperation.

Baoqing looked at his ma and then at his dad. Suddenly he recalled the old saying that before the bird dies it lets out a mournful cry. There had been a woman in their organization who committed suicide. Before she died she patched up and fixed the clothes her husband and children would wear for all the four seasons of the year.

He moved close to his father's ear and said loudly, "Dad, our home is more peaceful than most of the others. If you want to read your Bible, just go ahead over to Ah Ming's place. We won't object."

Ninth Brother, his eyes shut, was considering Baoqing's many good qualities. He would have loved to take his son in his arms but all he did was open his eyes and say rather flatly, "Just go on home. It's getting dark, so be careful riding your bicycle."

Baoqing didn't know whether his dad had heard what he said to him. He took out a piece of paper and pen and wrote, "Dad, I don't feel right about you. You can go to Ah Ming's and read the book you want to read."

Ninth Brother glanced at the slip of paper. "West Gate is peaceful and calm. Take care of yourself. And look after Wei'er. Feed him his three meals at fixed times and in regulated amounts," he said.

⌘   ⌘   ⌘

Baoqing still gave money to his mother. Second Sister caught sight of a five *mao* banknote[55] out of a pile of small change. Last year when she had given her grandson his New Year's Eve money present, someone had used a pen to mark the back of this bill with a small flower. She remembered it clearly. *Here's Fangzi embarrassing Baoqing again for sure. That Fangzi! From the day she went into the bridal chamber, she put on a new face. In every way, she makes things difficult for Baoqing.* As she thought of her beloved son swallowing these insults for the sake of his responsibilities and living in a marriage that was far from ideal, she became so sad that she felt her heart would break. *Why did Ninth Brother refuse to accept Baoqing's money? Is it that he knows something?*

At this moment, as he pedaled his bicycle back home, Baoqing thought and thought about his father's warm and affectionate gaze. And then this fellow who had served so meritoriously in Korea burst out sobbing.

---

[55]   A *mao* is one-tenth of a *yuan*.

2.

ARMED CLASHES NOW began in the streets as the two rebel factions started fighting with real guns and bullets. Whether in broad daylight or the dark of night, you could hear the bullets as they whizzed through the air. The ordinary citizens of Old Town, as always, showed great ingenuity in stocking away sufficient provisions and hiding behind locked doors and bolted windows.

The Lin family pussycat was above such mundane matters. As always, it pursued its lusty love life, every night crossing over the top of the wall to gang together with its male friends. The doctor was also above such mundane matters. Heart and mind, all he wanted was to go the thirty miles or more to P Town district office to visit his daughter and son-in-law. Capable, virtuous, and docile Second Sister spared no one's feelings as she exceeded her authority in handling matters. Locking the front gate and back door from the inside and gripping the keys tightly in her hand, she kept a vigilant watch over her husband. At night when they were sleeping she kept an ear pricked to monitor him. Every so often she would open the back door to let the doctor out for some air by the side of the city moat. And she stood behind, not too closely but not too far away either, as she kept her eye on him. The slums on both sides of this water were Old Town's dead space. It was a corner forgotten by the times, and always safe and secure.

The doctor did not negotiate directly with Second Sister but just quietly made his preparations to leave. He approached Ah Ming for a travel pass, but Ah Ming had already been reached by Second Sister. Ah Ming told him that the communications between Old Town and the outside world had been sealed off, and that, furthermore, he was the object of control. Therefore, never mind leaving Old Town; he wouldn't even be allowed to leave West Gate. But this didn't make the doctor give up his idea of going to see his daughter.

He continued to get ready for the journey. Looking in the mirror, he cut his hair short like Shuiguan, changing the style he had kept for decades, and now made it fall messily over his forehead. He also got Shuiguan to think up a way to buy a carton of cigarettes and a bottle of hard liquor. Within the family, people called the Public Security bureau chief "Big Zhang." Big Zhang's smoking and drinking hard stuff had been his most obnoxious habits. Now the doctor wanted to bring him cigarettes and liquor to restore the father-in-law-son-in-law relationship. Big Zhang had been in the cowshed for several months already, and these days the only news he could get about Baohua and Big Zhang came from their local rebel faction. Among the investigating personnel from P Town was a northerner who acted as a double agent. That agent would not appear for days on end and the doctor would just go crazy thinking about his daughter.

In a change from his fixed posture of sitting in the chair recharging his spirit, now all day long he stood in the main hall or the sky well looking up at the top of the wall. The cat jumped in and out of the house from the top of that wall. Sometimes it lay there with its head erect, and the two of them would look long at each other, as if each were guessing the other's thoughts.

One night, the doctor told his wife that he wanted to go off on a long trip early the next day, and if she didn't open the gate he would just have to pry open the lock. Husband and wife sat stiffly upright at the Eight Immortals table like two rival negotiators. Second Sister opened her mouth to dissuade him but she saw on his face the expression of thirty years before, when he was about to abandon wife and home in his single big roll of the dice. The Ninth Brother of this moment looked like both a willful, unreasonable child and a heroic martyr fervidly prepared to die. Words of dissuasion would have been superfluous, so she slowly closed her mouth. If I had not been there, Grandma would have gone with him to brave the dangers together. She thought it over, then untied the key to the main gate from her waist and thrust it into Ninth Brother's hand. He then got up and went out through the back door to get a travel pass from Ah Ming.

Just at that time, an unexpected visitor barged into the Lin home.

⌘   ⌘   ⌘

Department Head Li, Young Li in those early years, had a hidden personal history that was growing like a tumor in his body. Luckily both the tumor and he had passed safely through all the earlier political movements. With the Cultural Revolution now under way, batch after batch of city government cadres had been overthrown. Department Head Li was still teetering on the high wire. When one faction gave him a red armband to wear, the other faction "climbed to the heavens and burrowed into the earth" in search of some incriminating evidence on him. They concentrated their fire on him as a way of attacking the rival faction. The Li family's son and daughter wore their parents' old army uniforms when they went out to make revolution. His wife also wore her old uniform as she made revolution at the organization where she worked. Relying on Old Li (as he was now called) having been a meritorious official of the Revolution, they made revolution more vigorously than anyone. Only he himself knew how dangerous a situation his family was really in. Every minute of the day a feeling of treading on thin ice gripped his heart.

He had awakened his wife in the depths of many a sleepless night to persuade her to hang up her armor and go back to the countryside with him. Her own home place was a farming village amid the clear mountains and limpid waters of southern China. If they went there as a family and led a life free from outside strife, even if they worked the land as peasants generation after generation, it would still be better than this state of anxiety and fear. His wife would just laugh. "Before you go back to your old home place, we ought to first send you to a mental hospital for a checkup." As she saw it, all the cadres on earth could be overthrown, but Old Li's turn would never come. He was an orphan who had joined the Revolution before he was even eighteen years old. From squad leader, to platoon leader, all the way up to regimental commander— who could bring down this cadre who was Red, through and through?

This morning the four members of the Li family had the rare opportunity of getting together at the breakfast table and eating the rice gruel and fritters cooked by the housekeeper. Old Li said, "My mother used to say that you shouldn't laugh at the cripples you saw on the streets, that sort of thing. One day your own legs might become crippled. You are now smashing other people's revolution. It's very possible the day will come when people will smash yours."

His wife and two children looked at Old Li in amusement. They suspected he really did have a mental condition, after all. He tried to warn his family like this, lest the sudden descent of adversity upon them might prove too great a blow. He had an ominous presentiment that the tumor within him was going to burst out during this great Revolution. His daughter went round behind him and put her arms around his neck. "Daddy! How could you compare revolution to a cripple? If you go outside and say this, they'd arrest you. Besides, who could smash our revolution?" His daughter was the closest of all to him. *Oh, my precious daughter! If you knew Daddy's historical problems, would you still be this affectionate and loving with him?* At this thought, Department Head Li's eyes moistened. His wife put down her chopsticks. "Old Li, you're an old revolutionary who's come through thickets of rifles and storms of bullets. You've got to hold firm to the class stand." Old Li wanted so hard to make a clean breast of his painful secret, but looking at the complacency in his family's expressions, how could he make them believe that the heavens above this home were about to fall? How would he begin?

Old Li walked out the main gate of their group living quarters. Looking down, he drew from his pocket a red armband and was just slipping it over his hand when suddenly someone shouted out his full name. All these years, back to when he was a squad leader, his job was what people addressed him by and no one in public had ever yelled at him like this before. He felt the thin ice breaking up beneath his feet. The disaster of disasters had fallen upon him. At the same time, he discovered to his surprise a sudden calm coming over him and he felt quieter and more at peace than ever before. He pulled down the red armband that was half-on and gripped it his hand. But he didn't even have time to look up when the rebel faction knocked him down. More than ten big fellows laid into him with fists and boots. He closed his eyes. He didn't struggle. He didn't resist.

Beaten almost to a pulp, Old Li was dragged to the struggle session. The rebel faction that had originally protected him thrashed him even more fiercely than the other one had. Again and again he was beaten to the ground. Again and again he was pulled back up again. Deafening slogans bombarded his ears: "Down with the Guomindang reactionary faction!" He did not intend to survive this calamity. Just like during the war, every time he reached the battlefield he had been prepared to go to his death.

The slogan shouting grew more distant. A kind of lightness and release he had never before experienced washed over him like refreshing spring waters. He felt like he was sleeping, sleeping soundly and sweetly. When he came to, he found himself lying in ice-cold mud and the sky above was already pitch black. He dragged himself up to a sitting position and began to think. In this life, how many times had he brushed shoulders with death? This time, though, he surely couldn't avoid it, and he intended not to try. But no matter what, now that he was so near to death, he should go home and see his wife and children and apologize to them. The rebel faction had thought he couldn't move anymore and so didn't assign anyone to guard him. Being very familiar with the layout of the large compound of the municipal party committee, he knew which wall had a gap in it and he easily slipped out of the cowshed.

The home had been raided. No one felt like cleaning things up. The wife and daughter were crying in each other's arms. When Old Li, his body covered with the wounds from his beating, appeared in front of them, they never even looked up. He could hear their complaints and grievances against him, their grief-stricken laments over lost glories, power, and influence. His son sat in a daze on the sofa. When Old Li walked over toward him, the son stood up in a flash and went into his own room and slammed the door shut. Nothing need be said. He silently turned around and left. He walked to the doorway and stopped for a moment. It was as if he was hoping for something that wasn't clear to him, but from inside he heard his wife hurl abuse at him. "You still have the face to come home? You not only tricked the party and the people, you even tricked me and the children!"

Returning to the wall around the municipal Party committee compound, Old Li hesitated. If he now crawled back through the wall would he be able to survive? He had never feared dying.

Many times death would have been much easier than survival. His feelings kept their unusual calm. He thought of Tongpan District where he had been born and the hill behind this village where his father and mother were buried. To cover up his history he had never gone back. *The unfilial son is finally getting the retribution he deserves.* He decided to surrender his life to his home place...to sleep forever with his parents on the hillside. Suddenly though, he remembered that in this town there still was one person worth missing— Dr. Lin. *I wonder how he is now.* For ten years, from his hidden place, he had looked with concern after the doctor. Today, he could come forth into the open and say to him: "Sir, Young Li has never once forgotten you."

⌘　⌘　⌘

When the doctor heard the knock on the gate it was a very soft sound, as if it were a secret contact no one could know about. Rather fearfully, he went out to greet whoever it was.

"Who's there?"

"Sir, sir, it's me, Young Li."

People in Old Town who knew him well called him Dr. Lin or Mr. Lin. Only in those long gone years had Division Commander Zhang and Young Li called him "sir." The doctor felt as if in a trance and suspected he was hallucinating. Placing his ear up against the gate, he again asked, "Who are you?"

"Sir, do you still remember your medical orderly, Young Li?"

O heaven! What is this! It was a few moments before the doctor's trembling hands could unlock the gate with a clattering of the crossbar. Young Li opened his arms and tightly hugged the doctor. Sobbing in a sorrow which seemed bottomless he said, "Sir, sir, I should have come to you sooner."

The doctor stood there simply dumbfounded until he accepted that this man was the Young Li with whom he had lost contact so many decades ago. Then instantly he burst out uncontrollably in tears of joy and sorrow. "Young Li, I looked for you so hard!"

They weren't related by blood but they were closer to each other than if they had been. These two reserved and restrained Old Town men could no longer control their emotions.

The doctor touched the wounds and tracks of blood on Young Li. He brought him under the light in the main hall and looked him up and down and all over. Then once again sorrow overwhelmed him and he wept deeply.

Second Sister came back with the travel pass issued by Ah Ming and froze in fear at the scene before her. Her instincts told her that this battered stranger was very dangerous. *Will Ninth Brother be keeping this dangerous man in their home?*

The doctor didn't tell his wife who this person was and when he asked her to clear out all the various objects from the garret and lay down bedding, she didn't immediately respond.

Young Li stood up in front of Second Sister's frightened and suspicious gaze and said, "Sir, Madam, I only came to see you. Now I can go."

"Honored comrade, please go in peace. Take care of yourself."

The doctor, just then taking some medicine and instruments from the glass cabinet, spun around in fury. "Where do you want him to go? Don't you see his whole body's covered with wounds?"

In all the decades of their married life, Ninth Brother had never uttered such a strong rebuke. Second Sister bore this wrong in silence, and forcing a smile, said to the visitor, "Of course, let Dr. Lin bandage up your wounds before you go."

"Young Li, I don't allow you to go. I won't let you take one step away from me!" the doctor said with finality.

Suddenly Second Sister realized who this was. This was a person Ninth Brother could give up his own life for. She hurried into action. She locked the main gate and cleaned out the little garret. Since there was nothing in the house that this man could wear, she rushed to make him a set of clothes late that very night.

⌘   ⌘   ⌘

I didn't know a man was being hidden in the garret. What I could sense was different was that Grandpa's ears suddenly improved and, in fact, became especially sensitive. At the least suspicious sound outside of the gate he would bring his face up to the crack and peek out. He no longer mentioned going to P Town to see my mother and stepfather. Nor did he any longer sit in the rocking chair, eyes closed and spiritually recharging. Nor did he simply gaze blankly at the top of the wall.

One day, there was a furious pounding on the gate. Grandpa raced up to the garret as nimble as a rabbit and with a stranger in tow, told me to take him through the back door and find Shuiguan. After about an hour, Grandpa came to the side of the city moat to bring him back home. Grandma called me to the kitchen and made me swear never to tell anyone that there was a stranger hiding in our house. After she counted off all the people I was closest to, Rongmei, Chaofan, my cousins, also Uncle Baoqing, I solemnly swore this oath, keenly proud to be qualified to join in a mutual offense-defense pact with Grandpa and Grandma.

From that day on, the stranger no longer hid in the little garret. Our little family of three became a family of four. We passed the time with the deck of cards and the sets of military and elephant chess that my cousins had left here. The armed clashes out in the streets became more and more violent. Locked in the house, we played poker and chess. My happiness knew no bounds.

Grandma never told me what this man's name was, only that I should call him Uncle. I liked this amiable and approachable uncle and deep inside wondered whether or not he might be my real father. No one in the family had ever mentioned my real father to me. The first time my mother brought my stepfather home, she told me that *he* was my father. But I knew that northerner was not my father. Great-Auntie had long before told me in secret all about my life. She said my mother and father had divorced and my father was a big official in some far distant place. If this "uncle" were my real father, would I hate and resent him?

Little me, wracking my brains all by myself trying to solve the riddles of my life...and every time falling into clouds and mist eighteen miles long.

⌘ ⌘ ⌘

Just like that, all the fighting stopped. Perhaps the ordinary citizens of Old Town had quickly grown weary and disgusted at having to spend their days cooped up at home. Many people were beginning to experience shortages of the food they had stocked. The watery rice gruel my grandmother made became even more watery. *Could our rice jar now be in a critical state?* However, overnight the two factions that had been trading fire now shook hands and exchanged words of peace. This, nonetheless, left me with a deep regret.

In the veil of darkness, the main gate and the rear door were still locked. Under the 15-watt lights in the main hall, Grandma did her sewing off to one side while Grandpa, Uncle, and I played poker. I taught them to play Winner. Whoever lost would get their noses rubbed. Grandpa often lost and he would always obediently stick out his nose for me to rub. His nose was pronounced and bony. Even though I got used to his sober and humorless expression, every time I rubbed his nose I would invariably feel a bit tense as I hesitantly reached out my hand. Whenever I lost, shamelessly I would hide under the table or dash about to avoid my own nose rubbing.

I was just burrowing under the table when the sounds of fierce gunfire came in from outside. Suddenly everyone in the room just froze like statues, but after a few seconds like this, we recognized the sounds of firecrackers. These were followed right afterward by gongs and drums on every side. Outside the gate someone was shouting, "Dr. Lin, the highest instructions have come down from Beijing. It's the 'Great Alliance' now. No more fighting!"

I couldn't hold myself back and, snatching the keys from Grandma's hand, I burst out the gate to see what all the excitement was. The parading contingents came from the East Street crossing and passed through West Gate. Flags and banners were fluttering and the sounds of percussion and the shouts of slogans shook heaven and earth. A few hours earlier the two factions had still been at each other's throats. Now like brothers who had gone through all kinds of awful things together, they laid down their weapons, and with tear-washed faces, held each other tightly as they paraded through the streets. In the seething tumult I found Chaofan and Rongmei whom I hadn't seen in so many days. We had shaken off our captivity and now there was no controlling our fun and games.

Grandpa and Uncle didn't come outside. On the street I picked up several flyers and a big unexploded firecracker and jubilantly returned home. However, the atmosphere there was anything but reassuring. Grandpa had slipped back to his old ways, sitting over there, but a thousand miles away. Uncle was by his side. Grandma signaled me by her expression to go to my own room.

The next morning, Great-Auntie's uproarious voice awoke me. Old Town's buses today had resumed their routes and she had ridden the first bus over to West Gate. I supposed that Uncle would avoid Great-Auntie by hiding in the garret. After I finished breakfast, I grabbed our worn-out deck of cards and climbed upstairs to find him. But the place was empty. Even the bedding that had been spread out on the floor was gone.

My own period of happiness came to an abrupt halt at the same time as the violence in Old Town ended.

3.

THE GREAT CULTURAL Revolution was just like a raging wild-fire. The number of loafers on Old Town's streets grew steadily, and the Lin family's own Young Turks also became idlers. Baoqing had been fired from his job by the rebel faction, and right after him, Baosheng too. They had been only ordinary cadres in their organizations, so they never had their turn at being struggled and their bad family background disqualified them from struggling anyone else. All they could do was go home, cook meals, and take care of the children. Their wives were still on the firing line of the Revolution, though.

Bored in their inactivity, the two brothers often rode their bicycles, each with a child packed on his back, to meet at West Gate. Later, Old Town's idlers began to popularize cock fighting and Baosheng and Baoqing became quite skilled at raising these fowl. They would each buy a batch of newly hatched chicks and from these nurture a few fierce and aggressive cocks. Every few days they would bring cocks back to West Gate to fight and the ones that lost would become a tasty dish later that day.

The cockpit was set up at the gateway under the oleander bush and two multicolored cocks of a famous English breed would begin the combat. Those West Gate folk at loose ends all gathered around the Lin gate to enjoy all the fun and excitement.

The doctor sat expressionlessly in the main hall. Clearly his two sons had disappointed him again. Both had just passed thirty, that age at which Confucius said he had taken his stand. *How could they cast their youth away for no reason like this? With the world so disordered and many relatives and friends still shut up in the cowsheds, how could they just pursue fun and games like this and not feel that they were committing sin?* Second Sister said, "What can you make our two sons do?" *That's right, what can we do?* But he was firm about not wallowing in the mud with them. He didn't watch the cockfights, not one little bit of them. And he did not eat that meat either. While both sons ate and chatted away at the dinner table, he would just close his eyes and restore his spirit. He would open his eyes again only when, fully sated, they left West Gate.

⌘　⌘　⌘

First one, then another special-case team came to West Gate. They were the special mailmen during periods of emergency and Dr. and Mrs. Lin would welcome them in. The doctor sat over there, Second Sister right next to him. The investigators would ask something and she would loudly repeat it. When they asked a question you had to give an answer. Time and again the reply would not be what was asked. From the teams' questions, doctor could determine what kind of predicaments that Baolan and Ah Jian, Baohua and Big Zhang, Enchun, and even Young Li, were each in. And from his dealings with the various teams and their questions, the doctor could glean different bits of information. First, they would say that such and such a person was still alive. Next, they would explain this person's problem was not so great that he or she could never make a complete turn-around. Certain people had already been released from the cowsheds, one of these being Baosheng's old superior, Deputy District Chief Bai. Now he too was a layabout and a few days before had come to the Lins' gateway to enjoy the cockfights.

⌘　⌘　⌘

That night Young Li resolved to go back to the cowshed to give himself up to the authorities. His reason for this was the Party Central Committee's newly issued instruction, "Struggle verbally, not with weapons." So this was his moment to surrender. He was already resigned to what was in store for him and made mental preparations to return to his village and work the land. He had been the son of Tongpan District peasants. For peasants like them, even a trip to Old Town was beyond their wildest dreams. He had spent the greater part of his life following the tides of war in the north and the south and had been all over China. He was now content. If he died, he would have no regrets. He had gotten the doctor to believe in the Communist Party. His good achievements should be sufficient to compensate for his historical stain. He was sure he would quickly receive permission to hang up his armor and return to the fields.

The doctor listened to Young Li's analysis and, his eyes closed, wondered whether he should go on keeping him here. The reasons Young Li presented were indisputable, but he himself couldn't shake a feeling of unease. The times were just too anarchic. Who knew what would happen next? However, if he concealed him at home, how long would it take before all this ended? He stood up silently and went back into the bedroom, turned off the light, and said a prayer. In his heart he cried out "Father!" and his tears flowed. It had been a long time since he had last prayed. He had already felt there was no communication between him and God. Was it he himself who had turned away, after all, or was it that God cut him off?

He returned to the main hall with a bleak expression on his face. "Way back then, when we ran off from Division Commander Hu, we had God's protection the whole way, and everywhere we could take on and turn the dangers to our advantage. Now, though, I don't hear the voice of God. Will you join me in a prayer?"

Young Li looked blankly at the doctor. "Sir, I am a Communist. I joined the party when I was nineteen years old, more than twenty years ago."

The doctor didn't reply, but bowing his head he thought for a moment and said, "Then go. I'll see you off."

⌘　⌘　⌘

After all the revelry, the streets appeared unusually deserted, and bits and scraps of firecrackers rustling in the wind added to the dreariness. They walked in silence from West Gate to Drum Tower. Not a word was spoken between them, but each was immersed in the very same memory: the scene when they parted on the fisherman's boat on the Yangzi. This separation had lasted thirty years. And today—how long will this parting last before they met again?

Up ahead was the compound of the municipal Party committee. Stopping right where he was, Young Li said, "Sir, don't go any farther. Take good care of yourself. We will definitely meet again."

The doctor felt so sad that he couldn't speak. He didn't have the strength to wave farewell. Young Li strode along like a soldier setting out for battle, his head proudly held high. The doctor quietly followed him right to the main entrance of the compound. It was nighttime and there was a soldier armed with a rifle at the sentry post. All about was utter silence.

⌘　⌘　⌘

All he could do was wait for the arrival of the special-case team to get news of Young Li. This anxiousness was just like what Second Sister had felt so many years before when she had waited for the postman. The doctor was the only person who could vouch for

Young Li regarding that period in his history. He was going to relate this period of Young Li's life as it happened. Back then, when Division Commander Zhang's unit bivouacked at Tongpan District, Young Li was only fourteen years old. His mother tearfully sent him into the army so he'd have food to eat and clothes to wear. The doctor still remembered the boy's first day in the camp—he had been so hungry he wolfed down five bowls of rice.

The doctor waited days on end. Finally, Young Li's special-case team that he had so longed for, finally arrived. As she always did, Second Sister sat beside him playing the role of loudspeaker. When he heard Young Li's name, the doctor didn't wait for the loudspeaker to be turned on, but just stood up and with great feeling related the story. When he got to the part about the death of Division Commander Zhang, he started to cry. "After Division Commander Zhang sacrificed his life..."

A young member of the special-case team pounded the table and shouted, "You're not allowed to prettify the Guomindang reactionary faction!"

The three members of the special-case team clenched their fists and loudly shouted the slogan, "Down with the Guomindang reactionary faction!"

Baosheng and Baoqing, who were just then enjoying themselves by the gate, threw down their beloved cocks and ran into the house.

The doctor said, "Young man, you ought to learn a bit of history. That was during the War of Resistance against Japan. Division Commander Zhang gave his life for the country. So, how is it he doesn't deserve the word 'sacrifice'?" Ashamed, the young man flew into a rage and kept pounding on the table and threatening to arrest this reactionary old coot.

"Dad, you have to cooperate with the special-case team and report everything you know to the authorities," Baosheng said.

The doctor was infuriated. "What do you know?"

Baosheng also had an obstinate temper. "Dad, you should take the Revolution's stand and state the facts."

The doctor struck the table repeatedly. "Facts are facts!"

All of this frightened Second Sister half to death and she ran off to call for reinforcements. She told Ah Ming to quickly call for several "red armbands" to "arrest" the doctor.

Ah Ming brought a number of people and said to the special-case team, "This old reactionary geezer is under our charge. We were just getting ready to lock him up."

Several men pushed forward and carried him off.

After the Great Alliance, Old Town established a multileveled revolutionary committee. Ah Ming was the chairman of the West Gate Revolutionary Committee. The doctor wrote out the statements vouching for Young Li in the little wooden building of the revolutionary committee. For his statements to be effective, he came to terms and compromised by writing, "In this battle Division Commander Zhang died under Japanese artillery fire."

⌘　⌘　⌘

The testimony the doctor wrote for Young Li finally passed the check-and-approval process. Now Baohua and her husband once again became the heaviest weight on his heart. "Big Zhang's" special-case team was a long time in coming, and Baohua hadn't been writing home. He wanted to go see her and couldn't put it off one day more.

Early one morning, the doctor stood in front of his little mirror and got himself up as a worker. Second Sister knew where he was going and had already collected his cigarette carton and bottle of liquor, together with some clothes she made for Baohua, and packed all of this into a battered cloth bag. She also pressed on him a little money for contingencies. She went with him to the long-distance bus and ordered him to "arrive early and get back early." West Gate was now holding "study sessions," so, no matter what, he wasn't to create difficulties for Ah Ming. The doctor nodded his head in agreement.

The doctor rode in a rattletrap of a bus with the wind blowing in on all sides. He thought of Baohua when she was little and how delicate and pretty she had looked. His memories of how moved he had felt when he held her in his arms those many years ago were still fresh today. It was the tenderness he felt for a fragile little life. He thought if only he could stay alive he would prop up a serene piece of sky for her and not let her suffer the least bit of injustice. But over the past ten years or so he had watched wide-eyed his daughter's tempestuous setbacks without being able to do anything to help her. After Baohua's remarriage she rarely returned home. He had heard that she had adopted a boy. It would soon be two years and he still hadn't seen this adopted grandson. What kind of life did Baohua have now that Big Zhang had been detained?

⌘   ⌘   ⌘

When Baohua and her husband adopted their son, remote P Town had already begun its "Smash the Four Olds" campaign. Big Zhang had led the entire bureau's cadres and police force onto the streets in support of the Red Guards' revolutionary actions. He was an uncultured worker-peasant cadre who had always been prejudiced against intellectuals and was sincere in his support of this Revolution aimed at such people. This bureau chief with his police uniform and his red armband really strutted the limelight in little P Town. The only thing that marred this ideal situation for him was that he had no son playing at his feet. He was the son of a northern peasant and he took very seriously the matter of carrying on the family line. The reason he had divorced his first wife was that she couldn't conceive. Only after he married for the second time did he discover he was the one who was sterile. So while he was busy stirring up revolution he entrusted someone with arranging the adoption of an eight-month-old boy called Maomao. Maomao was both intelligent and lovable. Within two months of coming to the Zhang home, he could say "Baba!" and "Mama!" Every day when Big Zhang returned home from work Maomao would hold out his little arms and cry "Baba!" Hearing this word over and over turned the Public Security Bureau chief's heart to mush. He hired a "granny" for the house and nanny for the child. He also intended to adopt a girl child, for his salary was sufficient to raise a whole host of children.

At this time Baohua was already over thirty years old and it was only then that she knew the natural happiness of being a wife and having a family. Taking on the burdens with great gusto, she made an official's wife that people could admire, and enjoyed all the perks and privileges that came along with that. While the hospital staff also made revolution and they split into this and that faction, Baohua took no interest in any of this. She wasn't afraid of anyone saying she was ideologically backward. With the great tree of the Public Security Bureau chief behind her, who would dare provoke her? In this sweet and pleasant small-family life, her daughter and her West Gate family faded from memory.

Surprisingly, this intoxicating life amid the flames of the Revolution lasted a whole year. But the day that Big Zhang went to his office and didn't come back home, the columns supporting this home's cross beam came crashing down. Baohua's standard approach to anything was to cry, and with their lot in life so suddenly changed, this she did endlessly. The rebel faction saw this woman weeping and sobbing and couldn't get anywhere with her, so, as a punishment, they sent her to steam wheat flour buns in the mess hall. Every day, when she couldn't get the stove started, she cried. When the buns were not cooked properly, she cried. Big Zhang's salary had been suspended and Baohua's own salary also reduced by half. She was unable to pay the nanny and she cried over this too. The nanny packed a bundle of belongings and just resigned. The granny couldn't bear leaving the child and stuck it out for two more months. One day at the end of the month, she said that she ought to buy some rice, and Baohua got into such a panic at not having the money for this that tears flowed again. The old lady used her own savings and bought a few *jin* of rice. She told Baohua that from the look of things, Bureau Chief Zhang wouldn't be coming home any time soon. "Such a pampered wife like you can't manage a child, so I'll take Maomao back to the village. Whenever things are peaceful again at your home, I'll come back." Baohua took the child from the granny's arms and proceeded with a round of weeping and wailing. Then she took off her wristwatch and gave it to the other woman. In such a way did a lively and vibrant family come apart.

When the doctor arrived at the P Town hospital, it was just about time for the evening meal to be served in the mess hall. The stove where the buns were steamed had not yet been lighted, for it had rained heavily over the past few days and the firewood and the stove box were all sodden. When Baohua used alcohol to light the fire she scorched her eyebrows and hair but still the fire in the stove box was barely alive. She held the blowpipe and she cried as she blew onto the fire. Sometimes she would think of her mother. It was only now that she understood how capable her mother was and the difficulties she had been through. In those times her mother had raised three children all by herself as well as bearing the burden of the rest of the Guo family. *How come I can't raise even just Maomao?*

A ragged and skinny old fellow walked over to the stove. Whenever she couldn't serve the meal, a mass of people, their bellies rumbling with hunger, would come crowding around the stove. When she was in distress Baohua could not rein in her Big Missy temper and she often blew up, crying and shouting and losing her temper at the people waiting to eat. She looked at the little alarm clock that had been placed beside her. It wasn't yet time, but here was someone coming to make trouble. Depressed and resentful, she barked out, "Go away, go away! The steamers aren't hot yet. You want to eat uncooked buns?" The skinny old guy stood there dumbly without moving. "Didn't you hear me? If *you* don't go away, *I* will!" Baohua raised her tear- and smoke-streaked face and was totally stunned. "Dad, what are you doing here?" His own eyes were filled with tears, and without saying a word, the doctor took the blow pipe from the woman's hand and with total concentration got the fire in the stove going.

That evening, the father and daughter went to the cowshed to see Big Zhang. The special-case team was made up of his subordinates. That "double agent," Old Wang, who had gone to the Lin home, had grown up with Big Zhang in the same village. Over these several months Baohua could go and see Big Zhang anytime she wanted to. But not today. Old Wang said that he had been transferred to the provincial government. It looked like a serious problem. When he was young, Big Zhang had followed a certain leading cadre. And that cadre had been marked by Jiang Qing[56] as a secret agent.

---

[56] Jiang Qing (1914–1991), the last wife of Chairman Mao Zedong, played a major role in fomenting the Cultural Revolution (1966–1976) as a leader of the Central Cultural Revolution Group and the influential "Gang of Four" radical ideologues. Feared, reviled, and widely (if exaggeratedly) blamed for all the destructive chaos of the Cultural Revolution, her power ended with the death of Mao on September 9, 1976. Arrested shortly after this, she was tried in 1980 and given a death sentence that was never carried out. In mid-1991 she was released on medical grounds. Jiang Qing reportedly committed suicide days after her release.

Baohua cried the whole night long. Watching over his daughter, the doctor sighed the whole night long too. The walls were covered with photos of Maomao. Big Zhang was holding Maomao with an expression of love and happiness. So! This uncouth northerner *was* kindly and chivalrous. In an instant, a feeling of love which had never before existed sprung up in his mind toward this son-in-law whom he had only seen a few times before. The doctor decided to go bring Maomao back home. He wanted to stay in P Town and build a family for his daughter.

The next day, the doctor went to P Town's rural area and found the granny's home. When she heard that he had come for Maomao, she got very upset. She took off Baohua's watch and pressed it on the doctor, saying obstinately, "I love this child. I'm not seeking anything from you. Short of Bureau Chief Zhang himself coming for Maomao, no one can take this child away. Even if his mother came, I wouldn't let her take Maomao away. She can't raise children and I won't let Maomao suffer wrongs along with her." The granny's own children were running about wild, all in tatters and rags. But there in her arms Maomao looked in good condition. It was obvious that he received special love and care in this family. Although the world was in chaos, everywhere there were fine and good people. The doctor was so moved he wanted to cry. He said to the nanny, "Let me hold the child for a bit." Secretly he stuffed the watch and a few banknotes under Maomao's stomach bib and then said farewell.

Upon his return to P Town, the doctor went straight to the mess hall and became Baohua's assistant. The days passed, and with her father's help, Baohua learned how to light the stove and to steam fragrant and piping hot buns with ease. The workers in the mess hall all liked this taciturn, hardworking old fellow and nobody bothered to ask where he had come from. The doctor himself seemed to forget where he had come from. Looking at Baohua, tears no longer flowing down her face, and even occasionally laughing happily, he had been able to accompany this woman through a difficult period. For this he felt satisfaction and happiness.

4.

THE DOCTOR WAS staying on in P Town and did not return. This really alarmed Ah Ming. The West Gate revolutionary committee was holding study sessions and it had long since been Dr. Lin's turn to attend. Time and again, Ah Ming had handled this in a perfunctory way, and this gave rise to some comments. So he came to the Lin home and called in Baosheng and Baoqing to discuss how to get the doctor to return. The two brothers knew clearly that if Ah Ming's involvement in this led to his downfall, West Gate would lose its protective umbrella. But who could succeed in calling their dad back home? Baosheng and Baoqing knew well from their own experience that if the doctor saw them, just pretending to be deaf and dumb would be considered being polite on his part. Only Ma could take the field in this matter. Second Sister shook her head. She had just received a letter from Ninth Brother. In it were his thoughts on keeping their daughter company in P Town and mobilizing Second Sister to bring me as well, to P Town.

The tense meeting at the Lin home had not yet concluded when the doctor himself, wearing beat-up old clothes, suddenly appeared. He put down the empty sack he carried and peered furtively all around. Turning back, he fastened the bar on the main gate then gestured to me to leave the main hall. Several pairs of eyes followed me as I left. Who knew what drama was being acted out? The doctor sat down and, lowering his voice, told of Big Zhang's predicament. He only had to say that Big Zhang had been the bodyguard of that certain leading cadre, for Baosheng and Baoqing to know just how serious the problem was. That person had been convicted by Jiang Qing herself!

A blanket of silence descended upon them. After quite a while Baosheng said, "It's lucky that Big Sister didn't give birth again. Convince her to quickly break up her marriage with him."

"You impudent animal!" The doctor's eyes shot fire at Baosheng. "I'm going to find him and I'll see his face if he's alive, or his corpse if he's dead!'

Having delivered these words, he turned around and tilting his head back, closed his eyes. Waving his hand, he said, "You all just go. This matter has nothing to do with you. Just pretend you never heard it at all."

The two brothers brought Ah Ming to the gateway and asked him to order their father into the study session. Whatever else happened, he was not allowed to run loose like that again.

Second Sister brewed some hot tea for the doctor. She asked him who that leading cadre could have been. The doctor said without opening his eyes, "You don't need to know too much."

⌘　⌘　⌘

Big Zhang was convicted of being a member of a ring of public security secret agents. Yesterday, Old Wang went to the mess hall and called the doctor out for a confidential discussion. He had just gone to the provincial capital and heard that Big Zhang's attitude was arrogant and aggressive to the extreme. Even if he were going to be beaten to death he wouldn't admit his guilt. Old Wang just had to think of some way to persuade him to make this admission. If he could, Big Zhang's punishment would be determined, and Old Wang would fix it so he could be jailed in P Town. Otherwise, his violent temper really would get him beaten to death.

Old Wang had an old comrade-in-arms who was a section head at the provincial-level Public Security office. At the meeting table, the two men pretended they did not know each other. Halfway through the meeting, Old Wang used a toilet break to report on Big Zhang's situation. "Did you say that Big Zhang was a secret agent?" the doctor asked. Old Wang hawked up some phlegm and spit it onto the ground. "Pah! That's fucking rubbish. Big Zhang got to be bureau chief by *catching* secret agents. Now he's a secret agent himself—what a joke!" He didn't tell the doctor that the meeting at the Public Security office was precisely about catching secret agents, for they had caught a real one from Taiwan, and he had said that Big Zhang might be useful for breaking the case. The section head immediately notified the detention people that Big Zhang had to be kept alive and under no circumstances could they beat him to death.

Old Wang told the doctor to think of a way to get Big Zhang to change his attitude and act obediently. There was no way he could discuss this matter with Baohua, the cadre said. "Your precious daughter's useless for anything except crying," he said, and laughed bitterly. He gave the doctor a photograph. It showed two young army men: Old Wang and the section head when they had come south to liberate Old Town. He also made the doctor memorize the section head's home address. This photo gave the doctor an inspiration. He had found several photographs of Maomao at his daughter's home. He believed that Big Zhang would surely swallow all these insults and go on living for Maomao.

⌘   ⌘   ⌘

This discussion itself was like secret agent activity, with the doctor the newly inducted member in a special unit group. Second Sister sensed that ever since his return from P Town he had changed into someone devious and surreptitious. This wasn't the real Ninth

Brother. She privately expressed her misgivings to her sons. "Does your father have any mental problems?"

All the people who went into the study sessions were honest and decent. Being the dregs of the old society, they couldn't have been more grateful that they hadn't been struggled or put into jail. The whole thing was nothing more than to again shake out the history of each person that had been shaken out a thousand times already. None of them dared slip out the main gate of the revolutionary committee. But every day the doctor slipped out and slipped back in. Ah Ming thought he was going home for the noon rest, so he just closed an eye to this. It was all right so long as the doctor appeared in the morning for instructions and in the evening to give his report. When Ah Ming also speculated to Shuiguan on Dr. Lin's mental state, he got a real tongue-lashing from his father.

For several days, the doctor hurried to catch the noon break at the Public Security office where he sauntered about in the vicinity of its living quarters. Its main entrance was tightly guarded and you had to have a pass. Upon close observation, he discovered that a worker from the nearby coal shop brought coal to the living quarters daily at noon without having his papers checked at the guardhouse.

This day he asked Second Sister to try to get hold of a fifty-*jin* coal coupon. He went to the study session and after reporting in, slipped out again. On the road he borrowed some coal tools from someone he knew well and after buying the coal he blackened his face and swaggered into the Public Security Department dormitory. He couldn't help being secretly very pleased with his remarkable talent as a secret agent.

The section head himself opened the door. The doctor took out with his dirty hands the photograph that Old Wang had given him and introduced himself as Big Zhang's father-in-law. The two men then pretended to move coal into the cooking area. The section head said that he had lent Big Zhang to the department to assist in breaking a case, but there was a specially trained guard by Big Zhang's side, so he couldn't talk and didn't dare talk. Big Zhang was obstinate by nature and would rather die than to admit to guilt. Tomorrow he was going to be sent back to the detention center. If they didn't get a speedy sentencing, he was going to die in there. The doctor said, "I'd like to see him. Once I see him I'm sure I could get him to change his attitude." The section head stood by a pile of coal and smoked two cigarettes in quick succession. Pointing to the little building way off by the side of the wall surrounding the compound, he said, "That's where he is right now. The people guarding him are in the outer room and may be having their noon doze. There's a small barred window in the back. Just go ahead and give it a try. If he's asleep too there's nothing you can do about this, so please don't come looking for me again, all right?"

⌘   ⌘   ⌘

At this moment, Big Zhang was standing motionlessly up by the barred window, his mind in a daze. He couldn't figure out why he had ended up in this cell. Nor could he figure out how his most revered leader could possibly be a secret agent. He himself was the son of a destitute peasant in a northern village, and ever since he was little had hired himself out long-term to the local landlords. In 1938, that cadre was leading the Eight Route Army when it liberated his village. Thus at only sixteen years of age Big Zhang became a soldier of the Eight Route Army. The party's loving kindness to him had been higher than heaven and thicker than the earth, as they say. How could they make him admit that he was a secret agent plotting to overthrow the Communist regime?

A skinny old geezer bearing a shoulder pole with two empty baskets walked onto the patch of weeds outside the barred window. Big Zhang gazed idly at the scene in front of him, but in his mind he was thinking of the year when that leading cadre taught him to read. Hazily he recalled the vastness of the great plain where he came from and its stretch after stretch of tall, new crops.

The old fellow's eyes were flecked with tears as he came up to the barred window. When their eyes connected, Big Zhang didn't recognize his father-in-law. There was no way he would have expected Baohua's father to appear at this place at this time. He didn't have any good impression of Baohua's family, especially that father-in-law with his holier-than-thou air about him who had done all he could to oppose Baohua's marriage. Big Zhang had brooded over this and bore him a grudge. A few times Baohua had hopped a ride with Big Zhang back to Old Town and when the car stopped at the West Gate street crossing he hadn't gotten out. Last year when the news of the doctor's struggle session had reached P Town, his voice said to Baohua, "Bring your dad and ma to P Town," but his heart couldn't contain its pleasure at this other person's misfortune.

The doctor got right next to the window and said in a low voice, "Big Zhang, you've had a rough time of it."

Big Zhang was so astonished his scalp tingled, as if someone long dead was suddenly standing right there talking to him. He really couldn't tell if it was a man or a ghost standing on the other side of the window. Then he saw Maomao's picture. His son's adorable face thoroughly demolished Big Zhang's will. He lowered his head and, covering up his chin, his mouth, and his nose, wept with all his pent-up emotions.

The doctor unfolded a note that he had written beforehand and read, "For Baohua and for Maomao, you have to go on living. With a good attitude you can return to P Town to serve out your sentence. 'As long as the hills stay green, don't fear for a lack of firewood.'"

Big Zhang nodded, with tears in his eyes.

The doctor folded up the piece of paper and from inside his shirt took out the cigarettes, matches, and a small bottle of liquor and passed it in to Big Zhang. Then he hastily picked up his shoulder pole and walked off. Like some mischievous child, he had been in an exciting game and now, as he headed toward West Street, his unsettled nerves calmed down a bit. He pondered over Big Zhang. The tears of this tough and boorish northerner were daggers stabbing into his heart. As he walked along he wiped his own tears until half his face was black with coal dust. Passing West Street he forgot to return the shoulder pole and the empty baskets to their owner. He also forgot to return to the study session. Feeling quite light-headed, he walked to his own home.

Ah Ming was just then with the Lins reporting to his "auntie" and "big brothers" the doctor's odd behavior, when all of sudden he spotted the doctor coming home, face all black and still shouldering the pole with its two empty baskets. The four people sitting around the Eight Immortals table all came to the same immediate conclusion: *He really has gone crazy!*

Would Ninth Brother walk the streets from now on bringing coal to people? Is he strong enough to do something like that? Second Sister's heart ached as she wondered this.

She called him over to drink some water and to clean his face. "If you're thinking of doing labor reform, let Ah Ming assign you to sweeping the streets," she said.

Ninth Brother made no response. Utterly spent, he remounted his throne, closed his eyes and shut his ears.

⌘   ⌘   ⌘

One month later, Baohua sent a letter saying that Big Zhang had now been transferred to the P Town jail.

⌘   ⌘   ⌘

At the end of the 1970s, my stepfather held the position of deputy commissioner of P Town district. The personal misfortune of spending several years in jail hadn't done anything to improve his temper. After his release he learned that his adopted son, Maomao, at age four had been kidnapped from the granny's home and sold. This was really a great blow to Big Zhang. He left no stone unturned and experienced all kinds of setbacks in trying to find Maomao. Finally, he discovered that the child had fallen into a beggar band and within a few years had been thoroughly infected with all its evil ways. He was now a cunning and lazy little rascal. Disappointed to his very core, Big Zhang's temper became more violent than ever. His home was in a constant uproar and my mother would frequently return to West Gate crying to the heavens. The Lin family's relationship with Big Zhang stalemated at a new low point.

When the news of my grandfather's passing reached P Town, Deputy Commissioner Zhang was just then in charge of convening an important meeting. He immediately handed off this job and sent his secretary out to buy mourning apparel. My mother told him that hemp coverings and white sackcloth were not the fashion at Christian funeral services, but he insisted on this, and then rushed off, driving his own car the more than thirty miles to West Gate. There he fell on his knees with a thump, and, tears streaming down his face, knocked his head on the ground three times.

At that time, the two Lin brothers had a falling-out with their brother-in-law because in a fit of temper Big Zhang had smashed a thermos and scalded my mother's foot. When my two uncles raced in a fury to P Town to burst into his office and have it out with him, Big Zhang brought the police and police vehicles into play. At West Gate He paid no attention at all to Baosheng and Baoqing, but insisted on joining them in carrying the coffin in the funeral procession. His expression looked more imposing in its deep grief than anyone else's in our family.

5.

WITH OLD TOWN folk, happiness lies in being contented. They have always been optimistic in their belief that Old Town is a place blessed with riches. Look, in the beginning of the 1970s, the schools began classes, work started up at the factories, and food wasn't so scarce in the markets. All under heaven was peaceful and tranquil. Though the streets were still filled with slogans like "Vow to carry out the Great Cultural Revolution right to the very end!" in fact, the revolution no longer had anything to do with the citizens of Old Town. People had started to live orderly lives amid all the upheaval.

The little vessel that was the Lin home had weathered the tempest, frightened but unscathed, and like the rest of the people of Old Town, began a dull and contented life. Big Zhang was still in jail. Baohua returned to work in the maternity ward. With Old Wang looking after them, they were able to meet every week. Baosheng and Baoqing resumed work at their respective organizations. The lofty sentiments and grand aspirations of their younger years had long since felt like yesterday's dreams. Now they endured life with equanimity as low-level functionaries. Young Li's wish came true. He returned to his home village in Tongpan District where his fellow villagers chose him to be the local production brigade chief. Enchun was assigned to sweep and clean the school library and for him this was like putting a fish back in water. Everything went peacefully and smoothly. Everything exceeded what was needed and sought after.

Women with perms now began to appear on the streets. Grandma also kept up with the latest fashions and went to get her hair done. I let my hair grow long. Every day before going to school

I would comb it into braids and clip on butterflies of different colors and designs. The two uncles saw this but expressed no opinions. Perhaps they had simply forgotten the family revolution they had launched over my hair.

At some point, I don't know when, my grandfather retrieved that thick, calfskin book from Shuiguan's home. Now openly and honorably he sat in the main hall reading it and writing notes, with no one feeling uneasy about this.

At that time, my grandparents' biggest worries were about Pussycat, getting old but still restless. More often than not it would be off somewhere, and frequently got hurt in cat gang warfare. Every time it came home more dead than alive, it would jump up on the wall but couldn't get down. So Grandpa, himself over seventy years old, still had to move the ladder and climb up to carry Pussycat down.

⌘   ⌘   ⌘

When Baolan and her husband, Ah Jian, came to West Gate to visit their Ninth Uncle and Ninth Aunt, the two old folks were treating Pussycat's wounds and feeding it rice gruel with brown sugar.

It was an afternoon in early autumn. Baolan's face was lightly made up and she was wearing a pale violet-hued dress. As she stood there in the sunlight of the sky well, she dazzled everyone with her beauty. She was now a middle-aged lady over forty years old and though the past twenty years had been rough ones for her, she was still able to stay this attractive.

Grandpa was delighted at his niece's visit. As he dressed the cat's wounds, he looked up and said all in one breath, "Baolan! I'm so happy to see you. Stay a while, both of you. I'll boil a cup of good tea for you!"

Over all these years, the doctor had quietly kept a hotline connection with Ah Jian. He had never spoken a single word of comfort to Baolan and to date had never told her that he knew she had been designated a rightist and sent to do coolie labor in a factory, or that at the start of the Cultural Revolution both her legs had been broken by the rebel faction. In the cowshed she had insisted on treating her own wounds and doing her own physical therapy. She refused to end up as a cripple. His niece's indomitable character gained his admiration but also distressed him. Actually, he very much wanted to comfort her. He wished that she could be like Baohua and cry herself dry of all the injustices and heartbreaks she carried inside her. But every time he saw her she always appeared so cheerful and happy. It was as if all the information from Ah Jian were just so many rumors that didn't stand up in the light of day.

The doctor washed his hands and started the complicated tea ritual. Performing this was his highest level of hospitality to guests. Apart from Young Li, no one could enjoy the same level of courteous treatment as Baolan received.

Since that particular day was neither New Year's nor any other festival, Baolan and her husband's visit with gifts for her uncle must be "the arrival of good luck when misfortune has reached its limit." *Perhaps Ah Jian has returned to his teaching job or maybe Baolan has been transferred back to her newspaper.* The comfortable sight of Old Town's ordinary people enjoying whatever peace and ease they could had clouded the doctor's mind and he too turned into an optimist. He didn't even notice that Baolan wasn't laughing much on this day.

After three rounds of tea, Baolan said, "Uncle, from what I know, Christians have eternal life. The life they vest in Jesus is immortal, is that not so?"

It was as if a lightning bolt split the doctor's head in two. His feelings at this very instant were complex in the extreme. Ever since the West Gate church had been closed, he almost never talked about Jesus with anyone. For over two years now, he hadn't even the strength to pray. Right up to recently he would reread the Bible and still not sense he was in touch with God. Baolan's questions filled him with guilt and remorse.

"Oh, to be sure. Believe in Jesus and gain eternal life. Ninth Uncle owes so much to Jesus. Who knows when the day comes whether Jesus will be willing to take me to my heavenly home?"

Ah Jian said, "Ninth Uncle, you have given your love and warmth to so many people, Jesus surely loves you very much."

Oh, is this God telling me through them that he has not cast me aside?

Baolan said, "Ninth Uncle, Ah Jian and I have come to see you today to ask you to give us to Jesus, and thereafter we will have immortal life."

O God, is this real? Very excited, the doctor took hold of Baolan and Ah Jian's hands. "From this moment on, you are Christians. The Bible tells us if only we believe in Jesus in our word and in our heart, and we accept Jesus as the savior of our lives, we are Christians!" Then he closed his eyes and prayed, "O Lord, Heavenly Father, I bring Baolan and Ah Jian before you. Please receive them as your children, and grant them eternal life.

Only after eating dinner did Baolan and Ah Jian leave West Gate. Before their departure, Baolan embraced Ninth Uncle and Aunt with great affection. "Ninth Uncle, Ninth Aunt, after Dad and Ma departed from us, you have been my dearest relatives. Now that we have eternal life we will never be separated from you again. Even if tomorrow we should no longer be on this earth, we will be parted for only a short time, right?"

The doctor smiled lovingly and nodded his head. At that moment he thought of his own three children. *When will they suddenly come to their senses and repent?*

⌘ ⌘ ⌘

A few days later, Old Town's marketplace was rife with the story of the man and the woman who killed themselves in a double suicide south of the city on Black Mountain. The great tempest of the Cultural Revolution had passed. Suicide no longer would have happened for political reasons, so this couple's action caused a sensation in tiny Old Town. People gave full rein to their imaginations and came up with all kind of interesting tidbits.

Early one morning my grandmother went to the vegetable market and heard this news. On my way to school, I heard Rongmei give her own juicy account. Her father came to our house and babbled in deaf-and-dumb talk to my grandfather.

It was a middle-aged couple. They had on their best clothes as if going to attend a grand and solemn banquet. The time, place, and manner had been meticulously set out. Black Mountain was an oasis of serenity amid all the hustle and bustle of life. The time was on the eve of Old Town's return to life. They sprinkled one-*fen* coins from the foot of the mountain right to under the tree they hung themselves from. Early that morning, two middle school students on their way to school, book bags on their backs, discovered the coins at the road crossing. They picked them up all the way to the top of the mountain where they discovered the man and the woman hanging from the tree. At the time, their bodies had not yet stiffened and still held a trace of warmth.

This couple who had decided to go to their deaths had been so concerned with appearances. Every last detail was planned so that after their deaths their appearances would remain dignified to the extent that they could achieve this.

⌘ ⌘ ⌘

We are a family of intellectuals and scholars. From the time I was little that's how Grandma taught and raised me. Thus, we never exchanged news of what we heard out in the streets at the dinner table. The story of this couple was just like many folktales and legends, merely a light breeze blowing by the ears. We had no interest in chasing after phantoms.

Who would have expected it, though? The man and the woman were actually our Lin-family relatives—Baolan and Ah Jian. In the beginning, being designated a rightist had not caused Baolan to lose hope. Nor did she do so when the rebel faction broke her legs. After she came out of the cowshed and returned to factory labor, it seemed as if the storms surrounding her had calmed down and people had gotten used to the absurd time when white was black and black was white. With black and white all topsy-turvy, they found balance and enjoyment. Numb Old Town, content Old Town—*this* is what made Baolan lose hope. People always say that the more you think, the more torment it brings you. Baolan was not only the girl genius of the Lin family; she was also the girl genius of Old Town. She could not, nor would she have been willing to just drift along resigned to life like the majority of Old Town people. I heard that Uncle Baoqing received a several hundred thousand character-long letter that she wrote him just before she died. In it she spoke of her views on the conditions of the country and on Marshal Lin Biao[57] and Jiang Qing. He hadn't finished reading it

---

[57]   Lin Biao (1907–1971), an important communist military commander during the Guomindang-Communist Civil War, and subsequently a key figure in promoting the personality cult of Mao Zedong. During the Cultural Revolution, Lin emerged as the nation's paramount military leader and was officially designated as Mao's successor. Then, in 1971, Marshal Lin, together with his wife and son, were reported to have died in a plane crash in Mongolia while fleeing China. The exact circumstances of his death have never been definitively established, though rumors of plots and coups abound to this day. Along with Jiang Qing, Lin Biao has been a scapegoat for the worst aspects of the Cultural Revolution.

when his wife, my aunt, snatched it from him and stuffed it into the stove.

This bad news overwhelmed Grandpa. For several days straight he neither ate nor slept. He just lay on his bed without getting up. Grandma persisted in bringing hot meals to his bedside three times a day, and she sat beside him groaning and sighing. She waited until the food had gotten cold before taking it away, untouched.

My grandmother knew that Baolan and Ah Jian's decision to become Christians was to console their Ninth Uncle, so that he wouldn't take the news too badly. This husband and wife were so determined to end their lives, who could have held them back? In order to release my grandfather from his pain and grief, Grandma placed the Bible in his hand and said that Baolan and Ah Jian were now already in heaven and, compared to eternal life, this life today, long or short, was nothing. He took the Bible and shoved it into the cabinet drawer by the bedstead.

After my Grandpa could finally get up from bed, he immediately set out to uncover the reasons for Baolan's death. That winter he was like some unknown and coldly aloof lodger at the West Gate home. Even the pitiful cries of Pussycat crawling along the top of the wall couldn't distract him. Every day he got up early and came back late. He went to the printing plant where Baolan had worked, the school where Ah Jian had taught. He went everywhere and questioned people who had known this husband and wife. But he didn't find any "spider threads and horse hoofmarks." My grandfather had become enmeshed in an enigma from which he had no way to extricate himself.

I don't know if my grandfather went to heaven. Or whether he met Baolan there, who then released him from the endless mental tangles of that enigma.

Chapter Twenty-One —
Who's Roaming

1.

Are you so sure of yourself now? Has the Old Town story crumbled your notion about first impressions being the important ones? Is it sympathy you want to express, while at the same time an indefinable admiration has sprouted deep within you?

Most Westerners think that when it comes to Asia, and especially China, first impressions are the ones to go by. Even the humblest and most self-effacing of Christians think of China in terms of misery and suffering. So in the West, Chinese movies that are one long lamentation get a big box office and win awards. Yes, of course, we've been through a lot of suffering. But suffering has left us with not merely painful memories, but ones worth devoting a lifetime to understand.

Joseph's eyes narrow as he looks at me. "You ought to write down a history of the Lin family."

I laugh to myself. *Yes, I've had just such an idea.* I graduated from the department of literature. What student in a department of literature doesn't dream of becoming a writer? I once mentioned this to Uncle Baoqing on a visit back to see my family in Old Town. He was puzzled. "What's there to write about in our family? Your grandpa was poor and down-and-out his whole life. Your grandma was a housewife. Your mother, like most of that generation, is depressed and frustrated. Let's not even talk about your generation. Other than earning money and getting divorced, you're not looking for anything at all." At the time, my cousin Wei'er was going through an unpleasant divorce. Their little grandson was going to leave the Lin home with his mother, something that vexed and worried Uncle Baoqing and Auntie Fangzi no end.

Before I turned out the lights on my literary dreams, I did try putting something on paper. But if I tried once, I failed a hundred times. The longest thing I ever wrote reached fifty or sixty thousand characters, but still I walked away from it. Nowadays, my literary dream is just one more thing that I have walked away from. And at this very moment what I want to do most is turn right around and get back to Beijing to rally my defeated forces.

Joseph takes out a photograph of Helen from his document folder. I know that picture well. It is the youngest appearance of her that still exists. She was already an old lady of about seventy then, still in India doing voluntary relief work and teaching school. She is standing in the midst of a crowd of children and looking just like some old Indian mama.

Two years ago I bid farewell to Helen before returning to China, after which I then went back to see her again. On that last occasion, she was living in a nursing home in Lompoc. She and many old people were in their wheelchairs around the long dining room table waiting for the attendants to serve the meal. That scene really shook me. What shook me even more was the photograph on the front of each door. All the old people had put out a framed photograph taken during the radiant elegance of their youth. These photographs made you think of Hollywood stars. In fact, the word was that some former Hollywood stars really were there. Looking at the people in the photographs and then seeing the people in the wheelchairs who were totally out of it, their gaze glassy-eyed, their mouths drooling, their skin once glowing with loveliness but now like rotten old tree bark, all this was a reality that would really bring you down. To live our few short decades of life to old age is a matter of sheer luck, but here was what our twilight years looked like! I'd get depressed every time I paid a visit to the nursing home, and that's when I would long for eternal life and some deity.

Helen didn't have any pictures of herself when she was young. The one she put on her door was where she looked like the Indian mama. Her daughter, Lucy had told me that she knew very little about her mother. For several decades after leaving China, Helen had helped the destitute and desperate in the Third World, and from the time she was small, Lucy lived with an aunt in America. The wars and upheavals in all these countries time and again cleaned Helen out of everything she had. Her diaries, her photographs from her youth, all were lost and gone forever. She worked in India until she was seventy-five years old, right up until a stroke partially paralyzed her and she couldn't work any longer. So her daughter never had any evidence to document her mother's life in China.

Joseph studies the photograph and says, "I really hope that my grandmother is the person in your story. I hope she is the Guo family's Third Sister. Of course, it's only a hope."

Only a hope...Real life is never so coincidental. With an effort I recall the shape and features of Helen's face. Didn't she look a bit like my grandmother? But hers was a face that showed all too much the hardships of her life. There was no way of telling just how she really had originally looked. Also, Grandma had said that the so-called Third Sister Story was simply one among many others made up by Great-Auntie.

Suddenly, a melancholy hard to describe wells up within me. During the days spent at Helen's side, I often had these same piercing feelings. That old lady who never did find a home aroused my self-pity every time. Just what had made me wander so far afield to a little place even more of a backwater than Old Town was something I could never figure out.

To console a wandering ghost drifting through strange lands and on foreign shores, I ponder hard on who could still provide information about Third Sister Guo. Perhaps Great-Auntie in her own old folks' home still remembered her, though most probably she would improvise new "tales of marvels" and confuse me even more. I think of my Great-Uncle Guo's wife. She is already over eighty years old and still in good health. To this day she is still the real power in the Guo family. The thing that impressed me the most about her was at the time of Grandma's burial. Though out of respect for Grandma's beliefs none of us covered ourselves in white cloth and hemp, she represented the Guo family in leading the great ruckus in the mourning hall. However I explained it to you, though, would make no sense. They keened, they wailed, they beat their breasts and stamped their feet. And in the midst of their laments they bitterly accused my two uncles, Baosheng and Baoqing, of being unfilial to their mother. Just the year before last, one of the Guo family nephews got sick and died, and his widow took their child with her when she remarried. Although this was a girl child, she still belonged to the line of the Guo family. This Big Aunt Guo took a clutch of women, all professional troublemakers, with her and found the widow's new home. She brought the child back home and raised it with her own meager pension. She had met Third Sister and was a wealth of Guo family secrets. Would she tell what really happened?

Joseph laughed in relief. "Actually, what really happened has already come to light."

Out of love for Helen, why not turn a beautiful wish into irrefutable truth? I nod in warm agreement.

"They have reunited in heaven and at this very hour, at this very moment, are laughing at us. 'Look, those two children are still guessing at riddles.'"

Joseph jabbed his finger heavenward.

The concept of eternal life is truly baffling. If there is eternal life, all the vexations and perplexities of the present one are as easily understood as a blade splitting bamboo. But is it true?

Helen, I want to believe that you have returned to the heavenly kingdom. That is your real hometown.

⌘   ⌘   ⌘

With such thoughts, though, my mood now turns heavy. Chaofan once wrote a song called "Who's Roaming." It was one of the routine numbers he performed in the open air at Fisherman's Wharf. Is he still there this evening playing his one-man band? When the song is over and the people all leave, does he still have a woman to go home with him?

"Roaming"—once that was such a beautiful word. There was nothing to compare with how I felt when I imagined backpacking in alien lands and taking unknown roads. But this word, when I hear it now, trails in its wake bitter grief and sadness.

Chaofan has his own music studio for composing accompaniment to televised animation programs and advertisements. Our daughter says he's got several people working for him, so that makes him a boss. He doesn't need to sell his art on the street for a living, but he still wants to occupy that tiny spot on the Wharf.

I don't know whether he is as endlessly infatuated with his roaming as he had been. He stubbornly refuses to receive any news from China. He doesn't read Chinese newspapers. He doesn't make friends with other Chinese. Every last one of his studio staff are white people. What's all the more ridiculous is that he always uses his lame English when speaking with our daughter and every one of his sentences has at least three mistakes in it. The girl hardly understands him at all and feels nothing but disdain. In her overseas calls she laughs as she tells funny stories about her father. All kinds of feelings run through me as I hold the phone to my ear.

This is a severely damaged man. And it is undeniable that I myself am a scar on his memory. I don't have the confidence and the strength to accompany him through difficult times. I don't know what strength propped up my grandmother to love my grandfather through an entire lifetime. And *he* was not merely a man who had been "poor and down on his luck" but also someone who always brought calamity upon his family. I raise my head in admiration of Grandma. But *I* can't do it. I just can't.

2.

EVERY NEW YEAR Chrysanthemum makes a resolution: *This year I am definitely going to get myself married.* Year after year goes by and her seasonal love intermezzos are like old records. They go round and round again, never pausing, never stopping in their groaning and moaning. With the closing of the year, the ending goes back to the beginning. Comes the spring and she's all by herself again, so Spring Festival is a very trying period for her. She has to be on full-scale alert and early on plan her strategy for coping. For three years straight she signed up for travel groups and left Beijing as if she were seeking safety in flight.

Last year, just before Spring Festival, Chrysanthemum suddenly telephoned me to meet with her. She sounded unusually exhilarated and wanted me to come to her home to see something. She could barely control her excitement and sounded like an antique collector who obtained the thing she had most dreamed of having. Chrysanthemum was renting a spot in the northeast corner of the city, an out-of-the-way area I never failed to get lost in. I have been urging her all along to move out of there and get a place of her own, but she's convinced that her future husband now has the new home ready and is waiting to greet his bride. This was a day of sandstorms and I didn't want to face these conditions to go see her treasure. But hearing her sound so eager to see me, I arranged to meet at our old place—the coffee shop.

Chrysanthemum was clutching a laptop as she emerged from the murk of the storm and arrived at the coffee shop. The moment she entered she looked for an electrical outlet. "Got some great news for you! I now have hope. You also now have hope!

A rich guy with money to spend had hired Chrysanthemum to package some unknown singer for an MTV clip. He said it didn't matter how much it cost and once the contract was signed her reimbursements would definitely be deposited to her account. Now seeing Chrysanthemum beside herself with happiness, I had to remind her that signing such a contract could very possibly land her in a scam. "This sort of thing goes on everywhere. You pay the advance but when the time comes you don't get it back and you're just out of luck."

As Chrysanthemum's two hands worked the laptop, she waggled her chin impatiently. "This is nothing to do with business. It's almost New Year's! Who feels like talking business? I want to introduce you to a dating Web site. Here—look!"

On the screen appeared a long series of men's pictures. She scrolled down and browsed through the data on dozens of men. All around forty years old, with master's degrees, doctorates—everything you could possibly want, they had it.

"Ali Baba and the Forty Thieves' treasure is right here. This year I can hope to get married. Do you want me to set up a file for you? You should get married too you know."

It was a bit tempting, but I hadn't forgotten that I was still married. "Forget it. This year let me first get divorced so I won't be taken to court by someone for marriage fraud."

"Hmmh, so divorce! Fight a quick battle and win a quick decision."

Chrysanthemum keyed in for me several men she was especially cultivating. Over the past three days she had met three men, and actually felt that all three of them weren't too bad. Among these, the boss of a car repair shop especially aroused her interest. He was a middle-aged man who really knew how to create the romantic atmosphere. After dinner he took her in his SUV for a spin around the city's outskirts where there were still traces of snow on the ground. In just a few short hours he had Chrysanthemum head over heels. The man's screen name was Western Herdsman. She shut the laptop and stirred her coffee in her customary manner as she chattered on and on about Western Herdsman. Seized by an impulse, she had given him her cell phone data and invited him to come here and have coffee together. She gave me strict instructions that if Western Herdsman came, we would pretend we didn't know each other. Western Herdsman didn't respond to her invitation and Chrysanthemum looked rather crestfallen.

I realized then that that there was no hope for this turkey. She was only interested in pursuing the unattainable. And because unattainable, distances were only what she imagined them to be. So, in her mind a tiny minnow could be an enormous, heaven-spanning dragon.

This particular intermezzo was monotonous and tediously long. After hearing "Western Herdsman" for more than six months, my ears grew calluses. Always when Chrysanthemum was just about to lose hope, Western Horseman would drop old things in new guise down from heaven and create different romances, leaving her giddy and light-headed. After they dated he would then break off completely and vanish as if gone up in smoke. No need for anyone else to show her where she went wrong. She knew better than anyone. This man practiced what he preached and kept to the rules of the game. Dates were only dates. Don't get any bigger ideas. Don't overstep the boundary line even in the slightest.

This kind of game brought out the masochism in Chrysanthemum's underlying character. She suffered tremendously and she also found tremendous enjoyment as she sank into her unrequited love, like an imperial concubine of the rear palace longing for the emperor's favor. Day by day Chrysanthemum counted on her fingers the days until his summons came. Soon she was focusing on this alone and no longer felt like carrying out her vow to get married.

The period between his summons stretched out longer and longer. Chrysanthemum's game of unrequited love now had the acrid taste of a jilting. But the acrid taste was also a kind of enjoyment. In her Ah-Q way she said, "If these days there's still someone who can make me feel jilted, obviously such a man is a rare and precious animal." Chrysanthemum, to cite the classics on this, brought over some episodes of the sensational television serial, "Sex and the City," which had urban women all in an uproar. The female protagonist plays her cards out of turn and falls in love with a man she dates. On every date she tries to leave small feminine things in his bachelor apartment, like lipstick, hair clips, or a tooth brush. Each time, the man would "uprightly return the lost gold" to her afterward. Her unflagging love for him never abates and after the story develops through dozens of episodes, the director moves his heart in sympathy and shows the woman's clothing placed elegantly in the man's apartment.

So the possibilities were endless. Chrysanthemum was confident about bringing this game to a conclusion. She stood in front of the mirror, plucking up her courage. *Look, this woman, so attractive, so graceful and charming, cultivated, and able to earn money...she doesn't worry about the gorgeous powdered ladies in his six palaces. All she has to do is wait for him to finish inspecting all the spring colors of his world and suddenly look back, and in the waning lamplight there she is—my Chrysanthemum!*

Western Herdsman not only didn't suddenly look back, but, like a released fish, swished off free and easy, disappearing without a trace. He didn't return telephone calls or reply to messages left for him online. Miss Chrysanthemum was well and truly "banished to the cold palace," a major blow to her self-confidence. The game was over but the old recording still played "Western Herdsman." The white-haired maid of honor, cherishing the memory of those other years, repeated the ancient theme. "You can't imagine how nice, how delightful it was when he and I were together. It's not easy to come across two people so in love. I can't believe he could forget clean about me."

To find the answer, Chrysanthemum registered different information at the dating Web site and approached Western Herdsman in these new personas. When the melon was ripe enough to fall off its stem and a date was arranged, at the last minute she embraced the foot of the Buddha, so to speak, and sent *me* into the fray. She keyed in the online chat records and put me through a crash course. The things they had talked about were all over the place, from religion to loving and caring for small animals. In a sea so broad and under a sky so vast, she had found her match. Small wonder battle-scarred Chrysanthemum laid down her arms in surrender.

The curtain lifted for the prologue and I entered the stage as Chrysanthemum's understudy. The plot developed according to script. We had a romantic dinner on the weekend and Western Herdsman was attentive to me in every detail. After the meal, since he had not said all he had to say, the man suggested, "Let's leave the noise of the city and go to the outskirts to breathe some fresh air." So we set out for Huairou District, on the north side of Beijing, in a remodeled SUV. The night sights of the Great Wall, the bright moon, the stardust...

If there hadn't been a warning from Chrysanthemum's own chariot tracks, would I also have sunk into them, thinking I had encountered love? Western Herdsman spoke his lines from the script, but I went beyond the prescribed scene and asked, "Hey, you've got it all down about creating romance, but what if an online lady falls into your web and can't get out, then what?" He gave a big laugh, and not without some satisfaction. "My mission is to leave a little flavor in their insipid lives." I said that my life wasn't insipid, that it had all kinds of flavors all jumbled together, so one more or less wouldn't make much of a difference. "I really feel bad about wasting your time."

The practical joke that Chrysanthemum designed was for me to pretend to be intoxicated by romance. After we came down from the mountain, I would take him home, to Chrysanthemum's home, that is. Worried that I might get lost, she had drawn a map and put it into my pocket.

When Western Herdsman pointed to an airliner in the night sky, he said, "Doesn't that look just like a shooting star?" I thought how he had once said the very same thing to Chrysanthemum and was convulsed with laughter. He looked at me, puzzled. Time passed, minute by minute. Still I couldn't control my laughter. Western Herdsman must have groaned inwardly at his bad luck in running into this nutcase.

Sorry, Chrysanthemum, my laughing wasn't in the script and the performance died young. It was time to wind everything up before I ended up shaking everything out of the cloth bundle and giving her game away. Western Herdsman was still enough of a gentleman not to throw me out on the mountainside. He concentrated on driving the car and said not a word the whole way back to the center of the city.

I was giggling like some out-of-control motor as I pounded open Chrysanthemum's door. After letting me in, she peered all around me, as if Western Herdsman were following right behind. When she found out I had blown the performance, she furiously grabbed up a cushion from the sofa and hurled it at me.

"Oh, Chrysanthemum, don't get yourself into these one-sided love situations. The arrival of the Internet has created a borderless world, and so no one exists in his or her own special little sphere anymore. Even if you had double the charm, you've got to put yourself into perspective. Every day Western Herdsman can screen and select countless charming women just like you from the Internet. Why should he waste time on you alone? Who would just eye one course at a rich banquet and gorge himself only on it?"

Chrysanthemum looked at the ceiling uneasily, and after thinking for a long time, asked, "Don't people really need love anymore?"

This question was a bit academic, not like the thinking of a New Wave woman, and it took me aback.

Maybe it's not that people don't need love now, but the requirements for love have disappeared, like those organisms that became extinct on the earth. It wasn't that they sought their own extinction, only that the conditions for their survival no longer existed. Love was the product of agricultural society. In those times, people never knew very many other people over the course of their lives. If Lin Daiyu lived in the Internet age, would she have still hovered between life and death for Jia Baoyu?

"If there's no love in life, what's the sense of living?" Two brokenhearted teardrops rolled slowly down Chrysanthemum's face. "*Ai*, I shouldn't have been so obsessed with getting to the truth of this. Now that I have, the few wonderful images that remained are gone. I feel just like a total idiot. Never mind, I'll just marry my blockhead, Ah Mu."

Whenever verging on pessimism, she always thought of her computer repairman, Ah Mu. The guy still hovered moonstruck around her. This true love was worth protecting, like protecting an animal that was in imminent danger.

In fact, Chrysanthemum did not attain sudden enlightenment and marry Ah Mu. Rather, she began to go crazy making dates with Internet partners. In two months she saw over ten men. As she roamed about online, her luck went from bad to worse. She never dated anyone actually worth a second time. *Zhang Three's stare is too horny. Li Four's shoes are too dirty, and he's more of a blockhead than Ah Mu.* The last one she summoned was a software engineer. The software engineer told her that a certain company was currently developing a kind of software with which in the near future the Internet could send out pulses and link up with other Internet users' brains. All people had to do would be stretch out a finger and click on a key and you could get the feelings of the Seven Emotions and the Six Desires: love, fantasy, happiness, sadness, and even the feelings of floating like an Immortal after love and smoking dope. "The end of the world is here," mused the engineer.

Chrysanthemum had heaved a great sigh upon hearing this. "If such software hits the world, even Ah Mu wouldn't pay any attention to me. Everyone would just get married to their ice-cold computers. What a scary idea!"

She made up her mind to get out of these Internet games. It was as if by fleeing the Internet, she was fleeing the end of the world.

⌘　⌘　⌘

They say that God punished humanity for building the Tower of Babylon, but humans have never let go of their dream of building towers. Nowadays, the Internet, this present-day Tower, is going to break through the vault of heaven. How will God, if there really is a God who created and runs the universe, deal with rebellious humanity?

Chapter Twenty-Two – Farewell, West Gate

1.

SUDDENLY, "GOING INTO the mountains and down to the country-side"[58] had everyone stirred up once again in sleepy Old Town. The West Gate moat area was no longer the spot forgotten by time. Here, every pigeon coop of a dwelling had one or two young people who were mostly idle. Day after day this little corner resounded with drums, gongs, and firecrackers enthusiastically sending them off to merge with the tide of the times.

This deafening noise roused Dr. Lin from his fortress of isolation, and he and Second Sister busied themselves in sending off the West Gate youngsters. They had seen these young people grow up, and more than a few umbilical cords among them had been cut by the doctor himself. These children had grown like weeds but were now just hanging around West Gate Street with nothing to do. Some of them had even gotten into bad ways, like fighting and stealing, and this had always filled the doctor with worry. He

---

[58] A series of political campaigns throughout the 1950s, 1960s, and early 1970s, aimed at rusticating urban rightists, intellectuals, certain party members on the wrong side of internal political struggles, and, finally, the increasingly violent Red Guards and rebel factions, "to learn from the peasants."

supported these rustication movements, just as years before he had supported his own family's three children joining the army and the political side. Some of the neighbors couldn't make up their minds about sending their children to join this movement and they would come running over to ask the doctor's views. He always said firmly that the children should go.

He bought a lot of medicines for contingency needs, like *huangliansu* for diarrhea, Somidon, and mercurochrome, packed these in the local cowhide envelopes, and gave one to each young person about to leave West Gate. For several nights straight through to daylight, Second Sister rushed to sew together lined jackets for the children of poor families. Our old-style family sewing machine was bought at that time.

On this day, the front page of the provincial news displayed at the West Gate Street news board prominently featured the photograph of a female cadre wearing a big red flower. The article reporting her exemplary deeds was several thousand characters long and someone recognized her as the Lin family's daughter-in-law. People crowded two and three deep, commenting on this. "Look how she gave up her chance to be deputy director of the commerce bureau revolutionary committee. She intends to take her husband and child into the mountains and down to the countryside. This woman has long-range dreams. She must be aiming to be mayor or governor. The Lin ancestors were virtuous and their descendents have blessings and happiness."

Toward evening, the old codger in charge of the news board took down the newspaper and gave it to the Lins and, sticking up his thumb, said, "Dr. Lin, your family's daughter-in-law is something special. We West Gate people are going to produce a big shot, hey!"

The doctor and his wife were busy just then and after glancing at Fangzi's photograph, put the paper aside. A little while later,

Baoqing came in and the doctor handed the newspaper to him. "Fangzi has gotten a lot fatter. Tell her to go the hospital for a checkup. She may be suffering from an endocrine imbalance."

Baoqing stood blankly beside the sewing machine. Tomorrow he would be leaving Old Town and had come back here to say good-bye to his father and mother. He thought of the destitution and homelessness his mother had experienced in her lifetime. He looked at the wrinkles on her face and at her white hair. How could he bear to let her go through the pain of her family scattering in chaotic times again? For several days in a row now he had come back here, but he just couldn't say what he wanted.

Baoqing had never expected Fangzi to do this astounding thing. She was willing to pay so big a price to separate him from his parents.

Her satisfaction at being a part of officialdom never in the slightest diverted Fangzi's attention from her husband. When she discovered that Baoqing, under strict economic sanctions, had actually become an "inside" thief, lifting all the small change from the savings box, selling off old things, even a watch and heavy woolens, and bringing money to West Gate promptly every month, she gave up all hope. In her despair, her hatred of her mother-in-law was kindled to even greater heights and she thought of many ways to exact revenge. One of these was the frightening idea of sending Baoqing to jail. Just writing a big character poster exposing his reactionary comments would be enough to cause her mother-in-law to lose her son. *If I can't have him, then you can't either!* When she threatened Baoqing in this way, Baoqing showed no fear and only again calmly mentioned the word divorce. Just then, Fangzi, at her wits' end, received the Central Committee's internal document about cadre rustication. Right then and there, she decided leave Old Town and take Baoqing with her. In her application she signed for both husband and wife, and, fervid with revolutionary passion, requested a speedy departure to the toughest place possible.

Fangzi immediately became an important person in the Old Town news. "Learn from Fangzi and Baoqing" slogans were posted on the walls around the Commerce Bureau and colleagues trooped into Baoqing's office to congratulate him. Baoqing, like the proverbial mute who had eaten bitter herbs (and was unable to express his discomfort), could only voice some high-sounding words and slogans. The place that Fangzi had chosen was where Baoqing had fled to when he was a little boy, Nanjing County, that very same "it's a long story" place.

Baoqing pretended an interest on learning to pedal the sewing machine and help his mother do this work. He stalled to the last minute, and then he pulled from out of his shirt pocket a pile of banknotes, three months of support money that he had stolen from the drawer he had pried open.

"It's still early yet. Where did this money come from?" Second Sister asked.

Baoqing lowered his head and with some hemming and hawing replied, "Ma, you and Dad take good care of yourselves. I'm going away."

"Where are you going?"

Baoqing pointed his finger at the newspaper on the floor. Second Sister picked it up and brought it closer to the light to look at it. When she gathered what the article said, her anguished heart felt as if a piece had been cut out of it. She knew, of course, the real motive behind Fangzi's revolutionary act. *Oh, Baoqing! How could you have such a bitter fate, son?* Second Sister said nothing, though, and gathering up the material she had been working on, found a piece of cloth and hurriedly set out to make a little lined jacket for Wei'er.

That night, Second Sister couldn't sleep. The sky had not yet lightened as she stood at the gate of the commerce bureau, where small specks of lamplight shone in the bureau's living quarters. She had no idea which unit belonged to Baoqing's family. For many years now she had wanted to go see what building Baoqing lived in and how he passed his days, but she was afraid of causing trouble for him and so never went there. After she stood there in the cold wind for about an hour, Baoqing and his wife and child appeared amid drums and gongs.

Second Sister went forward and greeted Fangzi and covered Wei'er with the little lined jacket. Fangzi haughtily tilted her head to one side and didn't for one instant look at Second Sister. If Fangzi hadn't been surrounded by the crowd of people who were "learning from her," she certainly would have poured out abuse at this woman with whom she was struggling over the same man.

Baoqing came over to her and, putting his arm around his mother's shoulders, said, "Ma. Just go home. We'll meet soon."

He was thinking of divorce. He just had to leave this despotic woman who couldn't tolerate his mother.

"Son, be good to Fangzi, and treat her a bit better. You have to let her know that you belong to her. That from the day you were both married, you were hers."

Out of the corner of her eye, Fangzi caught sight of Baoqing's tears as he spoke with his mother. The jealousy that she had done all she could to repress exploded. She ordered Baoqing to go move their baggage. Fiercely she pointed at Second Sister's nose and said, "Do you know why your son has fallen this low? It was because of you! You'd better take a good look at him now, because you won't be seeing him again in this lifetime!"

Baoqing couldn't hear what Fangzi was saying, but he saw her expression and hand gestures. As he hastily and nervously turned back to take care of his mother, Second Sister said to him, "Fangzi wants Ma to make you a lined jacket. When you get there, write home as soon as possible and Ma will make you and Fangzi one each and send these to you."

Second Sister tried hard to look calm as she watched the long-distance bus depart. As it disappeared at the end of the road, she thought she was going to burst out in bitter tears and she took out her handkerchief, but not a drop fell. A vague presentiment within her was now gradually becoming clearer: *This was only the beginning. A new cycle of upheaval was beginning for the Lin family.* When her thoughts reached this point, she unconsciously straightened up. This was a strong woman who did not shed tears easily. When real difficulty hit, she would just straighten up and bear the weight of the crossbeam of their home. Even though she was now already an old lady of sixty-five, there was still no difficulty that could crush her.

⌘ ⌘ ⌘

Grandma's presentiment turned out to be true. Within six months, my Uncle Baosheng and his family, Enchun, and many relatives all left Old Town amid the drums and gongs. My mother was sent from the hospital in P Town and became a barefoot doctor in the rural areas. At that time, my stepfather was still in jail. Day after day, Grandma would stand under the oleander, looking out for the postman. Flowers blossom and fade in a very short season. Her hair was totally white now.

2.

THE REVERBERATIONS AND after-tones of the drums and gongs had not yet faded away when all of a sudden Old Town entered a Number One State of War Readiness. No one knew where the enemy was going to come from. The street idlers spoke to each other in low voices, just as if they were convening an emergency session of the Ministry of Defense, and each person was the most authoritative of military experts. Some said that the Soviet Union was going to drop an A-bomb on China. "Look, the newspapers are publishing popular science articles on how to defend against a nuclear war." Others said that American aircraft carriers were headed for Taiwan and that Chiang Kai-shek was going to counterattack the mainland. There were also rumors that the Number One State of War Readiness was connected with Marshall Lin Biao.

Before such "military secrets" had the chance to reach our home, Great-Auntie suddenly arrived, wiping her tears. "It's bad... this war business...We suffered through eight years of the War of Resistance, but this time for sure we'll never get through it. Second Sister, Ninth Brother, we'll only meet again in the next life in the next world."

Grandpa and Grandma looked at each other in blank dismay, unable to guess what was wrong this time with Great-Auntie. She leaned over the table and, between bouts of crying, told us the reason for all this. She and Rotten Egg had received a notice for emergency evacuation. In three days they were going to be sent to a little county about one hundred miles from Old Town. She drew from her stomach bib a piece of paper and read, "Little Bog Village, Bog Hollow Production Brigade, Bog Hollow Commune."

"Add Rotten Egg and me together and you get almost one hundred and fifty years. We'll never live through this war. Today is the last day we'll be meeting. Second Sister, Ninth Brother, I can't bear to lose you, really I can't. And then there's Hong'er..."

She pulled me toward her as she said this and took off a silver bracelet and put it on my own wrist.

The school was not holding classes now. Every day we dug air raid tunnels into the hill behind the Martyrs' Cemetery. This felt like a new kind of game. A bunch of us students of the same age would fill up a few baskets with earth, but most of the time we spent playing games and running around like crazy on the top of the hill. I thought Great-Auntie was teasing me, like that kid who played the joke of calling "Wolf!" She pulled my hand and was brokenhearted over our final parting. But I just laughed.

Grandma took the piece of paper and read over and over. "Is this true? With you two as old as you both are, too old for shoulder poles, and no strength in your hands, how can they order you to go out there?"

"It's not the mountains-and-countryside movement, it's an evacuation. There's going to be a war. Nowadays the bombs are much worse than during the time of the Japs. There won't be any more Old Town!"

My grandmother hovered between belief and denial. "You can't get out of going?"

"I thought of not going. I was born in Old Town, and here I'll die. But it's no good. The city government has issued the notice. When the time comes, they'll bring trucks and take us away. Second Sister, your older sister is going to become a lonely, wandering ghost. If you live through it, you've got to help me by looking after Ah Chang, shut up in the insane asylum. The Zhangs did evil things and are now receiving their retribution."

Grandpa sank into his throne with a long sigh and resumed his human vegetable state.

Pussycat was already senile now. The times it had torn up the roof tiles with its lovemaking had long gone. It wanted only to burrow into its master's chest and doze there. Even that height was more than it could manage, so it stuck by my grandfather's foot, mewing feebly. It didn't know its master had already shut his ears and closed his eyes.

My grandmother brought Great-Auntie to the No. 1 bus and when she got back home it was time to prepare dinner, but she just sat dully at the Eight Immortals table. The atmosphere at home made me uneasy and though my stomach was making hunger noises, I didn't dare ask Grandma for anything to eat.

Ah Ming came by when it was dark outside. He stood by the side of the sky well smoking cigarette after cigarette, and no sooner had he opened his mouth to say something when Grandma suddenly interjected, "Ah Ming, where is our family being evacuated to? Will you give us a few days to get ready?"

Ah Ming flicked away the cigarette butt. "Uncle, Auntie, I really would like to go in your place."

A military representative had come to West Gate. Ah Ming no longer had any real authority and couldn't protect Dr. Lin.

"Ah Ming, don't feel bad. No one can escape good fortune or bad. Just go ahead and tell us straight."

"I've put Mrs. Chen and her grandson together with your family of three to Nanping County. It's a commune not far from the train station. You have five day to get ready and I will help you by keeping watch over this house. With us in the house, not even one roof tile will go missing. Anyway, I really don't feel that war will break out. You're sure to come back soon."

After Ah Ming left, Grandma turned on all the lights in the house and went from room to room, not knowing where to start.

Suddenly, she thought before anything else she ought to send letters to her three children. In this home, correspondence was Grandpa's responsibility. She bent over and spoke into his ear, "Ninth Brother, can you write letters to our children and tell them where we will be evacuated to?"

Grandpa waved his hand slightly. "I'm not going anywhere."

She could think of nothing else she could do, so she just stood there, perplexed. All these years while she was coping with so many difficulties by herself, my grandfather not only *didn't* stand with her shoulder-to-shoulder through all this, but even baffled and frustrated her in every way. How did she provide the support to get through those years that were so beset with difficulties at home and outside?

⌘　⌘　⌘

Two days passed. Second Sister still couldn't calm down enough to organize the things they were going to take with them. She would open clothes closets and trunks and her mind would just draw a blank. She didn't know what to bring. When Baosheng and Baoqing left, not a tear had fallen from her eyes, for faith propped her up. She would hold the garrison at West Gate and wait for the children to come back. But the moment she received the evacuation notice, she really wanted to weep loudly and bitterly. To be suddenly uprooted at this age—would she still be able to return home alive? But she could not cry. A mansion was about to collapse. Her skinny shoulders, now enfeebled by age, were the final support columns. She had to hold everything up, right to the last minute.

The air at home thickened. The two old folks were preoccupied with their own separate matters as they numbly waited to be transported out. A scene hovered in front of Second Sister's eyes: The military representative of the revolutionary committee sending people to escort Ninth Brother out of the house and shove him onto the train. He lacked the strength to deal with reality. He might just turn against himself, or run off along the way, or not eat or drink or say a word. He was already seventy years old. How long could such a skinny old fellow hang on in the guttering-candle years of his life?

⌘   ⌘   ⌘

When Mrs. Chen received the evacuation notice she came to the Lin home with an old faded map that she spread out on the table. She appeared to be in high spirits, as if being given the chance to go to a place she had always dreamed of.

"Here, this is where we're going. Thirty years ago the pastor and I went there and preached the Good News. Back then, we set out from Old Town and walked seven days. Now by train it takes only a few hours. It's really convenient. Our fellow believers there are bound to remember Pastor Chen."

Second Sister looked at Mrs. Chen and smiled bitterly. She couldn't imagine why she was in such a good mood.

"Dr. Lin, it's a good place there, surrounded by mountains and water. The village people are extremely simple and unaffected. Take some medicines with you. They'll think you're Hua Tuo come back to the world."[59]

Her exalted mood stirred something in Dr. Lin. He opened his eyes and, just like his wife, puzzled over what she had to be so happy about.

"Dr. Lin, let's make a prayer to ask God to bless and protect us on the journey we are about to undergo. And let us also give thanks

---

[59]   From *The Romance of the Three Kingdoms*. Hua Tuo was a celebrated physician who met his end in 207 CE for refusing to treat Cao Cao, the great regional warlord and founder of the Kingdom of Wei.

that we're able to go to such a good place and that our two families can be together."

The doctor shook his head. "It's been a long time since I've known how to pray. I think God has forsaken me and Jesus doesn't want me."

"I completely understand how you feel. There was a time when I too asked the Lord Jesus, 'O Jesus, are you still with me?' Sometimes at night I would wake up in a sudden fright, thinking that there simply was no God in this world. That was really very, very frightening, for I had believed in God ever since I was little. I didn't know if life would have any meaning if there were no Lord. One night I dreamed of the Lord Jesus and seeing the blood flowing endlessly from him on the cross, I knew I was wrong. Our Lord has never forsaken me. It is only that our own faith weakens and goes astray."

"Lord Jesus," the doctor prayed in a choking voice, "ever since I was a boy I accepted you as the savior of my life. For many years I was very close to you. I beg you not to forsake me. Without your love, I am all alone and lonely."

"Amen!" The late pastor's wife clapped her hands joyfully. "Such a good prayer! Jesus has surely heard it! Dr. Lin, our God didn't promise that life on earth could be without difficulties, but He tells us that we will have happiness and peace by trusting in Him. Perhaps being evacuated to the mountain district is not just some chance matter. I myself don't understand why I feel so excited. It's like I've returned to my childhood years. When I was little and Mother would take me home to my grandmother's, the first night I was there I would be so excited I couldn't sleep. This is God working in me. As long as God is with us, the far corners of the earth are our garden."

Tears flowed from the doctor's eyes. "Yes, I was wrong."

Yes, how many years has it been now? I can barely feel my guardian angel, Second Sister thought. *What was it, after all? Did I leave my guardian angel, or did the angel leave me?* Forty years before, on the eve of her wedding to Ninth Brother, she was baptized in the West Gate church. From that time forward, she began to have a guardian angel by her side. Her guardian angel shared in her life's happiness and troubles. During those years when Ninth Brother had abandoned hearth and home, she would pour out her sorrows and anxieties to the guardian angel. She asked the angel to protect her missing husband and her three children. She clearly recalled that time when they were refugees and Baohua had been kidnapped and sold, the guardian angel had spread its wings and lifted her up. *O Angel, forgive me, please come back into my life and once again spread your wings and lift me up…*

That picture of them sending their son off to join the army was still hanging on the wall of the main hall. Starting then, she, an ordinary housewife, went into public life. She held the positions of committee head, women's representative, juror…all the various titles deluged her with work, while honors and recognition made her intoxicated and confused, and she could never spare the time or the strength to make a real prayer.

O God, O Angel, are you angry at me? Life has been so difficult over these past few years. Is it because this home has been without you?

In her heart, Second Sister called out, "Lord Jesus," and at that very instant, so many grievances welled up within her. *Lord Jesus, you surely have seen over these last years how perverse Ninth Brother's temper has been. I have looked after and cared for him day and night but I have no idea what he is thinking. I can't predict how he will behave. Day after day I am in a state of constant worry and alarm in case he might stir up some calamity. I often feel all alone and without strength, even more than during the War of Resistance when it felt like we were separated at different ends of the earth.*

The doctor sat there. His mind was replaying back his childhood. There were whispering sounds of Mr. Qiao's gentle voice: *Child, it was God who sent me to find you…O Lord, my life then was worth even less than a wild dog. If it hadn't been for your love, I never would have seen eight years. I wouldn't have survived the gunfire of the War, the butchery outside the walls of Nanjing. How could I have doubted you? But, Lord, if today you still love me, please receive me back at your side. I am not afraid of war and I refuse to go destitute and homeless if I am evacuated and have to become a refugee. Doesn't a person have the right to decide whether or not to be evacuated and to flee danger?*

⌘ ⌘ ⌘

The deadline arrived. Second Sister finally bestirred herself and set to organizing their travel things. The very first thing she thought of was to bring the old family cat, so she located a basket and tried putting Pussycat into it. "On the way, you take care of Pussycat, and I'll keep an eye on Hong'er," she said to Ninth Brother.

Ninth Brother raised his eyelids to look, but he didn't reply one way or the other.

Second Sister pressed the Bible into his hand. "You haven't read the Bible in a long time. When we reach there, let's read it together."

Ninth Brother again opened his eyes. "Second Sister, are you really so attached to this world?"

"What do you mean by that?"

"I don't want to go. If an artillery shell landed on my head, it would be because it had been fated to do so."

"Oh, you! Right up to now you still don't know that this isn't us fleeing. This is an evacuation. The government's issued the order. And obeying the government is Christian duty."

She also wanted to say. *If you don't go, you'll be staying here at West Gate all alone. I certainly don't want the government to send soldiers to arrest you at home tomorrow.* Heat roiled up within her and she really wanted to let fly with her temper, but all she could do was to clench her teeth and hold it in check as best she could.

At home the several hardwood boxes and crates were stacked up as high as a person. The sweat rolled down Second Sister's back as she moved these from this place to that. She had one last box to organize when suddenly everything went black before her eyes and she could see nothing at all. She felt her chest being all mangled and crumpled up as if by a steel claw. Then pain hit her like a typhoon and engulfed her like a tidal wave. Faintly she heard someone far, far off calling her name. In an eye-piercing ray of light she saw herself lying on the floor of the inner room. Two boxes were overturned and clothes scattered around. And Ninth Brother stood beside her, his face looking drained of all its blood.

Ninth Brother saw his wife, eyes closed and spitting out white foam as she lay on the floor, and was so terrified that he forgot that he himself was a doctor. The doctor who had gone through the gore and fire of war now stood there completely helpless. He had never expected that Second Sister would ever collapse like that. He thought that with her iron will she would keep a tiny safe haven for this family. But now she had fallen. It was only then that he realized that there were times when Second Sister couldn't bear the load. He thought of the worst possible situation, that they might be forever separated. Ninth Brother hadn't any recollection of his mother's death. He didn't know that his own misery and terror at this time was like that of a child bereft of its mother.

Second Sister saw Ninth Brother's two legs slowly bend down to kneel by the bed. She heard his heartbroken voice. "Lord, why are you punishing me this way? You can't have saved me time after time simply to make me suffer these blows."

She said, "Ninth Brother, I didn't die. I wouldn't abandon you."

Second Sister felt she was like a cloud of smoke or mist swirling around Ninth Brother and speaking comforting words to him.

Ninth Brother couldn't hear her, and kept on praying. "Lord, I don't know how I will go on living. Since you've taken Second Sister, please take me, too…"

"Ninth Brother, help me up."

Ninth Brother turned around and his eyes met Second Sister's tender gaze. He excitedly hugged her, "Second Sister, Second Sister, you can't go off without me, you can't."

"I'm thinking of just getting this all over with. The day will soon be light and the trucks will be here. I'll be going, but you just stay here at home."

Ninth Brother's eyes reddened and he laughed sheepishly at Second Sister. "Just now you scared me to death, I can't be without you…"

This was the Ninth Brother she knew so well, the Ninth Brother she hadn't seen in so long. This very scene made her think of that late summer night in 1943. She was right beside the well, washing clothes when all of a sudden she picked up the sound of Ninth Brother's voice behind her. She didn't dare turn around but stared hypnotized straight ahead at the moon through the tree branches. She was filled with doubt. *Am I dreaming?* Ninth Brother had walked over in front of her and taken her in his arms, laughing sheepishly.

"Second Sister, I'm sorry, I know this is more difficult for you than for anyone else. These years I have not felt the existence of God, nor have I felt your existence. There's a lot of things I really don't understand, nor do I want to understand. But so long as we can be together, that is my greatest happiness."

Second Sister reached out her hand and stroked Ninth Brother's wildly tousled hair. "It's late. Go get your own things organized."

Ninth Brother nodded his head obediently.

3.

YOU STILL REMEMBER that boss-lady of the rice shop who in one night lost both her sons? She was still an unchanging part of the West Gate crossroads. Somehow people all believed that the old woman set into the window like inlay was quietly mad. It was for just this reason that she had been able to avoid all the political movements. And so she also escaped this evacuation in preparation for war.

The boss-lady clearly recalled the last time that Huang Shuyi came to West Gate. It was two and a half years to this day. It was when Mrs. Chen talked with the vagabond woman under her window and so she found out that Huang Shuyi was Mrs. Chen's daughter-in-law. Her dried-up and numb eyes moistened as she recalled when Shuyi was the lively and attractive eldest miss of the Huang family and she didn't understand how Huang Shuyi could have fallen to such a state. All she knew was that Huang Shuyi came to West Gate to see her little son and so she sympathized with her as a fellow sufferer. After the pastor's wife moved out of the church with her grandson, every time the boss-lady saw the ragged woman appear at the West Gate street crossing, she would hurriedly call her husband. "Quick! Quick! Go out and tell Miss Huang that her son has moved to the side of the moat!" Her husband always obeyed her every word, but time and again he would fail to find the woman.

The doctor and Mrs. Chen came to say good-bye to the boss and the boss-lady. In over twenty years, these two were the only people ever to go to the upper floor of the rice shop. The doctor had treated the boss-lady and the pastor's wife had prayed for her, though the boss-lady still did not believe in God. Obstinately she told Mrs. Chen that if there were a God, why hadn't He returned her two sons to her? The boss-lady told Mrs. Chen to leave her address with her. Nothing on earth is more heartbreaking and tragic than a mother unable to see her own son. She would keep her eyes peeled and when Miss Huang reappeared, give the address to her.

On this day, a misty rain fell outside the window and a woman in a peasant's conical bamboo hat was loitering by the wooden fence around the church. The boss-lady grew excited and called to her husband, "Quick! Quick! Miss Huang is here! Go stop her! Her son is going away tomorrow!"

The boss squinted at the main street. He felt this woman didn't look like Miss Huang, but still he submitted to his wife's will and so he ran outside.

The woman in the conical hat was dressed simply and neatly. The boss decided that his wife had "faulty intelligence" and he was just about to turn back when the woman stopped him.

"Uncle, previously the Chen family lived here. Their daughter-in-law's surname was Huang. Do you know where they have moved to?"

Someone else was looking for Miss Huang too? I guess I didn't run out for nothing today.

"Who are you?" the boss asked.

"Do you know her whereabouts?"

"First you tell me, what is your relationship to her?"

"It's a long story. I was her brother's war comrade. I have a very important matter to tell her."

The boss was bewildered. *What important matter could be related to that crazed Miss Huang?* Those were incredible times when everybody looked crazy to everyone else.

"Her mind has gone bad. She has no fixed place to stay and has wandered about everywhere for a very, very long time now."

"Uncle, there's nothing wrong with her. I know what she's doing and I can help her."

⌘　⌘　⌘

Up at the window, the boss-lady saw her husband taking the woman in the conical hat in the direction of the city moat. She thought it was Miss Huang, so after feeling a great sense of relief, she immediately sank into self-pity. To date, her two sons had been away twenty years, nine months, and seven days. She had counted every day as she looked out.

After this, she went on counting for nine years, two months, and twenty-three days. Right when the count reached exactly thirty years, the boss and the boss-lady drank poison and their lives departed for the Yellow Springs. The West Gate folk never again saw the white-haired old lady who seemed a part of the window. However, their story didn't end with their lives, for just that year at autumn two travelers who had been away for almost thirty-one years returned to Old Town by way of Hong Kong. They got out of a car at the West Gate crossroads and threw themselves on the ground right in front of the rice shop. Old people of the neighborhood recognized them as the sons of the rice shop owner's family.

⌘　⌘　⌘

Huang Shuyi's luck was truly terrible. Heaven seemed bent on playing blind man's bluff with her, for every time she stretched out her hand within reach of her target and could just about grasp the historical truth, it would shift her line of vision elsewhere. In the 1950s, she found the Zhang family in the South Town district of Old Town. If she could have chatted just a bit with Great-Auntie, she would have found out the connection between the Zhang family and the Lin family at West Gate. Perhaps Great-Auntie could have stood up and borne witness on behalf of Huang Shuyi's brother. But she had been confused by the evasive replies of Old Rotten Egg Zhang, and let the opportunity pass by.

This woman in the conical bamboo hat held important proof in her hand. She was resolved to stand witness and prove that Huang Jian had been innocent and had died unjustly. But no one could locate Huang Shuyi. The only person who was concerned about her was Mrs. Chen. Sometimes in a fit of pessimism the pastor's wife supposed that Huang Shuyi may have become a wandering spirit and she felt very bad that she had not been able to save her.

⌘   ⌘   ⌘

The woman in the conical hat entered a dim little hut by the side of the moat. Before saying a word she wept quietly for some time. Mrs. Chen, thinking that she had come with bad news about Huang Shuyi, lowered her head and joined her in silent tears. In her heart she said, "Lord, all my life I have brought multitudes into your embrace, but I have been unable to bring my own off-spring to turn to you. I don't understand why this should have been so."

"Aunt, I have met you. Twenty years ago we used the church for cover and held our meetings there. I never imagined that I would bring a life of calamity to Enchun and Huang Shuyi."

Where to begin with all of this? The pastor's wife stopped her tears and looked at this unknown woman who had suddenly paid her a visit.

The woman smiled ruefully. "It's a long story. Originally, I was to have been Huang Shuyi's sister-in-law. Her older brother, Huang

Jian, was my teacher. It was he who brought me to join the guerrillas on Old Ridge."

She was an attractive woman. With all the wrinkles of a complex and event-filled life crisscrossing her face, traces of the beauty she once had still showed. The Old Ridge guerrillas and the locals had all called her "Dujuan," which means both "azalea" and "cuckoo," for they said she looked like this flower and like the bird.

Before that thing happened to Huang Jian, Dujuan had been assigned to the newly established liberated area to give literacy classes to the peasants. The two of them hadn't seen each other for several months. One day, one of the guerrillas, a Deputy Commissar Cao, crossed over the hills and mountains in search of her. He told her that Huang Jian had been a traitor and enemy agent, and had already been executed on the spot. Later, she married Deputy Commissar Cao and lived a peaceful ten years or more as an official's wife. During the Cultural Revolution neither of them was able to escape that unfolding catastrophe, and both husband and wife went into many cowsheds.

She was still suspected of being a traitor. Two months previously, her husband had been accurately diagnosed with late-stage liver cancer and the state of his disease worsened rapidly. When he was near death, he tearfully said to his wife, "I apologize to you. And I apologize to Huang Jian." As he said this, he kept pointing to underneath his pillow, but then sank into a coma which he never came out of. Under the pillow, she found a letter written to the organization department of the provincial party committee, and in it Deputy Commissar Cao stated the historical truth—"Huang Jian was killed by my hand. At the time there was no evidence at all proving that he was a traitor. This was a tragedy I created completely out of personal selfishness."

Dujuan, as she was known on Old Ridge, took care of her husband's funeral matters and then immediately began her efforts on behalf of Huang Jian's rehabilitation. She located the remaining few guerrilla leaders and, giving them Deputy Commissar Cao's letter to read, requested them to sign in testimony to the truth of its contents. She went to the provincial revolutionary committee, but in such chaotic times all the former guerrillas were suspected of being traitors, so who would take the trouble to distinguish between the real traitors and the ones who were not? She knew that over the past twenty years, Huang Shuyi was always going here and there crying out the injustice done to her brother. She had seen her standing at the gate of the provincial party committee bearing her written petition and calling out her claim of injustice. She too thought this younger sister of Huang Jian was insane and wiped the tears from her eyes quietly as she sidestepped by her. Today she was going to find Huang Shuyi and carry on the battle shoulder-to-shoulder with her.

Mrs. Chen took a packet of written materials from the other woman's hand and placed them in safekeeping upstairs at the rice shop. The boss-lady leaned on the windowsill looking out for three more years before she saw the form of Huang Shuyi.

After I married Chaofan I had the opportunity to read Huang Shuyi's letters. By that time Huang Jian was already at rest in the Martyrs' Cemetery. In her letters she recalled the endless road to rehabilitate her brother, and between the lines there radiated pride and happiness. On the address portion of each envelope she inscribed the single slogan: "Truth Shall Triumph!" She told her son that during the Cultural Revolution she had never ceased fighting for the truth and that she had wanted to go to Beijing to find Chairman Mao. Again and again she would be arrested on board some train and then escorted back to Old Town. In the end she decided to follow the train tracks to Beijing on foot. It took over two years for this broken journey, for she had to stop and earn money to keep herself going and for what she would have to spend on lodgings in Beijing. All along the railroad line many women earned money by breaking up rocks. They used iron hammers to break big rocks into small ones for use in road surfacing and after breaking up a cubic meter of rock they could earn a few *mao*. Huang Shuyi mingled with local women, making up a story of how her son had been lost playing by the railway and that she wanted to follow the tracks to find him. This story was the best way to get the women's sympathy and shield her from harm along the way to Beijing.

4.

THE WHISTLE BLEW and the dilapidated train began to wheeze and creep forward. On the platform were still crowds of people swarming around, shifting and moving all manner and sizes of packs and bedrolls. If you had thrust a camera lens into the dense mass of black-haired heads, you would have seen face after impassive, resigned face. One thousand people, ten thousand people, all had the same expression. That was the decade when the whole palette of human emotions had been forgotten.

All those scenes floating in my memory are surprisingly clear and complete. It's as if at the time my eyes had been some kind of adjustable movie camera taking close-ups and wide-angle shots in every direction. Actually, I couldn't see anything at all. My puny little body was jammed in between Grandpa and Grandma when an overwhelming force from all around heaved me next to the train. What I remember was Ah Ming lifting both me and Chaofan and shoving us through a train window. I didn't know at what moment the train started to move. When I next looked up, Old Town was way off in the distance.

The people in the aisle were standing chest to back. On the seats one person would be stacked up on someone else. Even when the windows were open, the air was still unbearably stinky. Some people had to pee very badly but they really couldn't squeeze through there, so all they could do was pull down the window and let loose. More than one woman wet her pants.

No one felt startled or dismayed by this. Nothing was thought to be very remarkable.

Once, in my comfortable home in Beijing while sitting on my comfortable sofa, I watched a foreign war film—an apathetic-looking woman, escaping some calamity in a horse-drawn carriage, is holding an infant to her breast; the infant slips out of her grasp; the woman simply raises her eyelids a little.

This scene reminds me of the so-called evacuation I experienced as a child. I can well understand that woman's exhaustion and indifference.

Ah Ming grabbed a seat for our two families. We hadn't fully settled in when we were inundated by one person after another. Three old gaffers stood squeezed in a tight bunch right between the two rows of seats, so Chaofan and I crammed underneath. Pussycat, packed into a small basket, saw us and meowed wildly.

I fished out of my pocket that deck of old cards. "Let's play Winner."

Glassy-eyed, Chaofan replied with something quite different. "We're all going to die. No one can survive when an atom bomb explodes. You can run away as far as you want but it's no use."

"Are you afraid?"

"Not afraid. It would be good to die. I hope the whole world dies."

As he said that, his two eyes shone cruelly. Now *I* became afraid.

I am not sure when this started, but my little playmate seemed to have turned into two totally different persons: one cold and even brutal, the other weak and tender. I often found myself entranced by this. I never knew which Chaofan I was confronting.

Just the night before, we were under the bridge that spans the moat. There we had earlier dug a little trench and buried what we considered our valuable possessions: remnants of stamps from after the catastrophe, candy wrappers, a few marbles...Now that we were going to say good-bye to West Gate we went there to dig up our treasures. With tears in his eyes, Chaofan told me many secrets of his life, about his grandpa and mother. He was worried that one day she would come back to West Gate, and not finding him, would go stark raving mad.

Whenever he was weak and tender, it felt like we were both playing house. He pretended to be my son and I pretended to be his mother. I would imitate the way Grandma coaxed me, patting him on the back and saying, "Be good. It's all right now." However, whenever I wasn't careful he would turn into the other person. I saw him burn a frog to death and catch a bird and pluck out all its feathers one by one. It was impossible for anyone to stop these cruelties. At times like that I got so scared I would run away as fast as I could.

At this moment, I also see that bleak but unyielding look on Grandma's face. I see her look like that as she stands on the ruins of the Lin residence and as she stands in the refugee passenger car. In this family of three generations, each person is a piece of her heart and from this heart piece after piece has been sliced away and fallen off to the ends of the earth. How could an ordinary housewife know how to bear such reality? But no matter where we were going to next, she could not collapse, she could not fall. So long as one person in her family needed her protection, she would stubbornly and tenaciously spread her wings as a shield to the death against the winds and rain.

⌘   ⌘   ⌘

Our destination was a mountain hollow where a mud hut awaited us. The dirt floor was spread with hay and the place had nothing, no water, no rice or food, no firewood. On top of the oven was a cooking pan as big as a bathtub.

This was to be our new home? I vaguely realized that this move meant the beginnings of new trials and tribulations and I sat down absentmindedly on the hay. When it turned pitch black outside, I automatically walked to the side of the door and groped for the lamp cord. I felt the mud wall, and lots of dirt came loose. Looking more closely, I realized that there was no electric light here and for a second I was totally stunned.

Painful sensations started from the palms of my hands and feet. It was as if feet and hands also have grown hearts that can sense what other people feel. Pains like poisonous snakes slithered through my veins and finally gathered in my chest. I thought of the silkworm eggs that I had forgotten at West Gate. By the time the spring thunderstorms came next year, the little worms would be crawling out of their eggs. Who would feed them mulberry leaves? I wept brokenheartedly.

⌘　⌘　⌘

We stayed in the mountain hollow only a little over two months. The war-readiness evacuation was suddenly cancelled and it was only after the various members of our two families returned to Old Town did we hear that the evil genius of this exercise had been Lin Biao. By the time we left Old Town he had already crashed to his death in the Mongolian desert. But Old Town's revolutionary committee was still carrying out his orders. We were that isolated.

The deepest impression those two months or so left with me was how homesick I felt. It's an ailment that's hard to put into words. During the days in the mountain hollow my homesickness was like a kind of illness. I thought of my home at West Gate, and always when I ailed like this, my mind would dwell on some small object, some kind of familiar smell.

After I left Old Town, I lived in different buildings, some big, some small, but none of them my home. My home is in Old Town, at West Gate. The old house that no longer exists there often appears in my dreams. To this day, whenever I hear the sound of cooking going on in other people's homes, I think of Grandma in the kitchen, bustling about.

CHAPTER TWENTY-THREE —
NOT 1,001 ARABIAN NIGHTS, REALLY

1.

IT WAS ALWAYS the same, that scene on the other side of the French windows. The white-haired old fellow with the pedicab appeared in the slow lane under the dappling shadows of the trees, while the old lady sat behind him, leisurely drinking tea.

And Chrysanthemum was, as always, daintily stirring her coffee with a tiny spoon. She was sitting across from me and gazing sidelong at that happy little vehicle until it passed from view.

This was just an ordinary day, mild, not cold and not hot. Miss Chrysanthemum wasn't mourning a love gone bad, nor did she have a new story to tell. Her calmness and reserve piqued my interest.

"I've heard that out in the western suburbs there's a peasant woman, a psychic who can see everyone's futures. Lots of well-known movie stars and business big shots go there to have their fortunes told. It used to be a session cost less than a hundred *yuan* but now it's jumped up to almost a thousand, and you've got to make an advance booking. I'd like to go take a look. You want to come?"

I thought this over for a second and then shook my head. Grandma once said that fortune-telling revealed God's plan and would anger him. Even though I wonder a lot about my future, I've never had my fortune told.

"I think I get into these situations only from lack of foresight. *Ai*, had I only known things would turn out the way they did, I would have acted differently. Look at the men I chucked out. Just take any one of them and he would be a hundred times better than the ones hanging around me now. I always thought the future was far off, but all my futures fast become my pasts. So I've got to go and see if I still have any future at all."

I guessed something had provoked Miss Chrysanthemum again. Those past lovers of hers actually had no intention of retaliating against her. If they still even thought of her, perhaps they clasped their hands in front of them and thanked their lucky stars at having escaped such a mixed-up lady. But the way they were getting on with their lives today always made Chrysanthemum lose her cool. For example, that time when she ran into her former husband, hand in hand with his daughter and going into McDonald's. That picture of father-daughter happiness gave Chrysanthemum a massive gut-wrenching. She had been pregnant three times by this man, and three times she had gone on the abortion table. In those days she dreamed too much of the future.

Chrysanthemum laughed as she said self-mockingly, "I'm the worst kind of tough-luck investor. I'm forever throwing away stock with real potential when it's at its low, only to watch it appreciate before my very eyes. I always end up losing my shirt. You still remember that artist I told you about?"

That was a painter without a *fen* to his name. Chrysanthemum loved him and they lived together. The place they rented was stacked with oil paintings that had interested no one. After several months of passion, she could no longer bear this loser of a man and moved out of the place they had been sharing, without a backward glance.

Three years went by, and Chrysanthemum had almost forgotten she once had an artist-lover. This morning she had passed by an art gallery when a familiar name on the billboard crashed into view. She just couldn't believe that *this* man had been *that* man. She bought an entrance ticket to see what this was all about, and there he was, her former lover. Those paintings once considered garbage were now hanging grandly in the exhibition hall and each one had a price tag that made her eyes bulge. Over there the artist was saying something, surrounded by television cameras, ordinary cameras, and several hot-eyed girls. She purposely slowed her pace as she walked by him. His expression didn't register any change.

"Would you say he didn't recognize me, or simply didn't see me at all?"

I so wanted to express my sympathy, but I just couldn't help it, I burst out laughing instead. Chrysanthemum started laughing too until her face was wet with tears.

Yesterday she passed through illusory dreams headed for the future, headed for today. When she opened her eyes, what she saw was a colorless reality. Fate was playing games and placed a similarly colorless Ah Mu in front of her, as if to say, "If you still want to get married, then just make do with this man."

The future is unforeseeable magic. It's like there's some willpower superior to your own, manipulating this magic. Whose willpower is that?

⌘　⌘　⌘

I thought of Chaofan and was pierced by pain. That slammed the brakes on my laughter. Because of my vanity and my Ah Q self-regard, I had never told Chrysanthemum that I had the very same experience and feelings. I had no right to laugh at her foolish conceits.

To keep my U.S. green card effective, every year, no matter how busy or hard up I was, I just had to fly to America and shut myself in Xiaoli's home for a few days in a sort of confinement. Then, without waiting to get over my jet lag, I'd fly muzzy-headed back to Beijing. Every time I shut myself up in Lompoc, I wrestled indecisively with whether or not I should see my lawful husband. I'd lift up the phone, only to put it back down again. Actually, it would have been extremely easy to get together. Every few days he drove the two hundred miles or so to see his daughter and, after taking her out for a meal, drove back the same night. I knew the restaurant where they had dinner and a ten-minute trip could take me there, but I never took that ten-minute trip. The shorter the distance the more deeply I felt my disappointment in him.

This spring, I was at a gas station in Lompoc when I unexpectedly ran into him. At the time I was driving Xiaoli's old junk heap. Right in front of me at the pump was a silver BMW sports model. A thought flashed through my head: *when would I too have a sports car like that one?* Out of the car stepped a man who looked Asian, and when he turned around after unhooking the gas nozzle, I just couldn't contain myself and shouted, "Chaofan!" He turned at the sound and looked over. He didn't show any surprise when he saw me. He casually finished filling his tank and paid by credit card. Then, like a real gentleman, he moved his car to the side and used his own card to fill up my car with gas. He asked me if I wanted to join him for dinner with our daughter. I shook my head.

After leaving the gas station, I couldn't remember what I had come out to buy. I drove the car to some secluded place and just let my tears of heartbreak and grievance flow freely.

I didn't know what I was so brokenhearted about or what wrongs had been done to me. Even if there were a hundred suppositions, not one of them could have made me stay by his side, enduring the long and utterly hopeless days.

He now had money. His music studio earnings weren't bad, plus he had received an inheritance from Taiwan. His grandfather on his mother's side had long ago been Boss Huang of Old Town's electric-light factory, who, on the eve of Liberation, had chartered a boat to escape from the mainland. In the 1980s, when he was on his deathbed, Boss Huang called in his lawyer to write his last will and testament. He placed one-third of his assets into a trust fund for Huang Jian and Huang Shuyi on the mainland, so, accordingly, Chaofan became a beneficiary as well.

If this story sounds so much like something out of the Arabian Nights, it really and truly happened during my lifetime.

⌘　⌘　⌘

Chrysanthemum's eyes grew bigger and bigger. The "willow leaf" eyebrows she had so carefully applied practically stood on end. "Heaven! O heaven! Is this true? You're still not yet divorced, are you? Either put the broken mirror back together again, or approach him for a part of the property."

I took a sip of coffee, and shook my head ruefully. Right then I was in urgent need of money but I wasn't about to go to Chaofan. In his eyes I was already a flunky, and I absolutely could not give him a new reason to verify his conclusion.

"Get a lawyer! If you can't split it fifty-fifty, at least get one-third!" Chrysanthemum was all worked up, as if she were party to a property lawsuit herself. "My dear elder sister, it's money, you know. We're rolling around in the market and our scars from being stabbed in front and in back are piling up. Hasn't this all been for the money?"

Bringing Chaofan to court and suing for money—this scene flitted through my mind as if the past years, my past life, were being uprooted and burned to ashes. I couldn't bear such brutal reality.

"Chrysanthemum, don't joke like that! It's not funny! It's not the least bit funny!"

"Who's joking? Oh, I see. You like to save face. You want to wait until he brings the money to you in humble, outstretched hands. And when he does, you're still going to pretend none of it's worth any of your time, so why bother?"

⌘   ⌘   ⌘

Early one morning, I was groggy from sleeping late when the phone rang. Beibei shouted "Ma," but after that there was a long pause.

I shifted the blanket and sat up. "Darling, what is it?"

"Ma, why did you write that letter?"

"What letter?"

"He's forwarded the letter to me..."

I was baffled. Over the past two years, I had written him only one e-mail. That was the time he wanted to take our daughter to study in San Francisco and I hadn't agreed to that. I couldn't let her witness his chaotic life-style. My wording had been completely businesslike.

"He told me to reply to you that he hoped that you weren't going to bring up the past. He said he had no history, no past, and he's never loved any woman."

I was pretty agitated now and I jumped out of bed. "You tell him, 'Don't flatter yourself!'"

"Ma, I really don't understand. Why do you both want to make everything so tangled up and puzzling?"

My mind then turned to Chrysanthemum. It had to have been *her*, that cluck who thinks the world isn't messed up enough. That day in the office, she borrowed my computer! *How was I going to explain this? Oh, Chrysanthemum, Chrysanthemum, I could just tear you to bits!*

"Beibei, I can say only that wasn't me who wrote it."

"So who's playing the big joke?"

"Forward me the e-mail and I'll take a look at it."

⌘ ⌘ ⌘

Five minutes later, I saw on my computer a deeply affectionate love letter. In it were things that Chaofan and I had experienced together in the past. My nose twitched, a sure sign of coming tears, and all the feelings of injustice and anger that filled me softly faded away.

Maybe subconsciously I did want to write such a letter. Only I understood Chaofan and what sort of feelings he would have. His reactions are more intense than I can imagine. His hatreds are more, much more, than I know about. I believe that he hates not just me, but the whole world. This world owes him. All the people in the world who are connected to him owe him.

How could such a person have gotten to be so sad and lonely?

I won't explain to him that I didn't write that e-mail, because I still ache for him. I'm just sad that I don't have the strength to go and warm his ice-cold lump of a heart.

⌘   ⌘   ⌘

When I met with Chrysanthemum again she looked at me with a worried expression. "Don't tell me that there's not the slightest hope now? He still hasn't fallen in love with anyone else, has he? Your luck is as tough as mine. Something always seems to cross us up..."

I kept a grim look as I complained about how she thought she was so clever but had made such a mess of things. In the end, though, I couldn't hold my laughter back any longer.

"Hey, people from Taiwan have been coming back to the mainland looking for relatives from as far back as the 1980s. How come your husband has only gotten money over these past two years?"

My husband? Who is my husband? What a strange term.

2.

WHEN SHE SAW the "Seeking Relatives" message in the newspaper, Huang Shuyi was then on the train headed for Beijing. She read: "Father and Mother's mounting grief from missing their son and daughter left behind on the mainland became an illness, and both passed away three years ago." For an instant there leapt before her eyes the long-ago scene of her mother and the serving girls kneeling before her. She felt a twinge of grief and sadness and her vision grew misty. Afraid that the two young people beside her would see her in this weak and teary state, she quickly got up and went into the washroom.

The train setting out from Old Town was going to cross the Yangzi River. The trip took more than twenty hours. Huang Shuyi talked about the greater part of her life spent in the Revolution. Her two young traveling companions were literature enthusiasts and said they wanted to make a movie of this marvelous tale of the female guerrilla fighter. Huang Shuyi really let herself go and, without knowing it, fashioned all kinds of embellishments and mixed in many fictitious details. For example, she said the other guerrillas had called her "Dujuan," and that she could fire a gun in each hand. When the local Old Ridge bandits and bullies heard the name "Old Ridge Dujuan," they just collapsed in terror.

She hadn't cried for years. At her brother Huang Jian's memorial ceremony many of her old comrades from those years had wept, and the real Old Ridge Dujuan had wept until she fainted. Enchun was there, supporting himself with a cane in one hand and wiping his tears with a tissue held by the other. Along with Huang Jian's rehabilitation, his party membership had been restored. Huang

Shuyi looked at him and thought: *For thirty years I fought a war single-handed and today you sit there reaping what you never sowed. Aren't you ashamed of yourself?* There were also several other war comrades present who likewise made her angry. They had distanced themselves from her campaign to safeguard the truth. She felt if only she could weep and wail now that the gross injustice done to her brother had been righted, but her eyes held only the flames of her anger.

Huang Shuyi looked in the washroom mirror at the two lines of tears on her face. *What are you crying for? Don't tell me you're sorry for having chosen the path of the Revolution? No, even though it's been tough and winding, I've never regretted my choice. When I entered the party, I took an oath to struggle for communism all my life. If I regretted that, wouldn't that make me a traitor? The day that my brother and I joined the Revolution, we completely broke off relations with our bourgeois family.*

At that time, the brother and sister were persecuted by their father. To stop her from joining the student movements, the father had locked her up at home and threatened Huang Jian. "If you let your sister join the communists I'll report you to the police. When the day comes that your head hangs from the city wall, don't blame me for being cruel." *They were counterrevolutionaries to the bone. To think that I lost my correct stance by shedding a tear over them!*

Huang Shuyi crumpled the newspaper up into a ball and threw it into the garbage pail. She turned on the faucet and gave her face a good washing, then returned to her seat. There she asked the two young people, "Where did I leave off just now?"

"On the eve of Liberation you were in a small coastal town doing underground work," someone prompted her.

"Ah. When I saw so many rich people chartering boats to escape from the mainland, I knew that the Revolution was just about to succeed, and that was real happiness. My father too had chartered a boat and on his way stopped by that little seaside town to fetch me. My mother brought the serving maids and they all kneeled down in front of me..."

"*Wah!*" exclaimed one of the youths. "Your family was really rich!"

"Oh, yes. You can't choose your background, but you can choose the path of the Revolution."

"You ought to put a notice in the paper to find them. A portion of your family's property is yours," said the other one.

How could these two kids think like this? Could they write a proper revolutionary story? she wondered.

⌘ ⌘ ⌘

Enchun arrived early on the day of the memorial service and saw an old woman, withered and bent over as a hunchback, arranging the place. He made no connection at all between her and Huang Shuyi. When he heard someone call out, "Shuyi," the old woman responded and went over to shake hands and catch up on old times. Enchun asked an old comrade-in-arms beside him, "Is that Huang Jian's younger sister, Huang Shuyi?" This other person sadly nodded his head. Enchun went forward and, putting out his hand, said in a choking voice, "Shuyi, you have suffered much." Huang Shuyi pushed aside his hand, her eyes bulging in rage. "You don't deserve to stand before a revolutionary martyr!"

Now that her brother had been rehabilitated and her Party membership restored, Huang Shuyi had no plans of settling down in Old Town. Her decades of pursuing this litigation had now become a way of life for her. Having won her own lawsuit, she also wanted to help other people do the same. She now had her hands full with twenty or thirty lawsuits. One of these was an appeal for redress which she helped put together for a peasant woman in

Hubei who had been persecuted by a township cadre. There was also a case of a certain department store in Beijing that had sold her a package of past-date biscuits. Her written complaint had been sent to the Ministry of Commerce but there had been no reply yet. She had already bought the train ticket and was ready to set out once again.

Enchun paid no mind to Huang Shuyi's harsh words. After the service concluded he followed her out. He said that the school had given him a three-room apartment in line with his full professor's salary. He could think of how to convert this arrangement into two small, one-room apartments and asked Huang Shuyi to stay and spend her final years in peace and comfort here. Huang Shuyi was scornful. "Chen Enchun! A full professor's salary, and three rooms, and now you can be pleased with yourself. I despise you. Losing the revolutionary will to fight is the same as losing your life. Though you're alive, you're no different from being dead."

This shut Enchun up. He stood there and watched Huang Shuyi's departing figure moving farther and farther away. The thought that this may well have been their last meeting filled him with a deep sorrow.

In the mid-1990s, the Huang family brothers on Taiwan, after much searching, finally located Enchun, and with the information provided by him, arrived in Beijing. For the next few days, the television program for seeking relatives broadcast the Huang Happy Family portrait and a photograph of Huang Shuyi at the memorial service.

A service attendant at a basement hotel realized that the person the television was looking for was that wretched old lady who had lodged there the whole year. She was so surprised she started yelling and shouting. The guests had no idea of what was happening and thought the hotel had caught on fire. When Huang Shuyi returned from traveling outside the city, she was mobbed and informed of the wonderful news. But Huang Shuyi calmly said, "From the day I joined the Revolution, I broke off relations with my family." The attendant chased after her to her room, a little windowless nook of about thirteen square feet in area. "Auntie Huang, you're going to be *rich*! Later, when you're living in a grand hotel and I come to take you out for some fun, will you still know me?" Huang Shuyi sat her down and gave her some ideological education. The girl went running off, giggling. Huang Shuyi then made her decision and placed a telephone call to the number provided by the television station.

She was true to her word. She insisted on living in this basement and no one could make her move. She stayed there right until that old building was demolished and only then did she move into a room with a window.

In order to improve their elder sister's life, the Huang brothers located Chaofan in America and sent her money through him. She accepted the money from her son, but used all of it for lawsuits and to help poor people pay for their medical treatment.

These years, her younger brothers take turns coming to Beijing to visit her. One of these has a very big business. When he had the time to spare he flew over to find her and discovered that she wasn't as forbidding as he had imagined. Sometimes he even envies and admires her. At least she has a life in which she never spends an idle moment and she is always so full of fight and high morale.

3.

Su'er was good at making money. He was the paragon for our third generation of Lins. He was also very lavish and generous. We all accepted his contributions with an easy mind and clear conscience. When my cash flow got tight, Su'er would help me. Even Big Aunt Fangzi, she of the revolutionary mind-set, began to "clothe in gold and dress in silver," as they say. People see wealth as something just like the big red flower that Grandma wore on her breast the year that she sent Baoqing to join the army. When Su'er first plunged into the sea of business, there was still some dissent about this among family members. Big Uncle Baosheng was very disappointed when Su'er dropped out of the university entrance exams, but gradually came around in his thinking.

Only my grandmother felt very uneasy about this. But who would take any notice of the views of a muddle-headed ninety-year-old woman?

Nowadays, my once very smug older cousin Su'er is serving eight years in prison for running private-channel goods. He's been in the clink for more than three years now.

How many times when I returned to Old Town did I want to see Su'er? I just never had the courage to do so. Once I dreamed I saw him locked up behind bars, his head shaven clean, and dressed in convict's wear. I woke up crying, and I went on crying after I was awake. He was such a vivid and dramatic person. For how many years had I grown used to seeing him in his big-name car with beautiful women and throwing money around like dirt? How could I face such brutal reality?

⌘ ⌘ ⌘

One time I went back to Old Town when it was Grandma's nine-tieth birthday and the old home at West Gate had not yet been torn down. Su'er held a sumptuous banquet for her at Old Town's best hotel. The Guo and Lin family members gathered there. All the relatives who were working in other places flew into Old Town at Su'er's expense to offer their birthday congratulations. I received even more favorable treatment: I flew first class. Su'er was afraid I couldn't bear spending the money and bought tickets for me in Old Town and had them couriered to Beijing.

Every time the waiter would bring a new course of food, Grandma would murmur, *"Zuiguo! Zuiguo!"* Now, this is a con-ventional way of saying something like "Thank you, but I don't deserve all this" for such occasions, but it literally means "sin" and "fault." Very satisfied with himself, Su'er patted his prosper-ous belly and laughed. "This is nothing! There's even more *zuiguo* to come!"

We drank and sang in praise of our beautiful and happy lives. Every one of the relatives and friends came over and toasted Su'er. He was the present-day hero of our Lin family.

In the middle of the night, I discovered that the lights were on in the main hall, so I got up to turn them off. Suddenly I saw a figure in the cane chair, and coming totally loose in space and time, I thought it was Grandpa.

Grandma was holding the Bible that Grandpa had kept and was praying there. "O Lord, I beseech you to forgive Su'er. Forgive him for not being aware of his *zuiguo*. Lord, I place him in your hands. Let him know that money is nothing. Let him understand that only you are the truth and that knowing you is the only true happiness. Su'er's *zuiguo* are also my own *zuiguo*..."

I never, ever expected Grandma to be so alarmed. In an instant the effects of the alcohol in me vanished, and for a long while I stood there behind Grandma, listening to her confess her sins and pray to Jesus. I didn't know how I ought to comfort and help her see what was right and sensible.

Grandma's last years were spent in that patched and re-patched rattan chair. Her hair which had turned all silver-white was now quite sparse. Her hands, covered with old-age spots, never stopped trembling. Day after day, year after year, she sat there reading the Bible. To her old-age glasses was now added a magnifying glass, and she read tirelessly with a hunger and a thirst that seemed never satisfied. But I don't believe she could understand what she read. After Grandpa passed on, she actually read it more than ten times—an old person over the waning years, nibbling away at an incomprehensible book from heaven. Obviously, she felt so alone and lonely. But Grandma put it differently. "If I am not a devout believer, how will I go to heaven and see your grandpa?"

I went over and crouched down by her side. "Ah Ma, go to sleep now. You've worked a lifetime for the Lins and the Guos. This birthday celebration was something you deserved. There was nothing sinful about it. You Christians talk of universal love. I can accept that, but everywhere you turn, there's sin. That's what I don't understand."

Grandma looked at me and there was worry in that gaze. "I don't feel good about Su'er. His squandering wealth like that makes me think that it wasn't proper to begin with. I'm old now, and nobody wants to hear my nagging and chattering. You'll have to convince him."

"The times have changed, Grandma." I pointed to that picture on the wall, the one of her sending her son into the army. "In those days, joining the army was something glorious. Now it's glorious to become a millionaire."

Grandma shook her head. "It's not right. I feel that's not right. Sooner or later, something is going to happen to Su'er."

All I could do was nod my head. People in our family said that Grandma had become like Grandpa, more and more stubborn and ignorant, and they found this both amusing and annoying.

⌘   ⌘   ⌘

Afterward, Grandma got even older and more scatterbrained. She didn't recognize money or Su'er. He again held several grand birthday banquets. When Grandma went, Su'er arranged a funeral ceremony that was lavish in the extreme. Nobody thought there was anything wrong with this and right up until that thing happened to Su'er, no one, old or young, in the Lin family mentioned Grandma's foresight.

Late one night, when Su'er was sleeping in the arms of who knows which one of his pretty confidantes, he was arrested and taken away by the Public Security Bureau. That woman then sold the apartment and the car, and then beat it out of there. To rescue her husband, my cousin's wife liquidated everything she could and took her daughter to live in a little courtyard place. Over the past three years, she has visited him in jail every month.

Deprived of his liberty, Su'er likes to write letters. At the start of the Cultural Revolution he was in the third grade at primary school, and after that he never seriously read or wrote anything. His character strokes are still at the primary school level, but between the unsophisticated lines an incongruous maturity and depth shows through.

In one letter he wrote, "Actually, a person doesn't need more than a three-foot-wide bed to sleep on, or eat more than half a *jin* of rice, so how could I have been so discontented? Be content, this is my advice to you. I don't complain about anything. The calamity of eight years in prison was really retribution for my wrongdoings. Every time I see my wife, I feel I really don't deserve to live in this world. Such a good wife, and yet for so long a time I just ignored her at home. I can hardly look her in the face. Later I just have to compensate her for all this. Although I won't be able to buy her an apartment or car again, just as long as we can be together as husband and wife, eating rice gruel and salted vegetables, that would be happiness…"

CHAPTER TWENTY-FOUR –
INFINITE IS THE BEAUTY OF THE SETTING SUN

1.

WHEN MY DRUNKARD great-uncle lurched through our gateway, bottle in hand, I was on the steps of the sky well, brushing my teeth. It was an ordinary West Gate autumn morning in 1976. People carrying vegetable baskets were rushing about the streets buying food for their daily meals, totally unaware that today was a day when everything would change.

Of course, neither did I know of a similar morning at the end of the 1940s when my mother, Young Miss Baohua, had stood brushing her teeth right on this same slab of stone I was now standing on. Her drunkard uncle came in, a bottle in his hand. That day also marked the beginning and end of an epoch— Old Town had been liberated.

I spat out my mouthwash and said quite impudently, "Old drunk, you've come to the wrong door!"

Great-Uncle crossed the sky well in a haze of alcoholic fumes and with considerable dignity sat down at the Eight Immortals table. "I suppose you all don't know, so far out in the sticks here at West Gate? There's been a big change! There's going to be a demonstration today. The boy at the Drum Tower provisions store gave me a free bottle of this. Real stuff, not a bit diluted. All these years,

I've had no swig of real liquor. So, all along, it was that goblin, Jiang Qing, who was to blame!"

He had once stood at the street-side news board and, pointing at Jiang Qing's photograph, said, "That woman looks like a goblin." For that he had been arrested and locked up for several days. Grandma in the kitchen heard Jiang Qing's name and ran out, her face taut with worry. "Just look at yourself! Drunk and talking rubbish! And even throwing that name around!"

This senior son of the Guo family muttered something as he took a few more slugs and then his whole body convulsed with laughter. "Second Sister, Jiang Qing has been brought down. Fuck her and her whole line before her! Wouldn't let me get a good drink...even arrested me..."

Grandma was so frightened she rushed over to shut the gate.

"Old Town's been liberated! For the second time! Everyone around Drum Tower is beating drums and clanging cymbals and you're still defending that goblin!"

The drunkard tottered up to leave. But Grandma worried he might stir up trouble and she tapped her hand on the table and shouted at him to stay put.

Grandpa was sitting off to the side like a wooden carving. He had gone deaf again for some time now. We all thought that this time it was for real. My two uncles got together and bought him a hearing aid, but he put it in the drawer and never used it.

After a while, my great-aunt knocked and entered. These days she was sulking with Rotten Egg and had gone to stay with her daughter who lived not too far from West Gate. Great-Auntie wiped her sweat and went straight over to Grandpa. "Ninth Brother! Ninth Brother! Something big's happened. It's really a big change!"

My boozing great-uncle laughed so hard that he swayed from side to side, sputtering and spitting, and the empty bottle fell with a crash on the ground. "You can call him 'Big Brother' but it won't be any use. You can call him 'Dear Daddy' and it still won't be of any use. He can't hear you."

Great-Auntie pulled over a chair and sat down. "Down through the ages, unschooled girls were considered virtuous. *That* one was pretty and read books, but she's been a disaster and a curse. Second Sister, back then if Mother and Father had sent you to school, you too would have been something special, someone who left her mark in the green bamboo strips of the histories. As for me, I've always been convinced that Third Sister became some big shot's wife—only she changed her name completely and would have nothing to do with us Guos."

My grandma, who was just then sweeping up the broken glass of the bottle, looked up at her sharply and cut her off. "Just what are you going on about?"

The two sisters and their brother were sitting around the dining table deep in conversation when they suddenly realized that Ninth Brother was nowhere to be seen.

⌘　⌘　⌘

The news of the fall from power of Jiang Qing's Gang of Four traveled far and wide, high and low. In a flash, West Gate, in normal times as placid as calm water, seethed and boiled as if it were an erupting volcano. The ordinary folk of Old Town who never looked any farther than the end of their noses saw this as a day of renewed liberation, after the first one in 1949.

Dr. Lin strolled about among the crowds of people. Men and women, old and young, everyone poured into the streets. It didn't matter if they knew each other or not as they gathered in fours and fives to give their own views on the affairs of the nation. The doctor would stop to listen to them from time to time. Everyone said that Jiang Qing tried to become a woman empress just like Wu Zetian, and so she created total chaos.[60] "China's been really lucky her plots never succeeded."

He walked from West Gate to Drum Tower, and then on toward the East Street crossing. Group after group of demonstrators passed by. His ears filled with all kinds of political slogans, but in his heart there resonated only one: Restore Order.

For ten years now he had never forgotten that obedience to authority was the Christian's duty, but every day of these ten years had passed in struggle and pain. All he could do was shut his eyes and cover his ears, and in this way escape reality. Restore Order told him that he hadn't been wrong. It was the world that had been wrong. All of a sudden painful memories arose in him and he thought of all the different things that had happened in those ten years. And in the midst of those crowds Dr. Lin covered his face and wept.

⌘ ⌘ ⌘

The sun had set but the city folk were still so excited they were unable to tear themselves away from the streets. My grandmother, Second Sister, stood under the oleander awaiting our return and every one of her neighbors passing by would stop to tell her the news. Now she was finally convinced that the world really had undergone a change of earthshaking and heaven-splitting proportions. Immediately a longing sprouted within her that in earlier

---

[60] The controversial Wu Zetian (c. 625–705 C.E.) ruled Tang dynasty China through her husbands and sons from 665 to 690, when she then founded a new Zhou dynasty with herself as China's first empress-ruler. This lasted until her overthrow by coup in 705. The Empress Wu appears to have been a harsh but capable ruler in times of great upheaval.

days would have been unthinkable—that the Lin family, all three generations, would come back to Old Town from wherever they were and gather at home. In her imagination she brought almost twenty people into the photo studio at Drum Tower.

She and Ninth Brother sit side by side in the middle, holding their little grandson and granddaughter. Baoqing and Fangzi in their mountain district now have a daughter whom she hasn't yet seen. *Fangzi wouldn't refuse to sit for a Happy Family portrait, would she?* Baohua is back from Xinjiang for this year's Mid-Autumn Festival. Everyone in the family has agreed to go to be photographed. Halfway there, Fangzi has gotten angry for some unknown reason and turned back, so the photograph is taken, minus one daughter-in-law. And Baohua holds a child but there is no man beside her. *This isn't a genuine Happy Family portrait then.* The only Happy Family picture, one with the whole family, that the Lins had is still the photograph taken during the War of Resistance.

Second Sister thought about the Happy Family portrait as if she were the studio photographer. Her eyes, hidden behind the camera equipment, focus on each face under the lights. She sees Baosheng, Baoqing, and Baohua. She sees them as they are today. She sees them as they were then. The faces of her three angelic children are now lined with wrinkles, and show their exhaustion from all the twists and turns of their lives. *All told, Baosheng was the one with the best luck. In the countryside where he had been sent, men didn't work the land. They just clutched their teapots and got together to yarn the day long as they waited for their old ladies to finish work in the fields and come home to cook dinner. Even more importantly, he enjoyed absolute authority at home. His wife behaved a bit oddly toward outsiders but she was utterly obedient toward her husband. His three children were all good and sensible kids. But, oh, Baoqing...how have these past several years been for you?* When they were refugees during the war, all she had to do was grab Baoqing's little hand tightly to feel she had something to rely on, to hope for. *And to think that nowadays when I want to see my son for a bit, it's harder on me than visiting someone in prison! Then there's poor, unlucky Baohua. Big Zhang is still locked up and Maomao kidnapped from his foster mother's home and nowhere to be found.*

Often in the dead of night when she thought of Baoqing and Baohua, Second Sister just cried and cried. She couldn't speak of this with Ninth Brother or me. She was this family's final point of support. Sometimes she would search out Mrs. Chen and the two of them would pray together. Mrs. Chen still firmly believed that Jesus heard her prayers. Every time Second Sister called on Lord Jesus, inwardly she harbored doubt: *Had Jesus, like Ninth Brother, shut his eyes and covered his ears?*

She sees Ninth Brother walk over to the lens with a happy smile on his face. *Now, this is truly something. He has never smiled when he had his picture taken.* The earliest picture of him was painted by someone his family had hired for this. He was only seven then and he still had that Manchu Qing dynasty queue. A deeply worried look hung over his clear facial features. How could a seven-year-old boy look so heavyhearted and worried? Maybe the child had a presentiment that his father, now well-advanced in years, would soon leave this world, and he himself would fall into helpless orphanhood. He still didn't understand what "the future" meant, but he already had an instinctive bewilderment and fear about it. The first time Second Sister saw that picture she had been terribly shocked. That was when she was his bride and she said to herself, "In this life and in this world *I* will be good to Ninth Brother. I will be a wife to him who will bring him only good and not harm." This was her idea of what marriage was, and she held onto this belief over the decades without a single complaint or regret.

"Second Sister, I've bought some crabs and aged rice wine."

Second Sister jumped when she heard Ninth Brother speak. She had almost forgotten that he could still speak of his own will, or even that he could still express a complete thought. So Second Sister was unable to say a word and she looked blankly at Ninth Brother.

"Today when I bought the crabs I just had to buy four of them, three males and one female. You know why?" Ninth Brother held up a string of crabs. "These crabs all have names. The female's called Jiang Qing…"

As if entranced, Second Sister revisited distant times and places. She sees Ninth Brother wobbling along on his bicycle through the streets around Drum Tower as they were forty years before. The Ninth Brother of those days had the most amazing sense of humor and was so mischievous. He always loved making sudden surprises. She remembered the time she returned from her own family home, when he and the three children, all wearing masks, jumped out of various hiding places at her. Ninth Brother himself had painted the masks. He really had a talent for painting.

Ninth Brother put down the crabs and guided Second Sister back into the house. "We have to Restore Order in our family too. But you rest today. I'll cook and wash up."

Second Sister wanted to say, "No, let me," when suddenly exhaustion robbed her of the strength to say the words that were right there on her tongue. Her feet seemed to be walking on clouds and fog and she surrendered herself to Ninth Brother.

⌘ ⌘ ⌘

This was a real Restore Order. When I had seen enough of the excitement outside I returned home with a stomach that was rumbling with hunger. I happened upon Grandma dozing away in the parlor just as Grandpa was coming out of the kitchen with a plate of bright red crabs. I was so shocked! In a voice filled with affection, Grandpa called me Hong'er, their pet name for me. But it was like I had been struck by a typhoon and I stumbled in retreat to the back of the house. Then, deep in my heart spread a glowing sorrow and I started to cry, still without understanding what had happened.

For several years before this, Grandpa's and my relationship had been extremely tense. I dearly loved Grandma and I often yelled at Grandpa, accusing him of faking deafness and dumbness and behaving perversely with Grandma in every way. I would say, "You may be the emperor of the Lin family, but I'm the rebel who braves the slicing death to unhorse the emperor." Most of the time I stayed out of his sight and he stayed out of mine. Or we would turn a blind eye to each other. If our eyes couldn't avoid a meeting, it would have come with gunpowder.

"Hong'er, come. Gramps wants to pick you a fat..."

The moment Grandpa opened his mouth, I was speechless. I turned away and wiped my tears. Then I walked over to the rocking chair to Grandma sitting the rocking chair. "Ah Ma, time to eat."

Grandpa said, "Your Ah Ma's got a sleeping sickness. The proper name for it is "hypnopathia." The last time she had this you weren't yet born. She slept right through Liberation. But never mind, let her sleep. Come, let's both eat."

How many years had it been since I had sat at the same table to eat with my grandfather? Now, out of the blue we're sitting across from each other, something I was really not used to. I bowed my head and tried hard to remember if he had ever loved me. A long-forgotten picture leapt into my mind—I am seated on Grandpa's lap, drinking cow's milk, and then many, many soft and warm pictures come tumbling in...the rice bowl pattered with the sound of my tears.

Grandpa shelled the four crabs and, picking out one of the fattest, put it on the plate and pushed it in front of me, and he also poured me a few drops of wine. "Today is a special day. Have a drink for Ah Ma, and see this as congratulating you on growing up."

How I longed to say something to Grandpa, something that would move him, but I was afraid of setting off an unbearable storm of emotions. Eyes all misty, I laughed loudly and, pretending that no one takes offense at children's words, rudely pointed at him. "Gramps, I guessed from the start that you were faking deafness! You fooled everybody. I was the only one who knew you could hear. You could hear everything!

"Everything you said when you scolded me I've kept in my heart."

Grandpa smiled rather awkwardly but also in a way that showed he was a bit pleased with himself. His smile held both an innocence and a naughtiness not at all in keeping with his age.

2.

WHEN GRANDMA WOKE up her eyes alighted on Wei'er. This child was the image of Baoqing when they fled during the War of Resistance, and unconsciously she called out "Baoqing!" She wanted to ask him, "Baoqing, what about your sister?" Grandma never fully got over my mother Baohua's disappearance at that time and whenever she became confused she would look for Baohua. She glanced up and saw Baoqing, now middle-aged and holding his daughter, and was baffled, unable to tell whether or not she was still in some dream.

All the family members who had scattered around the country continued to return home. One by one they entered Grandma's Happy Family portrait.

All three generations of Lins were in favor of going to the photo studio for a Happy Family portrait, but they felt there was plenty of time to do this, so everyone went happily about their busy lives. Finally, half a year later, the three generations finally managed to collect together at West Gate, and the studio photographer came with the equipment on his shoulder. But Grandma refused to have the picture taken. That was the day of my grandpa's funeral.

⌘　⌘　⌘

As a doctor, the first time Grandpa received his body's signal he clearly realized that the day of the Great Departing was near, and calmly and systematically he placed a period mark on his life. It was only during his final two weeks when he took to his bed for the last time that the Lin family members realized that a parting from life had silently descended upon them all, now gathered from the four points of the compass.

After it was all over, the rice shop boss-lady told us that during his last months she often saw the doctor walking along the crossroads all by himself during the darkest hours of the night. We couldn't guess what had been on his mind.

Everyone says that Christians see death as a homecoming. When life's final moment arrives, do they ever have an instinctive dread? Are they unable to bear leaving this home, this world? What do they feel, looking back over the years of their human existence?

What we saw was a hale and hearty old man. He was just getting started with preparations to travel northward once again and he was going to take Second Sister on this journey. This dust-covered intention of more than ten years again drew up its agenda. He had already contacted Mrs. Yang in Shanghai and Brother Yu in Hangzhou. These old friends who had gone through so many of life's storms and changes were still alive. There was truly no greater blessing than that.

He tried to achieve the realization of this travel plan. Late at night he would stroll along the street crossing, arranging in his mind the little time that was left for him. But he just had to give it up.

It escaped everyone's notice that he was planning his own posthumous affairs, for we all were taken in by his lively spirits. Also, during those several months our attention was centered on Grandma.

After Grandma recovered, she became ambitious about returning to public life. Just then the Residents Committee was holding an election for director. Grandma went out on her own initiative and tirelessly canvassed the voters. The people were all inclined toward the reinstallation of Director Guo; it was just that she *was* getting on in years. Thus she had to let the voters know that she was in better health than she had been ten years before. At home, though, there was general opposition. Baoqing shook his head. "Ma, can't you just stay at home and enjoy a leisurely retired life?" Baosheng put it more bluntly. "Ma, you really don't want to be lonely." Only my grandfather cast a vote in favor. One vote decided the fate of heaven and earth. There were no further objections.

When my grandpa fell, my grandma was already tied up with her many official matters as the Resident Committee Director. She sat by the sickbed, dejected and weeping. "Why didn't you tell me about all this?" she said reproachfully. Grandpa answered with a smile, "If you had known about it, would you have felt like running for election?"

⌘   ⌘   ⌘

Grandma could never forget a conversation she had with Ninth Brother on the eve of Winter Solstice. Every word he said was his last will and testament. But she actually hadn't the slightest inkling of this and later she felt annoyed at how very obtuse she had been then.

One day, Grandma was in the sky well grinding rice for rice milk—people in Old Town eat glutinous rice dumplings at Winter Solstice—and Grandpa was sitting inside, writing. She thought he was writing a letter to Mrs. Yang in Shanghai.

"Oh, Ninth Brother...Don't forget to ask Mrs. Yang what size she wears. There's still a length of satin in the trunk. I am rushing to make her a silk jacket..."

Grandpa put down his pen and walked over. "Second Sister, your eyes and hands aren't like they used to be. Don't do any more sewing."

"That's what I do to show my regards."

"Let's see about that next year, all right? Haven't you always wanted to have a Happy Family picture taken? One of these days we'll go together to visit Fangzi and give her that jade bracelet..."

Her grinding slowed, and after a pause she heaved a sigh, lowered her gaze, and continued with her work.

Everywhere was calm and peaceful. Only the Lin family's local wars continued, with the flames and gun smoke between Baohua and Baoqing's families even tending to escalate. The snow in front of Baoqing's gate had not been swept clean, so to speak, when he meddled in the frost on his big sister's roof tiles. A few days before, Baohua's two brothers made a special trip to P Town to give her their vocal support. This caused a falling-out with Big Zhang. The family members all kept a tight lid on this intelligence, and didn't let Grandpa know.

"*Hai*! Just seeing them all come back safely would be good enough. Taking the Happy Family photograph isn't all that important. And one bracelet won't necessarily win Fangzi's heart."

"There've definitely been times we could have treated her more nicely. I believe in the old saying, 'Complete sincerity can affect even metal and stone.' I hope to see her returning in happy spirits."

Grandma knew that in the Bible there was the line that went, "If a person strikes you on the left cheek, turn your right cheek for him to hit," and said, with some effort, "All right, then. 'God knows whose prayers are sincere.' I'll go with you to see her."

"We ought to see Maomao also...let him know that he too is our grandson and we love him just like the others. I'd like to give him my wristwatch."

"Give him the wristwatch and won't he have it sold within three days?"

"What I intend is to give the watch to Big Zhang in front of Maomao and tell him that after he's eighteen he can do with it as he likes."

"Now why do you have to do all that?"

In those years, a watch was a fairly valuable possession. It wasn't Maomao's turn for this among the several grandsons and grand-daughters of the family, so how could this be given to this bad boy that everyone disliked on sight?

When Big Zhang left prison he spared no effort looking for the vanished Maomao. This child, not yet ten years old, had already become a noted cat burglar in the world of hard knocks and quick wits. Back home again, his bad ways didn't mend. He ransacked Baohua's house and those of the neighbors. Again and again Big Zhang drove him out. Again and again he would come back crying to show that he had now changed, painfully and thoroughly. And each time Big Zhang's hopes would be dashed. Maomao was the source of the discord between Baohua and her husband.

"Actually, we ought to bring him back to West Gate. We'll use love to persuade him to change his ways. Too bad I have no more time now."

Grandma heard "bring him back to West Gate" and her scalp tingled. But she knew nothing she could say would be of any use. She laughed and said in resignation, "You're more Christian than ever. Jesus must really love you."

"Jesus has loved me all along. And his greatest love for me was in giving me a good wife."

Grandma's mind was so preoccupied over Fangzi and Maomao that she didn't detect from just what depths Grandpa said this.

He came over and helped her grind the rice for a while. "Second Sister, I want to put off the travel plans. I don't know if it'll work out. Maybe I've really let you down a bit in this..."

"You haven't let me down. I've also wanted to discuss with you that postponing it would be the best thing to do. The election for Residents Committee is still not over and the children have all just returned. How about if we invite Mrs. Yang and Mr. Yu to come to Old Town?"

"Tomorrow let's both go and visit Fangzi and after Winter Solstice we'll visit Maomao."

"Why so urgent?"

"'Time is an arrow.' I never thought our lives would go by this fast. This lifetime of being married to you hasn't been enough. If there's another one, I'd still want to be your husband."

Grandma laughed awkwardly. "I've got to think about whether or not I want to be your wife in the next lifetime."

The jade bracelet would be going to Fangzi tomorrow. She found this difficult to accept. *That was an heirloom passed down through the generations of the Lin family. It ought to be kept for Su'er's future wife. We really wouldn't have anything better than this to give her as a First Meeting gift.*

That night my grandma couldn't sleep from thinking about the jade bracelet. As she lay in bed she couldn't dispel the worry-ridden eyes of Baoqing that appeared before her. He was unhappy, even though he did his best to disguise it. She could still easily see that. It all came from the endless trials with Fangzi. She wouldn't let him come to West Gate to see his father and mother and she was unwilling to let them have the living allowance. Arguing daily, monthly, arguing to exhaustion, arguing until thick cal-luses grew on Baoqing's heart...He thought that Fangzi could no

longer hurt him, but Fangzi always came up with some new way to
do so.

Following Baoqing's return to Old Town, he had been given a
work position of some importance. From an ordinary section member he rose three levels to become a deputy department head. And
word had it that the superiors were going to break all precedent and
promote him to deputy bureau chief. But Fangzi had been demoted
to work in the mailroom because she had been too prominent during the Cultural Revolution. The change in her husband's position
put her in a state of constant fear and trembling and home life
became all the more contentious. Baoqing thought that the battle
was limited to their home only and so didn't let it get to him. He
never expected Fangzi would actually write to all the various office
heads that the suspicion about Baoqing's father having been a secret
agent had never been settled, and thus he shouldn't receive such an
important position. With this, Baoqing's candidacy was eliminated.

*How could a wife be so treacherous and underhanded toward her own
husband?*

Grandma tossed and turned to past midnight, when she finally
decided to make Baoqing and Fangzi's situation clearly known to
Ninth Brother.

The light in the inner room was still on. Ninth Brother was
writing something. Lately, day and night, he had been at it nonstop.
She didn't know what he was writing and didn't waste any energy
on guessing. Ninth Brother was an educated person. Educated people were always writing essays and composing lyric or heroic poems.

Grandma sat down next to the desk and after repeated sighing,
tirelessly related all that had happened to Baoqing.

Grandpa heard it through and then stood up and paced back
and forth across the little room. "We should have gone to see Fangzi
earlier. If you think about it, all along she had been a big star, then

suddenly she was a nobody. It was inevitable she would become unbalanced. And furthermore, did Baoqing have to place such importance on the bureau chief position?"

What my grandma had intended was to arouse my grandpa's righteous indignation and thus put aside the idea of winning over Fangzi. She never expected this kind of a reaction from him. The way Fangzi went about doing things struck her as utterly bizarre. But the way Grandpa put it struck her as equally bizarre. She couldn't contain her spleen and said sarcastically, "I see it now... Jesus saying to forsake the one we love and stretch out our arms to the stranger."

Grandpa gave this some serious thought. "Your metaphor has some truth to it."

"You've been able to do it. We couldn't. So only you will get to heaven and see Jesus."

Grandpa gazed at his wife with eyes brimming with love and affection. "I'll be waiting for you in heaven."

No matter how openly sarcastic or subtly you put it, he just can't understand. If I keep going on pestering him at this rate, won't I become just like Fangzi? There was nothing more she could do. *Just treat it as some unexpected loss. How many times in this life have we gone through poverty and ruin? What's one bracelet?*

"Don't stay up any longer," she said, yawning.

⌘ ⌘ ⌘

The next day, Grandma excused herself from paying respects to Fangzi, claiming that she was tired and headachy. Grandpa got the bracelet from her and went off alone.

What would Fangzi's reaction be when she saw the father-in-law she hadn't seen in so many years? Would she curse him to his face for being a secret agent? My grandma was worried about Grandpa, but she also wanted to see the old coot hit his head against the wall. Grandpa returned home in high spirits a few hours later and reported that the results of the talk had been excellent. Grandma didn't ask for details. She basically didn't believe that one conversation could turn Baoqing's home situation around.

⌘   ⌘   ⌘

When payday came that month, Fangzi, as always collected Baoqing's salary on his behalf. For more than ten years now, ever since his wife's relations with her in-laws at West Gate had broken down, Baoqing had not collected his own salary. Normally, husband and wife did not speak to each other. Fangzi washed the clothes and cooked. Baoqing fetched the children and washed the dishes. This cooperation was a sort of tacit agreement. If husband and wife needed to communicate while under the same roof, they would ask their son to be the messenger. Whenever they didn't require a messenger were the times for fusillades of gunfire.

Every month it had been routine for war to burst out over the living allowance for his parents. After work, Baoqing went to get his children and came home. Fangzi had already set out the bowls and chopsticks. Baoqing discovered that fifteen *yuan* had been laid at his place setting. Keeping a watchful eye on Fangzi, he hurriedly stuffed this money into his pocket, thinking that war was inevitable now. But Fangzi's expression never changed as she spooned food into their daughter's mouth. He didn't dare believe that Fangzi would on her own have set aside the money for his father and mother. He said to his son, "Tell your ma that Daddy's taken the fifteen *yuan* and in a little while will be going over to Gramps with it." The boy then parroted this to his mother. Fangzi's expression remained normal.

Baoqing still didn't believe it and made so bold as to speak directly to her. "I'll be taking the money to West Gate in a bit." "Go ahead," Fangzi said softly.

Baoqing didn't know that his father had met with Fangzi. As he rode his bike back to West Gate, he just couldn't figure out what had touched her heartstrings.

3.

WHEN THE DOCTOR and his wife went to P Town they encountered Baohua's own family war. Big Zhang had once again driven Maomao out of their home and the pictures of the boy when he was small were all torn up. Big Zhang now had been appointed commissioner of P Town, but as far as he was concerned, with the Zhang family having no descendents, even being secretary of the provincial party committee wouldn't have had the slightest meaning. In his despair, Big Zhang's temper grew even worse.

That morning, Big Zhang saw Baohua in the kitchen leisurely boiling rice porridge and frying dumplings. *Your son is gone, but you can still be in such a good mood.* All at once he flew into a terrible rage and started smashing up the kitchen. Baohua returned in tears to Baosheng's home in Old Town. Baosheng's home was her place of refuge.

The doctor and his wife arrived at Commissioner Zhang's new residence just when Big Zhang had locked himself inside and was drinking all alone. When he heard the knock on the door he roared out, "Beat it! Scram! I don't know you!"

Big Zhang's natural voice was unusually loud and clear. At meetings when he made reports, no matter how big the occasion, he never needed a microphone. Long ago, the first bad impression his future son-in-law had made on the doctor was that very same voice when Big Zhang had exploded at a taxi driver at the West Gate street crossing. His voice could terrify heaven and shake the earth. *Who had messed up heaven's marriage register and introduced Baohua to this northern oaf?*

Second Sister thought that Baohua was inside and called out in the Old Town dialect, "Big Zhang, listen to me! Don't hurt Baohua!"

Big Zhang calmed down. He was puzzled. *Baohua's only just gone. How could she have called my mother-in-law here?*

Before the Cultural Revolution, Big Zhang harbored tremendous hostility toward Baohua's family. But several years later, his father-in-law's daring visit to him in jail was a kindness he would never forget as long as he lived. These days, though he might feel every kind of dissatisfaction with Baohua, he still felt a deep reverence toward his father- and mother-in-law. When he and Baohua quarreled, he would often say, "Your mother could take three children out of danger, but *you* can't raise just one child."

He hurriedly put away the liquor bottle, scooped up some cold water and ran it through his hair a few times. After all, he was seasoned in the world of officialdom. He knew when he could let himself go and when he had to put on a mask. He opened the door and, smiling radiantly, welcomed in his wife's parents.

"Dad, Ma! Oh, I am so sorry for disturbing you. Look how silly that Baohua is. Is there any couple who doesn't quarrel?"

Second Sister noticed that Ninth Brother's face had turned white. "Oh, Big Zhang, look how upset you've made Dad. Nowadays there's no hard times we can't get through. How come your temper hasn't improved?" she grumbled in her distress.

The doctor took out a bottle of medicine. "It's nothing. I just take two vitamin B tablets and then it's all right."

During those several months, Ninth Brother was often taking medicine. He told Second Sister it was vitamin B and she never believed otherwise.

"Ma, you're an extraordinary woman," Big Zhang said. "If Baohua were half of what you are, even one-tenth, this family would be at peace."

The doctor waved his hand. "'Even the fairest magistrate has a hard time judging family matters.' We haven't come to judge your family matters. We've come to see Maomao."

The smile stiffened on Big Zhang's face. "I've kicked the little bastard out. Kicked him out ten times and ten times he's come back. This time I told him if he dared show his face again I'd have the Public Security Bureau grab him and send him to labor reform."

The doctor looked down and was silent for a long time and then said to Second Sister, "Go inside and rest. Big Zhang and I are going out to talk for a bit."

Commissioner Zhang's building was near the river. The two of them, father-in-law and son-in-law, sat under an old banyan tree by the riverside. The doctor took out the medicine bottle he had stuffed in his shirt pocket and told him that what he was taking wasn't vitamins and that he had only a hundred days at most left on earth. He said he wanted to make full use of this time to settle a few matters that weighed on him. And one of these was the relationship between Big Zhang and Maomao.

Big Zhang's face took on a deep and imposing look. "Dad, you have been very kind to me. If I could, I'd be willing to die for you. Even though I've given up on that child, for your sake, I'm willing to try one more time."

He called over his driver and they drove to P Town's long-distance bus station. That was Maomao's other home, and a gang of street-children beggars were his brothers and sisters. Whenever Maomao returned to his adoptive parents from this other home, "the lotus root would snap, but the fibers stayed attached."

They found the utterly filthy Maomao under a bench. Every time he had been kicked out of his home he would brazenly ask for forgiveness. This last time Big Zhang had given the final word. And when Big Zhang very clearly and plainly declared there was no blood relationship between them, Maomao despaired and in this despair a fierce hatred was born. Now, suddenly seeing Big Zhang and his grandpa from Old Town, he was so affected he started to cry wildly. Before, he had cried often but that had been all bluff and playacting. Today he didn't want to cry and in his tear-drenched eyes there was still hatred. He gnashed his teeth and his chin crumpled up in trembling and shaking.

If this child can be moved to cry, then he can still be saved. The doctor stroked Maomao's head. "Maomao, you're Daddy and Ma's son, and you're Grandpa's and Grandma's grandson. We all love you."

Maomao's facial features unclenched and he burst out wailing.

The doctor seated Maomao in Big Zhang's Shanghai sedan. Big Zhang made a big show of looking dour and sat in the front without turning around to look.

Can bringing Maomao back home solve the basic problem? I'm going to take him back to Old Town. Perhaps this is the thing I ought to do most of all before my life ends. We shouldn't have come to P Town just to seek a peaceful conscience. Second Sister said, "God knows whose prayers are sincere." This is far, far from good enough.

Second Sister boiled water and bathed Maomao and then presented him with the snacks brought from Old Town. She wanted to give him a talking to, but then she thought that she herself was only a guest here, so she let the idea pass.

Big Zhang came into the kitchen and took the thermos. Maomao was so panic-stricken he stuffed a whole egg tart into his mouth. Big Zhang couldn't help exploding in anger. "What're you scared of? Feeling guilty about something? You just can't change the bum looks of a dog rustler and chicken thief!" he roared.

"Oh, this child! He does give people a headache. Big Zhang may still drive him away again," murmured Second Sister.

The doctor gazed at Maomao and said to his wife, "We'll take him back with us to West Gate to live there for a while."

"What did you say?"

"Bring Maomao back to West Gate."

"Have you gone mad?"

Big Zhang sat there drinking tea and smoking, while a stream of curses poured out of him. "Listen, brat. If you want to become a bad guy, I'm not stopping you. Take me, for example—back then I'd have joined the bandits, you can be sure, if I hadn't run into the Communist Party. If you've got the guts to rob the highway then I'll say you're a man. What I can't stand is a sneak. How can I have someone like you as a son?"

The doctor said, "Big Zhang, we're taking Maomao back to West Gate to stay with us for a while."

"If Big Zhang can't manage him, I suppose you can?" Second Sister broke in.

"Just let me give it a try. How can you know if you haven't tried?"

Big Zhang looked with surprise at his father-in-law. *That old guy knows he hasn't got long to live. Where does all his love come from?* He thought of that time in the Cultural Revolution when he was behind bars in the provincial Public Security Department building and saw his father-in-law. For as long as he could remember he had never cried—even when he buried his father and mother he didn't shed a tear. But that day he cried, cried as if his heart would break. This old bag of bones in front of him was no ordinary man. *Maybe he really could change Maomao.*

Second Sister's mouth was half-opened, but she couldn't get a single word out, as if she had a sudden stroke. She was thinking, *there are so many rooms at West Gate, so many drawers. Even if I grew eyes on the bump in the back of my head I wouldn't be able to keep it all in view. Oh, Ninth Brother, you're always up to something and I really can't hold my own...*

She saw Ninth Brother lead Maomao out of the kitchen and sit down with him side-by-side in front of Big Zhang. He took off the watch and put it into the boy's hand. "Maomao, Grandpa has been poor all his life and never had anything that was worth much money. There was only this watch. Now I'm giving it to you."

Maomao looked fearful, not sure whether this was a blessing or a curse.

"Now you're still small and have no use for a watch. Give it to your Dad to put away safely and keep it as your eighteenth birthday present. Would that be all right?"

Maomao held the watch in both his trembling hands and gave it to Big Zhang.

Big Zhang didn't say anything as he took the watch. Grasping it in one hand, with the other he stuck a cigarette between his lips and took one big drag after another.

Second Sister thought, *How come Big Zhang is keeping it? Why not leave it with Grandpa to give to Maomao?*

After the busy day, they both went to bed. As she closed the door, Second Sister said, "If you bring Maomao to West Gate, I'll live here in Daughter's home."

Today Ninth Brother's reactions were pretty quick. He knew that Second Sister didn't like Maomao and so he didn't respond directly. "If you settle in here, what happens when the West Gate residents come looking for Director Guo?"

"Whatever you do you never discuss it with me first. For you it's all a command performance. It wasn't this way before. When you were deaf, the whole family had peace and quiet."

Ninth Brother laughed as he burrowed under the covers. "Now you don't know, but later you will. You're in good health. You're sure to see Maomao's future."

Second Sister lay down and then sat up. "Ninth Brother, we're both people over seventy. Before, I always said that when we get to this age, when we take off our shoes at night, we don't know if we'll be wearing them on the next day. So how can you undertake such a heavy responsibility?"

"Second Sister, even when we're young we don't know what tomorrow will bring. Reality is right there before our eyes. God wants us to extend a helping hand."

"You're always shifting everything onto God. God has a special love for you and you're the only one he speaks to."

"You're saying I can turn away and not be bothered?"

Second Sister had nothing to say to this.

⌘　⌘　⌘

The next day, Big Zhang himself drove his parents-in-law and Maomao back to West Gate. Then he turned in the direction of Baosheng's home to get Baohua. Baosheng stood blocking the doorway and demanded that Big Zhang guarantee he wouldn't bully his elder sister again. Big Zhang didn't utter a single word, but the smile on his face said he held the winning ticket. Baohua was quick to anger and quick to cool down. He believed that she would go with him. If Baosheng wouldn't let her go, it was possible she might still have a falling-out with her brother. And sure enough, when Baohua heard Big Zhang's voice, she immediately pulled off her own things from the clothesline and squeezed past her brother.

4.

THAT WAS A warm and bright Winter Solstice. The Dr. Lin we saw was an elderly kid in his second childhood. He took Maomao to play all around those fun places in Old Town and they ate wherever there were the tasty snacks Old Town was famous for.

In the evenings when we gathered at the dinner table, Grandpa would have Maomao describe the awkward and embarrassing things that happened during their rambles. For example, when they had rowed out to the middle of West Lake and couldn't get back to shore, grandfather and grandson yelled for help to the people walking along the lakeside. He told how Grandpa climbed up a children's slide but was afraid to come down. Everybody at the table laughed so hard they were spitting rice. Grandma picked up the thread and told of Grandpa's many misadventures when he was young. In the early 1930s he rode his bicycle on the streets around Drum Tower but couldn't get off, and charged right toward the trees, scared out of his wits and shouting the whole way. Director Guo not only didn't exclude Maomao anymore, she was very grateful for the joy this child brought to Ninth Brother. After her reinstatement she was totally swamped with her work. If Maomao hadn't been by his side, Ninth Brother would have felt very lonely.

Thus, when my grandma found out that Grandpa, burdened by certain thoughts, would frequently walk up and down the streets in the dead of night, she was both surprised and even quite irritated. She had always considered that she and Ninth Brother were the most harmonious married couple under heaven. "We haven't had so much as a cross word between us for decades now. What are these heavy thoughts of yours that you can't tell me about?"

Great-Auntie moved over to West Gate to keep her younger sister company. All the Lin family inside dope couldn't fool her. And naturally, she could never pass up the opportunity to let her imagination run wild. "You all never notified the Shanghai relatives, so surely Ninth Brother left with a troubled heart." She once dreamed she saw Ninth Brother turn into a bird whose wings drooped and couldn't fly away.

Second Sister firmly contradicted her elder sister, but she was a little puzzled and doubtful. Without letting anyone in the family know, she quietly looked through a big stack of letters for the ones that Mrs. Yang had sent to the Lins from Shanghai and studied each of these in detail. She was literate, for she had accompanied her younger brothers to their old-fashioned private school. But she always humbly kept a fair distance from writing. Before she was married, writing matters were done by her elder sister on her behalf. Afterward, anything connected with writing in the family was undertaken by Ninth Brother. During the War of Resistance she had Baosheng write her Letters from Home to Ninth Brother.

The address on every one of Mrs. Yang's envelopes was written, "Young Mr. Lin and Madam." She gave a bundle of letters to Elder Sister to read. "Take a good look at these. When you make up stories, don't go so far off track."

Ninth Brother spent several months arranging his posthumous affairs. Fangzi came back to the West Gate family she had cut herself off from for over ten years. Maomao returned to school. At the funeral he wept and rolled on the ground.

When the coffin was carried to the burying ground, standing next to Baosheng and Baoqing were Big Zhang, Young Li, and Enchun. They are big government officials now. From West Gate to Drum Tower all your patients came to send you off. Ninth Brother, you always said you were a ne'er-do-well and down on your luck your whole life long. Today you ought to have seen how honored and glorified you were. You shouldn't have any more troubled thoughts that you can't shake off.

The doctor, in fact, did have one unfinished piece of business that weighed on him and many nights he couldn't get to sleep on account of it. It was the sense of concern that stayed with him from the last time he traveled north.

He had gone to the hospital affiliated with his old Shanghai college and reproduced the X-ray films of Mr. and Mrs. Qiao's teeth. It was his wish to go to Shandong and look for their remains so that he could bury these in the courtyard of the church at West Gate. They were the father and mother who gave him his second life. Although in terms of Christian thoughts and beliefs doing this was of no particular significance, he still held the traditional Chinese moral and ethical concepts. He wanted to honor his filial responsibilities toward Mr. and Mrs. Qiao, just like all Chinese sons. Brother Yu, traveling with him at the time, shook his head and said this idea was just about unfeasible. The old bones in the vicinity of the concentration camp were piled as high as a hill. How could they identify those of Mr. and Mrs. Qiao?

After Ninth Brother retuned to Old Town, Pastor Chen heard of this and gave his firmest support and he himself wrote a report to the government. Mr. Qiao had been the founder of a school for girls in Old Town, a hospital for the poor, and the West Gate church. In the end, he died in a fascist Japanese concentration camp out of his belief that he should sacrifice himself for the sake of others. Pastor Chen proposed that a memorial tablet be set up at the West Gate church. The streets were already filling up with Red Guards when that letter was sent off, and for the past ten years the negatives of Mr. and Mrs. Qiao's teeth had stayed hidden at Shuiguan's home.

This was a matter that weighed on him alone. The doctor couldn't think of whom to pass the baton to. He had spoken with

Mrs. Chen. The pastor's widow was just then doing everything she could to restore the West Gate church. She was already almost eighty years old and her final hope was to once again play hymns there in the church. He sought out Enchun but Enchun was preparing lectures. The doctor sat for a few minutes in that room piled high with books and then said good-bye, never mentioning this matter. He even thought of Young Li. Young Li had just received notification that his party membership had been restored. Obviously he would not be an appropriate candidate.

He missed Pastor Chen. It was only then that he understood the Old Town saying, "Having a friend who understands you is all you need in life." At night he would often linger in the neighborhood of the church, calling to mind his many, many years of friendship with Pastor Chen. Sometimes he would close his eyes and meditate on what kind of world there would be after passing through death. Would he be able to meet Mr. and Mrs. Qiao and Pastor Chen?

Perhaps this streak of obstinacy in the doctor moved the spirits of Mr. and Mrs. Qiao. They floated down on the night streets of West Gate and, as when he was little, they embraced him and stroked his head, saying, "Child, that's not important, it's not important in the least. We are waiting for you in the eternal country..."

In short, he never mentioned to anyone the material he had placed in Shuiguan's home. He wrote a memorial speech for Mr. and Mrs. Qiao and gave it to Pastor Chen. Many years later a monument was set up in the churchyard at West Gate, its inscription telling the history of the West Gate church and quoting the writing left by Dr. Lin.

⌘   ⌘   ⌘

Shuiguan was already a very old man now. When the doctor passed on he had been lying semi-paralyzed in bed already for a long time and he made his son, Ah Ming, carry him on his back to the Lin home to say good-bye to the doctor. After the funeral, he recalled that the package the doctor had entrusted him with safekeeping ten years before was still on the roof beam of his home. He told Ah Ming to bring it down and again carry him to the Lins where he himself handed it to Baosheng.

Baosheng guessed that the package contained an important document connected with the fate of the Lin family. *Dad had been poor all his life, but the Lin family before him had been a great one. Might it be there was some inheritance that no one knew of?* He gravely assembled all the offspring of the three branches of the Lin family, and, gathered around the Eight Immortals table, opened the package. There was a layer of oil paper and one of cowhide, and he opened them layer by layer. All eyes were fixed on Baosheng's hands and everyone was surprised to see him drop out two black negatives from a small paper sleeve. Baoqing picked up the film and looked at it closely against the light. He said these possibly were his dad's dental records. Baosheng let out a guffaw of laughter. "Dad is playing a joke on us!" He put the negatives back into the little paper sleeve and handed it over to his mother. "Ma, we can't figure out what Dad had in mind. Do you want to keep this?" Grandma took the paper sleeve and sat down on the rattan chair and cudgeled her brains for some time. Then she said, "I know whose teeth these are." The brothers and sisters around the Eight Immortals table had now turned to other topics. No one was curious about whose teeth those had been.

As far as I know, my grandma gave those two negatives to Mrs. Chen. Some years later Mrs. Chen herself passed away and the church was dismantled and relocated. The negatives became ashes and smoke, along with the rest of West Gate's past.

CHAPTER TWENTY-FIVE — GRANDMA, I'M BACK

1.

THE TRAIN ENTERS the tunnel and the noonday sun outside the window is suddenly gone. It is dark and quiet. Like the soundless pause during a symphony concert. Like the blank connecting frames on a movie screen.

Ahead is my Old Town, that endlessly drizzling Old Town with its dripping eaves and soaking alleys...

It's not raining today in Old Town. The curtains are raised and the sunlight is as fierce as boisterous drums and gongs. Up on the stage flashes a silhouette of a modern city. The glass window-walls of the densely packed tall buildings are goldenly resplendent. A forest of construction cranes stand about the edges of a city vastly and mightily expanding ever outward.

Sounds crackle alive on the train's public-address system and amid soft music the female announcer languidly says, "Old Town, Old Town guest houses and hotels, Old Town's middle and outer ring roads." It sounds like an arrival in Hong Kong.

Indulging in Old Town's past is like wallowing in a compelling dreamworld from which I am reluctant to emerge. Something called Old Town's Modern City is rushing at us headlong, like the pitiless dawn that demolishes illusions of romance and sentimentality, and hurls me into this time and this place. And here and now I am no longer the sentimental and susceptible little girl at West Gate. I've got to exert all eighteen martial arts in the perilous wide world to seize a place in the sun.

I now think about Chrysanthemum. I haven't heard from this cluck for more than twenty hours. Has she secured some useful man? Hastily I pull out my cell phone. *Was it me who shut it off? This isn't my style at all.*

Chrysanthemum is shouting in alarm on the phone. In her anxiousness she has forgotten to cover up her Shanxi accent: "Damn you! I've called a thousand times. You've just got to fly back this evening! I can't close with that top executive—I heard that some other company has moved quicker than us. I still need you to come down from the mountains and peddle your old-schoolmate face!"

I glance sidelong at my companion. He's been organizing our bags and is painstakingly wiping his camera lens.

I want to say yes, certainly I'll rush right back, but another voice comes out instead: "That's impossible, absolutely impossible!"

"You've got to know that the fate of the rest of our lives hangs on tonight's meeting!"

"That's also impossible."

Chrysanthemum lowers her voice to a crestfallen level. "It's all over. You've ditched me and left me to fight this war all by myself."

I steel myself and once again shut off the cell phone.

We follow the flow of the crowd leaving the platform and stroll along the street. *Where am I? Why is it called Old Town?* I am perfectly aware that the Old Town of my memories no longer exists. But I'm still feeling stunned and in a daze.

A taxi stops. The driver sticks out his head. "Sir, Miss, where are you going?"

He speaks Mandarin with the Old Town accent. That familiar hometown sound brings me indescribable joy and I use my now very rusty Old Town dialect to answer him. "West Gate. We want to go to West Gate!"

The taxi driver is looking at me curiously. It's like he's in a daze too. *This travel-worn northern lady actually knows Old Town speech?* He gets out and helps us put our luggage in the trunk. "Oh, I know you want to go to the West Gate Hotel. The feng shui of that four-star hotel right next to Little West Lake is good. The place's doing great business!"

I don't know when a hotel had been built at West Lake. Every time I come back to West Gate it's changed. Every time I see West Gate it all seems like when I saw Chrysanthemum for the first time after her face-lift. What she spent on completely remaking her face and everything on it would have bought a house. She sat across from me, as always twirling the spoon in her coffee. As always, she put on that Hong Kong or Taiwan accent. I couldn't say a single word in reply because I didn't know whom I was talking to. This woman had the gestures and voices I was familiar with, but her face and its features and expressions were strange to me. I didn't dare look directly at her. I was so dumbfounded I felt mentally deranged.

The Old Town story isn't over yet. How does the Old Town story go on?

2.

THAT NIGHT, IT rains in Old Town. *Pitter-patter, pitter-patter.* I push open a window and smell the familiar faint odors of the wet earth. The fragrance of flowers wafts over from Little West Lake, our Old Town's unique White Jade orchids. Wave after wave of the bewitching scent seeps into my inner-most parts. Calm settles into this rattled and jangled heart of mine.

Walking out of the hotel, I stroll about in the rain around the West Gate crossing. I use my feet to chart the panorama of the past. Here was the rice shop. The window in the upper story of the rice shop was like a picture frame. The mother longing for the return of her sons was inlaid in that frame and grew old day by day. Here was the front yard of the church. Mrs. Chen weeded and watered flowers inside the fence. She would cut a few lush red roses for me to take home to Grandma...

In the main hall of the Lin home a young lady sat at an antique Eight Immortals table. Her chin was propped up in both hands and her eyes stared blankly at the soaked streets, the dripping eaves, the sodden branches. She thought of the world beyond southern Old Town. That was the world she yearned for. Why would she live in Old Town, she wondered. Why would she live in this house? These were things she thought about endlessly, without ever getting the answer. She ached to leave Old Town, an ache like a kind of home-sickness. She often felt a kind of sadness worse than anything she had ever known as she sat in this West Gate home in Old Town. Like a traveler in exile. She didn't know where she would ever feel at home.

A handsome young man walked in out of the rain. His name was Chaofan. He walked over to that young lady staring blankly, her chin propped up in her hands. The young lady's face suddenly radiated happiness. She didn't know yet just how long a life goes on, how many changes a life can experience, but she was dead-set on swearing to the mountains and the sea that she would give her own life to this young fellow. Who pointed to the top of the sky well and said, "I love you. If I break faith let me be struck dead by lightning from heaven."

The vows of youth are spells that a lifetime can never break. They split up. They live at opposite ends of the earth. They hold bitter grudges against each other. But in the coiled roots and twisted branches of their lives they stick to each other and possess each other. They never again can love another man or another woman.

For many years I have never told anyone. I have loved and I have been happy. That is a song buried deep in my heart that I have no way of singing. I cannot speak of it, for were I to do so, the tone and colors of the original would be lost.

At this moment, the mud that I am stepping on is our old house. Where the advertising lamp-box stands is where my grandfather planted the oleander tree. My grandmother would stand under that tree waiting for me to come home from school.

Grandma, I'm back.

Eyes closed, block by block I build in my mind the home of my childhood. After crossing the sky well you come to the parlor. Right in the middle of the parlor stands the Eight Immortals table. I lightly touch the tough grain of its surface. I slowly sit down and prop up my chin under my hands, my heart filled with warmth and gratitude. For my own life in Old Town. For my life in this home. For that handsome young man who grew up with me in our years of innocent childhood.

If I could return to the time of my youth, I would still be dead-set on marrying the young man from the Chen family. But I would ask him to vow to the heavens that he would never leave Old Town, that he would lead me by the hand in Old Town's endless drizzle and we would slowly grow old together...

Acknowledgments

I OWE A great debt to Lars Ellström for introducing Lin Zhe and her wonderful novel to me, and, of course, to Ms. Lin for accepting me, an unknown quantity, as her translator. In the course of this project, many people generously clarified certain linguistic and contextual expressions—I can only hope I have rendered these correctly. First and foremost, the author herself: her explanations were succinct, good-natured, and patient. It has always been a joy to communicate with Ms. Lin. Others include, but are certainly not limited to, Guan Yi of Beijing, Tom Ying-kuang Lin and Jiang Feifei of Seattle, and the many members of FANYI, a University of Hawai'i online list service of international Chinese translators.

A special thank you, as well, to Liza Danger Austin for the fine graphics, and for the several friends who read and provided valuable comments on the translation while it was in progress..

And finally, with this translation, as imperfect as it may be, I wish to pay tribute to all the people who taught me Chinese, beginning at Nanyang University, Singapore in 1970, and especially in Beijing in the early 1980s, where under the tutelage of the Guo brothers, I really did learn to speak the real Beijing Chinese.

About the Author

Photo by Time Out Beijing.

Lin Zhe (pen name of Zhang Yonghong) was born in 1956 of Han Chinese parents then serving in the People's Liberation Army in Kashi (Kashgar), a small frontier city in what is now Xinjiang Uyghur Autonomous Region. After graduating from the Chinese Language and Literature Department of Fudan University in 1980, she worked as a reporter and editor for Women of China Magazine in Beijing. She has written fourteen novels that focus on women's issues relating to marriage and personal and family life, as well as three TV drama series.

About the Translator

George Anderson Fowler lived and traveled widely in the Asia Pacific region for over thirty years, first as a US Marine, then as a student of Chinese and Malay, a writer, and finally for twenty-three years as a commercial banker. He co-authored *Pertamina: Indonesian National Oil* and *Java, A Garden Continuum* while living in Indonesia in the early 1970s. George received a BA from St. Michael's College, the University of Toronto, in 1975, and an MAIS (China Studies) from the Jackson School of International Studies at the University of Washington in 2002. He has most recently translated Marah Rusli's classic Indonesian Malay novel, *Sitti Nurbaya*, whose publication by Lontar in Jakarta is forthcoming.

George and his wife, Scholastica Auyong, currently live near Seattle, where he is a full-time freelance translator of Chinese, Indonesian, Malay, and Tagalog.

3

ML

/1